PRAISE FOR GAIL R. DELANEY

"GAIL R DELANEY CREATES SYMPATHETIC AND BELOVED CHARACTERS THAT PULL THE READER THROUGH AN EIGHT BOOK STORY ARCH ONLY TO REACH THE END AND WISH THERE WAS MORE, BUT *LIBER* REALLY IS THE RESOLUTION BOTH THE CHARACTERS AND READERS DESERVE. THE FINAL CHAPTER OF THE FUTURE POSSIBLE SAGA DELIVERS THE MOST IMPORTANT PROMISE STARTED IN BOOK ONE THAT LOVE IS THE STRONGEST FORCE IN THE GALAXY."

ANGELA LAVERGHETTA, AUTHOR

"ANOTHER AMAZING BOOK IN A SERIES THAT CONTINUES TO BLOW ME AWAY! BE PREPARED TO UGLY CRY, FOR ALL THE BEST REASONS!"

ESTHER MITCHELL, AUTHOR,
GUARDIANS, INC: WITCH HOLLOW
AND PROJECT PROMETHEUS

"GAIL R. DELANEY DOESN'T JUST WRITE NOVELS THAT TELL STORIES ABOUT CHARACTERS. SHE BUILDS MAGNIFICENT WORLDS FULL OF PEOPLE, HOPE, AND LOVE THAT INVITE READERS TO BE PART OF EPIC JOURNEYS. IT IS ABUNDANTLY EVIDENT THAT GAIL DELANEY CHERISHES THE PEOPLE AND PLACES SHE CREATES, AND DELIGHTS IN SHARING THE FREEDOM AND JOY FOUND IN THE PAGES OF HER MANUSCRIPTS WITH HER FANS. *LIBER* IS THE PERFECT ENDING TO HER FUTURE POSSIBLE SAGA WHILE LEAVING ROOM FOR FURTHER GLIMPSES INTO THE FUTURE... JUST BE SURE TO BRING EXTRA KLEENEX ALONG FOR THE MOST EMOTIONAL, TWISTIEST, TURNIEST, STOMACH DROPPING, ROLLER COASTER RIDE THAT PROBABLY HASN'T EVEN BEEN INVENTED YET, BUT WHEN IT IS...IT WILL MOST DEFINITELY BE NAMED THE GAIL R. DELANEY."

AMY ELIZABETH, AUTHOR

LIBER

LIBER

PHOENIX RISING BOOK FOUR

GAIL R. DELANEY

I'm glad you came along for the ride.
Gail R. Delaney

To: All those patient (and not so patient) souls who have waited for this conclusion.

To: Those who have encouraged me so much through their love of the Phoenix books—Esther Mitchell, Judy Tayson, Barbara Schroeder—It means so much to know someone else loves them as much as I do.

To: BookTok and all the BookTokers who stoked the flames of my writing fire that had been less than embers for years. They lit the fire again, they poured fuel on it, and they kept me going until I finished.

To: My beta readers Amy Dewey, Angela Canon, and Esther Mitchell. Each of you contributed to making sure this final book in the series is the best it can possibly be. And to Jenni Cole, for giving the book one last scrubbing.

And a special, heartfelt thank you to those who shared the names of people they wanted honored in this book. You know who you are, and I appreciate and am blessed that you shared this with me.

Copyright © 2022 by Gail R Delaney

All rights reserved.

No part of this book may be reproduced in any form or by any electronic or mechanical means, including information storage and retrieval systems, without written permission from the author, except for the use of brief quotations in a book review.

Cover Art by Jenifer Ranieri

CONTENT DISCUSSION AND AUTHOR INSIGHT

Throughout the whole of the Phoenix Rising quartet, there is a prominent character dealing with the trauma and emotional recovery from childhood sexual assault.

The events are in the past, and are not detailed anywhere in these novels. Doing so would not add anything but unnecessary shock value, and that isn't the type of author I am. I write enough so the source of the trauma is clear, and the reader can understand the extent of the physical and emotional trauma inflicted on this character.

There will be times when the memories are very raw and near the surface, and I recognize this may be very difficult for some readers when it parallels their own experience. Some books delve deeper than others, but the past events come into play in all four books.

There will also be a point when children are removed from a similar situation. Again, no details. I can't even go there myself.

I don't wish to blindside anyone. I hope perhaps the journey to recovery, very unique for the characters, will be worth the read.

THE FUTURE POSSIBLE SAGA

The Phoenix Rebellion Quartet

Book One: Revolution
Book Two: Outcasts
Book Three: Gaining Ground
Book Four: End Game

Phoenix Rising Quartet

Book One: Janus
Book Two: Triad
Book Three: Stasis
Book Four: Liber

THE FUTURE POSSIBLE SAGA STORYTELLING STYLE

The Future Possible Saga is a continuous timeline, in which any give book extends the story of the book prior to it and sets up for the next book while also telling its own story. The books must be read in order to have full understanding of the saga.

This means each book has its own story arc, but also extends the greater saga story arcs.

There will be cliffhangers, but as the author I will always provide you with a payoff within the book you're reading. Each book has its own plot, it's own storyline, and its own resolutions. Each book (with the exclusion of the final book in the saga) will have setup for the next book. These may or may not be considered cliffhangers by some. But, be aware, they exist.

The good news is the saga as told through The Phoenix Rebellion quartet and Phoenix Rising quartet is complete. You don't have to wait for a cliffhanger resolution. Just continue to the next book.

I hope you enjoy, and complete the journey with us.

*"Beauty, truth and rarity,
Grace in all simplicity,
Here enclosed in cinders lie."*

The Phoenix and the Turtle
~William Shakespeare

PROLOGUE

6 May 2052, Monday – Early Morning
Seattle, Washington

"I don't think I've ever been anywhere so beautiful," Lucy Santos said as she settled into the deep chair on her best friend's front porch, afghan wrapped around her shoulders and steaming cup of coffee in her hands. "Or so cold!"

Molly Tisdale laughed, tucking herself into her own blanket with her cup of tea. "It will warm up in a few weeks."

"I'm not complaining. I think I like it. Los Angeles is just so stifling in the summer and it's already hot. I don't want to go back tomorrow."

"Because of the weather?" Her lifelong friend tilted her head as a breeze came up from the bay, stirring her natural corkscrew curls. "I wasn't sure if you'd go back or decide to stay."

Lucy sighed, staring into her cup. "I need to go back and finish the term, then I'll have the summer to figure it out. All I know for sure is I *don't* know if I want to continue medical school or not."

"You know you are welcome here. It's why we got the house with the extra bedrooms. One for Mama, and one for you." Molly winked and took a sip of her coffee. "Have you talked to Ethan?"

Lucy sighed and rolled her head back to rest on the high back of the porch chair. "Yes, but . . . he doesn't have anything to do with this. Even if I went back, we both know we're not a couple anymore. Friends, but not a couple. No hard feelings."

The front door to the little house on Molly's other side came open with a loud squeak of the hinges, and Molly's husband Trevor joined them. Unlike the women who were bundled with coffee mugs, he carried a travel cup in one hand and his briefcase in the other.

"Hey, Rev," Lucy joked, grinning wide at her best friend's husband.

Trevor smiled back but didn't react to the ongoing joke. He wasn't a reverend, had no intention of being a minister of any kind – especially since churches and most organized denominations of faith weren't really a thing anymore – but he was a religious scholar and that was about as close as they were likely to get anymore. Abuela Gabi died refusing to accept her faith was obsolete just because the Areth and most of the world in general, said so.

He leaned over and kissed Molly, and she rubbed his new fade and short curl cut he'd gotten over the weekend. She wrinkled up her nose and whispered "sexy" before he stood again.

"Did I hear you ladies discussing an extended stay with us, Lucy?"

"Discussing, but not deciding." Lucy shook her head, no closer to a decision than she'd been when she'd left Los Angeles ten days earlier. She was infinitely thankful for Trevor and Molly and Mama Della, who welcomed her just as Molly and Mama Della had Lucy's entire life. "I'm finishing the term, but Molly says the offer of the bedroom still stands for the summer."

"Of course it does. The summer and beyond. Our home is open to you." He looked to Molly. "I thought I would pick up dinner on the way home, so you and Lucy have more time to—"

An alarm blared from inside the house, making all three jump.

"That's not the fire alarm," Molly said, unfolding herself from the chair. "What is it?"

"I think it's the emergency broadcast system," Trevor answered, holding the door open as Molly and Lucy hurried inside. "I haven't heard it engaged in years."

The three made it to the sitting room as the wall mounted monitor lit up on its own accord to the live image of a podium bearing the Seal of the World President. It was the press room of the White House in Washington, one of the many seats of power since 2017 when the nations of the world combined under one authority. Lucy's heart took up a sudden staccato and she sank into one of the chairs while the Tisdales sat on the couch. Nothing good could come of President Hargrave initiating the EBS like this. Nothing good.

The Chairman of the New World Congress gave a brief introduction, explaining that President Hargrave would be speaking on camera only, and would not answer any questions from the press. When the president stepped to the podium, he looked drained and anxious, deep frown lines bracketing his mouth and dark shadows beneath his eyes. He looked like he'd aged a decade overnight.

President Hargrave cleared his throat and braced his hands on the sides of the podium as he leaned into it. "Citizens of Earth, I speak to you today with a heavy heart and an angry soul. I have battled with myself for the last several days, trying to find some way to say what I need to say. I've concluded there is no good way, no way to ease the shock."

He raised his head and looked into the camera, and into the homes of billions of people around the globe.

"Should I get Mama up?" Molly said in a low, strained voice.

"I doubt this is good news. Let her sleep, in peace, while she can," Trevor answered. "She'll know soon enough."

"We have been lied to for the last forty-four years," President Hargrave said over them. "We were all so eager to embrace the possibilities of health, peace, and immortality that we willingly devoured the lies and turned our backs on what should have been obvious to us all.

"We are all to blame, but as leader of our world, I shoulder the responsibility and swear to you I will find a way to rectify the wrong done."

"Trevor . . ." Molly whispered, and in Lucy's peripheral she saw her friends grip their hands.

She wished she had someone to hold her hand because she felt ill.

President Hargrave straightened, squaring his shoulders.

"Irrefutable proof has been brought to my attention that the Areth, with whom we have shared our world and our lives for four decades, have been using our people in the most atrocious and sickening fashion. They have imprisoned men and women and have spawned children for the sole purpose of experimentation. They seek not a harmonious existence with Humans. They intend to use us to advance themselves, and when they are through, I have no doubt that all Humans would become expendable."

"*Dios Mio,*" Lucy gasped.

"All alliances with the Areth are hereby null and void. I reject all negotiations and cooperative institutions. I call upon all Humans to rally together and present a solid front to our enemy. We will once again return to the convictions of our forefathers. We will stand together. Strong against a common enemy!" He slammed his fist on the podium, his face blotched red. "Our numbers are many, their numbers few. We hold the power. We will rid our planet of their kind and return them to the stars from whence they came!"

President Hargrave paused, running his hand over his sweat-glistened upper lip. "Stay strong, People of Earth, and show no fear. We will prevail."

The screen went black, only to moments later be replaced with a message for all citizens to stand by for further information, advising people to stay in their homes unless it was necessary to leave.

"What does this mean?" Molly asked.

"I fear nothing good."

The weight of Trevor's voice sank into the stillness of the room.

Within half an hour, the message on the screen switched to media coverage and Trevor switched the monitor to a global news outlet. The anchors clearly struggled to gather information and report it without looking as frazzled as the three of them – and likely the world – felt. They barely moved, the thought of food or drink completely gone.

The Areth had been part of life and society for decades. Lucy, Molly, Trevor, and everyone in their generation had been born into their presence. Abuela Gabi told Lucy the stories of when the Areth had first arrived in 2008, making contact with every global superpower simultaneously. Just over a decade later, their presence was common and accepted. Depending on who detailed the history, some said the coming together of every nation on the planet to one central government had been miraculous and possibly the only way Earth would have been saved from itself; others said that after the wars and threatened wars of the previous centuries such a coming together was nothing less than suspect.

But what did it all mean now?

They watched for two hours. Eventually, Mama Della came from her bedroom with a smile until she saw their expressions. After a very quick rundown, Mama Della joined them in silence to watch the news. When Lucy's bladder could no longer allow her to sit staring at the monitor, Lucy unfolded herself from the chair and mumbled an "excuse me" to leave the room. She was halfway through the kitchen again, heading back to the living room, when Molly's scream made her freeze . . . then run.

"What? What happened?"

Molly had curled herself into a ball, crying, with Trevor holding her while simultaneously holding his mother-in-law's hand. He raised his head, his own cheeks streaked and looked to the monitor, and Lucy followed his gaze. She couldn't breathe.

"Reports are coming from all over the globe," the anchorwoman said with a trembling voice and wide eyes, her black makeup smudging beneath her eyes. "Washington is gone. New York. Geneva. London. Los Angeles. They have been destroyed."

CHAPTER ONE

4 August 2054, Wednesday
Protectorate Agricultural Cooperative Community
Bogota, Former Republic of Colombia
South American Continent

"Any time now, Forte!"

Pulse rifle blasts buzzed past David Forte's head to hit the stone and mortar wall behind him, and he ducked to avoid the flying debris, trying to continue his rapid typing. The windows had been blown out of the computer mainframe building an hour before, and little stood between him and a well-aimed—or damn lucky—shot.

No pressure. Right?

"I'm giving her all she's got, Captain," he shouted back to the newly promoted Colonel Connor Montgomery, doing his best Scotsman accent.

Despite the hellfire raining down on them from Xeno forces attempting to take over the compound, David chuckled at his own Montgomery Scott/Connor Montgomery joke. Too bad its brilliance was lost on his "hundred years behind the times" friend. He had a passing thought that Nick Tanner would have totally gotten the joke.

Connor shot him a confused, fuming glare before pivoting up and around to return fire through the broken window. *"Tu me gonfles*, Forte. Just do it!"

"Yelling at me isn't going to get me to work any faster!" David yelled back. He looked at Connor around the edge of the interface monitor, pointing a dusty finger. "And don't think I don't know what you said, Montgomery. I may not have taken French in high school, but Lorraine DuBois taught me all the good stuff. And some French, too."

Connor opened his mouth to come back with something, but the wall over his head exploded in a shower of dust when another blast hit home. Firebirds fought off invading Xeno forces all along the outskirts of the farming community, and the air reverberated with the battle. The ion residue left a metallic taste in his mouth. David punched in the last three keystrokes with hard jabs, because despite his arguments he was just as eager to get out of Dodge as Connor. Colombia was damn hot in August.

And humid.

And *hot*.

The power generator in the center of the bunker hummed to life with a crackle. The air came alive with an electronic vibration that made the hair on his arms stand up, and he pivoted on the balls of his feet to look through the back observation window—still intact since it was on the opposite side of the building from the battle—toward the center of the compound a mile away.

"Shields up in five . . . four . . . three . . . two . . ."

An iridescent beam shot straight up into the sky. Once it arced and came down again, meeting with the anchor units around the verge, the dome was invisible. Only those with knowledge of its existence and wearing the perimeter sensors would be aware, and those who chose to ignore the warnings would soon learn to pay attention to all posted signs. He'd designed the shield to emit a low-level hum and buffer to deter animals from inadvertently passing through it, along with any wanderers of the two-legged variety if they paid attention.

David pushed up to stand, the hydraulics in his body prosthetics hissing with the action. For once he was thankful for the support, his leg muscles twitching with the effort of maintaining his crouch. Tonight might be an extra dose of pain suppressant kind of night.

They couldn't see the outer edges coming down to meet the conductors, the contact points well beyond the mainframe bunker, but the screams of the Xenos standing in the wrong place at the wrong time echoed back to them through the thick foliage, muffled and mixed with the crack and thud of vegetation caught in the surge. Part of him winced at the painful way they either died or were left maimed, but a bigger part was thankful there would be a few less of the enemy to deal with. Besides, he doubted any of them mourned the lives they'd taken, today or any day previous.

The sound of weapons fire died down significantly as the Xenos inside the now-powered-up dome tried to keep fighting, some probably turning to run, only to come face-to-face with the invincible force field. With the dome activated, David took his service weapon from his thigh holster and pushed the capacity of his lower body prosthetics by crouch-crawling across the space to join Connor in returning fire against the few stubborn Xenos who kept up the attack. Within moments, the exchange of weapons fire died considerably, and the earpiece tucked into David's ear canal clicked once before Major Colton-Henry's voice came through on the open channel.

"Hostiles have been neutralized, Colonel. All clear on the east perimeter."

Connor brought his hand to his ear to open communications from his end. "Affirmative, Hank. All sections report."

"Clear on the west perimeter," came a second voice. He knew the face the voice belonged to but didn't know her name. A petite thing no bigger than a sneeze but could lay out any man three times her size. He'd seen her do it, and frankly, she scared him a little. Probably why he'd blocked out her name.

"Acknowledged, Vasquez. Stahl, report."

The familiar click accompanied a final weapon blast and a string of explicative-laced shouting a mix of English and what David thought might be Russian, or at least some Slavic language as hard but lyrical as Russian. "All the Xeno bastards have been neutralized. North perimeter is secure, sir."

"Roger." Connor stood, tapped the ear canal bud to close the two-way communication. He shifted the harness holding his long-range pulse gun so the gun hung along his side and used his forearm to swipe the sweat off his forehead, leaving a dirty streak. "We can probably get this wrapped up in the next couple of hours and head back to Alexandria. Weather reports say a storm may be brewing in the gulf; if we can get out of Baranquilla by dusk we can probably land jump from here to southern Florida and beat the storm system. If we don't, we'll have to stick to land and that'll add a day."

Montgomery delivered the plan with a deadpan expression, which said more than any smirk. The jerk. David wasn't sure if Connor was trying to provoke him because he knew David was less than thrilled with over-water travel in the high-speed military transport hovers, or if he jabbed at David about possibly missing his son Phin's wedding on Saturday if they didn't make it out and had to take the long way.

David slid his weapon into his thigh holster and used the wall as an anchor to push himself upright on his feet, his body protesting loudly despite the prosthetics. "Like you'd give a damn if we missed it," David poked back with a single chuckle. "You and Evie got married less than a week after—"

He stopped short when Connor's smirk dropped and he held up a finger to quiet David. He tapped the earpiece again. "Tambour, report."

A cold twist knotted David's gut when the same realization hit him that had clearly dawned on the unit's commander. Captain Sabrina Tambour—a new transfer to the Firebirds, and Captain Colton-Henry's fiancé—hadn't reported in. In the three days of skirmishes and all out offensives from the Xenos on the compound, they'd had only two Firebird injuries, one serious but neither life threatening.

Connor angled his head. "Tambour, report," he said louder.

"Sabrina!" shouted Colton-Henry, his desperate voice tearing through the commlink. "Sabrina!"

David and Connor turned together, likely sharing the same thought as they ran for the door, Connor easily outdistancing David when the hydraulics gave him the ability to run, but not much faster than a jog. They both were out of the building and headed for the south perimeter at a diagonal from their location when the line clicked again, followed by a nerve-scraping sound like someone scratching nails across a microphone.

"I'm here," came Tambour's ragged voice, weakened by heavy breathing. "Sorry, sir."

"Jesus . . ." Colton-Henry whispered in all their ears, and David had no doubt the word was far more a benediction than a curse.

Connor stopped running, and David caught up in time for Connor to hunch forward with his hands on his knees, huffing out a breath. Much like Hank, David figured it was more about relief than anything else.

"What is your situation?" Connor demanded.

"The hostiles had gotten a hundred yards inside the dome line before the shield engaged," she explained, still breathing hard. She paused, huffed, and ended with a chuckle. "It turned into pretty much hand-to-hand, but we've subdued them, sir."

David set his hands at his hips and shook his head, grinning when Connor's shoulders shifted with a quiet laugh. Captain Sabrina Tambour was a force to be reckoned with, and David wasn't sure if he should think Hank lucky or be afraid for the man.

"Any injuries?" Connor asked.

"Nothing keeping us from walking back to base, sir. Can't say the same for the Xenos."

"Understood," Connor said, rolling his head before looking toward the center of the compound. "Everyone head to base and we'll sort it out from there." He closed the link again and brought his hand down on David's shoulder. "Guess we might make it to the wedding after all, old man."

"Who you calling old man?" David growled back as they changed directions back to the center of the complex where they had told the civilians to gather. Safest place considering the situation.

"*You.* Aren't you something like eighty *technically*?"

"*Ferme la bouche,* Montgomery."

Connor barked a laugh.

7 August 2054, Friday
Alexandria Hospital – Private Nursery
United Earth Protectorate, Capitol City
Alexandria, Seat of Virginia
North American Continent

"*A*re they at risk?" Michael struggled to keep his tone level, to hide the worry stirring in his chest, but knew disguising it failed to prevent his wife from knowing his concern when she slid her hand into his and squeezed gently. She stepped closer, the firm curve of her stomach pressing against his arm. Victor set down his PAC tablet and pushed his hands into his pockets, adopting a relaxed stance. Michael appreciated his friend's effort, but wanted the answer, even if it was frightening.

"We've been monitoring them carefully the last five weeks, and there have been some minor scares, but I've seen a steady decline in their overall bio readings in the last twenty-four hours. Nothing to imply an immediate danger, but if this decline continues as it is, I will recommend we act."

"Jacqueline has another two weeks before her due date."

Victor was nodding before Michael finished. "True, but Michael, you know—and I know you've expressed to Jackie—the last three weeks or so of a pregnancy are for the sole purpose of growth. Baby Tanner shows all signs of doing just that. If you still wish to do as we've discussed and have us remove the infants from their artificial wombs to coincide with the natural birth of the baby Jackie carries, we may need to act on Jackie rather than wait for natural labor to commence and then act on the other children."

"I would like to see—"

Victor held up his hand, halting Michael's request. "You agreed to remove yourself from the daily process of their care. I am holding you to it. You are their father, and it's best if you allow me to do this."

Michael inhaled deeply and looked past his lifelong friend to the three gestational stasis containers holding the floating bodies of their children. Neither he nor Jacqueline had a say in their creation—another spiteful act by the woman who laid claim to his maternity, and yet, he considered their existence a gift like none he would have possibly ever imagined—but watching them made his heart squeeze. He stepped around his friend, drawing Jacqueline with him until they stood close enough to lay their hands on the thick glass of the first tube.

Victor had taken precautions, by their request, to shield the gender of each of the children from the pediatric medical staff who took shifts in the special, secure "nursery" by making the tubes opaque from mid-chest down on each baby. Only the trusted few who would attend their "birth" would know the sex of the three, just as only Jacqueline's attending physician and nurse, Jacqueline, and Michael would know the gender of the baby born of her body. In their hearts, there was no difference between their children separate from her and their child within her, and while Michael had no doubt those closest to them would feel the same, he and his wife wanted it this way. Even they didn't know the gender of the baby Jacqueline carried.

"What should we do?" Jacqueline asked, her voice low enough to stay between them.

Michael released her hand so he could wrap his arm around her shoulder and draw her to his side, kissing her black hair. "We don't need to do anything today," he told her, looking down at her when she tipped back her chin.

"But we will."

"Not today," Victor reiterated from behind them, walking across the nursery. "This weekend is a busy one with the final relocation back to the presidential residence, then Phin and Katrina's wedding. Unless something drastic happens—which I don't think it will—we proceed as we are and talk again in another week."

"You're sure?" Jacqueline asked. Her question might have seemed meant for Victor, but it was Michael she looked to.

"I agree with Victor," he told her, allowing his tone to soften. His mind, his knowledge told him his friend was right, and he could hold on to that understanding if it helped ease Jacqueline's fears. His heart had other plans.

She didn't say anything, her dark eyes fixed on him. Then her shoulders relaxed and she nodded.

"Go get some rest," Victor advised, his hand on Michael's shoulder as he focused on Jacqueline. "Now. While you can," he finished with a nod and wide grin. "Beverly and I will see you tonight."

Office of the President
Robert J. Castleton Memorial Building – The Castle
Center for United Protectorate Government
United Earth Protectorate, Capitol City
Alexandria, Seat of Virginia
North American Continent

"How many were lost?" President Tanner asked.

John Smith XXXIV, Areth Ambassador to Earth, sat hunched forward on the edge of a couch cushion with his head down, his hands together, and his heart heavy. The weight in President Nicholas Tanner's voice matched the weight in his chest. He closed his eyes, trying to hold at bay the colliding storm of emotions in the room. His own heartbreak for his kinsmen collided with fear, concern, and speculation from the others. Nick Tanner had no idea how fiercely he projected his emotions, and even if John were able to block out the bombardment, Nick's would make it through.

"Over seven-thousand Defense Alliance forces, including several hundred of the Areth Royal Battalion, our equivalent to your Firebirds. The Urdo Khantan attacked in the small hours of the mornin' and killed the entire civilian population of two outposts on the planet before the Defense Alliance forces could defend the population. The indigenous people of Abednego are not ones to seek war, which is why the Defense Alliance was there to protect them."

"There is no question these were the Urdo Khantan," stated Vice President Beverly Surimoto, her softened tone clearly a statement and not a question.

"None," John answered, jerking his head in a curt confirmation. "They're no' exactly easy to confuse with other races. The Defense Alliance captured a dozen before haltin' the attack with aggressive prejudice."

"Your ambassador-speak for the Defense Alliance blew them out of the sky?" Nick asked, the slightest yank at the corner of his mouth the only sign of his strained humor. "What have the prisoners given us?"

"Nothin'," John said on a hard sigh, pushing himself up from the cushion to stand so he could pace to the mantel where Jenifer stood.

She didn't reach for him, and he didn't reach for her, as much as he wanted to, but the way her gaze followed him was as reassuring as her touch. Her concern wrapped around him as tactile as Nick's outrage.

"The Urdo Khantan pride themselves on their brutality and their endurance under interrogation. They also have a strict code regardin' capture." He reached the dormant fireplace and turned his back on it, pushing his hands into his pockets. "Only two still survive. The others took their own lives through a rather imaginative array of means. One of the remaining two is no' far from death, and the other is under strict watch to thwart any attempts."

"There is no question they acted under orders from the Sorracchi," Colonel Connor Montgomery said from his post near the door. He had made it back to Alexandria very late the night before, along with David Forte and the Firebirds who had accompanied them to Colombia.

"Again, none," John confirmed. "All intelligence the Defense Alliance has gathered in the last few months indicates the only employer the Urdo Khantan currently report to is the Sorrs. This is preparation. I think what your military like to call a warnin' shot."

Nick stood from where he leaned on the edge of his desk and walked, head bowed and hands in pockets, to the double glass door looking out on the property behind the executive building.

Apprehension radiated from him. Beverly turned where she sat on the couch opposite from where John had been, watching Nick. When most attention was away from him, Jenifer stepped close enough to curl her hand around his wrist and he caught it, lacing his fingers through hers. He looked to her, not attempting a smile because it would have been a lie and useless with Jenifer. Beyond reading his face, she felt his heart as much as he felt hers, and it ached as much as his own.

Tomorrow would bring joy, but today was filled with heartache.

She released his hand and put her back to the mantel, standing beside him when Nick turned back, deep lines digging into his brow. "When?" was his only question.

"Soon. That's all we know. They've been preparin' for months, and these outpost attacks are essentially reconnaissance missions. It's been nearly four of your centuries since the Urdo Khantan dared challenge the Defense Alliance as a whole. They need to determine what they are up against, and it's a safe bet they believe if they can beat the Defense Alliance on our own grounds, they can wipe out any opposition they may have here."

"Because we aren't as advanced," Connor provided.

John nodded. "They seem to know Earth and the Defense Alliance are allies, but since Earth hasn't been officially brought into the Alliance, they may see you as vulnerable. There are no forces here. Your planetary defenses are limited in the wake of the war." He drew in a long breath through his nose, shaking his head as he expelled it. "A new war is comin', of tha' there is no doubt."

"Because the battles we're fighting here weren't enough of a challenge," Nick mumbled, referring to the skirmishes and attacks that took place at least twice a week all over the globe; Xenos and their followers protesting what they saw as alien involvement by killing their own people. "Seems our long-distance meeting with the Council in a couple weeks is more necessary than we thought." Nick snapped his attention to John. "Is that soon enough?"

"While I firmly believe the attack is forthcomin', it won't be in the immediate future. We likely have weeks, maybe even a few months, but no' longer than that."

Nick nodded and rubbed the fingers of his right hand over his mouth, his skin scratching over his late day beard. He was lost in thought for only a few moments before he visibly pulled himself from his musings. "Right. That's next week. *This* weekend, we've got things to celebrate." He clapped his hands together, rubbing his palms, and grinned when he looked to John and Jenifer. "Dinner at the residence tonight for the house re-warming. Everyone is welcome to stay for the wedding . . ." He stopped and looked toward John and Jenifer. "*Weddings* in the morning."

CHAPTER TWO

7 August 2054, Friday Evening
Presidential Residence
United Earth Protectorate, Capitol City
Alexandria, Seat of Virginia
North American Continent

The only indicator the large farmhouse that had been chosen as the residence of the World President and his family had been under assault a few months before was the lingering, faint smell of new paint and fresh cut wood. That mingled with the mouthwatering aromas of dinner was nearly enough to make David forget.

Little Nicole Tanner had been kidnapped from here, her whereabouts unknown for three months.

Nick Tanner had nearly died after being shot at point blank range.

And Gideon, a man David had learned only hours before was genetically his son—though the circumstances were beyond belief—was killed here protecting the little girl. Protecting all the children.

Through the hellish hours of that attack, David had been useless. Helpless. Unable to even stand, let alone come to anyone's aid.

He wasn't so deep in denial he didn't realize and accept that his invalidism that night had been the whispered voice pushing him hard in the weeks since, once the prosthetic robo-suit had been surgically applied to his body by the Areth doctor who claimed it would get him on his feet again. Most days that fact helped him ignore the constant ache in his muscles and joints that seeped into his bones.

From where he sat on one of the couches in the room, he focused on the laughter and conversation. If these people could move past it all and embrace the house again, he sure as hell should be able to. He wasn't going to live here, and if the whole of the Tanner clan could live here, then he could suck it up and deal.

Petite arms wrapped around his neck from beside him and Katrina Bauer kissed his cheek before resting her chin on his shoulder. "So, what do you prefer I call you, David? Dad? Papa? Pops?"

David chuckled and rubbed his palm over her freckled forearm. "Peanut, call me whatever you want as long as it's not old man."

She scoffed and came around the end of the couch to stand beside him, her delicate hand on his shoulder, her fingertips brushing over one of the prosthetic connections beneath his shirt. "I guess I won't know what to call you until after tomorrow."

David smiled and took her hand from his shoulder, ignoring the voice in his head calling him a vain idiot. Katrina had seen him at his worst, weaker than a newborn, and she had encouraged him every day since the first generation of the robo-suit had been applied. She had helped Doctor Olivia Cole with adapting the Areth computer language to the Earth computer operating systems, and knew every connection and circuit, better than he did and he knew them intimately. He squeezed her fingers and sighed, exaggerating so he could tease her.

"I guess if Old Man is what you settle on, I'll have to live with it."

She grinned, deep dimples popping in her cheeks, and kissed him again before leaving him to join Phin and Daniel. Anyone who didn't know them might wonder which brother she intended to marry, since they had created their own sort of triad since Gideon's death; it was almost always Phin, Katrina, and Daniel. But her heart, her love, belonged to Phin and tomorrow they would get married.

When David told Phin to not waste any time marrying her, the man took his advice to heart. Of course, David had still been in shock that Phin had reached out to him for counsel and advice, like a son would reach out to a father. There were moments when the whole concept still made his head hurt.

"How's the father of the groom doing?"

David looked to his right as President Tanner sank onto the couch beside him with a heavy sigh, handing David a bottle of beer. Considering the lack of liquor stores, David didn't know where the beers came from. Didn't care. So, before answering the question, David looked across the room of people again to Katrina and his "sons."

"Does what I am to him qualify as father of the groom?" David asked.

Nick snorted and took a long drink of his beer before answering. "Why? Because while you were in prolonged stasis your genetic material was harvested by a heinous bitch who created those boys to be the ultimate super soldiers?"

David laughed, shaking his head before he cleared his throat. "Not to put too fine a point on it, but yeah, I guess that's why."

"Hell, David, hardly anyone in this house right now has anything close to the *traditional* family, in any interpretation. The last hundred years or so included." He used the bottom of his beer bottle to sweep across the span of the room. "Probably *especially* the people in this house." He pointed toward Michael, who spoke with Ambassador Smith, Michael's very pregnant wife Jacqueline beside him. "The same heinous bitch deceived me into thinking she was just as human as I was and hid Michael from me for over twenty-five years. I'm still his father."

"Yeah, of course you—"

Nick ignored his agreement. "Michael and Jackie are going to have not just that one baby in the next couple of weeks, but three more created in artificial wombs in a lab by the *same* heinous bitch. How's *that* for not your traditional family." With each added point, Nick leaned toward David another degree, eyebrows arched. Then he chuckled. "I bet the fact we're all here having a party pisses her off. I *hope* it pisses her off."

"I'm happy with anything that might piss her off."

Nick nodded and said, "Aren't we all," then craned his neck to look around the room. He pointed, and David followed the direction to see Connor and Evie, with young Adrian asleep on Connor's shoulder with his thumb in his mouth. He was about a year and a half old and had lived with his grandfather only until a couple months earlier when Connor had found them. Now Connor was his father, with no "step" involved.

"She screwed up again when she stole Evie from her family, figuring new face and all. She even failed at that. She never expected the power of a mother's love, and now Evie works with the Child Rescue and Placement Agency using the information Jenifer *persuades* out of dirtbags to find kids. Another score for the home team, I say."

David huffed. "Okay, I get your point."

"Do you? Okay, forget the bitch."

He pointed at Ambassador Smith with one finger, the others wrapped around the neck of his bottle. "John adopted a human child because the boy had no one else, and tomorrow he's marrying a human woman and the two of them are adopting four more orphans because . . ." Nick shrugged. "Because the kids need them. See?" He drank again. "We're all one big, happy, *bizarre is the new modern* family." Just before draining the bottle, he mumbled against the open mouth. "Wanna know what beats all that?"

David swallowed several refreshing gulps of beer before sighing and looking to the man. "What's that?"

"I'm fifty years old, with a brilliant, hot wife and a six-week-old son."

David barked a laugh loud enough that several other guests in the house turned to look at them, and President Tanner chuckled low in his chest. A moment later, the combined laughter only little girls are capable of preceded Nicole Tanner and Amari, her best friend and soon to be Smith child, into the family room. Both Nick and David had just enough time to get their bottles up and out of the way before the girls launched themselves onto the couch, Nicole scrambling into her grandfather's lap.

"Lumpy say dinner, Gumpa," she declared, brushing her blond hair out of her face.

Amari didn't say anything, which David had noticed seemed to be her nature, but tucked herself into the space between Nick and David. Without the slightest hesitation, the little girl laid her cheek on David's arm and smiled up at him. He smiled back. Tiny arms wrapped around his, and little fingers rubbed his skin, smoothing over some of the healed but still visible and raised scars left by early versions of his robo-suit. A tiny frown turned down her lips and she looked at his arm, rubbing the scar with more attention. Inches away, Nick and his granddaughter carried on a conversation as Nick shifted forward, Nicole in his arms, but David found himself captured by this little girl's concern. He'd heard Amari's story, as much as any of them could determine. Whoever her family might have been, they likely sold her to a man in New Orleans who dealt in juvenile skin trade, for lack of a less sickening choice of words. How Jenifer Whatever Her Last Name Is connected to the man, David didn't know and got the impression he probably never would, but it didn't matter. Not to him. She had brought Amari back to Alexandria, along with her older "sister" Alexis, older "brother" Simon, and baby "brother" Toby. She was preschool age, far too young to have experienced what she had gone through, but despite it, the child was gentle and sweet . . . and had the power to hold him rapt without a word.

So, when she did speak, he couldn't help but tell her the truth.

"Do you boos hurt?" she asked, her voice as tiny as she.

David shook his head. "They happened a long time ago."

"Did you mama kiss dem?"

He had to press his lips together and swallow before his throat would work. "No, sweetheart. My mama isn't here."

Amari looked away, across the room, and back to him. "You need my mama to kiss dem?

The idea of making rough, tough, kickass Jenifer kiss his booboos because Amari asked her to was almost enough to make him say yes. Almost. But he feared the usually silent woman far more than he would enjoy the amusement. He chuckled and used the hand not held in place by the tiny girl to smooth her fine hair.

"You want me kiss dem for you?"

She asked with such innocence, such purity, it squeezed his chest and he could only nod. Without hesitation, Amari placed a loud kiss on the scar she'd been caressing so carefully. Then, apparently satisfied with the form of first aid, scrambled off the couch to follow Nicole. Nick waited for David to stand when First Lady Caitlin Tanner called for her husband from the dining room on the other side of the hall. Nick liked a full house. Even without dinner guests, the family living in the official residence consisted of Nick, his wife Caitlin, and their infant son Adam. Then Michael, Jacqueline, and Nicole. And as Nick had pointed out, they had another four arriving any day. The thought of it made David shudder. One at a time had been hard enough when he and Kelly had their boys just a few years apart.

Tonight, Nick had worked hard to fill the house, every chair at the table filled as they gathered in the dining room. David had come with Phin, Katrina, Daniel, and in an unusual turn Karl had come along. Karl Bauer usually stayed home, but Daniel had encouraged him to come along. Connor and his new wife Evie and her son Adrian, whom Connor had adopted, as much as the process existed in this chewed up and spit out world. The Smiths—the fact a man from a planet lightyears away would be named Smith was still hard for David to wrap his brain around—were two additional adults and their five adopted children.

He had to stop using that word. *Adopted.* Clearly, no one here wanted to use or reference the word. Their children were their children, and that was amazing.

Vice President Beverly Surimoto and her husband Victor were the last to fill the table, and were it not for the mix of faces, names, even races David would feel like he was back home for Thanksgiving.

"Potatoes, David?"

He almost laughed at the well-timed question and reached across the table to take the bowl of mashed spuds from Evelyn. "Yes, ma'am. Thank you."

8 August 2054, Saturday Morning
Presidential Residence
United Earth Protectorate, Capitol City
Alexandria, Seat of Virginia
North American Continent

"Jenifer, as the proxy ecclesiastic for your wedding to John, I feel compelled to ask you if you understand the significance of an Areth marriage," Jace Quinn asked in a whisper, after drawing Jenifer to the double door of Nick's office that looked on the backyard. "This may very well be the first documented marriage on Earth soil between a Human and an Areth, and you're committing to him under Areth law."

Jenifer shifted Toby on her hip and glanced back to the gathering of people in the president's office. John stood with Michael, and Michael held Jacqueline's hand. Other than the children, the only other people to be present were Nick and Caitlin Tanner. Normally, a child like Nicole not directly involved with the process wouldn't be present, but they had decided she would be good company for Amari.

"I'm good," she said, looking back at Jace. The serious dig between his eyes made her pause. "I mean it. I'm good."

Jace drew in a long, deep breath and some of the tension in his features eased as he released it. "Okay, I needed to ask."

Jenifer nodded and followed Jace back across the room. There would be no one else here to witness the proceedings that would make her John Smith's wife. The idea still made her stagger sometimes because of the sheer ridiculousness of it; the ridiculousness that someone would wish to be tied to her forever, and the ridiculousness that she actually agreed. That she would embrace the idea of raising five orphans with an alien man. An *alien* man.

John turned his head and met her gaze, and a slow smile tugged at one corner of his mouth.

The good reverend warnin' you of my nefarious intentions?

His voice was as tangible and calming in her mind as if he had spoken in her ear. Jenifer purposefully suppressed her smile and arched a single brow.

He's very convincing.

John's booming laugh made Toby giggle in her arms. As soon as they were close, Toby leaned away from her, trying to wiggle free from her hold to reach for his father. *His father.* When did the idea of family, of children, of a lifetime with someone become so easy to accept?

Once she accepted she loved him, the rest fell naturally into place.

I would hope you love me, too.

Don't get cocky, Ambassador.

John took Toby from her, kissing the boy's cheek. "You ready?" he asked the boy, but Toby already had his head on John's shoulder.

Likely he'd be asleep in five minutes. The little boy had a lot of healing yet to do, which meant a lot of eating and a lot of sleeping. Unfortunately, he seemed to prefer his sleeping during the day, and his eating equally day or night. While Jenifer had been programmed since she was Alexis' age to function on minimal sleep, she'd always been the dictator of when and how long. It was a challenge to have a fifteen-pound bundle of affection dictate those hours.

It was hard to be annoyed when he rested his cheek on her chest and let out a long sigh before drifting off, or when she found herself staring at Ambassador John Smith—warrior for his queen, and diplomat for his people—trapped in a chair because Toby had drifted off at an inopportune time.

With the hand not supporting Toby, John laced his fingers through hers and stepped closer. He waited until she shifted her gaze and looked him in the eyes. With their hands joined, he circled them behind her back and drew her against him. Instinct made her look toward the others in the room, conditioned to hide what she and John were to each other. It was safer that way. But the fact they were here to witness their covenant—what the Areth preferred over the word marriage—the proverbial cat was out of the bag.

Thank you.

She snapped her attention back to John, the weight of his unspoken words wrapping around the base of her skull to shimmer down her spine. *For what?*

For blessing me.

Before she could even form the thought to ask what he meant, John pressed his lips to her cheek. Jace Quinn made a show of clearing his throat, and John lingered a moment longer before moving away enough they could step together toward Nick's desk. Jace had laid out the documents that had arrived aboard the *Steppenschraff,* a Defense Alliance ship that had once carried her and John to Aretu, and now brought back from Aretu the contract that would make them a family.

Jace cleared his throat and took his place in front of the desk, facing all of them, with his feet set shoulder-width apart and his hands tucked behind his back. Despite the title *reverend*, his military training was showing. "I've had the pleasure of performing dozens of weddings since the war, including two couples in this room. It seems fitting that you, Nick and Caitlin, and you, Michael and Jacqueline, should stand as witnesses for the covenant of John and Jenifer."

He turned and picked up the first page of the covenant contract, as John had called it, and held it up. The writing was elegant, the paper a heavy parchment that rustled with age. John had also explained all covenant contracts were composed by hand on paper that was no less than three hundred years old. While artisans produced more parchment on Aretu each year, it could not be touched for this purpose for three centuries.

Jace wanted to know if she understood the significance. She understood it so well it had kept her up at night.

"In contrast to the marriage ceremonies we're familiar with, much like we'll celebrate later today, the joining of a family is solemn and small so one can get on with the business of building a life together. That sentiment in particular I appreciate.

"Traditionally, the couple is supported by their closest family, specifically their parents. In the absence of parents, as is the case today, the couple may ask another married couple whom they respect to stand with them in their decision. Nick, you and Caitlin have agreed to stand in the place of John's family. Michael and Jackie, you stand for Jenifer."

Jace put the document back on the desk and shifted his stance to clasp his hands in front of him. "As the proxy ecclesiastic on Earth for this highly traditional and binding ceremony, my responsibility is to assure all parties involved understand the tenets of the commitment between John and Jenifer.

"For the sake of this covenant contract, both John and Jenifer are considered as bringing children into the marriage; however, at John and Jenifer's request no child is designated as belonging to either one of them, but rather both of them. Another sentiment I also appreciate." Jace smiled. "Could all the children come forward as I explain their part in this joining?" With a wink, he grinned at Toby, asleep on John's shoulder. "We'll let the little one sleep. I don't think he really cares."

Simon and Silas, who were almost immediately inseparable the moment they met, scrambled forward to stand in front of John, wide grins on their faces. They were just old enough to understand today was important but had admitted they didn't understand how it made John more their papa than before, or Jenifer more their mother. Both had instinctively accepted those roles from the beginning.

Nicole and Amari joined them, hand-in-hand, but Michael picked up Nicole. Toby was asleep, and that only left Alexis. The teenage girl stood near enough to hear them, but not near enough to include herself, arms crossed over her body, her expression guarded. Without giving the girl a chance to argue, Jenifer took the single sidestep needed to reach her and tugged her wrist free. Alexis said nothing, and when Jenifer held her hand, she didn't pull away, letting Jenifer lead her to the desk.

"In Areth tradition, there are no such designations as step-families, or adopted children. When a family joins in marriage, they are whole. Complete. In that tradition, John and Jenifer have named Alexis, Silas, Simon, Amari, and Toby as their children and from this day forward they shall bear the name Smith."

Alexis' grip on Jenifer's hand tightened, and the tumult of emotions rolling off the girl was enough to make Jenifer's throat uncharacteristically tighten.

Jace explained—perhaps more for the benefit of the Tanners in the room, than her and John—the designation of property being without separation, and no single child would claim heir. She had questioned John when he'd told her the property on Aretu would be theirs equally; if there was no division of heirs, why was the property John's alone when he had a brother. It was one of the rare situations where property allotment could be changed. Since his brother was the prince regent, married to Queen Bryony of Aretu, he willingly separated himself from the lineage and granted all claims to John.

And now John had given it to her and five wayward children.

She blinked and swallowed hard, looking to John.

Thank you.

He glanced toward her, a small smile on his thin lips. *For wha'?*

For blessing all of us.

CHAPTER THREE

"*Hava Nagila! Hava Nagila! Hava Nagila! Venis Mecha!*"

David didn't know any of the words past *"Hava Nagila,"* but it didn't keep him from singing them as loud as he could while he kicked his legs and side stepped with the people around him as they all stumbled through the hora dance. Singing didn't matter much after a couple verses because he was laughing too hard to care.

Inside the circle was a smaller circle of children, from the tiniest being Nicole Tanner and Amari Smith, to the teens who laughed as they led the children in a dance that looked closer to "Ring Around the Rosies" than the hora.

"Uri achem! Uri achem! Belev sameach!"

The music ended, but the laughing didn't. Fighting to catch his breath from probably the most intense cardio workout he'd had since waking up, David set his hands at his hips and took a moment. As the wedding guests moved away in various directions, David watched with a smile that made his jaw ache as Phin and Katrina embraced, laughing and smiling.

It was the laugh that made David watch.

Phin couldn't help his stoic nature; he and his brothers had been conditioned to suppress and deny all emotion or attachment. It had been Katrina's affection for Phin, Gideon, and Daniel that had first cracked the fortress of his indoctrination. David had worried when Gideon died that Phin and Daniel would lose all they'd gained to the pain of his death, but if anything, that devastation had allowed Phin to embrace his new life with even more determination. But . . . while David knew his son was happy, a smile was rare and never, *never* had he heard his son laugh.

Not until today.

It was a pure sound, lacking any self-consciousness or restraint. Booming and deep.

"Hell of a thing to hear, isn't it?"

David had to force himself to blink and turn away to look at Nick, but still smiled as the sound of laughter overpowered every other ambient party sound. "It's right up there with the first time you hear your baby laugh." David squinted his right eye and winced. "No, it's different."

"I get it." Nick nodded, glancing around the backyard until his attention settled. Without having to look, David knew Nick had spotted his son. "It was a hell of a powerful thing the first time I heard Michael laugh." Nick looked at him again, his smile crooked. "Hell of a thing."

"Yes, sir."

Katrina Bauer—now Katrina Forte—ran toward them, one hand holding up the skirt of her white lace dress, the other hand pulling her new husband behind her, an infectious smile making her glow. Two steps away she released Phin to launch herself at David, wrapping her arms around his neck with a squeal as he lifted her off the ground in a fierce hug. She said something, but she talked so fast, and her face was pressed to the side of his neck, that he didn't catch it all. Something about "wonderful" and "so happy" and "thank you."

The moment her little feet touched the ground, she did the same to Nick. "Thank you so much, sir. Today was perfect!"

If David wasn't mistaken, he was pretty sure the President of the World blushed at Katrina's praise. "Sure," he said, clearing his throat.

David had only known Phin for a matter of months, and hardly felt he had any influence on the young man's integrity or authenticity, but despite that, he embraced the swell of pride in his chest when Phin extended his hand to President Tanner. Nick took it in a hearty shake. Some of the reserve and control had returned to Phin, but not enough to remove the spark in his eyes or the uptick of a smile.

"Katrina is far more eloquent, but my emotions and sentiments are the same, sir," Phin said.

"Yeah, well." Nick squinted his eyes as he looked back at the large house. "The place needs some good energy." He shrugged and pushed his hands into his pockets. "The more the merrier."

With another squeal and a kiss to David's cheek, Katrina took Phin's hand again and they were off once more as the musicians Nick had managed to bring together—with the greater miracle of working instruments—began another song. David smiled and shook his head, crossing his arms over his chest, the hiss of his robo-suit hydraulics muffled by the jacket someone had managed to find in a size wide enough to accommodate his shoulders and the prosthetics. He was still amazed at what the president and his people had managed to pull off for the wedding.

The huppah had been decorated with flowers and a prayer shawl, the shawl a small miracle since as David understood it, the practice of many faiths had fallen out of favor in the decades since his "big sleep" had begun. All over the world, faiths of all types were once again finding their way into people's hearts, and while David had been raised Catholic, he hadn't ever considered himself religious, there was something comforting in that fact. They hadn't been able to find a rabbi to perform the ceremony, but Reverend Jace Quinn had spent weeks learning everything he needed to know to perform the Jewish ceremony.

All that, and the food was amazing. First Lady Caitlin Tanner had seen to the baking of several loaves of challah bread, and somehow they had even managed to find a few mismatched bottles of wine for the blessing. Katrina's parents were gone, and it had been just her and her brother Karl for a long time, by what David understood. But every person here had embraced her like she was their sister, their cousin, their niece . . . and had done the same for Phin.

"You mind if I borrow you for a few minutes?"

Nick's question pulled David from his thoughts. "Of course not."

Nick canted his head toward the house, then led the way to the back porch. Probably more because he was aware the processing unit was there than hearing the low hum, David glanced toward the command box to the left of the backdoor. The backyard looked like any other backyard in any other Virginia suburb with a fence lining the property, a good acre and a half of grass and gardens and a simple swing set and sandbox for the kids. That was the point. Nick hadn't wanted the needed security to take away from his family. David had helped develop the invisible force field they'd designed for the residence, and he now deployed the same system on a larger scale at various bases and communities to protect citizens from Xeno attack.

Nick led the way into the house, then through the kitchen and to his office at the back of the house. Tingles of awareness—of what, David wasn't exactly sure—danced up the back of his neck. He followed Nick and waited in silence while the president leaned on the edge of his desk.

"Is there a problem, sir?"

Nick's head snapped up like he'd been lost in thought. "What? No. No problem. Just . . ." He tilted his head, studying David. "It hasn't exactly been easy for you, has it."

It wasn't a question.

David pulled in a deep breath, and let it out with a huff, looking past Nick to the windows that gave him a view of the backyard. The sun was setting, but in a few minutes the exterior yard lights would turn on and the party would continue. "Honestly, there are these random and quick moments when I forget just how messed up this whole thing is, Nick." He shook his head. "But then I really pause and think about it, and I wonder if I'm not still stuck in some twisted delusion."

"You're a huge asset to me. To us."

David shrugged and looked to Nick. "It's the least I can do. I don't have a whole hell of a lot to offer, but the most bizarre thing to me is that even though it's been decades, the core of a computer is still the same. And given enough time, I can make it do whatever I want. Even this new hybrid system you work on."

Nick chuckled and stood from where he leaned. He reached behind him to a PAC tablet on the desk, activating it as he walked toward David. By the time he reached David, several photos in a grid filled the screen. David took the tablet and glanced over the photos. A quick interpretation of the photos said he was looking at a community like the one he and Connor had been at in Bogota, except wherever this was it was less jungle in nature and more rural America.

The rural America he remembered.

He had to remind himself again that *America* no longer existed; not in any way he remembered.

The aerial photos spanned several hundred acres with the main settlement in the middle. There were three large, meandering farmhouses with juts and additions and attached barn structures, spaced far enough apart he figured they were probably once neighbors but were now part of a single group. All structures seemed to circle around a central farmhouse without attached outbuildings situated central to all, equidistant from the outer structures. It was an age-old means of protecting the center of government, or whatever, to place it in the middle to make it harder to overtake. Within the common space between the homes were large gardens and paddocks. From the altitude of whatever drone might have taken the photos it was difficult to tell what type of small livestock they held, but in other paddocks he recognized horses and some cattle.

In the perimeter connecting the houses were the small, semi-permanent looking structures that could have been conceptual bunkhouses. There were also a dozen Protectorate provided white shelters designed to house supplies or personnel and looked more like yurts than tents, some so large they could house several families. He'd helped Connor set up several at various locations over the last few weeks. They weren't fancy, but they provided needed shelter, privacy when warranted, and both heat and climate control depending on the location. There were clusters of what appeared to be repurposed RVs of various sizes, which made so much sense he wondered why someone else hadn't thought of it. They were designed to be all-inclusive homes. From the altitude of the images, it was impossible to determine the possible ages, but if they worked, they worked.

He tapped on the first picture and swiped through them. There were a couple burned out, half-collapsed shells of houses on the outskirts of the community, so wherever it was, it hadn't fully escaped destruction. Either from the war, or from more recent attacks. Sections of forest and land showed signs of fire and damage.

"Is this where I'm headed next?" he asked, raising his head. "Do we have a military presence there to cause Xeno issues?"

"Any community, camp, or cluster of people not under Xeno control has Xeno issues," Nick said, the sneer at his lip leaking into his tone. Xenos were the thorn in President Tanner's side. Mostly because their warped thinking made no sense.

But that was the way of zealots and terrorists. Always had been.

"They named their community Unity Valley. This is up north and west of here. Vancouver, British Columbia. Former country of Canada." He said the last with a tinge of sarcasm. "If you're up to it, I'd like to send you out that way later this week."

"Absolutely, sir. Whatever you need. But I thought the next planned outpost visit was overseas."

"A couple developments in the last few days have shifted our focus. Terra Force has secured the settlement in Stuttgart, and we've shut down the Xeno cells in the area. But we haven't located the base of the cell in Vancouver, and the settlement is being raided every few days. Crops burned. People hurt. Half a dozen killed. We have Terra Force there, but the area of coverage would do better with one of your domes."

David nodded, continuing to scroll through the photos. "Do you have a topographical map? I can start planning a layout before I leave. When do we go?"

"Probably Friday, but David, there's another reason I'm sending *you* to this one."

David stopped his study of the pictures and focused on the president. "Okay."

Nick took back the tablet, and after a few taps and swipes, handed the tablet back to him with an odd, snorted chuckle. "I was on the other side of this kind of conversation a few years back. Not any easier on this side. Not so much the subject, but the delivery."

David scowled at Nick's cryptic statement and looked down again at the screen. The photo was of a man David put in his fifties, with hair more white than the hints of brown laced through it, and an eye patch over his right eye, the edges of a scar sliding from beneath the patch down his cheek. His right arm ended above the elbow. He was seated on a tree stump, and despite the damage his body had survived, his smile was wide and genuine. If David had to guess, the smile was because of the kindergarten-aged boy sitting at the man's feet, playing with a large golden lab. Something curled in David's chest, like smoke from a campfire, spreading into his limbs. His pulse was suddenly so strong it made his vision swim, but he still stared. Familiarity . . .

Not that he knew this man. He couldn't know this man. He mentally ran the math. Whoever this was, he couldn't have been more than ten years old when David was captured.

Dear God . . .

Nick's firm hand on David's shoulder made him jump and suck in a breath. He'd stopped breathing. Stopped blinking. Eyes burning, he forced his chin up so he could look at Nick.

A tingle touched the base of his skull, fanning down his spine and along the top of his head. It wasn't chills; it came from the inside. Then another. Simultaneous touches in his mind, but he was too dizzy from the thoughts slamming around in his head like a tsunami to focus on whether he was on the edge of a full-blown aneurysm.

"Would it help if I said it?"

David nodded. In his head, he was screaming but he couldn't get his throat to work. He felt as trapped as when he was a prisoner in his own head, trying to escape the fabricated reality he knew wasn't real.

Nick's expression softened and he squeezed David's shoulder before speaking. "His name is David James Forte Junior, born September 9, 2000 in New York City to David and Kelly Forte."

The pounding in David's ears nearly muffled Nick's words. Were it not for the man's hand on his shoulder, he wasn't sure he would have kept his feet. He choked on air, his eyes burning with tears. Nick paused, glancing for a second past David. The dip of his chin was barely discernible. David was on the verge of demanding an answer when Nick's attention shifted back, and he continued.

"The boy is his grandson, David James Forte the Fourth."

Something deeper, something around David's soul, tightened.

"His wife Millie and their son, David James Forte the Third died in the war. He lives in Unity Valley with his daughter-in-law Felicia and his grandson. I'm sorry."

Through the fog of tears, David looked down at the tablet again, the image blurred further by the uncontrollable shaking of his hands. The next question formed in his head, but he didn't realize he had asked the question—"My son Anthony?"—until Nick answered him.

"We don't know. We're still looking. I hope your son can tell you when you see him."

The sob took him by surprise, choking him. A hand touched the back of his head, and arms came around him, supporting him. His sons—Phin and Daniel—gripped him while the joy and pain collided.

CHAPTER FOUR

14 August 2054, Friday
Protectorate Citizen Community — Unity Valley
Vancouver, British Columbia
Former Country of Canada
North American Continent

"Our community population has tripled since you were here last fall, Colonel," Trevor Tisdale said as he walked Connor and David away from the grounded hover.

"I can see that," Connor said, falling into step with Tisdale.

Connor had introduced Tisdale to David when the man reached the open hover hatch and had told David before they landed that Tisdale was the "unofficial" official leader of Unity Valley. A mayor or governor of sorts, and as such, he was their primary contact for civilian matters. Now that they'd landed, Connor was the highest-ranking military officer in the valley, but they would meet up with Captain Amad Azziz of Terra Force after the tour. Connor had told David that prior to a few weeks earlier, a guy named Pedadda had been top ranking, but he had some kind of weird accident that left him in a vegetative state, and he'd been sent back to Alexandria for rehabilitation. If possible.

Trevor Tisdale looked more like a grad student or maybe graphic designer – something "artsy" and "fulfilling"—than a guy just trying to keep a few thousand people alive under the daily threat of attack.

The one thing that deviated from his down-to-Earth, Millennial —*was that even a thing anymore?*—look was the scar; a slightly darker brown than his skin—that ran up the left side of his neck, in front of his ear and beneath the arm of his glasses, to disappear as a jagged line into the tight, wiry curls that extended out a good three inches from his head.

He wasn't quite as tall as David and Connor, but he was lanky which gave him an impression of height. Or maybe that was just his personality. He greeted them with a wide smile and a firm handshake before leading them away from the hover. He had a calming nature, like a social worker or priest. A good priest. Not the overbearing ones at Saint Ignacius Church and School where David got his primary education.

As they walked, David took in as much as he could of the complex, knowing he'd also get a separate tour to help better plan the dome parameters. They'd landed in an open area, probably a pasture when not in use as a hover parking lot, relatively centralized to the sprawling community made up of permanent structures, recently erected and semi-permanent structures, and a variety of Protectorate-provided tents, most in the shape of round yurts but made from materials that could withstand hurricane force winds.

Just not weapons fire.

"How are the water purifiers holding out?" Connor asked.

"Holding out is a perfect term," Tisdale said with a chuckle. He pushed his dark rimmed glasses up his nose. "Unfortunately, one is fully out of commission after either a well-aimed or incredibly unlucky hit about four months ago. We've used what's left for parts to keep the other two going. But we have been mindful, and the water is sufficient, even if not in abundance."

"We'll see what we can do," Connor offered, and motioned over his shoulder with his thumb to Lieutenant Maldonado, who walked a few paces behind them with Lieutenant Woolf. "Annie can fix anything with anything."

Connor and Tisdale fell into casual conversation as they walked, and David scanned the immediate area. To the east and south were rolling hills and fields, with trees a bit closer on the northwest side of the compound. Not close, but unfortunately close enough Xenos might be able to use them as cover to attack.

Probably had, based on the areas of burn David noted. He mentally worked through range calculations and geographic lay of the land, formulating how he'd best structure the security dome. They neared a large farmhouse, the kind that spread out in all directions with multiple rooflines, a fully closed in sunporch, and a deep farmer's porch that wrapped probably the remaining three sides of the building. It's what David's grandma would have called "a house that Jack built," because it had been added on to over the years. He would have considered the building vintage in 2008; now, it had to be nearly a hundred and fifty years old or older but looked sturdy and well-maintained. All around the perimeter of the house were small flower gardens providing bits of color.

The community was one in motion. People rode horseback or worked with horses in pastures set away from the central area. Others carried tools or baskets or hung laundry or whatever other tasks needed completion in a commune setting like this. In his day, the word commune brought up grainy images of the 1960s love fests where pot and sex were abundant, and bathing not so much, according to his much older siblings. Unity Valley seemed to be a commune in the best sense of the word.

The early 21st Century could have learned a lot from a place like this. David took in as much as possible as they walked, from the landscape to the people, and he saw every color and several clear sects of people. He was even pretty sure he saw a group of three women walking together dressed in the traditional clothing of the Amish, simple and practical, with white bonnet caps and long skirts with two other women wearing flowing clothing and hijabs.

Despite it all, the people of Unity Valley clearly embraced the beautiful. It wasn't hard to forget all the crap going on around the planet, when surrounded by green hills and lush forests and the smell of grass on the fresh breeze.

Whenever they neared any new people, David scanned for a familiar face, searching until he knew none of them were Davey. A bizarre mix of panic and excitement had warred in his chest since Nick gave him the news. How could he even begin the topic?

"Hey, so . . . I'm your father. Yeah, I know you were told I was dead. Not really. I was just frozen and floating around in a spaceship the last few decades."

Sure. That'd go over great.

"Yo, David!"

David snapped out of his daze, blinked, and focused on Connor and Tisdale, who stood on the porch of the farmhouse. They'd crossed the whole yard with David barely aware of the move. "What?" he snapped.

Connor scowled and shook his head once. "Trevor was just saying that after reviewing the specs you put together, he believes the dome controls should be in this building. It's considered the hub of the community, and centrally located. It would be the last building the Xenos could get to."

David nodded and started up the steps. "Sounds good. Let's check it out."

He moved past Connor and Tisdale, but Tisdale beat him to the door anyway, ushering them into a wide, bright entry hall.

"I understand your distraction, Colonel," Tisdale said in a low voice as David moved past him. "I am available for whatever you may need."

David nodded and kept going, both ticked that his personal business had been relayed to the guy and relieved it wouldn't be a total shock when Davey inevitably lost his shiz.

The interior of the house was slightly cooler than outside, but not chilled. Just less humid. The floors were wide, light-colored hardwood that gleamed in the sun and were quite possibly original. The walls were a cream color with white trim, and an oak staircase with white railing and risers led to the second level. The place felt old, but in a good way. In a reassuring "life goes on" kind of way.

Tisdale headed down the hall, motioning toward a wide pocket door entry to what David would peg as a front parlor in its original state, but as they approached it was obvious the space was now used as an infirmary. Running from the front of the house to the back, and a good twenty feet wide, the room was bright with sunshine from large windows on the three exterior walls. A dozen single size, mismatched beds and cots filled the room, along with rolling carts, and three of the beds were occupied. From somewhere in the house beyond the area they could see came the slap of a wooden screen door.

"I suppose it's obvious, but this is our infirmary. We are lucky to have two trained physicians in the community, and many gentle hands willing to help."

"Scouting for new volunteers, Rev?"

The low female voice came from behind the group, and David caught the uptick of Trevor's grin before they turned toward the sound. Coming through the kitchen beyond the hallway walked a stunning woman with thick, waved chestnut hair draping her shoulders, clipped back enough to stay off her morena-brown forehead. Her figure was suck-all-air-out-of-the-room shaped, her features full, feminine, and her smile was a solid punch in the middle of David's chest.

Damn . . .

With her was a second woman shorter and more petite of frame, except for the rounding of her belly that said she was at least six or seven months along if David remembered Kelly's pregnancies right, and darker of skin with her tight curls trimmed tight to her skull with a bright scarf wrapped like a headband over the top of her head and behind her ears to fall down her back like waves.

"I would say speak of the devil, but these are two of our angels," Trevor said, a teasing softness in his tone. Since the rest of the military group had been to Unity Valley before, Trevor turned his attention to David while reaching out to the soon-to-be mom, who crossed the space to them. "Colonel Forte, I'm happy to introduce you to my wife Molly and her longest and dearest friend Lucy Santos," Trevor said in way of introduction.

David stepped past Connor, making sure to bump him with his

shoulder as he did, ignoring Connor's grumblings, and extended his hand to Molly Tisdale. "Happy to meet you, ma'am." He somehow managed to swallow the lump in his throat when he looked directly at the angel Trevor said was Lucy, extending his hand to her as well. "Ma'am."

She had a way of smiling that never parted her lips but gave expression to her whole face, especially when she arched a single eyebrow. "Welcome to Unity Valley, Colonel."

"Molly, this is Lieutenant Colonel Forte," he said, motioning toward David again. "The colonel is here to help build a security system for us."

"We have family here named Forte," Molly said, her eyes widening with her smile. "I wonder if you're related."

A cold sweat danced across the back of David's neck, along with a sense of relief that his secondary reason for being there wasn't known to everyone and their brother. "Yes, ma'am. On . . ." He paused, swallowed, and looked up again. "On his father's side."

"Oh, that's wonderful. Have you said hello yet?"

"Not yet. I do *intend* to say hello," David said, clearing his throat. "Soon. But they don't know I'm coming, so I'd like to keep it a surprise."

"Oh, that will be wonderful." Molly turned her bright smile on Connor. "Did I hear correctly that you've gotten married since you were last here? And you adopted a boy?"

Connor's smile was instantaneous and unhindered. "Yes, ma'am. Evie's my wife, and Adrian is our boy."

Lucy took a step back to shift her path and walk around them all as they stood blocking the stairs. David did his best to still seem interested in the conversation, but knew he'd failed when she looked back and they made eye contact. Her dark brown eyes held his gaze, and that closed-lip smile edged up on one side of her mouth, then the other, before she looked away and walked into the infirmary, around a corner, and out of sight again.

David stayed silent until Tisdale showed them down the stairs to the cellar that would be David's "office" for the next couple of weeks.

Unknown Mountain
Approximately 20 miles from Unity Valley

"But soon," he cried with sad and solemn enthusiasm, "I shall die, and what I now feel be no longer felt. Soon these burning miseries will be extinct. I shall ascend my funeral pyre triumphantly and exult in the agony of the torturing flames. The light of that conflagration will fade away; my ashes will be swept into the sea by the winds. My spirit will sleep in peace, or if it thinks, it will not surely think thus. Farewell."

Tessera read again the circled paragraph from the closing page of *Frankenstein or The Modern Prometheus*. The page was inserted into a notebook as forgotten as the aged shelter she now called home. The writing in the notebooks was in a fluid script she couldn't read, sometimes clearly neater and more focused and sometimes harsh and hard. Sometimes she was able to decipher some of the words, but the handwriting was a style she simply didn't know.

She assumed the notebooks had been filled by the previous resident of the cobbled together shelter. A few feet from the entrance, after staying in the shelter a few days, she found skeletal remains; a hole in the skull and a rusted weapon on the ground beside them, still held in curled bony fingers. Considering the few pieces of clothing she'd found, she assumed it had been a man and he had been the only inhabitant.

With the notebooks had been several other books. Some on survival off the land, which had already proven helpful, some that seemed little more than rantings of the insane – disjointed and scattered – about the impending end of the world, and some works of fiction.

Among the fiction had been the Frankenstein novel with the final page missing. When she'd first heard any kind of reference to the book she had no idea what it was. Her education was limited, going barely beyond language. No history. Anything she knew now she had learned from Mama Della and the people of Unity Valley.

Before she had to leave.

"All I'm saying is resources are damn limited. Why should we waste what little we have on not us."

"So, define not us."

Tessera didn't raise her head, or even shift her eyes, to look toward the two Terra soldiers standing just outside the infirmary in the downstairs hall. She focused instead on the careful task of re-bandaging the pulse blaster wound on Zhang Wong's shoulder and arm. Even though she restrained herself from showing any acknowledgment of their conversation, she listened intently.

Only when sure she wouldn't be noticed did she shift her position on the pretense of reaching for more bandages. It wasn't just the words; it was the thick press of hostility and anger pushing out from him so intensely she felt it in the next room. He sought out those he didn't trust, anyone not human enough to warrant his consideration.

"You know exactly what I mean, Molina," the taller said, scowling. "The husks. The lab rats. The freaks. The sympathizers. Why the hell should we take food off the plate of a natural born human over one of them."

He didn't word it as a question.

"Yeah, because the Sorrs haven't been screwing with our natural evolution for the last forty years. There aren't a whole lot of people who can claim their genetic soup wasn't stirred by Sorracchi interference."

"There's a big difference between being made better and being made a freak."

"Geez, Pedadda, could you sound like more of an ass? If you don't have any interest in helping, why did you sign up for Terra Force?" Molina asked Pedadda.

"Three hots and a cot. Ever hear your great grandpa say that?" Pedadda shifted, taking the cigarette between his fingers so he could motion with his hands. Ash fell from the tip to the wood floor. "We got it pretty damn good out here, except for the occasional Xeno crap to deal with. Plenty of food, plenty of women. And besides, I'm out here helping us. All these people are people. Humans."

When he paused in speaking, Tessera dared to glance again. Pedadda's cheeks sucked in as he pulled air through the skinny cigarette. He blew it out in a gray cloud over his head.

"Not supposed emancipated whatevers. You can't tell me once one of those slugs have been in your head that you can be trusted. And not like those freaks they've got guarding Tanner."

Tessera scowled. Information about events around the planet didn't always make it to Unity Valley. She didn't know who they meant, only that the Tanner they referred to was President Nicholas Tanner. Pedadda's opinion wasn't new. Tessera had heard it before, and it still left her chilled. It wasn't the majority, but it was the loudest.

"Those freaks were created by the Sorrs," Pedadda continued, then coughed. "Indoctrinated from the day they were hatched, or however the hell they were created like some damn Frankenstein."

"Frankenstein Monster," Molina said.

"What?"

"Frankenstein Monster. Frankenstein was the doctor who created the monster. Frankenstein wasn't the name of the monster."

"Who the hell cares? Point is, Tanner is an idiot for putting his life in their hands." He coughed again, the sound turning to a rattling hack. After a few barks, he cleared his throat. "Pay attention, Molina. If we don't watch our backs, all us real humans will find ourselves stabbed in the back by the soulless freaks Tanner thinks we should be saving."

Now, having read the book full of blasphemous science, pain, revenge, and isolation she wished she might have left the parallels a mystery. Was she destined to the same fate? Wasn't she already on the same path?

It hadn't been long after she'd overheard that exchange that Pedadda had discovered her deception and she had become the monster he so viciously hated. She had become that which even *she* hated. She had fled Unity Valley under the veil of darkness with no destination other than away, and no purpose other than to protect those who had trusted her when she didn't deserve that trust.

No one knew where she'd gone.

She'd found the empty shelter built partially into a rock and soil mound, camouflaging it effectively, purely by accident and at first, she'd thought it was an illusion of her hunger and fatigue. After several days of walking, the only reason for her direction that it was away from Unity Valley, she had fallen into an exhausted sleep beside a flowing stream and had woken when cold pellets of rain hit her face. To find some shelter, she'd moved away from the water to where the trees were denser when the cabin seemed to emerge from the mountainside. Had she really been so close to shelter the night before, so close to a roof and protection?

Nothing from the outside indicated anyone lived there; she'd confirmed the abandonment of the structure once she was inside. Years of dust and wildlife remnants dirtied every inch within the single-room structure, but it was dry. She had fresh water from the creek nearby and had found a variety of pouched and canned food in a cabinet that might well have been beyond any time they should have been eaten, but they renewed her strength until she found a way to feed herself. She knew nothing of how to survive, but she still lived and had determined within herself she would figure it out. In the weeks since, she'd made the single room structure as clean and safe as she could and had found some level of self-reliance.

She wouldn't starve.

She wouldn't freeze.

And she wouldn't ever risk her life around humankind again. She'd promised her sisters she'd live. The only way to assure she kept her promise was to stay away from everyone.

CHAPTER FIVE

ALEXANDRIA HOSPITAL – REHABILITATION WING
UNITED EARTH PROTECTORATE, CAPITOL CITY
ALEXANDRIA, SEAT OF VIRGINIA
NORTH AMERICAN CONTINENT

Katrina Forte paused at the door to the exercise gym in the rehabilitation wing of Alexandria Hospital, toeing up to look through the square glass window. On the exercise mat on the far side of the room were Michael Tanner, Phin, and Daniel, all dressed in loose linen pants bound high at the waist by knotted belts and no shirts. Phin wasn't required yet to return to duty after their wedding, but today he was meeting with his brothers for a training workout.

While Phin and Daniel had spent their lives honing their fighting skills with each other – against enemies – and with their third brother Gideon, they hadn't been able to fight as a triad since Gideon's death. Michael had confided with them how he hoped to learn their ability to move as a single unit, and this would be their third training session.

Just on the edge of the visible space in the room, Katrina caught sight of Jacqueline Tanner sitting on one of the high piles of workout mats, one arm bracing her with the other resting on top of her stomach. Her official due date was still two weeks away. While Michael and the boys stood in the middle of the mat in a circle, heads down, in silent communication Katrina knew well from the outside, she pushed open the door and walked toward Jackie.

"Hey," she said as she got to the mat and scooted to a spot beside Jackie to sit cross-legged. "How are you feeling?"

Jackie looked at Katrina's legs and chuckled. "Jealous. I'll be so glad to be able to move again." She sighed. "And pee less. And see my toes."

"You must be so excited, though."

Jackie's smile said everything, and she rubbed her hand over the tee shirt stretched over her waist. "I am. This sure isn't something I ever saw in my life just a couple years ago, but now that it's here, it feels like this is what was always supposed to be. And yet, with a twist."

"Or three."

Jackie laughed, but movement on the exercise mat drew both their attention. Ignoring the two of them, the three men took stances around the perimeter of the mat with their backs to each other, arms at their sides, three-foot-long batons in each hand. She'd observed martial art classes, but they held no comparison to what these three men did together. Without a word or other audible signal, they simultaneously launched into motion. For a few moments, Katrina was taken back to months before when she witnessed the original Triadic in action.

Without even slowing down, Phin attacked the nearest man to him, both deflecting their attack and taking the offensive in two swings of his arms. He grabbed the bat the man held, and with a twist, snapped it around to knock it against the side of his attacker's head, using the man's weight as leverage to pivot through the air and take out two other men with kicks from his bare feet.

Daniel yanked the stun bolts from his chest and shoved away from the wall in time to defend himself against two of them. Katrina's pursuer shot her one hard, cold glare then turned away and entered the fight. With men blocking the door, she had no escape. But she refused to just stand by and watch. She shot past the end of the couch to the fireplace and picked up the wrought iron poker used to stoke the embers. One of the men saw her and cut away from the *fighting to grab at her. Katrina swung wide, screaming out all the power she could put behind the blow, and clocked him across the jaw. He stumbled back, wide-eyed, then dropped hard to the floor.*

The two blocking the door suddenly flew forward into the fight, landing on their faces, and Gideon grabbed the next nearest him. With no visible effort, he tossed the man away, taking down another two like bowling pins.

And then there were three.

Katrina could only stare—in dumbfounded shock—at what she could only describe as a perfectly choreographed dance. Though there were three, they moved in perfect harmony, perfect unity, perfect precision, taking down permanently every man who dared approach. They moved around each other as surely and as accurately as a single man in battle. Weapons were turned on attackers and exchanged between brothers like runners in a relay race, and they arched, flipped, and leveraged both each other and the attackers to their advantage. Katrina held her breath, and in what seemed seconds unconscious bodies littered the floor around them and they stood, back-to-back and shoulder-to-shoulder.

The three men now weren't fighting anyone else, but their choreography was still as impressive. The batons cracked loud against each other as they feigned blows their brothers deflected. They used each other's bodies as weapons, tools, and points of leverage. She couldn't blink, couldn't look away; with each minute their movements grew faster until the three were a blur of movement. Only occasionally could she differentiate Michael from Phin and Daniel, and only because his hair was longer. In every other physical way, and at this speed, they were almost completely indiscernible.

They "fought" for nearly twenty minutes, until finally and with a unified, loud "Hah!" bark from all three, they slapped all six batons together in the center of the circle they formed and fell silent save for their slightly elevated breathing, Michael a bit more than his brothers. They were created for this; he wasn't.

"Damn," Jackie said under her breath.

"Yeah," Katrina said in agreement.

She had been so engrossed in the show, she hadn't noticed the rapid increase in her heartbeat and the warm flush over all her skin. Studying her new husband as he spoke with his brothers, locked hands with them, and shifted the batons to one hand, she enjoyed the flutter deep in her belly his nearness inspired.

At that moment, she wanted nothing more than to be somewhere alone. With her husband.

Alone.

When silence settled again, Phin looked toward her, winked, and smiled.

Jackie chuckled but Katrina couldn't look away from her husband.

"How are *you*, Katrina?" Jackie asked. "Enjoying married life?'

"Uh huh," she answered, scrambling off the pile of mats to jog across the room to Phin. He met her in a deep, breath-stealing kiss.

AMBASSADOR RESIDENCE
UNITED EARTH PROTECTORATE, CAPITOL CITY
ALEXANDRIA, SEAT OF VIRGINIA
NORTH AMERICAN CONTINENT

The building used to house the Smith family, as well as other individuals who may require increased protection such as when the president and family had been there temporarily, had been built two decades earlier when every citizen owned one or more private vehicles. The lower levels were well ventilated but completely enclosed, and the Smiths had claimed a portion of the first level below street level as an exercise area.

John and Jenifer warmed up their quarterstaff training with several repeated motions of rutter swing with rising strike, blocked by low guard thrust snaps, alternating between moves so each gained the center space advantage. Their contact was firm enough to send vibrations down the staff into John's hands, but not enough to knock anyone's grip free of the weapon.

After several minutes of warm up, a mutual nod was their silent indicator their next move would not be practice but as close to the real thing they came. It was possibly the only time they mutually blocked off the other from their thoughts to make the exercise interesting.

Both came from high guard, but this time John swung his forward thrust and Jenifer stepped away, blocking with a low guard swing to steal the advantage. She only had it a second before he slid the staff along hers to swing upward. Her block was fast and precise, swinging into a half-circle snap with enough force the breeze stirred his hair. He sidestepped, nearly losing his nose to her down snap, spun through his coil and punctuated the swing over the bridge of her nose as she arched away.

"Geez! Don't break her face!" came a shout from the edge of their exercise mat.

At least on his part, John had been so focused on the physical training he'd been unaware Alexis had returned with Captain Doli Bravebird, Alexis' protection on the rare occasions she left the family. Today, it was for her twice weekly counseling meetings at the hospital. Had he not closed himself off for the exercise, he probably would have. John swung the quarterstaff away from his wife, tucking the short end against his side and the far point in the opposite direction from their eldest daughter. Jenifer took a step backward and spun her staff with enough speed it whistled in the air before she slammed the tip onto the mat by her foot.

"You two always go at it that fierce?" Alexis asked, stepping away from the statuesque Firebird who stood her post near the door, her hands tucked behind her back.

"An opponent isn't going to go easy on you," Jenifer answered, walking to the containers of filtered water they'd brought down with them, using the quarterstaff like a walking stick so it tapped the floor with each stride of her left foot.

Alexis watched; her arms crossed over her body in what was her common stance.

Have you considered—

Yes Jenifer answered in his thoughts, even while tipping back her head to drink.

John went to a rolled carpet set against the wall of the space they'd cleared to serve as an exercise room and dropped heavy to sit on it with a long sigh.

"What's wrong, Old Man?" Jenifer teased.

"No' fair bringin' up my age."

Jenifer smirked and took two steps toward Alexis before bringing the quarterstaff parallel with the ground and tossing it toward Alexis. The young girl caught it, but only after flinching and shooting a scathing look at her mother. Jenifer didn't take her eyes off Alexis and extended her hand toward John. He relaxed his hold on his own staff and it flew across the space at Jenifer's powerful command, slapping into the palm of her open hand. Alexis took another step back, eyes wide. She knew John and Jenifer had Talents, and he knew Alexis had witnessed Jenifer using them when she discovered Freddy Casper, but she was often caught off guard to see them in action.

Eventually, it would seem natural to her.

"Come over here," Jenifer said, returning to the mat.

Seeming to understand, Alexis followed, the downward tip of her staff dragging behind her. Once she reached the center of the mat, Jenifer pointed to where she should stand. The same place John had been before the practice began.

"Your stance is the most important thing," Jenifer explained, shifting naturally into the proper position. "Set your feet just a little wider than your shoulders, with your dominant foot a little forward toward your opponent. That's me."

"How do I know which is my dominant foot?"

"Are you left-handed or right-handed?"

"Left."

"Then your left foot is your dominant foot. Set it forward a little. Like this." Jenifer shifted to place her dominant foot toward Alexis. She then held up her staff to show Alexis the hold. "Your right hand should be at the base of the staff, and your left about a quarter way up. Like this."

Alexis nodded and shifted her hold.

Within a few minutes, Alexis was both blocking Jenifer's gentle swings and making some thrusts of her own. She was clumsy and rushed, with a little too much anger behind her motions, but already a good student. John continued his tired farce and watched his wife and oldest daughter teach and learn together.

He glanced toward Captain Bravebird, smiling himself at the small, almost invisible bowing of the silent woman's lips. She caught him watching, and while her smile didn't change, she nodded to him with a slow dip of her chin.

This might be just what Alexis Smith needed.

16 August 2054, Sunday
Protectorate Citizen Community — Unity Valley
Vancouver, British Columbia
Former Country of Canada
North American Continent

David startled awake, disoriented, scrambling to sit up and focus, his hand going to his waist for his weapon. His pulse raced with a ghost on the edge of his awareness, the dissolving remnants of a dream. He was outside, and darkness had settled over the community, forcing him to squint. Silver moonlight made everything monochromatic.

"Sorry, Colonel. I didn't mean to startle you."

He jerked toward the soft voice, his eyes finally adjusting enough that he made out Lucy crouched beside his chair, her hand resting on the arm close enough he felt the warmth of her fingers once he was aware enough to process everything. Strange facts registered in the fog of his brain: she wore a red scarf wrapped around her head to hold back her hair and a cardigan at least two sizes too large. So much so the rolled cuffs fell past her wrists.

"I thought you might prefer to sleep inside," she added, her eyebrow raising just enough to add the spice of a tease to her softly spoken words, probably so she wasn't announcing to anyone within earshot that he'd fallen asleep because he was too damn tired to get any further.

If it had been daytime, with more sounds of life around them, he might not have heard her voice. But then again, he probably wouldn't have fallen asleep in a chair on the porch in the middle of the afternoon. David shifted forward to rest his elbows on his knees, pressing the heels of his hands into his eyes. The catch of stiffness in his back reminded him that he'd come to the porch to sit in one of the Adirondack chairs after working in the basement for hours, lying on the cold concrete. Like he had the last two days. Just walking up the stairs to the main floor had been a challenge, his abused and ancient muscles screaming in protest, so much so the prosthetics were little help. His muscles had spasmed with overexertion.

He'd made it to the bottom of the stairs going to the second floor, dreading each step, when he'd glanced out the front windows and saw the deep Adirondack chairs. He'd only meant to rest, but exhaustion must have gotten the better of him.

A surprise since he hadn't expected his body to let him sleep at all.

"No, it's fine," he said, then tried to sit up as he lowered his hands from his eyes. The motion made his back catch, and he groaned, using the pain as motivation to try to stand.

Try being the operative word.

Half-hunched and half-tipped, David nearly lost his balance, but was saved from falling over like a drunk when Lucy came to his side, sliding under his arm to support him. Given any other time, any other situation, he would have enjoyed her proximity. Pain radiating up the spinal nodes kept him from saying anything, and frustration made him groan low in his throat. Despite his bruised pride, he circled her shoulders with his arm beneath the dangling corners of her scarf and tried not to dig in his fingers or tug on her hair.

"Sorry," he managed to say through clenched teeth.

Lucy raised her chin, looking up at him from the level of his shoulder, one hand pressed to his chest and the other behind his back. He had to fight hard not to flinch when her hand came close to the spinal connection points, and probably only managed not to because he'd fall on his ass if he lost her support right then.

Way to impress a lady, Forte.

He probably would have wallowed deeper in his self-pity if she didn't smell so damn good, like wildflowers and fresh air.

"Wow, you're in bad shape."

David tried to smile but didn't have to see his face to know he didn't succeed. "Thanks."

"Honestly, that's more a compliment than an insult. Let me help you inside. Maybe Tessa left something in the infirmary that can help."

David chuckled, but only because yelling wasn't an option. "If she can help, it'd be a miracle."

"Unfortunately, Tessa isn't here anymore," she said on a long release of air. "She left behind a lot of her concoctions and mixes. She had a real talent for natural treatments."

"No human or alien science has managed to do more than get me on my feet. The pain is part of the cure."

Lucy scowled, then shifted her focus to helping him walk into the house. After the first step or two, the protesting muscles eased and the hydraulics apparently remembered their job, and he was able to stand a bit more upright by the time they reached the door into the house. He tried once to lower his arm, to let her know he had it, but she didn't move away so he kept in step with her.

Once inside the infirmary, Lucy took him left, away from the other patient at the far end of the room. At the furthest bed, she eased away from his side so he could sit on the edge of the narrow mattress.

"I'll be fine in a few minutes," David assured, attempting to convince himself as much as Lucy. "I'll walk it off getting upstairs. A couple hours sleep, and I'll be good."

He mentally worked through each major muscle group. The walk in from the porch had loosened up his limbs, and while he'd move like the eighty-year-old man he was, he could make it. At this point, any chance of impressing the beautiful Lucy was dead in the water. He'd only managed to see her a couple times since they arrived a few days before, spending all his awake hours and some of his sleeping ones in the basement of the house.

"Maybe," she said, crouching in front of him with a nimble ease of youth that made him jealous. "Just sit here for a couple minutes. Will you tell me what happened to you? Might help with figuring out what I can do or what Tessa might have left."

The sincerity in her voice pressed something into his chest. David chuckled and pinched the bridge of his nose. "It's one hell of a story, and pretty hard to believe."

Lucy laughed, raising a single eyebrow. "We've heard some pretty hard to accept stuff in the last couple of years. You'd be surprised what I'm willing to believe."

David sighed, rolling his shoulders. The brutal pain was easing its way back to the usual, persistent discomfort he lived with all the time. "That's fair. My story is a hell of a hard pill to swallow. Even *I* find myself thinking *what the actual hell*." He gave another short chuckle. "The world is a crazy-ass place."

"Exactly," she said with a quick nod. "Honestly, being truly shocked and surprised by something would be refreshing at this point."

"You say that until it happens. Trust me."

Lucy rose from the crouch to go to the bedside table and turn on a small light. It was only bright enough to illuminate the small area where they sat, but David still squinted until his eyes adjusted. Lucy came back to sit on the mattress beside him to wrap her hand around his bicep, her thumb resting near one of the exposed contact points for the arm braces. The skin around the bracket was raw, tingling, and itching, which was fairly common and widespread. His muscle clenched at her touch, which both hurt – and didn't – at the same time.

"I was in a form of suspended stasis for a very long time," he explained, figuring either she'd believe or she wouldn't. It wasn't a state secret or anything. At least he didn't think it was. In the grand scheme of things, the real-life Buck Rogers didn't seem so inherently top secret. "So long that when I woke up my body was in a severe state of atrophy. An Alliance doc hooked me up with this sort of robo-suit to get me moving and stimulate my muscles so they work again." He used the hand furthest from her to wave at the arm she touched. "This is the latest generation."

She never looked up from his arm, her focus fully on examining what she could touch or see, even though the network of nodes disappeared under the tee shirt, some actually under his skin to the spinal network.

"How long were you in stasis?"

"Over forty years."

Her attention snapped to him, and she stared for three thumping beats of his heart until she canted her head and stated, "Sorracchi."

"How'd you guess?" he asked, struggling to hide his surprise.

Up here in God's Country, he knew the citizens of communities like Unity Valley knew of the Sorracchi – they all lived in a post-global war world—but their greatest enemies now were the Xeno cells. Home grown terrorists, as they called them in his past life.

"I've seen the aftermath of their abuse. People have come here to escape the horrors. Some talk about it. Some don't."

David nodded, understanding both sides.

"May I see?" she asked, the entire tone of her voice changing to something more delicate, gentle. Soothing.

"It's not pretty . . ."

"I understand."

He wanted to say no, if only for the sake of his pride. Why did it matter? Since waking up months before, he'd been poked, prodded, Borgefied, and paraded in front of panels of doctors and interested people. Why did one more matter?

Because somehow it did.

He looked away from her and reached behind his neck to grip the back of his tee shirt, yanking it up and over his head. As he focused on making sure the shirt was right-side-out, Lucy stood and walked around the foot of the bed so she was behind him, and turned on another bedside light. He felt the slight shift of the mattress when she knelt behind him, closed his eyes, and swallowed hard.

He'd only seen the cyborg matrix of nodes, connections, and metal fused to his skin in photos, and even then it had been hard for him to accept it was his own body. The only thing that had made him sure he looked at his own mangled body was the tattoo on the back of his left shoulder – the names of his boys and their birthdates.

"Will it hurt if I touch you?"

David had to swallow before he choked out, "No."

Her touch was so tentative, he wasn't completely sure he felt her at first, then the warmth of her skin registered. She touched first with one fingertip, then two, until both hands examined his back. His physical exams were always kind but lacked the gentle care Lucy used.

"What does all this do?"

David inhaled deep through his nose, and released it on a huff, straightening his spine. The movement effectively pressed her hands firmer against his back. Not unpleasantly so. "I'm not a physiology guy, but I know the gist. The implants continuously stimulate my muscles, even when I'm resting, to increase their strength and remind them how to work." He reached across his body to point to the hydraulics bracketing his elbows. Similar brackets attached to his legs and hips to his lower back. "These are supports. They were a lot bigger at first. I looked like RoboCop for weeks. It was like a suit. But as my muscles improved, the suit got smaller."

Lucy took one hand from his back to touch the shoulder near where he had motioned. She ran her thumb along his skin beside the bracket. The nerves sparked beneath the touch. David had to swallow before continuing with his explanation. "I take off the brackets and supports when I sleep, but . . ."

"But what?" she led.

David turned his head so he could see her over his shoulder. Even though her hands still examined his contraptions, her gaze met his.

"But I perpetually feel like I've survived the worst workout of my life. I ache, all the time. And the brackets irritate the skin. Doc does what she can, so I live with what she can't."

"Do you have a hard time sleeping?"

David huffed and smiled, shaking his head. "You mean other than in wooden chairs on the front porch?"

She smiled, that closed-lip grin that popped dimples in her cheeks and tipped her eyes, her voice laced with amusement. "Yes, other than on front porches."

"Yeah, it takes a long time to get to sleep most nights, unless I'm just beyond the point of exhaustion. Which I was tonight, but I—" He snapped his jaw shut and looked away from her into the dark edges of the room. "I couldn't make it that far."

"I think Tessa has something here that might help, even if just a little. She's told me about her studies into homeopathic approaches since pharmacology isn't exactly easy to access out here. It might take a few days before you really feel a difference, but—"

"I'll try it," he cut her off, looking over his shoulder again. He smiled and winked. "I'm in your capable hands."

Lucy nodded and scooted backward off the bed. She shrugged off the oversize cardigan and laid it on the bed before turning away, and David would swear to anyone who asked that he made a valiant effort to look away from the sway of her hips as she crossed the long, dark room to the far end. Only when she was out of view did he wonder what he'd agreed to.

Logically, it didn't make sense there was anything here to help him that wouldn't have been available in Alexandria, and Michael and Doc Cole had done all they could with what they had. Doc Cole had regretfully explained the pain was almost necessary. They had tried some approaches to treating the discomfort, but David didn't like how the medications messed with his head. He only allowed himself to take anything when he wasn't on location like this. He needed focus. So, he pushed through, until he couldn't.

Like tonight.

"You're a real prize, Forte," he mumbled, leaning forward to rest his elbows on his knees, the task of sitting up straight wearing him out.

He didn't hear her until she was nearly to the bed, managed to straighten before she sat beside him and held out a mug with some steaming liquid inside. The scent was odd, but not unpleasant, like Christmas in Little India.

"Drink this. Be careful. It's hot."

David inhaled again. "What's in it?"

"This has clove, turmeric, cannabidiol, and willow bark." She smiled. "I added some honey to help with the taste."

"I don't suppose you've got any Cheetos to follow this up?" David took a sip, bracing himself for whatever hit his tongue. The whole *bark* thing had him worried. It wasn't exactly delicious, but it wasn't exactly terrible either. Tasted like chewing on a piece of wood. She picked up a small bowl he hadn't noticed she'd set on the bed, a pale salve inside.

"I can make you more tea in the morning, just without the willow bark. That's the part that will help you sleep. I can make you more in the evening before you go to bed. Turns out Tessa left us a pretty good supply before she took off."

While she explained, she dabbed her fingertip in the salve and leaned in close to his arm to smooth it on the angry red skin around the bracket contact points. The salve was cool, and immediately the itchy, hot sensation eased. David sipped again and looked down to watch her apply the cream. A slight floral scent drifted to his nose, mixing with the clove and turmeric.

"That feels good."

She glanced up to meet his eyes, smiled, and went back to the application. "I can help with this as well. I'll put some on your back each morning and evening, and you can take this to apply where I . . . can't."

He took the last swallow of the tea, the sweetness of the honey that had settled at the bottom of the cup coating his tongue. Lucy stood to move behind him again, starting the process of applying the salve to all the hot spots on his back. When she used her thumb along the tense trapezius muscle David couldn't help his groan.

"I'm sorry," she said in a rushed whisper, and withdrew her touch.

"No, no. It's good. That felt good."

She went back to the application, and David closed his eyes to enjoy the soothing, calming sensation.

CHAPTER SIX

"*H*ey! Forte!"

David came awake with a jerk, sucking in air. He looked around, realizing he was on one of the narrow beds in the infirmary, and groaned. "Geez, I gotta find a better way to wake up," he mumbled, squinting until he could focus on Connor Montgomery standing over him.

Connor took a step back, hands at his waist, glaring down at him. "You okay?"

With another groan, David moved his legs off the bed to sit up, automatically bracing himself for the morning ache and weary weakness for not having on the prosthetics. But the deep bone ache didn't come, and while his groggy mind registered the fact he'd slept with the prosthetics in place, the sparking nerve irritation didn't follow the movement.

"David," Connor said firmer.

David looked around the sunlit infirmary, with no sign of Lucy, and tossed aside the blanket partially covering him. His tee shirt was draped over the foot of the bed, and he grabbed it, pulling it over his head as he stood.

Easier than he recalled standing in a long time.

Wow...

"David, *alors aide-moi, Dieu...*"

"I'm fine," he explained, tucking the shirt into his waistband, glancing around for sight of his nurse. "I worked late, and I was just too damn tired to get up the stairs." David set his hands on his hips and grinned wide at Connor, who still looked worried. Or pissed. Hard to tell. "But you're sweet for caring." He winked and grinned.

"So you crawled into the infirmary?"

"Kind of," David responded with a smirk, then winked and inhaled deep through his nose. There was a whole lot of goodness coming from the kitchen, but above it all he smelled coffee and . . . *bacon*. "Smells like breakfast."

It took maybe fifteen steps to get from his bed to the wide archway to the kitchen, and when he rounded the corner by the door leading to the cellar, the sounds of fellowship greeted him. The long table teemed with people, from the very old to the very young. David scanned the length of the table for the familiar face of a man who would have no idea who he was but didn't see Davey amongst those gathered.

He wasn't sure if he was disappointed or relieved.

Guilt at his procrastination slammed his chest. Yeah, he was a chicken.

In that moment, he decided he had to step up and deal with the real reason he'd come to Unity Valley.

"Connor. David. Come," Trevor called over his shoulder, motioning with a hand holding a thick slice of toast to two empty chairs to his left. "We don't have a breakfast like this every day, so come sit and eat before the day begins."

"Don't mind if I do," Connor said, moving past David to take the nearest chair.

Without needing to be asked, people passed plates of food to their end of the table and David snagged the plate of bacon as he sat, and before Connor could get it. His mouth already watered at the smell. He hadn't had bacon since . . . since the morning of the day he got orders from President Heyward to investigate the new "visitors."

That deserved a few extra slices.

"Save some for the rest of us, Forte," Connor grumbled, reaching for the plate.

David grabbed one more, shoving it in his mouth. "You weren't alive the last time I ate bacon. I deserve extra."

"Likely excuse."

David laughed and took the next plate that came his way, teeming with pan-fried potatoes. With his plate full, he paused to take a deep breath and one more glance down the table. There was no sign of Lucy.

"Looking for me?"

He practically snapped off his own head spinning it around at the sound of Lucy's voice and the touch of her hand curling over his shoulder. She leaned around him to set a mug beside his plate. "I was making it when Colonel Montgomery woke you."

When she reached to set down the mug, a long twirl of hair fell forward and brushed his arm.

Goooooood morning!

"Thank you," he managed to choke out without sounding like a prepubescent teenager.

She gifted him with her lovely, closed-lip smile and pressed his shoulder with her fingertips for just a moment before dropping her hand and stepping away to find a chair on the other side of the table near Molly Tisdale.

"Something I need to know?" Connor asked around the potatoes in his cheek, motioning with his fork toward Lucy and Molly.

"Don't be jealous. It doesn't suit you," David chided before digging into the best breakfast he'd had in nearly fifty years.

ALEXANDRIA HOSPITAL, SECURE WING – PRIVATE NURSERY
UNITED EARTH PROTECTORATE, CAPITOL CITY
ALEXANDRIA, SEAT OF VIRGINIA
NORTH AMERICAN CONTINENT

"Who would have thought deciding on eight potential names at one time would be a real-life problem?" Jacqueline huffed as she reclined on the chaise her husband had brought to the "nursery" for her. She rested the tablet she'd been using on the highest point of her expanded abdomen.

Michael sat on the edge of the chaise beside her, rubbing his palm along what had once been her waistline. "Were this a more natural situation, I would say the likelihood of all four children being the same gender at birth would be so low we wouldn't need to consider it."

"But it's not." She sighed again and shifted. "So, it's four of each."

The remainder of her pregnancy could be counted in days, and she was 150% ready for this baby – and the three waiting in their dimmed, environmentally-maintained wombs – to come into the world. Yet, the idea of four newborns and a toddler left her sleepless. She looked again at the tablet, reading through the names they'd written to distract her.

"I suppose if needed we could split up some of the names so both the first and middle aren't a name after someone. Just the first, and the middle somehow goes with it." She groaned, shaking her head. "Again, never thought running out of names would be a problem. Can't we make up some names from way back relatives or something? Like Dorcas or Hortense. Or for boys Elmo or Aloysius."

Michael laughed as he stood and leaned over to kiss her. "We will choose when the time comes and pray we won't need to resort to Dorcas Hortense and Elmo Aloysius."

Jackie smiled and raised her hands to hold his face in her palms. "If we do, I'm swearing under oath the names came from your side."

From her playing spot a few feet away, Nicole pushed herself up to her feet and toddled over to them, her single stuffed toy – a beanbag frog with dark green spots and big eyes she'd affectionately named "Froggie" – clutched to her chest.

"Daddy, beebees music," she told them, pointing toward the artificial wombs.

Michael chuckled and retrieved his violin from the foot of the chaise. "I'm coming."

Jackie relaxed into the soft cushions as Michael walked toward the three tubes that protected their children. They had repeated this routine nearly every day since Victor and Katrina had determined the babies were biologically theirs, the outcome of a vengeful experiment by the monster they knew as Kathleen.

The irony was beautiful.

Every time Heinous Bitch had tried to steal not the lives, but the joy, of the Tanner family she had ultimately failed. The most spectacular failure of all were the three unnaturally conceived children waiting to join their sibling. Three gifts to add to the gift she carried; a child she wasn't sure she'd ever conceive.

Found through a chain of events so remarkable, so unbelievable, so miraculous they seemed guided by an invisible hand.

As her father-in-law said, the cosmic timing was impressive. And God had one hell of a sense of humor.

Jackie just wished the heinous bitch would die already and leave them all in peace in a world free of her special form of insane.

But her control was gone, her power to hurt them now impotent.

Instead, they spent their evenings preparing for the soon-to-be exponential growth of their family. They had moved with Michael's parents back to the now-remodeled presidential residence, and once the babies were born they would be a combined family of ten, half of which would be under the age of three months.

Michael seemed completely nonplussed by the idea of four newborns; either that or he was just *really* good at hiding it. Jacqueline, on the other hand, broke out in a cold sweat whenever she thought about it too long.

Sometimes Michael played music for all of them. Sometimes they brought Nicole so she could talk and play with her future siblings listening. They each responded in their own ways, some with activity and some with a noticeable calming of their tiny heartrates like the music soothed them just as it did the baby in her body. As he drew the calming notes of Brahms Lullaby from the violin, Jacqueline closed her eyes and ran her hand over her stomach.

The baby moved – a jerk of his or her foot against Jackie's palm – and she smiled. Then a rolling tightening of her lower abdomen muscles made her inhale and hold her breath, waiting for the cramp to pass. It was the third similar pain in the last day, but they only lasted a short time, and then let her relax again. She closed her eyes and let her husband's beautiful music wrap around her.

>PROTECTORATE CITIZEN COMMUNITY—UNITY VALLEY
>VANCOUVER, BRITISH COLUMBIA
>FORMER COUNTRY OF CANADA
>NORTH AMERICAN CONTINENT

Lucy couldn't pinpoint the exact moment her mind realized she'd been handed a puzzle, or when she subconsciously began solving it, but she knew when it all came together. She stood, transfixed, at the fence surrounding the common lawn where the community's children tended to come together to play, watching one family in particular.

Felicia, Davey, and DJ Forte.

Felicia sat on a blanket watching while grandson and grandfather played with their dog Duke. She smiled and laughed when Davey got the ball away from Duke and tossed it away with the only hand he had left and then took a tumble when he knocked himself off balance. DJ ran after both dog and ball, and after snatching up the ball, ran back to his grandfather.

"Here, Grandpa," DJ yelled, because like every child that ever lived he only knew whispering and yelling, there was no in between.

Davey took the ball, his smile as wide as his grandson's, and threw the ball again.

Lucy stared. Transfixed.

"*I was in a form of suspended stasis for a very long time. So long that when I woke up my body was in a severe state of atrophy. An Areth doc hooked me up with this sort of robo-suit to get me moving and stimulate my muscles so they work again. This is the latest generation.*"

"How long were you in stasis?"

"Over forty years."

David Forte didn't look over forty, but if what he said was true he'd be over eighty years old. He'd be older than Davey Forte, the fifty-something-year-old playing with his grandson and their dog. Old enough...

"We have family here named Forte. I wonder if you're related."

The question Molly had asked that afternoon when they had first met Colonel Montgomery and his team in the hallway of the main house was simple. It wasn't intrusive. Everyone in this new world wanted to find that family connection again, especially when some people had no idea what might have happened to their family. Her grandmother who raised her had been gone before the world imploded, and Lucy didn't know the fate of anyone else. Trevor and Molly were the closest she had to family now, and if luck or whatever she could call it hadn't put her here she would have been desperate to find out their fate. Reconnecting was always considered a miracle.

Yes, ma'am. On... On his father's side."

"Oh, that's wonderful. Have you said hello yet?"

"Not yet. I do intend to say hello," David had said and cleared his throat. *"Soon. But they don't know I'm coming, so I'd like to keep it a surprise."*

"Oh, Dios mio," Lucy whispered under her breath and forced herself to blink.

Davey returned to the blanket where Felicia sat, stumbling as he tried to sit and caught himself with his remaining arm. Lucy didn't know the whole story, but what she didn't know she saw. Davey and his family had been living in Portland, Oregon when the Sorracchi had given up any mask of duplicity and turned on the world, and Portland had been hard hit. His wife and his son had been killed, and he had been left maimed and damaged. Medical care was hard to find, and those found did everything they could with what they had. He'd lived, but he had lost an arm, an eye, and much more. Those that remained of the Forte family had found Unity Valley after The War when the Sorracchi threat was gone; only the three of them. Felicia was his daughter-in-law, now a widow, and they remained a family no matter how broken.

But... David had said his story was pretty unbelievable.

Lucy gripped the top fence rail, her chest squeezing with heartbreak. She closed her eyes, remembering the tattoo on the posterior of David's shoulder when he'd removed his shirt so she could see the extent of his injuries. It had been simple, but beautiful in its simplicity. At the time she hadn't tried to attach meaning to the sentiment, but the possible significance hit her in a cold flash.

David James Junior
8 ~ 22 ~ 2000
Anthony Mason
5 ~ 15 ~ 2004

"Oh, David..."

"Is something wrong, Luce?"

Molly's question, especially since Lucy had been oblivious to her friend's approach, yanked her from her thoughts and she had to blink to bring the evening into focus. She had been so overwhelmed by the potential ramifications of her suspicions she hadn't realized the Forte family had gathered up their blanket, ball, and dog and had left the lawn. She inhaled and centered herself before turning her head to look at Molly.

"No, nothing's wrong. I just..." She paused, then shook her head, completely without the right words to explain. "I realized something I need to take care of. Are you headed back to the house?"

Molly smiled and nodded, her hand smoothing over her high tummy. "Yes. I was walking with Mama but she wanted to visit with Tiffany and Samantha."

"Then I'll walk with you."

The walk to the house was a slow one since Molly was nearing the end of her seventh month and the baby overtook her petite frame. Any other day and any other hour Lucy wouldn't have minded at all, since she and Molly had been friends since elementary school, but a sudden, real need to find David fluttered in her chest. Though, she wasn't sure what she would say or how she would say it. How did one broach such a subject? Did she even have the right to? Just because she'd figured it out – or thought she'd figured it out – it didn't give her the right to ask for confirmation.

Sound filled the house, coming mostly from the kitchen. Dinner had ended a couple hours before, but preparations for the next day had already begun. People took turns prepping, cooking, and cleaning since the kitchen in the main house fed not only those living in the house proper but provided meals to those in Unity Valley who couldn't prepare meals themselves. Or needed temporary help. Mothers with new babies or families with ill members, so they could focus on taking care and not cooking meals. Their elderly citizens were provided a day's worth of meals each morning. Meals were prepared and provided for a variety of reasons, because Trevor insisted as long as there was food no one in Unity Valley would be hungry. Sometimes it was simple when supplies were scarce, and sometimes they had an abundance to share. Everyone was equal, and everyone was worth the effort.

Lucy steered Molly away from the kitchen, telling her to go rest and put her feet up. Once convinced Molly would do as she said, Lucy took the long way to the cellar door by going through the kitchen. David had been absent from the evening meal, but she heard Connor talk to Trevor about taking a plate down to David because he was hyper-focused on his work. She only understood the basic mechanics of it; that David had developed a program to create a protective dome around Unity Valley to keep the inhabitants safe and the Xenos out. She'd heard enough chitchat to know how many in the community were hopeful and thankful for the possibility of safety, but what caught her attention the most keenly was that David had been the one to create the dome. That was, of course, if the gossip was true.

Either way, he was committed to his work.

"Hey, Luce," called a couple of the people at work in the kitchen, and she nodded and smiled in response. She was afraid to say much for fear someone would want to chat. Normally she wasn't antisocial, and it wasn't so much about being antisocial as seeking someone else.

On a hunch, she scooped up three of the remaining shortbread cookies left from after dinner. A brief touch to the side of the stoneware carafe on the sideboard told her the coffee was still warm, and she poured a mug. She had no idea how he might like his coffee, but since sugar was saved for cooking she decided to take it down black. The door to the cellar was at the back of the house, reachable either from the kitchen or the central hallway. Lucy opened the door, the presence of someone confirmed by the light and the sound of work, and took the first step down, the old stairs creaking.

"About time, Montgomery," David yelled out. "I was beginning to think you went back to Alexandria for the part."

Lucy smiled and continued down the stairs. As she cleared the header that served as both floor for the main level and ceiling for the cellar, she leaned forward enough to see the console in the center of the space and chuckled at the boots sticking out from beneath. "I'm not Colonel Montgomery. Should I go look for him?"

The boots jumped, something clattered, and David cursed.

"Oh, I'm sorry!" Lucy hurried down the last couple steps as quickly as she could without spilling the coffee as David shifted out from beneath the structure. "I didn't mean to—"

"Nah, it's okay," he said, leading with an extended hand as he came visible. He reclined on a rudimentary plank on wheels to let him roll along the pitted concrete floor, and once he was clear of the console edge, he sat up and grabbed a nearby rag to wipe his hands. "I'm starting to think he's not coming back tonight, which is okay," he said, the last word swallowed up by a groan as he shifted to stand without the plank being more a hindrance than help. Lucy moved to assist, but he held out one hand again as he used the other to grip the console to gain his feet. "I didn't actually need the part I sent him to find. He's apparently bored because he was down here for over two hours talking my ear off. I don't know how Evie isn't deaf."

His smirk made her smile back. She'd witnessed the brotherly harassment nature of their relationship, and knew he was teasing. It was amusing. But she was glad she hadn't found Colonel Montgomery in the cellar keeping David company. Lucy couldn't deny, didn't know if there was any reason to deny, the warmth that spread over her skin when she talked with David Forte. She found him compelling, beyond her fascination with his medical condition.

"Would you prefer I leave you alone to work?"

"No," he said, barely letting her finish. Then cleared his throat. "I'm not right in the head sometimes, but I'm not so far gone I'd send away a beautiful woman who offers to keep me company. Especially if she comes bearing gifts of cookies and coffee?"

Lucy held out both, and David took the coffee but only two of the cookies, leaving the other in her hand. "I don't have much in the way of comfort down here, but I've got a couple old camp chairs I don't think are in danger of collapsing." He motioned with a tilt of his head toward the far wall on the other side of the console.

Several old-fashioned LED lamps hung from the first-floor joists, casting a decent amount of light in the middle of the space with shadows around the edges. Decades of what could only be described as *stuff* filled the corners, took up shelf space, or hung on the walls. Everything from winter coats to stacks of maps to more of the camping equipment David had utilized. Probably the treasures of past generations who had inhabited the house before it became the center of Unity Valley.

The camp chair creaked enough as she sat to make her flinch, but when it didn't give out beneath her, Lucy relaxed, smiling as she caught David's low groan of appreciation as he bit into one of the cookies she'd grabbed on her way down.

"Thank you," he said, saluting her with the remains of the cookie in his hand.

"You're welcome." She sighed and studied the console he'd been beneath. "How's it going? Are you making progress?"

"Not as fast as I want. I'm usually making do with what I can bring from Alexandria and what I can get my hands on whatever I can MacGyver wherever we go to build the dome system. It's not like I can run down to Best Buy or AutoZone for what I need."

Unfamiliar with either of the places he mentioned, she just nodded and took a bite of the cookie he'd not taken from her. "Did I hear right that you designed the ... *dome?*"

He curled his upper lip and canted his head. "Yeah, I guess. The idea kind of hit me after—" He practically bit off the last word he might have said and took a sip of coffee. "A few weeks back, I witnessed some pretty amazing people protect an entire house with nothing but the power of their minds." David shook his head and looked toward her, his usual smile gone. "Have you ever witnessed anything like that? People who are more Jedi than Human. I guess most now call it Talents."

She shook her head. There was a lot he said she didn't quite understand but guessed the gist of it. "No, I haven't. Not up close anyway. I've heard about it, though. There are more people with – Talents? – than I think most of us realized until recently. It must be amazing."

"It is." He lowered his chin, staring down at the remaining bite of cookie held between his fingers. "Back in 2011, when I lost everything, I wouldn't have ever imagined the crazy shi-stuff," he corrected, clearing his throat and a small smile ticked at the corner of his mouth when he looked at her sidelong. "Crazy stuff like what I woke up to. I could spend days explaining it all."

"I look forward to it." She held her breath for the two seconds it took for him to glance toward her and hold her gaze. His slow smile made her cheeks warm, and she smiled back.

"Good," he said, then nodded and took a deep breath, looking forward again. "Good," he repeated. "I've got something to take care of tomorrow. Something I've been putting off, mostly because I'm a coward – don't hold that against me," he interjected with a crooked smirk. "But maybe after that I can . . . buy you a cup of coffee." David held up the cup she'd brought him and finished the contents.

At that moment the question she wanted to ask didn't seem as pressing. If he decided she was worth telling, he'd tell her. "I look forward to that, too, David."

CHAPTER SEVEN

It took David nearly an hour and three circuits around the inside perimeter of the compound before he worked through his inner dialogue enough to convince himself he was ready to see his son.

His son . . .

Thinking those two words were enough to derail an hour of contemplation and fortification. Why he was so concerned – no, *terrified* – to see his son he wasn't sure, but he was.

No, he did know. Maybe actually admitting it would help him not be such a wuss. One of the last conversations David had with Kelly had been one filled with yelling and accusations, and predictions on Kelly's part. She told him one day he'd come home from one of his "missions" and his boys wouldn't want to see him; or worse, he'd not come home at all, and they wouldn't miss him in their lives. She'd said it to hurt him. He knew that, and he'd refused to rise to the bait, but that didn't mean there wasn't some part of him that worried she was right.

Who needed the disruption of their four-decade-absent father showing up out of nowhere with a Deadbeat Dad excuse to beat *all* Deadbeat Dad excuses?

He held a small bit of hope they didn't hate him or resent his absence since two more generations of Forte men bore his name. You didn't name your son after someone you hated, right? And your grandson had to have heard okay things to continue the tradition, right?

Right?

Cursing himself out under his breath in a tirade that would have made his drill sergeant proud, David marched toward the steel-enforced canvas yurt he'd been told housed in part his descendants. The yurts were three-thousand square feet each, divided into family quarters with a central hallway. The outer framework was metal with wooden doors and beams inside. When erected properly, the yurts would last up to four years through all types of weather, giving communities time to build permanent homes. When access was available, they had heat, cooling, running water, and power. For now, David was glad his family had the protection.

He went to the inner doorway Tisdale told him was the one he wanted. On the door was a sign written in juvenile penmanship, with strange capitalization and spelling included.

Felicia Forte

Davey Forte

David james Forte 4th

This must be the place.

David braced his feet, bowed his head, and raised his hand. Beyond the door he distinguished three voices: a woman, a young child, and a man. The words didn't form, but the tone was easy. With one strengthening breath, he knocked three times.

"Hang on," came the woman's voice, along with a couple sharp barks from a dog followed by "Duke, hush," and moments later the door opened. He was met with a wide smile from a woman about the age he was when his old life ended, with dark blond hair and green eyes. "Hello," she said, but he saw the slightest second take in her expression.

Did she see it already? Could she?

"Hi," he said, every rehearsed and formulated word completely evaporated from his head. David cleared his throat. "Hello."

He hadn't seen a photo of her, but he assumed this was probably Felicia, his granddaughter-in-law. The world got freakier every minute. Her smile widened a little further.

"I think we established the proper greetings. Can I help you with something, sir?" she asked, angling herself to keep the dog from pushing past her.

"Who is it, Mum?" called the young voice from inside, and the pounding of feet only a six-year-old could manage echoed on the wooden floors before the youngest of the family appeared at his mother's hip. "Hi!" he said with enthusiasm.

"Hi."

Felicia chuckled. It helped ground David a little.

"Um, I'm looking for David Forte," he managed to say, tagging "Junior" on the end. "I'm . . . family. I just found out he was here, and—"

Felicia blanched and her eyes widened. "DJ honey, go back in with Grandpa, okay? I'll be right in," she said to her son, stroking his hair.

DJ's answer was to bolt back into the six hundred square foot space beyond the door, the dog deciding to follow him instead of guarding the door. Kids that age had two speeds: sonic and sleeping. With the boy back inside, Felicia stepped into the hall and closed the door behind her, not looking at David again until it was shut. A lead ball sat in his gut. There was more going on than he knew, and he had the distinct feeling he was about to be ambushed.

Felicia walked with purpose toward the door he'd used to enter the interior hallway of the yurt, not bothering to ask him to follow but he did, catching up with her right outside. The tendrils of twilight had just begun to stretch across the community and the air was a little cooler. It shifted quickly here, dependent wholly on the sun. Once they left the structure behind by several dozen feet, Felicia stopped short and pivoted to face him. He pulled up short of running into her.

"Am I crazy?" she demanded.

"I—"

She spoke so fast he almost didn't keep up, punctuating every few words with a cut of her hand through the air or a finger pointed at him. "I've seen pictures. *And* videos! I mean, how else would I have *any* idea what you – if you're you – if you're who I'm *nuts* for thinking you are – how could I possibly know what *you* look like. If you're you. Or him. Or—" She stopped herself, shaking her head. "Because you either are, or you're the most impressive doppelganger ever. Don't even answer because I've got to be crazy."

At any moment either his head or his chest was going to explode. He just didn't know which would go first. He'd lost the plot and didn't know what to say or do.

Ah, hell . . .

"I'm David James Forte. Senior," he choked out. "The first one."

She shook her head before he got out his last name, staring at him with wide, round eyes. "How is that *possible?*"

He laughed, though it nearly choked him, and looked up at the darkening sky, shaking his head. "Damned if I know," he answered. When he looked at her again, tears brimmed and slipped down her cheeks, but he was pretty sure she hadn't blinked. "It's a hell of a story, and most days I don't believe it myself. But I swear to you I am David Forte. And I'm looking for my son. I assume you're Felicia."

She nodded. Then just as quickly closed her eyes and shook her head. "I'm sorry." More tears fell when she opened her eyes and looked at him, sadness plain as day overtaking her shock. "I'm sorry, but you can't just go in there and tell him who you are."

"Look, I know there's not any *easy* way to do this—"

"You need to give me time," she said, cutting him off. "He can't . . . he can't understand. If you're confused and think *I* can't understand, there's no way *he'll* be able to. Didn't anyone tell you what happened to him?"

A cold flush shot down his reinforced spine, splintering into his limbs. "Reports are iffy at best. It's taken months just to find him, and I don't know a hell of a lot more. I saw pictures . . ."

Felicia shook her head and pressed her lips together. "Pictures can't show you everything. My father-in-law is . . ." She swallowed hard, and with more of her tears David's throat closed in tighter. "He's gone.

Whoever you thought you'd find here, isn't here. He's mentally not much older than his grandson."

David wandered into the main house kitchen after the table had been cleared, prep for the next day was complete and everyone had gone their separate ways for the evening, and the kitchen was nearly clean. It was the sound of his boots scuffing on the floor and the subtle hiss of his suit when he stopped in the doorway that drew Lucy's attention. She stepped back from putting dishes in the cabinet to look toward the door and smiled when she confirmed it was him.

He looked her way, but his expression was distant. His eyes were red rimmed, and he looked away just as quickly. A cold bullet of concern shot up her spine.

"Hey," she said, wiping her hands on a towel and walked toward him, hoping a little tease might lighten whatever load he carried. "You're a little late for dinner."

David looked confused for a moment and looked at the watch on his left wrist. "Damn," he mumbled.

"I can make you a sandwich."

David looked up from his wrist, making eye contact with her, and the pain in his eyes, even though he obviously tried to mask it, made Lucy's chest squeeze. She instinctively took a step toward him, though she had no idea what she'd do if he said no and left. Lucy held her breath, waiting for him to say something.

Finally, he nodded, and she relaxed.

"I appreciate that."

Instead of going to the long, now empty table he walked with her into the large kitchen prep area and sat on one of the tall stools along the island they used to prep dinner. Fighting the urge to watch him over her shoulder, Lucy took some of the food from dinner – leftovers were rare, but existent tonight – and set to making him a sandwich.

When she turned with plate in hand, he sat with his head down and his hands linked together on the countertop.

Sadness emanated from him like a wave of cold air.

None of her suspicions about his connection to the Forte family had been confirmed – though she couldn't imagine being so wrong – and if her suspicions about today were correct, a visit to them was probably the commitment he needed to take care of. Too many scenarios from that possibility clamored in her head, but only a small few could result in this emotionally beaten down man.

Could they have rejected him? With so many people having lost so many people, it would be unthinkably cruel to turn him away.

"We don't have a whole lot in the way of sandwich fixings, but I've learned to really love butter as a condiment. We have plenty of that." The talking filled the silence as she made the basic sandwich of wild rabbit. It hadn't been a protein source ever on her list – short or long – of preferred meals when life was normal, but here they ate what they had. The forest had rabbits and the streams and creeks had fish, all in abundance. Lucy set the plate on the island and slid it toward him, leaning forward on her elbows once he reached for it. "If you're a good boy and eat your dinner, I might be able to find a piece of apple pie."

David smiled, but it was forced and incomplete. "Thank you," he said before picking up half the sandwich and taking a sizeable bite. "Butter works great," he mumbled around the food in his cheek. "It feels like whenever we talk you're giving me something to eat or drink."

"I'm holding out until a bit later for your evening tea."

The upward tip of his mouth couldn't come close to being called a smile, but it was something.

She turned away to let him eat, finishing her chore of putting away dishes while he finished. By the time she heard him push away the plate she had dished out the apple pie as promised. Without speaking yet, she swapped the empty plate for the new, full one.

"I'd normally offer coffee, but I don't think the sleeping tea could fight back the caffeine if you drank coffee now."

"Thank you," he said again, sounding so much more than tired it made Lucy's chest ache again, even though she didn't know why yet.

"I haven't had apple pie in . . ." He trailed off and made a dismissive chuckling sound, shaking his head. He cut away the tip of the slice with the side of his fork, and scooped up the apple chunks and crust, shoveling it into his mouth.

Lucy smiled when David closed his eyes and groaned. "I'm glad you like it. Culinary school wasn't exactly my professional calling, but Abuela Gabi was a good teacher."

He shifted his fork in his grip to rub his thumb across his lower lip, then cut away another piece. "You made this? It's amazing. She'd smack me with a dishtowel if she ever heard me, but I'd say it's better than what Nana Forte used to make."

"That's quite possibly the most earnest praise I've ever gotten for my attempts." She scooted up onto the stool beside him, set her elbow on the counter, and rested her chin in her palm to watch while he devoured the pie. With each bite, she thought maybe some of the weight on his shoulders eased.

"What was your calling?" he asked, glancing at her while he worked closer to the crust of the slice.

"Professionally?" she asked, and he nodded. "Medical school, actually, which came in handy when I ended up here." She hitched her thumb over her shoulder to the dark hallway that led back to the infirmary. "My course of study was supposed to be . . ." She paused because it really seemed ridiculous now. "Ophthalmic surgery."

"Like . . . eyes?"

She nodded. "I had finished three terms, almost four, and was at the 'questioning my life choices' stage of medical school, so I decided a visit with Molly and Rev might help me clear my head." Lucy shrugged and sighed, sitting straighter to drop her hands into her lap. "That was two years ago this past May."

A hint of understanding crossed his features, and Lucy arched an eyebrow. "Yeah, you get it. All plans I might have had, or changes in plans I guess, went up in smoke quite literally. I was in Seattle with them when the Sorracchi destroyed Los Angeles, where I would have been in another day. We left Seattle shortly after because Rev worried about our safety in the city. Completely justified since Seattle was hit a few months later. We ended up in a small town not far from here, and eventually Unity Valley came together as the need grew. I've been with Rev and Molly ever since, and nearly four terms of medical school gave me enough training to be helpful in the infirmary."

"You've been great for me," he said, looking away again, his head hanging so he once again looked tired and worn. "Might be the medicine, might be the caregiver, but I think it's both." He raised his head and met her gaze as he finished the compliment. "I'd say thank you again, but it feels like that's all I've said." David stared at her, but she wondered how much it was intentional focus on her, or actual lack of focus. He tilted his head and his forehead creased. "I heard you call him Rev before; is it some kind of nickname from Trevor?"

Lucy grinned and shook her head. "No, it's more of an inside joke, I guess. Trevor was studying for a doctorate in theology, which one might argue was useless in the 21st Century. I called him Rev all the time, and it stuck a lot firmer than I think he likes."

"That explains things for me," David said. "He's got this way of calming people. No wonder he's the one taking care of everyone.

Lucy winked and grinned – because he'd just summarized Trevor Tisdale as efficiently as anyone she'd known in Unity Valley – as she slid off the stool and took his dishes to the sink to rinse them quickly. While she washed, she tuned in to the subtle hydraulic hiss of his body suit as he moved off the stool and walked to the back door that opened onto the third side of an open-air farmer's porch that wrapped almost completely around the house except for the sunroom off the perpendicular side. She flipped off the single solar generator-powered light in the kitchen as she left, joining David on the porch.

He'd found one of the bench swings and sat in the darkness, his silhouette coming into focus as her eyes adjusted to the low light. The chains holding the swing creaked softly with his slight movement. Lucy debated whether she should leave him with his thoughts or sit with him, but in the end, the tug in the center of her chest drew her to the swing.

As she walked in front of him he braced his feet on the porch floor to stop the swing's movement, letting her climb on beside him. She sat with her back to the armrest, facing him sideways with her feet tucked between them. Once she settled, he pushed off and put the swing into motion again.

They sat in silence for at least twenty minutes, Lucy watching his profile as he stared into the yard. The community was relatively quiet; it was somewhere between late evening and early night now and families had gone to their respective homes, such as they were, to rest and be together. Despite the danger that always skimmed around the edge of every moment, people here embraced their peace any way they could. The soft mingle of conversation sometimes carried on the evening breeze, seasoned with an occasional laugh or the sound of some of the animals in their stables nearby. Night insects chirped to each other, and the aromas of evening flowers tickled her senses.

It was the peace of Unity Valley that had kept many of them sane in the weeks and months following the whole world being turned upside down.

"February 13th," he said, catching her off guard. "Friday the 13th this year. That's the day I was found frozen in this dying Sorracchi ship. Another couple of weeks and we would have been dead."

"We . . ." she led.

He chuckled with another one of his humorless laughs. "That's another story. Important, but hell, most days I can't process it myself."

Lucy rested her arm on the back of the swing and set her curled fingers against her temple. "Okay," she said simply, hoping he understood the offer.

"I woke up February 26th. Nearly died in the process. Couldn't sit up on my own. Couldn't move my arms, my legs, nothing. I'm told this crazy ass story about it being 2054 and I've been 'in stasis' for over four decades." He stopped and cleared his throat, looking down at his hands. "Forty-three years for the rest of the world. But for me, it had been a couple days."

His voice cracked harder with each word, and each word tightened around Lucy's throat.

"My boys were eleven and seven."

"Oh, David . . ." she whispered.

He raised his head and looked out into the night. The minimal moonlight glistened off the wet trails on his cheeks. "I saw Davey tonight. My oldest boy. I came here to meet him. I have to believe if Nick had known he would have told me . . ."

Lucy closed her eyes and held her breath, swallowing hard, and chastised herself for not talking about the older David Forte the evening before when she'd found him. She'd assumed – incorrectly, she realized now – that if David knew his son was here, he knew about the severe brain damage that had left the fifty-something year old man with the mind of a child.

"I couldn't talk to him because he wouldn't understand. He can't —" His words died, strangled by the raw emotion. He sucked in a hard breath, bowing his head again.

Unwilling to consider any other action, Lucy rolled forward onto her knees to close the small space between them, wrapping her arms around him to lay her cheek against his shoulder. He shook in her hold but kept talking.

"Felicia told me Anthony, my youngest, died thirty years ago. Of cancer. I wasn't there. I wasn't there for him. For any of them. If I had just—"

Lucy shook her head, trying to move closer. She laid her hand on the side of his head to draw him toward her, pressing her tear-slick lips to his temple. "No, no," she whispered against his salty skin. "No, David. Don't."

He turned into her embrace, pulling her hard against him to bury his face over her heart. He cried in silence, only the ferocity of his hold and the shake of his body revealing the pain tearing through him.

CHAPTER EIGHT

19 August 2054, Wednesday
Protectorate Citizen Community — Unity Valley
Vancouver, British Columbia
Former Country of Canada
North American Continent

"Gadamnit!" David yelled and tossed the useless, irreparable part across the basement space where it bounced off a rusty bucket with a ping. He braced his hands on the edge of the control console and dropped his head forward, clenching his jaw to rein in the frustration grinding in his chest.

"That bad, man?"

David inhaled deep through his nose and pushed it out with just as much force before he looked up to the staircase where Connor stood six or seven steps up from the cement floor.

"I'm trying to build a Ferrari out of a John Deere, an old combine, and a twenty-year-old hard drive and I'm holding it together with chewing gum and fertilizer." He picked up another useless part he'd burned out an hour earlier and chucked it in the same direction as the pail. "MacGyver couldn't pull this off with all the damn paperclips in the world."

"Who's MacGyver?"

David closed his eyes and shook his head. "No one. Never mind."

The stairs creaked as Connor finished the descent. "If he's someone who can help—"

"He's not – he's a guy from an old tv show," he tried to explain, then saw the smirk on Connor's face when he moved enough into the light cast from the ceiling fixtures and stopped with a low groan in his throat. "You can be a real son of a bitch, you know that?"

Connor shrugged and chuckled and picked up an unused fuse. "Not having much luck, huh?"

"If it weren't for bad luck, I'd have no luck at all. Every time I do this it's like a new project. No blueprint. No schematics. No plan beyond 'make it happen.' I brought the pre-programmed computer core with us I need, but it's a real pain in the ass not having the exact equipment each time. I'm making a miracle every damn time."

Connor tossed the fuse back into a pile of other fuses. "Yet, you've pulled it off every time. It impresses the hell out of me."

"Did you come down here to give me a pep talk, or do you need something?" David asked. "Or are you just bored?"

"Pep talk, no, but I did want to check in with you. Don't get all weird on me, but it seems you're . . . *off* . . . today. Everything go okay yesterday? I know you were going to talk to your son."

David turned away from Connor and went to one of the camp chairs he'd set up against the wall, dropping hard into it. He'd done his damnedest to not think about the afternoon before, but every time he let his mind drift away from the erector set of a computer console it went back to his conversation with Felicia.

She asked him to stay away. At least for a few days. Until she could figure out a way to explain things to Davey. He'd agreed.

It had broken him. Nearly completely broken him.

"What did Nick tell you about my family?" he asked, realizing a second too late he'd snapped out the words.

Connor stared hard at him, and David stared back, hoping he knew Connor well enough at this point to know if he was lying. Then again,

Connor had to know how to lie to do his job, though he'd argue it's not lying if the information is confidential. Didn't mean he didn't know how to lie through his teeth if needed.

"I don't think anything more than what I needed to know, that they were here. Your son, his daughter-in-law, and your great-grandson."

"Nothing else?"

"No," Connor said with the same firmness as David's question. "Come on, man. What happened? Did he not believe you?"

David shook his head and huffed. His gut told him yesterday, and kept reminding him today, that if Nick Tanner knew the full extent of the truth, he would have told David. He wouldn't have sent him in blind to something like that. Nick wasn't that kind of man.

"I didn't talk to Davey."

Connor didn't say anything; just watched David while he worked a broken machinery bit between his fingers. David knew he had to get used to saying it, but damn, it hurt like hell. He took another deep breath to fortify himself and cleared his throat.

And rattled off the story of the day before the fastest he could without sounding like a county fair auctioneer and without his voice cracking in the process. He managed to get it out in six sentences or less but stared across the basement at the pail he'd attacked instead of looking at Connor. When he finished, silence filled the basement like smoke, making David's eyes burn.

"*Merde*," Connor finally said. "Damn, man. I'm sorry."

David could only nod, not ready to say anything else. He braced his hands on the worn aluminum and nylon arms of the camp chairs and pushed himself forward and upward, his hydraulics hissing and his body protesting at the movement. He needed to do something other than curse about his lack of parts or waiting for Connor to say something profound.

"I'm going to go scavenge in the barns and outbuildings, see what I can find," he said as he moved past Connor.

He was four steps up the stairs before Connor said his name. He stopped and looked back.

"Nick would have told you if he knew."

David clenched his jaw and nodded before turning away and starting back up the stairs. "I know."

"What do you think of Colonel Forte?"

Lucy glanced up from the freshly washed bandages she was busy rolling to look at Molly. "That's an out of the blue question. We were talking about baby names. Are you considering David as a name?"

Molly smiled, leaning back against one of the railings on the main house back porch off the kitchen. She rubbed a hand over her belly. "David is a nice name, but that's not why I ask. I just noticed you're spending time with him."

"If I didn't think highly of him, I wouldn't be spending time with him," Lucy said with a noncommittal shrug. She glanced sideways at Molly. "Now would I . . ."

Molly curled her smile into a mock-annoyed smirk and shook her head, tossing a handful of bandages at Lucy they'd decided to discard because they were too worn out to use. "Fine then. You *think highly* of him. How highly?"

Lucy finished up the roll she had and put it in the special container they had to keep them sanitized. She sighed and shifted to match her best friend's position, her back to the railing on the other side of the wide steps.

"Am I crazy, Mol?" she asked, deciding to cut through the teasing. "He's been here days, not even a week, but . . ." She smiled, knew it was a ridiculous grin, and didn't care because this was Molly and she wouldn't be able to hide from Molly how she felt for long.

Molly laughed. "Wow, that smile says everything."

"Maybe it does. He's easy to be with, but at the same time he keeps me out of balance. Does that even make sense?"

"Makes perfect sense, Sis. Sounds to me like you're falling fast."

"Oh, don't be silly. I enjoy spending time with him, talking to him, but it's nothing—"

"Serious? Why not? Why can't it be?"

"Because it's been five days!"

"So. Honestly, Luce, who cares how long it's been? The whole world changed in a matter of days; why can't your heart."

Lucy shook her head and stood, offering Molly her hand to help her stand. "Come on," she said. "I have to work the evening shift in the infirmary and want to take a walk before then."

Molly groaned as she stood. "Fine, but we're not done talking."

"Fine."

Molly said she wanted to find Trevor, so Lucy dropped off the bandages in the infirmary and went to her bedroom to retrieve her sketch portfolio and pencils. When she reached the bottom of the stairs, she considered going down another level to the cellar to see how David felt after the heartbreaking news he'd learned the day before. But decided against it. He was trying to finish the dome generator and she didn't want to do anything to distract him. She'd find him after dinner to make sure he was okay.

She went out the front door and down the steps, turning right to head toward the trees. They'd been cautioned not to go too far into the forest because the threat of a Xeno attack was always there, but her favorite spot wasn't more than twenty feet from the edge of the cleared property. They'd had rain overnight, so the stream ran fresh from the source somewhere up the mountain. The air under the tree canopy was cooler and smelled more crisp right at the stream edge.

Tucked just into the woods was a massive Victorian home with twin chimneys and turret rooms at two corners sitting idle and unused. It was solid but had long been left to sit silent by whoever had lived on the land decades before the world changed and because of the much-needed repairs the community had decided to leave it unoccupied. As Rev had said once, she – the house – had good bones but needed time and resources they didn't yet have. Perhaps someday. She'd wandered more than once through the rambling building with spacious and oddly shaped rooms with high ceilings that made her footsteps echo, huge windows with window seats and bookshelves, and fireplaces in nearly every room and wondered what lives had been lived in those walls.

She'd heard the children telling stories about it being haunted, but she felt nothing but a peace and calm when she stepped inside. They'd probably been told it was haunted to keep them from wandering around alone inside the old walls. Sometimes she imagined she still heard the laughter of years past, but it was probably just her imagination.

Today the house didn't call to her, though. Today, the water did.

She walked the path by memory, going right to her favorite spot to sit on a fallen tree trunk. On hot days, she liked to dangle her feet in the water, but the day wasn't warm enough and the water was probably ice cold. So instead, she found a perfect spot of sunlight coming through the leaves and opened her portfolio on her lap. She had precious few blank pages left, but she wanted to fill the book with memories while they were still fresh and sharp.

She had no real idea how much time had gone by when she heard someone coming through the trees from the direction of the old Victorian. Figuring it was someone coming to find her, she worked on finishing the spot she'd been focused on since she'd have to quit soon. Other than the stream and the sound of the forest beneath their feet, there was little other sound, so when she heard the distinctive hiss of hydraulics she smiled.

Lucy stilled her pencil and looked up, watching where she thought he would come into view. He stepped clear of the trees closest to the stream maybe fifteen feet downstream from her and stopped with his hands at his waist, breathing deep like the trek in might have winded him. He told her there were days the simple act of moving was exhausting and walking the uneven forest floor must have been a challenge. He inhaled deep, opened his eyes, then slowly crouched at the water edge, dipping his fingers into the stream. Lucy smiled when he cupped his hand and brought the water to his lips, drinking. He hummed in appreciation.

"Delicious, isn't it?"

David startled and almost fell, twisting on the balls of his feet in her direction. Lucy gasped and reached out a hand in an instinctual need to try to help, despite the fact she was too far away.

"I'm sorry!" she cried. "I didn't mean to—I thought you knew I was here."

David righted himself on his feet again, his boots now wet, and shook the water off his hand while he chuckled. "So much for be aware of your surroundings, right?"

Lucy turned down her lips and tried to look as apologetic as she felt. "I really am sorry."

With a low groan and strained movement, David stood again. Water darkened spots on his olive utility pants, but didn't soak them, and he ran his hands down his thighs to dry them as he headed upstream toward her.

"Not a problem, but no, I had no idea you were out here." He looked back out the way they both had come. "I was scavenging in one of the garages for anything I can adapt for use in the control console. I thought I heard running water, so I took a walk. I saw that house. I never knew it was down here. I was surprised to see it." When he looked back at her, his smile was slow ... and dare she admit sexy. "You're an even better surprise."

"I love that house," she said, looking past him to the faded white clapboard siding and deep porch she knew wrapped all the way around the house. "Did you go inside?"

"I did," he confirmed, looking back to it. "I was surprised it's not being used, but I can see why. She needs a lot of love, but she's got–"

"Good bones," Lucy said with him, and laughed when he grinned. "Rev says the same things. I thought I was the only one who referred to the house as a she. She really is beautiful."

That slow smile spread his lips again. "Yeah, she is."

She smiled wider and moved the bag holding what remained of her precious sketch pencils to the other side of where she sat so he could take a seat on the trunk beside her. He sat close enough his hip pressed hers.

"Can I see what you're working on?"

Lucy didn't often share her sketches because they weren't for anyone but her, so she surprised herself when she easily handed over the portfolio and her partial sketch. "I'm working completely off memory," she explained. "This is Uncle Ignacio, my mother's younger brother, and his husband Leo. Ignacio was only about ten years older than me, so growing up he felt a lot like a brother."

David took the sketchpad and angled it so the sun coming through the leaves let him see it better. "This is great," he said. "How long has it been since you saw them?"

"About three years." When he looked from the drawing to her, she shook her head. "I don't know what happened to them. If they're alive, or . . ." She stopped to swallow hard.

"Ignacio . . . Santos or something else?"

She nodded. "Santos."

"Can I look at the rest? It's okay if you say no; I know artists are sometimes protective of their work."

Lucy chuckled. "I'm not an artist. I just like to sketch. Go ahead."

David flipped backward through the sketchpad. Some were of people in Unity Valley like Trevor and Molly and Mama Della, and a variety of other community members. There were even sketches of the Victorian and how she imagined some of the rooms looking when she was a home or might look when someone could bring the home to life again. Some of the older sketches were of Abuela Gabi, of neighbors, and of some of her classmates at university. She explained with each who they were, and he just nodded and studied the images.

"I wish I had spent more time when Abuela Gabi was with me, and maybe drawn her then rather than trying to remember. Same as Uncle Ignacio. Hardly anyone has something as precious as a photograph anymore. I think we all took things for granted, and I don't want to forget them now."

David nodded, then looked up from the sketches. "If I've figured out anything in all this, it's not to take anything for granted." He took a deep breath and released it on a sigh. "Do you have brothers or sisters?"

Lucy shook her head, then gave a wry chuckle. "Not that I know of." At David's confused look, she rolled her eyes. "My mom got pregnant with me way too young, and Abuela Gabi raised me. She was my maternal grandmother. My mother only stayed with us until she was eighteen, and then wasn't around much, if ever. I don't know if she had other kids, or if my father had other kids. Abuela Gabi told her to stay away until she knew how to be an adult. She stayed away," Lucy finished with a shrug. "Honestly, it never bothered me because Abuela Gabi was everything I ever needed."

"I can tell. It's the way you talk about her."

Lucy rocked on the trunk and bumped David's shoulder with her own. "What about you? If we're sharing family stories . . ." She immediately realized the weight of what she asked and shook her head. "I'm sorry. I didn't even think about the fact you've been—"

"On ice for forty years?" he finished and waved his hand to dismiss her worry. "Hell, sometimes I forget. Then I look around, think 'holy crap,' and remember."

"I've tried to imagine how strange that had to be."

"Strange doesn't even start to cover it and gets stranger every day." David sighed and smiled, the lopsided kind she'd already learned to recognize as just a way to skirt whatever he was probably really feeling. "To be honest, I didn't ask anyone to find them. You were born when your mom was young, and I was one of those late-in-life-oops kids. Mom was in her mid-forties and Dad was in his fifties."

"Wow."

He chuckled and it sounded more genuine. "I doubt that's what either one of them said. Mom probably figured baby making was in her past. My youngest brother was already sixteen when I came along. By the time I was in kindergarten, I was pretty much an only child."

"In an odd way, I bet we had similar experiences growing up. You were raised by elderly parents, and I was raised by an elderly grandparent."

David nodded and looked across the stream to the dark woods beyond. "I suppose so. Anyway, both Mom and Dad were already gone in 2011. I had two older brothers and two older sisters, but even the youngest of them would be in their nineties by now. Even if the world hadn't gone to hell in a handbasket, the chances of any of them being alive would be pretty damn slim."

"They could have kids, or grandkids . . ."

"They've been without Uncle David for decades. I'm that weird, unexplainable leaf on the Ancestry.com family tree that everyone just ignores. They don't need me showing up now."

Lucy tilted her head, studying his profile. After a few moments, he turned and looked at her and she smiled. She'd wanted him to see her face when she said, "Their loss is my gain. I'm glad you showed up now."

David's genuine smile was her reward. He looked away and focused again on the sketchpad. "These are amazing. You shouldn't undersell yourself. You're an artist," he said, handing back the portfolio.

Her cheeks warmed and she looked down, closing the book. "Thank you. I need to go back to the house. I'm working in the infirmary this evening and I should change and eat."

David moved away from the trunk, his hydraulics barely audible over the running stream, and waited for her to finish gathering her supplies and draping the crossbody bag across her shoulders, then offered his hand. Instead of letting go when he'd made sure she cleared the obstacles along the stream's edge, he shifted his hold to lace their fingers and walked beside her. After a few feet, he stopped, and she stopped with him, turning her head to see why.

His head was down, his attention on their hands, and Lucy waited until he finally raised his chin and looked at her. "Thank you."

Lucy tilted her head. "For what?"

"For last night. I was . . . I *wasn't* prepared for any of it."

Lucy raised her free hand and laid it on his cheek. "I don't think anyone could have been. I'm glad I could be there. I don't know if I helped, but—"

"You helped," David said, cutting off her sentence. "You helped."

"Good." She started to lower her hand from his cheek, but he brought his own hand up to hold hers there, turning into the touch to kiss her palm, his eyes closed.

Her pulse jumped and an immediate flush of heat spread from her hairline to her toes. She had to take her next breath deep and slow, releasing it just as slowly. He held his lips to her palm for several racing beats of her heart before he opened his eyes and looked at her. Still holding her hand, he brought it down from his cheek and studied her, the way his eyes shifted from her eyes to her lips making her flush hotter.

"You can call me a dirty old man if you want," he said with a slight uptick of his mouth. "I want to kiss you, Lucy."

She smiled back. "So, kiss me."

The last word was barely spoken when his lips came over hers, drawing a soft sound from her throat. Lucy leaned into him, and when he brought up both his hands to hold her face, she parted her lips to encourage him to kiss her deeper. He didn't hesitate, leaving her heart pounding and her head light. David slowed the kiss, finally stilling with his mouth pressed to hers, giving one final touch before drawing back. Lucy drew in a steadying breath and opened her eyes again as she released it, to find him studying her again with a lopsided smile.

Still smiling and watching her, he took her hand again, and they walked out of the trees together.

17 HOURS 36 MINUTES LATER . . .

"They're on the west ridge behind the tree line!"

"Brilliant observation, Sherlock," David mumbled, ducking his head as shattered masonry dust showered down on him from yet another blast hitting the barricade wall along the west property line of Unity Valley.

"Forte, can you confirm?"

David groaned, and twisted to put his back against the wall, tapping the earpiece to answer. "I'm pretty damn sure they're on the west ridge." Another blast blew out a chunk of the concrete ledge. "Yep! Absolutely sure, Montgomery!"

Connor threw out a list of orders, but most of them were lost in the cacophony of weapons fire and blasted structures around David. He caught enough to get that Connor was shifting coverage from the east perimeter to the west perimeter. Wiping dust from his face, while trying not to scratch his eyeballs with it, David shifted to his knees to squint and check out the tree line.

Damn Xenos were smart to attack in the middle of the day and from the shaded side of the community. The sun above the treetops, just enough to shine right into the eyes of anyone trying to defend Unity Valley. Sitting in the shade, the Xenos sights were clear, and their positions weren't given away by the flare of their weapons when fired. Even with his visor on, he couldn't make out the flashes, or shapes of anyone moving in the trees.

He inched up, and a bullet whizzed by his head, nearly parting his hair before it landed deep in a tree behind him. *Geez, bullets!* These guys were scavengers. If he saw bows and arrows, he was going to . . . well, he didn't really know what he'd do. But it changed the playing field.

More than anything, he was kicking himself for not getting the dome powered up before the Xenos attacked. They knew it happened every few days, and he'd been busting his hump for four days, but he wasn't even close. He'd joked with Connor, but even MacGyver would have had a hard time getting anything up and running with what he had to work from – spaghetti wire, burned out spark plugs, and bubblegum. Not much more.

Shouting to his left drew his attention, and he checked the charge level on his pulse rifle with the tip of his tongue as half a dozen Terra soldiers ran toward him – fully crouched. A bizarre flash of envy punched him in the chest before he pushed it aside. No time for pity parties.

Coming up from behind the row of soldiers came Connor, and he motioned for each of them to take up a position as he moved straight to David. "What are we dealing with?"

"I'd guess nine to twelve in the trees, then one on each side fanned out," David explained, motioning in the direction over the wall before slamming his charge pack into his rifle. "They've got old fashioned projectile weapons out there, along with whatever else they're using on us. They're either going to back down in another three minutes, or they're going to come in hot."

"How do you figure?"

"The sun is to their advantage right now," David said with a jut of his chin. "Just try looking at the source of the weapons fire. You can't, even with a visor, because of the sun position. And it's too bright to see the weapon flares."

Connor nodded, clenching his jaw. He wore a visor, but David noted the pinched lines fanning from beneath them. Looking into the light probably hurt like a son of a gun since Connor had been injured with severe flash burn a few months prior.

"If there are only a dozen or so, they're not going to rush us," Connor theorized. "They're ballsy but they're not stupid. They're inconveniencing us."

The air filled with a high-pitched whistle. Both Connor and David looked up, but the sun blinded them. "Missile!" they both shouted at the same time.

As a unit, everyone along the wall bolted away from the barrier. David pushed up and away, an instinctive move born of muscle memory, except his muscles had also forgotten four decades of immobility. Connor and the other soldiers were just a second faster, but it was enough they made it clear of the blast and he felt the slam against his back as he was thrown forward into the ground.

It knocked all the wind out of him, and he fought to see through the black miasma in front of his eyes. He sucked in as much dirt as oxygen, coughing while he tried to rise to his hands and knees. *Damn, that hurt!* As he squinted through the grit and pain he looked to the north. Through the debris and dust, he caught a glint of sunlight off something leaving the area fast. With herculean effort, David propelled himself forward and onto his feet, running as best he was capable of toward two hoverbikes, hoping they weren't damaged in the attack. He doubted he could catch the Xenos, but he might be able to track them long enough to get a bead on their base of operations.

"Forte!" Connor yelled, running up to him as he swung his leg over the bike and tried the ignition. It fired up no problem. "Where the hell are you going?"

David jutted his chin to the northwest in the direction he'd seen the flash. "I'm going to follow as long as I can! We might figure out where the hell they're hiding and deal with them head on," he shouted over the O_2 churn of the engine.

The bike lifted off the ground, kicking up more dirt and dust in its wake, and David set the balls of his feet on the foot pegs. Before the Xenos gained too much ground, he shot forward to catch up. He hadn't ridden one of the hoverbikes, but he'd spent many hours on the back of a Harley and figured it couldn't be much different when it came to balance and control. If anything, the hoverbikes were more versatile because they could navigate groundcover like a motorcycle never could.

With a slight tip upward of the nose, he navigated the bike over the perimeter wall, swearing long and hard when he nearly slid off backward like a rider on a rearing horse, but gained his seat again and headed for the tree line. Fighting still went on behind him, but it had already begun to wane which meant the Xenos were in retreat mode.

Once within the trees climbing the mountain to the north/northwest of the community, he slowed his speed to both allow for better control – he didn't need to plow himself straight on into a tree – and to listen. The O_2 engine was relatively quiet once started, and probably hummed like a dream if the machine was at peak performance. Once he honed-in on the sound of movement, he advanced, but always hung back in hopes of not drawing attention.

He was a good fifteen or twenty klicks from the community, easing over a cluster of fallen trees in a small clearing, when the hairs on the back of his neck stood on end. Too late he realized the Xenos had to have heard his approach and laid in wait for him. He pulled up hard and banked right, barely averting the mix of bullets and pulse weapon fire singeing the air around him.

"Damn it," he cursed.

"David!" Connor shouted into the earpiece still nestled in David's ear. "Report! What the hell are you doing?"

"Trying not to die!" he shouted, riding the hoverbike like a jet ski on a turbulent ocean, hanging on for dear life while he tried to get to the trees again. He'd be able to find cover there. Maybe twenty-five-hundred feet into the trees he tried to bank the bike and dive toward a cluster of foliage with the idea of hiding under cover until the Xenos thought he'd retreated, but as he twisted the bike a blast hit the tail end, sending him into a hard spin.

Somewhere in the flight, David lost his grip and slammed into a tree before he fell hard to the forest floor. Once again, all air left him and pain jolted through him before his vision swam black. He held consciousness only long enough to see the bike slam into an upcropping of rock and burst into a fiery ball.

CHAPTER NINE

"I need help now!"

Lucy's stomach clenched and she snapped her attention to the infirmary entrance from the main house hall at Connor Montgomery's shout. Her heart seized and jumped forward in an adrenaline-fueled jerk. An incompatible clash of relief and dread slammed together when she identified the Terra soldier being carried between Colonel Montgomery and Sergeant Molina, her head hanging limp and her hair dark with blood and debris.

The clash of emotion was immediately followed up by guilt when she acknowledged she was relieved the wounded soldier wasn't David.

Lucy blinked and forced herself back to the second – a moment was too long – and took hold of Isaias' hand, guiding him to hold the folded bandage to his own forehead. The slice was long, but not deep or damaging, and bled like a typical head wound. "Hold the bandage, Isaias. You're going to be okay."

He nodded. "I'm fine. Go ahead."

She scrambled up from kneeling beside the bed where Isaias rested and stumbled toward the three soldiers, reaching them at the same time as both Nathan and Doctor Dardashti, and the two men took the wounded woman from Colonel Montgomery and Sergeant Molina. Before following, Lucy glanced toward Connor. Sweat rolled down his cheek through smudged dust and dirt and he breathed hard, his hands set at his waist. His blue eyes shifted, and his gaze connected with hers, and what she saw made her gut clench once again. He shook his head, the tiniest of movements, then looked down and away before turning to run from the house into the aftermath of the Xeno attack.

Lucy blinked hard and shoved aside the cold dread to return to the infirmary. A dozen citizens had been injured, with two in critical and one they knew wouldn't make it more than a couple more hours. His injuries were extreme, and they didn't have the capability to help; he might not have made it even in a city like Alexandria. All they could do was put him in a room with his family and do their best to ease his suffering. He wouldn't open his eyes again.

The woman soldier Connor and Sergeant Molina had brought in was one of two soldiers who had been brought to the infirmary. The other had serious injuries, but not life threatening. But she had been through the aftermath of enough Xeno attacks to know the final count of injured and lost wouldn't be known for hours.

She didn't have any memory of going back into the infirmary or joining Doctor Dardashti to help the woman, and her conscious reality only clicked back into place as she saw her own hand wiping blood from the woman's forehead to expose some of the wound. Lucy forced herself to not lose attention again and pushed hard through the next two hours until the infirmary had calmed, and the smell of blood had been replaced with the cleansing scent of disinfectant now that the floors were clean again.

It was near dusk, but no one had been able to stop to eat, and with the ugliness of the day momentarily stilled, she took one more look around to the patients filling every available bed and walked with tired feet to the kitchen. At that moment, anything she could find to eat would be welcome, whether it was a piece of fruit or just a slice of bread. Anything that might calm the acidic battle in her stomach.

A handful of people worked around the large island, not speaking a word to each other as they prepared small meals likely going out to the residents who had no other way to receive food. Those who remained still needed care.

"Hey, Luce," Molly said, coming around the side of the island, holding her arms wide to embrace Lucy.

Lucy willingly complied, not realizing until that moment how much she needed the hug from her longest friend. She had to lean forward to compensate for Molly's belly, but it was worth the angle. Molly rubbed her back and kissed her cheek before drawing back.

"Sit down. Let me get you something to eat."

"Don't do anything special," Lucy said, sinking into the closest chair. "I don't have energy to eat much. I just need to fill the hole."

Molly nodded as she walked away and returned just moments later with a sliced apple and some farmer's cheese and a glass of cold water.

"Thank you," Lucy said on a heavy sigh. She'd known before that moment she was tired, but the simple act of sitting with her friend drained her to her core.

Molly eased into the chair beside her and rubbed her arm. "You were amazing today. Doctor Dardashti came through a bit ago, and told us you never paused, never slowed down. He says you're a gift to him."

Tears welled and burned, and Lucy pressed her lips together to suppress her chin trembling. She hid her eyes behind her hand, the tears too vicious to hold back. "Oh, honey," Molly whispered, scooting closer to drape her arm across Lucy's shoulders.

The release valve had opened, and Lucy couldn't close it again until she'd let herself weep. She usually managed to keep it all in check until she was behind the closed door of her bedroom, though on the days they lost someone it was hardest, but today . . . today was too much.

When she was finally able to take a breath and lift her head, Molly handed her a linen towel to dry her cheeks. "I'm sorry," she whispered.

"You know you don't ever have to apologize."

Before Lucy could say more, footsteps descending the stairs in the hallway made her look. Molly stood when Trevor came into view, and her small gasp matched the tightening in Lucy's chest at the downfallen sadness in his eyes. He crossed to them in three long strides and embraced his wife. Lucy imagined he needed the strength of affection as much as she had moments before, perhaps more, and Molly always seemed to have a full well to share.

Lucy looked away, not wanting to impose on their moment, and tried to take a bite of the apple and cheese. Molly knew one of her favorite snacks was sliced apple with cheese, and the thoughtfulness gave her a moment to smile.

Moments later, Trevor pulled out the chair adjacent to where Lucy and Molly had sat, and folded his hands together on the tabletop. "We just lost Jed."

Molly sniffled and gripped her husband's hand on the tabletop and Lucy set down what remained of her apple, any trace of appetite gone. This was often the hardest part of any attack . . . the aftermath. The tally.

"We lost no other of Unity Valley," he added. "We have many wounded, as Lucy knows, but Doctor Dardashti doesn't believe any are at risk. Colonel Montgomery's people have two minor injuries, and one serious. She was brought to the infirmary earlier, and Doctor Dardashti has expressed how grateful he was for your help."

Lucy swallowed and tried to meet Trevor's eyes, knowing he tried to make her feel better. She smiled and nodded. "I do what I can." Then something he said looped back into her thoughts. "None of the military died?" she asked.

"No." Trevor held her gaze and rolled his lips together before adding, "But Colonel Forte is missing."

A cold chill slid down her spine. "Missing?"

Trevor nodded. "He took a hoverbike in pursuit of the retreating Xenos, Connor said with the plan of finding their location and then returning to Unity Valley, but . . . they lost communication with him and haven't been able to locate either him or the bike."

Lucy had to force herself to breathe.

Unknown Mountain
Approximately 20 miles from Unity Valley

The sun had set an hour before, but it had taken her hours to find the man, return to her home for what she needed, return to him, and begin the trek to shelter. The sky opened when they were less than fifty feet from the cabin, but every foot Tessera dragged the makeshift litter behind her was a battle between the size of the man and the unforgiving terrain, with her ever mindful of the severity of his injuries and her mental and physical strain to move him. By the time she stumbled into the dark shelter both were soaked, and a deep chill had already attacked her.

Tessera barely managed to lift him from the litter and onto the cot. As his right arm came away from the back of her shoulders, one of the broken pieces of machinery somehow attached to his body scraped across her neck, burning as it dug at her skin. She hissed but ignored the pain to make sure he was on the cot sufficiently.

The rain pelted the small window behind her and soaked the wooden floor just inside the open door. A chill shook her, and gooseflesh rose on her exposed arms. She grabbed the one sweater she owned from the back of the only chair in the room and pulled it on over her wet clothes before opening the iron door of the small wood stove in the opposite corner.

Some embers still glowed at the bottom of the stove from her cooking fire the night before, and she stirred them with the iron bar she'd left leaning against the inner wall. Soon the low glow bloomed until the charcoal left behind by the last fire were red again. Her hands trembled as she grabbed a fistful of leaves she'd brought into the shelter to dry as starter fuel for the fire. As soon as they burned well, she laid some dried twigs and small pieces of wood she found helped get the fire burning.

While waiting for the fire to be strong enough to add larger chunks of wood, she stood and went to the small chest that held every piece of clothing in her possession, which wasn't much. With a glance over her shoulder to confirm the man was still unconscious, she shrugged off the sweater and peeled the wet tee shirt from her skin and over her head. She would deal with the wet shorts later. She grabbed one of the few tee shirts she'd found left in the cabin and covered herself, the shirt hanging loose from her shoulders. By the time she put the sweater on again, the fire was burning well and the red glow from the open stove door gave her light to see by. The wood pile in the cabin was shrinking so she did her best to remain judicious with what remained and added a single large log to the stove. The space was small and would warm up quickly. Whoever had built the shelter had put considerable thought and planning into the structure; in the warmest days of the summer the shelter had been cool and comfortable, and in the chill of the nights as the weather cooled, she remained warm and dry.

With the cabin quickly warming, she took a steeling breath and turned to face the cot. He hadn't moved from where she'd dropped him. Mostly on his back, he was turned slightly toward the cot edge, his left arm hanging off the side and his right arm draped across his chest. One leg hung off the side as well, the booted foot resting on the floor, with the other leg spread toward the wall, only the foot off the end of the cot.

She had heard the weapons fire while exploring the forest within an hour or two walk of the shelter. She never liked to go far, and never so far she worried about knowing the way home. She'd headed west that day, climbing upward. If she did get lost, she knew if she found the stream it would bring her back home again. When the sounds of blasts began, she dropped into the undergrowth to avoid being seen from above just as the air bike zoomed overhead. The kill shot came from the ground some distance away from her, hitting the back of the bike, and it flew into a horizontal spin.

That's when the rider had fallen, crashing through the trees, seconds before the bike hit the side of the mountain and burst into a fiery ball fed by its oxygen engines. She'd considered not trying to find him. In the end, the lesson of kindness Mama Della had taught her won out and she followed his flight and fall path until she found him in an unconscious, bleeding lump on the forest floor.

The stranger fascinated her.

He wore the standard work uniform most people in the military forces beneath President Tanner seemed to wear. His jacket had torn mostly off him, but there had been enough for her to recognize the emblem of the Phoenix on his sleeve, indicating he was of the elite Firebird branch. They had come to Unity Valley a couple times, and by what she understood they were highly trained and highly loyal to the Protectorate. Beneath he wore a dark shirt with short sleeves. His utilitarian pants were a heavy material with large pockets, and weapons had been strapped at his waist. Like most military men, his hair was cut short and close to his scalp, but there was enough for her to know it was dark brown. He spent time outside, because his skin held the kind of color only the sun could give, and he had telltale paler lines at his temples where he must wear his solar shades. Whatever eye protection he'd worn was gone when she found him, and likely had caused some of the damage to his face. He had a sizeable cut above his right eye, along with many other abrasions and possibly broken bones.

What confused and gripped her was the visible, mechanical apparatus that originated somewhere beneath his shirt, how far up she couldn't know yet, and extended down his arms to brackets around his elbows. Now her hands shook not because of the cold, but because of the fear tightening her lungs.

What if he was one of the Xenos who had attacked Unity Valley again and again? What if he discovered what she was?

Tamping down the fear until she knew she had something to be afraid of, Tessera struggled with all the strength she had left to better situate him on the bed. Now that the room warmed, she took the sweater off again but didn't return to the stove to close the door. Her lamp oil was dangerously low and if she could get by with the light of the fire she would, even if it got warm.

He might need the warmth.

From her meager possessions, everything but the clothes she wore when she arrived belonging to the man who left them behind, she took a pair of dull scissors and tugged the wet cotton away from his chest to cut away the fabric. There was no way she could possibly remove the shirt, not in his unconscious state. The dull blades made it even more difficult to cut the wet material but eventually she managed to expose his torso and arms. A deep purple and blue bruise had already bloomed around his left side and up his sternum that aligned with bruising on his shoulder and left jaw. His torso and arms seemed saved from but just a few of the cuts and abrasions she saw elsewhere, likely because of the heavy jacket and clothing he had worn, taking the brunt of the damage as it was ripped off in the crash.

With the shirt cut away, she saw more of the apparatus she'd seen broken and exposed before removing the shirt. A band wrapped the top of each of his forearms, just below the elbow, with extension arms connecting the pieces. Tessera realized with a twist in her stomach that parts of the mechanisms were fused to his skin. And the mechanism spread further than she originally believed.

What devastating injury befell him to force such barbaric prosthetics on his body?

She couldn't confirm the extent of the prosthetics because they were either on his back or beneath his trousers. While there were spots of blood, she'd seen no blood soaking the heavy canvas material to make her think he had any open wounds she didn't see yet. She didn't suspect injuries that couldn't wait until a more convenient time of inspection.

She spent the next hour treating the wounds she could with what few supplies she had, making do by sacrificing some of the rags she'd kept for washing. Some of the remedies in her arsenal might help, but she needed more information before she dared treat him. Finally, she removed his shoes and socks to allow them to dry. And perhaps, if he was able to gain his feet when he woke, he wouldn't be as likely to leave until she could figure out what to do.

When Tessera felt she'd done all she could, she gathered the rags left of his shirt and set them near the stove to be burned at some point.

His socks draped the edge of the table nearest the stove, and she set the boots near enough to dry before finally closing the front of the stove. The inside of the shelter was overly warm, but it was best for him.

The rain had stopped. Finally, before trying to find some rest for herself, she took the single weapon she found with him and hid it outside the walls of her home.

Having him here complicated things. His return to Unity Valley, because she was sure that's where he had come from, would likely mean she would have to move on again. She didn't trust him to not reveal where she was and how to find her. She was here not only for her protection, but for Trevor, Molly, and Mama Della. If he proved to be a good man, perhaps he would stay silent for their sakes.

But how would she know?

*C*onnor looked up from his PAC tablet to his recon team as they came through the door of the military command base in the community, one of the smaller, generally unutilized homes on the property. Lieutenant Annie Maldonado led the march of Firebird and Terra soldiers returning from their search.

"Report," he snapped.

Annie shook her head as she removed her ocular helmet. "I'm sorry, Colonel. We only made it a couple miles up the mountain before we came under attack. With the rain and the unfamiliarity with the terrain, we had to retreat."

Connor pinched the bridge of his nose, trying to push back the headache that had threatened to bloom hard since David's comms had gone silent. "What about his comms signal? What about the tracker on the bike?"

"We tracked the bike and his comms to just over twenty miles up the mountain, and that's where they went dead." Sergeant Molina, one of the Terra soldiers stationed at the community, said in response. He winced and shook his head. "Bad choice of words."

"The surveillance drone? What did that see?" he asked, shifting his focus to another sergeant stationed at the community, struggling to remember her name. Right now, details were a blur. He'd barely slept since the attack. *Delgado.*

She shook her head, looking reluctant to answer. "We received back images of a burned section of forest. The drone was flying in the rain, so the image isn't clear, but it looks like that's where the bike crashed."

Dread sank in Connor's chest. "Any sign . . ."

Sergeant Delgado shook her head. "No, sir. No sign at all."

"Damn it," Connor cursed, slamming his hand on the table in the Terra command center building. "The rain stopped. Prep another drone." Connor twisted his expression in anger. "Damn it. First light."

"Yes, sir," everyone in attendance said in unison.

The stranger's deep groan yanked Tessera from her shallow sleep, and she raised her head from her folded arms on the edge of the cot. She had spent the night watching over him, checking his wounds, and doing what she could to reduce his pain. The exertion drained her. It had been a long time since she'd given of herself to help someone else, and even then, she had restrained herself for fear of her ability being discovered. She and her sisters had even hidden it from their creator and captors. Had they known, the experimentation might have been worse.

It was early dawn. She had managed to urge him to swallow some oregano tea, but he'd not opened his eyes or made a sound. The room was gray at best, but enough light came through the single window to let her see. Tessera rose to her knees and leaned over the edge of the bed, studying him.

He'd turned his head in his sleep, a small but significant act. Until he woke, she couldn't know how extensive his injuries were, or what the mechanisms attached to his body did. Tessera laid her hand across his brow; his skin was clammy but not warm enough to imply he had a fever. With her palm over his heart, she focused on its beat. While slightly elevated from what it had been since bringing him back, it wasn't so fast it worried her.

"You're safe," she said softly, smoothing her thumb across the space between his brows. "You can rest as long as you need."

CHAPTER TEN

21 August 2054, Friday Morning, pre-dawn
Forte & Bauer Residence
Civilian Employee Housing
United Earth Protectorate, Capitol City
Alexandria, Seat of Virginia
North American Continent

Katrina drew in a long, deep breath through her nose as she stretched, moaning as she rolled from her side to her back. She reached out to the space beside her, expecting to find Phin, but only found empty space. It hadn't taken long at all to become accustomed to his warm presence beside her at night. Blinking, she tried to focus in the dim light of the bedroom and caught movement. With her other outstretched arm, she instinctively found her glasses on the bedside table and put them on, sitting up.

Her eyes adjusted in time to catch Phin's slender, amazingly perfect, and naked form as he finished crossing the small bedroom. She smiled, loving the warm flush over her skin his cute butt created.

"Why are you out of bed?" she asked, drawing up her legs to sit crisscross with the bedding over her lap. "We only have a couple more days before we go back to work."

"Something is wrong," Phin answered as he dressed.

Katrina threw back the blankets and scooted from the bed, rounding the foot before Phin opened the bedroom door. Since she was dressed in sleep clothes, she didn't have to grab anything as she went, or she wouldn't have been able to catch up. She didn't ask what was wrong; if he'd known, he would have said. One thing she'd learned about her now husband in the months she'd known him was that he spoke with honesty. He sensed something, but what wasn't clear.

She followed him into the hallway of their three-bedroom apartment where he met his brother. The two faced each other in the wide doorway leading to the main portion of the residence, the only indicator of their communication the slight angling of Phin's head.

"Words, please, boys," Katrina reminded, resting her hand on Phin's arm. "What's wrong?"

Phin looked toward her and shook his head, a single movement to the right and left. "We both sense it, but neither of us can determine the source or the problem. Only that it is significant and eminent."

"President Tanner," Daniel stated, and looked toward the apartment door.

A cold chill skimmed up Katrina's spine and she crossed her arms over her stomach, gripping the loose material of Phin's tee shirt she wore to sleep. "Something is wrong with President Tanner? Wouldn't someone have come for you if—"

The knock at the door made her gasp, but Phin was already across the room. Katrina's stomach twisted with a sense of panic she couldn't name yet. Behind her, one of the bedroom doors opened and she heard Karl's long, exaggerated yawn as he stepped beside her. "What's going on?" he asked on the end of his yawn.

"I don't know yet."

When Phin opened the door and President Tanner stepped in, flanked behind by his off hours detail, she wasn't sure if she felt relief or a new wave of fear. Daniel's saying of his name had been an announcement, not a theoretical statement. *What would bring the president to their door?*

"Oh, god . . ." she whispered, suddenly cold. She wanted to move closer but couldn't get her feet to cooperate.

President Tanner cleared his throat and shut the apartment door with his detail standing guard outside. He glanced toward Katrina and a tight wince pinched at the corner of his eyes. "Sorry to get you up," he apologized, turning his full attention to Phin and Daniel. "I've got a transport waiting downstairs when you're ready to go. I got word this morning that your father is missing."

"Missing?" Katrina repeated, finally finding the ability to move. She stumbled across the room to where the men stood. "How can he be missing?"

"The community he's at was under Xeno attack. Happens once a week according to Trevor Tisdale, the guy running the place. Connor says David thought he saw signs of what direction the Xenos were leaving in, so he tried to follow."

Phin's hand closed around hers and she realized she was holding her breath.

"He took a hoverbike. Connor lost contact with him after several minutes and tracking on the bike was lost about twenty miles up the nearest mountain. Connor sent out a reconnaissance drone, and it was shot down by the Xenos, but not before sending back images of the bike pretty much destroyed after impact."

Even though President Tanner's voice was level as he explained, she saw the tension around his eyes and the anxious bounce of his hands in his pockets. He focused hard on Phin and Daniel, his mouth set firm.

"They can't risk sending a team up the mountain. The Xenos seem to know their moves."

"Understood, sir," Daniel said. "We appreciate the opportunity to assist."

*D*avid startled awake, disoriented, scrambling to sit up and focus, his hand going to his waist for his weapon. Pain gripped his ribs and he cried out, falling back again. His pulse raced with a ghost on the edge of his awareness, the dissolving remnants of a dream. Lying on his back to catch his breath again, David took the forced moments of stillness to take in his surroundings. He was in a room lit with sunlight coming through a small window and open doorway, implying it was at least midday. But the sun wasn't bright, and everything cast in gray. A chill hung in the air and the petrichor tingled his senses.

What else he saw confused him even more.

He was on a long, narrow cot, covered with a worn but whole blanket, his shirt gone. A quick glance confirmed he at least still wore pants. His side was dark with a mottled bruise over his ribs and under his arm, with more bruises crawling up his shoulder. Based on the tenderness of his neck and jaw, he guessed the bruises went further than he could see.

With a long, painful groan and exhausting effort David forced himself to sit up and shift his legs – boot free – off the narrow bed to rest on a small, braided rag rug on the wooden plank floor. His vision swam, a high-pitched whine shrieked through his left ear, and the effort broke sweat on his exposed skin.

He was in a room no larger than a hundred, maybe a hundred-twenty-five feet, sitting on the only bed tucked into one of the corners so his feet were toward the open door. A very small cast iron stove sat in the opposite corner, venting up out of the ceiling, a cooking pot with lid on top of it. Seeing the pot seemed to engage his olfactory nerves, and the aroma of cooking food hit him with a loud grumble of his stomach. A table was against the wall between the bed and the stove, with a single wooden chair angled to face the bed. A large bucket sat on the table, and a variety of cups, plates, and utensils were laid out on a worn piece of fabric. Shelves lined the wall the width of the table, with a variety of jars, cans, and stacks of MRE packets on the shelves. There was also a hurricane lamp with a very low level of oil in the glass well. On the opposite wall from the bed was a rough hand-built chest of drawers, with a variety of books and notebooks across the top like a makeshift bookshelf.

The three interior walls were a mix of fieldstone and brick pieced together like a makeshift jigsaw puzzle with clay filling the spaces between. The floor, ceiling, and front wall were wood planks, no bit of sunlight showing through except for the window and open doorway. The structure was well built and sturdy, but there was no way he could place an age on it. Nothing he'd seen thus far gave him anything to work with.

"What the hell . . ." he said to the empty room. His voice cracked, making him aware of his dry throat.

He had the sinking feeling he'd just woken in the shelter of a doomsday prepper.

Approaching footsteps on leaves and twigs outside the open door made David tense, and he did a cursory look around the space for his weapon, not remotely surprised when he didn't see it. He raised his hand to use the edge of the table to stand, pausing when he realized only sections of his braces hung useless and broken from his forearm. He tried to stand but doubted there was any part of his body that didn't protest the move, and he lost the two inches he'd gained and dropped back onto the cot. David panted through the pain gripping his side. Sweat beads ran down the side of his face despite the cool air, leaving him feeling both flushed and cold.

The footsteps stopped.

"Well, I'm not dead yet," he mumbled under his breath before clearing his throat. "Ah . . . you probably know I'm unarmed in here. I'm not going to do anything stupid," he said loud enough his voice would easily carry. "I don't remember much of what happened after my face made contact with a tree trunk, so I figure I owe you a thank you more than anything."

Twigs and gravel crunched as the approaching person took a couple more steps. The voice that followed caught him completely off guard. "Who are you loyal to?" asked a distinctively female voice.

David scowled. "I'm not sure—"

"Who are you loyal to?" she asked again, her voice stern.

He ran a hand over his mouth, trying to clear the final, muddy details of what had happened, hoping something would tell him what she needed to hear. Nothing came. Hell, if he pissed her off, he pissed her off. He wasn't going to lie. "Ultimately?" David cleared his throat again, realizing how thirsty he was. "President Nicholas Tanner and the Protectorate."

She moved into full view from the doorway, but a foot or so back so the sun kept her in silhouette. She was maybe five and a half feet tall, but that's about all he could determine. The tee shirt she wore hung over her frame, and the pants were just as baggy, not conforming to any part of her.

"Your jacket bore an emblem of the Firebirds."

"If you know that emblem, you know where my loyalties are."

"Uniforms lie. Men lie."

"Sure. But I'm not. My name is David Forte. I'm a lieutenant colonel with the Firebirds. I was defending Unity Valley against an attack by the Xenos, and I was following them when I was hit."

"They left you for dead," she said, taking a step toward the door. "They flew over and saw your bike burning and left."

Feeling the need to move, David reached for the table edge again and grit his teeth as he attempted to gain his feet. He only managed a few inches before his thigh muscles protested and he fell back on the bed, leaving him shaky. She never moved toward him. Sweat from effort chilled his skin.

"How long ago did that happen?"

"Two days."

He closed his eyes and shook his head. "I don't remember getting here. How far are we from the crash site?"

"It took three hours to get you here." From the corner of his eye, he caught the slight relaxing of her stance. Probably when she realized he was about as much a threat as a newborn. "I made a litter . . ."

He tried to stand again but wavered and tried to keep himself from pitching forward. Every muscle twitched with exertion without the support of his robo-suit, and the deep aches and pains of bouncing around the hillside like a steel ball in a pinball machine weren't helping. She came through the doorway in a rush, but then she stopped halfway across the short space. He managed to raise an arm enough to push back against the table edge nearest him, giving him the ability to sit up again and find a steady seat. His muscles twitched with the minimal effort, and the impact on the bed stole his breath as his ribs throbbed. The room teetered, making his stomach flip. Lucky for him it was empty.

"Some of your mechanisms are damaged, but I didn't know how to remove them. Or whether it would be more harmful to do so."

She spoke eloquently when she used more than two or three words. Certainly not like some backwoods hillbilly conspiracy theorist. Then again, Ted Kaczynski was supposedly a genius, and he was the Unabomber and the king of all conspiracy theorists. Did people willingly live off the grid these days? Some days he was painfully aware of all the things he didn't know.

Before she finished speaking, he focused on the bit of bicep connection hanging loose from his elbow. He reached for it, the mechanics coming away effortlessly when he gripped them. The skin over the internal connection was red and raw, looking like rug rash. "It's some kind of bio-psycho-mumbo-jumbo connection," he explained on a long sigh. "Don't ask me to explain other than it's a mix of Areth tech and something Jenifer worked up so nothing could be stolen. Took me four days and a hell of a headache before I mastered being able to put them on and take them off."

As soon as he said Areth, he tensed. If she wasn't part of Unity Valley, and it appeared she wasn't connected with the Xenos, she might just be a Separatist. People who wanted Humanity to remain separate from anything and everything alien.

"Who is Jenifer?" she asked.

David relaxed and chuckled. If the name Areth didn't set her off she probably wasn't a Separatist. So, who the hell was she and why was she out here alone? *If she was alone.* "Jenifer is what would happen if Terminator, Inspector Gadget, and Lara Croft had a baby."

"I don't know who that is."

"Don't worry about it." He tried to straighten, his back muscles protested, and his side hitched, stealing his breath. There wasn't a part of him that didn't hurt now that he was awake and moving. "She's brilliant, *terrifying*, and makes cool toys. We can leave it at that." He took a deep breath and let it out. Whoever she was, she didn't seem prepared to kill him; though the way he felt, she probably could without much trouble. "Could I get some water?"

She went to the bucket on the table and dipped one of the cups into it, bringing it back to him. He hated the tremor in his hand as he took it and brought the cup to his lips. She let go of the cup but kept her hands close in case he dropped it. The water was cool and was perhaps the purest water he'd ever tasted.

"Thank you."

She crossed the small space to stand as far away as possible without leaving, crossing her arms over her body as she watched him, and he finally had a chance to really see her. The loose clothing looked like they belonged to a man more David's size and showed many years of wear with frayed hems and worn through at the knees, though the knees of the former wearer were below her own knees. The tee shirt sleeves hung past her actual elbows and the neck hole gaped to expose some collarbone. The pants were stained but otherwise clean, and she'd pinch-rolled them to be above her ankles. Her sneakers were dirty but didn't show the same years of wear as her clothing. When she'd walked away, he noted the long braid of light red hair down her back, and the corkscrew ringlets around her face implied the hair was likely very curly when free. She was fair skinned, though the freckles on her cheeks and nose were prominent.

The clothing was too large for her, but she was also too thin for her frame. Her elbows and the line of her jaw showed not a slight build, but possibly a malnourished one.

"Do you know Unity Valley?" he asked.

She nodded. But offered nothing more.

"How far am I from there?"

"I don't know how to measure distance," she answered, shaking her head. "It would take several days to walk from there to here up the mountain."

Until he had a better understanding of the landscape, he couldn't estimate the distance, but he thought he'd gone maybe twenty or twenty-five miles up the mountain before being knocked out of the sky.

"I won't take you there," she added, her voice stern again. "You can't bring them here."

"Kind of limits my options." Not ready to fight that fight, he tried to shift and sit back but the cot was just wide enough he couldn't without putting himself in an uncomfortable position that would probably pull at all the wrong muscles. "Can I know your name?"

Her internal argument played loud and clear across her features. She pressed her lips together before she finally answered. "Tessera."

"Tessera. Like the number four?" She nodded, and David curled his lips in understanding. "Great name. Sounds like a story."

"Not one you want to hear," she said without a pause.

She turned and went to the stove, taking a bowl from the shelf as she went, and scooped some of the contents from the cooking pot. His stomach growled loud enough he pushed his hand to his gut, and she glanced over her shoulder at him, the slightest hint of a smile on her lips. She came back and handed the bowl to him with a spoon.

"It's not much, but it will help you gain your strength."

"Thank you." He tried to reach for it, but tremors took over his arm halfway to the bowl.

Tessera saved him the humiliation of not even being capable of taking a bowl of soup, and sat beside him on the cot, setting the bowl on his thigh. He refused to let his mind wander back to a few months prior when he couldn't feed himself, wiggle his toes . . . or save his son. The content looked to be a basic broth with chunks of fish and greens. It was just warm enough that steam rose from the surface. With the spoon she gave him, David scooped up some and ate it. There was little flavor beyond the fish, maybe a hint of something like oregano, but right then it was the best thing he'd tasted in a long time.

"Thank you," he said again.

He glanced at Tessera as he brought the next spoonful to his mouth. Tessera held her hand hovered over his shoulder, moving it an inch above his skin as if smoothing her fingers over the bruises and abrasions. Deep worry lines dipped between her brows and her mouth turned down in a small frown.

"What?" he asked.

She didn't answer his question, but instead whispered, "You are in so much pain. I didn't realize while you slept, probably because your unconsciousness shielded you. I can feel the pain all around you."

Another lifetime ago someone speaking of his pain like it were a tangible thing to them would have had him giving side eye and wondering about their mental stability. In six months' time, hearing things like that was almost commonplace. It seemed more people around him had some kind of Talent, as the Areth called it, than didn't. Like him. Nothing special here.

"Banged and bruised from bouncing off the side of a mountain is likely to do that to anyone," he said, taking another bite. His hunger was screaming louder than anything else right then. "I didn't exactly show up in perfect health."

"The mechanisms you wore . . ."

"Wore being the operative word," he said around the next bite of fish. "Not a whole lot of it left that I can see. Feels like the lower ones are mostly attached, but I haven't checked yet. Attached or not, they're not working." He scraped the bowl for the last chunks of fish and drank the broth. "Have you been taking care of me by yourself the last two days?"

She nodded and without saying another word, scooted off the cot and quit the cabin, leaving him alone. Though, he'd bet a Benjamin she hadn't gone far.

PROTECTORATE CITIZEN COMMUNITY—UNITY VALLEY
VANCOUVER, BRITISH COLUMBIA
FORMER COUNTRY OF CANADA
NORTH AMERICAN CONTINENT

"We won't leave until we find him. Safe," Phin added, firming his embrace to hold Katrina against his chest.

She nodded, her cheek rubbing against the rough denier of his jacket. She tried to hide her sniff, hoping the battering of rain against the wall of windows in the main house sunroom would disguise the sound but knew it was pointless to hide her sadness from her husband. Besides, she knew he was as desperate to find David as she was. The idea of losing David, like this, after so much they'd all gone through seemed pointless and wrong.

Katrina drew in a deep breath, the smell of rain and soil filling her senses. It had been raining since they arrived shortly after dawn. It rained in Alexandria, but she never experienced rain that went on this long. It was frustrating. All she could imagine was David out there, hurt, unable to make it home.

"I know," she managed to say, doing her best to absorb his calm.

Even though she knew it was just on the surface.

As much as Phin always knew how she felt, she knew him just as well. Better than anyone. Except maybe Daniel. She had been there every moment as he let himself open up, let himself feel, and let himself express his truest self, and when he nearly died because of it. Phin rubbed his jaw along her hair and lowered his chin until he kissed her temple.

"Daniel and Connor are waiting."

She nodded again, really trying to be brave.

What if he's gone?

"We would know if it were otherwise, Katrina," he assured, answering the question she didn't need to ask. She tightened her hug.

"I know," she whispered again.

Phin laid his hands on either side of her face to urge her to tip back her head. When she looked up at him, he first kissed the middle of her forehead, then each cheek, and finally pressed a long, simple kiss to her lips. "I love you, Wife."

She smiled, a warm peace moving through her despite her worry. Some men chose terms of endearment like "honey" and "babe," but Phin simply used her new position in his life. Wife. And it felt more precious than any other name he could have mimicked. "I love you, too."

His gaze shifted to look over her head and behind her. Before she could turn out of his touch to look, he kissed her again. "Felicia would like to speak with you. I will find you upon my return."

As he walked out, Katrina turning to see Felicia Forte standing near the second entrance to the sunroom looking embarrassed. Probably for interrupting their parting, but Katrina accepted early and easily that Phin had little to no qualms or hesitation in expressing to her what he felt, regardless of whomever would be watching. She would never tire of his affection. She never doubted it.

"I'm sorry. I didn't mean to interrupt . . ."

Katrina walked across the sunroom to stand closer while they talked. Felicia Forte was tall, several inches taller than Katrina, but that wasn't uncommon. A lot of people were taller than Katrina. Before he left Alexandria, David had told his family about his son Davey being in Unity Valley and showed them pictures of two members of the Forte family. Not Felicia, but it hadn't been hard to figure out who she was.

"It's okay. Phin was on his way to meet Daniel and Connor to talk about looking for—" She almost just said David, like he was just a missing member of the community. ". . . for your, I suppose he'd be your grandfather-in-law."

Felicia huffed a strained chuckle and shook her head. "I'm having a very hard time wrapping my mind around it all, and I know Papa Davey will really have a hard time. David Forte – the *first* David Forte – has been more a family story than reality. He remembers his father, but—"

Katrina laid her hand on the woman's lower arm, squeezing. "Trust me, I understand. I've been there since David woke up, and I watched him struggle with figuring out everything. I'm pretty sure he thought *we* were the crazy ones. And then to find out about the boys, and—"

"Actually, that's why I came. Can I ask you a question?"

"Of course," Katrina answered.

Felicia glanced toward the door Phin had exited. "We've all heard reports and stories about these . . . super soldiers . . . who were created by the Sorrs. Some of the soldiers have talked about them because we don't get a lot of recent news reports here. We heard these Sorrs creations now serve as bodyguards to the president. Is he – I mean – are they—"

Katrina nodded, her nerves prickling. "They used to be known as the Triadic."

Color flushed Felicia's face from her collar to her hairline and she avoided making direct eye contact with Katrina. "We were told they were monsters; not in the physical sense of the word, but—" She stumbled over the words; her reason for hesitation obvious. "But in how they were trained. Killers. I mean, what else could the Sorrs create? Why would President Tanner trust them?" Only then did her eyes shift to Katrina. "I'm sorry. That probably sounds xenophobic, which is ironic considering the world right now. I'm just confused, and the whispers in the community have been growing once people heard *they* were here about how coldhearted they are. But . . ."

"But I'm married to one of them," Katrina said, probably a little more coldly than necessary. She'd seen and heard the prejudice before, but that didn't make it easier. "You saw yourself he's far from coldhearted."

"I'm sorry," Felicia said barely above a whisper, the color in her cheeks deepening.

Katrina crossed her arms over her abdomen, gripping her own sides, and tried to understand people like Felicia Forte and other residents of places like this might either be getting incorrect information or no information at all. Phin and Daniel made no attempt to not be seen, yet they weren't there to be seen. They were there to protect Nick, and they had proven themselves, but those stories didn't always filter out to everyone. It was the way news had always been; slanted, incomplete, incorrect. Only those living it knew anything close to the truth.

"There were three of them when we found them. Three brothers; like I said, the Triadic." She lifted her chin to look straight at Felicia. "They were only known by the designations given to them by the Sorracchi scientist . . ." The words stuck in her throat because demon spawn was more appropriate. ". . . who created them. Alpha. Beta. Omega." She shook her head. "I can't even think of them that way anymore, not that I ever really did. From the beginning, they've been Gideon, Daniel, and Phin to me. I'm the one who gave them their names."

"There are only two . . ."

"Their brother Gideon died a few months ago protecting President Tanner's family. I don't know how many reports of what happens in the world reach here—" It was hard to say, but she managed to do so without her voice cracking. Felicia nodded and mumbled she knew what Katrina was talking about. "They earned our trust that day." She shook her head, correcting herself. "No, that's not right. They had already shown where their true loyalty would be, but that day Gideon proved it with his life."

She hated the flash of satisfaction she felt when Felicia swiped a tear from her cheek and looked away toward the dark windows. "How does David – the *first* David – fit in here? Is he really their father?"

Katrina puffed her cheeks with a huffed breath and closed her eyes for a moment. She'd never had to explain everything to someone not involved. To the new mind, it probably did all sound insane. "If you go by the strictest definition of the word, some people might not see them as father and sons, but as far as David and the boys are concerned, that is their truth. Run a paternity test, and he'd come out their father. The scientist who created them used David's DNA along with her own." She smiled. "I like to believe their true selves, that goodness and love for each other that made them unacceptable to her to accomplish her purposes, came in part from him. Nature won out over nurture. The good in them is the good in David."

"You seem close to him. To David. The first David." Felicia shook her head. "Just trying to talk about them is confusing."

"He's very special to me," Katrina said, smiling again. "Just like with the boys, I was there when we found him and I was there when he woke up. I'm trying really hard to help him get better, too."

"Get better? Do you mean those things I saw on his arms?"

"Don't worry about that part," Katrina added. "It is, yes, but it's temporary. He's doing great but being in stasis for as long as he was made it hard."

"It doesn't bother you that they're not . . ." Felicia rushed to speak but stuttered off the end of whatever she wanted to say.

"That they're not *what*?"

Again, Felicia looked away, unable to face Katrina when she said, "That they're not real. Real people. Humans."

The words were as effective as a slap across Katrina's cheek.

CHAPTER ELEVEN

22 August 2054, Saturday – Early Morning
Presidential Residence
United Earth Protectorate, Capitol City
Alexandria, Seat of Virginia
North American Continent

"Is your conversation confidential, or may I join you?" Nick looked down the porch to where Michael stood, just coming out the front door of the residence, a steaming cup in each hand. "Nah, your brother and I were just having a father-son talk about how he should let his mom sleep."

In response to Nick's voice, Adam drew in a deep breath and released it with such force it made his little body shudder. Nick laughed, trying his best to stay quiet enough to not wake the infant he'd managed to get to sleep just minutes before.

Michael walked the length of the porch to where Nick sat in one of the deep Adirondack chairs, set one of the mugs of coffee on the wide armrest, and sat in the chair beside him. "Has there been any word about David?"

He shook his head. "Connor is keeping me updated, but he said it's been raining like crazy. Makes it tough to keep up the search, even for the boys. He confirmed Phin, Daniel, and Katrina made it fine."

"I've no doubt Phin and Daniel will find him. I know Connor must welcome the help."

"He's beating himself up pretty bad about it. Not sure why. By what I hear, David took the initiative to follow. No fault there, either. Just a bad turn. Bad results don't always mean it was a bad decision."

With a little shift, Nick situated himself better in his chair to let Adam continue to sleep on his chest, but he could both see Michael and drink the coffee.

"What has you up?" he asked after taking a drink.

Michael released a long breath, not quite a sigh. "I was having trouble sleeping, and I didn't want to keep Jacqueline from resting."

Nick smiled and angled his head so he could look down at his son. "See, Adam? Moms need sleep." When Adam didn't stir, Nick took a moment to watch the profile of his firstborn son.

Michael hadn't drunk any of the coffee he'd brought for himself and stared instead into the misty landscape beyond the edge of the yard and the fence surrounding the house. It looked like any other front yard, but that was intentional. Yes, the house was the residence of the "First Family," but Nick had made sure the property was protected and protected well before he brought anyone he loved back to this place. The house was shielded by one of David Forte's domes, monitored by constant security, and guarded by Connor's elite Firebird Guard.

This was more than a home; it was a safe haven.

"What's on your mind?" he asked.

"Names," Michael said without any of his usual hesitation.

Nick canted his head. "Huh. Not what I was expecting. Not sure *what* I was expecting, but it wasn't names. Like . . . baby names?"

Michael nodded and finally looked at Nick before taking a drink from the mug. He cleared his throat as he set the cup back on the armrest. "I am about to be a father of four additional children, and I fear the world they might inherit if the threat of war with the Sorracchi comes to fruition, and the Urdo Khantan John says are ruthless. Heartless. Xenos who are prepared to kill to prove a false point."

"That's a lot to worry about," Nick said after Michael paused, then cleared his own throat. "But worrying about all that is kind of *my* job, not yours."

Michael smiled, slow and incomplete, before he looked at Nick. "Perhaps I believe you shouldn't bear it alone."

"What does that have to do with names?"

"With all we face, I feel somehow guilty for focusing on names, but Jacqueline has made me promise we won't name one of our children Dorcas Hortense or Elmo Aloysius."

Michael delivered the statement with such a straight face Nick barked a laugh, and immediately stifled it when Adam jerked on his chest. He rubbed his baby's back until Adam sighed again, then looked to Michael, whose smirk told the truth. His son had pretty much mastered the skill of dry humor.

"Those are a hell of a couple names."

Michael nodded before taking another sip of coffee. "They are, but I'm hoping you can help." He focused for a moment on his little brother and the smirk slid into a smile. "Adam. It's a family name."

Nick nodded. "My father's middle name."

"You don't speak about your parents."

Michael's straightforwardness still had the power to throw him off guard sometimes and coupled with the immediate punch in the chest when he made himself think of his parents left him dry mouthed and hot.

He drew in a slow breath through his nose and looked out into the same mist Michael had studied minutes before, struggling with how to explain. "Might as well be honest. It's hard," he started, but had to stop one more time to swallow against choking. "My mom and dad were . . . great. They were great parents. I just wasn't a great son. I've been living with that for a long time and finding out just how much the Bitch manipulated me makes it worse."

"I didn't intend to bring up pain–"

"No," Nick said, cutting him off, but immediately followed with the best smile he could manage when he looked at his son. "You deserve to know about them. I should have told you sooner. It just . . . didn't seem like a good time, I guess. Or an easy time."

"Okay."

Taking one more breath and downing the last of the coffee, Nick found his focus by rubbing his hand up and down Adam's blanket-covered back. "Dad was in the Army. He went in right out of high school, but in 2001 my grandpa had a stroke. He was limited to a wheelchair and lost most of his speech. Dad got an emergency release from his commitment so he could go home and help Grandma take care of him."

"Your grandparents were Sean and Sara," Michael said. "You told me the story about Great Grandfather Sean's dentures in the campfire."

"That's right. I did," he confirmed with a chuckle. Michael nodded, his silence as encouraging as talking. "So, Dad returned to Maine with them and went back to college while he was there on the G.I. Bill. You heard of that?" He glanced toward Michael, who nodded. "Dad was in school and met Mom there. He was her tutor. I think in Calculus. Dad said more than once that Mom's problem in the class wasn't that she didn't get it. She got it too well. He said her brain worked several steps ahead and it messed her up. Like they say, I guess the rest was history." He paused to figure out where to go with the story, finding it easier to stick to the early stuff. "That was 2001, though, and right after 9/11. How's your history?"

He asked it with a smirk, knowing full well Michael probably knew more about world history than most historians. If he read it, if he'd been told it, he remembered it, and chances were good he'd read it. Michael read everything.

"It's the designation given to an attack on what was then the United States of America by a terrorist group named al-Qaeda. It's known as 9/11 because the attack was on September 11th, 2001."

Nick nodded. "Dad carried a lot of guilt about not serving his country after that. He was torn, ya know? He wanted to be at home taking care of Grandpa, but he also wanted to be with his team wreaking justice on Osama bin Laden." Nick chuckled, but it was a release valve more than anything else. "What the hell would Dad do with the world now, I wonder."

"Adam was his name," Michael said, not quite asking it as a question.

Nick shook his head. "Nah, well yeah. Matthias Adam, but most people called him Matt. Mom didn't. She said she'd always preferred Matthias."

"What was my grandmother's name?"

"Grace," Nick answered, not surprised his voice cracked. He cleared his throat. "Grace Meridian. Meridian was her middle name. She didn't like it very much, though."

"It's unique."

Nick nodded, squinting at the blurry mist. It would clear soon when the sun started to come up. "Long story short, they got married early 2002, just a few months after they met, and Dad returned to active duty. Mom was training to be a physical therapist, and Dad always gave her 100% credit for Grandpa's recovery. Within a couple years he had regained most of his speech and could walk with a cane and lived way longer than any doctors thought he would. He moved slow, but he could do it. I was born a little over a year after they got married. I was about five when Dad left the military for good. That was shortly after first contact and the world practically imploded."

"You were their only child?"

Nick nodded, appreciating his son's easy way of drawing out the conversation. Sometimes it was with silence, sometimes with well-placed questions. He wondered if Michael intended his questions to work that way, or if it was completely natural to him. He was more inclined to believe it was natural because Michael had also developed a deep empathy he'd rarely seen in anyone else. Remarkable considering the life Michael had led.

Another stab of guilt hit Nick's chest.

"Yeah, just me. And I screwed up."

Protectorate Citizen Community — Unity Valley
Vancouver, British Columbia
Former Country of Canada
North American Continent

"The truth doesn't change simply because someone doesn't wish to see it. Perhaps she will with time. She is David's family, and as such we will welcome her."

Lucy heard the voices the same second it was too late to halt her entrance into the dimly lit kitchen. Sunrise wasn't for another two hours, but since she hadn't slept all night anyway, she'd planned on making some strong tea before finding some way to feel useful. The small gathering of people in the kitchen caught her off guard, but especially the statement she'd heard from one of the two men who had arrived in Unity Valley the day before with more Firebirds and one young woman.

That young woman stood with the brothers – because that much was obvious – along with Colonel Montgomery and half a dozen Firebirds and Terra soldiers, prepared to again go in search of David.

Just the thought of David still lost and likely hurt made her heart clench painfully in her chest. She tried to take a step back in retreat, but the young man who had spoken turned his head toward her and effectively froze her in her spot.

"Sorry," she said, still trying to back out.

"Lucy," Colonel Montgomery said when he saw her. "Hang on."

With a word and nod to the men he'd been standing with, he came to join the woman and two men who stood together. The one who had spoken, and had caught her trying to slip away, set his hand on the woman's arm and she looked back at Lucy when he said something softly. Her smile was melancholy, but genuine. He motioned to Lucy to join them.

"I wanted to find you yesterday after they got here, but I didn't have a chance before we headed out again." His tone was upbeat, but the strain around his eyes was obvious. He looked to the men. "This is Lucy Santos."

She was confused. Why would Colonel Montgomery need to find her when they arrived? "Is there something I can help with?"

Connor shook his head. "Nah, I just thought all of you should meet." He motioned between her and the three. "Lucy, this is Phin and Daniel and Phin's wife Katrina." He paused. "Forte."

Whatever Connor saw in her expression seemed to satisfy him and he nodded, one brief movement. "We're heading back out to look." *For David* didn't need to be included. "You and Katrina should talk."

Phin kissed his wife's cheek and whispered something that made her smile, though there was no hiding the melancholy behind it, before the three men and other soldiers left to leave her alone with Katrina.

"I apologize Connor dumped and ran," Katrina said once the group was gone. "He probably didn't mean to be so shockingly vague, but he's got a lot on him. He's really worried about David."

"So am I," Lucy said, then cleared her throat and crossed her arms. "We're all worried. David hasn't been here long, but I think a lot of people liked him. I'm sure Colonel Montgomery is happy to have the help. Did you come from Alexandria as well?"

Katrina nodded. "As soon as we could after President Tanner told us David was missing. Um . . ." She paused, her young features pinching in thought. "I don't know how to ease into this conversation, so I'm going to borrow a page from Phin and Daniel's book of bluntness. Connor told us you've been spending a lot of time with David. He thinks maybe something is happening between you. Is that true?"

Lucy was thankful the kitchen was fairly dim and she had her Abuela's complexion, hoping the flush that hit her cheeks wasn't as obvious as it felt. Didn't do any good to deny it, but still . . .

"Something, yes, but not enough for either of us to define it. Like I said, he hasn't been here very long. You're family?"

Katrina nodded. "Here's where I have to be really blunt, I'm sorry. But there's no real way to not get to the point. Did David tell you anything about . . ." Even though she said she'd be blunt, the poor girl looked as uncomfortable as Lucy felt.

"That he's been in a kind of suspension for over forty years?" She nodded to answer her own question. "His body is still recovering from it, and that's why he has the prosthetics. And he came here because he found out one of his sons is here." The memory of the evening before David went missing – how devastated he was, torn apart inside – made her throat tighten. "It's been hard."

"I found out after we arrived about Davey." Katrina's voice was softer, carrying just as much strain as Lucy felt. "I'm excited, though, to meet him. I've only met Felicia." The tone in her voice hardened just a fraction, but enough to make Lucy wonder if Felicia had been the topic of discussion she'd initially overheard. "Did he tell you anything else?"

Lucy shook her head. "Only that he had more he wanted to tell me, but . . . we lost the chance. I'm guessing that's where you come in."

Katrina drew in a long breath through her nose and motioned toward the empty kitchen table. "David would say it's a hell of a story, so maybe we should sit down. Do you have something you need to do?"

"I came down looking for something to keep me busy. Let me make some tea, and we'll talk."

"Yes. Tea sounds perfect."

As Lucy moved from the table to the kitchen to make two cups of tea, she had the undeniable feeling the story she was about to hear would be even more fascinating than the one David had already shared.

Alexandria Hospital – Private Nursery
United Earth Protectorate, Capitol City
Alexandria, Seat of Virginia
North American Continent

Victor had turned on the low-level lights and was three steps into the nursery before he realized someone other than the three unborn Tanner children occupied the room.

"Michael," he said, pulling up short. "It's early yet. Is there something wrong?"

Michael stood with his back to the door, his hands pushed into his front pockets, with a full view of the three artificial wombs that had kept his unborn children safe since being brought to Alexandria. "Wrong, no," he said, turning.

Victor immediately recognized the lines at the corners of Michael's eyes; lines not often seen in a man so young. Michael's soul was so much older than his twenty-eight years, so much so Victor often forgot his friend was so young. Which was probably a strange irony since Victor had known Michael practically since the day he was born.

"Then what weighs on you so heavily."

Michael looked past Victor, contemplating, composing, ingesting himself whatever it was he felt before expressing it. "My father told me today about his parents."

Victor canted his head, scowling in thought. "I can't say I've ever heard anything about them. I suppose, like with so many, I assumed they were no longer alive but beyond that . . ."

A sharp pierce of pain hit the back of his right eye, and he flinched at the suddenness of it. Just as quickly, it was gone. Michael's attention was still somewhere else, so Victor swallowed against the lingering ache to keep his focus on the conversation.

"Dad told me they died a few years before I was born. He carries a suffocating amount of guilt, not for their deaths but for what he perceives as his part leading to the accident that killed them."

"He had to have been fairly young if it was before you were born. Likely younger than you are now. How could he have caused their death? I can't imagine Nicholas Tanner doing anything willingly."

Michael finally shifted his attention from the shadows of the room to look at Victor directly. "He had recently become involved with Kathleen, knowing her then as Kathy. In ways he still cannot understand, his parents were adamantly opposed to a relationship with her. He told me the more they tried to convince him to end the relationship, the more he felt driven to go against their wishes. He realizes now with clear recollection that Kathleen guided him even then in such subtle ways he never saw it at the time. She was a master orchestrator."

"Dear God," Victor said, a cold flush skimming up his spine. "Knowing now the extent of her deception and evil, I can only imagine how he must feel looking back."

"He admitted he had carried guilt for the last thirty years, but yes, it has been worse since he learned the truth. He's hidden it. I don't believe even Caitlin knows the extent of it." Again, Michael's gaze drifted to some point Victor couldn't see. "He had already gone against their wishes by joining Earth Force. Both of them, but most especially his mother, had asked him not to join the fairly new military branch formed after the unification of the planet under one government. He had met Kathleen within a few months of joining. On the night they died, he told me they had driven to the base he was stationed on not far from here in Virginia. While they were at his apartment, Kathleen arrived, and they argued. He finally demanded they leave."

A tear slid from Michael's eye. His empathy was a deep well Victor knew he could drown in if he was allowed to sink too deep. But in this, Victor wouldn't advise him to keep a distance. This was his father, and if Michael sensed his father's pain, he would willingly accept some of the burden to carry it.

"They died an hour away in a horrendous car crash; one so bad they barely had remains for a funeral. Kathleen had consoled him, and despite the fact it had been his relationship with her that had fueled the argument, he married her within a few weeks." He looked to Victor again. "He wonders, knowing now what we know of her deception and the extent she and the Sorracchi went to manipulate him, whether his mother and father died as part of their plan. They were in the way, and thus, they had to die."

Victor's stomach twisted and he had to look down or deal with the angled shift of the room. "Of course. It's clear why he would believe that to be true." When his stomach calmed, and the room was still, he raised his head again. "I cannot speak to fact, but yes, I believe it was quite likely her doing that brought about their death. Of what I know, she was ordered by Barnabas to carry out their orders and death meant nothing more than a means to an end."

"I wondered if you had knowledge of any of it—"

"No," Victor said quickly, but made himself swallow. He shook his head. "No."

Michael nodded. "I doubt you would have kept it from me if you'd known. You've already shared so much. I know it isn't easy for you."

Victor shook his head. "I never want to withhold anything from you, but I also know not all my memories are at the forefront. They are there, that much we've learned since I was emancipated from the demon in my mind. I swear to you that if I *should* recall anything . . ."

Michael nodded, his lips pressed together as he looked over his shoulder toward the children awaiting introduction into the world. "I know. I didn't come to ask you about it; I just found myself here. It's peaceful here." He looked back to Victor. "Thank you."

"For what, my friend?"

"For caring for them. And for me. You have been my constant."

A headache bloomed behind his eyes. "Always, Michael. Always."

CHAPTER TWELVE

Unknown Mountain
Approximately 20 miles from Unity Valley

Panic and indecision churned in Tessera's stomach in an acid ball, leaving her nauseated and weak, shaking with fatigue. She sat on the floor of her home, knees drawn to her chest and held there by her arms, staring at David Forte with tears burning her eyes.

He had been in a restless sleep for hours, neither resting nor aware. His pain was increasing, even though he didn't speak of it. He still couldn't stand or walk. A low-grade fever warned some type of infection grew somewhere, but the oregano tea – her only tool to battle it – had done nothing to help. When awake, he was coherent, but if he couldn't travel how would he recover? How long could he grow worse before it was too much for his battered body to take?

She'd been sharing her strength for hours, trying desperately to heal him enough he could travel. Perhaps if she had ignored her fear and headed down the mountain as soon as she'd gotten him to the cabin, perhaps if she'd tried to return to Unity Valley, she could have gotten him help.

For two days she had sensed the mental energy of someone – perhaps two, she wasn't sure – searching with more than just their eyes. Their energy hummed in the air, and she had blocked the search for fear she would be found. The only creatures with the ability to find her that way would be assassins sent by those who spawned her and her sisters, created for death only.

They would have no interest in David. They sought her.

Tessera rolled onto her knees, pain from kneeling lancing up her thighs. Every joint hurt and every muscle ached. She'd given so much to save David, she had wasted away in just days. Perhaps this was her penance. She'd heard Mama Della and Trevor speak of God; perhaps this was what He demanded for her blasphemous existence.

She would give her last breath to give David Forte a chance to live. She would give everything and continue to give until it destroyed her.

23 August 2054, Sunday
Protectorate Citizen Community—Unity Valley
Vancouver, British Columbia
Former Country of Canada
North American Continent

"Katrina! Katrina!"

Lucy nearly lost her balance twice trying to both run down the basement stairs and crane her neck to see the slight woman. The clatter of some tool finally alerted her Katrina had heard her call. She scrambled out from beneath the console, and for a heartbeat Lucy remembered the night she'd visited David and he'd come out from beneath the same machine. Now the lights were on, and the console gave off a low hum.

"What?"

"They found him. Your husband and his brother . . . they found him."

She tried to catch her breath to keep talking. She'd been out by the barn when one of the community teenagers had run to her to tell her Colonel Montgomery had taken a Firebird hover up the mountain with Doctor Dardashti and they were coming back with David. To be ready. She'd run all the way back to the main house and straight to the basement where she knew Katrina had occupied her time by continuing the work on David's device.

"David?" Katrina asked, coming to her feet.

Lucy nodded. "They'll be here soon." She turned and pulled herself back up the stairs before finishing the statement.

Nathan Harshbarger came through the front door as Lucy reached the doorway to the infirmary. One glance in his direction, and the nod he gave her as he followed her into the room, told her he'd already heard. All they knew was David would be here soon. They had no idea what to expect or how to prepare. She hurried to the supply room, scanning the glass door cabinet and the sparse collection of medicines inside. The attack just days before had nearly depleted their supplies. Some of the most common medicines for pain and infection were at dangerous levels, with no reliable way to restock.

Lucy both prayed they would have enough, and hoped none of the medications would be needed, even while knowing there was little hope of that. She had heard enough and knew his physical condition before he even went up the mountain, to know the worst was possible.

"No," she whispered to herself as she opened the door and grabbed precious bottles of antibiotics. "They wouldn't be rushing back here if there was no hope."

A screeching roar sounded outside the house, and a shower of leaves and dust pelleted the infirmary window. Lucy gasped when she witnessed the Firebird hover Connor and David had come to Unity Valley in just a week before now practically drop vertically at a speed that made her heart flip before it stopped short of hitting the ground. She had no idea if the hovers were supposed to be piloted that way, but whomever did it was a master. Before the wind kicked up by the fast approach could calm the side door opened, the bottom of the ramp it created slamming into the ground.

"They're here!" she shouted, at the same second knowing everyone else in the infirmary would have witnessed the breath-stealing descent.

She wanted to move, but her feet held her in place when Daniel and Phin – which was which, she couldn't guess – exited the hover, each carrying the rails of a hand stretcher.

The sight of David's arm hanging limp from the side was enough to slap her into action and she grabbed her tray of supplies. The house door slammed open with shouted orders for action. Phin and Daniel Forte carried their father with both a speed and delicacy that appeared unnatural and yet caught in Lucy's throat, easing the cot directly onto a bed already prepared for him.

She had seen citizens of Unity Valley carried into the same room with limbs burned, mangled, and sometimes missing. She had witnessed more gore than she ever thought she would when she entered such an innocuous field as ophthalmic surgery, but none had affected her so violently and viscerally as David Forte battered, bruised, and unconscious.

He was shirtless, and even while she responded to Doctor Dardashti's commands, she mentally itemized what she saw and what it meant . . . if that could even be defined.

A long, angry red cut slashed his forehead over his right eye. It had knitted some, and wasn't bleeding, but there were mild signs of redness.

The left side of his face, jaw, shoulder, and upper arm were bruised, with the largest and darkest hematoma enveloping his shoulder and upper arm, spreading down his ribs toward his sternum.

His prosthetics were gone, but she could only see a couple of the contact points that had begun to look less irritated before he'd disappeared but were now red and angry.

Had they been torn off him?

Doctor Dardashti ordered a massive dose of the antibiotic she'd made sure to have on hand. She nodded and grabbed a swab and antiseptic to clean his skin for the needle.

"Lucy, try to start IV hydration, two lines if you can. I don't know if you'll get a vein—"

"I'll do it," she promised as she gained her feet and ran for their meager supply.

It wasn't until she stood that she saw the other patient. At the other end of the infirmary in one of the few other empty beds . . . was Tessa. Two other infirmary staff members worked on her, though it didn't seem with quite the same urgency as needed with David. One had already put her on an IV while the other seemed to be documenting her vitals.

Lucy couldn't take even a second to process what that meant.

She grabbed four bags of fluid and one of the only three IV poles in the infirmary, rushing back to David's side. It took her two minutes – that felt like five hours – to both find and pierce two viable veins, one in each arm, to begin the rapid infusion of fluid.

"Push antibiotics once you know you have a solid flow," Doctor Dardashti said over his shoulder, his attention not breaking from David.

Lucy nodded, even though she knew he didn't see.

She paused for a breath, crouched at David's side once the final IV was in and secured, taking that moment to take him in. He was gaunt. In just a few days he had lost weight, but he had the sallow look of dehydration. Pale. Gray, even. Tears burned her eyes, but she kept her focus on David, giving up any real hope of keeping herself distant.

It was too late for that.

"He is in extreme pain."

She looked up, caught off guard by one of the men Katrina had explained was David's son, but which she didn't know. She didn't know how to tell them apart. Beside him stood the other brother. The one who had spoken continued.

"It radiates from his ribcage; I perceive broken ribs. He experiences an intermittent ringing in his ears when he attempts to move and battles to maintain equilibrium. He has attempted to eat and drink, but nausea has been a detriment."

"Phin—" Katrina said on a gasp, coming to the side of the other, silent brother, who took her hand without looking away from the man on the bed.

"He struggles, but he isn't without hope," the one Lucy now assumed to be Phin said to his wife.

His attention shifted from Katrina to David to Daniel. Daniel looked to him as if he'd spoken, nodded, then turned again to Lucy and Doctor Dardashti. "He has been unable to stand since waking after the crash. The woman who was with him has done her best."

"Her name is Tessa," Lucy said, barely managing to speak above a whisper.

"He was able to tell you this?" the doctor asked.

"We are aware," both brothers said together.

Doctor Dardashti didn't seem to hesitate in his acceptance of their explanation, and gave Lucy more instructions for David's care, including something for his pain. With hydration his nausea would ease, but until then they would give him some nutrients intravenously as well, just to give him some strength until his treatment could be fully determined.

Hours later, after making her rounds to the other patients remaining in the infirmary, Lucy sank with a weary sigh to the chair someone had brought to the side of David's bed. Whomever it was had also left a sandwich and glass of water on the bedside table, but as much as she knew she should eat her stomach rejected the idea.

The infirmary was dark except for the two small lamps spaced through the long room so the remaining patients could rest but those responsible for their care could move about as needed. They hadn't lost anyone else that day, and two community residents had moved out of the infirmary to convalesce with their families.

Tessa was still at the far end of the infirmary and hadn't shown any signs of waking since she'd arrived. She was pale and thin, and much like David, they had been administering hydration and nutrition steadily. She hadn't shown any significant signs of improvement.

David had, and for that small gift Lucy was thankful.

His color had warmed, and his skin turgor had improved with each bag of fluid they'd administered. He hadn't woken up yet, though

Doctor Dardashti confirmed it was most likely a sleep of exhaustion and recovery and nothing to be concerned about. The mild fever had broken, and either Phin or Daniel had come to the infirmary at regular intervals to give her and Doctor Dardashti updates on David's pain levels. She wasn't sure what it meant that despite not having any actual understanding of how either of the men could know, she accepted their word, and so did Doctor Dardashti.

Reality shifted daily.

Lucy leaned forward to rest her elbows on her legs and rubbed her palms over her face, ending with a sigh as she tried to smooth down the whisps of hair that had long since escaped the braid she wore to keep her hair off her face in the infirmary. She probably looked like a forest witch, frazzled and wild.

She lowered her hand to rest on David's lower arm, exposed outside his blanket to allow access for pulse checks, the IV attached to his far arm. He was warm. She ran her thumb over his skin, feeling the roughness of the hair and the firmness of his muscles beneath. They hadn't dressed his upper body to allow for medical access; his arms, shoulders, and chest were bare, with the blanket tucked over his chest. She hadn't realized how natural it had become, so quickly, to see his prosthetics and attachments as part of him, but his bare arms struck her as odd now. The areas near his elbows where some of the connections had been still showed red and looked raw, irritated, possibly from whatever outside force had ripped the appendages from their housing.

I should apply some salve . . .

"Lucy . . ."

His voice, raw and rough, startled her and she looked up. He'd shifted his head on the pillow just enough to angle his face toward her and the nearest light cast the angles of his features in shadow, making his bruises darker.

"Hey," she said, scooting to the edge of her chair until her knees pressed against the edge of the narrow bed. "It's good to hear your voice again."

His eyelids hung low, and each blink was slow, but his lips curled just enough to hint at the dimple in his cheek. "I had these vague, um, memories maybe of being here," he forced out then paused to swallow, the scratch of his voice making Lucy wince, "but I didn't believe it until I opened my eyes and saw you."

Lucy reached for the glass of water someone had left for her and took a chance by opening the drawer of the bedside table in hopes to find some of the reusable drinking straws they often kept close at hand for patients since frequently positions and injuries made drinking difficult. There were three in the drawer, and she shifted from the chair to the narrow bit of bed beside him. She knew she couldn't help him sit up alone, and didn't think it was wise with his injuries, but with a hand behind his shoulder she helped him roll just enough he could accept the straw and take a long drink. When he released the straw from his lips and groaned, she helped him recline again. David managed to shift his arm over her knee, and she stayed in her spot, only leaning forward enough to put the water back on the table.

"You are definitely here," she assured, smoothing her fingers over his forehead before returning her hand to his shoulder. Where it rested, she could just feel the beat of his heart against the heel of her palm, and it was oddly comforting. "Your sons found you earlier today."

His nod was slow, and barely enough movement to qualify as a nod, his eyelids moving even slower as he likely slid back into sleep again. But then his eyes opened, and he focused on her. "You met Phin and Daniel..."

Almost everything he said trailed off, like he was too tired to manage a period. Lucy smiled and stroked his cheek with the back of her fingers. Perhaps it was to comfort him – perhaps it was to comfort her – but it felt as natural as anything she'd ever done.

"And Katrina. She's what Abuela Gabi would have called *chiquita pero picosa*, tiny and feisty, but only in the best sort of way. She's tiny but spirited."

David's smile grew and he made a small sound that might have been a chuckle. "That's Katrina."

"How is your pain?" she asked.

David winced and made a low noise in his throat before swallowing again. "Um, I'm feeling kind of numb and floaty right now."

Lucy couldn't help but smile. "Then the medication is helping. Daniel said you were experiencing ringing in your ears. Are you still?"

"Some, I think," he said and added a chuckle, his eyes sliding closed. "Kinda hard to tell. Did they talk to Tessera?" he asked as his lids closed completely.

"Tessera? Do you mean Tessa?" He nodded slowly. "She's here. She was unconscious when they found her. One of your sons said it was a sort of cabin where they found you."

His eyes snapped open, and he blinked, squinting at her. "Unconscious? What's wrong with her?"

Lucy shook her head. "We don't know. She was very dehydrated and malnourished; we've been giving her fluids and nutrition, but she hasn't woken up yet."

Before she could finish, David rocked his head on his pillow. "What day is it? How long have I been gone?"

Lucy laid her hand on his shoulder, hoping to calm him because he looked about a second away from trying to get out of the bed. "It's Sunday. They found you today. You've been missing since Thursday."

"That can't be right." Whatever sleep had tugged at him he'd visibly pushed away, wincing with pain as he tried to lift his head off the pillow. "I know I was pretty useless, but I would have known if she was—" He shook his head, confusion twisting his features. "She said she dragged me to the cabin from the crash. How could she have—"

His voice ticked up with each word until Lucy laid her palm on his cheek to get his attention. He turned into the touch, taking a breath before shifting his focus to her face.

"That doesn't make any sense," he reiterated.

"I'm sorry. I wish I could explain more. Maybe Phin or Daniel can shed some light."

He released a long breath through his nose and relaxed into the bed, confusion still pulling at his brow. "I need to know something else," he said, the weight of his voice tangible and he shifted his focus to her again, swallowing. "That attack was pretty bad. Davey—"

The question made her throat tighten, or perhaps it was the painful concern in his eyes. "They're all fine." Lucy smiled, leaning forward hoping he'd see her face better in the dim light. "None of them were hurt."

David's eyes shifted down, focusing on her mouth as she spoke. "Thank you."

She leaned further and pressed her lips to the center of his forehead; his breath warmed her throat as he inhaled and exhaled. Shifting back, she licked her lips and smiled. "You should rest. There will be plenty to catch up on tomorrow."

His fingers resting on her leg pressed slightly into her thigh, and a flush raced up her throat to her cheeks. "Is it wrong for a patient to ask his nurse to sit with him until he's asleep?"

Lucy grinned wider. "Maybe, but not wrong for a friend to sit with a friend to make sure he rests."

David closed his eyes and with a long release of breath, his body relaxed and within moments sleep had taken him again.

Lucy sat beside him for another hour.

CHAPTER THIRTEEN

24 August 2054, Monday
Protectorate Citizen Community — Unity Valley
Vancouver, British Columbia
Former Country of Canada
North American Continent

Father . . . wake up.

David's awareness slipped in before he opened his eyes, the sounds of conversation nearby mingled with the diminishing buzz that hadn't gone away yet and the smell of disinfectant and linens filling his senses when he inhaled. Then the ache in every joint and muscle came to the forefront, and he wished he could slide back into whatever oblivion he'd been in moments before.

"He's waking up," came Katrina's voice. "David . . ."

He blinked, immediately regretting the assault of daylight that shot straight through his eyes to his brain, turning up the volume on his headache several notches. He groaned and tried to lift his arm to shield his eyes. It was halfway to his face when he realized he had an IV and dropped it again to the bed.

"Yeah," he mumbled. "I'm up."

"I'll have someone disconnect those," came a relatively familiar male voice, but it hurt too much to look quite yet.

"Oh, it's so good to hear your voice," Katrina said to his right and he smiled when she smacked a kiss on his cheek. "We were so worried."

"I'm alive." David forced himself to open his eyes again, blinking and squinting until they adjusted and the sun wasn't a spearhead anymore.

He was in the same infirmary bed he'd been whenever he'd woken up last, but Lucy had been beside him then. Now, several people stood around the bed. None of them Lucy. Katrina was on his right, with Phin and Daniel along the side of the bed. On the other side, Connor stood but a bit further back. And closest to David on his left was the doctor he'd seen working in the infirmary. Darwin . . . D'artagnan . . . Dardashti . . . something like that. Probably a voice he'd recognized. And a young woman he'd seen working in the infirmary the few times he'd been here with Lucy worked at removing the IV drip line from his arm.

"Why do I suddenly feel like Dorothy Gale at the end of *The Wizard of Oz*?"

The blank stares reminded him he was way, way, *way* past that particular pop culture reference.

"Katrina is correct. It is good you're awake and talking. Can you tell me how you're feeling?" Doctor Dardashti – that's what he was going with until someone corrected him – asked.

"Sore," David answered. "Everything aches."

"Your sons mentioned you had ringing in your ears and lack of balance. We can't test the equilibrium until we get you on your feet, but how is the ringing?"

"There, but not as bad as at first."

Doctor Dardashti nodded and made a note on the tablet in his hand. "I suspect you had a concussion and possible inner ear damage. Unfortunately, there isn't much we can do here in Unity Valley, but I'm sure they can help with that in Alexandria if it doesn't self-resolve."

"Yeah, well, bouncing off a tree tends to do some damage."

"Is that what happened?" Katrina asked.

David nodded. "Yeah, pretty much. The Xenos hit the hoverbike and I lost control. I went one way; the bike went another. I hit a tree and the bike hit . . . something else."

"If you feel up for it, I'd like you to sit up and maybe even stand," Doctor Dardashti said with raised eyebrows.

David chuckled, but it wasn't out of humor. "I'm pretty sure my robo-suit is FUBAR, so I doubt—"

"We will assist," Phin and Daniel said in unison.

"I'll help get him up," Connor offered, stepping forward.

David figured Connor would expect a snarky response, but his heart wasn't in it. He'd been "less than" for months, and the idea of being dependent again landed in his gut like an ice cold, lead ball. Connor came to the left side of the bed, moving around the doc, while Katrina stepped back, and Phin came to his other side. With a groan on his part as dull pain wrapped around his ribs, and with a friend or son on each arm, David curled forward until he sat upright. Phin kept his hand on David's shoulder, giving him just enough support to stay in the position while he caught his breath.

"*Ca va?*" Connor asked and David nodded, gritting his teeth.

On his own he shifted enough to lower his legs off the bed and his bare feet to the floor, grateful when he confirmed he at least had on infirmary pants and wasn't about to do an awkward flash dance. The room tilted slightly when he let his legs fall over the side of the bed, but his son's hand on his shoulder helped.

"How is your equilibrium?"

"Busted," David mumbled, fighting the wave of nausea that came with the pain and room tilting.

"Did you have equilibrium issues before?"

"No," David answered, lifting a hand to rub it across his face. The movement was slow, but he managed it. "Guess the universe thought I needed some new challenges."

"Do you want to attempt standing alone?" the doctor started to ask.

"Not gonna happen," David snapped, probably too quickly and with too much edge. Anger flared, hot and vicious, in his chest and heat crawled up his spine.

When exactly was enough going to be enough?

He motioned to Phin and Daniel to get on with getting him on his feet, because being pissed took his ability to talk. His boys braced his arms on each side, and with minimal effort, propelled him to his feet. Minimal for them; it took all he had to straighten his knees. His shoulder – the one he knew had taken the brunt of the impact – zinged with sharp, prickling pain but he refused to acknowledge it. The room shifted, but his sons kept him from tipping over. Each breath pushed against his aching ribs, but something in the back of his mind told him it should be worse.

Maybe I just don't feel things right anymore . . .

With his jaw clenched and his lips pressed hard against each other, David forced his spine to straighten and stood to his full height. His legs trembled beneath him, but Phin and Daniel had him in a solid hold. When he raised his head, he looked forward across the room.

And made eye contact with Lucy.

She was at the far end of the room, one arm crossed over her body, the other bent so her fingers covered her lips, watching him. From here, he didn't know if it was pity he saw but it didn't matter. The anger slammed hard into humiliation, which amped up his rage. It had been one thing to let her see the brackets and appendages when he could at least gain his own feet and walk across a room, but to be held upright by his sons was too much. David clenched his jaw until it hurt and looked away.

"Let me down," he snapped.

They did without a word, and once on his ass again, David gripped the edge of the mattress on each side of his legs, his arm muscles spasming as much as his legs.

"I'm sorry this is so difficult for you—" began the doc behind him.

"You don't have an effing clue," David ground out, only curbing his language for Katrina's sake. At least those lessons had stayed with him while he was a human popsicle.

Katrina crouched in front of him, forcing him to make eye contact. Ultimately, he wouldn't have denied her anyway. He was probably alive because of her. "We want to take you back to Alexandria," she said, touching his cheek. "Doctor Cole is back on the planet. She can help."

"When do we leave?" *The sooner the better.*

"I can have your hover prepped in thirty minutes," Connor answered. "Phin or Daniel, I assume you'll pilot him back."

"Yes, Colonel," Daniel answered. "We will assist in preparation."

"I can pack up your stuff upstairs," Katrina said, bumping his shoulder with her hip, he knew, with the intent of getting him to relax.

"Sure," he said, looking up at her with the best cocky grin he could manage. "If you don't mind folding my skivvies."

"I've seen Karl's. Yours can't be any worse." She smirked, winked, and headed for the hall.

"Would you like assistance reclining again, Father?" Daniel asked, and David shook his head.

Now that he was up, he intended to stay that way. "No, I'm good. I'll just sit here until you're ready to retrieve your invalid old man."

When neither of the boys moved, David looked up. Their expressions were often hard to read, especially to those who didn't know them well, but he recognized the confusion and concern. He lifted one hand and waved them off.

"I'm fine. I'll wait here. I'm done being in bed."

Together, they turned and left, following Connor from the infirmary. David released a long, weary sigh and let his head fall forward, eyes closed. After Gideon's death he'd been driven, powered by his need to never be in a position of helplessness again.

*E*ven across the room, Lucy felt like an intruder.

When she'd spoken to Katrina about David, the love the young woman had for him had been without question but seeing David with his family awakened in her a sudden ache of loss she hadn't let herself think about or acknowledge in months. Even though the young men had been described by other people in the community as stoic, even cold and disconcerting, she easily saw the affection they had for their father.

Lucy swallowed and forced herself to look away. They all spoke for a minute or two more. He was going back to Alexandria, which was, without question, the right thing to do. Unity Valley barely had the medical means to take care of their own people. David's care required exceptional skill and access. So why did her chest hurt, and her throat tighten at the acceptance he'd be leaving?

She knew she should return to her duties. She knew she should stop watching him. She knew she should turn away.

But she couldn't.

Group by group, they left him. Katrina ran up the stairs. Doctor Dardashti moved on to another patient. Connor, Phin, and Daniel went out the front door to prepare to depart. David still sat on the bed, his head down.

"Stop being a child, Lucinda Gabriella Bautista Santos," she scolded herself under her breath, rubbing the ache above her eyes. "Good grief. Get over yourself."

She steeled her nerves, raised her head with a deep breath, and prepared to put on the best face possible to go talk to him. But when she looked his way, he watched her, and her stomach tumbled. David shifted a hand to his knee to push himself to sit fully upright, his eyes never shifting from her. He canted his head, his lower jaw working.

"Come here."

She wasn't sure she actually heard his voice across the space or saw the words on his lips and knew what he said, but it didn't matter. Lucy pushed away from the wall that had been her support and moved toward him. When she was a few feet away, he raised a shaking arm, hand extended to her, and she took it to sit beside him. He brought their joined hands to his thigh to rest it there, staring down at their fingers.

"I'm going back to Alexandria," he finally said, still looking down.

"I know," she said barely above a whisper, and cleared her throat before she could continue. "Katrina told me you have a doctor in Alexandria who built your prosthetics. She can help you."

"Maybe," he said.

"No maybe," she rushed to say, leaning closer until her shoulder pressed to his and her forehead nearly touched his temple. "The sooner you go, the sooner you can come back."

David raised his chin, bringing their faces close; so close her heart jumped. "This question is going to make me a real son of a bitch, because not five minutes ago I reminded myself of the pathetic excuse of a man I am—"

"Stop it," she scolded. "David, don't."

"Do you want me to come back?"

"Yes." Lucy rolled her lips together, gathering her courage, and his gaze shifted down, distracting her for a thundering beat of her heart. "I wish you didn't have to leave, but . . . I know you have to."

"Come with me."

It wasn't exactly a question, but the effect was the same. It wasn't a demand, and she knew she could say no . . . but did she want to? She couldn't breathe for several seconds, especially when his gaze finally shifted from her lips to her eyes. Lucy blinked several times, hoping the burn in her eyes didn't manifest in tears because she felt them threatening.

"Would that be okay?"

His smile ticked up, popping the dimple in his cheek she'd learned to appreciate shortly after meeting him. "Why wouldn't it be okay? I'm pretty sure I can work out the details. Come with me." His warm hand came to her jaw, and as soon as she felt the tremor in his fingers she covered it with her own hand, holding his palm to her cheek. "I know you have people here—"

"I need to grab a few things . . ."

David's smile widened, reaching all the way to his eyes. His gaze lowered again to her mouth and his thumb brushed the corner of her lips before he closed the space between them and pressed a slow, firm, closed kiss to her lips.

Lucy leaned into him, into his touch, into the kiss, and when his lips opened over hers, she couldn't help the small sound in the back of her throat. David's fingertips pressed to the side of her head behind her ear, drawing his lips closed again. He moved his mouth away from hers, resting their foreheads together, and their breath mingled between them.

David pressed a kiss to her cheek near the corner of her mouth. "Go pack. The bus leaves soon."

"Okay, I've let Alexandria know you're on your way back and to expect you in a few hours. Michael said Doctor Cole will be waiting at the hospital for you and the other patient here."

Connor stood in the open hatchway; one arm raised over his head to grip the edge above him and jutted his chin toward the platform where Tessera had been moved to from the infirmary. David was in one of the deep seats across from her, security straps crossing his chest to help him keep his posture, though the longer he sat upright the less weak he felt. He had flatly refused to make the journey on his back. Traveling in these damn sardine can/bullet train, deathtraps was bad enough sitting upright. On his back was a hard no.

"Thank you, Colonel." Daniel finished checking the fasteners holding Tessera securely in place.

Lucy stood near Tessera's head, scanning her brow for some basic bio-readings. Once she had heard Tessera was also going to Alexandria, she'd slipped effortlessly into her caregiver persona.

After all Tessera had done for him, David liked the idea of her going back to Alexandria. Not that Unity Valley didn't do everything they could with what they had, but she looked in a bad way. He was confused as hell when he got a good look at the woman who had effectively kept him alive for the time he was on the mountain with her. The woman who had, on her own, managed to somehow drag his deadweight ass who knew how far to her small home. Sure, he'd noted she was thin when he'd woken up the first time and figured she could put some meat on her bones, but the woman was covered to her chin in blankets because her body temperature was too low was practically a skeleton. Her cheeks were sunken, dark shadows under her eyes, and her skin was ashen.

"Wasn't sure what to tell them," Connor said. "Why she was coming back, too. I mean, happy to help, but this is her community—"

"Michael will wish to see to her care," Phin answered, walking up the ramp behind Connor with Katrina beside him.

"Yeah, that still doesn't answer my question. Michael doesn't even know her. Why would he need to oversee her care?"

"Michael will understand," was the only clarification he provided, walking around Connor.

He headed toward the cockpit of the hover and Katrina took one of the other seats directly across from David, facing him, with her back to the cockpit. *Apparently motion sickness and the fear of dying wasn't a problem for her. Brat.*

"*D'accord,*" Connor said with a shrug and took a backward step down the ramp. "Have a good flight. David, I'll catch up with you when I get back. Since Katrina got your super dome turned on while you were on holiday, we're going to stay another week or so then head back to the capitol to figure out the next destination."

"Will you miss me?" David asked with a pout.

"*Tais-toi, connard,*" Connor tossed over his shoulder as he went down the ramp.

"You say the sweetest things!" David yelled after him, earning a single-finger salute and he laughed.

Lucy left Tessera as the ramp hydraulics engaged to close the hatch and scooted between David and Katrina's knees to take her seat on the hull side of the row. He enjoyed the view and stuck his tongue out at Katrina when he knew she'd caught him, and she smirked.

"You can just . . . hush," he scolded, and she smiled wider. As Lucy buckled in, he tilted his head toward Tessera but spoke to Katrina. "Do you know what Phin and Daniel mean? About Michael having some interest in Tessera?"

"I'm not super clear on it," she said with a shake of her head that bounced her curls off her cheeks. "But Phin said when they found you, they recognized her somehow. Did she say anything to you that would make that make sense?"

"Honestly, our conversations were limited. Either I didn't have the energy to talk long, or she wasn't willing to say much. She was absolutely adamant she couldn't return to Unity Valley, though, so when she wakes up, she might be glad not to be there."

"We thought she had gone back to wherever she'd originally come from," Lucy explained. "She just up and disappeared a few months ago. No one knew why. She didn't say anything, not even to Mama Della and Mama was the one who had brought her home right after the war. We were in town still, and to Unity Valley shortly after. Tessa was always quiet and kept to herself. She was closest to Molly if anyone. Mama Della didn't know where she'd come from, and said it never mattered. She needed a home."

"That's another weird thing." David looked from Tessera to Lucy. "You call her Tessa. She said her name was Tessera. I mean, not a huge thing but . . ." David shrugged. "Maybe it's nothing. My name is David, but someone might call me Dave."

"Maybe."

"How was Molly when you told her you were going to Alexandria?"

She paused, blinking, then a small smile bowed her lips. "She said she'd miss me, especially with the baby coming soon, but she was very happy. She likes you."

"We are departing," Daniel said from the co-pilot seat up front.

Simultaneously the O_2 engines came to life and with a tiny pop, the hover lifted off the ground. Lucy snapped out her arm and grabbed David's hand.

"Sorry," she whispered. "I've never been a fan."

David squeezed back. "Me neither, darlin'. Me neither."

CHAPTER FOURTEEN

24 August 2054, Monday
Alexandria Hospital – Private Nursery
United Earth Protectorate, Capitol City
Alexandria, Seat of Virginia
North American Continent

The nursery was dimly lit, as usual, with the steady rhythm of the babies' hearts reverberating off the walls. The choice to amplify their heartbeats was in hopes of helping the infants connect with each other just like they would if they shared a womb, through the sound of each other's heartbeats. The babies could hear the voices of anyone who came into the nursery, and when Michael played his violin for them. They couldn't replicate the comfort and protection of a mother's womb, but they hoped in the last few weeks of the babies' gestation could be as realistic and calming as possible.

It had been a busy day, and Michael had spent much of the last few hours helping Doctor Cole prepare for David's return.

And a mystery woman his brothers felt needed to be in Alexandria. Connor had relayed the information, but it was not complete enough for Michael to understand the reasoning. Only that Phin and Daniel wanted the woman in Alexandria, and that Michael should be involved. He trusted their judgment but was intrigued. Time would tell him why, and likely soon since their arrival was eminent. While he was more consultant than treating physician for David, he wanted to be sure to be available as needed. In the short time he had before they reached Alexandria, he wanted to seek some peace in the calm of the nursery.

"I knew I would find you here."

Michael smiled at the sound of his friend's voice and twisted at the waist enough to glance over his shoulder at Victor who stood just inside the double door.

"I like to come and talk to them," he explained. "Just spending time in here with them. It's soothing."

"Very soon these moments of calm will be harder to find, especially once you have four newborns."

Michael chuckled and turned to fully face Victor. "I doubt Nicole's infancy has adequately prepared me."

"Not even close, my friend."

"Were you looking for me?"

"I came here first, so I'm not quite sure that constitutes looking." Victor grinned and walked toward him. "I was, however, asked to assist in finding you. Did you leave your PAC somewhere?"

"My office, yes. I only intended to be away for perhaps quarter of an hour. Is someone trying to reach me?" Apprehension skittered up his spine and he took a long stride toward Victor. "Is something wrong?"

"Wrong, no. But your wife has been trying to reach you. She is on her way to the hospital with Caitlin. She began having consistent and frequent contractions mid-morning, and about an hour ago her water broke." Michael tried to bolt for the door, but Victor gripped his arm. "Michael, she assured me she is fine. Caitlin has been with her all day, and called ahead to let us know it was time for them to come in."

Michael didn't realize he was staring, unblinking, until his eyes burned, and Victor clamped a hand on his shoulder to break his daze. "You are about to be a father again." He looked past Michael. "And again. And again. And again. Let's go find your wife, speak with

Doctor Eaton about timeframes, then discuss the implementation of our birth plan for these three."

No matter how many times he and Jacqueline had discussed and planned the various possibilities and scenarios for this day, Michael found his mind entirely blank. The general obstetrics wing was in a different wing away from the secured wing, but because of the extenuating circumstances around the birth of the four Tanner children, if it was time to discuss delivery, she would be in a specifically designated room in the secure area not far from the private nursery. He had to allow Victor to lead, because he'd drawn a blank of how to get there.

Victor opened a door, motioning Michael through, and the moment and reality snapped back in place when he saw Jacqueline reclined in a chair with her feet up, dressed in her favorite robe from home.

"Hey," she said with a smile, rubbing her hand over her stomach. Her expression was slightly strained, but not enough he worried she was in pain. "I was beginning to wonder if you'd skipped town on me, handsome."

"I'm sorry," he said, kissing her cheek before kneeling beside the chair. "I didn't intentionally make it difficult to find me."

She smiled and rested her head on the cushion behind her. "I know. Besides, Victor was pretty sure he knew where to find you."

"How are you feeling?" Victor asked, standing near her feet with his hands in his pockets.

"Good," she said with a nod. "I was able to nap for a bit earlier this afternoon. I'm just ready."

"Of course. When Doctor Eaton returns, we will discuss the rest of the day."

Jacqueline laughed. "That's such a casual way to put it. Like you're asking if I want to get lunch first."

"I am grateful you were able to make it back to Alexandria before we got to this step," Victor said as he scanned the readings of the three infants, all data scrolling parallel to each other on his screen practically in unison. His voice was muffled by the surgical mask he – and everyone in the room – now wore, along with full surgical gear. The babies couldn't be moved, so the nursery had been sterilized. "We are all grateful David was found, and in relatively good health, and your family can enjoy his return. Your gift with the stasis systems, and these Areth-based technology pods, will be integral today and I'm not sure I would have wanted to do it without you."

"Of course," Katrina said as she headed to the space behind the artificial wombs to check on the access drains for when the time came to remove the babies. "It's been such a crazy few days. Who would have thought everything would be happening all at once."

"Quite right."

Through the door came Doctor Eaton's practice partner and three pediatric nurses who were highly trusted by the Tanners and loyal to the concept of secrecy. Everyone wore the same sanitary attire as Victor and Katrina: full body suits, skullcaps, masks, and gloves. Katrina knew she would be part of a larger secret known only to those present. Not even President Tanner would know the outcome of today's births. Michael and Jacqueline made it abundantly clear these four babies – the three in the artificial wombs and the one Jacqueline carried – were to never be seen as separate. That included the manner of their births.

She felt honored for being included. But also, a bit weird that she couldn't even tell her husband. Not that Phin would ever ask. If anyone understood the significance of the babies being considered no different for their origins, it was Phin and Daniel.

Even then, all she would know was the gender of the three in the room. It wasn't like they came out saying their names.

Victor stepped away from his monitors to speak with Doctor Cyn Carr and the three nurses and be sure they knew where they could find everything they needed, including the stainless-steel bassinette carriers for each baby and any emergency infant medical equipment. Victor and Katrina would be responsible for the proper shut down and preparation for extraction of the wombs. Doctor Carr and her nurses would take over from there. Katrina shifted from the first womb to the second, running through the same diagnostic and system prep.

An alarm went off like a claxon that made Katrina jump back with a gasp. A red warning light flashed rapidly on the third womb. Katrina pushed the cart beside her out of the way and scrambled to the womb as both Victor and Doctor Carr bolted from the other side of the room. From her side of the womb, she couldn't see any of the forward facing panels, but she saw the baby inside suddenly thrash and the artificial amnionic fluid inside churned.

"They're seizing," Doctor Carr shouted. "We need them out. Now!"

"Katrina!"

Victor shouting her name over the claxon alarm was all the instruction she needed, and she retrieved the cart she's shoved aside. She didn't need to mentally run through the checklist for shutting down the pod, engaging both the new life support systems while disengaging the existing systems and engaging the drain of fluid and breaking of the pod seal.

Another alarm went off.

Katrina's heart stopped.

"You are doing great, Jackie. With the next contraction, I want you to bear down. Okay?"

Jacqueline nodded, her glistening lips pressed tight together, sweat running down her temple. Michael patted her brow with a washcloth and braced her shoulders with the other arm so she could lean forward. She groaned and huffed several breaths.

"Bear down with it, Jackie."

Michael had tried to draw the pain from her when it amped up, but worried he was drawing strength as much as pain, so instead he tried something he'd only done a handful of times, the first time out of desperation to save his friend's life, and that was to shift his strength to her. Anything he could do to help, knowing few men could give this way, and likely many wished they could, he was willing to give for her.

Perhaps that was why he felt the sudden shift. The change. The sudden rush of panic that made his blood go cold.

"Something is wrong!" Jacqueline screamed.

"No, Jackie. You're doing fine—"

"No! Something is *wrong*!"

"Jackie—"

"Listen to her," Michael snapped. "Something is wrong!"

"Get a trauma team in here now!"
"We need anesthesiology! Stat!"
"Code Red! Code Red!"

Two hours later . . .

"Michael . . ."

Michael raised his head and opened his eyes, seeing his father's reflection in the NICU window where his four children slept beyond, each in their own isolette. His father stepped behind him and rested his hands on Michael's shoulders, squeezing gently.

"Victor came down to the waiting area to tell us we could come up.

Your mom went to Jackie's room. I said we'd be down when you're ready."

"Thank you."

"How are they?"

Michael inhaled deeply through his nose and released it slowly through his mouth before he felt ready to speak. "No one knows exactly what happened, but I have suspicions only because everything I've experienced dictates I cannot rule out the fantastical. Kathleen wanted them to exist for a reason, and likely for the same reason she conspired to create me; to harness whatever abilities she believed could be harnessed to her benefit. That being the case and knowing the level of connection Phin and Daniel shared with Gideon, and on a level with me, I believe they are all somehow connected at a cerebral level. Including, through proximity and genetics, the baby Jacqueline carried. I believe the first baby to fall into distress quite literally drew the other along with them. Or they felt the fear and panic, and in turn, felt fear themselves. The timing for events in the nursery coincided too closely with Jacqueline's birth."

Nick chuckled, but it sounded sad and Michael felt the weight of his father's concern. "I know you needed to say that, but are they okay . . ."

Michael nodded. "Yes, or they will be. Victor and Doctor Carr immediately called in additional help, so they acted swiftly and removed the babies far faster than intended. Victor said Katrina was indispensable in the process. And Doctor Eaton acted quickly to take the fourth baby by cesarean. They will likely stay in the NICU for a few days longer than anticipated, but they will all be fine. Jacqueline is sleeping after the surgery, and I'll let her know all our children are well when she wakes."

His father wrapped an arm around him from shoulder to shoulder, and held him in support and in that moment, Michael realized he was crying. Perhaps he had been since he was able to breathe again.

"Good. That's what matters. They'll all be fine, Jackie is fine, and we'll have a house full of babies. Tanner and Tanner Daycare."

Michael chuckled, appreciating his father's ability to ease the weight in his chest. "None of us may sleep again."

Nick Tanner barked a laugh and shifted to stand beside Michael, leaning forward to look through the glass, so close his forehead almost touched the window. "Okay, so what've we got?"

"Three boys. One girl."

"Oh, boy. She's going to have a hard time dating in . . . thirty or forty years."

Michael laughed again and slid his fingers across his wet cheeks, sniffing. "Undoubtedly." He took a deep breath and sighed. "When they are home, we'd like to bring those closest to us together and introduce them properly."

"Sounds good." His father turned his head to look at Michael along the line of their equal shoulders. Moisture shined in his eyes, mirroring the tears still threatening in Michael's. "When we heard there were problems, I had this flashback to the day you were born . . . and they told me you died."

Michael just nodded. He understood. But he had no words.

*J*acqueline's hospital room was dark, the sun had set an hour earlier, with only a low-level light along the ceiling edge to allow him to see. Her bed had been adjusted so she didn't lie flat, providing some relief by not straining the surgery site, and she was nestled amongst several pillows and blankets. An IV pole was on the far side of the bed, delivering fluids, antibiotics, and mild pain relief. Her surgical incision had been knitted shorty after delivery and an SB stimulator would be utilized over the next twenty-four to forty-eight hours to heal the scar and reduce the pain. But for now, she would be tender.

Caitlin stood from the chair beside the bed and embraced Michael when she reached him. "She hasn't woken up yet," she whispered before kissing his cheek.

"Dad is waiting in the hall. Thank you for sitting with her."

"Of course. Now that everyone is okay, we'll probably head home.

We left Nicole and Adam with your dad's bodyguards on duty." She chuckled. "I don't think it was the evening they planned on."

Michael chuckled and nodded. Caitlin squeezed his hand as she walked away, heading for the door. He walked on soft feet across the room and stopped to stand beside the bed and watch her rest.

She was amazing.

He realized most fathers looked upon the women who created and birthed their children with a sense of awe and admiration, and yet somehow, he felt uniquely humbled and blessed this woman was his wife. He wasn't so foolish or blind not to know Jacqueline had stepped away from a life at such a drastic juxtaposition to the one they lived now – from being a warrior, a soldier, and a fully independent woman to a mother and wife – but she had done it without pause and for that he was blessed. He wouldn't have ever asked her to leave a life he believed she loved, or at the least enjoyed, but she had stepped into his family and become Nicole's mother. She had become his wife. And now she had become the mother of four more children.

How could she not be amazing?

She inhaled slow and deep, rolling her head in his direction, her brow wrinkling with a cringe just before she opened her eyes. Michael set his hand on her shoulder, and she blinked, bringing him into focus.

"Hey . . ." she said, her voice heavy with sleep and medication. "Did you get the ID of the hover who hit me?"

Michael smiled. "More like four small hovers."

Her smile was slow and her eyes slid closed again, only to snap open again and she gasped. "The baby!" She tried to sit up faster than Michael could attempt to stop her, and cried out, falling back.

"The baby is fine, Jacqueline," he said softly, moving his hand from her shoulder to her cheek, shifting to bring himself into her line of sight. "All of them."

Tears welled in her eyes. "Something was wrong."

Michael nodded before she could finish the statement and used his thumb to wipe away her tears. "One of the babies in the nursery went into distress and it was a cascading effect. I believe the babies share a connection like Phin and Daniel and I." He leaned in over the railing and kissed her forehead, holding his lips to her warm skin. "We have three sons and a daughter."

"But they're okay?"

"They are all okay." As he spoke, he stroked his thumb across her brow, hoping he could share with her some of the calm he'd found since speaking at length with the pediatrician they'd chosen to care for the babies. She was already Nicole's pediatrician, and they knew her well. She also understood the complexities of their unique situation, as well as the need and requirement for privacy. "Doctor Longbow has completed all her preliminary exams and tests and assured me they are all strong and thriving and doing well despite their exciting entrance into the world."

His wife watched his face as he explained, her eyes barely shifting. When he finished, she took a long, deep breath. "I would ask you to swear to me you're telling the truth, but I've never once questioned what you say. But you sometimes leave out things you don't think people want to know or hear."

"I swear to you, on everything I am," he said with a smile. "They are beautiful and strong and doing well. Doctor Longbow wants to keep them for a couple extra days. Not because of specific concerns, but because they are unique and out of an abundance of caution."

"They can't go home with me?"

"Not tomorrow, no. But likely by the end of the week."

Jacqueline sucked in a shaky breath and nodded, tears welling in her dark eyes. Michael leaned in to press a long kiss to her forehead.

CHAPTER FIFTEEN

25 August 2054, Tuesday
Alexandria Hospital – Rehabilitation
United Earth Protectorate, Capitol City
Alexandria, Seat of Virginia
North American Continent

"I don't know if this is the news you wanted or expected to hear or not, David, but at least we have a point to move forward from."

Lucy paused in the doorway of the hospital room she'd been directed to, instinctively knowing she'd just stepped into a very private conversation. David sat in a wheelchair with his head down, his elbows on the armrests and his fingers linked in the space between over his lap. A woman stood between Lucy and him, her back to Lucy, wearing the universally recognized white lab coat of a doctor, with her blonde hair with slight gray streaks twisted into an ornate coiffure at her crown.

David sighed and lifted his head. Before Lucy could step out of the doorway and his line of sight, he saw her. Despite the strain evident in his features, he smiled, though it was less than convincing.

"I'm sorry . . ." she said, taking another step back. "I can come back."

"Nah, come on in," he said, motioning with one hand for her to come into the room. He gestured toward the woman, who turned enough to look at Lucy. "This is Doctor Olivia Cole. She's the top cybernetic prosthetics doctor with the Defense Alliance. She designed and built my robo-suit to get me back on my feet. Doc, this is my friend Lucy Santos."

Lucy crossed the space and took the hand Doctor Cole extended, shaking it. While sitting alone in David's apartment overnight, she'd used his data access system in as much as she could without delving into coded files and systems to research the true state of the world, learning about alliances and key players – information that never quite filtered its way to Unity Valley. It was a lot like she imagined her Abuela Gabi meant when she said she used to "surf the web." They didn't call global open access the "web" anymore, but it seemed the equivalent. Regular reports and updates were broadcast to every continent, but if you didn't have the technology or knowledge of the information's existence, it didn't reach you. She doubted Trevor didn't know, but also didn't feel like he'd intentionally held back anything. She had learned about the Defense Alliance and numerous races and worlds throughout and beyond the Milky Way Galaxy including the Areth and Umani, who most directly assisted Earth during the War. It had been a lot to absorb, and she'd been up well into the small hours of the morning reading and watching archived broadcasts, but she felt she had at least a stronger understanding of the true reality of their battered and bruised existence.

"Nice to meet you," she said with a nod, quickly processing the woman was not human . . . and if David hadn't said so, she would have never known. No wonder the Sorracchi and Areth had slid into their lives so easily; the Sorracchi through deception and the Areth through common genetics.

"I'll leave you now," Doctor Cole said, turning her focus back to David. "We'll talk later this week once I've spoken with the proper doctors here at the hospital to get you on the right path." She rested her hand on his shoulder in a "bedside manner" move Lucy had seen

Doctor Dardashti do countless times. It had to be in the DNA of a physician, no matter the planet they came from. "I don't want you to be discouraged. I believe this is a positive development."

David nodded and the doctor stepped away, dipping her chin to Lucy with a smile as she headed for the door. Lucy stepped aside and into the room to let her pass, then moved to the side of David's chair and crouched beside him, gripping the armrest for balance. His expression was strained, and even though he offered a smile, it was far from convincing.

"I can't tell if she told you good news or bad news," she said.

David sighed and gave a small chuckle that was as unconvincing as his smile. He sat up straighter and brought his palm to his chest, rubbing the cotton shirt he wore like he tried to work out a sore muscle. He was in street clothes, not any hospital garments, that made her suspect he wasn't staying.

"I haven't figured that out yet," he said more to the open door than to her, then finally shifted his position in the chair and his attention to Lucy. "The suit was designed for rehabilitation and recovery, not bouncing off the side of a mountain. It's tough to fix something when parts of it are still up on that mountain somewhere."

"She can't build a new one?"

"It's more than that. The whole thing has a neurological interface, and there are subdermal nodes and parts."

Lucy nodded. "I suspected when I treated the contact points. Had to be something under the skin to keep them there. There have been developments in eye care that use neurological interfaces and subdermal connections, but much more low-key than what you have."

"Yeah, well, a bunch of those got seriously screwed up in the crash. Parts were forcibly ripped off, and the ones that were left were hanging on by practically nothing. She can't fix those." He made a low, rough sound in his throat and shook his head. "I'd have to go through the whole surgical process again – having these removed and new ones put in, neural coding, all that – to get a new suit."

"Okay . . ." she led.

"A couple problems there. We don't have this kind of tech just hanging around on Earth. This isn't human tech at all. She'd have to get the parts from Aretu. With the current tensions, that could be weeks."

She let the tensions comment go, knowing it was significant but at that moment David was more important. "What's the other side? She mentioned doctors here and a treatment path..."

"That's going to be a longer story. Pull up a chair."

She rose from the crouch and looked around until she spotted a chair. Lucy intended to pull it back to him, but by the time she reached it and turned around David had swiveled the wheelchair and faced the chair she sat in so they faced each other, knees to knees.

Rather than nudging him to continue, Lucy just sat and waited because the play of emotions over his face said he was battling with whatever he had to say, whether it was how to say it or how to process it. Or both. She'd been around patients enough who had to process a diagnosis they'd just been given to see the signs. It wasn't always because the diagnosis was bad; sometimes, it was just unexpected and thus required a shift in perspective.

"For a few weeks, I've felt like I was losing ground. Walking and lifting was exhausting. I wasn't getting the support from the prosthetics the same way I was at the beginning, when I first got my feet back. I thought something was wrong; Doc Cole even had Michael check them out. They said everything was fine. Every reading from the equipment was spot on and to spec. So, I put up with it. Part of being busted up, I figured."

"Sounds like maybe something else was going on."

David winked at her, and she smiled, seeing some of the tension ease around his eyes. If she served no other purpose here, maybe it was just to help him smile. She was okay with that.

"Theoretical outlooks gauged my recovery at a certain pace, figuring in how long I'd been in stasis, how old I was physically – not chronologically, because if we go by that I'm a really creepy old man flirting with his young, sexy nurse – all that."

She smiled and returned his wink.

He chuckled and that was her reward.

"The reason I was fighting so hard to use the prosthetics is because the suit wasn't helping, it was hindering. It was like I was working a bench press 24/7. My muscles were stronger than the suit expected."

"But . . . that's a good thing, right?"

David tilted his head back and forth, wrinkling his nose. "Yeah, but not great. I guess we could have adjusted if it weren't for the whole crash; now, I have to work with what I've got and see how far I can get on my own. That's what Doc Cole suggests. I'm not going to climb mountains or chop wood any time soon, but I'm going to start at a point better than if I hadn't had the suit at all."

"David, that sounds wonderful to me," she declared, scooting forward to put her hands on his knees. "If you made that kind of physical progress with the restriction of the suit, you can make physical progress now that you're free of it. Right?"

He laid one of his hands over hers and squeezed. "Well, dang, woman. I was all set to wallow in my own self-pity for at least a week. How am I supposed to be miserable with you cheering me up?"

Lucy smiled and leaned up from the chair, kissing his cheek. "You didn't ask me to come because I make an amazing apple pie, did you?"

"Now that you bring it up—"

She laughed and kissed his lips – quickly, because she found with each kiss they shared, she wanted more and here wasn't the place – before sitting down again. "So, what's next?"

David didn't answer right away, his gaze fixed on her mouth with a slightly crooked grin on his own lips. Heat slowly crept up her throat to her cheeks, even warming her lips, and she smiled, enjoying his scrutiny. David cleared his throat and sat back in the chair.

"Today, I go home. Get up. Move around. Try to walk a bit. Don't do anything too crazy like taking the stairs to my floor. Doc Cole is going to talk to a few people and make a plan and let me know when to come back in for, probably, another evaluation . . . and go from there, I guess."

"I have very little physical therapy experience – just what I did with Doctor Dardashti – but I'm glad to help."

"My own personal PT nurse." David acted like he was trying to suppress his grin and failing. "I'll take it."

Alexandria Hospital – Private NICU

"This little boy is a little underweight, but not enough to concern me. He's already proven he has a solid appetite," Doctor Rowena Longbow said as she leaned over Jacqueline, who was feeding the baby boy in question. He eagerly devoured the super-fortified infant formula created by Doctor Longbow and the quadruplets' care team. She smoothed her hand over his hair. "He's going to catch up to his siblings just fine."

"But what about whatever caused his distress?" Michael asked, rocking in one of the cushioned rocking chairs in the nursery, his arms supported from beneath so he could hold a baby on each side. He had one of the boys and the girl.

The third boy had already finished eating, had been swaddled, and immediately went peacefully back to sleep.

Doctor Longbow straightened and slid her hands into the pockets of her white coat, shaking her head. "Truth be told, Doctor Tanner, I find no indication of anything happening to him. Yes, I know something did, but if you handed me the brain activity and plethora of medical tests we've run on the children since their birth I would be hard pressed to pick out which one experienced the seizure." She smiled and looked from him to the babies in his arms. "That being said, as their pediatrician I will be very mindful and will never dismiss anything of the slightest concern. These children are wholly unique in every right, even between the four of them, and caring for them will be an adventure."

"Thank you, Doctor," Jacqueline said, removing the now empty bottle from the baby's mouth. She set it aside and shifted him to her shoulder to pat and rub his back. "We know you'll keep an eye on them, but four of them is a bit . . ."

"Daunting?"

Michael looked toward the sound of Victor's voice, who had just come into the nursery. "One word of many I might choose."

Victor chuckled and crossed to them, pausing beside Michael to look at the two sleeping children. He stepped to the open bassinette where their full-belly, sound asleep son slept. "Everyone looks hearty and strong today. Well fed and well loved."

"I will come by this evening to check on them again," Doctor Longbow said, taking a step back to leave. "I have assigned two nurses to be here through the night, and if at any point – no matter the hour – you want to contact them for updates, please feel free."

Jacqueline's response was interrupted by a loud, satisfying burp from the baby on her shoulder. She laughed and turned her face away from him, wrinkling her nose. "He's his grandfather's grandson."

Michael laughed and smiled, watching his wife hold their son. Nicole was a toddler, and Michael had spent many hours watching with ever expanding love as Jacqueline became a mother; watching her nurture their newborns was an equally beautiful sensation for him.

"Don't rule out his father's influence," Victor said, winking at Michael. "I recall some hearty belches coming from his father in his youth."

"Not fair telling my secrets, Victor."

Victor's smile widened, and yet Michael sensed something about the pinch near his eyes. "What else am I to do with all those glorious stories but embarrass you fully? It is my duty as the keeper of the secrets of your youth." He came back to Michael and crouched beside the chair, bringing him level with the head of the only girl in the bunch.

"They are beautiful, Michael. Truly beautiful."

"I will never be able to thank you for all you've done to bring them to us, my friend."

Victor made a dismissive sound and stood. "Now I feel utterly ashamed for coming here on other business. Before you leave the hospital today, would you come see me?" He pivoted on his heels enough to face Jacqueline more than Michael, raising his right hand. "I swear to you I will not keep him long, and I only ask because I believe it necessary."

"Do you want to go now?" Jacqueline asked, shifting the baby into the bend of her elbow so she could stand.

Victor closed the space between them to help her stand, for which Michael was thankful since he was essentially pinned to the chair where he sat. Only a slight pinch of pain played over her features, the treatment she'd received since the day before already progressing her healing to a point where her physical discomfort would be minimal.

"I can put this one down, and I'll feed the ones you have," she said, tilting her head to Michael while she took the baby to his bassinette. "Just come back and rescue me when you're done."

"I don't want to abandon you."

Jacqueline smiled as she leaned over to take the boy from his right arm and feeling rushed back into his fingers. He hadn't realized they'd fallen asleep. "I'm pretty sure I can get help quick if needed. Once we're home, though, you're never to leave me."

Victor willingly took the girl while Michael shook out his arms and stood. He watched Victor for a moment, the little girl bundled to his chest as he spoke in whispered words that Michael couldn't hear.

He would be a natural father. He had been a father to Michael throughout his childhood when there was nothing else but fear and pain and uncertainty, even at the risk of his own life. It was a cruel truth that Victor would never be a father in any biological sense, because the centuries of body cloning by the Sorracchi had taken away his current body's ability to be a father by natural means. Victor and Beverly hadn't shared any decisions about being parents otherwise – there was a world of children – but Michael sincerely hoped they would.

Until then, Victor was the best possible extended family the Tanner children could ask for.

With a final kiss to the girl's forehead, garnering a long sigh from her and a soft chuckle from Victor, he laid her in her bed until Mama could gather her up for dinner. Michael waited for Jacqueline to settle again in the feeding chair, a new bottle and a new hungry boy in her arms, before he leaned over to kiss her.

"I will be back soon."

"I know," she said, looking up at him. "Do what you need to because I mean it. You're never leaving me alone with all four again."

He kissed her forehead and headed toward the door, where Victor stood holding it open for him. Together, they walked side by side toward the elevator, just as the day before with Michael letting Victor lead. This time, he didn't know their destination at all.

"I do apologize for taking you away from your wife and new progeny," Victor said as they walked. "While I debated whether I should approach you with this today, I did decide ultimately you would want to know what I need to show you even if time passed before you could be actively involved."

"You have me curious."

"It is about the woman Phin and Daniel brought with David from Unity Valley."

Michael's step hitched as he realized the mystery of the woman and her significance had been completely lost to him in the sudden arrival of the babies. Victor laughed and patted his hand on Michael's shoulder, steering him toward a hallway to their left.

"As I thought. I assumed you might have had your mind elsewhere. You will, however, want to know who she is."

"Do you know who she is and why my brothers thought she needed to be here? For me to care for, specifically?"

Victor nodded, pressing his lips together before he spoke. "I do. I knew the moment I saw her this morning."

His features tightened, but Michael only saw it because Victor turned to open another door. They were still within the secure wing of the hospital, but a non-specialty ward for general, non-intensive care.

"She is from New Mexico . . ."

No other conclusion made sense. Michael and Victor's lives had been intrinsically coiled while they were prisoners of different forms in New Mexico, and since absolutely no one came to mind for Michael since he'd found his freedom, the connection had to be from their common hell. *But who?*

Victor nodded, stopping outside the closed door of a private room. "Yes. I haven't spoken to Phin or Daniel since I saw her to determine just how *they* know her, how all the pieces come together, but somehow they not only know who she is but how she is connected to you."

"Well, let's find out."

Victor nodded, lips pressed in a straight line, and pushed down the door handle to allow Michael entrance into the room. The lighting was low, and the only sound in the room was the steady beep of monitoring systems indicating her heartbeat was steady, her blood oxygen levels were acceptable, and all other systems were functioning. From the door, he couldn't determine any details as she was swathed in blankets and IVs and other medical apparatuses.

It only took two steps toward her before reality slammed his chest, taking his breath, and nearly knocking his legs out from beneath him were it not for his lifelong friend who gripped his arm and kept him standing until he reached the side of the bed. He clenched the railing, a riot of thoughts and indiscernible emotions slamming in and around him with a miasma of light and color that made him dizzy.

"Ranae . . ."

"Not Ranae, Michael—"

Michael nodded rapidly, looking away from her sallow, sunken face to Victor and back again. "I know. I understand. I just never imagined . . . It was just months ago we learned she'd been cloned by Kathleen. How is it that something so miraculous as this could happen? Didn't Connor report she had been caring for David when they found him?"

"Yes, but little else is known. She has been in a deep coma since they brought her to Unity Valley, so she can offer no explanation. David said he was in a bad way while with her, only speaking with her a couple of times, so he knows nothing himself other than her name and that she had some type of connection to Unity Valley."

Michael looked to Victor, trying to gather his thoughts. "Her name. What is her name?"

"David calls her Tessera, but David's friend Lucy said they knew her in the community as Tessa. She joined them days after the War, but no one knows her past."

"Tessera . . ." Michael said slowly, absorbing the name as he looked back to her. "Tessera. That's Greek. It's like a stone or tile or glass used to make a mosaic. It almost sounds like four in Greek as well. Four. Number four?" He looked to Victor again.

"Your conclusion is far more eloquent than anything I imagined," Victor said with a slow smile. "But it might make sense. We know from records we've found that Kathleen made six clones of Ranae. We found record of two dying, and Connor and Olivia found one deceased in Boston a few months ago. That leaves three yet unaccounted for. Perhaps they were designated in this way."

"Perhaps."

Finding his focus again, Michael went to the foot of the bed to remove the medical tablet and access the records they'd created for her in the last roughly twenty-four hours. She came in having mostly recovered from severe dehydration due to the treatment given to her in Vancouver, but she was visibly malnourished. Layers of blankets covered her to her shoulders, matching the notes indicating her body temperature was slightly low and the blankets were to keep her warm. The sunken cheeks and eyes and stark features spoke to the lack of nutrition. She had been receiving nutrition directly since arriving, high protein and high calorie.

"Her brain activity is low but present," Michael said aloud as he read the notes. "But there has been no response to her environment or stimuli."

"Correct. At this point, we are maintaining her until we can determine a course of action. Honestly, until there is a change, I don't see how we can make any decisions for her long term care. David may have more information, and simply hasn't been asked the right questions."

Michael nodded, looking from the tablet to the familiar face of a woman he knew a lifetime ago, though his heart and mind knew she was an absolute stranger. "I will speak to him as soon as the opportunity can be made."

CHAPTER SIXTEEN

Interstellar Secure Communication Chamber
Robert J. Castleton Memorial Building – The Castle
United Earth Protectorate, Capital City
Alexandria, Seat of Virginia
North American Continent

The chamber was dim when John stepped inside since the long-distance meeting with the leaders of the Defense Alliance wasn't slated to begin for another quarter of an hour. This meeting had been delayed twice already because of immediate emergencies – a surprise attack on another Defense Alliance outpost being one of them – and it was his sincere hope the meeting would happen today.

The accelerated attacks from the Urdo Khantan, mercenary soldiers to the Sorracchi, had him concerned. Whispers of information through the Alliance Intel society solidified the theory the Sorracchi wanted revenge on the Defense Alliance and their newest allies . . . Earth. The Sorracchi alone were formidable and powerful enemies, but they lacked the bloodthirst the Urdo Khantan brought. The Urdo Khantan were brutal and without souls, ready to die as viciously as they killed others in the name of their employer. Their cultish mindset believed each life was a tier to a higher existence where they would be rewarded for their brutality, a disgusting juxtaposition to the beliefs of so many societies across the galaxy.

He took the few moments of stillness to center his thoughts for the next couple of hours, since this discussion would surely not be a quick one. The space was designed to appear as part of a much larger conference hall where all attendees sat at the same level around a circle, facing each other with no single spokesperson elevated over any other. There were hierarchies within the Defense Alliance, but only in that some spoke for groups as a single voice, but all voices were on equal standing.

Earth was not yet a vetted and assimilated member of the Alliance, but the time would come and soon.

For the attendees from Earth, a semicircle table sat against the wall to his left when he entered. The meeting would be transmitted instantaneously through three-dimensional laser technology with such clarity if someone were to enter, they wouldn't know who was in the room, and who was fifty-thousand lightyears away. He stepped to the center of the room, currently illuminated with a circle of light from the projection system in the ceiling, although the images would be from multiple sources to create the three-dimensional effect.

John stopped in the light and tipped back his head, closing his eyes.

He hated the fear curling in his chest.

He had been a soldier and had accepted the risk of his chosen profession when he left his physician education to serve his queen. When she asked him to set aside his weapon and be an ambassador to the people he'd lived with and come to care so much for, he'd done so willingly, and would choose nothing else even now; but knowing the truth of war with the Sorracchi terrified him for a world that had known war, but not anywhere near the scale they could face soon.

He feared for his friends. He feared for the race his people had protected from a distance. He feared for his wife. His children. This was their world and their people, and thus, it was his as well.

The door behind him opened and he pivoted on his heels enough to look, seeing President Nick Tanner enter, with Phin walking first and

Daniel behind. Phin acknowledged John with a nod, and once Nick was in the room, joined his brother as they stepped outside. Just like Jenifer when her duties were as his bodyguard – a position he'd asked her to reconsider, but she stood stubbornly firm – and she could not attend meetings of Defense Alliance leaders, Phin and Daniel were required to remain outside the chamber.

Somehow, he didn't see them falling into chatter. They weren't prone to what the English language called "chitchat," and Jenifer despised talking in general.

The thought made him smile.

"Congratulations to the Tanner family," John said as he turned and walked to Nick, his arm extended.

Nick met his forearm-to-forearm greeting, gripping each other at the elbow, and John patted Nick's shoulder with his free hand. "Thank you, John. We were scared as hell for a good hour and a half, but they're all doing good today."

With Nick in the circle of light John had stood in, John saw the signs of fatigue in Nick's expression. The thick hedge of concern, and a very old fear, buffered around him and pushed into John. John firmed his hold on Nick's shoulder. Those close to the Tanner family knew how Nick had been tricked over twenty-eight years before when he was told his "wife" and son had died in childbirth, stealing Michael from his life for twenty-five years.

"Remember tha', my friend. The sadness of years past is behind you, and you have been gifted beyond most can imagine. A new son of your own and four new grandchildren."

Nick inhaled slowly, meeting John's gaze, and nodded as a genuine smile eased his features. "Three boys and a girl."

"That's fantastic!"

Nick nodded again and the tension eased a little more. "They're going to be at Alexandria Hospital for a couple more days just because of their . . ." He smirked and the Nick Tanner John recognized most edged out of the fatigue. ". . .unique situation, but when they come home Michael and Jackie want people to the residence for proper introductions."

"I look forward to the introductions."

The next two or three minutes consisted of the entrance of the Earth commanders and leaders who would attend, including Vice President Beverly Surimoto, and their subsequent rounds of congratulations for Nick and the Tanner family. The Firebird tech manning the long-distance comms-array system announced via the comms the meeting was scheduled to begin shortly, so they each moved to their seats.

Nick took what constituted the center chair at the Earth-based table, with Beverly to his right and John to his left. Chief Security Advisor Phillip Ebbon sat to Beverly's right. Normally, Connor Montgomery would attend as Firebird Commander, but John understood he had requested to stay in Unity Valley until they felt more secure in leaving. Beside Colonel Ebbens sat Colonels Conrad Corchan and Helen Bertrands, Earth Force Terra Commanders and Colonels Roberta Castleton and Merin St. John, Earth Force Sphera Commanders.

In his usual show of grandeur he felt fitting his station, Raxo Ambassador Drucillus Clodianus Hiacyntus swept into the room, flanked by his guards and trailed by his concubines who halted at the door short of entering. In his garish robes and outlandish accessories, he walked through the ring of light and took his chair beside John without any acknowledgment of anyone else in the room.

Because Aretu and Raxo were the only other races with which Earth had yet to have direct contact, they were the only planets with ambassadors on Earth. For the time being as the relationship between Earth and the Defense Alliance expanded, so would the ambassador contingent. Eventually, Earth would send ambassadors across the galaxy as well.

John had frequently questioned the wisdom of the Council of Seven for their choice of Drucillus Clodianus Hiacyntus for the position, but the leadership role of the Council would shift in the next year to another sovereignty which would likely change the ambassadors as well. Ambassadorships from Raxo tended to be based highly on personal favor and wealth over viability, with admittedly some sovereigns worse than others.

"Why do we delay?" Drucillus Clodianus Hiacyntus demanded to know, declaring clearly and loudly he would not be inconvenienced.

Seconds later the light shifted and the room filled virtually with a host of Defense Alliance leaders. John couldn't help but smile when his brother's wife – Queen Bryony the Fourteenth of Aretu – appeared in full, solid color. He supposed some would see his assignment as ambassador to Earth as based in nepotism and favor as that of Drucillus Clodianus Hiacyntus, but John served with pride.

Speaker for Council of Seven Constantius Dionysius Franciscus of Rome sat beside Bryony, but like his Earth ambassador, did his best to sit a bit taller and straighter to try to appear of more import. He only succeeded in looking foolish. Bryony came from a long line of regal rulers, he did not. Rome was known for their pretention; nearly any other sovereign would be an improvement in John's opinion.

He personally was inclined toward Eire or Bagdaghir himself.

John had read about and witnessed the undesirable elements of Human politics, but Earth was far from singular in their political scandals and unpleasantries.

Politics had never been an aspiration of his.

Not every race in the Defense Alliance had representation in the chamber, as the chamber would need to be much larger, but the races most likely to be involved in any direct fight were all present. On the other side of Bryony from Constantius Dionysius Franciscus was Gozzo Torroni of the Ilgen, his moisture-infusing mask releasing a cloud of vapor around his nostrils and mouth. The atmosphere of the Ilgen planet of Oknayil was so moisture saturated, the Ilgen people required protective clothing to keep their skin from cracking after even short exposure to anything below 97% humidity, and vapor masks to irrigate their lungs.

Also present were the Lundraids, Qacrin, Pehemau, and Zibalan representatives. Zibala had only recently gained sufficient inclusion into the Alliance to be included on the leadership council, having been protected by the Alliance for nearly two-hundred Earth years.

Nick had a writing tablet in front of him, and John glanced toward it long enough to realize Nick was writing himself notes about the members of the Council. He'd seen Nick do it many times to solidify details in his head.

John leaned a few degrees toward Nick and spelled the name of the

Lundraid planet since Nick had started, crossed out, and tried again half a dozen times. To be fair, it wasn't an easy planet to spell in Lundraid or any other language. "K-a-o-s-i-u-m-t-zed-i-esh-t-a. Kaosiumtzishta"

Nick nodded with each letter, pausing when he said zed and esh, but immediately picked up again. "Hell of a name."

John chuckled. "Agreed."

"That's at least a two-thousand-point Scrabble word. What about the Quacrin?"

"Qacrin."

"Right. Qacrin. My English teacher drilled Qu into my brain."

"Planet spelling is B-e-r-a-apostrophe-a-apostrophe-d-a-p-t-a-s-i. Bera'a'daptasi."

"Damn."

Councilmember Gozzo Torroni stood, garnering the attention of all to begin the discussion.

Civilian Employee Housing
United Earth Protectorate, Capitol City
Alexandria, Seat of Virginia
North American Continent

"How are you doing?"

Exhausted doesn't even start it . . .

David ignored the answer in his head, focusing instead on the monumental task of continuing to put a foot forward and keep walking. He'd made the brilliant decision before leaving Alexandria Hospital *not* to take a wheelchair, insisting if he didn't walk he wouldn't keep walking.

"I'll be glad to get there," he said, also fighting to keep his breathing steady. He glanced down the hall toward where he knew his apartment door would be, and it looked a mile long. "Next time I try to look all macho in front of you and do something stupid like refuse medical equipment, do me a favor and just smack me."

Lucy jogged a couple steps ahead of him – *showoff* – and turned to walk backward so she faced him. "If I'm going to smack you, it won't be for something like that."

David stopped walking, leaning heavy on the canes that held him upright, and raised his head to look her square on. An evil, and damn sexy, grin tipped up one corner of her mouth in that close-lipped smile he'd appreciated from the minute he met her. She winked, took a step backward, crooked a finger and beckoned him to her.

He chuckled and tipped back his head to look at the ceiling. He sighed and focused on her again. Her grin had grown. "You are a truly evil woman to tempt an old, fragile man."

"Is it working?" She took a step backward, away from him.

"Damn it, woman."

Taking a deep, hopefully fortifying breath he forced the exhausted, shaking muscles of his legs to take that next step.

Sometimes his only recourse was edging on insanity, or so he figured was how most people saw him, so why hold back. With each step he managed, lyrics rolled through his head until he started singing them under his breath.

"Are you singing?" Lucy asked, slowing her backward progression.

"Maybe," David answered, taking another step. "Call it motivation."

"Sing it." She paused. "I dare you."

David shook his head. "You asked for it, Ms. Santos." He cleared his throat and lifted his chin, making no effort to sound like anything but the bleating goat of a singer he was. "Just put one foot in front of the other, and soon you'll be walking 'cross the *floor*." He smiled as he sang, dragging out the word when Lucy made a theatrical wince. "Put one foot in front of the other . . ." He took another step, finally seeing his apartment door within a few more steps. "And soon you'll be walking out the door."

"Now you're a songwriter, too?"

"Nah." *Six more steps, Forte.* "I don't even know who wrote it, but Fred Astaire did a good job singing it."

"Who is Fred Astaire?"

"Geez, woman . . . way to make me feel all eighty of my years. I know he was old when I was a young'un, but damn."

She pulled her lower lip through her teeth before spinning away from him, both tempting and taunting him simultaneously. The sleeveless sundress she wore ended just at her knees and reminded him of all the curves and enticements he'd noticed the first time they met, and other than a bright scarf tied around her head to hold her hair off her face, her chestnut hair fell around her shoulders and down her back. When she twirled, the hem of the dress teased him with a fleeting view of the back of her knees.

By the time he reached the apartment door, she had it open and was holding it for him. How pathetic and weak would he look if he just stumbled to the couch, collapsed, and stayed there for the next forty-eight hours?

He took a step into the doorway . . . and stopped.

And looked over his shoulder to confirm the right number was on the door. Was this his place?

"Um. . . I hope you don't mind I did some cleaning and rearranging. *Not* that your place was dirty!" she declared, coming back to him from the small kitchen area. "I was just . . . restless."

He'd been in the military long enough, and married long enough, and a bachelor long enough to know how to keep a place relatively clean but David wanted to know what kind of sorceress magic she'd used to make it feel *brighter*. It smelled good, too.

"Nah, I don't mind. I'm crippled, not crazy."

He took the last few steps to the couch that she'd turned so he didn't have to walk around it to sit, and it now faced the wall with the mounted monitor. He'd used the system to access data and broadcasts a couple times, but most often when he was here it was to sleep, clean up, or eat. Not much else.

At the thought of food, his stomach grumbled, and he recalled the cardboard toast and reconstituted eggs the hospital had brought him for breakfast. He couldn't stomach it then, but now his stomach wanted to be recognized.

Lucy laughed and stepped around him to close the apartment door.

"Sit down. Katrina connected me with a sort of goods and supplies *'guy'* who delivered some food yesterday. It's not Abuela Gabi's recipe, but I made a chicken and white bean chili and some biscuits. Do you want some?"

David inhaled deep through his nose as she explained the mouthwatering aromas hanging in the air. "Marry me, woman."

Lucy laughed again and motioned toward the shifted couch. "Sit down and I'll warm up some for you."

"Did you make apple pie, too?" he asked, sinking onto the couch, his long sigh releasing the exhaustion in his muscles as he finally relaxed.

"No," she said from the kitchen, followed by the beep of the 2054 version of the household microwave. "I did ask, though. Lieutenant Dinh said to give him a couple weeks, and they'd be bringing in fall produce from surrounding farms for the city and for distribution to areas where they didn't have access. In Unity Valley, I was using some of our fruit from storage."

The warmer-appliance-thing, because he couldn't remember what it was called, beeped again and when she opened the door a fragrant steam curled into the air. The apartment was an efficiency apartment designed for small, simple living so the smell hit him quickly. His stomach grumbled louder.

"I did, however, manage to scrounge up enough ingredients to make a batch of very simple peanut butter cookies."

"Marry me, woman," he said louder this time.

"You haven't tasted the chili yet." She came out of the kitchen carrying a bowl in one hand, with a towel in her palm to protect it, and a small dish in the other hand with two huge biscuits.

She sat on the couch beside him, sideways so she faced him, and balanced the dish of biscuits on her exposed knee. "Can you hold the bowl okay?"

The question was innocent, but it was a jab to his chest. He knew the intent, and the reason, but it dug deep. He just nodded and took the bowl from her. Just a few days before, Tessera had held the bowl for him and practically fed him. At least now he could feed himself. He stirred the chili, releasing some more of the fragrant steam, blew on it and brought a spoonful to his mouth.

Flavor like he hadn't tasted in weeks – not to bash the mess hall at The Nest or anywhere else he grabbed food, but most of it was produced in huge quantities for nutrition, not taste – exploded in his mouth, and he more groaned than hummed in satisfaction. David closed his eyes, enjoying the chili, and when he finally had to swallow took a spoonful of just the broth. "This is amazing," he said, slurping up the liquid.

"I did what I could with what I could get. I'm glad you like it."

"Best thing I've eaten since your apple pie."

Lucy gifted him with her sexy, closed lip smile and raised her arm to place it on the back of the couch, resting her temple against her knuckles. "Katrina rushed back to the hospital yesterday after getting an urgent message. What does she do there? I didn't realize she was a doctor."

He slurped up some more chili, then shook his head until he could speak without looking like a four-year-old. "She's not, but she works for Victor who is a doctor at the hospital. She and her brother Karl are his tech gurus, though it's more Katrina than Karl. She was helping him with Michael's babies, and they were born last night."

Lucy squinted one eye, looking puzzled. "She's tech and helped with babies?"

He lowered the bowl to balance it on his lap and take one of the biscuits she'd also warmed up. It was fluffy and delicious, and she'd buttered it, too. *Damn.* "It's going to take a long time to explain it all, darlin', but I'll try. Like I told you once, I'm still trying to process most of it, and I've been here awhile."

As he finished his chili and biscuits, and she brought him cookies, he did his best *Cliff's Notes* version of the craziness that was the Tanner children, though agreed it would take a few more conversations to make it all make sense. She sat silent at times, staring with a slightly slack jaw in probable shock at the story, and then she would find her bearings and fill in the holes in the story with questions.

"So, these babies were born last night?" she finally asked, a natural end to the convoluted yet short history lesson.

David nodded, leaning back after having eaten every bite of the chili and crumb of the biscuits. He hadn't eaten that much in a very long time, but damn, it tasted and felt good. "Yeah, Katrina stopped in to see me last night before she headed home. Three boys and a girl. I guess Michael and Jackie want to have people out to the house to tell us all their names."

"The house? Doesn't he live with his father?"

"Yeah."

"President Tanner . . ."

David nodded. "Yeah, but Nick isn't like anyone I ever imagined holding an office like that. I mean, in my day most presidents were, well, not great people. Let's just leave it at that. But I get the impression Nick really likes to have the house full of those closest to him and the family. I don't know when that'll be, but it will be after all the babies are home. Might be later this week."

"But, at the house of the World President . . ."

David grinned and rested his head on the back of the couch so he could look at her better. "You're gonna want to get past that look of shock and awe, darlin.' He's a cool guy."

Lucy's eyes widened. "'Why do I have to get past it? I'm not going."

"Why wouldn't you? Don't you want to go with me?"

"I'm not someone who just *goes* to the presidential residence, David," she declared. "He doesn't even know me. Why would he?"

"But he will," David said, only realizing how deep the tired had set into his body when he lifted his hand to touch her cheek. Every inch was a struggle, but as soon as he touched her, she held his palm to her jaw with her own hand. "You plan on sticking around a bit, don't you?" She nodded, staring at him. "Then he'll know you, and he'll welcome you. Trust me on this."

She still looked perplexed, but nodded, then tilted her head. "You look really tired."

"I am. I hate to admit it, but yeah."

"Too tired for peanut butter cookies?" She arched her brows and grinned.

David chuckled, something he found so easy to do with Lucy

Santos, and sighed. "Too tired. And . . ." He patted his stomach. "Too full. I haven't eaten this well in a very long time."

"Do you need Tessa's tea? I brought both recipes."

David shook his head before she finished. "I'm so tired, I'm not going to have trouble sleeping. And I might just be too tired to drink a whole cup," he ended with a chuckle.

"Come on." She stood from the couch and took the bowl from him, making the quick trip to the kitchen and back, moving in front of him to offer her hands to pull him to standing. "We'll get you in bed and resting. And we'll discuss a walk in the morning."

David shifted forward and accepted the help to gain his feet, groaning a little more theatrically than needed, but it was worth a laugh from Lucy. Once on his feet and feeling a bit more energy after the hearty meal, David circled an arm around her waist and brought her against him. Memories from their kiss by the stream slammed back into him, and the day felt like both yesterday and an eternity ago. Much like his life. But, *hot damn*, she felt good.

She wrapped both arms around his ribs, tipping her head back to look up at him. He loved her smile. It could be everything from pure happiness to pure flirtation. Feeling steady now that he stood, he brought his free hand to her face again, enjoying the calm stroking her cheek brought him. Lucy leaned into his touch, still watching him.

David inhaled deep, taking 2.3 seconds to process the rapid shift in his life in less than two weeks. Two weeks ago, even entertaining the thought of . . . did he dare think a *love life* . . . in his life wasn't a blip on his radar. Not even remotely so. And now . . .

She tilted her head slightly, shifting how he had to look at her. "What are you thinking about?"

David grinned slow. "I'm running an argument through my head."

"An argument?"

"Yeah, darlin'," he said with a wink, and looked past her to the partially open doorway of the only bedroom in the apartment. "More like a discussion. I insist you take the bed because I'm nothing if not an absolute gentleman." She made a low, amused sound in her throat and he chuckled, looking down at her again. "You say something like 'Oh, I'll be fine on the couch'—"

"It's a fine couch."

"And I say absolutely not," he continued. "We go back and forth for a little longer until we both agree it's silly, we're both mature adults—"

"Speak for yourself."

David hummed and focused on her lips, because why not torture himself at this point. "I'm not asking for anything, and I don't expect anything, but . . ." He cleared his throat because casual conversation was growing more and more difficult.

Lucy toed up and pressed her mouth to his, and as much as the kiss along the stream two-thousand miles away had been a powerful precursor for kisses to come, the impact was still devastating in the best possible way. It surged from first touch to consuming in a breath, and like a man starved David devoured the rush. One of them made a sound of need, he wasn't even sure who only that he felt it, and David opened his lips to kiss deeper, Lucy matching every breath, every stroke of their tongues, every slide of their lips.

He fisted his hands into the back of her dress, both desperate to feel more and desperate to not take too much. Lucy raised her arms to wrap his neck, pushing her fingers against the back of his head.

Only the sudden sway of his treasonous legs broke the kiss, and the burn of need was almost destroyed by the burn of anger and frustration. David tightened his embrace, but only enough to keep himself upright, and turned his face away from her, clenching his jaw.

"David," she said softly, her voice uneven with her rapid breathing. She brought her palms to his cheeks, trying to make him turn to her again. "David . . ."

Jaw still clenched and lips pressed together, he consented and looked to her. Shining eyes shifted to take in his expression and she stroked the corner of his mouth with her thumbs. "I think we both know what we want, but we both know tonight isn't the time. I didn't come to Alexandria with you because I felt like a vacation. I came because, regardless of how long we have or haven't known each other, I want to be with you more than I want to be anywhere else."

David had to take in air slow and metered before he could speak, his throat suddenly tight. "I don't know if I'll ever be right again."

She smiled, a small curve of her lips but enough to tease her dimple. "You will be. You'll be as right as you need to be, and I'm going to do everything I can to help you. But until then . . ." She stepped back from his hold, but not too far and he knew it was to make sure he didn't fall. "We go get some rest. Okay?"

He couldn't say anything until his jumbled, crazy thoughts managed to Tetris themselves back into some semblance of coherency. David nodded and linked his hand with hers. "Okay."

CHAPTER SEVENTEEN

26 August 2054 – Wednesday
Office of the President
Robert J. Castleton Memorial Building – The Castle
Center for United Protectorate Government
United Earth Protectorate, Capitol City
Alexandria, Seat of Virginia
North American Continent

Nick walked around his desk to the two couches arranged to face each other, perpendicular to the fireplace. Tossing a pillow out of the way, with his back to the windows, he sat on the couch opposite his vice president Beverly Surimoto to face her. Talking from behind his desk felt weird, especially with Beverly.

"Queen Bryony has committed to sending several machines on behalf of the Alliance to help us with mass production of pharmaceuticals." He shifted, trying to get comfortable. He'd fallen asleep holding Adam and had woken with a hitch in his back. "They were developed for use specifically in battle theaters and on planets recovering from war."

Beverly's expression brightened slightly, and she smiled. "Oh, that's wonderful. So many have been left for too long without what, for some, is a daily need. I fear how many people we've lost just because we didn't have the knowledge of their need and the means to help them even if we had known."

"Yeah." Nick nodded and rubbed his fingers across his mouth. "Keeps me up at night, to be honest. Among other things."

"We've done the best we can. I know not everyone knows that, but just as many if not more understand."

"Doesn't mean I like it."

Beverly canted her head and smiled, the sadness sliding in again. "Which is why you are the man to lead us. You know the true weight of every decision." Her expression shifted again, back to curiosity. "How do the ... what would we call them, replicators? ... work?"

He chuckled, half a dozen scenes from *Star Trek* he'd watched as a kid running through his head. "I'm going to leave it to the geniuses like Victor and Michael and others about the actual process. I'm sure there are ingredients, or something, but we'll work it out when it gets here. The next time a ship comes this way."

"I've no doubt Victor will not only be thrilled to help, but excited to see the technology."

"I'm going to depend on him to build a team to take the machines and run with them. Maybe not him directly, but he knows how to find the best people for these things." She nodded in agreement. "I've sent word to Unity Valley for Connor to come back to Alexandria by the end of the week. They've confirmed David's dome is in working order – Katrina made sure of that while David was out of commission – and they've narrowed down the location of the Xeno cell who has been attacking the community."

"Oh, that's excellent."

Nick nodded. "They're going in tomorrow, kicking ass, and taking names. Everyone they apprehend is being brought back here. We'll deal with them in Alexandria."

"I only wish stopping one would stop them all."

He grunted. "I'd really prefer dealing with one group of asshats at a time. If Xenos aren't enough, we've got the Sorracchi and Urdo Khantan."

He motioned toward the stack of papers on his desk. He'd been thought mapping all morning; a technique his mom had taught him when he was a kid. He had a tendency to get marked down in school for skipping right to the answer in math or leaving out key points in essays because he figured everyone already knew so why explain. Thought mapping helped him pay attention to the connective parts his brain knew was there but skipped over to get to the results. She told him once it was probably a tendency he got from her.

"I've been processing yesterday's conference since yesterday afternoon. The big picture is perfectly clear, but there are a lot of moving parts to get lubricated here on the ground before we find ourselves in the middle of an atmosphere battle. I know the Defense Alliance has our backs as the new kids in town, but I'm not inclined to just sit back and let them take charge."

"Agreed. Perhaps when Connor returns a conversation with the military division heads is in order. We need people ready to protect and fight. I don't like the idea of recruiting, but we need people everywhere ready to, at the least, defend themselves if we are attacked globally." She closed her eyes and swallowed before looking at him again. "Just saying the words terrifies me."

"Me, too, Bev. This is going to be a different fight than last year."

"We had the advantage of surprise that time. This time, I feel we're all walking on eggshells waiting for a moment we have no idea when will come. Other than I believe the Defense Alliance will do their best to give us as much aid and forewarning as they can."

Nick sank back into the cushions of the couch, rubbing a finger across his mouth. He jutted his chin in her direction. "Let's put all that away for a minute. You okay? Anything wrong?"

She smiled, but it wasn't one of humor. "You're very perceptive, Nicholas. As if our current discussion wasn't enough."

"It's not just today. I've been meaning to ask."

For the first time since their conversation began, she looked him straight in the eyes. "Something is troubling Victor, and it worries me. Not just because he's not sleeping well, and is frequently lost in his own thoughts, but because often when he struggles like this it ends in some memory coming forward. That can be a blessing or a curse."

A cold ball landed in Nick's gut. She was right. Sometimes Victor's revelations were great, sometimes not so much. Always useful, but not always good. "What is he remembering?"

Beverly shook her head, looking away again. "He doesn't know. I've tried to help, but until I know the right questions to ask, I'm of no use. He says there is something right at the surface of his memories but hasn't broken through yet." She motioned near her temple, a sign for memories. She spent a long time in silence, using manual language and sometimes the habit returned. "He has so many hundreds of years sorted and stored away in his mind, he can't just pull it up like a computer file. It's like he needs a password or the right metadata to search," she said with a small smile. "I don't know if his apprehension stems from the memories, or just not being able to access them yet."

"Well, keep me posted if it's anything I need to know."

She nodded and sighed, folding her hands in her lap. "Of course. As always."

"I need to shake his hand when you come to the house for the babies' introductions. I know he thinks what he did wasn't anything to be praised since he'd do whatever he can for Michael, but he saved the lives of my new grandchildren as far as I'm concerned." Nick was kind of amazed he managed to get through all he said before the choking emotion started. He cleared his throat and rubbed his hands together. "There are days I regret questioning his motives when we first brought him out of New Mexico with Michael. He's proven himself a hundred times over."

Beverly's smile softened, some of the strain relaxing. "He has never begrudged anyone their doubt. How could he when he doubted himself so much?"

"Yeah, well . . . he's good people, as my father would have said. Good people. He's good people."

"I'm inclined to agree," Beverly said with a wink and a wider smile.

Nick chuckled and slapped his hands on his knees, shifting forward to stand. "I want to get your take on yesterday's conference, but I haven't actually eaten anything yet. You hungry?"

She nodded. "Actually, yes."

"Good. I'll see what they might have just lyin' around."

Civilian Employee Housing
United Earth Protectorate, Capitol City
Alexandria, Seat of Virginia
North American Continent

After months of going to bed well after dark and waking up before dawn even in the long days of summer, waking to the sun already being up and bright made Lucy panic for a moment before she remembered where she was. She wasn't in Unity Valley anymore and wasn't immediately needed in the infirmary or kitchen or for other tasks. She was in Alexandria, the new capitol city. Sun came through the spaces in the blinds of David's bedroom window, and she lay on her side facing it, so the warmth and light slowly pulled her awake before her jolt of realization.

Once she reminded herself of where she was, she took a breath and let her other senses fill in the spaces. The next sensation to slide into her morning was David's warmth behind her in the bed. He radiated heat under the blankets, and she smiled at the thought of how nice it would be to sleep beside him on a cold winter night.

Just in case he was still asleep, Lucy shifted to her back trying not to jostle the bed so she could look at him. He slept on his back with his far arm tossed over his eyes, the light blanket covering him to midtorso. He'd slept in a loose pair of cotton shorts, so his chest was bare, and not for the first time Lucy fully appreciated his form. For a man who months before had been unable to lift his arms or move on his own – as he'd described himself – he was well defined. Looking at the entire picture, even that made sense. He'd pushed himself beyond a physical point anyone had anticipated. He'd been driven to be capable, and in doing so, he was far stronger and healthier than any of his doctors would have anticipated.

And yet, he felt weak.

Lucy was confident his struggles would be short-lived. He had the need to be better, and she had the need to help him.

She was tempted to touch him, just to lay her palm on his bicep, to see if he felt as warm as she thought. Not feverish, just the type of person who emanated heat. But she also didn't want to wake him before he needed to be awake. Sleep, real rest, was as important in his healing as food and exercise. Watching him to make sure she didn't wake him, she slid backwards from beneath the covers, taking light steps in bare feet to leave the bedroom. She left the door open just enough she'd be able to hear him if he woke up and needed help.

After a quick shower and comb through of her wet hair, and a pause at the door when she left the bathroom to make sure he still slept, she went to the kitchen. When he did wake up, she wanted him to have a strength-building breakfast. She couldn't make any bacon – which was a shame since he'd been very vocal about his love of it back at the community – but she had eggs and other basic ingredients.

With chickens being one of the easiest sources of protein to renew, there was plenty of chicken and eggs to be found. Along with a good supply of fish. Cooking fish wasn't her strong suit, and she wasn't sure his opinion on the matter, so she'd stuck with what she felt was safer foods to cook for him. There were biscuits from the night before she could toast in a pan and fry him some eggs when he woke up. There was coffee in the cabinet, but she wanted to be sure he had some of Tessa's tea as well.

Lieutenant Dinh had provided a variety of goods from fresh to canned – including some clearly canned recently based on the glass jars they used repeatedly in Unity Valley, and she'd helped Abuela Gabi with canning many times as a kid – and powdered foods requiring reconstitution. It was hard to stomach the idea of powdered foods after eating all fresh and homegrown for months, but this was the world they lived in. The canned peaches looked good, though, so she opted for them as a side. They might even make a good cobbler or pie if she had the right ingredients.

She was about done when a knock at the door startled her. She contemplated for a moment going to the bedroom but went to the door instead. After releasing the inside lock, she opened the door to find a young man of probably around her age, maybe a little younger than thirty, in the hallway with light brown hair in need of a cut dressed in jeans and a yellow tee shirt.

"Hello," he said with a wide, genuine smile. "Lucy Santos?"

She canted her head, arching an eyebrow. "Yes . . ."

The man extended his hand, and she took it. Rather than shaking it, he just held it. Not forcibly, but firm. "I'm Michael. Tanner. I'm a friend of David's."

Lucy gasped and took a step back, realizing with a snap who he was. *All* the designations of who he was. Not the least being son of the World President. Immediate concern drew down his forehead and he took a step toward her.

"I'm fine," she spit out, then shook her head and closed her eyes for a second. "I'm sorry. I just wasn't expecting . . ."

"I apologize if I came too early. I'm on my way to Alexandria Hospital and hoped I might be able to check on David. To see how he's doing, but I also had some questions for him." When he spoke, his entire focus and attention was on Lucy. She wasn't sure if he studied her, or watched for a reaction, or what but it was both strangely unsettling and calming at the same time. "It's about the woman you brought back to Alexandria with you."

"Tessa?"

Michael nodded. "I understand she's known by both Tessa and Tessera. Do you know her?"

"Yes. She lived in the community for a long time. Well, as long as any of us." Lucy took another step back and opened the apartment door wide, motioning for him to come in. "Come in. I don't know if David is awake yet—"

"I'm up," came David's sleepy voice.

He stood in the bedroom doorway, one arm raised to brace against the doorjamb, rubbing his eyes with the other hand. "Hey, Michael," he mumbled. "Give me ten."

Lucy almost asked if he needed help but held back. He'd gotten from bed on his own and might not welcome the help with someone else there. She didn't know him well enough yet to know what would be unwelcome, but she'd figure it out in time. He shut the door of the bedroom, and Lucy headed for the kitchen.

"Would you like some coffee? I'm making breakfast, too, if you're hungry. I have biscuits and eggs and some canned peaches."

"Don't eat my biscuits!" David shouted from behind the bedroom door. "They're mine!" After a pause he added, "Or the cookies!"

Both Lucy and Michael chuckled. She leaned toward Michael and winked, speaking low. "I made a double batch of the biscuits. They'll go stale before he can eat them all. Would you like some?"

"Thank you," he said with a simple nod. "I appreciate your hospitality."

He took a seat at the table Lucy and David had foregone the evening before, thanking her again when she put a cup of coffee and two warm biscuits in front of him.

She took the three steps needed to be back in the kitchen so she could start his eggs, but gasped and turned back. "Oh, congratulations! David told me last night about your four new babies. It's wonderful."

"Thank you," he said again, licking his lips after taking a bite of biscuit. "These are delicious. I hope to hear today when they will be able to come home. Jacqueline and I hated to leave them at the hospital but know it's necessary."

The bedroom door opened again, and David came out with slow steps. He held up a hand, holding up two fingers, before taking the three steps to the bathroom door and going inside. Lucy smiled and went to the stove to crack his eggs into the hot pan.

Michael ate the biscuits and drank his coffee while she finished cooking, timing it well for when David made his own way to the table to sit adjacent to Michael.

"Doctor Cole would like you to come to the hospital this afternoon. How are you feeling today?" Michael asked as David settled with a heavy grunt in his chair.

"Hard to tell just yet," David said with a crooked smile before he took a drink of Tessa's tea Lucy had put on the table, humming as she put his plate in front of him. He looked at the biscuits, fried eggs, and peaches and looked up at her. "Marry me, woman."

"Stop it and eat," she said, tapping his shoulder. She turned away before either man caught her grin. David's teasing was just that – teasing – but it still made her smile. "Drink your tea. I've got coffee here for you, too."

"I keep asking," she heard him say to Michael. "She never says no, so I guess that's a good thing."

Michael chuckled. "I will say, the biscuits are delicious."

David barked a laugh, sounding more awake already. Lucy made herself a plate much like David's, but not quite so focused on feeding his healing, and sat at the opposite end of the table from Michael with David between them.

"I hoped you both might be able to tell me more about Tessera." Michael nodded toward Lucy. "Or Tessa."

"Lucy can tell you more than me," David said, dipping the edge of a biscuit into the yolks of his eggs. "The way things were with me up on that mountain, I don't have much to offer."

"Tessa was very quiet," Lucy explained after taking a drink of the coffee she'd made for them. "We – Trevor, Molly, and me – were in a small town near where Unity Valley is now when *everything* . . . happened." She stuttered over trying to put a name to those days, even though they were generally known as The War, and twirled a non-committal hand in the air. "Mama Della, Molly's mother, basically brought Tessa home like a stray pup who needed someone to take care of her. Mama said she knew Tessa had been through some hard things, but until she wanted to tell us, we just let her find her way with us. So we did."

"She never said where she was from?" David asked, licking peach juice off his lips after eating a chunk.

"No," Lucy confirmed. "She stayed to herself most of the time and preferred to help in the evening and night shifts in the infirmary. I know she was even more nervous around the soldiers in the community, you could just see it when they were around. She read every book and resource she could find, which is how she came up with the tea I give you. There was a used bookstore in the town, which most of the books came to Unity Valley when we left the town, and she educated herself."

Michael looked puzzled, and David held up the now empty cup.

"This stuff is great. Lucy can tell you what's in it, but it helped with the pain almost immediately. And she adds something—"

"Willow bark," Lucy provided.

David pointed at her and winked. "Willow bark. That helped me sleep. And she's got this salve she put on the contact points. Awesome stuff."

"We didn't always have actual pharmaceuticals, and we often filled in with some of the balms and tinctures and teas she made. They were a big help."

"So what happened?" David asked.

Lucy shrugged. "She was just . . . gone . . . one day. She didn't tell anyone she was leaving, not even Mama Della. We didn't know where she was from, and certainly didn't know anyone to reach out to even if we had a way to do that. It was a shock when she came down the mountain with you and your sons."

"How long was she on her own up there?" David asked.

Lucy paused to think, counting backward. "Probably four months?"

"And you knew her as Tessa," Michael stated.

She nodded. "Yes, that's how Mama Della introduced her to everyone and she never said anything different. I would have remembered a name like Tessera."

"She told you her name is Tessera," Michael said to David.

"Yeah. I think I said something about the number four and sounded like an interesting story. She said it wasn't one I'd want to hear." David sat back, his plate empty. "We didn't talk about much. She asked some questions about my robo-suit, my injuries, and very specifically where my loyalties were."

"Your loyalties?" Michael asked.

"Yeah. She pointed out the Firebird emblem on my jacket. It didn't impress her, which based on what Lucy said about her not liking the soldiers, I guess I get her question. I said I was loyal to your father and the Protectorate. That seemed to be an acceptable answer. She also made it very clear she would not take me back to Unity Valley. She wanted nothing with going back."

"That makes no sense," Lucy said, shaking her head. "She was part of our community, like anyone else. There are plenty of people there who don't share their life stories. They don't have to."

"What I don't get is how bad a way she was in when Phin and Daniel found us," David said, crossing his arms over his chest.

Lucy suppressed her smile, wondering if he realized the relative ease he'd had in making the simple move. She had seen him when they brought him down the mountain. Lifting his hand had been a struggle. That had only been three days before, and he'd already markedly improved.

"If she was alone up there for months, it makes sense she might be malnourished," Lucy offered. "She was absolutely gaunt, easily a good twenty or thirty pounds lighter than when she left."

"That's what I mean," David said, shifting again to sit forward, setting one arm on the table to motion with the other hand. "I mean, the first time I woke up and saw her I noticed she was thin. Too thin, really. She's not much bigger than a flea's sneeze, but she wasn't emaciated. I saw her in the hover. She's emaciated. And she sure as hell wasn't pass out weak. She somehow managed to get me to that cabin on her own. It doesn't make sense she went to that extreme in a couple days." He looked to Michael. "Have you talked to her yet?"

Michael shook his head, but his focus had drifted away from them. Lucy could practically hear the wheels turning in his head. "She hasn't woken and has shown no sign of waking. I had hoped one of you would have some small bit of insight to help."

"I wish I did," Lucy said, scraping together the last bite of her breakfast. "I will help in any way I can, though."

"Why were Phin and Daniel so adamant she needed to come back to Alexandria?" David asked, motioning toward Michael.

Michael visibly pulled himself back from his thoughts, drawing in a long breath through his nose before looking between them. "She is one of six duplicates made by my mother of a young woman I knew and cared deeply for while I was held captive in New Mexico, who ultimately died at my mother's hands."

Lucy dropped her fork, the utensil clattering loudly on her plate before it bounced and hit the floor.

David sat back hard. "Well, damn."

CHAPTER EIGHTEEN

Alexandria Hospital, Secure Wing – General Care
United Earth Protectorate, Capitol City
Alexandria, Seat of Virginia
North American Continent

Victor opened the door to Tessera's quiet room, his head down as he reviewed that day's health data, pushing it open with his hips as he turned into the dark room. He looked up and stopped short when he saw Michael standing at the foot of the bed.

"I wasn't expecting to see you at the hospital today," he said, stepping in so the door closed behind him. "Or perhaps I should clarify. I didn't expect to see you anywhere other than the NICU."

Michael looked his way but didn't move. He stood with his feet set slightly apart and his hands pushed into his pockets. "I spent much of the morning there with Jacqueline and Doctor Longbow."

Victor's nerves rushed. "Is there something wrong?"

"No, not at all. Each baby had a thorough physical today." He smiled wide. "They are doing very well, so well Doctor Longbow has decided they can come home tomorrow morning."

"Oh, that's wonderful!" Victor declared, taking the last two steps to his lifelong friend with his arms extended.

Michael welcomed the embrace, patting Victor's back before they stepped away from each other. "Thank you. We will likely have everyone to the house Friday evening for a meal together and introductions."

"I am beyond pleased." Victor stayed close enough to keep his hand on Michael's shoulder. "I cannot wait to meet each one of them properly and be able to spoil them by name. As any uncle would."

"Of course. They will be thoroughly and fully loved, of that Jacqueline and I have no doubt."

"So why are you here?"

"I haven't been able to solve the mystery of Tessera's condition," Michael said with a dip of his chin toward the bed.

Victor chuckled and joined him, going to the foot of the bed to look at Tessera's data from overnight. "Tessera's medical state is a mystery we all would like to solve."

Like every other day, there was little change of note. They maintained her weight now, having managed only a seven-pound gain, but it was only through a constant delivery of high calorie nutrition and fluids. Her cerebral activity was only present enough to rule out brain death but had shown no increase or fluctuation since she'd come to Alexandria. The low-grade fever had passed, so they had stopped antibiotics. It was all maintenance, with no substantial progress.

"I have a theory," Michael said after Victor reviewed the records. "Unfortunately, I don't yet know how to test it."

"What's your theory?"

Michael walked around the bed to stand near the windows looking out of the central garden area. It was damaged and closed off to visitors since the attack on the city, but the sunlight coming through the blinds might offer some soothing effect for Tessera. At least, that was what Victor hoped and certainly knew it would do no harm. Michael put his back to the light and leaned against the sill with his hands in his pockets.

"I'd like to share the facts that inspired my theory and see if the path is clear to you. If there is logic in my thoughts."

"I've never known you not to think logically, Michael."

"Perhaps at one time, but more and more I have thought with emotion that overrides logic." He inhaled a deep breath through his nose and focused on the frail, pale woman in the bed.

She was a reflection of the Ranae Victor remembered from Michael's painful youth in New Mexico, he saw remnants of the girl in the woman's face. Ranae had passed over a decade earlier at Kathleen's hand, but her legacy still lived somehow in this woman. Even if it weren't the case, Michael would want to find the reason for her condition and that was a reality Victor understood without question. For that reason as much as any, Victor wanted the answers for him.

"Fact one, when my father found me on the Sorracchi ship near death, my body instinctively pulled strength from him, and Jacqueline, and even my uncle to keep me alive."

"A price they all would have willingly paid if asked, because it was likely because you did that you survived at all." Victor returned the tablet to its place and crossed his arms over his body. "Even that small bit of strength was enough the Areth doctors were able to revive you later."

Michael shook his head. "I can't argue with that. I know that. But it leads to fact two. I hated the idea I could have potentially harmed the people I cared about to keep myself alive, even knowing it had been purely instinctual. So much so that when I woke from my surgery last year and learned of Jacqueline's collapse, I had assumed I'd done it again."

"Of course, we now know you likely didn't at all. It was early days of her pregnancy combined with her concern that caused her collapse."

"All facts we learned later." Michael pushed away from the window and returned to her bedside on the opposite side of where he'd begun the conversation. "Do you remember when I came back from Florida and told you I'd been able to give strength to help people heal? And I gave to David to bring him back?" Victor nodded and Michael paused, drawing in a breath before adding, "I only knew I could do any of that because I attempted it before I had learned how to control myself."

Victor scowled, searching his memories. "Before you went to Florida?" He shook his head. "Who?"

"You."

A sudden thrust of cold hit Victor's veins, and he stared.

"In Tennessee you were near death when we found you, and despite everything I did with medicine . . ." Michael's voice faltered. "I couldn't save you. I believed you'd given up and I wouldn't allow it."

Victor closed his eyes against a sudden onslaught of visceral, vivid memories of pain and fear and resolution. He had intentionally bound himself to prevent his demon from taking control and hurting anyone, and he had determined his life was forfeit. When he woke in the Areth med bay lightyears from Earth, he only knew he lived and Michael was again Kathleen's captive. The cold in his veins chilled deeper.

"Why didn't you tell me? Why didn't anyone tell me?"

He opened his eyes again when Michael didn't answer immediately. The strain around Michael's eyes made them shine. "Jacqueline was the only person with me."

"Untrained and with no control, Michael, you could have died trying to save me—" The admonition stuttered quiet when Michael's point began to become clear.

Victor looked from Michael to Tessera, his brow pulled down as he thought. "David said she was in relatively good health when he woke in her cabin. He described her as thin, but–"

"Yes," Michael confirmed.

"He said she had physically brought him from the crash site."

"Yes."

Victor snapped his attention to Michael again. "Is it possible?"

Michael shook his head and shrugged. "I don't know. I have no knowledge of what she may or may not be capable of, but if she lived under Kathleen's experimentation it had to be for a reason. While I've no doubt Ranae fell victim to her because of me, the duplicates she created served a purpose, which logically says she and the others like her have some level of Talents."

"But . . . to continue to the point of her own death?"

"I don't know. If my theory is right, that she somehow shared strength with David, it would explain his rapid and unexplainable improvement, but there are so many more questions. Was it her intent for it to go this long? Did she intend to bring herself to the point of death? And most importantly, how do we break the cycle?"

Victor shook his head. "I fear while the light is visible, the path to reach it is still impossible to see."

Michael looked toward Tessera again and shifted to lean forward, his hands on the footboard of the bed. "I know I won't likely be able to participate in her care for a few weeks, and I suppose I hoped I might be struck by some realization or inspiration to help before we take the children home. I spoke with David and Lucy this morning, hoping one of them might be able to provide insight, but both are confused as to why she is in the physical state she is in. Lucy said Tessera was quiet and kept much to herself, and simply . . ." He waved a hand toward the still woman's form. "Disappeared one day. No one knew where she had come from, so no one knew where she might have gone. She apparently found a way to survive alone in the forest several miles from the community."

"Where she somehow managed to find David in his hour of need."

Michael made a sound similar to a chuckle, but not quite. If Victor had to guess, it was to mock the serendipitous nature of the events. "And then to be found at the point of death by the sons of the man she saved, who happen to be half-brothers of the man whom the original woman whom she was created from had a relationship with over a decade ago while both were captives in a facility twenty-nine-hundred miles away from where they find her."

Victor barked a laugh. "Okay, well, when you put it that way it does seem a bit fantastical."

"I've learned not to question the hand that has guided my life, because many of the events that brought me to this point should never have happened, but the current state of this development has left me confused. I have to believe she is here for a reason, and she is my responsibility."

"Don't take on yourself responsibilities you need not own," Victor said, shaking his head. "You are not responsible for everyone."

Michael turned his head abruptly to level his gaze on Victor. "But aren't I? Responsible for her? We know from the records we've deciphered, and from what both you and I know on a very painful level, that my mother not only was responsible for Ranae's death, but she created the clones out of pure vengeance and revenge. Even if she never believed I would know of their existence. What did this woman endure at Kathleen's hands before the War? Before she somehow found freedom?"

"Michael, Kathleen is responsible. Not you." He took a step closer, ignoring the sudden crawl of pain at the back of his skull. It wasn't the first time in the last few days the pain had hit, but pain was familiar, and he would push past it. "You are her victim. Just as Ranae was. Just as Tessera was. Just as so many have been. I commend you for wishing to help her and would honestly be surprised if you felt any other way, but I caution you not to carry blame."

"An easier promise to speak than commit to."

"That is because you are a born healer, a testament to the strength of your soul considering what plans Kathleen wanted for you. If Tessera has any knowledge of you at all, I sincerely doubt she holds you responsible for what may have occurred in her life before now."

Michael stared at him for several moments, and Victor held his stare waiting for the young man to process his words. As much as Michael was close to his family, Victor understood and accepted the memories of Michael's youth were his alone to cherish.

Finally, Michael looked away and back to Tessera. "David said when he woke the first time after the crash he noted she was thin, but not at a point of malnourishment like we see here."

The conversation of responsibility was done . . .

"Knowing she physically dragged him from the crash site to her home, looking at her now with that event less than a week ago, I don't understand how she could have deteriorated so drastically in health."

"None of us understand yet."

"There are no signs of infection or virus."

"None. We have been providing her nutrition and hydration, as well as a vitamin and nutrient supplement, but we've stopped all antibiotics because they seemed unnecessary. We have halted any further weight loss, but even with increased caloric input, she hasn't gained any weight back. Her color is slightly improved, however, and we have picked up some minor increases in brain activity."

Michael stared at her in silence, then with a deep sigh, took a step away from the bed and toward the door. "I realize I will be otherwise occupied in the coming weeks, but if there are any notable developments—"

"Of course. I know you will want to know."

As he walked past, Michael patted Victor's arm. "Thank you, my friend. As always. Thank you."

As soon as Michael was gone from the room, Victor stumbled back and sank into an empty chair, a final wave of nauseating pain slamming into him with such force it nearly took him to his knees were it not for the furniture. He hadn't experienced this level of pain since well before the demon Sorracchi had been eradicated from his soul.

What demon haunted him now?

Alexandria Hospital – Rehabilitation Wing

"I am absolutely amazed, David. Your improvement is astonishing, and it's been less than twenty-four hours. I don't know how it's possible," Doctor Cole said, standing a few feet away while he exhausted himself on the leg extension machine.

David lowered his legs as slowly as he could manage without letting the weights fall with a clang and grunted out a breath as soon as the resistance eased, breathing heavy. Sweat ran from his temples and made his tee shirt stick to his back.

"Sure doesn't feel like an improvement. Right now, I don't know if I can stand. My muscles are twitching."

"The point is when you arrived two days ago you absolutely could *not* stand. That's the amazing improvement for me. I . . ." She shook her head and waved a hand in his direction. "My entire area of expertise is physical rehabilitation for catastrophic injuries, and in my seventy-five years of practice I've never seen such improvement in such a short period of time."

David tried not to laugh at the sudden, wide-eyed look Lucy shot Doctor Cole from behind, out of view of the doctor. Considering Doctor Cole didn't look much older than maybe her early forties, she certainly didn't look old enough to have practiced medicine that long. *Gotta love the longevity of Areth genes.*

"Maybe it's Lucy's cooking," he said, waiting for her to look at him before winking at her.

Doctor Cole looked back to Lucy, who hadn't yet lost her wide-eyed surprise. "Well, whatever you're feeding him double his portions. It's doing wonders." She turned back to David. "I had anticipated establishing a physical therapy regimen of having you here once or twice a week for evaluation while keeping your exercise at home simple, nothing more strenuous than walks and such. Honestly, I believe that's wholly unnecessary and inadequate now. Do you think you can be here every other day?"

"Not like I have a whole lot else going on," he said with a tired shrug. "Your schedule open, Lucy?"

She'd regained her composure and gifted him with one of her slightly crooked, closed lip smiles that made him warm up. "I can check, but I think I can clear my calendar for a bit."

Doctor Cole laughed and nodded. "Good. If you could wait here, I have asked Doctor Koharu Noguchi to consult on your care. I am returning to Aretu in a month, and I honestly believed your physical rehabilitation would extend beyond that. Now, I am not so sure, but she will be your primary doctor."

"Sounds like a plan."

She nodded. "Be sure to drink some electrolytes while you wait. I will go see if she is available a little early."

Doctor Cole nodded to Lucy as she left, and as soon as she was gone Lucy retrieved a cup of the electrolyte blend always on hand in the gym. Coming back toward him, she snagged an exercise ball and rolled it with her free hand until she reached him. He took the cup and she sat on the ball beside him.

He kind of envied her the ease of the movement.

And he envied the ball.

David cleared his throat and swallowed half the contents of the cup. It was salty, and not much else.

"How are you feeling?"

"Tired," he said, slumping back onto the back support of the machine. "I told you shortly after we met how I felt like I had just survived the worst workout of my life."

"I remember."

"Yeah, well . . . that was nothing compared to how I feel right now. I did a workout, competed in a triathlon, climbed a mountain, then did *another* workout. The idea of standing up right now is too much."

"You know that salve of Tessa's I brought with me? I saw her use that once when giving a muscle massage. She mixed it with some other lotion. I bet they have something around here I can use as a carrier, and I'll give you a good rubdown at home."

David groaned and chuckled. "Woman . . ."

The gym door opened before he could finish his lecherous thought, and Doctor Cole returned with a slight woman, perhaps a little taller than Katrina, with black hair generously laced with silver strands braided against her scalp. Unlike Doctor Cole, the woman he assumed to be Doctor Noguchi did not wear the obligatory white coat, but instead jeans and a cotton shirt with her nametag clipped to her collar. She appeared to be well into her forties, though hell, how could anyone tell anymore? Doctor Cole already said she'd been practicing medicine for nearly as long as he'd been alive, and he'd technically be eighty-one on his next birthday.

Technically . . .

"David, this is Doctor Noguchi."

"It's a pleasure to meet you, David," she said with bright enthusiasm before Doctor Cole could complete the introductions, crossing the gym with her hand extended. She gripped his hand in a solid shake and turned immediately to Lucy. "I'm happy to meet you both."

"David, Doctor Noguchi would like to run some specific exams on your affected muscle groups. She has developed a method of tracking muscle improvement beyond presentation of strength or weakness. I've read over her findings with other patients, and I believe it will provide some needed insights."

"Sure," David said, shrugging one shoulder. "Whatever we need to do, and if it gets me moving like something younger than my eighty years, I'll take it."

"You may not feel that way when we're done. Unfortunately, the tests run a scope from the non-invasive to the highly invasive and unpleasant."

David drew in a slow breath, then released it with a huff. He shook his head and waved a hand in the air. "What the hell. My last few months have ranged from the non-invasive to the highly unpleasant. Why shake things up now?"

"That's a great attitude. Let's get started."

CIVILIAN EMPLOYEE HOUSING
UNITED EARTH PROTECTORATE, CAPITOL CITY
ALEXANDRIA, SEAT OF VIRGINIA
NORTH AMERICAN CONTINENT

"We aren't going to stay long," Katrina said, leaning across the space between her and David and resting a hand on his arm. "We wanted to see you're doing okay. You look so tired."

David raised his head, his eyelids heavy. Katrina's words were inadequate for how he looked. When Doctor Noguchi said her tests would be extensive, she had also been inadequate in her preparation. Lucy had watched, wincing often, and forcing herself to hold back from saying something. David had been determined – perhaps driven was a better word – to complete the tests to see a clearer picture of his future.

It had been hard to watch.

"I'm tired, but I'm glad you stopped to check in."

Even his voice was heavy and slow.

Phin and Daniel stood behind Katrina's chair, and they exchanged silent looks. David had further explained how they communicated just as easily, or perhaps more easily, telepathically as with spoken words. It helped her understand the few times she'd heard Katrina say "Use your words" to them like a mother scolding her children.

"We are concerned the tests today may prove to be too much considering recent events," Daniel said.

She was getting better at telling them apart. As long as she could get a good look at them, she differentiated Phin by the scar on his lip. But there were minor differences down to the way they stood, and sometimes spoke, that helped give them each their own identity.

David waved off his son's concern, though the motion was singular before he let his arm rest on the table again. She had made him something to eat, and he'd made some progress on it before his family had arrived. Now it sat waiting. Katrina had noted the food, and so Lucy knew she wouldn't stay long.

"What did they do to you?" Katrina asked, and the indignation was abundantly clear.

"Ummm," David began, but didn't finish.

Lucy reached out to touch his arm on her side, and he nodded, keeping his head down. "They performed electromyography while actively having him perform physical tasks. Exercises. Various movements," she explained for him. "The nerve conduction tests were the most invasive I've ever seen, even when I was in medical school. I understand some of the technologies are adaptations from Defense Alliance tech, but it was tough to watch."

David didn't raise his head but lifted a hand to lay it on top of hers, where it still rested on his arm.

"This new Doctor Noguchi agrees with Doctor Cole that David is much stronger than they would expect." He made a snorted sound, and she smiled, but continued. "She intends to do this same series of tests at least every two weeks. At least twice a week, when David is in physical rehabilitation, they have a type of . . ." She stuttered over how to describe what she'd seen. "Jumpsuit, I guess, that he will wear when doing the exercises and it will detect changes in muscle density. They mentioned some other test types, but nothing they used today and a bit beyond my medical education."

"I don't like how hard it is on him," Katrina said in a softer voice.

"It's necessary," David said, slowly raising his head. "Trust me, Peanut, I don't particularly *like* it, but the end should be worth the pain to get there."

"You say that now . . ."

"I do. I mean it. You know I mean it. Now . . ." He slowly sat up straighter, dropping his hands into his lap. "Get out of here so I can get some sleep."

Katrina nodded and stood from her chair, leaning over to kiss his cheek as she stood. Each son silently laid their hand on his shoulder before following their tiny queen to the door. There was no question who was in charge in that trio, whether she even knew it herself. Lucy stood to walk them to the door, pausing to slide the mug on the table closer to David.

"Finish your tea. I made it good and strong tonight."

"I doubt I'll need the help to sleep."

"No, but the rest of it will help you heal."

She went to the door with David's young family and watched from the doorway as they went down the hall to their own apartment. She'd yet to meet Katrina's brother Karl, who supposedly lived with them as well, and had teased David whether Karl existed at all. Karl had his own life, David said, but stayed around to make sure Katrina was being cared for. He hadn't been a fan of the Forte brothers at first. For good reason, by what Lucy understood. Though David implied Karl's opinion, especially of Daniel, had shifted dramatically. Not so much that anyone wanted to put a label on things, but a shift had occurred.

He'd finished the tea as she'd told him to, and with a long groan from David she got him on his feet and headed toward the bedroom. He barely opened his eyes as he stripped down to his shorts and laid, stomach down, on the bed. Another night, a full muscle massage might be more fun for both of them, but tonight her goal was to help him rest, sleep, and heal.

He awarded her efforts with a couple low groans when she hit especially knotted spots, or places where the muscles radiated heat, but within five minutes' work on one calf he was sound asleep. Lucy finished the massage, giving the same attention to every muscle group she could, and applied the pure salve to some of the electrode connection points, and left him in his place to rest.

As the sun set, she changed into her night clothing and slid into the bed beside him, lying on her side facing him to watch him sleep.

CHAPTER NINETEEN

28 August 2054 – Friday
Presidential Residence
United Earth Protectorate, Capitol City
Alexandria, Seat of Virginia
North American Continent

"I'm never going to remember everyone."

David squeezed Lucy's hand, bringing it to his mouth to kiss her fingers, and she did her best to try to smile without looking as panicked as she felt inside.

"You'll be fine. No one expects you to remember everyone. You already know Katrina and Phin," he said, winking at Katrina who sat across from them. "Daniel, Connor, and you met Michael. You've got a head start. You're not walking in completely unprepared."

The hover transporting them to the Presidential Residence slowed and Lucy wished there were more windows in the back so she could see, but it was a military transport so fewer windows were likely more secure. Through the front shield she saw only trees and the road stretching out in front of them. She knew they were leaving Alexandria proper, but the rurality of the area surprised her. Not that she was any kind of strategist, but it would seem it would be easier to protect the president and his family within the city.

"We're almost there," Katrina offered. "I'm glad we're going together. I always feel weird when they send a hover just for me because Phin and Daniel are already at the residence."

"Just don't head home without us," David said with a chuckle. "I'm lucky if I could walk to the end of the driveway, let alone back to Alexandria."

"How many people will be here?" Lucy asked.

David shrugged. "Don't know. The Tanner family alone, including all the kids, is ten. Connor and family is another three. Forte family and guest is five. Smith family is another six. Victor and Beverly. Have you heard if the Quinns are coming?" he asked of Katrina.

She nodded. "They arrived this morning."

"Another three, then."

"Who are the Quinns?" Lucy asked, doing a terrible job of hiding the rising panic in her voice. She felt like she was being thrown into the fire. Or the deep end. Or both.

"Reverend Jace and Lilly Quinn," David said. "Old friends of the Tanners from before the War. Jace was a pilot."

"It's a beautiful story. You should tell her, David," Katrina said with a wide smile. "I bet Lucy would love it."

"Do I need to know it tonight?"

Katrina shook her head. "No, I don't think so. But you should. It's beautiful."

"So, how many is that?" David asked

"Twenty-nine," Katrina provided.

"*Dios mio* . . ."

David chuckled again. "Sorry, baby. I didn't mean to make it worse."

"We're here, Colonel," said the Firebird navigating the hover as it slowed and stopped before settling on the ground. Lieutenant Graves was out of his seat and into the back, opening the ramp before Lucy or David could unbuckle their safety belts.

David rose slowly, but mostly on his own. It had been two days since the rigorous exam by his new doctor, and she said he didn't have to return to the hospital until Monday. Lucy was glad because he'd needed the days to recover physically. He moved at a stroll more than a stride, but he moved. For that she was thrilled. She'd spent some time when he rested studying up on physical therapy techniques using the access available through his apartment access system. She was far from certified, and nothing near even intermediary trained, but at least she knew how to help and not hinder him in his progress. At least her past medical training gave her some advantage.

They exited the hover, Katrina leading, and Lucy paused at the bottom of the ramp. Once again, the contrast between what she expected and what she saw was startling. The home where President Nicholas Tanner lived would have looked just as natural in Unity Valley. It was a large, sprawling farmhouse that had to easily be one hundred or more years old with large windows and a deep covered porch wrapping around all sides she could see. There were hanging porch swings and deep porch chairs and the sound of life and festivities already drifted through the open windows.

There were outbuildings and barns, but they were set a distance from the house. A white fence stretched away from them in both directions and seemed to fence in a minimum of a one-acre yard. The house was three stories, but by the placement and size of the third level, she thought it was likely an open attic rather than living space.

"Are we the last to get here?" David asked of Lieutenant Graves.

"No, sir. Lieutenants Foren and Cupero will arrive shortly with Vice President Surimoto and Victor."

"Good. At least we're not the only ones fashionably late."

Katrina ran ahead, bounding up the steps to the deep porch, and straight through to the house beyond as if she had just gotten home from school rather than arriving at the home of the President of the World.

President of the World . . . Dios Mio.

As if summoned by her benediction, President Nicholas Tanner stepped through the open door like any man would, with an infant resting on his shoulder who struggled to hold up their head. "Hey, David," he said in welcome, taking his hand from the baby's back only long enough to wave them up the steps. "Hurricane Katrina swept through so I figured you couldn't be far behind."

"Hey, Nick," David said, but kept his head down to focus on the process of raising each leg to take the next step.

Lucy stayed beside him but offered no help. President Tanner seemed unbothered by the time it took him to take the few steps to reach the porch. What struck Lucy was the appearance of new wood planks, though stained and carefully patched in, amongst the original. Once on the porch, President Tanner took the step to meet them and rested a hand on David's shoulder in a solid pat.

Having met Michael already, the resemblance between father and son was striking. She could easily imagine Michael aging to the silver haired with only touches of brown and laugh line marked face of this man. Just as easily, she could imagine Nicholas Tanner when he was a young man. They both stood over six feet tall easily, and in frame and form were practically identical.

"It's good to have you back with us, David. You look damn good for a guy who bounced off a mountainside a week and a half ago."

David chuckled. "I'm getting there." He motioned toward Lucy. "This is Lucy Santos. She came back from Unity Valley with me."

President Tanner extended his free hand, and she took it. His hand engulfed hers and she suddenly felt very small. "Great to meet you, Lucy. I'm glad you came with David. I hope you like food, because I'm pretty sure Caitlin borrowed half the Nest's kitchen staff to cook today. There's a houseful."

"Thank you for having me, President Tanner."

He pulled a face and shook his head, waving her off. "Not here, I'm not. Just Nick, please. Come on in. I like a crowded table."

Lucy glanced sideways to David, who had been waiting for her to look at him because he was watching. He winked, smiled, and followed Nick into the house. It was a beautiful kind of chaos inside, and as much as she couldn't forget this was the home of the President of the World, she immediately knew this was just that. A *home*. Immediately inside the door in the foyer was a wide staircase to the second floor and a hallway leading to the back part of the house. To the immediate right was a dining room already set with a huge table. To the left was a living room that looked to run from the front of the house to nearly the back, and it was brimming with people.

It seemed half of the occupants were children.

And one very shaggy senior dog who wandered from person to person to have his fur ruffled, back pet, and then he'd moved on. He seemed unbothered by new people, or people in general, and when they stepped inside he trotted away from three little girls all of maybe two years old or so, who were immediately on their feet following him, as he came to greet David and Lucy. Two of the girls shouted a version of "David!" and ran for him, each hugging a leg while the third followed by didn't act quite as familiar. He swayed, but kept his feet, laughing. But he didn't try to pick up either one of them.

Moving a hand from one girl's head to the other, he introduced them. "Lucy, this is Nicole, Michael and Jackie's oldest. And this is Amari. She belongs to John and Jenifer Smith. They are two peas in a pod. And the shy one there is Jamie Quinn, which means her Mama and Daddy are around here somewhere."

"Ewww, peas," Amari said, wrinkling her nose.

"Dey're not as bad as c'rats," Nicole said.

"Carrots," David mouthed to Lucy. "And that is Dog."

Lucy arched an eyebrow. "I know it's a dog—"

"No, his name is Dog," David said with a laugh.

"Yeah, I'm not that creative when it comes to names," Nick said, coming back from stepping away to speak to a group of people. "You want me to introduce you around?"

"Nah, I'll do that," David said, waving off the president's offer. He leaned back to look at the face of the baby still struggling to hold up his head, making small sounds like a baby does when they just like to make noise because they can. "Speaking of which, that little one is Adam, Nick and Caitlin's son."

"We were thrilled in Unity Valley to hear of your son," Lucy said, trying very hard to push down her nerves. She wasn't typically a nervous person with new people, but there was a difference between new people and meeting the ruler of the entire planet.

And twenty of his closest friends and family.

"Thanks. Make friends," he said, winking before turning away.

The little girls ran away again, the dog on their heels. They darted between a tall, lanky man with short, light brown hair and striking blue eyes and an absolutely beautiful woman with dark brown hair braided over one shoulder, nearly as tall as the man she was with. On her hip she carried a young boy of no more than a few months.

"Easy," the man called after them, his soft voice having a slight lilt she'd describe as those she'd heard from people of the European continent. "Amari . . ."

The girls slowed and the one he'd called after turned back to him, then smiled. "Yes, Papa." She, Nicole, and Jamie walked to the other side of the room.

He turned back and saw them, his smile stretching his expression. "David," he said with enthusiasm, crossing the room to them with hand extended. David took it in a still grip. "It's good to see you."

"Thanks." David drew Lucy forward by their joined hands so she stood beside him and facing the couple. "Lucy, this is Ambassador John Smith of Aretu and his wife Jenifer. And the little one is Toby."

Toby stared with wide, dark, monolid eyes as he sucked his thumb, a thick thatch of dark hair covering his forehead. He glanced up at his mother, then his father, and back again to smile around his thumb. Lucy smiled back, fighting the urge to ruffle his hair, but his mother gave off an undeniable badass vibe. Lucy knew the story between them and decided not to risk it.

She spent the next forty-five minutes smiling, shaking hands, and memorizing faces to go with the names and stories David had told her. He had told her so much, it was overwhelming. Everyone in this house was somehow larger than life, somehow superhuman, somehow astonishingly unique and would be forever remembered in history.

By the time the introductions were done, and she and David found an empty couch to sit on, her face hurt from smiling but she had the distinct feeling of being part of something amazing, but something she still didn't quite belong in.

"I knew you'd do fine," David said, patting her knee. "I don't know why you were worried."

"That's easy for you to say. You're from . . ." She waved in the general direction of the full house of people. ". . . all this. There's not a person in this house that isn't extraordinary in some way. I mean, right down to the children! The children we are here to meet are in their own, completely unique ways absolutely extraordinary."

David snorted. "I'm about as far from *all of this* as Buck Rogers in the 25th Century." She must have looked confused because he chuckled again. "I woke up in the middle of a crazy science fiction movie and I didn't have a copy of the script. Or some fanfiction mashup between *Robo-Cop* and *Demolition Man*, but I feel more like *Encino Man*. The only reason I'm of any use is I'm decent with computers."

Lucy stared at him wide-eyed and slack jawed. When she could finally blink her way into cognizant thought, she shook her head. "You're kidding, right? David, your very existence is extraordinary, and what you call being decent with computers has saved countless lives. Your dome is phenomenal. It's amazing! You're a walking miracle, *literally* with the fact you're walking. You're a piece of history. You're—"

"Okay, okay," he said through a laugh. "Fine, I'm an oddity." She scowled and he grinned. "I'm usually just looking around, wondering how the heck I got here and if I'm going to wake up again. Like the repeat dream they programmed into my head went on the fritz, so they plugged me into The Matrix and this is a bizarre video game or D&D quest. Like those Pick Your Own Path books I read in school."

Lucy laughed and rested her cheek on his shoulder so she could still see his profile. "I don't understand most of the references you make sometimes, but I think I get it."

Nestled against him, she took a moment to watch the gathering of friends in the house. David had told her Nick liked the house full, and she believed it when she saw everyone. They were the faces of humanity, across creeds and colors and what would have been called nations at one time in a history she didn't remember or know. And one non-Human who could be mistaken for one without hesitation. Then again, wasn't that the new truth? They were all – every human on Earth – some amalgamation of what was here and what came to be here, John's people included?

It made her brain hurt, and at the same time, left her in awe.

What would Abuela Gabi have thought of all of this?

"You're pretty extraordinary, too."

David said it low, and for a moment she wasn't sure she'd actually heard him. She tipped her head to look at his profile. He watched her, a smile tipping one corner of his mouth.

"I get the impression you don't think you're extraordinary. You are." He pressed a long kiss to her forehead and said against her skin, "You took a broken, old man and made him feel human again. That's pretty extraordinary to me."

"Thank you for helping us," Michael said as he eased one of the boys into Katrina Forte's waiting arms.

She grinned so wide he thought her cheeks might split and scrunched up her nose to rub it on the baby's hair. "Of course," she said in a singsong voice. "I'm happy to hold one of these little ones for a bit."

"It just seems safer to walk down the stairs with only one baby at a time," Jacqueline said, handing their little girl to Victor, who looked nearly as smitten as Katrina.

"As Katrina said, I am more than happy to help."

With the two designated babies handed off to their intended recipients, Michael retrieved his baby from the bassinette and Jacqueline picked up hers. With a glance between them to assure they were all ready, Michael led the way out of their bedroom where the babies were sleeping for now until they were more comfortable with them moving to the nursery. Multiple voices, laced with laughter of adults and children alike, filled the stairwell.

This was exactly the homecoming the babies deserved.

Michael went first with Jacqueline immediately behind him, and Victor and Katrina followed. The naming of their children had been of the utmost importance to honor so many they loved and was intrinsically coiled with so many people in this house right now, their official introduction needed everyone here. Michael hadn't even told his father the names yet. As he reached the foyer his parents came down the hallway from the kitchen, Caitlin holding Adam and Nicole holding Gumpa's hand talking at rapid speed. As usual.

"Look, Gumpa! Babies!" she shouted.

Her enthusiasm for her younger siblings was contagious. She bolted ahead into the living room, heralding their arrival with "Babies! Babies!"

Michael smiled. His heart was so full he couldn't breathe sometimes.

By the time they entered the room, every person in attendance was aware of their arrival. Perhaps out of forewarning, or because many there were parents themselves, no one cheered. Of that, Michael was thankful. The babies were well tempered, and hardly fussed, but a room full of loud people was a test they had not undergone quite yet. The four adults, each bearing a child, passed through the room to the mantel where it seemed so many significant moments had occurred, not the least of which was the moment when Michael had realized his failings and asked Jacqueline to be his wife. And she accepted.

There had been sadness in this house. But there had also been so much joy.

Michael put his back to the dormant fireplace, and Jacqueline took her place beside him, then Katrina on his other side and Victor beyond her. With his free arm, he reached for his wife's hand and held it as he spoke. He had to clear his throat first, because the well of emotion nearly overpowered him.

"When I was young and had no knowledge of who I came from other than the woman who abused me, all I knew was my name. Michael. It wasn't until my father rescued me that I learned my full name. Michael Sean Tanner. I learned I share my father's name, and my great-grandfather, and I belonged to the Tanner family line.

"So, when Jacqueline and I knew our family would grow by four, we knew each name we chose was important. From these names, our children would know from where they come."

He released his wife's hand and kissed his own fingertips before he reached across to rest his palm on the head of the baby she held. She smiled, looking down at their son, then looked at him.

"This is our son Sean Anders Tanner," he managed to say, deciding it would be impossible to hide the effect of the words on his own soul. "My middle name is Sean, named after my great-grandfather, and I pass that name to my son. His middle name is Anders, after his mother's family Anderson. These children are not just of the Tanner line, but the Anderson line."

He took his hand from Sean's head and touched Jacqueline's cheek before focusing on the baby in his own arms. "This is our son Matthias Matthew Tanner." He looked to his father, who nodded with a surprised, emotive smile. "Matthias was my father's father, and my grandfather. The name Matthias means Gift from God. As does the name Matthew. By giving him two names that mean Gift from God, we are acknowledging we are truly blessed with the gifts we have been given."

He turned enough to face Katrina, who both smiled and had tears glistening in her eyes. She looked up at him as she rested her cheek against the downy head of the baby boy she held. Michael had to take a moment to shift Matthias from one arm to the other so he could touch his third son's head. Of the three, his hair was the lightest and softest, often sticking out straight like fluff after his bath.

"This is our son Gideon Paul Tanner."

Katrina sucked in a sharp breath, the tears rolling from her eyes.

"Gideon was my brother, but his name was given to him by Katrina because he had no name and she said he deserved one. For his existence, he had only known the name Alpha, but Katrina gave him a name befitting him. Gideon means Warrior. And my brother Gideon died, giving his life for his family."

Katrina closed her eyes and pressed a long kiss to Gideon's forehead. His eyes were open, and he stared at her near face. He was too young to see much detail, but he seemed mesmerized by her.

"Paul," Michael continued, "is in honor of Jacqueline's father Paul Anderson. He fought for truth, and he protected his daughter at all costs, leaving her within the safety of Phoenix when he knew he couldn't protect her anymore. Gideon Paul is named after two selfless men."

With a shift, Katrina moved closer to Jacqueline and Michael took his place beside Victor, who already had emotion pinching his dark eyes. The little girl – the only girl of their four – was sound asleep in his hold, bundled in her pink and yellow blanket Victor and Beverly had gifted her with just the day before when they prepared to leave the hospital. All the babies were given gifts, but Michael wondered if somehow Victor knew.

"This is our daughter Victoria Grace Tanner."

Victor stared at him, wide-eyed, his own cheeks streaked. The room vibrated with emotions, but Michael couldn't – didn't dare – look around. He might not finish.

"She is named first and foremost after my longest and dearest friend, often my savior, and forever as loved by me as any brother. She is named after the man who swore to me our children would be safe in his care, and for the man who I am proud to call family.

"And she is named after my father's mother, my grandmother, Grace Tanner. Our children will never know most of the people whose names they carry, but they will know whose love brought them to us all."

His last words barely made it clear of his throat because it was finally too much. Too much to say. Too much to express. Too much to breathe.

Victor rested a trembling hand on Michael's shoulder and whispered, "Thank you, my friend."

Michael nodded and cleared his throat, reaching deep into the evaporating well of strength he had remaining. As blessed as they were to introduce their children to those closest to them, it was still far more draining to his and Jacqueline's emotional strength than he imagined. Ending the introductions with the final name would be the most difficult of them all.

"Everyone here, those closest to us, know the story behind finding the babies and how they came to be, but something we have not widely shared beyond those there that day is there was another baby, but he was already gone. He was our son as much as any of these, even though we never had the chance to bring him home. We have chosen to honor him with the name Gabriel, which means angel."

Somewhere in the room someone sniffed, and someone cleared their throat.

"Okay," came Jace Quinn's voice from the gathering as he stepped forward. "Michael, now that you've got every single person in this room practically weeping, do you mind if I finish?"

Michael just shook his head and smiled.

Jace cleared his throat and rubbed his hands together and took a deep breath, squaring his shoulders. The soldier who became a Man of God.

"While the Good Lord had a great many things to say about the blessings of children in our lives, I think I'd rather fall on some of the lyrical Irish blessings I heard growing up. They're as good as any prayer I've ever said, and as true."

He stood closest to Michael and Victor, so he stepped to them first, laying a hand on the head of each baby.

"May strong arms hold you, caring hearts tend you, and may love await you at every step. May you bring light to the home, warmth to the heart, joy to the soul, and love to the lives you touch."

He moved on to Katrina and Jacqueline, touching their heads again.

"May God surround these children and bless this day. May God hold you in the hollow of His hands, forever and ever. May you have a sunbeam to warm you, good luck to charm you, an angel to protect you, laughter to cheer you, and faithful friends near you.

"Amen."

Michael's father snuffed the side of his nose with his thumb and cleared his throat. "After that, I think we're all ready to eat."

As people shifted from the living room toward the dining room, his dad joined Michael and Victor where they stood together. At first, he just nodded, his lips pressed firm together, as he put a hand on each of their shoulders. He took a breath, huffed, nodded again, then simply said "You did good, Michael. You did good."

CHAPTER TWENTY

28 August 2054, Friday
Civilian Employee Housing
United Earth Protectorate, Capitol City
Alexandria, Seat of Virginia
North American Continent

"Isn't he beautiful, David?" Katrina whispered, sliding the bundled baby into his arms.

He couldn't speak, only able to nod, looking down at the sleeping face of the four-day old baby named after a son he'd only known as his son for hours before he was dead. When Michael had announced the name of the third baby, the intense pressure in David's chest had been instantaneous and smothering. He had closed his eyes, trying to calm the waves of sorrow he knew he would never shake, pride he knew he didn't earn, and some tangled, undefinable mess he couldn't name but it choked him.

"I know they're all beautiful and wonderful, and don't tell Michael I said so, but I think Gideon Paul will always be my favorite."

He nodded again, unable to say a word.

. . .

"You look a thousand miles away."

Lucy knelt on the couch beside him so her knees came against his hip, her arm draped across the back behind his head, as she held his evening tea mug in front of him with the other. Not ready yet to say anything, he took the steaming cup and swallowed half of it, even though it burned on the way down. He needed the scorch to ground him in the moment.

"Not a thousand," he said, leaning forward enough to put the half-full mug on the table in front of him. "About ten. My head is still back at the residence."

She ran her fingers through his short hair, her nails scraping his scalp in a way that both soothed his fractured nerves and stirred him at the same time. David let his head fall back to rest on the cushion, eyes closed, as she continued her ministrations.

"You had no idea Michael would name one of his children after Gideon."

She didn't make it a question, but it felt like one. David rolled his head on the cushion, stopping with his face angled toward her before he opened his eyes. "The idea he might never even crossed my mind, but it makes complete sense he would because . . ." He shrugged. "That's Michael. From the minute he found out the boys were biologically his half-brothers, they were nothing but his brothers."

"Just like they are your sons."

Another non-question.

"I don't feel qualified to say I'm their father, but I'm happy to be whatever I can be to them. They can't help where they came from."

She smiled slow, her focus on the point of contact between her thumb and his forehead. "I'd say you are infinitely qualified because you're here for them. Biology connects you, sure, but you don't have to be anything more and I think if you hadn't accepted them, they would have probably understood. But you did, and they are all the better for it. That says so much about you. Don't you think?"

David couldn't answer, so he rolled his head away again to stare up at the ceiling. His chest hurt. Lucy smoothed her thumb across his brow, the motion hypnotic and calming in a sharp juxtaposition to the twisting turmoil behind his ribs.

"Katrina told me you asked if the boys could have your name, so when Gideon was honored, he had a family name. They all have a family name. Even if the e is useless," she added with a soft chuckle behind the phrase that had been a constant in his family for generations.

David smiled, but it felt heavy.

"Tonight, before Michael and Jacqueline came downstairs and when you were talking to Connor, I was watching everyone in the room. All in their own conversations with different people. Phin and Katrina were talking to Victor and the vice president. Katrina said something that made them laugh. Instead of laughing like the rest of them, Phin looked down at Katrina and he smiled." She paused, and David opened his eyes to look at her. Lucy tilted her head, her lips tipping up. "He smiled. Right then, like I hadn't yet seen, I saw you in him."

David inhaled through his nose, forcing himself to meter it out slowly to help process everything curling and battling in him. There was so much. For a month he'd been struggling to find his footing, jerked around from one catastrophic event to another with only brief moments of calm to catch his breath, like cresting the peak of a rollercoaster for two seconds before being plunged into another adrenaline rush that threatened to either kill him or remind him he was still alive.

Lucy was a constant calm.

Even when she made his heart race and his blood thicken.

"Thank you," he finally managed to say.

"For what?" she asked. "I'm just talking."

"You know what I need to hear, even if I didn't know I needed to hear it." He shifted his head so he could look at her better, but it took him just outside her touch range, so she curled her fingers and rested her temple against her own hand. "You sure you didn't study psychology in school?"

She smiled, the slow, sexy, closed-lip grin he'd noticed the first time he met her in the hallway of the main house in Unity Valley. It was a smile that said she knew so much more than she said, or she knew something you only wished you knew.

"Dunno," she said with a shrug of one shoulder. "Maybe I'm psychic. Maybe I do fit in with your superpower crowd."

"Or maybe you're just perfect. And I'm one lucky S.O.B. that you decided not to leave me on that porch to sleep all night." He raised a hand to rest his palm against her cheek, stroking near her mouth with the pad of his thumb like she had to his forehead. She leaned into the touch, and the heavy weight in his chest shifted to be something lighter, but definitely warmer. "And you didn't think I was nuts when I told you I was a meat popsicle for forty years."

"You just love me for my cooking," she said with a wink.

"Nah, I love you because—" He stopped short when the reality of the words he's chosen hit him. He tilted his head and let them sink in, realizing that he'd surprised himself, but they were absolutely true. "I love you because I love you."

She looked as stunned as he felt, so before either one of them tried to work it out David decided to grab onto one of those moments that made him feel alive and drew her down to him as he raised his head. Her position kneeling beside him put her above him and the angle was devastating to any control he might have pretended he had. David shifted again so he could hold her face in both hands, and she leaned into him. Lucy pressed her hands against his chest, and he wondered if his heart would pound its way free of his ribs.

When she parted her lips and their tongues touched, David had to groan to keep from jolting at the rush that hit him; instead, he dove in deeper to the kiss.

Then she rose on her knees, breaking the contact of their lips, and David stared up at her, trying to catch his breath. Her hair fell around her face, and his, in a rich curtain. Then her shining lips ticked up in the smallest of smiles. Holding his gaze, she moved the hem of her knee-length dress up her thighs and she shifted into his lap, her knees settling again into the couch cushions on each side of his hips.

As her weight and warmth pressed onto him, David groaned again, momentarily resting his head on the back couch cushion before meeting her mouth in a soul-wrecking kiss.

29 August 2051 – Saturday, early morning hours
Vice Presidential Residence
United Earth Protectorate, Capitol City
Alexandria, Seat of Virginia
North American Continent

Victor barely managed to slip from their bed and make it to the bathroom before his stomach tried to turn itself inside out, leaving him shaking, on his knees, and soaked in sweat. His blood pounded in his ears like tsunami waves, but the rush wasn't enough to drown out the voices overlapping and clashing in his mind.

"*I have been trying to get my hands on this family's damn bloodline for decades! I won't let them destroy my plans. Kill them. Tonight.*"

No matter the body she occupied, or the voice she spoke with, Tosk Rak'blon of the Sorracchi had the power to make his blood run cold, even if her words played only in memories he'd long since buried so deep he'd forced himself to never acknowledge them again.

Until tonight.

No, it had begun before tonight. Now that he understood, now that the memories drowned him in sensory overdrive like a hundred monitors playing all at once at maximum volume. Only the worst memories came back to him like this, an assault on every sense and every nerve until it left him wasted and ruined.

But even then, the memories didn't stop.

Victor hunched on the floor, forehead pressed to the marble tile like a supplicant in prayer, screaming in his own mind for the memories to please stop. They wouldn't. This was his punishment for the sins his hands had perpetrated.

Torrential rain made it nearly impossible to see more than a few feet, except for the flickering headlights of a car off the road in the ditch, the beams pointed at an angle toward the sky. Victor walked toward the lights, ignoring the cold rain plastering his clothing to his skin. Ikor and Leonid, Kathleen's blood soldiers, walked behind him subservient to the rank he held over them. They reached the edge of the ditch, and Victor shined the brilliant beam of his flashlight onto the SUV they'd run off the road.

Through the driver's window he saw Matthias Tanner hunched over the steering wheel, the window smeared with blood. He raised his arm above his head to change the direction of the light and saw the unconscious – possibly already dead – body of Grace Tanner.

"I will ignite the vehicle," Ikor spoke, taking two steps into the ditch.

"Should I assure they are dead first?" Leonid had asked as he followed Ikor.

Victor shifted the flashlight to his non-dominant hand and reached behind his back to remove the M18 handgun from where he'd hidden it in his waistband at the small of his back. "No need."

He raised the weapon and fired twice in quick succession.

Then set about to finish the task.

"Victor?"

Beverly's voice barely made it through the miasma before her gentle touch yanked him back from the terrifying edge of his past. Victor flinched away from her touch, desperate not to let her feel the evil drenching his soul even though he knew simply moving away from her would never be enough. It had never, ever been enough.

"Please, *Cusbibil*, my love," he whispered through the bitter bile lodged in the back of his throat. "I cannot . . ."

He slid away from her until he came against the glass enclosure of their large shower and managed to sit with his back to the glass. The enclosure was cool against his bare, sweaty back but it did nothing to quell the disgust in his chest. Finally, when supported by the glass, he blinked against the stinging sweat in his eyes and looked at his wife.

His beautiful wife whom every day he asked what he might have done – with every sin he had committed – to somehow earn a moment of her love and compassion.

She said she didn't care what happened before he helped them rescue Michael because she knew he'd been quite literally a man of two minds, but when he remembered the blood on his hands, he hated himself more for defiling her with his sins.

"Please, Victor," she begged, the tears glistening in her eyes enough to crush him. "You've been troubled for so long. Please tell me what it is. You know it's the past."

He shook his head violently before she could finish, clenching his jaw to keep himself from speaking. Victor drew his knees to his chest and pressed the heels of his hands into his eyes until he saw spots and pain shot through the sockets.

"Will I ever be free of this?"

He hadn't meant to ask aloud, but his tolerance and his control was slipping too quickly for him to manage.

"Only if you share the weight of it with me, my love," Beverly said softly, and he sensed her slow approach.

"No!" he snapped, slamming his head back into the glass.

He'd done that once before, what felt like a lifetime before, and had woken hours later distraught that the shattering glass hadn't slit an artery and let him die. Had it really been so long ago? Before he understood the demon raging within him to be free, before he'd had it purged away, leaving him with the sins.

"Please . . ." she begged.

Victor swallowed against the raw pain in his throat from vomiting, and lowered his hands, forcing himself to look at his wife again. She knelt within arm's reach, but just like in early days when he'd fought so hard for control back in the mountain base in Colorado, she kept her hands in her lap as he asked. Her wish to help him vibrated off her, both soothing him and scraping across his sparking nerves.

He panted each breath as the sob curled in his chest, but swallowed it down, only allowing the tears to burn his cheeks like acid. His lips tasted of salt and bile and his body shook with the toll the memories left behind.

"You are the most beautiful soul in all of existence," he finally said, sniffing as the tears fell.

She tilted her head, her eyes sad. "You're frightening me, Victor."

He shook his head. "I don't think I ever truly frightened you, did I." He didn't intend it as a question and knew she wouldn't either. "Even when I was terrifying to myself and everyone else, even when I hurt you, you were strong and brave and never wavered."

"I did waver," she admitted, "and I regretted it. I swore I would never, ever question you again. Please, Victor, tell me. I beg you."

"I can't," he choked through the tightening of his throat. "Not now. Not yet. Not until . . ." He shook his head, not knowing what to say because he didn't know what the truth would bring. He took a deep, shuddering breath. "I have to go. I can't tell you where, because it wouldn't be right or fair to put the weight of the truth on you."

"I'm your wife—"

"And you are Vice President Beverly Surimoto of the United Earth Protectorate," he finished for her, the swell of pride in his chest giving him a moment of reprieve from the heartache. "I cannot ask you to choose between me and—"

"There is no other choice but you!" she shouted.

His heart broke, for what had to be the hundredth time, and each time he wondered if he would recover. "When I come home, I will share everything. Whatever that truth may be."

CHAPTER TWENTY-ONE

31 August 2054 – Monday
Forte & Bauer Residence
Civilian Employee Housing
United Earth Protectorate, Capitol City
Alexandria, Seat of Virginia
North American Continent

"Can I ask a question? It's probably silly."

Phin stopped shaving, leaving a single stripe of bare skin down his cheek where he had just dragged the blade. His far cheek was already smooth and clean. He looked at Katrina for a moment before looking back to the mirror. "You can ask anything."

Katrina wrinkled her nose and shifted a little on her perch on the bathroom counter, her back to the mirror so she could watch her husband shave. And appreciate his bare torso with the heavy steam of the shower still clinging to his skin. She'd seen his bare chest before he'd ever woken from his stasis pod, and while she'd always appreciated it, knowing it was her *husband's* bare chest made her appreciate it even more. Katrina cleared her throat and looked down to focus her thoughts before looking at him again.

"I know but that doesn't mean it's not a silly question."

Phin stared at her for three beats of her heart before he leaned over and kissed her, the smell of his shaving cream filling her senses. She kissed back but giggled when she felt a smear of the cream stuck to the end of her nose. Phin moved away with a lopsided smile – something she liked to believe happened so much easier now – and handed her the small towel he'd left on the counter between them so she could clean away the foam.

"Ask your question," he said, tilting his head to drag the blade along his jaw.

The crackle the sharp blade made on his skin sparked her senses in all kinds of pleasant ways. She had to take a sip of her coffee to compose herself before she could manage to spit out her question. Phineas Forte was downright distracting.

"Why did she . . ." She sneered because she didn't even like referring to the monster. ". . . manipulate or modify or *whatever* you and your brothers so you hardly ever shave? I mean, that's something she did, I assume."

He finished the strip he had started and shook the razor in the sink of warm water, even though his focus was on her. He tapped the razor on the side of the sink and started on his throat. "She wanted our appearance to be uniform and intimidating to her enemies. That was best achieved by assuring things that changed our appearance be limited. We were also expected to be in adverse conditions for extended periods of time." He finished the last section of his face and rinsed the razor again. "To a smaller extent, it is much like our reduced need of food or sleep or protection from the elements. It was about efficiency."

"Yeah, well, I like to watch you shave and I only get to do it a couple times a month."

Phin bent forward and rinsed his face with the water in the sink, drying it as he straightened. "I have a question."

"Okay."

"Why do you enjoy watching me shave?"

Everything from Katrina's chest up flushed hot. She rubbed her lips together and fought the urge to break eye contact. He was her husband, and she knew she didn't have to be embarrassed, but being a wife with all the intimacies and casualness that was supposed to come with their changed relationship was still new. Kisses and embraces before they were married didn't adequately prepare her for how much she would like ... *no, love* ... being married.

"I don't know why," she answered, shaking her head. "Not exactly. I just do. I like watching you do a lot of things."

Phin shifted so he stood in front of her, holding eye contact as she tried to explain. She had to tip back her head because even sitting on the counter, he towered over her. The scent of shaving cream and soap clung to his skin. Barely blinking, she enjoyed the way the flush spread from her throat to her whole body, and the catch of her breath when he slid his hands up her legs to her hips and pulled her closer to him so he stood between her knees. Then he took her face in his hands – hands she knew had strength like no natural human could claim, but always touched her with gentleness – and kissed her.

Katrina hummed into the kiss, wrapping her arms around his shoulders, loving the feel of the warm, damp skin against hers. He kissed deeper, firmer, and Katrina answered by crossing her ankles behind his hips. Phin reached out and opened the bathroom door, the humid air inside clashing with the cooler air of their bedroom and carried her back to the unmade bed.

Forte & Santos Residence
Civilian Employee Housing
United Earth Protectorate, Capitol City
Alexandria, Seat of Virginia
North American Continent

"*D*avid..."

David hummed a reply because that's all he really wanted to do. More would require he opened his eyes. If he opened his eyes, he might have to wake up. And if he woke up, he might have to give up his hold on the warm, sexy woman tucked against him.

"David..."

"Shhhh," he whispered against her hair.

She laughed, and he felt it against his chest pressed to her back. "It's not my alarm going off, it's yours."

David groaned and reluctantly flopped onto his back, immediately feeling the loss of Lucy against him. The alarm was louder and clearer, and he flailed his hand until he found the watch on the bedside table. Without looking, he turned off the alarm and chucked the watch across the bedroom. It hit the far wall with a satisfying thud.

"Remind me why that was on?" he asked, staring up at the ceiling. Now that he'd forced himself to open his eyes, he scowled at the daylight seeping in the window.

The sheets and blanket rustled as Lucy rolled over to face him, one hand sliding over his side to his chest as she rested her cheek on his upper arm. "Because your doctor wants you to go into the hospital this morning, and we've gotten way too used to waking up whenever we want to trust getting out of bed on time."

"Right," he said, dragging out the word. "Bad idea."

She laughed again, and sat up, tossing aside the blanket.

"Aw, no. No, no, no," he groaned, reaching for her.

"Yes," she said over her shoulder as she stood and walked around the foot of the bed toward the door. "I'll be out of the bathroom in ten minutes. Breakfast will be ready in about twenty."

"Or I could just join you—"

"The goal is to get *out* of the apartment," she said as she went out the bedroom door, leaving it open.

David stared up at the ceiling, listening while the water in the shower turned on, failing miserably at not imagining Lucy Santos under the water as she washed her hair. The idea of sharing the shower wasn't unique in the last three days, and sure as hell made it a challenge to stay put until she finished, and the bathroom door opened. Through the doorway, he watched her head for the kitchen, tempted by the glimpse of the back of her knees below the hem of her sundress.

When did summer dresses get so damn sexy?

The smell of her soap drifted to him, and he inhaled deep as he forced himself to sit up. Whether it was the tea Lucy gave him twice a day, or the deep massage she'd worked into their routine, or their extra *exercise*, but he felt stronger than he had a week before. Not strong – he was miles from strong – but he was strong enough to stand on his own without worrying he might fall over, and strong enough to walk rather than shuffle from room to room.

By the time he left the bathroom, the aroma of eggs and fried potatoes filled the small space. Eggs were easy protein, and by all rights he figured he probably should be sick of them by now, but Lucy managed to take the simple supplies given them and make them delicious every time. David pulled a tee shirt over his head as he walked, tucking it into his waistband as he reached the kitchen and stepped behind her while she poured hot water into a mug with his tea blend.

David wrapped his arms around her waist and nuzzled the side of her neck, using his nose to move her hair. "I think we messed up the days," he said against her warm skin. "I'm pretty sure today is Sunday."

"Nice try," she said, setting the kettle back on the cooktop. "We can sleep in tomorrow."

David kissed her cheek in front of her ear and stepped away, picking up both their plates to carry them to the table while she brought the mugs. Glasses of juice already waited. Perhaps months of cooking for dozens of people at each meal with limited resources had honed her skills, perhaps she was just that good, but when he took his first bite of the steaming potatoes David closed his eyes and hummed around the savory goodness of potatoes fried in butter.

"Marry me, woman," he said once he'd chewed enough to speak.

"Are you going to propose every time I cook you a meal?"

"Yes," he said, nodding as he used the side of his fork to separate a bite of egg. "I've asked you to marry me other times, too."

She snorted. "Hardly a unique moment to shout a proposal."

David grinned and finished the bite in his mouth as he scraped together his next bite. He paused to take one of the two pan-toasted biscuits she'd set on a plate between them. They were the last of her biscuits, and damn they were good. Especially toasted. "If I'm not careful, I'm going to gain twenty pounds."

"You're healing," Lucy said, taking a sip of her juice. "You're burning calories." She winked over the edge of the glass before taking another sip and setting it down. "As long as you ease up on the peanut butter cookies, that is."

David smirked and pointed at her with the tines of his fork. "You made them, so it's your fault."

"Fair enough. Did you know you had a slow cooker buried in the back of your cabinet over the refrigerator?"

David shook his head. "I don't even know what a slow cooker is, other than the obvious being something that cooks slow. The apartment was semi-furnished with whatever was available, so who knows what else is hidden up there. Why?"

"If it works, I might try a few recipes. Abuela Gabi loved her slow cooker, so she taught me. Granted, a lot of her recipes were what we could make with what we had available."

"Your eyes change when you talk about her. They light up, like you're smiling." David used half his biscuit as a saucer for the eggs left on his plate. As he made the perfect bite, he watched a slow smile bow her lips as she swirled the juice in the bottom of her glass. "She raised you, so she had to be pretty damn special."

Lucy nodded, her gaze cast on the glass and not looking at him. "She wasn't like any grandmother my friends had, that's absolutely true. Maybe because she was younger than most of the other grandparents. She glanced at him and smiled. "I loved every minute of it. Losing her was one of the hardest moments of my life."

David pushed his plate out of the way and slid his arm across the table to squeeze her hand. "I wish I'd met her."

"Me, too. She would have loved you."

Presidential Residence
United Earth Protectorate, Capitol City
Alexandria, Seat of Virginia
North American Continent

"You're up early."

Michael snapped his head up from its resting place on the back cushion of the sunroom couch, startling at his father's voice. Nick chuckled and took the single step down onto the sunporch, setting a cup of coffee on the table closest to Michael. Not that Michael could reach for it yet. He'd dozed off feeding one of the babies.

"I'm up because they all decided they were hungry," he mumbled, shifting to find a better sitting position. The bottle was empty, and Sean Anders had fallen back asleep, so Michael set the bottle aside and shifted his son onto his shoulder. "I'm not sure if it is a blessing or a curse that they seem to do all things in unison. They wake up together and go to sleep together. They cry for attention together and want to be fed together. We fed Victoria and Gideon first, and Jacqueline was feeding Matthias when I came downstairs for a fresh bottle."

"I'm not sure if it's helpful or just a little creepy."

Michael smirked and nodded. Time would tell which way his children's synchronized living would play out, or whether it would change when they got older. What amazed him was the fact all four of them were in unison, not just the three who had been together in the special care nursery. All four, including the one Jacqueline had carried.

"How is the rotating feeding working?"

Before answering, Michael picked up the mug of coffee and took a long drink. Feeling a slight revival of his senses, he nodded as he put the mug on the table and began patting Sean's back.

"Jacqueline would be a better person to answer, but I have concerns. I understand her wish to breastfeed each of them and rotating through them is the only way to accomplish that, but I worry about the toll it's taking on her."

"It's tiring enough with one. Twins would be a challenge. You've got twice that." His father finished the contents of the cup he carried. "I know you want to do it all, but it's still two of you and four – five if you count Nicole – of them. We can find help."

"Ask me in another week."

"Fair enough. I'm heading out. I think I heard my ride pull up out front. See you at dinner."

"Okay, Dad."

A minute later, Sean let out a hefty burp and long sigh. Michael shifted deeper into the cushions and closed his eyes again.

ALEXANDRIA HOSPITAL – REHABILITATION WING
UNITED EARTH PROTECTORATE, CAPITOL CITY
ALEXANDRIA, SEAT OF VIRGINIA
NORTH AMERICAN CONTINENT

"I've seen some amazing things, especially in the last two years since we've had exposure to Areth research and technology, but I have no problem saying you are quite possibly the most remarkable patient I have ever worked with, David."

David guzzled down half the bottle of salty electrolytes Doctor Noguchi had handed him, wincing at the taste but at least it was cold. "Sure doesn't feel that way from this side, Doc."

"I don't know how you can think that," she said, shaking her head with such fervor some of her haphazardly pinned hair came loose from her clips. "David, when I met you last week you barely shuffled into the room *before* any of my tests. Today, you walked. Not shuffled. Walked. And I don't need to run the analysis to know your improvement is impressive." She smiled and twisted to find Lucy where she stood a few feet away. "I don't know what you two have been doing in the last few days, but it's working wonders."

While the doctor's attention was off him, David grinned waiting for Lucy to look his way. The second she did, he winked and gave her what he hoped was a truly lecherous grin and relished in the flush of color in her cheeks. She flustered and shrugged.

"I don't know . . ." she stuttered out.

"She bakes my biscuits," David provided, drawing Doctor Noguchi's attention back to him, who looked puzzled. "I mean, she bakes me biscuits. Lucy has been feeding me very well. And we've been exercising, like you said."

It was almost painful to keep a straight face watching Lucy's wide-eyed expression beyond the doctor's view.

"Then I think I need your biscuit recipe, Ms. Santos, for all my patients." Doctor Noguchi stood from the exercise ball she'd been using as a seat near the exercise bench David had been working on. It rolled toward him and he reached out to stop it. "I'm going to take one more look at these numbers. I will be back shortly. It won't take long. Rest while I'm gone."

Lucy crossed the room as the doctor left, waiting until the gym door closed behind the woman before she scrunched up her face and gave David's arm a light slap as she took her own seat on the ball.

"You are awful," she declared in a loud whisper.

David laughed, pretending to wince. "Ouch, woman. That's elder abuse."

Before she smacked him again, David cupped his hand behind her head and pulled her to him. Without resistance she moved to him, and he fell headfirst into the kiss. Every kiss . . . *every damn kiss* . . . hit him square in the chest and reminded him all over again he was alive, and this beautiful woman was with him.

Lucy touched his cheek, her thumb brushing their joined lips and she drew back, smiling at him. She could speak with her eyes and her smile as much as anything she ever said. Maybe that's why he'd fallen so fast.

"What?" she asked, her dark eyes looking down at his mouth before meeting his gaze again. "You're smiling different."

"Just smiling," he said, running his fingertips along her cheek as he took his hand from behind her head. "How am I smiling different?"

She shook her head, but not enough to move away from his touch on her cheek. "Just different. Good. Happy."

David chuckled. "Well, hell, woman. I'm damn happy."

She smiled wide and turned into his touch, kissing his wrist. "Good."

"Marry me, woman."

She made a noise in her throat and slid back until he had to lower his hand. "What are you going to do the day you ask me that, out of nowhere and for no reason, and I say yes?"

David took in a deep breath, enjoying the warm spread in his chest. He sat back, straightening his spine from the slightly slouched position he'd needed to reach her and curled his lower lip into his mouth so he could run his tongue across it. He swore he could taste her. Damn, he was a lost man. He knew it. He didn't give a damn.

"I'd marry you."

Her mouth parted and her eyes widened, but before she said anything the gym door opened and Doctor Noguchi returned. Lucy stood and rolled the ball away from him, stepping back a couple feet. David watched her until he had to look away, wondering how to read the color in her cheeks and the wide sheen of her eyes.

"Well, David, I was correct. Everything shows a marked improvement in your muscle strength, nerve conductivity, and recovery time. You've improved in a few days what I would expect, being generous, in a month to six weeks." Doctor Noguchi didn't look up from the tablet she carried, still managing to not only find the exercise ball again but sitting on it without falling. She finally looked up, shaking her head. "Honestly, I am completely stumped. Often that isn't a good thing, because as a doctor that usually means we don't know how to treat someone, but in this case, I'm feeling rather useless."

"So . . . what next?"

She scrunched up her face enough to make her glasses shift, and she put them back in place. "I want to continue monitoring you, but I honestly don't believe we need to be as aggressive as we had planned.

Continue doing what you're doing and come in once a week to check with me. Does that work?"

David glanced toward Lucy and winked. "Works for me."

Doctor Noguchi stood and held the tablet to her chest. "Then I'll see you next Monday. Ms. Santos, bring me the recipe for those biscuits," she said with a smile and wave as she headed for the door.

David stood, the muscles of his thighs and back protesting some but he had to admit even to himself the ache was nothing like it had been when he first came back to Alexandria. The ache wasn't what it had been the end of the previous week. He held out his hand, and Lucy took it falling into step with him as they left the gym.

MILITARY TRANSPORT VEHICLE – ALEXANDRIA PROPER
1.75 MILES SOUTH OF
ROBERT J. CASTLETON MEMORIAL BUILDING – THE CASTLE
CENTER FOR UNITED PROTECTORATE GOVERNMENT
UNITED EARTH PROTECTORATE, CAPITOL CITY
ALEXANDRIA, SEAT OF VIRGINIA
NORTH AMERICAN CONTINENT

"Why didn't you reach out? Let me know?"

Beverly shook her head, staring out the tinted side window of the military transport. Not a tear had fallen, but Nick felt the grief buffering off his vice president much stronger than he'd felt it the week before when she'd shared her worries about Victor.

"I had nothing to say. Victor may have said he couldn't force me to choose between telling you and keeping the secret of whatever it is, I know deep down he wouldn't do anything against the Protectorate or you."

"Bev," Nick said, shifting forward to rest his elbows on his knees. She didn't react so he reached out and tapped her knee where she sat across from him. "Bev, look at me."

She swallowed before turning from the window, meeting his eyes.

"I'm not talking about the vice president calling the president to tell him she thinks we have a situation. I'm talking about a friend calling a friend to tell him she's upset and worried."

She pressed her lips together and nodded, looking down at her hands. "I should have."

"You don't have to be alone. Come out to the house—"

"Sir," called Daniel from the front of the hover. "We have a situation."

Nick pivoted from the seat and headed toward the front of the hover. The military units were much larger than street hovers, allowing for several people to fit or for a few to move. He knew Beverly followed and went to the space between the two pilot seats. Phin navigated the hover but glanced toward his brother.

"What's going on?"

"We have an urgent message coming from Colonel Montgomery, sir." Despite his calm, Nick's nerve prickled. "Global radar just picked up several crafts coming into the atmosphere at high speed. They appear to have been cloaked."

"Give me the headset."

Before he finished his order, Daniel's headset was in his hand and he clipped it over his head. "Speak, Connor."

"Sir, they're coming in fast. At least two dozen. Unidentified. We don't know who they are. We're scrambling fighters from all points—"

"Engage domes."

"We are, sir. We don't know what kind of weaponry, if any, we're dealing with. They're coming in hot and unannounced. I'm guessing they aren't friends."

"We're a half mile from the Castle," Phin provided.

The silent message was the capitol dome couldn't be engaged until they were within the parameter.

"Punch it."

The power surge in the hover engines lasted half a second, but the thrust hit his veins before it thrust through the hover and it jumped into maximum street-level speed. His gut clenched. Nothing good came from sudden visitations from the sky.

Nothing.

"Nicholas—"

"Incoming!" Phin shouted.

A screeching wail pierced his head before the hover slammed sideways, sending both him and Beverly bouncing off the interior of the craft. Pain blinded him as his head made impact, but Nick tried to hang on to consciousness long enough to see Beverly move. More screeching sounds cut the air before everything went black.

CHAPTER TWENTY-TWO

"*L*ucy!"

David's voice echoed through the pounding in her ears, but she didn't know where it came from. She tried to push up from the stone pavers surrounding the fountain where they'd been sitting, dust and smoke scraping her throat and making her eyes burn. She squinted and lifted her head, trying to see, but everything was a fog.

"Lucy!"

His hands were frantic on her back, her hip, her shoulders until he rolled her into him against his chest and she looked up at him. His face was dirty, and dust clung to his hair, but the panic in his eyes pushed her to speak more than anything else.

"I'm okay." She nodded, shifting so she sat, still in his hold as he knelt beside her, water from the fountain soaking into her sundress.

Lucy raised her hands to touch his cheeks and saw the blood on the back of her knuckles and long, angry scrapes from her impact on the stone. Reality thundered in again, assaulting every sense. The smell of smoke, dust, and fire in the air. The grit of stone. The sound of screaming, and above them a wailing screech. They both looked up to the hazy sky as five black crafts ripped through the clouds over them.

"Those are ours," David said. He used the edge of the fountain closest to them as point of leverage to push himself to his feet, then offered his hand to help her stand. Once she was on her feet and knew she could stand he wrapped her in his arms and held her so tight she almost couldn't take a breath. "Sweet Jesus, my heart nearly stopped when I saw you," he said against her hair.

Still holding her against his chest, David looked to their left, right, and behind them. They were no more than fifty feet from the hospital entrance having just walked outside. With her cheek against his shoulder, Lucy stared at the hospital and the tears burned their way from her eyes. One section had been hit directly, and smoke billowed up from the top floor. She had no idea what might have been housed in that part of the building, only that it wasn't the wing they'd been in just half an hour before.

They were on the street and all around them were the sounds of fear, of crumbling structures, and she feared, of people dying.

"Who the hell did this . . ." David whispered.

"David!"

He twisted away from Lucy to the sound of his name, and Lucy gasped when she saw Katrina running at them from the hospital, breaking away from the crowd that stumbled into the daylight. Lucy gasped and covered her mouth as David tried to run to Katrina. She was faster, and perhaps more afraid, and reached them in hysterical tears. David swept up the tiny woman, lifting her feet off the ground in his hold.

"What's happening, David," she cried into his shoulder, Lucy hearing the smothered words as she reached them. "Who would do this?"

"I don't know, Peanut," he said, setting her down. He smoothed his dirty hands over her hair in a quick inspection. "You okay?"

Katrina nodded, tears still falling. "I don't know who's inside. Victor isn't here – I was going to his office – when the building shook." Her eyes suddenly widened, and she spun around, looking off toward a billow of smoke rising from the skyline. "David!" she screamed. "The Castle! Phin is with the president!"

"Sir, we need to examine your injuries."

Nick waved off the Firebird medic, then paused long enough to take out of the man's hand the bundle of gauze he carried. "I'm fine," he snapped, holding the gauze to the throbbing spot over his right temple. "Connor!" he shouted to the room, not knowing where he was.

"I've got her!"

Nick looked up to see his Firebird Commander – but at that moment his highly motivated brother-in-law – coming fast through the gathering of leaders and officers in a bunker three levels below The Castle they knew would be inevitably used but had been in no hurry to open for business.

The War Room.

"Audio only. Can't get a clean connection," Connor explained as he reached Nick, holding out a headset. As soon as he had it, Connor was off again.

Nick whipped off the one half on his head and put on the new one. "Caitlin..."

"Nicky!" she cried, the tremor in her voice punching him in the chest. "Connor said you were okay, but I couldn't believe it until I heard you."

"I'm fine," he lied. If Connor didn't tell her about the bangs, bruises, and gashes from the hover crash he wasn't about to. "You're all okay?"

"Yes. Nothing happened here at the house, but we heard the explosions and saw fighters overhead. I felt the house shake." In the background he heard the wailing of more than one infant.

"Firebirds are coming for you," he said, fighting with everything in him to keep his voice steady. Mess with his planet, and he'd nail you to the wall with a grin but messing with his family stole any kind of calm he had. "They may not have hit the house, but that doesn't mean they won't. You're too exposed."

Connor came back. "Villarreal and Singh are on their way."

"Did you hear Connor?" Nick asked into the mic.

"Yes. We'll be ready."

"They're taking you to the bunker."

"Nicky—"

"Caitlin, you can't be here. This building is protected, but it's a target."

"How bad is it?" she asked, her voice dropping.

Nick clenched his teeth and pressed his lips together before he could answer, because in this there was no point in lying. "It's bad. I just don't know how bad yet."

"Please, Alexis, we can' argue about this right now," John said, trying to stay calm as he comforted Amari who cried into his shoulder.

"You're leaving us alone!" Alexis yelled, but while her tone was angry the fear came off her like ripples on Llynne Callondia Lake after a storm.

"*Sidan.*" He reached for her, intending to touch the side of her head, but she flinched away from him with a scowl.

"Don't call me names I don't understand," she bit out.

She was afraid. They were all afraid. Amari and Toby had been crying since the bombing began, and Silas hadn't moved since his initial scream and John feared his son relived those first few nights of horror when he had come into John's life. Simon sat with him, silent but close, having no idea what to do for his brother.

"I'm sorry," he apologized and shifted Amari so she could wrap her arms around his neck. "We won't leave you alone. You won't ever be alone. But we *need* to make sure you are safe. We must go and help. Stop this if we can. We need to know you're safe to do that."

Her lips pressed together and her chin shook. She looked away from him before the first tear fell and swiped at it angry enough the contact of her hand to her cheek was almost as loud as a slap. Weighing her anger over her need for comfort, John reached out again. This time, when he touched her hair she didn't pull away, but sucked in a sharp sob and curled herself into his chest, her arms crossed and tucked between them. He couldn't hear her crying, but felt it in the shake of her shoulders, and he smoothed his hand over her hair, wishing he could embrace her but the poppet in his other arm wouldn't allow it.

He wished he could embrace every one of them at once.

He wished he could secret them all away to a ship that would take them home. Back to Aretu. Back to Callondia. Back to Devon on the Hill and his family home. Back to peace and quiet.

She's afraid.

John looked up and across the room to where Jenifer stood, holding a relatively calm now Toby on one shoulder, a large satchel in the other with clothing and other needs for the children. He nodded, not ready to release either child in his arms though Alexis would argue she was far from a child.

In experience, yes . . . in age, she was young and to be protected.

"I promise you, Alexis, we will come for you as soon as we can and we will all be together wherever that may be," he said against her hair. "The soldiers you will be with will protect you, and we will be able to check on you through them. You will be with people you know."

She twisted away from him, head down so her hair hid her face, and took the few steps to the nearest couch where she dropped hard. The only sound she made was a single sniff. A sharp knock at the apartment door preceded a loud shout.

"Ambassador, we're ready to go!"

The children would go in one direction, and he and Jenifer would go the other, until hell had passed.

"Captain!"

The Firebird cluster ahead of them turned at David's shout, and one man stepped away from the group as the rest moved on to their destination; a downtown building with blown-out windows as civilians stumbled into daylight. David had seen transports and clusters of both Terra and Firebird soldiers but was thankful it was Firebirds they'd reached first. At least they were more likely to recognize him. Terras wouldn't. Especially since he wasn't exactly in uniform.

"Colonel, sir," the Firebird said with a salute as they approached.

David recognized him as Captain Jan Nebaba from the Eastern European Continent contingent. He released the hands of each woman who walked with him, each holding a hand, and motioned for them to stay where they were while he approached the military personnel.

"Do you need medical attention, Colonel?" Nebaba asked, looking past David as he approached to where Lucy and Katrina stood. "Any of you? We are searching for injured."

"We're okay. Just bruised. Give me a status report, and don't worry. I know information is probably coming in hot and fast, and probably in pieces."

"Yes, sir. I can't say much about what happened beyond Alexandria, but I understand the attack was global. We're in damage assessment."

"Where is President Tanner?"

"He's in the Castle, sir. The unknowns attempted to hit the capitol, but the dome was nearly fully engaged so damage is minimal. I understand President Tanner's transport was hit, and they took damage, but the president is fine. Vice President Surimoto was injured and is receiving treatment at the capitol as Alexandria Hospital took a direct hit."

Intel on the Urdo Khantan, hired guns for the Sorrs, had been spread through the upper ranks of the military in all branches. David didn't question who was responsible, but it wasn't information he could casually toss around. Not even to Lucy when she asked.

"Yeah, we know. That's where we were." David's chest squeezed at hearing Beverly was hurt. Things were a scramble, but Victor would see to it she was well taken care of. "How about President Tanner's guards?"

Captain Nebaba looked confused at the question. "His guards, sir?"

"Yes, his guards," David repeated. "Phineas and Daniel. Forte." He put just enough stress on the name to make it as clear as a bullhorn.

Captain Nebaba's expression shifted from confused to recognition to surprise. It wasn't that Nebaba didn't know how to put together one and two and get three, but if he didn't have all the parts of the equation until now, he couldn't be expected to know. Hell, there was probably a good chunk of people who didn't know their names. They didn't need to be known on a personal level. They just needed it known they were there to make sure nothing happened to President Tanner.

"Yes, sir," he said with a sharp jerk of his head. "To my knowledge, they are not injured."

David took half a step toward the man, leaning in. "Captain, I'm going to explain something real quick. This isn't on you, but I need you to understand when I go back to those two ladies I'm going to need to know for sure. See the little one?" Captain Nebaba started to look, but David stopped him with a warning sound. "Don't let her size fool you, and she happens to be the wife to one of those men."

Captain Nebaba gave another nod and raised his hand to the comms earpiece hooked around his right ear. "Nebaba to Montgomery," he said. It took a few seconds for him to nod. "Yes, sir. I'm downtown. I'm here with Colonel Forte." He paused. "Yes, sir. He says he and the ladies he's with are fine, one being a Mrs. Forte. He's inquiring about President Tanner and his guards." Again, Nebaba listened and nodded, his eyes cutting to David at one point. "Yes, sir. Thank you, sir. I will see to it immediately."

Nebaba lowered his hand and cleared his throat. "Colonel Montgomery has informed me both men are without injury and are with the president now. He also asked I relay a message. Verbatim."

"This should be good."

"He said that just because you bounced off the side of a mountain doesn't mean you get to sit this one out, and to get your lazy ass to the capitol *tout de suite*. I'll have a transport take you immediately, and we will take the ladies to safety. Also per Colonel Montgomery's orders."

David barked a laugh and patted Captain Nebaba on the arm. "Thank you, Captain. Appreciated."

*A*lexandria was still mostly a strange city for Lucy, having only seen the areas around the hospital and their housing, and the streets they traveled leaving the city to go to the president's home. She didn't need to know streets and neighborhoods and landmarks to know this city was forever changed.

Alexandria had become the new governing city for the continent after the Sorracchi had destroyed Washington. By default that President Tanner was from the North American Continent did the governing city stay in the general area. If he had been from anywhere else, things would be dramatically different now.

Still, what she saw through the tinted glass of the transport window made her chest hurt and her throat ache from holding back the tears. The attackers seemed to have picked targets as they went over the city, with the area around the hospital and the capitol building – which she'd learned was called The Castle – hardest hit, but destruction could not be brought down on a city without having widespread effects.

There were soldiers everywhere, some gathering up or helping civilians on the street and others trying to put out fires or clear damaged buildings. She recognized the differences in uniform emblems between the Terra soldiers and the Firebirds, since both were in Unity Valley, and there was a third emblem she didn't recognize but would find out as soon as she could.

At the thought of Unity Valley, her heart pounded viciously behind her ribs, making her head swim. Were they okay? Had they been attacked? If they hadn't been, did they even know? David said there had been attacks all over the globe. Where did they attack and why? Maximum damage, loudest message, or random beyond the capitol?

"I lived in Boston when the first wave of attacks happened," Katrina said beside her, surprising Lucy.

They had both been silent since saying goodbye to David so he could go do his job while they waited. Lucy wasn't accustomed to just sitting and waiting when people needed help and doing it now just because she was here didn't sit well. She pulled her attention from the devastation outside to look at the young woman who looked ready to jump out of her skin.

"Our parents had this idea that the best way to hide was in plain sight. My brother Karl and I had 'shown promise' from when we were little." She emphasized the word choice with air quotes, but her knuckles were white from clenching her hands for so long. "Computers and stuff just made sense to me. Mama and Papa didn't like the way the world was going, with the unified government and the way the Areth – because that's who we thought they were – discouraged traditions and religions."

Katrina seemed to need to talk, so Lucy let her. Maybe she just needed to listen.

"They took us to Boston to live near family in a neighborhood that was still mostly Jewish. They wanted us to keep the traditions, to never forget, but they wanted us to be hidden. They were afraid for us." She paused and took a long, shaking breath.

"They died when Boston was bombed."

"I'm sorry."

Katrina finally looked at her, eyes shining. "I hoped we'd never have to go through that again. Then there was the War, but that was over so fast. I thought finding our way here and working with Victor, we'd find ways to keep everyone safe. I thought we'd be okay now."

Lucy swallowed and reached for Katrina's hand, holding it so Katrina wouldn't dig her nails into her palms again. "If we've learned anything from history, there's always someone who thinks they have the right to take what isn't theirs."

*J*ackie fought the equal urge to punch a wall or scream. Maybe both. But the bunker walls would break her hand, and sure as hell no one other than the poor people trapped with her would hear her scream. Instead, she paced the length of one of the primary rooms in the secure bunker hundreds of feet below the surface somewhere beyond the perimeter of Alexandria.

The air in the bunker was filtered and cycled, but it was heavy with the fear and anxiety of the half dozen adults and dozen children occupying the space; so much so Jackie felt it like a buzz on her skin. It had taken half an hour to calm the quads once they arrived, and now they slept, leaving her to simmer in her thoughts. She didn't even have Nicole to distract her because once Amari and the other Smith children arrived, Nicole was with her best friend.

So, she paced.

She made it to the far end of the room nearest to the kitchen kept fully stocked for any inhabitants and turned to march back in the other direction. She'd nearly traversed the length when she lifted her chin to look ahead and saw her husband standing, waiting for her, with hands in his pockets and an unreadable expression. Jackie continued walking and slowed when she reached him. The moment they made eye contact, a new twist of emotions battled for priority.

Jackie shook her head, keeping just outside his reach. "You have no idea how hard this is for me, Michael," she said, both hating and needing the anger in her tone.

He didn't answer at first, his gaze shifting over her face and stance as he contemplated his response. She didn't need to be in his head to know that's what he was doing, because that was what Michael did. He never spoke without choosing every word with care.

"I do understand, but perhaps in a different way," he finally said, moving half a step closer, his hands still in his pockets. "I believe I know what you battle with, because I know you."

"Yeah?" She crossed her arms over her body and leaned back a few degrees, not distancing with an actual step, but the turmoil was vicious in her chest. "You think you do. I'm not made for this."

"I know. You are a soldier. You were a soldier the day I met you, and despite everything since then, you're still a soldier."

"You're approving of your wife and the mother of your children wanting to—" She threw her arm out in a wide arch, encompassing pretty much everything everywhere. "Go find a fight? Kick some ass?"

Another damn pause. "My approval isn't . . . relevant. And besides, how could I disapprove of who you are when who you are is who I love?"

"They bombed the hospital," she said through clenched teeth, bitter fear at what could have been churning with the hot rage. "A week ago, our children were in that hospital."

Michael swallowed and nodded. "I know. I haven't been able to shake that thought. I want . . ." The weight of his voice when he spoke chilled Jackie's anger, replacing it with shock. "Revenge."

She had to look away, taking in a carefully metered breath because Michael was so slow to anger when she saw it and felt it, it shook her. Not once, not ever, had she ever seen his anger focused on anyone other than those who absolutely deserved it, but she had also witnessed the power of his rage. God help anyone who inspired that in him.

Nothing, no words, would form. It was all chaos and fear and fury and panic in a rolling storm she had no way to harness. There was nothing left but to do what she had done since the day she met Michael Tanner . . . she turned to him, and he wrapped her in his arms and they said nothing at all.

CHAPTER TWENTY-THREE

2 September 2054 – Wednesday, early morning
War Room
Robert J. Castleton Memorial Building – The Castle
Center for United Protectorate Government
United Earth Protectorate, Capitol City
Alexandria, Seat of Virginia
North American Continent

"Twenty unknowns broke the atmosphere and disbursed, with two to three crafts staying together except for Alexandria where five total attacked the city," Connor reported, head down as he scrolled through information on his PAC tablet. "They attacked six major populous locations, including Alexandria: Helsinki, the area around the ruins of Los Angeles, Nairobi, and Perth.

"Sphera deployed out of Alexandria, Honolulu, Melbourne, and Nigeria and engaged the unknowns," Colonel Merin St. John, Sphera Co-Commander, added. "Seven unknowns were eliminated in the atmosphere, and an additional eight were shot down either into oceans or exploding on impact. We confirmed four retreated and are actively searching for evidence of the remaining craft."

"Where did we lose tracking on it?" Nick asked.

"Scotia Sea, thirty miles north of the Antarctic Peninsula," Connor answered.

"Keep me updated." He looked the other direction around the table to Colonels Conrad Corchan and Helen Bertrand the Terra leadership primarily responsible for civilian aide, support, and assistance distribution. "I don't want to hear it, but what are our numbers?"

"We have 2,478 confirmed deaths," Colonel Bertrand answered. "We know of 798 injured, and as of right now an additional 584 unaccounted for. The largest percentage of deaths and injuries occurred here in Alexandria as it seemed to be their primary target and we have the most geographical and structural damage of other locations."

"How does that break out between military personnel and civilians?"

Colonel Bertrand didn't bother referring to his notes, which didn't surprise Nick. It was more than just his job to know; it was his conscience to know. "Of the 2,478 deaths globally, 1,030 were military. Of the injured, 504 were military. Of the 584 unaccounted for, only 20 are military."

Nick nodded. It didn't help knowing the breakdown, but he needed to know. "I want a list of names, all categories."

"Yes, sir. I will have it to you within the next few minutes."

Colonel Corchan continued. "We have deployed an additional 200 Terra to Helsinki and Perth, and 300 Terra to Los Angeles and Nairobi. Honolulu has reported the least amount of damage and casualties, despite the location, and have stated no additional personnel are needed. We are, however, dispatching a shipment of medical supplies and food to them. While souls weren't lost, one of the areas hardest hit was a storage warehouse so they lost much of what they had on hand."

Nick's head was still stuck on the nearly 2,500 deaths from the attack. Yes, they still called the attackers unknowns, but everyone knew who had invaded their airspace. He'd have confirmation once whatever wreckage remained was brought to Alexandria for examination and identification. How they'd gotten so damn close to

Earth without setting off alarms from here to Raxo he didn't know but intended to find out.

He bowed his head for a moment, the exhaustion of the last twenty-four hours sitting between his shoulder blades, with his hands linked in front of him. "How is the vice president?" he asked the room in general.

Doctor Richard Anson, a doctor on Victor's team who had stepped up in Victor's absence, cleared his throat. "Her head injuries were moderate, but sufficient for us to insist on further bedrest. We have completed the second stage of knitting the broken bones in her arm and shoulder. She is anxious to be released."

Nick tapped his fingertips on the tabletop and sat back, the chair creaking with the movement. "Yeah, I'm anxious to have her here, too. But I'm not willing to risk her recovery for it. You can tell her that."

He shifted again, antsy with the need to do something now and the knowledge no answers would come soon, and no action could be taken right then. He sighed and looked across the table to where David Forte sat beside Connor.

Nick jutted his chin in their direction. "How are *you* feeling, Colonel."

"Feeling ready to do whatever needs doing, sir."

"Domes," he said simply at first. "I want them bigger. Stronger. Faster to power up. In fact, I want you to think bigger than you ever have."

David was nodding before he finished, tapping the pinkies of his joined hands on the tabletop. "Already doing that, sir. I need to get into Victor's research lab with Katrina and the rest of the computer technologies, mechanical engineering, and reverse development experts. I have the theories, just need to see if we have the resources for it."

"Good. Keep me posted, and let Connor know what you need and when you need it."

"Yes, sir."

"We're keeping a closer eye on the long-range radar, and since the unknowns left the system, we've had no sign of them coming back," Chief Security Advisor Colonel Ebbens added. "We are also investigating why their approach wasn't observed and reported prior to them being on this side of Mars."

"Yeah, that's a damn good question. One I'm not happy we don't have answers for. If it's a flaw in our technology, fix it. If it's a personnel issue, cauterize it."

"Yes, sir," Ebbens said with a scowl and nod.

"Opinions . . . can we send our families home?"

There was only a brief exchange of glances around the table before multiple people turned to face him again, answering with a variety of nods and affirmations.

"Good. Connor, see to it. Get some transports out there to take everyone home. I'm sure they're all anxious to see the sky again."

The PAC tablet in front of him blinked on, showing a notification he had the list of names from Colonel Bertrand. He tapped it for the document to open. Seeing the names segregated by geographic location and either military or civilian standing made his stomach twist all over again. He had a brief memory of something his father once said about the presidency aging a person, and while the previous fifteen months had been exhausting and thought-consuming, this was possibly the most aging day of his life.

"Ambassadors Smith and Drucillus Clodianus Hiacyntus are waiting to discuss next steps with the Defense Alliance," Connor said, drawing his attention away from the file.

"That's fine. We'll break for now and I'll talk with them. Let's come together this afternoon after some of these to do items are taken care of."

As everyone stood and broke into smaller groups of conversation, Nick went back to scrolling through the list of names. Most would be strangers to him. That didn't mean he didn't feel it necessary to read each and every one of them to somehow honor their lives.

When he hit the Alexandria list, his heart dropped, and another hit of acid hit his gut. He looked up and scanned the room as people left. "David," he called out, and David stopped.

"Yes, sir."

"Hang on a second."

He pushed back his chair and stood, twisting at the waist to look in the direction of Daniel and Phin, the two silent men who had not been more than fifteen feet from him since the shitshow began. Not that they were ever far, but he'd been possibly even more aware of their presence in the last day. What most people didn't know – or didn't talk about – was not only how bad the hit to his transport had been the previous day, but how bad it could have been except for the two men. When he made eye contact, he motioned for them to join him as David pushed upstream against the departing crowd to make it back to him.

Phin and Daniel reached him first, but David was only a couple seconds behind. Considering how he'd looked when he'd gotten back to Alexandria, the man was recovering like Clark Kent after someone moved the green kryptonite away from him.

"Yes, sir," David said when he reached them.

Nick looked past him, waiting a couple more moments until the rest of the meeting attendees left the room and Connor shut the door with one last glance in their direction. Once alone, Nick looked down at the tablet whose screen had gone dark again and drew in a long, deep breath before raising his head to answer David's curious – and his sons' stoic – stares.

"I just looked at the list of people we lost in Alexandria. Karl Bauer is there. I assume he was probably lost when the hospital was hit."

David let out a long chain of curses and turned away with his hands at his hips and his head down. With his focus on David, Nick almost missed the slight shift in the brothers' stances. Daniel's ramrod stature swayed, and Phin put his hand on his brother's shoulder. Nick mentally gave himself hell. The men were so stolid most of the time, it didn't occur to him they would feel Karl's loss just as David or Katrina. Not in the same way, but the four of them lived together. Of course, the men would feel the loss. And he'd just dumped it on them.

"I don't think she should hear it from anyone other than the three of you. Other than Karl—"

"We're her family," Phin finished.

David circled back to his sons and set his hand on the back of Daniel's bowed head, saying something low to the young man Nick couldn't hear.

"I'm sorry. I'm sure it's not easy for any of you to hear either, but it's going to be hard as hell for her. You three go talk to her as soon as they're back in Alexandria. I'll let Connor know you'll be out of pocket for the next day or two," he said specifically to Phin.

"Thank you, sir," Daniel and Phin said in unison.

Three knocks came at the door, and it opened as Connor stuck his head in. "The ambassadors are here, sir."

Nick waved Connor to come in. "They can wait a minute."

Connor came into the room, and shut the door, his eyes squinted slightly as he looked between them. David stepped back from Daniel, but only enough to face Connor as he reached them.

"How soon will you have everyone home?" Nick asked.

"I've sent Alvarez, Granholm, Hayes, and Paskialski out to the bunker in two transports. One will take the Tanners home, and the other will bring everyone else back into Alexandria. I'm guessing within the hour. I also sent a message ahead, so they know to pack up."

"Rotate in whoever would be duty relief for Phin and Daniel. They're going to need to get back to their place, along with David, as soon as possible." Nick paused and sniffed. "Karl Bauer is among the lost."

Connor's expression shifted from curious to serious, and without a word he put his hand on David's shoulder closest to him. With a couple sharp nods, he took a step back. "I'm on it," he said before heading to the door.

"Go ahead with him," Nick said, motioning toward the door with his chin. "Connor will have your replacements here in a few minutes, and he'll probably have a hover idling and waiting for you by the time you get to the front door. And . . ." Nick cleared his throat. "Tell Katrina I'm sorry."

Civilian Employee Housing
United Earth Protectorate, Capitol City
Alexandria, Seat of Virginia
North American Continent

The windows along the eating area and living room had been blown out in the attack, but the building itself wasn't fundamentally damaged. The plywood nailed over the windows blocked out the sun and left the apartment so much darker than Lucy was used to. The space felt foreign, like she had walked into the wrong apartment.

She shut the apartment door and set down the small bag of clothing she'd brought back from the bunker. The clothing she now wore wasn't hers but had been provided for her since there had been no time to gather anything, much like every other person in the bunker. Some had been picked up from their homes after the attack but some like her, and Katrina had been rushed there with only the dirty clothing on their backs.

With an anxious tumble in her stomach, she walked through the apartment and turned on every light she could find. The window in the bedroom had not been damaged, probably because it was on the opposite side of the apartment from the downtown blasts, so she opened the shade to bring in the only other source of sunlight she could.

Once she reached the kitchen, she noted whoever had covered their windows had done a passing job of cleaning up the mess left behind, but bits of glass and dust and dirt covered almost everything. With a deep sigh, she retrieved their broom and dustpan, and some cleaning rags, and did the only thing she could until David came home.

Whenever that would be.

Two hours later, the apartment was possibly cleaner than before they left two days earlier, and she'd taken a lukewarm shower to clean away the grime. They'd been warned some utilities had been affected, so she was happy to be able to wash up at all.

She opened the bathroom door and gasped when she realized David stood in the living room, staring at the covered windows.

"I didn't hear you come in," she said, crossing the space. "How long have you been here? How long can you stay?"

She walked around to face him and stopped short. His expression was devastating, his lips pressed together in forced control, his eyes shining. David raised his chin and turned his head enough to look at her, and Lucy's throat tightened so viciously and quickly she could barely breathe.

"What's wrong?" she whispered.

He didn't say anything, but when she raised her arms he pulled her to him in a hard embrace and buried his head into her shoulder. Lucy hung on because there was nothing else to do.

FORTE & ~~BAUER~~ RESIDENCE

Does each loss feel different?

Phin looked up from making a peanut butter sandwich for Katrina while their teapot boiled water for tea, to look toward the archway leading to the bedrooms. He set down the knife and went to the hallway, finding Daniel standing outside Karl's closed bedroom door. None of them had entered the room yet, and Phin was unsure who would be the first. If it alleviated either his brother's or his wife's pain, he would be the one when the time came.

Daniel turned his head to look at Phin.

Gideon's loss did not feel like this.

Phin went to him, resting his hand on Daniel's shoulder. *Every person has a different place, so their absence is different.*

Daniel turned away and lowered his chin, clenching his fists at his side. Anger and confusion battled for dominance with the sadness in Daniel's heart. Phin was helpless to provide any advice or guidance, to either his brother or wife. With nothing else to communicate, Daniel stepped away from Phin's hand and into his room.

When they had been three, they always had balance. They always knew what was expected and what to do, but since Gideon died the balance had been skewed. Michael filled some of the gap, but both Daniel and Phin had been left navigating emotions and situations without the third part of themselves. He wanted to help, wanted to alleviate the soul pain the way they had alleviated the physical pain for each other so many times. But it was beyond his power.

For anyone he loved.

Phin returned to the kitchen to finish making the tea and sandwich for his wife. It felt inadequate and insufficient, but he had no knowledge or experience to tell him what to do for Katrina. He understood the hollow sense of loss she felt because he and Daniel had felt the same when Gideon died, and only because of that did he feel he had any insight. He empathized with his wife on a level he couldn't with his brother.

She sat on the edge of their bed, staring at their windows that had survived the attack. Windows throughout the building, depending on the direction they faced, had been blown out during the attack but their apartment had made it through without damage of note.

Phin stood beside her and held out the cup of tea and plate holding the sandwich. She looked up at him with shining eyes, took the cup, and shook her head at the sandwich. He set the plate on their dresser and returned to the bed to sit beside her.

After nine minutes and twelve seconds of silence, she took in a deep breath and released it as a sigh. "When Mama and Papa died, it hurt in a way I never could have imagined. They were so strong in what they believed, and they loved us so much, we thought they'd be with us forever. I think I cried for a week, but Karl took care of me and told me we'd be okay as long as we were together."

Her voice trembled with the final words, and she lowered her head. Teardrops fell to leave dark spots on her pants. Phin took the tepid cup of tea from her shaking hands and set it on the floor, unwilling to leave her side even long enough to put the cup with the sandwich. As he straightened again he wrapped his arm around her shaking shoulders and pulled her to his side.

"I thought I knew how you felt when you lost Gideon because I'd lost my parents," she whispered. "I'm sorry. I didn't understand how much more it could hurt."

"There is nothing you should be sorry for," he said against her hair. "You offered me comfort and gave me peace, two things I had never known. You were a blessing to me, and you are now. I will do all I can to take care of you in a way Karl would approve."

Forte & Santos Residence

"I think that was probably the hardest thing I've ever had to do in my life," David said, taking the cup of evening tea Lucy offered. "Thanks. And that includes learning to walk again."

"We spend our lives trying not to hurt the people we love," she said, sitting in the chair adjacent to him. "Having to tell someone you love that someone *they* love is gone . . . it's not a pain you inflict, but it feels the same."

"The look in her eyes . . . I'm never going to forget it."

Lucy curled her hand over his wrist, rubbing her thumb on the back of his hand. "President Tanner was right to tell you and the boys so you could tell her. I'm sure he knew it would hurt, but he seems like someone who understands."

David nodded and lifted the mug to his mouth with his free hand. He was used to the odd mix of flavors now, and since returning to Alexandria he'd not needed the extra whatever it was she added to help him sleep. He slept great now. At least, when he was home with her. The last two nights he'd only managed a couple hours in a row on a cot in a room of cots with other military personnel trying to catch some rest between the marathon of frantic, straight-out hours of doing the job of recovery. He knew he didn't know everything, because it wasn't his place to know, but he knew enough. Nick and the upper echelons of command knew who had done this, and knew this day might come, but every piece of intelligence they'd received indicated two days ago should not have been that day.

Something felt wrong. He knew it. Connor had said as much. There was a fly in the ointment somewhere.

"We've been getting reports in from all over the planet. Other than in some places just hearing the unknowns' fighters or ours, there are a lot of places that didn't even know something happened before they were contacted for updates. Unity Valley included."

Lucy drew in a sharp breath and closed her eyes as she released it. "Oh, thank God. I have never missed the ability to speak to someone within seconds like I have in the last few days."

"In 2011, before I went into the deep freeze, the smart phone was the new thing. Surf the web and look at pictures of cats." He chuckled. "I expected the damn things to be fully implanted by now. I wanted to check on you and Katrina—"

"We understood why you couldn't," she said, shaking her head. "We got reports every now and then and those were enough to tell us you were okay. When you and the boys have to go back to The Castle tomorrow, I'll go see Katrina and make sure she's not alone."

David shifted his hand so he took hers and brought it to his lips, kissing her fingers. "Thank you."

She smiled and rested her temple against the knuckles of her free hand, her elbow on the table. "I'm sorry I don't have anything tasty to offer you. I'd only just gotten past cleaning up; I hadn't had time to think of making anything and I didn't know when you'd be here. The cookies from last week are stale now."

"I've got something better in mind." He stood, leaving the nearly empty mug on the table, and drew her out of her chair, kissing her as soon as she gained her feet.

CHAPTER TWENTY-FOUR

3 September 2054 – Thursday, late evening
Interstellar Secure Communication Chamber
Robert J. Castleton Memorial Building – The Castle
United Earth Protectorate, Capital City
Alexandria, Seat of Virginia
North American Continent

"I don't like how this feels, Your Highness," Nick said, pacing a six-foot swath in front of the full-reality projection of Queen Bryony the Fourteenth. "Our long-range radar picked them up around Mars. I know our radar array isn't as impressive as the Alliance tech, but we still should have gotten a blip when they were on this side of Saturn. A forensic deep dive shows someone *off planet* was helping mask those crafts."

He stopped and pivoted to look directly into her realistic eyes.

"Off planet. Do the Urdo Khantan have tech on their own to do that? Do the Sorrs at this point?"

He didn't like the crawl of suspicion he'd been battling against since the facts had begun to surface. It twisted and clawed at the base of his skull and churned acid in his gut. Bryony canted her head at an angle, probably the Areth equivalent of a head shake, or just the way a queen would deny knowledge.

Yeah, he really hated seeing enemies everywhere. Hell, where else was he supposed to look?

"Every piece of information we have from all contacts within the Defense Alliance span say the Sorracchi Empire has been reduced to bare rubble with only the ships and limited resources they managed to keep hold of after the fight for Earth. Most of the survivors have slinked off to hide and allow themselves to be poisoned by the venom of their failure and rage. They don't have the capability to come to your part of space or to affect your radar to that degree."

"So, what does that mean, Bryony."

He wasn't asking a question. Not really. He knew it. She knew it. But the answer needed to be found.

"A full investigation has been initiated from the top levels, which is why I have come to you alone. There are those amongst the higher echelons of the Defense Alliance who resist the inclusion of Earth, and those who support the inclusion but are pressured by their constituents to refrain. The investigation is being managed by those who believe Earth and Humanity belong with us, and who knows we need to find the truth."

"A few decades back, that would be called a non-bipartisan investigation."

She canted her head with a small dip of her chin. "Nicholas, we will do all we can to find the answers. We are gathering and organizing forces to be sent to you, but it takes time to move a fighting force of that size."

"Yeah, well, keep a watch for anyone making that more of a challenge, too. We're not feeling the warm welcome here. I get that this wasn't exactly planned on *anyone's* part, but we're here and we have to move forward. There's no going back."

"Agreed." She paused and took a breath. The realism of the interstellar projection was so impressive he swore he could feel her exhale between them. "What can Aretu do to help? The medical replication devices were scheduled to be on a stellar ship tomorrow, but I can have a scout ship on its way to you within the day, with those and anything else you may need."

"Faster delivery of that equipment would be a Godsend right now, Your Highness. We have a lot of people hurting in a lot of ways, and I want to help them. Other than that . . ." Nick shook his head and turned to walk a few feet away from her projection. "Thank you, but more than anything I want to find the truth for all the people who lost someone to this. That can't be brought on a scout ship." He turned back to face her again. "I appreciate the offer, especially if there are anti-Earthers on the council."

"The help offered by Aretu is by my command, not the council. We are independent parts of a whole, not governed by the whole."

"Good, because I'm not considering joining up just to have someone else tell us how things get done. I see the benefit of an alliance, but I'm not handing over the governing of Earth to anyone." He intended to make another point, but a jaw cracking yawn stole his thunder and he cupped his hand over his mouth. Shaking it off, he tried to chuckle. "Sorry."

Queen Bryony smiled and linked her hands in front of her. "I have yet to learn the correlation between Aretu's day and Earth's night. Is it morning or evening for you?"

Nick extended his arm to reveal his watch past the end of his sleeve and turned it to look at the watch face. "Evening. Getting late. I promised Caitlin I'd be home tonight if I could."

"You should go. It is days like this when you need those you love close to you, to give you strength before the next battle must be fought." She smiled wider and gave a small hum. "Be sure to kiss your new son for me. And your new grandchildren. Your home and heart must be so full."

Nick chuckled, but already felt the weight of exhaustion and absence settling on his shoulders. Once he allowed himself to think of home, he missed it with a vengeance. Had it only been four days since he saw Michael feeding a baby before he left for Alexandria? It felt like a month had passed since then.

"Very full," he said, nodding, then looked at her beautiful but projected face. "I love it."

He closed the transmission from the handheld switch he'd retrieved since his Comms people were gone and he'd wanted this conversation to be as off the record as an interstellar projected conversation could be. Pocketing the switch, he fought another yawn as he left the chamber. Any other Thursday evening of any other week, he'd be home by now and Phin and Daniel would be home as well. Once the fear of another eminent attack had passed, he'd insisted the young men return to a regular schedule especially since Katrina needed them close.

His heart hurt for the young woman.

The rotation cycle through Firebirds had been different in the last few days, and those not necessarily his usual guards had taken up the role. Tonight, it was Levi Colton-Henry, Connor's Second, and Sabrina Tambour. They were talking about something in hushed voices that had them both smiling wide, but as he came out of the room, they went silent and bolted to attention. With a grin, Nick remembered Connor had told him the two were engaged to marry. There had been a time the military would have thrown a fit over the relationship, but Nick didn't give a damn. People deserved to find whatever normalcy and peace they could, whether they wore a uniform or not.

"I'm ready to get out of here," Nick said, motioning down the hall. "The sooner you get me back to the house, the sooner the two of you can go home, too."

"Yes, sir," Colton-Henry said, and led the way down the hall while radioing ahead for Nick's new transport to be ready.

Tambour fell into step behind him, but he purposefully slowed his pace and stepped sideways. She got the hint and stepped up to walk beside him, hands tucked behind her back.

"I know things are a bit shuffled right now," Nick said, jutting his chin toward Colton-Henry. "But you two figured out when you're getting married yet?"

Her dark eyes widened for a moment and her head jerked so she looked at him, and she just as quickly looked away. Nick tried not to chuckle, because he doubted it'd help.

"Connor told me. Congratulations. Good for you."

"Thank you, Mr. President," she said, but her voice practically squeaked.

"Sure."

He dozed off in the transport once they were clear of the city limits, so it felt like only a moment before the transport slowed again outside the residence. Colton-Henry escorted him to the porch and into the house. From that point, the Firebirds watching the house were unseen and non-intrusive, but there, nonetheless. Nick mumbled a thank you and entered the house that was mostly in darkness. A single light from the kitchen in back gave light in the central foyer and staircase. The light tap of toenails came from the living room, and Nick crouched to greet Dog as he came to say hello. Dog had given up trying to climb the stairs, so he made himself comfortable in the living room at night.

"Hey, Dog," Nick said, ruffling the fur on top of the old mutt's head. Dog sat and nuzzled Nick's hand, giving it a lick. "Good boy. Go on back to bed."

Dog turned and went back into the dark room. By the time Nick took the first step up the stairs, the exhaustion was smothering. He hoped he managed to say hello to his wife before he collapsed into a deep sleep. At the top of the stairs, he looked down the hallway toward the rooms occupied by his son and family, and saw no lights beneath the doors. Hopefully everyone was asleep. With five infants in the house, sleep was precious. Nick walked the other direction and eased open the bedroom door. For now, Adam's crib was in their room until he got a little older and from the doorway Nick saw the still form of their son sleeping beneath a light blanket.

"Nicky?" came Caitlin's low whisper from their bed.

"Shhhh," he said, crossing the room. "I sure hope it's me, otherwise you've got some explaining to do."

She was out of the bed by the time he reached the foot, and nothing had felt so good in a very long time as embracing his wife.

*4 September 2054 – Friday, early morning
Alexandria Hospital, Secure Wing – Medical Research
FacilityMedical Research Facility
United Earth Protectorate, Capitol City
Alexandria, Seat of Virginia
North American Continent*

The pre-dawn light made Alexandria Hospital appear silver-gray against a darker gray backdrop, like the historical archive films Michael had watched while trying to absorb as much history and knowledge as he could. He walked toward the front entrance but knew the lack of visible damage from this angle belied the actual damage done to the building in the surprise attack. He had only come once since Monday, not wanting to leave Jacqueline and the rest of the family for too long, and knew the destruction left on some floors.

A total of thirty-seven people had died from the hospital attack. Of those souls, four had been medical staff, nine civilians at the hospital for a variety of reasons but most simply there visiting patients, two were hospital employees, nineteen patients, and three civilian employees. Of the nineteen patients, three had been children.

Learning of the loss of the most innocent had torn apart something deep in him he hadn't felt in a long time. It had been hard to push down the rage. The only thing that finally, although even then he had fought the sorrow, was holding Matthias Matthew and Victoria Grace as they fell asleep on his chest. They knew they were safe and he would always make sure that fact stayed true.

He wouldn't have left them now, but one of the few people who could compel him to leave the house before dawn, was Victor. Victor, who had left Alexandria for reasons no one knew. Who had been gone since, without a word and who now had returned, and needed Michael.

The medical research section of the hospital was dimly lit in comparison to the floors and wards where patients were cared for directly, because most of the space was occupied by labs and offices and storage spaces with little need for individual care except in most rare cases. Such as when Gideon, Daniel, and Phin had been still within their stasis pods and under Katrina's watchful eye. Michael walked the halls by rote, nodding to the few guards he saw along the way, until he reached the room designation Victor had requested he come to specifically. It was on the same level as the research labs, and near to where the now empty pods still remained, but the space was primarily an open-air patient care space with glass windows along the wall that could be covered by curtains if needed. Mostly, the room wasn't utilized.

Until this morning.

Michael saw the low-level lighting as he rounded the corner, and his pace slowed as he realized the room was occupied. By what appeared to be two horizontal pods similar to the ones that had held Michael's brothers and David Forte, but reclined.

Then he saw Victor, slouched forward in a chair near the foot of the pods, with his elbows on his knees and his head in his hands. Michael reached the door and pushed down the handle, pushing inward.

"Victor . . ."

Victor startled and sat up, nearly falling out of the chair as it rolled away from him in his attempt to stand. Dark scruff covered his jaw, and his hair was disheveled. More than anything, he looked exhausted and drained. The five-day beard didn't hide the hollow of his cheeks and the darkness under his eyes.

"Michael," he called, stumbling toward him.

Michael met him, accepting Victor's embrace as much to assure himself the man was there as to support him from falling over. "Where have you been?" Michael asked. "We've been worried."

Victor withdrew, shaking his head. "I didn't know what happened or I would have – I just didn't know. I didn't realize until I came into the city." His dark eyes filled with tears, and his sincere regret and sadness rolled away from him, assuring Michael he was sincere. "I've been terrified to find out – to ask – I—"

"Beverly is well," Michael said, not forcing him to ask the question.

Victor tipped back his head and released a sound like a sigh and a song and a benediction all at once and covered his face with his hands. Not since before his emancipation had Michael seen Victor so distraught, so desperate, so unbalanced.

"She will want to know you're home," Michael said as gently as he could. "She was hurt, but only minor and treated immediately. She was with my father on the way to The Castle when the attack happened."

Victor's eyes widened and his shoulders slumped. "Your father... anyone..."

Dad is fine. Bruised." He paused, knowing the name would hurt. "Karl Bauer was lost."

Victor's jaw fell open and he stumbled back until he bumped the edge of a table and he leaned into it, his palm pressed to the tabletop. He released a long, pained sigh and ran his other hand over his face.

"I should have been here. I should have never left. I didn't know—"

"How could you have?" Michael asked, approaching his friend. Victor's state of mind had him concerned. "Victor, *where* did you go? Why? Who is in the pods?"

Victor dropped his hand from his face, his arm falling limp into his lap in a clear sign of his exhaustion, both physically and mentally. His breathing was rapid and shallow; he needed sleep and at the minimum hydration. Victor slowly raised his head and looked toward the pods.

"They are a memory I had pushed down impossibly deep in a desperate fear my demon would never, ever suspect what I had done. In retrospect, I know now I acted in the early days of my own consciousness pressing through and battling for control."

He pushed away from the table and Michael took a step closer, in case his friend needed his support, but Victor's focus was on the pods. He walked with shuffled steps until he reached the foot of the nearest to them and braced his hands on the top dome. Michael stayed close but moved along the side until he could see inside.

This pod held a man who, by appearance, was probably early fifties, though without knowing how long he had been in the stasis pod his appearance could be deceiving. His hair was either dark brown or black, and his facial features were angular. There was a slight crookedness to his nose, implying it had been broken at some point, and a scar near his hairline. Michael could tell little else for sure but based on the size of the pod and the way the man filled it he was likely over six feet tall.

"The memory has been trying to claw its way free of its own volition, because whether my conscious mind knew of the events, my subconscious mind chipped away at the walls around the existence of these two people since the morning you and I spoke in the nursery. When you told me the fate of your grandmother and grandfather."

A chill . . . a tingle of possibility . . . ran up Michael's spine and over his skin. He snapped his head from looking at the man in the pod to Victor, but he couldn't find his voice. Couldn't form the question.

"It is a story I do not know if I have the strength to tell more than once, because I am tired, Michael. So very tired."

Michael moved to his friend and wrapped his arms around Victor's body to keep him on his feet, helping him to one of the long-forgotten beds in the room. Reaching one, he helped Victor sit, then helped him lift his legs to the mattress as he reclined.

"Your father," Victor said, his eyes already mostly closed. Michael physically felt the energy draining from him. "Bring your father. Your family."

"I will," Michael promised. "Victor, tell me their names."

Victor struggled to open his eyes again, blinking slowly as he looked at Michael with blank eyes. On a long release of breath, he said "Matthias and Grace Tanner. Your father's parents."

CHAPTER TWENTY-FIVE

4 September 2054, Friday – Mid-Morning
Alexandria Hospital, Secure Wing – Medical Research Facility
United Earth Protectorate, Capitol City
Alexandria, Seat of Virginia
North American Continent

"He looks so pale," Beverly said, smoothing her hand over Victor's forehead. She looked to Michael when Victor didn't respond to her touch. "Tell me honestly, Michael. Will he be okay?"

"You know I wouldn't lie to you," Michael said, walking along the other side of the bed to take some biometric readings through the interfaces he'd applied to Victor while he waited for Beverly to arrive. He had kept Victor's return between those he felt needed to know immediately, so he had seen to Victor's care himself. The IV beside the bed provided hydration and some nutrients to help him recover. "I find nothing physically wrong beyond exhaustion and dehydration. I suspect his focus was so intent on his goal, his own care was secondary."

"That's physically."

Michael looked to her when she didn't continue and found Beverly watching him with deep intent. He lowered the PAC tablet he'd been reviewing and focused his attention on her. "I am concerned about his mental and emotional state, but I can't make any judgments on that until he has recovered physically. He was distraught when I arrived, but that could be just as much the exhaustion as anything else. Anyone who had been awake as long as I suspect he has been, and under the stress he has been, would not be themselves." He reached across the span of the bed to lay his hand on her wrist. "Give him time. We are all here for him, and I will not let him battle anything alone. Nor will you, I know."

Beverly turned her head and looked toward the pods behind them. "Do you think they are who Victor says they are? Your grandparents?"

Michael shook his head and set aside the PAC, satisfied with the improvements in Victor's readings. "Honestly, I don't know. I have no way to know. I've never even seen photographs or any other images of my grandparents. Dad may have some at the cabin in Parson's Point, but until recently I didn't know their names."

Beverly smiled, but it was still sad and tired. "I think you, and your dad, look like her."

The same thought had crossed his mind, but he wasn't ready yet to accept the reality of what it all meant. Not that it was unbelievable, because if he knew anything it was as strange as something may seem that didn't exclude the possibility of it being real. He wasn't ready because if they were his grandparents, his father's life was about to change dramatically. He hoped for the better. It was an invaluable gift. But if they weren't Matthias and Grace Tanner, it could be a devastating blow. Victor believed them to be who he said, that was abundantly clear. But Kathleen's hand had been in the events, so nothing was trustworthy.

The sound of voices in the hallway drew his attention, and he looked to the windows to confirm his family had arrived. He had debated with himself if he should have them all come, or just his father, but ultimately, he knew his father enough to know either way he would want family with him. If it were true, his father would want to share it. If it proved not to be true, his father would need them.

"Stay with Victor," he told Beverly, though he doubted he needed to say it, and left the side of his bed to meet his father, mother, and wife at the door.

Michael had waited until after he'd seen to Victor, and after contacting Beverly, before reaching out to his family. His father had finally come home the night before, and Michael had wanted to allow him rejuvenating rest in his own home for as long as possible, but he didn't want his father to leave for The Castle before speaking with them. It wasn't practical to bring all the children, and each hour that passed gave Victor more time to recover himself and be prepared to have the conversation they needed.

But Michael would lay the groundwork.

He met them at the door, opening it so they could come inside. He had left the details vague; only that Victor had returned and the reason he left was important to all of them. His parents walked past him, and as Jacqueline came through the door Michael reached for her to bring her to his side for a kiss. When she drew back, she studied him with drawn brows.

"What's going on, handsome," she asked in the space between them.

"Far too much to explain quickly."

"She's asking the question we all want to ask," Nick said, stopping a few steps into the room with his hands pushed into his pockets.

He glanced down the length of the room, to where Victor rested and Beverly sat vigil, then his eyes darted to the two stasis pods. It would take more than Michael to prepare the pods for extraction. Victor needed to be on his feet, and likely they would need at least Katrina if not more members of the team. This technology was complicated, and their care would be specialized.

"Is Victor okay?" Caitlin asked.

"Yes, but he was near collapse by the time I arrived. I doubt he has slept much since he left Alexandria. He is sleeping, but I know he will want to be woken soon so he can explain himself what made him leave."

"You don't know yet?" his father asked.

"Only in the sparsest of details. He said he would explain everything once you were here."

"So, who is that?"

Michael pressed his lips together and swallowed, not having any idea how to say, or ask, what needed to be said. There was no approach that wouldn't be a shock. Jacqueline squeezed his hand, without a word giving him strength and support.

"I can only tell you who Victor believes it is. You are the only one who can confirm it, Dad."

"Me?"

Knowing they had to be there eventually, Michael led them toward the pods. The room was moderately long, so the few feet walk gave him a few more moments to collect thoughts. He'd hoped clarity would come when the family arrived, but it hadn't. He stopped before any of them would have clear views of the people within the pods and turned back to face his parents.

"Geez, Michael, spit it out," his father said with a shake of his head and motion toward the pods. "I'd say I'm imagining the worst, but there is no scenario – even a worst-case scenario – I can imagine that would explain any of this."

"I don't doubt any of us could have imagined this, and I apologize for my hesitation. I just . . . don't know how to explain." Michael met his father's confused stare. "Victor told me the people in those pods are your parents. Matthias and Grace Tanner."

The moment Michael said parents, the shift in his father's expression was instant. His lips parted and his eyes widened, unblinking.

"What?" Caitlin took a step forward. "Michael, how is that possible?"

"I don't know," he answered, but didn't look away from his father. "Before Victor collapsed, he told me who he believes they are and asked me to bring you here so he can explain."

"Nicky . . . is that possible?"

His father finally blinked and shifted his stare beyond Michael to the pods. Then he took a single step. And another. Moving past Michael to the pod closest to them. The pod that supposedly held

Matthias Tanner. The apprehension radiated from his father like heatwaves off the sidewalk in August. All Michael could do was turn and walk beside his father.

Until they knew, there was nothing else to do.

Nick went to the space between the pods so the man was on his right and woman on his left, bringing both into view at once. Michael waited at the bottom with Caitlin and Jacqueline, unsure if any of them breathed. Waiting.

His father sucked in a sharp breath that made his shoulders draw back with a jerk, and he raised shaking hands to lay them on the glass. He didn't have to speak. Michael felt it almost as real as his father. They were who Victor said. They were Matthias and Grace Tanner. Michael nodded, and kept nodding as he looked to Caitlin, knowing his father couldn't say the words. His heart was both tearing apart and healing in the same moment, and it stole his ability to speak. Michael had to say it for him.

"It's them," he said, his vision blurring with tears for his father. "It's his parents."

Nick bowed his head and cried.

"I don't usually advocate for more coffee, but I think you need it."

Caitlin's arms slid around his shoulders from behind as she lowered a steaming mug in front of his chest and kissed his cheek. Nick took the mug, then closed his eyes and tipped his head into her touch. He had been sitting at the foot of the pods for . . . he didn't even know how long. An hour? More? Watching, like one of them might move and he'd know they really were alive.

But other than the almost indiscernible rise and fall of their chests, because even in stasis they had to breathe, there had been nothing.

"Thank you," he said, opening his eyes again.

She stood and slid her hands up to his shoulders before stepping away from him, walking around to stand between him and the pod that held his mother.

Mom.

Grace Meridian Pryor Tanner.

"Do you need to get it out?"

Nick smiled and took a drink of the coffee. It wasn't the good stuff at home, or maybe it was just better at home because it was at home, but if it delivered caffeine he didn't care. He shifted forward to rest his elbows on his thighs, staring down into the cup.

"I probably do, but all that's going on in my head is this really long scream. Not an angry one. Just . . . aaaaaah!" he finished, waving one hand by his head. "There's a part of my brain that says I'm still asleep, and this crazy-ass week is playing havoc with my brain." Nick looked up at his wife. "But it's not. I'm not asleep."

Caitlin shook her head and reached out to run her fingers through his hair. "No, not asleep. I don't know if even the deepest part of your mind would come up with this one."

Nick set his mug on the floor and stood from the creaky chair, walking to the heads of the pods again. He'd returned to the spot half a dozen times, but each time seeing his parents punched him in the middle of his chest. It had been nearly thirty years since he saw them, but they looked *exactly* like the night they had fought, and he told them to get out of his life.

The memory of it now made his heart hurt, actually *hurt.*

Mom's light brown hair was mussed, with some of it around her face than in the loose bun she often wore it in at her crown. Same freckles he'd counted when he was a little boy, spattered across her nose and cheeks. Same cheekbones and complexion both he, and then Michael, had inherited. He always took more after the Pryor side than the Tanners. At least in looks. Mom used to say, "You are more like your father than you will ever know." In his youth, he'd been proud when she said it because Dad was a superhero; in his cocky twenties he took it as an insult.

And then he would have done anything – *anything* – to take back every angry word and thought he'd ever had.

"I don't understand what the hell I did to earn . . . *this.*" Before

Caitlin could offer an answer, Nick turned to look back at her. "I'd given up, you know. Not like off myself given up, but I didn't give a damn. Not one damn. Three years ago, the world could have exploded, and I wouldn't have flinched. I was done. I was alone, and I was done."

Caitlin tried to smile, but her eyes shined too much to be convincing. He took the two long steps to reach her and took her face in his hands. "Who the hell am I to be given back so much?"

"Has it really been only three years?" she asked.

"Yeah," he said with a half-laugh. "Hell of a three years."

"Nicky, if anyone deserves to be given back what they love, it's you." He shook his head, but she threaded her arms up through his to match the hold, her palms on his cheeks. "You saved the world. You saved all of us. Maybe the universe gave you Michael because you needed a reason to fight. And the universe gave you them for fighting."

"I don't have them yet—"

She nodded, smiling as tears slid from her eyes. "You do. Michael will move heaven and earth to make sure of it. Victor saved them then, so Michael can save them now."

"You're assuming Victor saved them somehow. We don't know how he knew about them, how they got into stasis. I'm curious as hell to hear what he says about this."

"I've no doubt, and I'm happy to oblige."

Nick hadn't heard Victor wake or whatever conversation had to have gone on between him and Michael and Beverly, but he was on his feet. Not steady, but on his feet, and with Beverly holding his hand he made his way to them. He was still rumpled, and except for the first few weeks in Colorado when Victor's battle for control had been craziest, Nick couldn't recall ever even seeing Victor with facial hair.

"I owe everyone a sincere apology," he said when he got to them, bracing his hand on the nearest pod to help him stand. "I admit my departure alone from Alexandria was out of sheer cowardice. I had an overpowering fear that I would have been too late, or my efforts to care for them had been lacking, or that my memory was so defective I was quite possibly finally insane."

"I wish you had trusted us," Beverly said.

Victor shook his head. "It wasn't about not trusting any of you. It was wholly about not trusting myself."

"Well, you're here. *They're* here." Nick left off the "start talking" in his head, because he knew he was torn between joy and anger. Less said the better.

"Right."

As he moved to the chair Nick had previously vacated, the door to the room opened and Jackie came back from wherever she'd gone. Hell, they probably could have all left at some point and Nick wouldn't have noticed. She looked between them and crossed her arms over her body before joining them. Nick had been picking up a different vibe from Jackie all day; the first time he'd seen her since the attack was that morning after Michael reached out to them. She had a buffer around her, and she was tense. Nick couldn't figure it out because he'd never picked up on that from her. Ever.

With Victor seated and Beverly beside him, Nick and Caitlin standing between the pods, and Michael and Jacqueline nearby, Victor leaned back to look him in the eyes and took a deep breath.

"The Sorracchi were on Earth, amongst you, years before anyone knew. Barnabas and Kathleen knew they would eventually make themselves known, but they spent those years investigating, watching, and determining if their goals could be accomplished. From the beginning, they wanted to both create superior husks for the consciousness transfers and create super soldiers like the Triadic that they could control. Humans were going to be little more than cattle for them."

"We know that much," Nick said.

"Yes, however, I'm not sure just how far ahead of 2008 when First Contact was official that they were here. *We* were here. I'm sorry if by excluding myself I sound disingenuous."

"We understand, Victor," Michael said.

Victor nodded. "The first time your planet was observed to determine whether the time was right was late 2001, weeks after what is known in your history as 9/11. The world was in chaos. Wars were happening, threatening to happen. There was racial division and hate crimes. Nations taking sides. Terrorism on the rise. And this was . . . perfect. None of you were alive then, or not old enough to be aware, but shortly after First Contact was public there were a variety of conspiracy theories saying the 'Areth' had been here far longer. As is sometimes true, theories can be real. The Sorracchi had Humans willing to help them find out what they needed to know." He shifted his attention fully on Nick, and his nerves sparked. "What they needed most was access to the most gifted amongst you, whose DNA carried the greatest potential to create . . . power. One name was repeated. Again, and again. Matthias Tanner. While his official military record made no direct mention of it, his highly classified record did."

"What the hell are you talking about?" Nick demanded.

Victor stared at him for several moments, his eyes slightly pinched, and he canted his head. "You don't know."

"Don't know what?"

"Your father's Talents were some of the most impressive – if not *the* most impressive – of his generation."

"Talents?" Nick repeated, shaking his head. "Dad didn't . . . I would have known if he . . ."

"Where do you think Michael's Talents come from?" Victor stood so he could look at both of them, his hand still on the back of the chair. "Michael, I know you have battled for years with the idea that Kathleen *created* you. That she twisted and manipulated your DNA to make you who you are. But she didn't. You were more than she ever anticipated. And that is fully because of the blood that runs in your veins. Tanner blood."

"That's crazy. It's wrong. If Dad had Talents, I would have known."

"I'm sorry, Nick," Victor said, taking a deep breath. "I have relived a great many months and years in the last few days, and I saw the proof. Your father didn't overtly display his abilities, but there was documentation. I'm sure he never intentionally allowed himself to be documented, but those who wanted to know found ways. He came to Kathleen's attention, and she wanted . . . access."

Nick's heartbeat thumped in his ears like ocean waves and his vision blurred. He felt like the top of his head was about to blow off.

"I don't understand," Caitlin said. "If Kathleen wanted Nick's father, why did she wait for so long to deceive Nick? If she knew about his father years before Nick was born?"

"She tried," Victor explained.

Nick turned away to brace his hand on the wall between the pods. He heard their words, but his brain didn't want to hear, and was actively trying to make him ignore them. He bowed his head but forced himself to listen. As absolutely insane as it seemed . . . *what if?*

"Because they weren't known to the world, even if by the name they stole, Barnabas told Kathleen to keep a low profile. A man like Matthias Tanner couldn't just go missing. He would have been missed too quickly, and the search for him too intense. Which meant getting to Matthias Tanner in the most basic way. As a woman. But, by the time she attempted contact Matthias had already met Grace Pryor, and . . . he had little interest in another woman. And once Kathleen knew who Grace Pryor was, she determined it was best to wait."

Nick turned back. "What the hell does *that* mean?"

Victor looked sympathetic when he looked from Caitlin to Nick. "I'm sorry. I realize all this is new information. I suppose I assumed you knew, at least in part, some of this information. At least enough to understand why she chose you to father her . . ." He winced when he finished. ". . . experiment."

"Nah," Nick said through tight lips, his jaw aching from clenching his teeth. "All new information to me."

"Then I am truly, truly sorry. I realize I've said this before when memories come to me, but had I remembered *this* before now – perhaps this more than anything else – I would have spoken sooner. I never would have kept them from you. Any of you."

"Just finish," Nick ground out.

He was pissed. He wasn't exactly sure who he was pissed at, but he was pissed.

Victor nodded, and with his wife's silent urging, he sat again. "Your mother, though on a much smaller scale, had her own Talents. What I recall from the time was that all indicators were that she herself didn't know. And how Kathleen determined this fact, I cannot say, but she decided to allow things to play out naturally between your mother and father and . . . determine a course of action later."

"Meaning did they have kids."

"Yes. I am aware she attempted to gain access to you when you were young; however, it was a failure that enraged Barnabas to such a degree that she was beaten to the point of death for her body before being transferred to another."

"That's a damn shame."

"It was not long after that when David Forte was captured, and she turned her attention to other means of reaching her goal. First Contact had been made but was still in early stages. The Sorracchi were not yet ready to play their hand. She spent years on the Triadic, and as we know, they also were failures in the eyes of Barnabas and his equals. She was ordered again to attempt to resource the Tanner line, and at that point you were an adult."

"And I met Kathy." Saying her name was like licking a urinal.

"Yes." Victor paused, lowering his head. When he looked up again, his features were pinched and strained, and apprehension buffered around him. "Your parents were an obstacle she needed removed. When she feared their influence would possibly sway you, she ordered them killed with the thought it would weaken your resolve."

Nick sniffed, not realizing until he did that the tears had started again. His chest ached and it was hard to breathe. He'd carried guilt for nearly thirty years about the way he had sent them out of his apartment, told them his life was his, and never saw them again. The idea they died *because of him* was suffocating.

"They didn't die, Dad," Michael said, drawing his attention. Michael shook his head, his own eyes full. "You can let that go now. They didn't die, and they're not going to."

Nick shook his head, not ready to take it easy on himself. "So, how did they get from Kathleen's hit list to these pods?"

Victor shifted in the chair, leaning back with his hands together in front of him, working the palms with a scrape of skin against skin. "This . . . body, this version of this body is the last one I received and the transfer of the Sorracchi consciousness occurred just a few decades before the Sorracchi collective reached Earth. We know now that the last transfer was either defective or my mind . . . *my mind* . . . had found some strength to fight the overwrite, and I was breaking through.

"I can't yet explain, and I'm sorry for that, but I don't know the answer. What I know is an order was given to two of Kathleen's blood soldiers and I inserted myself into the assignment without her knowledge. When the time came, I didn't allow it to happen. I killed those sent to do it, I staged the accident as intended with sufficient forensic destruction no one was the wiser, and I secreted them away. Kathleen had no idea I had any connection to the events. I buried that memory so deep, so very deep, the Sorracchi demon commandeering my body never, ever knew. I didn't know, or remember, until Michael told me you had told him how you lost them. It was the first chip in the wall around the knowledge."

"Nicky." Caitlin laced her fingers through his when she said his name, squeezing until he looked at her. "We don't need all the answers right now. We'll figure it out. We'll do it together. Right now, I think the important question is . . . will they wake up okay?" She shifted her attention from Nick to Victor as she asked the question.

Once again, Victor took a deep breath. He looked like Nick felt after partying all weekend when he was in Basic, ready to drop in a bed for three days straight.

"I have every confidence we will be able to draw them out of stasis successfully. Unlike when Kathleen put David into stasis, haphazardly and without actual care for his survival, I had the mental wherewithal and scientific knowledge to complete the process correctly based on all the data stored in the pods. It may be a slow process, because they have been in stasis for a very long time, but it will happen."

Nick nodded and inhaled deep through his nose. "Twenty-four hours ago, this wasn't even a possibility. I guess I can wait."

Caitlin wrapped her arms around him and put her cheek to his chest, and he returned the embrace.

"After all this, I'm going to need a damn vacation, though. Damn it, but it's been a hell of a week."

Caitlin laughed and squeezed him tighter.

One hell of a week.

CHAPTER TWENTY-SIX

4 September 2054, Friday – Some time before midnight
Forte & Santos Residence
Civilian Employee Housing
United Earth Protectorate, Capitol City
Alexandria, Seat of Virginia
North American Continent

Lucy shifted in bed and reached out to David's side, finding an empty space. She opened her eyes and blinked several times to get them adjusted to the dim light in the bedroom and looked to the spot in the bed where he should have been. His side was undisturbed. She sat up and looked to the closed door. Light shined beneath it.

There was nothing in the bedroom to tell her the time, but she thought she had been in bed at least a couple hours, having waited to see if he came home until her eyelids were heavy and she'd almost nodded off while reading on the couch.

Lucy pushed aside the blankets and rose from the bed, pausing at the door before opening it, waiting to hear anything beyond. It was silent. Maybe he fell asleep, so at least he was resting. Once she opened the door, the small hope she had was gone. He sat hunched forward on the couch with papers, notepads, and a large PAC. The large monitor mounted on the wall she'd used her first night in the apartment to educate herself now had streaming data she had no hope of understanding. There were numbers, some letters, but mostly a lot of highly advanced mathematical and scientific symbols that could have just as easily been Egyptian hieroglyphics as much as she knew what they meant.

"David . . ." she said just loud enough he'd hear without startling him.

He looked up and took the pencil out from between his teeth, looked at her, then flipped his hand to read the watch he wore on the inside of his wrist. "Did I wake you up? I was going to just . . ." He trailed off, made a contrite face, and shrugged. "I'm sorry."

She moved around the table to kneel beside him, glancing over the array of work he had spread out, covering the whole tabletop. More stuff she didn't understand. Before she sat, she touched his jaw so he looked at her and gave him a solid kiss. "Are you making any progress? This looks really . . . high level," she asked, sitting back on her bent leg.

David flopped back into the couch and tossed his pencil into the pile. "It's a lot of mechanics and programming I'm trying to mesh together. I have this *big picture* concept of what I need to do." He arched his hands up and out like one of the domes he'd created. "But getting a model worked up to run through some sort of beta prototype is hanging me up."

"Is that something you can do here?"

"Here, like here in the apartment?" He looked at her, groaned and rolled his head. "No. Point taken. I came home a couple hours ago, but my brain doesn't want to shut down and let it go. It's like the answer is right there." David chuckled with a crooked grin. "I remember this scifi show about this Earth guy who was slingshot across the galaxy, and he spends all these seasons trying to figure out how to get home. He'd write equations on walls and floors and stuff. That's what I feel like I'm going to be doing soon."

"This is an expansion of the dome you built in Unity Valley?"

David nodded, raising a hand to rub the top of his head. "Yeah, and the one in Unity Valley is the fifth I've set up, but Nick wants it bigger. Stronger. Preferably global. The plans I have work for a community or city, but I'm skipping right past region and continent."

"Wow."

He gave a single chuckle. "Yeah. Wow. Global had kind of always been the plan, but what happened this week put those plans into overdrive. I've been perfecting on a small scale so it would translate, but I need to skip all the middle parts and get to the end. And by yesterday."

"Is this what you did . . . before . . ." she asked, stuttering over the question, waving one hand at her shoulder to some long past date behind her.

"Building invisible forcefields?" He smirked.

Lucy shook her head, smiling back. "Not that specific. I don't even know what this is. Engineering?"

"This is more programming than engineering, but either way, no," he said, moving his hand to his face, rubbing like it would keep him awake or revive him. "I went to college for criminal justice and had a computer science double major. Then I joined the military after 9/11. I was stationed in the Middle East, but my focus was computer forensics, hacking, that kind of thing. Then Homeland Security, when became Home*world* Security after First Contact. I always had a knack for computers and computer language. If you can get a computer to understand what you want, it'll figure out how to do it for you."

"And this is what you're trying to do . . . figure out how to tell a computer what you want."

"Yeah, basically." His last word was lost in a long yawn. "I'm sorry," he said at the tail end of the yawn. "It's been a hell of a week. I know none of this was what you planned when you came to Alexandria."

Lucy chuckled. "David, I don't think any of the last couple of weeks would have been what anyone planned. Besides, I didn't come to Alexandria for the culture or night life. I came to Alexandria to be with you."

He dropped his hands to rest in his lap and focused on her,

drawing in a long, deep breath through his nose. "I keep thinking about what could have happened on Monday. You could have been hurt, or worse, just because you came with me. Unity Valley didn't even know anything happened until *we* contacted *them*."

Lucy was shaking her head before he finished, shifting closer to him so she could lean in, close to his face. "Stop it, David Forte. Nothing happened to me, and since the past isn't going to change, it doesn't matter."

He tilted his head so it rested on the couch cushion, but still watched her, his gaze shifting over her face. Lucy inhaled and laid her hand on his cheek, rough with the day's growth of beard. "Besides, here I can at least see you and know you're okay. If I were in Unity Valley, and heard about the attack, I'd never sleep until I saw you again." Lucy raised up enough she could press a kiss to the center of his forehead. "Because I love you, too."

One corner of his mouth tipped up, creating the deep grin dimple she loved when he really smiled, then the other corner. "Yeah?"

"I don't bake my biscuits for just anyone, you know."

"You'd better not," he said with a wink. "I'm jealous about my biscuits."

Lucy laughed. "Okay, this is getting weird."

The tentative knock at the apartment door made Lucy jump. David was off the couch and halfway to the door when Katrina's soft voice came through the wood. "David? Lucy? Are you awake?"

Lucy followed David, getting off the couch just as he opened the door to reveal the petite woman, red eyed and wet cheeks, standing in the hallway with her arms wrapped around her own body. Before David could say anything, she sucked in a shaky breath and her face contorted into a sob. David pulled her into the apartment and into his embrace.

"Aw, Peanut," he said, shutting the door as she cried. "Where is Phin? Why are you alone?"

Lucy couldn't get every word but managed to pick up enough from the girl's muffled answer to understand something had kept Phin and Daniel with the president and they wouldn't be home for a couple more hours. And she just didn't want to be alone.

"Come sit down," David said, drawing Katrina to the couch. He looked up at Lucy as she took a step back. "Maybe Katrina would benefit from some of your tea."

Lucy nodded and backtracked to the kitchen. The poor girl could use some calm and rest.

5 September 2054, Saturday
Alexandria Hospital
United Earth Protectorate, Capitol City
Alexandria, Seat of Virginia
North American Continent

"I was just barely getting used to walking through a city without seeing as many hovers and other vehicles in the streets. The last time I was in a city was before the War, and the streets were full. Then here, there were so few of them, and most military. Now ... it's just eerie."

David glanced sideways to Lucy as they walked through the city. They had seen very few people, most of which were either military or citizens working with the military to clean up, fortify, or rebuild what had been damaged.

"So, not long before I went into the deep freeze there was this television show about some kind of plague wiping out most everyone in the country, making them into zombies."

"Eww!" Katrina declared, making him chuckle. "Why would you make a show about that?"

"It wasn't so much about the zombies, but the people trying to survive and not become one. The zombies aren't the point here, Peanut. The point is I watched some of the early episodes and the cities and towns were like this. Quiet. Empty."

"Oh, that makes me feel so much better."

David laughed, despite Katrina's side-eye glare. "Okay, so maybe zombie apocalypse wasn't the best comparison. My bad."

The walk from the apartment complex to Alexandria Hospital only took forty minutes, despite having to divert around areas of construction or damage. On a normal day, it would take less than half that time, which was why so many citizen employees lived in the same building. Easy walk. They entered through a secure, employee and approved personnel access only and not the front entrance where David and Lucy had been when the attack happened days before. From this entrance the damage was less noticeable, which led David to think the ones attacking were going for big picture hits and not fine points. The Urdo Khantan could have destroyed months of research and development with a well-placed hit. They still did plenty of damage in the way of lives lost and facilities damaged.

Katrina slipped her hand into his as they went through the doors, and he realized with an internal curse that this was probably the first time she'd returned to the hospital since Monday and since Karl had died here.

"I'm sorry, Peanut," he said as gently as he could.

She didn't look at him, but nodded, her mouth set firm.

"Where do we go first?" he asked. "We're a little early to meet Phin. He said one, so we've got almost forty-five minutes."

"Let's go see your friend," Katrina offered quickly.

David nodded. The next stop after checking on Tessera would be the medical research facility where Katrina and Karl had worked with Victor. They had learned Karl wasn't there when he died, but it didn't mean his ghost of memories wouldn't be. David was only slightly familiar with the layout of the hospital, and it was fairly limited to where he'd recovered after waking up and where most of his rehabilitation had happened. He knew where labs and offices were in relation to that space and had a general idea of where patient rooms would be in the secure wing where Tessera was being kept – because of both her condition and her relationship to Michael – so he let Katrina lead the way.

Both David and Katrina were known by military personnel, but they had to sign Lucy in as a visitor and asked that she remain in patient areas only. The hallway where Tessera was being cared for was quiet, and David assumed it was probably because the general care area of the secure wing wasn't as utilized as other parts of the hospital. The parts hit hardest by the attack.

He still wondered whether that was intentional or not.

Tessera was in an ICU-type room with glass windows rather than walls, so any doctor or nurse could see what might be happening in the room, but despite it being mid-day the room was dim with the blinds drawn. The only light sources were the monitors situated around the bed and a low-level light above the headboard. Katrina led the way, pressing the hydraulic button to slide open the door with a hiss and cool, oxygenated air blew in their faces. A low, steady beep came from one of the monitors.

"*Dios Mio,*" Lucy whispered. "She's so . . ."

"She's fading away," Katrina said, moving to the side of the bed near the foot. "I mean, I only saw her briefly in the infirmary when they brought you down, but she looks so . . ."

"Small," Lucy finished.

She didn't respond when they spoke, didn't react at all. The room was cool, but not cold, and she was covered to her neck with blankets. Electronic lines and IV tubes disappeared beneath the blankets. Her head was raised slightly, and when David took another step closer, his heart jumped to his throat.

Tessera had been thin the first time he remembered seeing her, up on that mountain, but nothing he didn't think a good cheeseburger and fries on a regular basis wouldn't help. He'd been amazed such a slight woman could have somehow gotten him back to the cabin. But now . . . she was emaciated.

He looked down and away. "Geez, can't they give her more . . . nutrition or whatever it is they do? She's starving."

"They are," Lucy said, and he glanced toward where she stood at the foot of the bed scanning the tablet that had hung at the bottom. Of the three of them, Lucy would be the one to have any kind of understanding of her treatment. "They keep increasing her caloric input. They're giving her over six thousand calories a day right now."

"What the hell? What's wrong with her?"

Lucy scowled, her dark eyes shifting back and forth as she read. "She's been running a low-grade fever for about four days now, but nothing of concern. They are keeping her hydrated and nourished as best they can, but they've had to increase it every day since she arrived. Her brain activity is low but present. She isn't reacting to any sort of stimuli. She's just . . . wasting away. Quite literally."

David moved to the head of the bed, studying Tessera's ashen, sunken features. He stared at her, trying to equate her to the woman who had stood her ground making sure he understood she was the boss in her house. That she would not go back to Unity Valley. Told him she had somehow brought him to the cabin. The woman who fed him and treated him as best she could. Much of it was a haze, but he knew – *he knew* – this woman was a pale shadow of that woman.

What was wrong?

"How does this work," he said, not really asking a question because it was a question that would have no answer. "Since we came back from Unity Valley, I've gotten stronger. *Every* single day. I shouldn't be, but I am. It's 2054, medicine and technology are way past anything I could have ever imagined, and doctors don't know why I'm thriving and she's dying. Not to lessen the benefit, but I'm pretty damn sure it's not just the tea."

Lucy's small gasp made David turn. Her cheeks had gone pale and her eyes wide. "Lucy . . ." he said, and she raised her chin to look at him. "What? What does it say?"

"I'm not sure I understand it completely, but . . ."

He took a step toward her and she focused again on the tablet, blinking rapidly before she read. "Hypothetical diagnosis of psychokinetic transference of life-sustaining electrical activity from patient to second party, resulting in patient levels incompatible with life. No course of treatment determined. The notation was made by Victor just a couple days prior to the attacks."

David went cold.

"There's an attached annotation." She looked up at him. "Should I open it? I mean, am I breaking some rules?"

"Open it," David choked out.

She blinked again and tapped the screen. Lucy read for a moment, her eyes shifting, before she cleared her throat. "Anecdotal evidence based on conversation with Doctor Tanner has produced a hypothetical scenario based on shared experience and knowledge of patient's origins that patient known as Tessera may have utilized extreme psychokinetic abilities otherwise known as Talents to transfer life energy from herself to David Forte who suffered life threatening injuries. It is unknown if patient Tessera intended for transfer of strength to be permanent or at such an extreme level to diminish her ability to sustain her own life. Current treatments have only succeeded in maintaining life without further decline, but no marked improvement. No known treatment options; no known method of halting process while patient remains unresponsive. Anecdotal parallels indicate that since patient initiated the process, patient must initiate termination of process."

"Oh, no . . ." Katrina's cry broke his dazed silence.

"She's dying because of me?" His voice boomed in the room, and he flinched at his own shouting.

"I-I-so much of this is hypothetical medicine—there's nothing I would have or could have learned in medical school to explain this—"

"She's dying because of *me*," he snapped again.

Lucy looked up, her eyes shining, and when she blinked tears streaked her cheek. "She's dying, but David—"

She stopped, staring at him wide-eyed. David gripped the safety bar on the side of Tessera's bed, lowered his head and closed his eyes trying to push down the undefined rage in his chest. He didn't know if he was angry because he was the cause or because she was stupid enough to think he was worth dying for.

He slammed his hand against the rail, turned, and left the room. Lucy called after him, but for once he needed space more than he needed her. Maybe by the time he got what he came for he'd be able to talk again.

Alexandria Hospital, Secure Wing – Medical Research Facility
United Earth Protectorate, Capitol City
Alexandria, Seat of Virginia
North American Continent

Katrina walked with purpose to the storage room of the shared office spaces in the research wing, in the opposite direction of the office she had shared with Karl. She knew she would eventually have to go into the room, transfer Karl's work and research into her own workspace, and remove his personal items amongst the clutter on his desk, but not today. She wasn't ready today.

She didn't know when she'd be ready. But it wasn't today.

David followed close behind. He'd been silent since leaving Tessera's room, and she'd had to run to catch up with him in the hallway. She was in shock after what Lucy had read; she couldn't imagine what David felt.

Her heart hurt for him. She wanted to hug him until it was all fixed but knew it wouldn't help. Not really.

The lights illuminated as they moved into the rooms. With Victor gone, and since it was Saturday, no one else was there. Though, she wouldn't have been surprised if Ngoju had been in his space. He seemed to always be there. Sometimes she wondered if he lived anywhere else. Kind of like thinking the teachers lived in the schools when she was little.

"Carmen thought this might help with development of our own galactic travel ships," she explained as she took a tablet from the wall by the door and it engaged. She scanned to the inventory grid until she found the technology in question. "She'd made some progress with Ngoju, but some of our focus shifted and it got set aside. I'm pretty sure she won't be coming back to the project until after things calm down."

"Probably not, no." David said, standing at the door as she went to the designated storage locker. His voice was so much heavier than usual. "You said it creates holographic schematics?"

"Yes." She typed in her code and pressed two of her five fingers to the biometric scanner, waiting for the lock to disengage. The volume of technology in that room alone was staggering and kept under extensive levels of security. "Expandable, too. You could probably easily fill your living room with it. Or a bigger space if needed. She said eventually she could program a space where you could walk around and see everything like you're really there. It would shift as you move and stuff."

"So, like a holodeck. Cool. Captain Picard would be jealous."

Katrina removed the holovid projection platform and computer interface from the safe and turned, holding it out for David. He came forward with two long steps and took it. "Who is Captain Picard? Is he a Firebird?"

David made a weird sound between a snort and a chuckle. "Uh . . . no. Never mind. Wrong century. I keep forgetting."

"Okay."

"I appreciate this, Peanut. I hope it can work for what I need."

"Anything we can offer to help," she said, her throat tightening so fiercely it surprised her. "We need to be safe, right?'

"Right," David said with a gentler tone that only made the choking emotion worse.

A noise from the main space drew their attention, and David turned to clear her view. Phin walked to the middle of the room and looked in her direction. The corner of his lips tipped up in the smallest of smiles, but it was enough to make Katrina's heart expand.

"Have you completed what you needed to accomplish?" he asked, looking from her to David. "We have a few more minutes if needed."

"I don't know," David said, nodding to the tech equipment he held. "Is this everything you wanted to give me?"

"Yes. I'm sorry. I don't have a manual or anything."

"Nah, I'll figure it out. Not a problem." He leaned toward her and kissed her cheek. "See you later, Peanut. Have fun doing whatever it is you're off to do."

"I would question your definition of fun, Father."

David pulled up short and dropped his jaw open, staring at Phin. "Did you . . . did you just use *sarcasm*?"

Phin canted his head and raised an eyebrow. David barked a laugh and shifted what he carried so he could pat Phin on the shoulder as he passed. "I don't think I've ever been prouder," he said with a false hitch in his voice.

Katrina followed David until she reached her husband, and once David was out the door, she raised herself up on her toes for a kiss and her husband obliged. He wrapped an arm around her to hold her close but looked down at her with small shifts of his eyes.

"What troubles you? Is it the same that troubles my father?"

She drew in a long breath through her nose, nodding, not even remotely surprised Phin knew something was wrong despite David's joke as he left. She did her best to explain what Lucy had read and how she understood it, and how David had reacted.

"It sounded like maybe it all tied back to . . ." She tried not to make a face but failed. "Her. You know who. Does that make sense? Do you think it's possible?"

Phin released her and took her hand leading her toward the door. "It's possible. My brothers and I don't share this ability; however, we were also created and engineered with the bionanetic technology to heal us when injured. Though, I cannot imagine she would intentionally assure one of her creations would have this ability because it would require compassion. An emotion she stifled with prejudice."

"Oh, don't say creation like that. I don't like it," Katrina said with a scowl. "You're not a creation. You're my husband."

"Nonetheless, I exist because of her."

Katrina shook her head and squeezed his hand as they walked. "So, what is it you needed me for here at the hospital?"

"I am delivering you to the one who does. It's not far; just down the hall. Which made finding you here quite convenient."

"Hmmm . . . color me intrigued."

"Victor, I'm worried about you. If you don't rest, you won't be able to do all it is you want to do." Beverly stepped beside his chair and laid her delicate hand on his shoulder, sending a warm, comforting wave through him and he raised his head to look up at his wife. "And I miss you at home."

Victor laid his hand over hers on his shoulder. "I know, *Cusbibil*. I intend to be home today once I feel our patients are stable and without concerns until we are ready to act. Phin is bringing Katrina here shortly. Other than myself, Katrina is the most knowledgeable of stasis equipment and technology amongst my team. Together, we will work this out."

"Do you promise you will come home to me tonight?"

Victor stood, his chair rolling away from him as he gained his feet and wrapped his arm around Beverly's waist to draw her to him. "I promise, my love."

"I have returned," came Phin's voice from the main room where the stasis pods holding Matthias and Grace Tanner still waited.

Victor gave his wife a far too short kiss before taking her hand as he moved aside the privacy curtain he'd used to shield the desk he'd set up. They had drawn all curtains along the glass window walls that normally would be opened to theoretically give medical staff visibility to patients. It had been before the war when this part of the hospital had been used for patient care, which had been one of the reasons he and his team had taken over the rooms for their research. Now the room returned to its original purpose.

Katrina had only made it a few steps into the room, her full attention trained on the pods. Unlike many other people, she would have known what they were the moment she stepped into the space. Victor watched, silent, curious of what her response would be. She left her husband's side, so focused she hadn't looked around the room to see who he might have called out to when they entered and went to the end of the pod holding Matthias Tanner. Katrina canted her head, studying the man, then just as Victor predicted she moved to the panel along the side with continuous streaming biometric data.

"Once again, I call upon your knowledge and assistance," Victor said.

Katrina's head snapped around and she stared, wide-eyed, for three solid seconds before running across the room. Victor had no choice but to open his arms and accept her embrace, but he did with a chuckle. But the chuckle died when he realized the girl holding on to him shook with silent tears and he recalled with a slam to his chest that her brother – a member of his team – had died in his absence. Victor wrapped his arms tighter around her and pressed his cheek to her hair.

"I am so sorry, child," he said, closing his eyes. "I am sorry I wasn't here for you. For any of you."

Katrina drew back from him, looking up with wet cheeks. "Where were you? Are you okay?"

"I'm fine." Victor nodded toward the pods. "I was retrieving our newest patients, a story which is quite long and most likely more confusing than would be helpful. As I said, I hope you might be willing to assist me with the process of removing them safely."

Katrina swiped her fingers across her cheeks and went back to the pods, Victor following. Beverly touched his arm only long enough to draw his attention to say she would see him at home. He nodded and joined Katrina where she stood between the ends of the pods, the same position Nick Tanner had taken the previous day. From there, she looked at the biometric readings for Grace just as she had Matthias.

"Their readings look very good. How long have they been in stasis?"

"Nearly thirty years."

She looked at him again, wide-eyed. "Thirty years? Who put them in stasis? These pods are different than the ones from the *Abaddon*."

"I did," Victor answered.

Her wide-eyed surprise shifted to confusion, and she looked again to the people in the pods. "But . . . who are they?"

Victor took the last few steps to bring him to the pods and set his hand on the one holding Grace. He inhaled deeply and released it before answering. "Before I tell you, please forgive me for reiterating a fact you already know. But sometimes the question of who knows what can be unclear. I ask that you not speak of their identity to anyone I do not specify."

"Of course."

"The only people who know the true identity of our patients are the whole of the Tanner family, including Connor Montgomery and his wife, and Phin and Daniel and Beverly." Victor smiled, hoping it would ease the shock. "It would be quite mean of me, I think, to force you to keep secrets from your husband."

Katrina looked over her shoulder to Phin, who stood back with his hands tucked behind his back. She grinned. "Oh, I know my husband has secrets." Then she focused on Victor again, waiting for his answer.

It grew easier with each telling, but still stirred something deep in Victor's soul that ached for the truths connected to the revelation. More than just the events around Matthias and Grace Tanner were released with this influx of memories; dark and haunting and would likely keep him awake many nights. He didn't know – yet – if any of the memories were beneficial to anything in 2054, but until then he would keep them tucked away from the hearts of those he loved.

"They are Matthias and Grace Tanner. The parents of President Nicholas Tanner, whom he believed to have died when he was a very young man."

Her already wide eyes widened more, and he held his breath until she blinked, then she blinked rapidly and looked back to the two people frozen in time.

"I don't think I ever thought about his parents," she said, her voice low. "I mean, so many people have lost so many people . . ." Her voice broke over the last words.

"So many of those losses are because of the Sorracchi," Victor said, giving her a reprieve from trying to say more. "I know you are aware of only parts of my history, other than I was amongst them for centuries and emancipated before the war."

She looked back at him, her eyes shining, and she nodded.

"The Sorracchi we call Kathleen—"

"Heinous bitch," she mumbled with a shaky smile and a flush of pink to her cheeks for saying a word usually beyond her vocabulary.

Victor smiled. "Yes, one and the same. She ordered these people murdered, and in a battle – a moment – I only recalled recently, I stopped the order and did the only thing I could think to do."

"Place them in stasis."

He nodded. "Yes, and then promptly and quite literally forced myself to forget the entire thing." Victor swallowed and pushed his hands into his pockets. "I realize this may cloud your opinion of me—"

"No!" she declared, stepping toward him. "No, Victor, not at all. You're amazing. This is . . . amazing. I'm happy to help. Thank you."

Victor nodded, forcing himself to swallow before he took a deep breath through his nostrils. "Thank you. The process of removing them will hopefully be easier and less stressful on *them* than David experienced, or even Phin and his brothers." He glanced toward Phin again. "The Tanner children were in a different type of stasis, but some of the principals remain."

"When do you want to remove them?"

"They are stable, and other than Nick having a strong urge to see them awake, I don't wish to rush the process. If we manage within the next week or two, I will be pleased."

Katrina nodded. "Yes. Okay." She smiled, but it was soft and touched with sadness. "Thank you for giving me something good to do. I know none of this was done for my benefit, but I appreciate it all the same."

Victor lowered his chin in a single nod.

CHAPTER TWENTY-SEVEN

29 September 2054, Tuesday – 7:17am
Forte & Santos Residence
Civilian Employee Housing
United Earth Protectorate, Capitol City
Alexandria, Seat of Virginia
North American Continent

Lucy came awake at a sound that was enough to break her sleep, but not distinctive enough she knew what it was when she opened her eyes. She blinked against the sun coming through the blinds and took in a deep breath. It wasn't necessary to check the other side of the bed. She knew it was empty.

She got out of bed, showered and dressed, and braided her damp hair while she pan fried a couple slices of bread for breakfast from a loaf she'd made over the weekend. It wasn't worth making much more for just herself. Lucy had spent months cooking for dozens of people, and when she'd cooked for herself and David it was often more than enough for a couple days. Without him at home, the process of cooking seemed excessive.

David had slept at home, in bed with her, four times in the last near three weeks. Sometimes three or four days went by without her seeing him while she was awake, though she often found proof he'd been home while she slept. She made sure there were always cookies, biscuits, or other grab-and-go foods for him, and the depletion of her supply was sometimes the only sign he'd been there.

That and the notes he would leave. They weren't very long, and sometimes just telling her she was beautiful and he missed her. Always signed *"Love you . . . David."*

She didn't want it to bother her, but in truth, she missed him. She understood. She knew he felt he had to find the solutions the president asked for. He was driven to do whatever he could, even if that meant pushing himself to exhaustion, and that worried her more than anything else. She also worried he felt the need to be worthy of the life Tessa might ultimately give so he could live. He'd regained his body because of her, but how far could he push before it was too much?

But she missed him.

8:42 AM

When the world changed and Lucy became a part of Unity Valley, she just assumed things like entertainment programming and global broadcast news no longer existed. One evening, when she sat alone in the apartment trying to educate herself on all the changes in the world, she discovered 24/7 news feeds.

There were dozens of channels, and it took her three days to shift through them all. There were streams by region, streams by continent, and streams that consolidated everything. In a matter of a week, she learned some heartbreaking truths. First, the life she lived in Unity Valley was idyllic in comparison to so many. Second, she had been naïve to imagine her life after the war was somehow the norm. They didn't have many of the medicines they wanted, and had to make do, but no one ever went hungry, and everyone had shelter and care and support.

So many in the world did not.

There were places left decimated.

Some news streams applauded the Tanner administration for their efforts. Some focused on shortcomings, saying President Tanner wasn't doing enough.

Regardless, the world had so much healing to do.

9:36 AM
ALEXANDRIA HOSPITAL, GENERAL CARE
UNITED EARTH PROTECTORATE, CAPITOL CITY
ALEXANDRIA, SEAT OF VIRGINIA
NORTH AMERICAN CONTINENT

"What had occurred since, calculated to change and my relative positions? Yet now, how distant and far estranged we were! So far estranged, that I did not expect him to come and speak to me. I did not wonder, when, without looking at me, he took a seat at the other side of the room, and began conversing with some of the ladies.

"No sooner did I see that his attention was riveted on them, and that I might gaze without being observed, than my eyes were drawn involuntarily to his face; I could not keep their lids under control: they would rise, and the iris would fix on him. I looked, and had an acute pleasure in looking – a precious yet poignant pleasure: pure gold, with a steely point of agony: a pleasure like what the thirst-perishing man might feel when who know the well to which he has crept is poisoned, yet stoops and drinks divine draughts nevertheless.

"Most true is it that 'beauty is in the eye of the gazer.' My master's colourless, olive face, square, massive brow, broad and jetty eyebrows, deep eyes, strong features, firm grim mouth, – all energy, decision, will, – were not beautiful, according to rule; but they were more than beautiful to me; they were full of an interest, an influence that quite mastered me, – that took my feelings from my own power and fettered them in his. I had not intended to love him; the reader knows I had wrought hard to extirpate from my soul the germs of love there detected; and now, at the first renewed view of him, they spontaneously arrived, green and strong! He made me love him without looking at me."

"What is that from?" asked Aolani, one of the nurses on the floor that Lucy had talked with several times, standing in the doorway to Tessa's room.

Lucy paused in her reading, using her thumb to hold the spot in the worn paperback novel she'd managed to find. "It's *Jane Eyre*," she answered. "I'm not sure if it's the type of novel she'd like, but I wanted to try something. And my choices were limited. It was either this or *Moby Dick*."

"It's really good of you to come visit her. Do you know her?"

Lucy nodded, looking back to Tessa who had yet to acknowledge her presence in the two weeks she had been coming to visit. "We were both part of the same community in Vancouver before coming to Alexandria. I can't say I knew her well, but I did know her."

"Well, it's still good of you to come."

"Thank you."

11:47 AM
PRESIDENTIAL RESIDENCE
UNITED EARTH PROTECTORATE, CAPITOL CITY
ALEXANDRIA, SEAT OF VIRGINIA
NORTH AMERICAN CONTINENT

"Your help is appreciated so much, Lucy," First Lady Caitlin Tanner said as she settled on the blanket they had spread on the side yard of the presidential residence.

She sat crisscross with her son Adam, just a few weeks older than his younger nephews and niece, sitting in her lap leaning against his mother's body. The age gap was small, but at this stage things seemed to happen overnight, and Adam had mastered holding up his head and looking around while gripping his mother's fingers.

Lucy looked up from making faces at Gideon Paul as he tried to lift his head from the blanket and focus on her features. His eyes were wide, his mouth open, and he managed to hold up his head for several seconds before resting again. She rubbed his back and smiled.

"Oh, I don't mind at all. I love babies. We were a small community and only had one or two infants at any given time, but I always was happy to help with them." She sat up, then rolled Gideon Paul onto his back, with tummy time being done, and switched her attention to Matthias Matthew. "I also appreciate feeling like I'm contributing somehow."

"I don't care who wants you for anything else," Jackie Tanner said at the end of a jaw-cracking yawn. "If you want to move in, I'm cool with that. I knew, logically, four babies would be a lot of work but damn..."

Lucy exhaled and shook her head. "I doubt anything could have actually prepared you for this. Except perhaps someone else who also had quads and could explain."

"Even then, I don't know anyone else would understand," Caitlin said, offering a compassionate smile to her daughter-in-law.

Who didn't see it because she'd leaned back and braced herself with her extended arms and lifted her face to the sun. Caitlin turned the smile on Lucy and gave a small shrug.

Lucy had been coming to the residence for a week and a half to help the two new mothers to keep them from being overrun by five newborns and a toddler. It had been an odd chain of conversation to get her there, beginning when Katrina and the boys had stopped at the apartment to check on her, and Katrina casually mentioned how she'd heard the struggles of the two ladies. Messages shifted through various chains of communication, but within two days Lucy's presence at the residence was a daily thing.

They'd also been ecstatic when she said she could improve on the supplemental baby formula they had to resort to since there was no way Jackie alone could feed four. Even with breastmilk donations they'd been able to set up, there sometimes seemed not quite enough. When the Quads were born, the hospital had means to provide special formula to help, but since the attack they hadn't been able to provide as much. A few months before in Unity Valley, a new mother had been unable to produce enough milk for her baby and Lucy had helped Doctor Dardashti create a supplement. It wasn't a primary source of nutrition, but it served as a great addition.

Jackie Tanner wasn't the only mother in the city who needed milk supplementation. John and Jenifer Smith had a little one and donations of milk along with the baby formula were their sole source of nutrition for Toby.

What else did she have to do? She meant it when she said she wanted to contribute somehow.

But what she had observed very quickly, and the Tanners confirmed, was the Quads acted and reacted to everything in tandem. It reminded her a small bit of what she'd seen with Phin and Daniel, but not nearly at that level. Not like they were psychic, or talented, or whatever it was called. She was both in awe of the concept of Talents, but also hadn't quite wrapped her head around the same concepts. The Quads were only reminiscent Phin and Daniel in that the babies slept at the same time, fussed at the same time, were calm at the same time. It was wonderful when they were happy but harrowing when they weren't.

The sound of running feet on the porch served as vanguard for Nicole's return, and moments later she ran across the yard toward them with Dog beside her and her father not far behind.

5:47 PM
UNITED EARTH PROTECTORATE, CAPITOL CITY
ALEXANDRIA, SEAT OF VIRGINIA
NORTH AMERICAN CONTINENT

Lucy chuckled at Katrina's wide yawn as they rode in the transport hover together from the residence back into Alexandria proper. Katrina must have heard her because her cheeks flushed and she smiled as she managed to finish the yawn.

"It's not the company, I swear," Katrina said. "Just a really busy day."

"You've been working hard for a few weeks now."

Katrina nodded. "Yeah, but it's a good kind of busy. I feel like I'm doing something really good."

Lucy smiled at the parallel to her own thoughts earlier in the day.

"You're helping David," Lucy led.

"For part of the day, yes. But I'm also helping Victor with . . ." She caught herself, her eyes widening behind her glasses. "With a project he kind of brought back with him."

Lucy held up a hand. "Don't worry. It didn't take long to figure out I'm often around people who can't openly chitchat about work around me. I know what David is working on, but then again, I'm pretty sure I don't know everything. And . . ." She canted her head and tried to look amused and convinced at the same time. "I'm okay with that. I guess I have to get used to it."

Katrina looked over her shoulder to the front of the hover where Daniel and Phin navigated. It had become a routine, once Lucy started going to the residence every day, that Phin and Daniel would bring Katrina with them when they took President Tanner home in the evening – ending their regular time with him – and would pick up Lucy to take everyone home. Her days were pretty similar. Walk to the hospital to see Tessa, then catch a scheduled transport set up for her from the hospital to the residence where she spent the afternoon helping. Then ride back to the apartments with the Forte family. Maybe eat. Maybe read. Sleep. Repeat.

"I know there are a lot of things Phin can't tell me," Katrina said, and when she said his name, her husband glanced back to her with the tiniest tip of his mouth. "I mean, the stuff I do the president knows and since he knows they probably know, too."

She was grinning when she looked back at Lucy.

"I like our daily commute together." She smiled wider, the kind of smile that lit up her eyes. "Hey, if you and David get married you'll be like my mother-in-law."

It took the remainder of their ride to even begin to process the information.

6:10PM
CIVILIAN EMPLOYEE HOUSING
UNITED EARTH PROTECTORATE, CAPITOL CITY
ALEXANDRIA, SEAT OF VIRGINIA
NORTH AMERICAN CONTINENT

"Good night, Lucy," Katrina said with a wave when they split directions at the elevator. "See you tomorrow."

"Good night," she said back, waving.

Even when she was tired herself, Katrina had a way of energizing those around her and as soon as they parted ways the tired settled over Lucy again. The Tanners always offered to have her stay for dinner, but she never did because they deserved the time together, so as she walked toward the apartment door, she mentally ran inventory of what she had on hand to eat. Not much. Maybe she'd have more toast.

She smelled something savory and mouthwatering when she reached the door and paused to inhale. If it was coming from one of the other units, the smell inside their apartment had to be intense. Garlic and oregano and tomatoes. Lucy envied her neighbors and put the key in the lock to open the door.

To be greeted by a succulent wave of aromas.

She stopped in the open doorway, her hand still on the doorknob, caught off guard by what met her. David was at the stove, his back to the door. Because of the half wall dividing the kitchen from the living area, she only saw him from the waist up, but he had a hand towel tossed over his left shoulder and his head bopped side to side to music she only heard when she stepped inside. It was something old, so old she couldn't name the performer or song. The lyrics were a mishmash of bullet points that David only seemed to remember parts of because he mumbled parts and sang others.

Lucy stepped in and closed the door, David so enthralled in his solo performance he didn't hear it.

"Wheel of Fortune, Sally Ride, heavy metal suicide, foreign debts, homeless vets, AIDS, crack, Bernie Goetz," he sang along, then mumbled a bit before singing again, "Rock and roll, the cola wars . . ." Then David tipped back his head and shouted with the song, "I can't take it anymore!"

She laughed and he spun around, stumbling, then smiled wide when he saw her. He tossed the towel on the counter and met her halfway. Before she could say anything, David took her face in his hands, the sweet smell of oregano mingling with the tang of garlic on his skin, and only paused for a second to look her in the eyes before he kissed her. It had been days since they'd been able to share more than brief touches, and in that moment, she realized how hungry she was for him. How starved she was for his touch. How quickly she'd become addicted.

Lucy wrapped her arms around him to lay her palms on his back, pressing against him to give fully to the kiss. What might have been intended as a kiss of greeting, a kiss of hello, shifted into a kiss to quench a thirst, to feed a need. She tilted her head and parted her lips to him, a low purr curling in her throat when his tongue slid along hers. Instantly, every part of her hummed.

When David stopped the kiss, still holding her face between his warm palms, a sharp wave of disappointment dulled the spark. He moaned in a sound that matched her feelings, and she opened her eyes as she inhaled again.

"I have missed you," he said in a low voice between them, stroking his thumb across her lip. "Damn, woman, I've missed you."

"I've missed you, too. How long can you stay?"

His smile curled up enough to reveal the dimple in his cheek she loved. "Until tomorrow morning." The grin widened. "The program is running a simulation, and I get the night off. So, I made dinner for you tonight for once." David ran the tip of his tongue over his lower lip, his gaze shifting down to her mouth. "And trust me, if it weren't hot on the stove, I'd forget about it." He slid the side of his nose against hers, and as simple a touch it was, it made it hard to think.

"We have all night?"

He hummed his affirmative. "Yes, we do. Sit down. I'll have everything served up in a few minutes. It's nothing fancy, and Nana Forte probably would roll over in her grave knowing I used boxed pasta, but Trader Joe's was out of the fresh stuff."

He gave her one last, far too brief, kiss that was too short and too light to ease anything before going back to the kitchen. Lucy went to the table that was already set with two plates, some sliced bread, and a bottle of red wine. Whoever Joe was, he might have been out of pasta but the fact he had wine was impressive.

David gave voice instruction for the music to change and decrease volume, and soft, jazzy music played. Jazz was timeless.

"Are you just getting back from the Tanners'?" David asked, stirring the fragrant pot of whatever he'd made.

Lucy nodded and poured the wine into the two glasses he'd set out. They weren't wine glasses, but the wine would taste just as good. "I'm going almost every day now," she said more over her shoulder than directly at him. "I'm glad to help."

"I told you they're just people and you'd get used to them."

Lucy chuckled and set the bottle on the table, picking up both glasses to join him in the kitchen. She stepped behind him, standing close enough she pressed against his arm so she could look around him at the pot. The aromatic steam rolling up from the meaty sauce made her stomach grumble.

"I still get flustered when President Tanner comes home," she said as she held out one of the glasses to him. "This smells amazing."

He took it with his hand not stirring the sauce and leaned over for a kiss before taking a sip. "Like I said, nothing fancy. But it will taste good. I just need to drain the pasta. Sit. You've had a busy day."

She conceded and went back to the table, taking his glass with her. The wine was light, dry, with just a touch of sweet. It had been so long since she'd had any kind of alcohol, she figured she was a definite light drinker now. Once she sat, she realized he'd even set out shallow dishes of olive oil for the bread.

"What did you have to give Joe in trade?" she asked.

David looked over from the sink where he drained the pasta, billows of steam curling around his face. "What?"

"Wine. Olive oil. I can smell the garlic. What did you have to trade with Joe to get this?"

He looked confused, then grinned and laughed. "Don't worry about it. Joe the Trader is my secret."

She took a piece of bread and dipped it in the olive oil, watching David work in the kitchen. Maybe it was the two sips of wine, or maybe it was because she'd missed him so much, but there was something intensely sexy about watching him cook. He finished his preparations and returned to the table with a massive bowl of pasta and meat sauce.

"There's enough there to feed half of Unity Valley," she teased.

"Yeah, well, I never quite mastered the art of cutting back on recipes. By the time I was old enough to watch Nana in the kitchen, she was set in her ways, and I told you we had a big family. My brothers and sisters had a bunch of kids, so a lot of food was how we ate."

He scooped a hefty serving into her plate, and Lucy leaned over to inhale the steam, her mouth immediately watering. David dished out his own and sat down, motioning with his fork for her to take the first bite. It was quite possibly the most delicious pasta dish she'd ever eaten. Whether it was his Nana's way of cooking, or David's spin, the sauce was heavy with garlic and oregano and pepper, and it was amazing. She hummed in appreciation around her first bite.

"You're going to have to cook more often," she said, finally managing to finish the bite.

"Not sure if I have anything to impress after this."

Lucy paused in preparing her next bite to take a moment and look at David. He must have felt her pause, because he stopped and looked up, meeting her gaze.

"What . . ."

She smiled. "Just . . . enjoying the moment. Did I mention I missed you?" Lucy took in a quick breath through her nose and let it out as she focused on her food again. "So, are you making progress?"

"Some, yes. I'm missing something, but I can't figure out what."

"You'll get it. I know you will."

"Thank you. I'm pissed because I feel like the answer is right in front of me. I'm just not seeing it."

They talked through dinner, and the heavy melancholy Lucy had felt for days lifted off her until she could breathe again. Conversation had always been easy with David, even when highly laced with flirting, and she enjoyed laughing again with him. All the fatigue was gone, and she soaked up the energy being with David created. When they were finished, Lucy reached for David's plate but he beat her to standing and put his hand on her shoulder.

"Just sit," he said. "I'll take care of this."

"I can help—"

He stopped her argument by bending down and giving her a solid kiss. "Just sit," he said against her lips before smacking a loud kiss and walking away from the table with their plates.

"Okay, fine."

She turned her chair so she could lean back and rest her arm on the table, cross her legs, and sip the last of her wine while she watched him clean the kitchen and put away the leftovers that would easily be enough to feed them both for a couple days. He even washed their dishes and put them in the strainer on the counter.

"Are you trying to soften me up so you can tell me something I'm not going to like?"

"No," David answered, tossing the dishtowel he'd been drying his hands with over their two plates and her one from breakfast she hadn't put away yet. He came back to the table and crouched down in front of her, one hand on the table edge and the other on her knee. "If anything, I'm trying to tell you I'm sorry."

"For what?"

"For not being here. I want to be."

Lucy laid her palm on his cheek, rubbing her thumb over the late day stubble that stood as proof he'd shaved at some point earlier in the day. "David, everyone is doing what needs to be done. I'm proud of you. You don't need to apologize." She leaned forward, and he rose from the crouch enough to meet her kiss.

"Can you forgive me for having so much to say and do, I keep forgetting everything?" he asked against her lips before sliding into his chair again. He reached across the table to a tablet sitting on the far corner away from them and tapped the screen to activate the tablet. "A message came in from Unity Valley today, and Connor asked me to pass it on."

As soon as he said Unity Valley, gooseflesh raised on her arms.

David scrolled through a couple screens before setting the tablet on the tabletop again. He turned it and slid it across to her with a smile. Lucy managed to blink, then looked down at the tablet. On the screen was the most beautiful baby with glowing dark skin, full cheeks, bright, wide eyes and a full head of black curls bundled in a blanket and held in the arms of her lifelong friend.

Lucy gasped and covered her lips with her fingers.

"Her name is Della Lucinda Tisdale," David provided, and Lucy looked up, his face blurred by her sudden tears. "She was born yesterday. Six pounds, twelve ounces and twenty inches long." David chuckled. "She's probably all elbows and knees."

Lucy sniffed and picked up the tablet to look more closely at the photo. "She's beautiful. Thank you."

He stood again and held up a finger as if she should wait and jogged across the living room toward their bedroom door. If she hadn't known him when he first arrived in Unity Valley and hadn't seen him confined to the prosthetics that helped him move, and then to see him struggle so hard to walk in the days after they'd come back to Alexandria, she'd never believe the physical, strong man she saw now was one in the same. There was something miraculous about it. She'd seen too much to believe in true miracles, but if there ever was one, it was David Forte.

She went back to studying the picture while he was gone.

Della Lucinda . . .

He spent moments in the bedroom, and when he came back out, he carried a bundle hugged to his chest that looked like it was wrapped in one of his tee shirts. Whatever it was, he was grinning wide when he got back to the table.

"So, as it turns out, gift wrapping is hard to come by these days. Harder than getting what I would have liked to wrap, and that wasn't easy." He set the bundle on the table beside her and sat down in the chair he'd left earlier. "So, pretend my shirt is fancy wrapping."

Lucy uncrossed her legs and sat up, turning in the chair. "Is this something else you traded with Joe for?"

"Worse than that. Connor," he said with a chuckle. "Or people Connor knows. I asked him to see what he could do about getting his hands on . . ." He waved at the pile. "Whatever he could get his hands on, especially since I didn't really know what to tell him to find. He ended up finding a few options, and I took what I thought was the best. Go ahead."

Watching him for a moment longer, trying to read the mix of excitement and maybe even nervousness in his expression, Lucy finally reached for the cotton shirt and tugged it away from his gift.

She gasped.

Beneath the shirt he'd hidden three different types of sketchbooks. One was larger with a spiral binding, one smaller with a similar spiral binding, and on top a beautiful hardcover notebook bound in black moleskin. She picked up the moleskin notebook and slid aside the elastic closure and opened the book, the binding making a thrilling crackle sound to expose the heavyweight ivory paper inside.

"Oh, David. These are beautiful."

"There's more."

He moved the smaller of the spiral sketchbooks to reveal a black canvas zippered pouch and a rolled pouch held closed with a snapped leather strap. There had once been a cardboard label on the zippered pouch, but the label had been torn and water damaged at some point, but she saw the remnants of the words 'watercolor pencils.' Her vision blurred behind tears when she reached first for the case and unzipped it. It was full of dozens of watercolor pencils, a media she'd once dabbled in but had never owned a proper set of her own tools. The rolled case was full of charcoal pencils in different textures from soft to hard and different thicknesses, along with kneadable erasers and other artist tools.

"I've never owned anything like this," she whispered, unable to project her voice anymore. "These are wonderful."

She raised her head to look at him, smiling even when tears rolled down her cheek. David reached out and stroked her skin with the pad of his thumb.

"I didn't mean to make you cry."

"These are the best kind of tears. Thank you. I don't know how Connor found these, but they are wonderful."

"I remembered when we talked down by the stream, I noticed your pencils were really short and it looked like your notebook was full. I wanted you to be able to draw more." He shrugged a shoulder. "It meant a lot to you to sketch the people you loved, so—"

Lucy pushed out of her chair and leaned over the table to kiss him, careful not to rest on the gifts. Still leaning over so she was eye level, Lucy sniffed and wiped at her own cheeks. "Thank you so much."

"I'm glad you like them."

"I love them." She stood and stepped away from the table, holding her hands out to him. "I love you."

David stood and instead of taking her hands, he wrapped his arm around her waist and brought her into his embrace. "I love you, too. I like to make you smile."

"Then kiss me again."

David slid his hand up her spine, urging her to circle his neck with her arms, and cradled the back of her head in his large, strong hand to kiss her until her body hummed again. They would both be exhausted by morning, but there were many nights apart to make up for.

CHAPTER TWENTY-EIGHT

29 September 2054, Tuesday Evening
Ambassador Residence
United Earth Protectorate, Capitol City
Alexandria, Seat of Virginia
North American Continent

John knew Alexis stood in the doorway behind him, knew the moment she'd arrived, but didn't say anything and continued talking to Toby as he fed the poppet. The baby was still a wee bit behind yet for what Doctor Longbow would like to see for a human child his suspected age, but all things considered, he was growing and thriving. And loved it when John or Jenifer talked to him.

"If you keep eatin' like this, *gigri*, your Papa won't be able to pick you up soon," he said with a wide smile that Toby returned, the nipple of his bottle still between his gums and tongue and bubbles of the fortified baby milk dribbling on his chin.

"What does that mean?" Alexis asked.

John made a small show of being surprised she was there, looking over the back of the couch where he sat. "Wha' does wha' mean?" he asked.

"Whatever you just called Toby. Gigi or something."

She stepped away from the doorway, arms wrapped around her abdomen in her familiar, defensive stance. It had been over three months since Jenifer had returned from New Orleans with Alexis and the other children, and while there had been some easing of the girl's apprehension, it was still always present. John knew she waited for the day he, more than anyone else, betrayed her. It hurt his heart. Alexis came around the end of the couch and stood a few feet away.

"*Gigri*," he repeated. "It translates roughly to ravenous toy, but on Zibal it was a term of endearment for very hungry children."

"Is Zibal a planet?"

John nodded. A conversation initiated by Alexis was a rare thing, so he wasn't about to let the opportunity pass. "Yes, near Seta Gemii. I spent a lot of time there and loved their language."

"Is *su'ista* their language, too?"

"Yes. It means beautiful soul and precious treasure."

She arched one eyebrow, looking skeptical. "That's a lot of meaning in one word."

John nodded. "Zibalan is like that. Their language has nearly three hundred thousand words, and many of them are to express some combination of other words."

"Do you speak their language, or do you just know some words?"

"I speak it," he answered. "I speak several languages."

She took a step sideways and sat on the arm of one of the chairs, arms still crossed. "That's how you think of . . . Jenifer?"

Alexis seemed to struggle with using the name of whom, on Aretu, would be without any other definition her mother. Toby made a solid popping sound when he released the nipple of the now empty bottle, so John laid it on the cushion beside him and lifted Toby to his shoulder to pat the baby's back. He wanted to encourage the conversation by making it seem normal, just like burping a child.

"It is," he answered simply once Toby was settled.

Alexis slid from the arm of the chair into the chair itself, the piece of furniture seeming too large for her slight frame. She didn't say anything for a few minutes, just sitting silent, watching John take care of Toby. When Toby finally let out a solid belch, she laughed, and John grinned when he looked toward her.

"He's no' one for holdin' back."

She shook her head, still smiling. Toby laid his cheek on John's shoulder with a long sigh, which meant he'd be sound asleep in less than two minutes. The two things Toby Smith had mastered were eating and sleeping.

"What does *sidan* mean?"

Her pronunciation of the name was perfect. Since he'd only used it one time, in the middle of high emotions after the Urdo Khantan attack, he was surprised she remembered so clearly. And for a split moment he debated whether he should tell her the true meaning, since he'd used it without considering how she'd feel about it and wondered now if she would accept the name. No trust could be gained if he lied. He turned his head and met her gaze without waiver, taking in a slow breath before answering.

"First daughters are God's Gift," he answered.

Her light brown eyes widened, and John held her stare with intent, so she knew his words were truth. She blinked and looked away, her chin dipping down. Toby was asleep, making small snoring sounds in John's ear with his breath warming the side of John's neck. Normally he would take the baby into his room to sleep, but not this evening. He would stay where he was until Alexis decided the conversation was over.

"I'm not your daughter," she said with some of the sharp edge John often heard in her rebuttals. "I'm not anyone's daughter."

"I know you feel that way, so I won't use that name aloud again until when and if you tell me I can."

She didn't move her head, but her eyes shifted to look at him in what he presumed she thought to be surreptitiously.

"In my heart, Alexis, you are my daughter. You are my oldest daughter. My first daughter. And you are a gift. After your mother brought you back to Alexandria," he explained, intentionally using the designation, "I told President Tanner the greatest gifts are the ones you never expected. Each of you are gifts to me."

A part of him fully expected Alexis to push herself from the chair with an angry flounce, snap out some snide remark in hopes of garnering an equal response, and quit the room. But she didn't. She didn't look at him but drew her legs up into the chair so her bent knees came to her chin and partially hid her features.

John didn't push, but also knew it wasn't time to leave.

"Why does Silas call you Papa?" she asked, her voice so small he barely heard her.

He drew down his brows, looking toward her again. She still hid behind her knees but had lifted her head enough to look directly at him.

"I wan' to make sure I answer properly," he began. "Do you mean why does he use the name Papa, or why does he call me Papa?"

She shrugged one shoulder, offering no other answer.

"I suppose the answer is about the same. He just . . . started callin' me Papa, and I was proud to be called his Papa." He had to pause to clear his throat, taking the moment to look down at Toby curled against his shoulder. "I don' know why he chose Papa. Perhaps he heard someone else use it."

"Simon and Amari call you Papa."

John nodded.

"Toby probably will, too."

He nodded again. "Seems likely."

"Do you expect me to call you Papa?"

He looked up and she still watched him from behind the safety barrier of her raised knees. "Alexis, I expect you to call me whatever you feel comfortable callin' me, whether it's Papa or John the Alien."

That earned the smallest smirk from her. It had been a joke the day Jenifer brought the children back to Alexandria, and he usually brought it up to get a chuckle, maybe not always from Alexis but at least the younger ones.

"But know this, Alexis . . ." He waited until he knew he had her full attention again. "In my heart you are my daughter. Six weeks ago, I did more than swear to be Jenifer's husband. I became your father. And Simon's, and Amari's, and Toby's. And Jenifer became mum to all of you. You are a Smith. You are my child. No matter how you see me, tha' is how I see you. I will protect you. I will defend you. And I will care for you as such, and that will no' change."

She stared at him, unblinking, until the tears welled up and slid down her cheeks. Alexis looked away from him, finally blinking, and nodded before she unfolded herself from the chair and headed for the hallway leading to the children's bedrooms. Moments later he heard her bedroom door shut – much softer than usual – and the door lock engage. John closed his eyes and released a long breath as he laid his cheek against Toby's dark hair.

The moment of introspection was short lived when Simon and Silas, who were as inseparable as any brothers raised together since birth, came charging down the hall calling his name.

"Papa!"

Toby jerked in his hold but settled again almost instantly, and the second the boys were in his view John held up his hand and they stopped running and shouting. He swore sometimes they completely forgot there was an infant in the home.

"Can I help you?" he asked.

"When is Mama going to be home?" Simon asked.

"Later," he answered, not knowing for sure since he knew what business she was busy with and knew there would be no specific timeframe. "I realize this is likely a foolish question, but can I assume you might be hungry for dinner?"

Both boys nodded, and John sighed. "The Smith family is going to singlehandedly wipe out the food supply in all of Alexandria," he mumbled as he rolled forward off the couch. "Let me put down your brother and I'll see what we've go' to eat."

DETAINMENT AND INTERROGATION FACILITY
UNITED EARTH PROTECTORATE, CAPITOL CITY
ALEXANDRIA, SEAT OF VIRGINIA
NORTH AMERICAN CONTINENT

"He hasn't quit complaining since we moved him here from the prison facility," Connor told Jenifer, and she appreciated his satisfied smirk. "Since I know for damn sure it's not because the prison is a five-star luxury hangout, I'm pretty sure it's because he knows you like to come visit when he's here."

"Maybe I should remind him where I'd put him if it were my call"

"Oh, no," Connor said, completely flat and dry, zero tone fluctuation. "Don't do that."

She smirked, momentarily forgetting her annoyance at having to relinquish Damocles before she was allowed to the interrogation area of the facility. Staring down the Firebird commander, she withdrew her weapon from the thigh holster and held it in her open palm.

"We're doing this again." She didn't put it as a question.

"You know I have to. If a prisoner—"

"Got this weapon, the worst they could do would be to throw it at you. No one . . . *no one* . . . fires this but me."

"Okay, and if you get pissed enough at Casper—"

"I'll kill him with a thought."

Connor sighed but didn't look away. She gave him credit. Still holding her stare, he took Damocles. Only when he had to turn away to lock up the weapon did he break eye contact to place Damocles in the security shielded safe. Jenifer followed him out of the office and to the locked door leading to the high security section of the facility. This portion of the building had been remodeled, redesigned, and fortified after Heinous Bitch had managed to escape in Evelyn Amon-Chevalier, now Montgomery's, body and lead an attack on the presidential residence that left many dead and Nicole Tanner missing.

Like with so many things, events inspired the "never again" mindset.

In Jenifer's view, people had to stop thinking about never again and start thinking never at all. But she wasn't paid the big bucks to make those decisions. Her job was to keep the Aretu ambassador alive. Good thing she had proper motivation.

"He's already waiting for your visit. He's excited. I can tell."

"If you say so."

"I like to think I'm a good reader of people."

Freddy Casper's shouting was just a muffled whimper through the thick door of the interrogation room. As was the routine for these visits, Connor stopped at the observation room door and gave Jenifer a nod before going inside. At the next door a Firebird stood guard, who offered the same nod of acknowledgment but didn't say anything. He pivoted to face the door and entered the security code to the keypad. A click and hiss disengaged the lock and he pulled the door open, stepping aside to allow her entrance.

"How long are you gonna keep me in here!"

"Until I say you can leave," Jenifer said with a calm in sharp contrast to the rage and sudden feeling of sick that hit her at the sight of the man who had murdered her childhood.

She felt sick at the thought of how many other children had been victims of his perversion and immorality, and every time she faced him, she had to fight the urge to picture his spine snapping with one thrust of her mind. John trained her to control the Talents she'd denied the existence of for decades, but there were moments like now she wished she didn't hear John's voice whispering about control.

What if I slip?

But she didn't, and she wouldn't. Instead, she embraced the satisfaction of seeing Freddy Casper immediately shut up and cower at the sound of her voice. His pasty, sallow face flushed and beads of sweat almost immediately appeared on his pock-marked forehead. They'd shaved off his wild, wiry, infested hair and he'd lost some of the alcohol and street drug bloat, leaving him as nothing more than a pathetic, weak, old man with hanging jowls and sunken eyes. She'd been kept informed on his stay at one of the few functioning prison facilities on the continent, and how horrible his detox had been, and hadn't felt a single second of sympathy.

Now, he sat cuffed to the one table in the room. The table was bolted down, and his chair was so heavy it was impossible for a weakling like Casper to push it back to stand.

"Time to give me a new list of names," she said, dragging back the other chair in the room with an echoing scrape of metal on metal that made him wince.

"This is inhumane," he said in a much gentler tone than of moments before, bordering now on the pathetic she knew he really was. "You can't keep—"

"Do you *really* want to get into a discussion about humane treatment?"

She met his watery eyes with an unblinking glare and relished in the red deepening over his whole head as pain twisted his features. Jenifer smirked. She probably shouldn't enjoy it, but as far as she was concerned, cutting off circulation to the part of his body he probably held most dear was a small pleasure she was allowed without guilt.

He let out a strangled string of curses, crying out, "Ya damn witch! You're of the devil hisself!"

"You have no idea." She sat back, letting go with her mind so he could slouch and pant for breath. "Now that we're past the pleasantries, let's take care of business so I can wash my brain of your filth."

Forty minutes later, Jenifer walked out of the interrogation room. In the hall, she stepped out of line of sight from either Casper through the small, metal mesh enforced window in the door or from Connor when he came out of the adjacent observation room. Jenifer leaned back against the wall and hunched forward with her hands braced on her knees as she sucked in deep breaths of air not tainted by his presence. She hated sharing space with him, but if it saved one more child . . . just one more child . . . she'd do it again and again.

She needed a scorching shower.

And John. She wanted John.

A year earlier she would have felt weak and inadequate if she ever admitted needing someone else, but she understood now she didn't need him out of weakness. She wanted him out of strength. She was stronger than she'd ever been since she left Sister Mahalia.

The observation door opened, and Jenifer pushed away from the wall, composed and clear again by the time Connor looked her way. He held up the PAC in his hand. "I got it all. I'll clean it up and send to CRRPA."

Jenifer nodded, falling into step with Connor as they headed back out the way they came. "What's the number now?"

"Thirty-two," he said with a proud smile. "That's from what you've gotten from Casper. But Evie has helped place over two hundred in just a few months."

"That's great," she said, hoping she sounded convincing.

Yes, thirty-two kids saved from whatever hell Casper had sold them into – and anyone involved taken into custody because Nick Tanner had no sympathy for people who hurt kids – but Jenifer knew they'd gone looking for a whole lot more than that. She'd take the thirty-two as a battle won, but far from the war.

Back up front, she reclaimed Damocles without any further banter with Connor, and left. The short ride across the city on the hoverbike she'd claimed for solo travel not nearly long enough to free her of the cloying stench she swore lingered on her skin after being around Freddy Casper. This wasn't her first time making a late day visit to the detainment facility for the purpose of getting information from Casper, so the routine was well established for them.

She left the children to John, no matter what time she came home, and used the back entrance into the suite that had been home to the president and his family for weeks while the main residence was repaired. Every entrance had the usual security, but she'd added her own layers just as she had when she first became John's bodyguard. The back entrance let her slip into the apartment without the kids hearing her and allowed her to cleanse herself as much as physically possible before any of them knew she was home.

Logically, she knew no trace of his filth and poison came home with her, but their children had endured too much of him to even be near her when she had been near him. They didn't know where she went, and that was the way she wanted it to stay.

Laughter came from the kitchen on the other side of the apartment when she moved into the hallway with all the bedroom doors. She paused only long enough to differentiate between Amari and Simon and Silas. Toby was likely asleep and would be for a few hours. Just as Jenifer reached for the doorknob of their bedroom, an unfamiliar laugh – yet one she knew immediately – joined the others.

Alexis.

Jenifer smiled and risked being caught just long enough to listen.

All the voices mingled together, talking over each other, with John's voice domineering once in a while to remind everyone to be polite and it was time for bed. She smiled.

I'm glad you're home, su'ista.

Of course, he knew she was home. She should have put up more walls, more filters, so he didn't know the way Casper made her feel. She should have, but she didn't. John's voice was as tangible and clear as if he'd stepped up behind her and whispered in her ear.

I'm glad they're laughing.

She slipped into the bedroom and didn't turn on any lights that might be seen under the door. Jenifer paused in the dark room to safely store Damocles – because even though none of the children could fire the weapon, she wanted no chance of them accidently finding it – and then stripped off her clothes. She wouldn't even put the tainted garments with their usual laundry. Her head told her she was being illogical; Freddy Casper wasn't a virus she could bring home to her family. Yet, she did it all the same.

In the bathroom, she cranked up the temperature in the massive shower and let it run to get hot with the multiple showerheads flowing. There was something to be said for living in an ambassador's home.

Long, hot showers were a luxury available to them but not an indulgence she would normally allow. She'd taken plenty of cold showers, and sometimes gotten by with a bucket of water when nothing else was available, but she needed the burn. With the room full of steam, she opened the glass door and stepped under the forceful stream to let it pelt her skin. It stung, but it purified.

She couldn't see through the heavy haze that fogged every surface but felt the curl of cooler air when the glass shower doors opened. Before she could turn, John stepped behind her and slid his hands over her hips to her waist and up her stomach, eliciting a low groan she didn't try to control. John moved against her, his chest to her back, his palms slick on her skin. He kissed her shoulder, and she raised her arm to reach back, pushing her fingers into his wet hair, tipping her head to stretch her neck beneath his mouth. The benefit of huge showers with multiple showerheads was no one had to be cold.

He spoke her name against her skin, the word *su'ista* in her mind.

Jenifer turned in the circle of his arms, her breath fast and hard to match his. The water shut off, the hum of John's Talents reverberating within the tile and glass shower like an echo chamber, and Jenifer smiled. It was a new sensation, and it left her skin tingling. Worth exploring later. When the tile wasn't quite so wet.

"Interestin'," John said with a wicked grin before taking her head between his hands to kiss her deep again.

They both had gooseflesh from the shift in temperature by the time they reached the bed, but by then neither cared about anything other than each other.

CHAPTER TWENTY-NINE

30 September 2054, Wednesday
Alexandria Hospital, Secure Wing – Medical Research Facility
United Earth Protectorate, Capitol City
Alexandria, Seat of Virginia
North American Continent

"We are ready to disengage the final systems," Victor explained, looking from his PAC to the monitors positioned beside each open hospital bed.

"They aren't going to wake up right away," Michael said to his father, sensing the wave of concern and apprehension. "This final stage is just to stop the stasis function of keeping their minds dormant. I'd compare it to the autopilot function in your glider. The stasis program allowed the mind to complete all necessary functions without the need for conscious intervention."

"Did they experience anything at all? Dreams?"

"Based on the record of data we have for the last three decades, nothing at all. Because any brain activity would be very distinctive, it was very easy to scan the entirety of the records, and there is nothing for either one of them."

"Why would—" His eyes shifted briefly to Victor, who was locked in deep concentration, and didn't see the glance. "Why do that?"

"By what I've researched, the idea of dormant life suspension, stasis, suspended animation, whatever name applied to it has had a variety of views about mental function. In this situation, Victor halted mental activity because he didn't know how long they would stay in this state of existence."

"What would have happened if their minds weren't . . ." His father pulled a face and huffed, "Dormant like that?"

"They would likely wake insane. They're different than both David and my brothers. The Triadic were created to endure torture far worse than stasis, and David was given a loop, but it kept his mind active enough he became aware. Much longer, if his life was maintained, he would have likely lost his sanity, too."

"There but for the grace of God, go they . . ."

Michael nodded, looking from the two scientists working on his grandparents to his father. "Every reading, scan, and data analysis says they have been completely unaware of anything in the last thirty years. Just like for David, and even my brothers, reality will be a shock and we will have the challenge of helping them understand."

"Tell him our thoughts, Michael," Victor said, not looking up from his readings, and his tone made clear his focus on the task at hand.

"Thoughts?" Nick asked.

"David told Katrina after he came out of stasis that he was aware of her reading to him, even before he was conscious. When the memory loop began to glitch, and changing to events not programmed, he described being in a blank room. The only thing he heard was Katrina reading to him. It's the same theory that coma patients, who are in that state for a variety of reasons, are on some level aware of what's happening around them. They hear and recognize voices."

"So, we should talk to them . . ."

"You more than anyone, Dad. Of any of us, you are the one they will know. You are the one who will be familiar. You can speak to them about things only you would know. That might help ease them into their new reality when they wake up."

His father stared at him as he explained and seemed to process the concept before nodding. Slowly at first and then with conviction. He looked past Michael again to the beds.

Victor and his specialized medical team, who had worked on Matthias and Grace without knowing their identities, and along with Katrina Forte's assistance with the technology, had removed Michael's grandparents from the pods ten days earlier. Since then, they had been cared for by a limited medical staff, and every few days when Victor was convinced they were stable in their new medical state, another stasis system had been disengaged. Today was the final step.

The beds were just far enough apart to allow someone to move between them. Each bed was equipped with an EEG node halo that allowed them to have a constant reading of brain activity without the trauma of prolonged electrode attachment to their skin. The halo was mounted to the head of the bed and hovered over their heads at about eighteen inches. No contact, but theoretically, perfect readings. They would know soon.

Once they knew the halo worked to their satisfaction, the neural connections implanted at the time they were placed in stasis could be removed. Hopefully that would be in the next day, and before Matthias or Grace woke.

"They're fine, physically, right."

It was more a statement than a question because Michael had assured him for over two weeks of the success at each new step. Michael nodded, understanding the need to hear the reassurance. He had come to accept that his part in the process was not to assist with the medical or technological side, but to support his family in this newest version of their ever-changing lives.

"Yes. We don't know how long it will take for them to wake up on their own, or who will wake up first, but once this final system is effectively turned off all we will need to do is wait."

"Functional electroencephalogram is on and ready," Katrina said, positioning herself between the two beds so she could see the monitors for both adults. "Ready to deactivate stasis cerebral function hibernation program."

"She just likes to say the big fancy words," Nick said just under his breath.

Michael smiled, and while he knew Phin and Daniel would have maintained their expressions, felt the nudge of humor from both of them. Which was exactly the reaction he knew his father had intended, whether he felt or saw it, or not. It was a release valve for him.

"Deactivating Matthias . . . now," Victor said, tapping his screen.

They all collectively held their breath. Moments later, the F.E.E.G monitor beeped. Followed by another. And another in a steady rhythm. Michael slowly released the breath and looked to his father when Nick Tanner put his hand on Michael's shoulder.

"Activity is steady," Katrina said, leaning closer to the monitor. She nodded and drew back, looking to Victor. "Node halo is working great, Victor."

"Excellent," Victor acknowledged, his attention still on the tablet in his hands. "Let's proceed. Deactivating Grace . . . now."

The grip on Michael's shoulder firmed. Once again, they waited. It was only moments, but after nearly three weeks of preparation, even those seconds felt elongated and unnaturally protracted. Katrina made the small move to watch his grandmother's monitor. "Activity also steady and node halo functioning perfectly."

Victor looked up from his tablet with a long, relieved sigh and smiled, looking toward Michael and his father. "And now we wait."

"Awesome. I'm so good at that," Nick said, his tone flat and dry.

"You appear thoroughly engrossed in your work, Katrina." Katrina turned her head toward Victor's voice but didn't disengage her eyes from the information on her screen until she absolutely had to and had to focus on closing her mouth and gather her thoughts.

"I'm still working on translating all the files we downloaded from the *Abbadon*. Most of it is just HB's notes – we haven't been able to productively use anything since we were first treating the boys – but

I'm finding something . . . I don't know if interesting is the right word because it's messed up, but—"

"HB?" Victor asked, leaning against her office doorjamb with his hands in his pockets.

Katrina smiled while her cheeks burned. "It's short for heinous bitch," she said, whispering the name like her mom would hop out from the closet and wash her mouth for swearing.

"Ah. I see. What did you find?"

"Well, I've found some records that weren't necessarily hers, but they related to hers and I've been building a timeline. Maybe you might remember something—" She immediately regretted saying anything, knowing how difficult it was for him sometimes to remember.

Difficult and unpleasant.

"Tell me what you found," he said, and the kindness in his voice almost made her feel possibly worse.

She took a deep breath and scooted back from her desk so he could see the information on her large screen, although what showed there wasn't enough to begin to explain.

"I came back to her records because of what you told me about President Tanner's parents, that HB found out about Matthias Tanner and his Talents – though that's not what they were called, for obvious reasons like the Areth not being the Areth and that's what the Areth call them—"

"Katrina," Victor said firmly. "I understand."

"Sorry. Knowing that information, I kind of did some key word searches as best I could with the Sorracchi translations, and that just spread out into all the records like a spiderweb. I found the original references to Matthias Tanner, how she wanted access to him as part of their bigger plan. Of course, we know those plans changed because of Grace and HB wanted to see if she could get an even better DNA pool to work with."

"Carrying all the way through to the point of trying to abduct Nicholas as a child."

"Right." She swiveled her chair to look at her notes she'd scribbled out on a paper tablet. "President Tanner was born in 2004, and we think the abduction attempt was somewhere around 2009. David was captured in 2011 and placed in stasis. It was after that when she created the boys, and spent years putting them through hell." She didn't even try to hide the anger in her voice. Victor got it.

"When they were deemed a failure, and in turn so was Kathleen, she turned her focus again on the Tanner bloodline by going after Nick directly."

"Yes," Katrina declared, jabbing a finger toward the screen. "But I found these records that fall kind of in and around there. I guess it was like a Plan B? Plan C? It's hard to keep track of how many things she tried to do but failed at. And this is what I wanted to ask you about.

"Somewhere around '27 or so – Michael was born in '26, right? – the Sorracchi learned about a human child who was young, I mean not even in school yet, who showed evidence of *astronomical* Talents. There was no evidence it ran in her family, but she was just . . . wow." Katrina paused and looked at Victor, still processing what she'd read. "Victor, her father basically sold her to the Sorracchi. They promised him power and wealth – but I think he was wealthy already – but he took it. He promised his daughter to the Sorracchi for . . ." Her stomach churned. "Basically, like breeding stock." She shook her head. "Do you remember anything about this?"

His eyes pinched at the corners like he was deep in thought and his gaze angled off to the empty parts of the office. "There is some familiarity to this, but I was not held in close confidence. Often, what I knew and what I learned was either by accident or my presence was specifically required for other reasons." He shifted his attention back to her. "Did you find a name? Or what happened? I certainly don't recall any young girl being introduced to her experimentations."

Katrina squinted at her screen. "Um, yes . . . Genevieve. Genevieve Moffett. I don't think you would have seen her because I did an archive search with her name. I know historical archives can be really spotty, but I found a mix of news stories. She disappeared for two and a half weeks when she was eleven years old, and everyone thought she'd been kidnapped because her family was a wealthy family. Then she was back, and her father said she'd run away. Two years later, all mention of her stops. Like she disappeared for real."

Victor shook his head. "No, I don't recall the name at all. You don't believe she was turned over to the Sorracchi as promised? She would have been a teenager, and as crude as it may seem, she would have been at the age Kathleen would want her."

Katrina shrugged and shook her head. "No idea. But I found news footage from a couple years ago that show the Moffett mansion burning. Seems people found out this Moffett guy was in bed with the Sorracchi, even knowing somehow he'd given his daughter to them, and they . . . they killed him."

"Seems a fitting end if the accusations are true."

"This is so sick, but Victor, what if HB planned on using Michael and this Genevieve as her next evolution of super soldiers? I mean, based on what I'm finding this little girl was Michael level powerful, and they knew it even when she was little. Can you imagine what HB would have done with those genetics?"

"Thankfully, we shall never know."

Detainment and Interrogation Facility
United Earth Protectorate, Capitol City
Alexandria, Seat of Virginia
North American Continent

"How has he – he? – been since your people brought him back?" Nick asked as he and John followed Connor down a corridor to the secure lift to take them down to the maximum-security levels of the facility.

"I'm not going to be the one to figure out their physiology, but Victor has referred to our guest as he, so," Connor said with a half-chuckle. "Not exactly on their best behavior, let's put it that way. Victor's people used enough anesthesia to take down a herd of elephants, and that only kept him down long enough they could examine him for suicide devices. Since then, he's been restrained except for humane reasons and he's still bitching up a storm." He looked back at John. "At least, I assume he's bitching. Sure sounds like bitching. I guess that's what you're here to tell us."

"Goin' to attempt to, at least."

"You really speak his language?"

"Speak it, no. I don't have the right throat structure to speak their language. I do, however, understand it. I have means to communicate in reverse."

"They as ugly as that picture in the Mona Lisa you showed us?" Nick asked, his wince twisting his lip.

"More now," John said, trying not to chuckle when Nick's expression twisted more. "That image was hidden over five hundred years ago and based on da Vinci's memory and stories he'd heard. I have seen reports from the last couple centuries, and they have evolved into something more grotesque to attempt to be more intimidatin' I assume. I've no' been of the pleasure of seeing one alive."

"Sorry to end that streak," Nick said, this time adding a chuckle.

They reached the secure lift and Connor typed in his code, pressing his hand to the bioscan to call the car. Once it arrived, they all entered including Phin and Daniel Forte who had followed them in silence through the facility and Captain Bravebird who was John's security contingent for the afternoon. He wasn't sure who was more silent, the Forte brothers or Doli Bravebird.

From the street, and even upon entering the facility, most casual visitors would have no idea there were five levels down for the worst of the worst prisoners. Very few had been held down here.

Few, thus far, being one.

Even Kathleen, while still inhabiting Evelyn's body, didn't make it this far down.

The lift bumped to a stop and the doors opened. Connor led the way and Nick and John followed with their guards behind. The walls were reinforced cinderblock, and the corridor light brighter than daylight. CCTV cameras monitored every inch with wide lenses so there were no gaps. No way to hide. Even if their prisoner of war somehow managed to escape his cell and tried to leave, he wouldn't get any further than the corridor before a variety of safety measures stopped any progress.

Forty feet from the lift stood two Firebirds at attention outside a cell door and greeted Connor with silent nods. John had seen a range of formality in military command structures from a variety of planets and cultures, and of them all he commended Connor Montgomery and his Firebirds the most. There was an informality and yet the highest level of respect he could recall seeing. One of the guards sidestepped to clear the security panel for Connor. He entered his code and submitted to the palm bioscan. Three beeps preceded the hiss and pop of the security measures releasing. Bravebird and the Forte brothers took position in the hall as Nick and John followed Connor inside.

The cell was a 12' x 12' cube of foot thick clear, shatterproof, weapon proof, and brute strength proof material twenty times stronger than the strongest polycarbonate produced in the last thirty years, courtesy of Alliance technology. The much larger space holding the cube allowed for another ten feet of space on all sides and a gap of just a yard from the top of the cube to the ceiling. Inside the cube, preemptively restrained for their visit, was the sole Urdo Khantan in captivity.

Mottled brown leathery flesh stretched over a flattened facial structure with jagged bone ridges beneath long scars, indicating this one had seen many battles. The Urdo Khantan had no nose structure like many races, instead with what looked like a sliced wound for a mouth, and when they stepped into view it pulled back the edges to snarl and expose the rows of teeth they filed to vicious points. John had only seen images of the Urdo Khantan, and always in full armor. This was the first time he'd seen one without their smooth helmets and body plates.

Many races used armor to look larger and more menacing, but even without his armor, this enemy soldier was massive. They were bred for strength, endurance, and possibly a level of psychosis.

He threw back his head and released a guttural sound that echoed off the walls, throwing out his arms in a primitive show of power. The length of his restraints didn't allow for any leverage, and any attempt at intimidation was lost.

"Ooooh, I'm scared," Connor mumbled. He took his weapon from his thigh holster and tapped the butt of the grip on the wall. "Yo, Skippy, don't be rude."

The Urdo Khantan slid his orange tongue past his razor teeth and hissed, spittle running down his chin with his guttural language.

Connor looked over his shoulder, one eyebrow raised.

"He promises death," John said with a shrug of one shoulder. "A grotesque death through a variety of means his people like particularly well. Death on you. On your slaves. Your females. Your spawn."

"My goats, too?" Connor asked and Nick chuckled.

"A lot of big words for a naked guy in a glass box," Nick said and took a step toward the cell. He kept his stance relatively relaxed, hands casually in his pockets, his feet shoulder width apart.

John recognized the anger buffering away from the president, but as much as Nick Tanner sometimes let his thoughts play in his features, he was also skilled at projecting the exact image he wanted. Unfazed. Untouched. Unconcerned with the figurative chest-pounding of an impotent blowhard.

Perhaps it would do the Khantan to feel the rage the way John did. This enemy, and his compatriots, might actually flinch if they understood the potential for vengeance they had awakened in Nicholas Tanner.

"Time to have a little talk," President Tanner said with a chilling calm.

CHAPTER THIRTY

2 October 2054, Friday
Forte & Santos Residence
Civilian Employee Housing
United Earth Protectorate, Capitol City
Alexandria, Seat of Virginia
North American Continent

𝓟hin, Daniel, Nick, John, Jenifer, and Michael stood silent, shoulder to shoulder with eyes closed and heads bowed like deacons at a prayer meeting. They weren't praying – maybe they were – either way, they were the only salvation for everyone inside the house as hellfire and brimstone rained down from the Xeno attack. The walls shook, the air rumbled, and with each blast the six of them swayed. Nothing came through the invisible, awesomely powerful hedge of protection their combined Talents created.

David was trapped where he had been placed, on the floor cowering like a dog, his heart in his throat and a ball of acid in his gut. He could do nothing but hold his breath and watch in silent awe. With each blast that hit the house, the air around him pulled inward toward the small group keeping the rest of them alive. The hair on his arms stood up and his nerves prickled.

Another volley hit the house, this time coming straight at the front porch and windows closest to him. David pushed himself up on shaking arms and looked out, catching the split-second shimmer of genesis energy created not from some artificial source . . .

From them.

David jolted awake, already sitting up with his feet on the floor before he opened his eyes. He fought to breathe, a vise squeezing his chest, scrambling to plant himself in the present.

"David? What's wrong?"

Lucy's hands on his shoulders registered the same second he slammed fully into reality. He hunched forward, fighting to catch his breath with the heels of his hands pressed against his eyes until lights flashed behind his lids.

He didn't realize he was talking out loud until the bed shifted and seconds later Lucy was in front of him, pulling his hands away from his face. She knelt in front of him, eyes wide and brow furrowed, her beautiful dark hair wild around her face.

"David," she said, her voice firm.

"How stupid can I be? Damn it! I thought I'd come out of that damn stasis coffin with *most* of my brain cells." He stood, marching away from her and the bed, a rush of angry energy pushing him to move. He reached the open door of the bedroom and slammed his fist into the wall, the plaster cracking. "Damn it!"

"David, if you don't tell me what's wrong—"

He pivoted. Lucy stood where he'd left her, one hand on her hip, her cotton shorts and tee shirt rumpled from sleep.

"The whole godda—" He snapped himself back, clenching his jaw to hold in the string of foul language he wanted to shout. Even pissed as hell, his Mama raised him better than to curse in front of a lady. David fisted his hands until his knuckles ached and sucked in several deep, rapid breaths before he dared look at Lucy again. "The dome. My concept for the dome came to me after the Xenos attacked the residence."

Lucy nodded. "You told me that. John, Nick, your sons . . . they used their Talents to protect the house and you created the dome to mimic them."

"Mimic!" he shouted, tossing a hand toward her as if the pile of crap that was his plan was in his hand for her to see. "Perfect word. I've been trying to replicate with wires, chewing gum, and solar batteries a level of *power* you can't just . . ." He fumbled for the words. ". . . yank out of the air! *God* created this kind of power. No wonder I haven't been able to find an energy source strong enough to protect anything more than a few square miles. There *is* no energy source because the mind is the source." He tapped his fingertip rapidly against his temple.

She raised her hand to her forehead, rubbing it before she pushed back her hair. "What does this mean?"

He tipped back his head and huffed out a heavy breath. "Hell if I know, darlin'. Hell if I know."

Alexandria Hospital, Secure Wing – General Care
United Earth Protectorate, Capitol City
Alexandria, Seat of Virginia
North American Continent

"Good morning."

Victor looked up from the tablet he rested on the nurse's station when he heard Michael.

"I wasn't expecting you to be at the hospital until later today, as usual," Victor said. "I thought Jacqueline had expressly forbidden you from leaving too early."

Michael chuckled, remembering how his wife had pointed and scowled at him that morning. "She says I am too difficult to live with when I have something on my mind and ordered me out until later to give her some peace."

"What is on your mind? Your grandparents? I'm heading there shortly after I check on Tessera."

"She is why I'm here."

"Then walk with me and tell me what you've been thinking."

"Once you eliminate the impossible, whatever remains, no matter how improbable, must be the truth."

Victor pushed his hands into his pockets and tipped back his head, pausing his step on a heel. "That's . . . ah . . . Conan Doyle, correct? From the *Sherlock Holmes* books?"

"Yes, but it seems appropriate. Not that we have removed the impossible, but we *have* removed anything explainable by modern science. Infection. Physical injury. Even poisoning. As illogical as it might seem to the general study of medicine, I am convinced there is a psychokinetic source."

"I agree."

They reached Tessera's room, and Victor put his back to the door, pushed down the door handle, and stepped backward into the dark room.

"And the more I think of my own situation and experience, the more I am convinced the only way we can stop this is that we can't at all. She has to do it," Michael said, following him in.

"Do what?"

Both pulled up short, surprised to find David Forte in the dim room standing at the foot of Tessera's bed, hunched forward with his hands curled around the footboard. Michael and Victor exchanged looks, and Michael approached the bed.

"We have a theory about what triggered Tessera's failing health—"

"She somehow transferred her life to me so I wouldn't die?" David snapped out the statement, making it far more than a question. He nodded his head. "Yeah, I heard that was your theory."

Michael wanted to ask how he could know, but in the same moment realized it didn't matter how. If anyone deserved to know, it was David, and they had been negligent – possibly even cruel – to not tell him.

"I'm sorry," Michael conceded, reaching the bed. "We should have told you. It's a theory, but the more I consider it the more I believe it's the likely answer."

"But *how*? How do you even *do* that?"

"I realized last year that I had the ability, with focus and discipline, to share my strength with someone who needed it whether to help them heal or save their life if needed. The first time I did it, I didn't know how to control it, but I learned. Because Tessera and I have some shared . . . history and experiences . . . I suspect she might be able to do the same. If, like me, she didn't know how to control it she might have gone too far."

"How do you stop it? I'm fine. I don't need – is that what you were talking about? She has to do it?"

Anger and frustration emanated from David and Michael was amazed he hadn't felt it just approaching the room. Had he been so distracted?

"That is my suspicion."

"So, unless she wakes up, she can't stop it. And unless she stops it, she's probably never going to wake up?" David pushed back from the bed, striding across the small room until he reached the windows, and turned back with his hands set at his waist. "Because of *me*?"

"She must have believed it was the only way to save your life. Even with her intervention, my understanding is you sustained extensive injuries, and with the damage already done, you may not have survived another day if Phin and Daniel hadn't found you. What she did gave you time."

"At what cost!" David thrust a hand toward the bed with his shout.

"David—" Victor began, but Michael raised his hand.

They had no right to try to change his response. In the same situation, Michael knew he would likely feel the same. David dropped his head forward, taking several rapid breaths before he looked up again. He said nothing as he crossed the room until he reached them, pausing in the light from the hall. His jaw was set, his lips tight, and he pointed back to the bed.

"Figure it out, Michael. She can't—I don't know her, and she didn't know me. She can't die for me."

He pushed past them into the hall, his boots echoing as he marched away. When the sound died, Michael released a slow breath and walked to the side of the bed. She was slightly moved whenever he came but based on the constant monitoring of her vitals and brain activity, he knew the perceived movement was not by her own power but by the nurses caring for her. Her color had perhaps the slightest improvement, but it was nominal.

"No change of note. We are successfully maintaining her weight, but no further gain. The fever has stayed away. But brain activity shows no change. Existent but not responsive."

"This is quite possibly the most frustrating medical situation I have faced," Michael said, speaking as much to Tessera as Victor. He turned his head and looked to his friend. "Not that I have the years of experience you do."

"Ah, but you have more years of experience caring for the health and recovery of others," Victor said with a heaviness settling in his voice. "I have been given the privilege to provide care and healing for barely a year. It will be a very long time before my scale is tipped."

Michael wanted to argue what he saw as the obvious, as most of them saw as obvious, that Victor had nothing to atone for. He knew it wouldn't change the weight on Victor's heart any more than telling David the guilt wasn't his with Tessera's situation. Instead, he bent forward and crossed his arm on the safety rail, bringing him closer to Tessera's resting face.

"Hello, Tessera," he said, on a long exhale. He extended his arm and brushed his fingertips across her cool forehead. "I'm Michael. I would very much like to know you. You are safe. You are welcome here. And you did what you wanted to do. David Forte is alive and well because of you. You can stop giving so much. Wake up and stop."

He didn't expect her to open her eyes, but a part of him hoped.

"Come with me to check your grandparents," Victor said as he returned the data tablet to its place at the foot of the bed. He tipped his head toward the door. "When Katrina arrives, I will also ask her to do some focused data searches in Kathleen's file. Perhaps we can find a small detail somewhere that will put us on the correct path."

"Anything would be helpful. I worry how much longer we can maintain her life. She deserves a chance to live."

"Agreed."

Katrina arrived just as they reached the room, and upon entering Victor took her aside to explain the details of their conversation. While they talked, Michael went to the beds where Matthias and Grace rested. They were close enough that if one or both woke, they would be able to reach out and touch the other. Or at least the bed of the other. It had been a request his father had made very specifically. He said they had always been affectionate, holding hands whenever they were near each other. They were even set the way he instructed, saying Matthias always slept to Grace's right and that was how the beds should be. The space was just wide enough for someone to move between them for care.

He turned to his grandmother first. They were moved regularly and cared for daily. Her hair was washed and brushed, her face clean. They were dressed in comfortable bedclothing, out of the torn and dirty clothing they had worn the night of the accident. Color had returned to her cheeks after having been kept in the dark for so long. They had both been slightly underweight, which wasn't surprising. Even in his altered mental state thirty years before, Victor had accommodated for their ongoing care. It wouldn't have been indefinite, but for the time they had been in stasis, they had been cared for as best as possible.

She was beautiful. Michael recognized small parts of her features that had been passed to her son, and in turn to him. He wondered what traits his children would inherit, and from whom. Michael reached out to smooth his thumb over her brow and move some of her light brown hair off her cheek.

He turned to look at his grandfather. Michael had yet to see much physical similarity from father to son and wondered if the comparison would be in mannerisms rather than looks. Time would tell once they awoke. Matthias Tanner had long, angular features and very little gray showed in his dark, almost black, hair. The stubble that had grown over the decades had been shaved away, but even before then Michael had noted the gray was minimal.

In the quiet calm of the room, a slow realization crept over Michael and he tilted his head, giving himself a slightly shifted perspective as he looked down on his grandfather. Matthias' head was turned into the pillow so his face was angled toward his wife, and his left hand – the one closest to her – had been moved away from his side toward the rails of the bed. Close enough his fingertips hung over the edge.

Almost reaching for her.

Michael stepped backward, keeping his eyes on his grandfather until he reached the foot and retrieved the medical tablet left there for review. He tapped it on and scanned the overnight readings. Brain activity, which had been steady since they'd been removed from stasis, showed several jumps during the night. Michael returned to the side of the bed, his heart racing at the possibility.

He leaned over, bringing himself closer to his grandfather's face, seeking some sign of awareness. Michael opened his mind, hoping that if Victor's facts had been accurate that his grandfather had extensive Talents, he might feel Matthias' mind awaken.

"Are you with us?" he asked. "Can you hear me?"

The shift was so small, so slight, Michael didn't trust it to be anything more than his desire to hear his grandfather's voice. He laid his hand on his grandfather's cheek the way his father had to him more than once, because he always found comfort in it. His grandfather's skin was warm and slightly rough from the beard growth from when he was last shaved clean. Michael leaned in closer, bringing his face within inches.

"You are safe. Your wife is safe." He stopped and swallowed, a suddenly intense wave of emotion hitting him. Whether it was Matthias' or his own, he wasn't sure. "Your son is safe. Time has passed, and we will explain everything. But know . . . everyone you love is safe. And we are waiting for you."

With his heart racing and his vision slightly skewed, Michael straightened as Victor and Katrina approached the bed. Victor was speaking, but only his voice registered and not the words. Michael gripped the railing on the side of the bed to keep himself upright, finally pushing through the fog.

"Michael," came Victor's voice again, sharp and demanding.

Michael blinked and raised his head, looking to his friend.

"Call the Castle. Tell my father to come. He's going to want to be here when they wake up."

Katrina gasped, the sound of pure glee, and Victor pivoted on the balls of his feet to return to his desk. Michael blinked through the haze in his eyes and looked to his grandmother.

Her hand now hung off the edge of the bed, reaching out.

CHAPTER THIRTY-ONE

3 August 2024, Sunday
Lincoln Military Housing
Virginia Beach, Virginia

"Nicholas, we aren't trying to control you. Your father and I are just asking you to take a break, step back—"

"I don't *want* to step back. It's my life!" Nicholas shouted, slapping his palm against his chest several times. "You didn't want me to join Earth Force. You don't want me dating Kathy. When do I get to decide, huh?"

Grace winced at their son's shouting, and Matthias had to push back his anger. Nicholas was angry enough for all of them. He stepped between them as a buffer and set his hand in the center of his son's chest, not pushing him but not letting him move any closer. "You're going to stop talking to your mother that way. Now."

Nicholas pressed his lips together until they were white and stepped back, twisting away as he raked fingers through his short hair. He marched to the far side of the sparsely furnished living room, anger, frustration, confusion, and fear rolling off him like the rain on the windows. Matthias clenched his jaw, closing his eyes when Grace slid her hand into his and rested her forehead on his arm. She felt it, too.

She felt everything. While Matthias had his severe doubts about Kathy, Grace knew it far more intuitively. He'd learned long ago not to question her. She'd saved their son – all of them – more than once.

But how could they make Nicholas understand without saying too much? Revealing too much? Exposing the very facts they'd worked over twenty years to keep veiled? He'd be ready someday, but not yet.

"I just don't get it," Nicholas said, each word heavier and harsher as he turned to face them again, hands planted at his waist. "My whole damn life I heard about how you met in October and got married in March and oh how beautiful it was and you just *knew*. Guess it just hits different when it's your kid, huh?"

"It's not about how fast—" Grace tried to say.

"It's about her? About Kathy?"

"Yes!" Matthias snapped. "She's—"

He stopped short, the painful prickle of awareness clawing at the back of his neck like claws of a cat dipped in acid. He turned with his wife to face the door, where Kathy Slater stood, her hand still on the knob as she looked between them with deceptively wide eyes. Her brown hair hung in wet tendrils around her shoulders, her tan jacket darkened by the rain. Even her makeup was smudged to give her the look of a helpless, drowned kitten. Everything about her shouted liar. Matthias hated the way she'd somehow tricked their son. Nicholas was more intuitive than he knew, and yet, she'd tricked him.

"What am I?"

A liar. A contemptible, heinous . . . bitch.

"Answer her, and we're done," Nicholas said through clenched teeth.

"I'm sorry." Kathy came into the apartment, leaving the door open behind her, crossing her arms over her body. "I never wanted to cause so much trouble. I never imagined you would disapprove of me so much. I know I'm not anyone special. I just—I love Nicholas. I wish I could make you understand."

"You know why," Grace said in a whisper intended only for Kathy, her body shaking with her struggle not to say more.

Kathy canted her head, effectively blocking her face from Nicholas' view by using them as a barrier. The wide-eyed, sad expression shifted to a mocking sneer for just a moment.

"I won't ask Nicholas to choose me over his parents," she said with a voice that dripped with venom.

"I'm making my own choice, Kath," Nicholas said behind them.

The tears in his wife's eyes were too much for Matthias, and he turned on his son. "*This* is your choice?"

Nicholas looked him square in the eyes, unflinching, just like Matthias had taught him. Don't back down when you're fighting for something you believed in, and that fact was the answer Matthias didn't want to hear. But it was an answer.

"Matthias . . ." Grace whispered, her voice breaking his heart.

For a heartbeat, he thought he saw the same heartbreak in his son's eyes, but just as quickly it was gone. He raised his hand to touch his only child's cheek with his palm. "Don't do this."

"It's my life," Nicholas said, snapping his head away from his father's touch. "If you can't accept who I love, you won't be in it."

Matthias turned from his son and put his arm around his wife's shoulder, leading her from the apartment, past the woman who made his skin crawl. In the last moment she remained in their line of sight, a smirk curled the corner of her mouth. Just as quickly, she reverted to the wide-eyed victim and ran to Nicholas. His voice, attempting to soothe her, followed them down the hall to the elevator.

It wasn't until the elevator doors closed that Grace turned into him and Matthias wrapped her in his arms, holding her while she cried. His own tears burned as they escaped to slide down his cheeks.

"He'll change his mind," he whispered before kissing her hair. "He didn't mean what he said. He'll figure that out and come home. She'll slip. She'll show her true face. He'll see it."

By the time they reached the car, the rain was a downpour and lightning flashed, turning the night into day, the rolling thunder making the car shake.

"I'll get us home," he said to the question she didn't ask, squeezing her hand before he pulled out of the parking space.

Three and a half miles from the housing complex he knew the lights behind him weren't coincidental and a familiar apprehension crawled over his nerves. He pressed his foot to the accelerator but failed to be subtle enough Grace didn't notice. She looked to him, then twisted in her seat to look through the back window.

"Go faster," she said, and he obliged.

2 October 2054 – Friday
Office of the President
Robert J. Castleton Memorial Building – The Castle
Center for United Protectorate Government

"Why reinvent the wheel? The Constitutional Law of the United States worked for over two hundred years—"

"Did it? Are you sure about that? It worked for some, but not—"

"It worked, but it wasn't without its flaws. Why just do something the way we've always done it just because that's the way we've always done it?"

"This is no longer the United States of anything, Doctor Murdock. In the grand scheme of the world and history, the United States was a very short blip. The way the United States *did it* wasn't the way it was always done."

"I'm not trying to rewrite history here, but I'm saying we can learn from it. Take from it the good—"

"And learn twice as much from the bad. We can do better, to rebuild and rebuild stronger. We can be better. Regurgitating the past doesn't fix the future."

"The past *created* the present we're stuck with! I'm just saying there have been a lot of forms of government—"

"Like the monarchy, Attorney Barclay? Hey, wouldn't you be

something like the 17th in line if the monarchy were still a thing? Trying to restore the royal—"

"Enough!" Nick shouted, slamming his palms down on the conference room table as he shot to his feet, his chair rolling back from him so fast it slammed against the wall behind him.

Every one of the fifteen jurists, legal historians, civic historians, judges, parliamentarians, and legal analysts gathered around the table jumped and silenced. Judge Sergey Viagedor, who had gained his feet to shout across the table at Dr. Shondavia Iannucci, slowly sank into his chair again. Parliamentarian Jean-Phillippe Sauvageon and two jurists – Zelda Braun and Aadarsh Bhatt – faced off at the far end of the table, and like the judge, also diverted their eyes, lowered their hands, and took their seats while he stared them down.

Even after the silence was complete, edging on the uncomfortable, Nick waited. Then the tension broke like surface tension on the pond at Parson's Point, and the rigid posturing of each of them eased. Nick straightened and pushed his hands into his pockets, taking in a deep breath himself. He'd spent the last four days in this room listening to arguments, discussions, valid points, invalid points, more arguments . . . and felt no closer to any kind of restructure plan than when he'd stepped into his office well over a year prior. They'd been here less than an hour before the shouting started.

"This . . ." he said, taking a hand from his pocket to wave out over everyone in general. "Stops. We don't have time for 'My degree is bigger than your degree' pissing matches."

A few of them had the sense God gave an ant to look at least moderately contrite, looking away, down, at their glasses of water, just about anywhere but at him or each other.

Doctor Amy Dewey, one of the most educated legal historians on the panel who happened to be seated closest to Nick, took a deep breath and stood to face him. He gave her credit. She had hutzpah, and while she wasn't one of the screamers, he'd seen her shut down the loudest with a look and a couple stern words.

Reminded him of his kindergarten teacher. No one gave Ms. Hastings grief. Ever.

"Ideally, Mr. President, changes like these would be done after years of review, study, analysis, debate, and then following the proper course of acceptance."

"We don't have time for that," he said, doing his best to keep the groan of frustration out of his voice. "Look, I get it. I don't want to just slap some chewing gum on the massive crack in our crumbling dam of society. That's not the plan. But the muddy cement of bureaucracy isn't an option either."

"Sir, may I ask what you see as our first priority?" Dr. Dewey asked. "That might give us all a road to at least start down."

Nick stood and walked away from the table, hands pushed into his pockets. The conference room was on the same side of The Castle as his office, giving him a slightly different angle view of the property. The dome had protected it on the day of the attack. Staring out on the simple garden reminded him of Parson's Point. He needed a day on his dock, listening to the water ripple and the wind in the trees.

He wasn't in the right headspace for a meeting like this. Not today, anyway. He was tired. Drained to the bone tired. What he once heard his father call soul tired. It wasn't about staying at the hospital later than he intended so he could talk to his parents while they slept in silence. It wasn't about wringing every possible moment he could from his days to be with Caitlin and Adam, and to see his new grandchildren. It wasn't that all those things sometimes meant he slept all of three hours.

It was the waking hours in between.

It was trying to rebuild, but not just cover the cracks and holes to make things *look* whole again. He was determined to do it right. This was their chance to not just do it different but do it right.

It was waiting for the unknown attack that would inevitably come.

It was wondering who the new world's version of Judas Iscariot was, because his gut told him without a doubt there was one.

It was the guilt of knowing he hadn't done enough.

It was the fear he'd never do enough.

"Law," he finally said, turning around again to face the room of people. "I have detention centers full of criminals – *suspected* criminals – and we need to deal with them. Civil law. Criminal law. Military law."

The statement of goal propelled him back to the table. "I want a fair system with clear definitions. No damn loopholes. Loopholes exist to get *out of* justice. What is a law, and what happens when you break that law. Start with the obvious. Start there."

"Thank you, sir," Professor Michone Dixon said before clearing her throat. She had been seated beside Dr. Dewey and took the moment to stand. "The Rule of Law is a solid basis on which so much else can be built."

"It is still going to take time," Judge Cameron Kyle said, sounding like a grumpy old man. "You can't just pluck law out of the air."

"We have a pretty empty slate," Nick said, shaking his head. He wondered how many ways he had to say something before some of the people around the table got it. "That doesn't mean we can't take examples from the past. Society has had established law for centuries. A lot of it builds on the same foundation. Someone . . . one of you yelling a few minutes ago," he paused to make sure the point was clear as he scanned the group, "said we can learn from mistakes, too. Do that."

That seemed to kick a few in the ass, and knock a couple down a few pegs, and they returned to discussions with more talking and less yelling. Nick was about to take his seat again when there were three rapid knocks at the door before it opened, and Phin let Beverly into the room. She had her own round table session going on down the hall with a panel of medical and scientific experts working toward widespread initiatives all over the globe. There were so many councils and panels and planning sessions, the two of them needed to divide and conquer to come close to getting anything done. He trusted her judgment as much as he trusted his own. Hopefully, there wasn't as much yelling in that group. What was there to yell about? *Antibiotics good, broken bones bad.*

Nick left the table and sped up his walk when he caught her expression. It wasn't panic or anything that screamed "Oh, no!" but something was definitely up.

"How's it going down your way?" he asked when he reached her.

"We're making progress," she said with a smirk. "I could hear your meeting down the hall."

"Yeah, wish I could say the same. They're waving around their degrees to prove who is smarter. Something up?"

Beverly glanced toward the table and turned slightly so anyone seated would see her back. "Victor tried reaching us, first you and then me, but was told we were busy. He insisted until someone finally called me from the meeting. You should head to Alexandria Hospital." Her smile widened. "Michael suspects you may have someone to speak to very soon."

Alexandria Hospital, Secure Wing – Medical Research Facility
United Earth Protectorate, Capitol City
Alexandria, Seat of Virginia
North American Continent

"I hope I didn't take you away from anything necessary."

"Nah," Nick said, using every spare measure of focus he had to keep from sprinting down the hall to where Mom and Dad slept. "I'd rather be here waiting than have them wake up with me not here. Besides, I was about at my limit with the panel of highbrows waving around the letters after their names and shouting at each other."

He looked over his shoulder at Phin and Daniel walking behind them. The truth was most of the time he forgot they were even there because they were so silent. Not that other guards were loud and obnoxious, but if you looked up stealth in the dictionary, their pictures would probably be there.

"I was almost relieved when Phin opened the door and let Beverly in. Another couple of minutes I was going to send to the kitchen for some damn cookies. Maybe that would have helped."

Michael chuckled. "I'm glad we could *help*. The truth is they could wake up within the hour, or it could be another day. I just know they are closer, especially your father."

"That's good to hear. I'll feel better when I know—"

Whatever he had to say was cut off by a crash and shouting from the room just thirty feet ahead of them. They all ran, with Michael and one of the brothers hitting the doorway just ahead of him. His father was out of bed, and despite the dangling train of connections hanging from his temples, he had Victor by the throat.

"Dad!" Nick shouted.

Everything slowed for half a heartbeat as his father staggered, looked up, and his grip eased enough on Victor's throat he stumbled back, coughing. Michael caught him, and Nick realized his father's full attention was on Michael. He stared . . . unblinking. Then he swayed and caught himself from falling by gripping the footboard of his now empty bed. Nick moved forward with slow, careful steps. His father looked confused, then raised his head and saw Nick.

The air hummed and the hair on Nick's arms stood straight up like he was caught in a static storm.

Without the conscious thought to do it, Nick had raised his hand to stop Phin and Daniel from intervening. They stopped, their expressions unchanged, but kept back.

Victor motioned Michael back toward his grandfather, moving to the far part of the room. "It's alright," he rasped out. "He's confused. And possibly recognizes me on some level."

Nick took another step forward, his voice stuck in his throat like a handful of pills he couldn't swallow. His father's eyes shifted from him back to Michael.

"Nicholas?" he asked, his voice rough like he needed a drink. "Where's your mother . . ."

He turned enough to see the other bed and tried to get to it, his knees folding as he rounded the end to Mom's side. Michael went to him, giving him support to sit on the edge of the bed, but looked to Nick. "Dad . . ."

Swallowing hard, Nick forced himself to move. He'd run a dozen scenarios how this moment would go down but not one damn one of them prepared him for the actual moment. His father . . . not in stasis, not unconscious, but awake. And confused as hell, based on the way the air vibrated. A perception that confused the hell out of Nick.

Matthias pulled himself along the side of the bed, using the safety rails to propel him, until he reached his wife's shoulders and he hunched over the bars, stroking her hair. "Gracie," he whispered.

"It's okay, Dad," Nick finally made himself say, drawing his father's confused attention again. He raised his hand and wiped his finger over his damp upper lip. He hadn't had nerves like this talking to his father since he dented the pickup driving home one night. "A lot has changed, but . . . it's okay. Mom's okay. She'll wake up soon."

Matthias Tanner squinted, then closed his eyes and gripped his forehead, swaying. Nick closed the space, going to his father's side opposite Michael, supporting him. As soon as he laid his hand on his father's shoulder, something invisible but almost visceral slammed into him and his father jerked. Not away, but in response to the same sensation. Matthias stared at him, his breath rapid. He glanced at Michael, but only briefly before bringing his attention back to Nick.

"Nicholas . . ."

Nick nodded. "Yeah, Dad. It's me." He tried to smile, but it was hard, and the tightening of his throat was making it hard to talk. "It's been a while." The last word caught, and he sniffed, working his lips together as he tried not to squeeze his father's shoulder too hard. For a few moments all he could do was nod. "It's good to talk to you, Dad."

His father pushed up off the edge of the bed again, standing his full height that was just an inch taller than Nick, and Nick shifted his hand from his father's shoulder to his arm to support him. Still staring, still silent, Matthias raised a shaking hand and laid his palm against the side of Nick's neck . . . just like he had more times than Nick could count in his life.

"How . . ."

Nick chuckled, trying not to break into a full out, insane cackle. "That is a long story, Dad."

Matthias' movements were slow, and the waves of exhaustion buffered off him, so Nick knew they'd have to let him rest, but he still turned with unblinking eyes and focused on Michael again.

"This is your grandson. Michael."

Nick was pretty sure his father had mistaken Michael for him. They were near the same age when . . .

"Grandson," Matthias repeated, with the confidence of a statement and not a question.

Michael moved to be more in his view, smiling. "I'm looking forward to . . . everything."

CHAPTER THIRTY-TWO

Alexandria Hospital, Secure Wing – Medical Research Facility
United Earth Protectorate, Capitol City
Alexandria, Seat of Virginia
North American Continent

The clawing sting of annoyance wouldn't let David go.

Lucy had done her best to encourage him and shift his thinking, and he loved her more for it, but he was the idiot and homemade biscuits wouldn't change that. Lucy's biscuits did a lot of things, but they apparently didn't make him less an idiot.

He'd tried to excuse himself by saying he was distracted since he'd learned what she might have done, and the reality of what she might give up saving his stupid ass, had messed with his head but the idea for the dome went back months before he'd even met her. If anything, realizing now how much time he'd wasted figuring it out made him even more angry she'd chosen him over herself. He sure as hell wasn't worth it.

He'd tried to focus on the fact he'd realized his screw up, and could now figure out how to fix it, but he couldn't let go of the personal disgust that it had taken him so damn long to figure out what should have been so obvious.

It was equivalent to Isaac Newton being inspired to make pie instead of discovering the laws of gravity after getting bonked on the head by a random apple. Completely missing the point.

As his grandfather used to say, "If it were a snake, it woulda bit ya."

There was no justification.

"Hey! I didn't know you were here," Katrina said, bouncing through the door of the lab. "I would have come down sooner."

Even her jubilance and kiss on his cheek wasn't enough to yank David out of the muck he was stuck in. She leaned against him, resting her arm on his shoulder and her chin on the back of her hand, oblivious to his dark mood.

"How's it going?"

"Not a good day to ask me that, Peanut," he grumbled, dropping his stylus to scrub his hands over his face, groaning into his palms before dropping his hands onto the table again. "I've been an idiot for weeks, and my own brain finally Gibbs-slapped me this morning."

"Um, okay."

He motioned at the display in front of him. "This might as well have been a million-piece puzzle after the dog ate the most important piece. Useless."

He'd set up a to-scale holographic prototype on a massive table in what had been a relatively empty lab off Victor's research area to help him with running scenarios and visualizing the span and effectiveness of the dome on a larger scale. The prototype allowed him to see smaller geographic areas like Alexandria and its surroundings all the way out to a global level. Not that he'd come close. He'd barely come close to Alexandria, and while he could create a stable dome it drained every power source they had. Solar, hydro, wind . . . hell, he'd even considered geothermal. They were all sources of energy widely used, but the massive level of output needed couldn't be produced even when combining them. Especially when not every natural power source was available everywhere, and he would need a consistent net of energy to do what he wanted. He didn't know if there had ever been a power source since nuclear power was a thing.

And it hadn't been for a very long time.

Nor would it be again.

"Can I help?" Katrina set a foot on one of the rungs of the stools he kept around the table, pushing herself up to sit. "I'm good at puzzles."

"I don't think so. Not unless you have a degree in psychokinetic energy I didn't know about. Hell, does *anyone* have a degree in psychokinetic energy?"

"You mean like Talents?"

"That's what the kids are calling it these days."

He sat up straight, his back notifying him he'd been sitting hunched for too long. While a long cry from where he'd been physically a few weeks earlier, he was still almost eighty and his body liked to remind him.

"I don't understand."

"Neither do I. And that's the problem." David sighed and tapped in the commands needed to switch the hologram to a closer view, representing the control devices and power connections he'd been setting up for the last few months. "I designed this after seeing the Tanners et al save our collective asses at the residence. But my head was stuck back forty years ago when psychics were charlatans and talents included tap dancing and baton twirling at the county fair."

Katrina looked from him to the hologram, her forehead creasing enough to shift her glasses on her nose. "Is that why you haven't been able to find enough power?"

"Yep. Except how do you harness something like Talents? I mean, I can't exactly strap down every person with Talents to power up a planetary forcefield. I'm pretty sure there'd be some sanctions against it, and I don't know how I'd do it anyway since – duh – I don't know how they *work*."

"Yeah, but you know that's what you need to do, right? So, ask John."

David shook his head and crossed his arms over his chest, huffing. "Just because John is Areth doesn't mean he'd know a way to be a giant, biological battery. I mean, humans breathe and . . ." he practically stuttered, trying to find an explanation that made sense. "We're not all pulmonologists. We drive cars – or hovers, or whatever – without being mechanics. You can use something without understanding exactly how it works. Like I said . . . I don't think there are degrees in this."

Katrina turned away from the table to look at him. "Don't they? I mean, kind of? Maybe not here, or yet, but John was a physician before he was an ambassador, right? Wouldn't *his* people maybe know more about how Talents work? And if they do, wouldn't a physician maybe know how it works? Didn't they design their ships to enhance Talents? Maybe they *do* know how to harness it." She shrugged. "If John doesn't know, maybe he can talk to someone who does."

David stared at his sprite of a daughter-in-law, feeling both profoundly stupid and profoundly proud at the same time. He inhaled a deep breath through his nose and said "thank you" as he exhaled.

Katrina grinned. "For what?"

"For being a hell of a lot smarter than me." He stepped off his stool and offered her his hand so she could get down. "I have a phone call to make."

She arched a single eyebrow and smirked. "Phone call. So obsolete, old man."

"Today, Kiddo, I'm inclined to agree."

"*H*ave you seen any change?" Michael kept his voice soft, calm, as he approached his grandmother's bed, stepping to the side opposite where Matthias sat.

His grandfather raised his head and looked across to Michael, the same look of recognition and surprise in his expression he'd worn every time he looked at Michael since waking. His forehead pulled down for a moment, then he shook his head with one small motion and looked to his wife again.

"No. I've been asking her to wake up. I feel her trying—" He stopped short and glanced at Michael again. "That must sound strange."

Michael shook his head. "Not at all. It might surprise you how much I understand." He smiled, hoping his grandfather felt his assurance. "Victor told us there are some traits that run deep and strong in the Tanner family."

Matthias sat up straighter but kept his hand on his wife's. His eyes pinched. After decades without movement sitting in a chair caused him intense discomfort. He tried to mask it, but Michael felt it, and had tried to get him to rest but he wouldn't leave Grace's side.

"Victor. He's the one—"

"Who was here with you when you woke up, yes."

"He's the last face I remember."

In the few hours Matthias had been awake, Michael already recognized his grandfather was a man of few, but weighted words. His meaning came from everything else about him, from tone to eyes, to body language. Michael kept his body relaxed, despite feeling the tension around his grandfather, and walked around the bed to stand near him closer to the head of the bed. It let his grandfather angle himself in the chair to see both wife and grandson. Michael could see the majority of the room, including if Victor returned.

"Victor is a good man. You'll believe that in time."

"I don't know what to believe since I don't have much to go on."

"I realize that. I'm not avoiding the answer," Michael finally said. "It's not a simple history to relay and there are so many things to explain. Having lived them, it's very difficult to know where to begin."

He paused, trying to choose the right words. The weight of importance held his tongue. Matthias never looked away from him, and perhaps for the first time he understood when Caitlin or Jacqueline had tried to explain how his penchant for study made people uncomfortable.

"The race that called themselves the Areth, the race you knew . . . were not. You *will* meet more than one *true* Areth. The liars stole the name just like they stole the lives of thousands of Humans. Victor is, in essence, one of their victims. You were to be murdered – the majority of that story should belong to your son – but Victor stopped it. He saved you. And could not bring you back until now."

"Who is your mother?"

The sudden shift in conversation initially caught him off guard. Michael inhaled deep, using the exhale to attempt a suppression of the visceral reaction he knew Matthias would probably feel if his Talents were as powerful as Victor believed. Matthias never looked away.

Michael also felt the shift in the room, the nudge. The awareness.

"You would know her by the name Kathy Slater."

"That wasn't her name."

The sentence lacked the inflection of a question.

"These days we leave it at heinous bitch."

Michael looked past his grandfather to his father, who had returned from calling home to let Caitlin know what had changed. He'd also sent Daniel to pick up her and Adam, leaving Phin with him who remained by the main door into the room. The full introductions of the rest of the family would wait until another day, probably when both Matthias and Grace could go home.

Matthias turned his head to watch as Nick took up the place where Michael had stood minutes before, on the other side of the bed. He looked down at his mother, giving a small smile as he took her free hand, then looked at his father.

"This is when I say what I should have said thirty years ago." Nick paused to press his lips together, working his jaw before he spoke again. "You were right, Dad. You were right all along about her. She was everything you said, and . . ." He shook his head, his expression twisting with the anger he always harbored against Kathleen. "A hell of a lot more."

"She's one of the other alien race. The one you say lied."

Nick nodded, and Michael let him take over the explanation while he surreptitiously looked to his grandmother's scrolling medscan data.

"Yeah." He cleared his throat and shifted his attention to Michael. "If there were ever any actual epitome of evil it's her – we'll get into all that – but, at the end of the day, I have Michael because of her." He looked back to his father, the smile replaced by cold fact. "It's the only reason she'll see any mercy from me when she dies."

"Damn," Matthias said, adding a low chuckle that sounded so much like the sound Michael had heard his father make hundreds of times.

"Yeah, well, nothing is about her anymore." He looked at Michael and winked. "We're going to start introducing you to what it *is* about."

Beyond Nick's shoulder, Michael saw Phin dip his chin and speak low, likely responding to a message transmitted to the effectively invisible earpiece he, Daniel, Connor, and other Firebirds wore. He crossed the room, approaching them with an acknowledging nod to Michael and Matthias.

"Sir, a message has been relayed. Your presence isn't requested, but Colonel Ebbens has asked you contact him. He realizes you are attending to family matters but has stated it will be brief."

While they spoke, Matthias turned to Michael and spoke in a low voice. "Who is he? He hasn't left since you got here."

"His name Phin Forte," Michael answered. "He is one of Dad's primary protection details. He and Daniel, his brother who you probably saw, stay with Dad during the day."

"Protection detail."

"I need to step out for ten," Nick said, interrupting their exchange. "Ebbens needs me to say it's okay to buy paperclips or something," he added with a smirk. "I'll be right back."

"Hang on," his father said, and Nick rocked back on his heels. "Seems like a good time to ask—"

"Probably," Nick said before he finished with a pressed lip grin. "Hope you're proud, Dad." He hitched his chin at Michael. "You fill him in, since most days I can't believe it myself."

He followed Phin out of the room, but Michael's grandfather had his focus back on Michael before he was out of sight.

"Dad is humble," Michael added with a smile he knew expressed his pride. "He's also amazing. He is quite possibly the single, sole reason any of us are here right now. He saved mankind, and that is not in any way an exaggeration. Dad – your son – is president of our world. Elected in war, and he's doing everything he can to assure peace."

Matthias' unblinking eyes expressed what he didn't say.

Michael smiled and looked at his grandmother. Her face was still relaxed in sleep, but he felt the shift. Every few minutes, she reached out even if she didn't realize herself she did it. He had felt it strongest when his father had come to the bed, and when he'd touched her hand.

"She's almost ready," he said, laying his hand on her hair above her brow. "I think she's listening."

"You're aware of her. I thought maybe, but I knew better than to talk about it."

"Those strong Tanner genes Victor spoke of." Michael nodded, looking back to his grandfather. "It's one of the many different things now. We call them Talents. It's what they are called on Aretu, where the true Areth people come from. It's exceptionally common amongst them and becoming more common and accepted here. Now that it's not seen as . . ." He paused, trying to find the right word for how it had been viewed decades earlier. "Freakish."

Michael sensed his grandfather wanted to take a step back from the topic, so Michael let it go to silence while he studied the medscan data and let Matthias rest, even if it was just in the chair beside the bed. The fact he had been on his feet, upright, and communicating so clearly was likely more a testament to his need to be present than the care he'd received in the stasis tube. Victor had seen to their care, and it showed in their overall health, but even then most lesser men wouldn't have been able to stay conscious, let alone actively engaged.

His father was in the hallway approaching the room, and Michael looked to the glass windows at the same time as his grandfather. Caitlin walked with him, with Adam in her arms. Daniel walked ahead, and Phin behind. Although Adam was only a few weeks older than the youngest Tanners, his growth was obvious. He held up his head now, easily looking around as Mom or Dad carried him. He napped, ate, and now played. She smiled and talked to Dad as they walked, and Dad smiled, too.

"Who is that?" Matthias asked.

Michael probably should feel some sort of guilt whenever he explained Caitlin's relationship, but a part of him enjoyed the surprise. "The woman you asked about may have given birth to me, but she . . ."

He dipped his chin to indicate Caitlin as they came through the door. "Is my mother."

Dad crossed the room, one arm behind Caitlin. Her smile was beautiful, and Michael soaked in the waves of happiness coming from both of them.

"Dad, this is Doctor Caitlin Montgomery-Tanner. My wife. This is our son." He smiled wider. "Adam Nicholas."

"I'm so incredibly happy to meet you. This is such a gift."

Matthias braced one hand on the bed, and Michael stepped in to take his extended arm and help him to his feet. Once standing, Matthias moved by his own accord and Michael followed just close enough to be near if his grandfather needed support. Matthias' focus was entirely on Adam, who was busy with both sucking his own fingers and staring at his grandfather. Eldest Tanner raised his hand, only the slightest tremor of fatigue shaking it, and touched his fingertips to Adam's hair.

"I have so much to find out," he said, his voice adopting the higher pitch that seemed to naturally happen to any adult when speaking to a child. "Are there more Tanners I need to be introduced to?"

Nick laughed, inspiring a deep, rolling sound from the baby. "Oh, we're just getting started."

Michael turned his head and looked down to the bed as gentle fingers wrapped around his, a comforting warmth spreading up his arm. When she looked at him, he knew who she thought she saw, and didn't want to startle her just yet, so he smiled and gave her hand a comforting squeeze.

CHAPTER THIRTY-THREE

Ambassador Residence
United Earth Protectorate, Capitol City
Alexandria, Seat of Virginia
North American Continent

"Abuela Gabi taught me you never show up at someone's door without a plate in hand," Lucy said, hoping the sudden wave of embarrassment didn't manifest as brightly in her cheeks as the heat felt.

At that moment, showing up at an alien ambassador's luxury apartment with a plate of marmalade cookies seemed as gauche as it got. Fully committed with no other way to explain the cookies, she held them out to Ambassador Smith. She also had a fleeting thought she should have offered some to the Firebirds standing guard outside, but just as quickly wondered if they would be allowed to eat cookies while on duty.

Her brain needed to calm the hell down.

"Lovely," he said, taking the plate. He lifted the cloth covering them and inhaled. "Thank you. The children will love these. Sweets were never my strong suit."

With her hands now unoccupied, David took one to walk with her into the Smith's home. They followed John down a short hallway that opened into a larger living space with a couch and some chairs. The Smith children were spread out on the furniture, watching a very old, animated movie Lucy knew was several years old when she was a child about a little girl and her best friend who happened to be a blue alien. The irony was amusing. But all the children were thoroughly engrossed. The two boys, Silas and Simon, sat on the couch, with the little girl Amari between her brothers. The eldest daughter Alexis was in the chair holding Toby but was just as focused on the movie as her younger siblings.

"Come sit," John said, leading them past the family room to a long table off the kitchen.

The apartment was beautiful, though not nearly as fancy as she had expected for someone of Ambassador Smith's station. It was certainly larger than anything in their building, and David had told her the space had once been where President Tanner and his family stayed while the official residence was being repaired.

Everything came around full circle, since that attack had been the inspiring moment for David, and they were here tonight in hopes he'd gain some clarity from Ambassador Smith. David had tried to explain further his thoughts, but psychokinetic genetics weren't exactly something covered in her medical courses.

Jenifer Smith exited another hallway leading away from the common area, and Lucy had all she could do not to stare. She was accustomed to seeing the stately, silent, pretty much terrifying woman dressed in military clothing and usually armed. Even when they were at the residence. But instead, she wore a sleeveless tunic that fitted to her torso, then hung long and loose over loose pants with slits in the sides and front of the tunic that flared when she walked. The material was a beautiful cobalt blue and looked like it might be silk, but she couldn't recall ever seeing clothing like it before. Either way, the usually stoic woman appeared far more relaxed than Lucy had ever seen her, possibly because this was her home.

"Lucy brought us cookies," John said as he set the plate on the table. "I haven't told the children yet, so you might wan' to get some now." He added a wink and took one as he motioned toward two chairs.

Jenifer smirked as she walked by and grabbed a cookie, bumping John with her hip as she did. He chuckled. Lucy felt like an intruder. David pulled out a chair and she sat, then he took the chair beside her while John and Jenifer took space across from them. Jenifer bit into the cookie and groaned.

"Wow," she mumbled around the food.

"I attribute Lucy's cooking for my speedy recovery," David said, reaching beneath the table to take her hand again, resting it on his leg. It felt different now that they knew the truth behind Tessera's sacrifice, but he still used it.

"Of tha' I have no doubt. So, wha' can I help with?"

David sighed and sat back, using his free hand to rub his hair. Lucy knew she was just here to be company, and probably wouldn't understand much of what they talked about, but she was intrigued by the possible discussion, nonetheless. Genetics had always been interesting, and alien genetics even more so now that she had the chance to learn.

"I'm not really sure, John," David admitted. "I'm trying to figure out the power source for the domes and had kind of an a-ha moment this morning. Except I don't know what to do with it."

"Fair 'nough. Tell me wha' you know, and we'll go from there."

"Okay, so, the whole idea of the dome came to me after that night at the residence. I saw what you and Jenifer and the others did, and . . . I thought I could replicate it somehow."

"You've had some success, clearly."

"Some, yeah sure, but not on the scale we need. I've been trying to create from manmade power something that can't be duplicated like that. Your power. Talents. Maybe it's not anything I can do at all, but Katrina thought if anyone could shed light it'd be you. At least, anyone I can talk to about it."

John sat back and crossed his arms over his body, using a thumb to rub his lower lip. Jenifer watched him and reached for another cookie. His eyes cut to her and she smiled, the kind of smile that if he'd spoken implied he'd said something cheeky or off color. Once again,

Lucy felt like they were intruding on something. Then John sat up again and laced his fingers together on the table.

"I'm no' an engineer and can't explain the full science behind it, but did Katrina explain how our ships – like the *Steppenschraff* – are designed to enhance Talents? Magnify them? The theory is to make it less work to use them, thus creating a more comfortable travel experience or whatno'."

"She did, and she gave me some schematics. To be honest, initially I thought it was interesting but irrelevant. But today, after my 'light dawns on Marblehead' moment, I took a deeper look. I don't have all the pieces because I don't have the education to back it up, but I see the theory behind the construction. The ships are built like massive power conduits. Amplifiers."

"Exactly. Like I said, I canno' speak to the engineering element but I can speak to the biology of Talents. There are elements tha' are still hypothetical, but we're growin' our understandin' every year. But I think one thin' to understand is Talents come from a prominent recessive gene."

For the first time in the conversation, Lucy had a rush of excitement at comprehending the topic at hand. She didn't realize she'd visibly responded until David looked toward her.

"You understand that?" he asked.

Lucy nodded. "It's probably the first thing I've understood in all this, but yes. There are a lot of human traits most people would consider the norm, or if asked, would say they must be dominant traits. They're not, they're just more prominent in the gene pool. Like having five fingers."

"Having five fingers?"

"Yeah," Lucy said with a laugh. "For a long time if someone had six fingers it was thought of as a defect, or having webbed or fused fingers, but they're actually the dominant gene. Having five fingers, or separate fingers, is recessive, but so many have the recessive genes it's just the norm."

"That's freaky." He looked to John. "That's how Talents work for the Areth?"

"And likely Humans with time and generations. More and more

Humans show the Talent gene, which is really what the Sorrs were trying to weed out. Bring forward more dominant genes to suppress Talents, while encouraging other genes whether they were dominant or recessive. They were trying their own Human recipes. What would have taken generations to happen through careful breedin', for lack of a nicer word, they tried to force with genetic manipulation and filterin'."

"Okay, so Talents and five fingers are dominant recessive." David shifted in his chair to join his hands together, then stopped and raised one hand to look at his fingers. He cleared his throat and put his hand down again. "How does that translate to the amplification structure of the ships?"

John took the next hour to explain the concepts – both theoretical and proven – about how Talents interacted with surroundings. It was all related to the energy, both kinetic and potential, the individual was able to influence. Every action, every sensation, even every emotion was intricately connected to either kinetic or potential energy, or both. Talents could affect energy, or sense and interpret energy, and in some cases all of the above. Ships, weapons, homes, everything on Areth was geared to the use and wielding of those energies. With each generation, fewer and fewer Areth were born with the dominant genes that suppressed Talents and even those without full-fledged Talents often had some minor level of skill. John explained how Talents could be present, but also muffled either by choice or by suppression and grown with exposure to the energy of others.

That part confused Lucy the most, but she found herself completely enthralled by the entire concept.

"So, just by being *around* people with Talents – if you have Talents, but don't know it – you suddenly can use the Talents?" David asked.

"Of a sort, yeah."

Lucy caught the subtle shift of eyes between John and Jenifer. He didn't look directly at her, but his eyes moved down and in her direction. She sat sideways in her chair, knees raised, watching him, and never moved but a moment later he dipped his head in the very tiniest of degrees and his attention was again on David.

"Jenifer is a perfect example. She is quite possibly one of the most gifted Humans I've ever met, next to Michael and your sons and they all are exceptional, but she herself was unaware of her potential until she spent time on the *Steppenschraff* and it enhanced the Talents she already had, allowing her to learn and grow and harness them. Now, she doesn't need that amplification, bu' anyone with Talents would feel an amplification on a ship like that. Anyone, with any degree of Talents, known or unknown. You yourself would likely feel an increase almost immediately—"

"Me?"

John smiled and tapped the table with his fingertips. "Why do you think Phin and Daniel and Gideon are so powerful? It's recessive, tha' is true, but there are levels of strength. Known or unknown. Awakened and trained, or not. Just like Michael to Nick, those boys to you, the power didn't happen by accident. It happened by genetics."

David shook his head, leaning back in his chair. "Nah. I can't do the stuff you do or come close to the boys. I couldn't bend a spoon if my life depended on it."

"Talents manifest in all kinds of ways, and they can be strengthened," John said, his smile telling Lucy he'd had similar discussions before and with other equally skeptical people.

David waved him off, clearing his throat. "Whatever. Let me ask you this – hypothetically – could the concept of Talent amplification be converted into a power source for a planetary defense system?"

"The Areth have developed numerous forms of weaponry and defense utilizing Talents because it virtually eliminates our enemies' ability to steal our weapons and use them against us. Much like Jenifer's personal weapon Damocles. To anyone else it's a fancy paperweight. Weaponry and design is no' my area, but . . ." He paused, thinking, then grinned. "Fortunately, I happen to know how to find someone. I canno' guarantee I can get them here, but I can get you talkin'. Tha' work?"

"Hell yeah. That'd be amazing."

"Will you be at the Tanners this weekend for Nicole's birthday?"

"Not originally, but I got a message from Nick that he wants us to come by for something else and said we should stay for cake." David grinned. "Nothing can beat Lucy's cooking, but I'm not one to turn down cake."

"I hope to have an answer for you by then."

Alexandria Hospital, Secure Wing – Medical Research Facility
United Earth Protectorate, Capitol City
Alexandria, Seat of Virginia

"So, the guys we thought were the bad guys really *were* the bad guys, but they aren't the real Areth, who are the *good* guys." Matthias Tanner hunched forward to rest his elbows on his knees, hands loosely linked, to look at Nick. "Along with a whole Federation of Planets of other aliens who you skipped across the galaxy to say hello, brought them back, and kicked the bad guys' asses and now you're president of the whole damn world. That about right?"

Nick cleared his throat and shifted in the too deep, too low vinyl upholstered chair that seemed to be standard issue in hospitals since the beginning of time. Once Mom had woken up and gained her legs, Phin and Daniel had found and brought chairs and a couch from some storage room somewhere for them to use and catch up. At Victor's urging, his parents would need to stay in Alexandria Hospital overnight, minimum, but until they needed to rest again, he would take every minute he could with them. Thanks to the attention Victor had apparently put into their stasis preparation, they awoke more like they'd been asleep for a couple days not unmoving for decades. Caitlin sat at an angle to the couch, staying near while Adam napped in his grandmother's propped up and supported arms. Mom didn't look interested in giving him up any time soon.

Nick found himself, every once in a while, fighting to breathe when he looked at them for too long, his youngest son in his mom's arms. A thing he wouldn't have ever imagined.

"In a nutshell, yeah, I guess that covers it."

"How many people died?" his mother asked.

She hadn't said much since he'd begun to explain everything a couple hours before, only asking questions his father hadn't. As always, they worked together with a beautiful choreography, and Nick accepted he hadn't appreciated it enough when he was young and could learn from them and their beautifully woven personalities.

"By the time everything was done, and we felt we could claim victory, eighty percent of our population was gone," he managed to say with a fairly steady voice. "Near extinction level, and I've been fighting to keep people alive ever since."

"He doesn't see how much he's accomplished," Caitlin said, watching him with a smile when he looked at her. "How much he does every day. Nicky doesn't see himself as a diplomat either, but he is our voice with the Defense Alliance."

Dad looked from him to Caitlin and back to him. "Defense Alliance, that's the Federation of Planets basically."

Nick chuckled. "Yeah, close enough. We're kind of the kindergarteners in the mix, but we're making our place."

"I've got to ask . . . aliens. Are we talking Roswell Grays? Vulcans? Klingons? Mon Calamari?" He paused with a shake of his head and grin. "Ewoks? Furlings? Wookies?"

"I've only met the Areth and Umani face-to-face, and they're both uh . . . humanoid? That sounds very humancentric. Bipedal? Whatever. Variations on a theme. We do these trans galactic conference calls and I've . . ." He fumbled over the right words for 3D long distance chat rooms. ". . . interacted, I guess. Yeah, some are pretty crazy looking. The Areth really do look like us, or we look like them. Which makes sense." He motioned to Caitlin. "You tell them. I'm not the sciency brain here."

Caitlin smiled and winked, clearing her throat. "Genetically speaking it's not that they look like us, or we look like them, but at a certain level we *are* them. The Areth and Umani were here centuries ago, not to take over or conquer, but to live with us. Like pilgrims. Modern Mankind is a combination of all of us. Original Humans, Areth, and Umani. Many, many generations of mingled origins have made us who we are now." She canted her head and shrugged a shoulder. "It's difficult to tell what part of who we are is who we would have been without the Areth and Umani, and what part of who we are is because of them."

His dad fell back in the cushions, the vinyl hissing with the shift, and looked at his mom. There was a silent communication when she looked up from Adam and smiled, and he shifted again to drape his arm along the back of the couch so he laid his hand on the back of her neck. "I've got one hell of a wicked headache. You?"

She shook her head, lifting tired eyebrows. "I'm sure it will all fall into place eventually. As crazy as it sounds, I think I'm ready for a nap. But I'm afraid *this* is the dream."

"No dream, Mom," Nick said, having to stop to clear his throat for the umpteenth time. "Trust me, I've thought the same thing more times than I can count since Victor brought you back. I want to show you everything and everyone, but it can wait another day."

"Victor and Michael think you should be able to come home with us tomorrow," Caitlin added. "My field of medical study isn't anything near theirs, but with both Michael and I at home we will know if anything of concern comes up."

Matthias shook his head, but it was with a wide smile. "Doctors and presidents. We're in good hands."

CHAPTER THIRTY-FOUR

2 October 2054, Friday – near midnight
Firebird Command Barracks – Former Hotel District
"The Nest"
United Earth Protectorate, Capitol City
Alexandria, Seat of Virginia
North American Continent

Captain Isaac Bennett jogged into the Nest command center, breathing hard as he stopped short near the end of the monitor console. "Sorry, sir," he panted, planting his hands at his waist while he tried to catch his breath. "I—"

Connor held up his hand, and Bennett stopped talking, dropping his chin toward his chest while he tried to breathe. Connor chuckled and looked up from the screen he'd been hunched over and stood straighter.

"At ease, Bennett. *Laisse tomber.* Don't worry about it. You've got a damn good reason for not being here a few hours ago."

"Yes, sir." Finally catching his breath with a final huff, he smiled crooked and shrugged a shoulder. "In Earth Force, even with a damn good reason my ass would have been in a sling and I'd be scrubbing toilets with my own toothbrush for being late."

Connor made a face and shook his head. "Nah. Not here. And sure as hell not for the reason you're late. How's Lacey?"

The crooked, uneasy smile broke into a huge grin. "Great. She's doing great. Honestly, sir, I don't know if I could have done what she did."

Connor chuckled and took a sidestep to glance at another monitor, scanning the information. It was a quiet night. "That's why God gave women the job. Us men are wimps. So, boy or girl?"

"Girl," Bennet said, and Connor was afraid his face would break soon he was smiling so wide. "Seven pounds seven ounces. She looks so tiny. We're naming her Elizabeth Jane."

Connor popped up his eyebrows. "Elizabeth Jane?"

"Yes, sir."

"Elizabeth Jane Bennett."

Bennett squinted, looking confused, and Connor chuckled. "Is your wife a reader, Captain?"

He nodded. "Yes, sir. Why?"

Connor shook his head and extended his hand and Bennett took it, his grip firm. "Nothing at all, Captain. Congratulations. When is she going home?"

"Probably tomorrow, sir."

"Well, take her home and take a week. We'll make it without you."

"Thank you, sir. Very much. Thank you."

Connor waved him off and went to the chair where he'd draped his jacket. October came in with a definite bite in the air at night. "I'm heading home. You know how to get me if—"

"Sir!" shouted Captain Laramier from her station across the room. "Incoming! Appears to be SSM, medium range ballistic coming from south of here, coastal."

"Trajectory," Connor snapped, tossing his jacket in the general direction of the chair as he sprinted to her station.

She scanned her screen. "Multiple targets. Alexandria. Coastal harbors north and south, Quebec City—" Another alarm blared. "More

SSM from Cuba. Trajectories to Las Vegas, Los Angeles harbors, and toward the equator. Unable to yet determine possible target."

"Coltraine, defense maneuvers," Connor ordered over the low divider to the seated Firebirds on the other side. "Launch ABMs now. Alexandria. Santa Rosa Island. Santana, get me Santa Rosa Command. Trigger the claxons," he ordered to the command center in general and a second later, sirens sounded throughout the Nest. "Sonofabitch. Tapia, inform POW security commander on duty."

His 2IC Levi Colton-Henry burst through the door from the hall, breathing hard from running from wherever he'd been in the building. "What's going on?"

"We're under attack. The whole damn planet." He straightened and shouted across the space. "Boost power to dome over Downtown and the residence."

A "Yes, sir" answered.

"More SSM, sir," Laramier said beside him, the level calm of her voice a sharp contrast to the adrenalin rush in Connor's blood. "Launching from Aasiatt, Greenland. Trajectories indicate Cairo, Hanover, Helsinki. Confirming remaining SSM from Cuba on target to Manta, Equator."

"*Bordel de merde,*" Connor cursed. "Defensive ABMs from all available launch sites." He looked to Hank, who'd moved to a nearby monitor, taking in the chaotic flow of data. "Contact POW and the Veep."

"Yes, sir."

He hated leaving the conversation to Hank, but he couldn't step away from the situation at hand. The next ten minutes felt like ten hours before all SSMs in motion were, in one way or another, out of the sky and fighters had been deployed awaiting further orders.

Exceedingly more exhausted than he'd been half an hour before, Connor took a deep breath and motioned toward Hank to send the open calls to his private office. Hank nodded and hunched forward at his console and Connor went into the room, closing the door behind him. The hum of voices and the follow up noises of the assault and defense immediately silenced. Connor wanted to sit, but not yet. He went to the monitor on the wall and tapped it on. The split screen showed POW Nick Tanner on one side, and Veep Beverly Surimoto on the other, both looking rumpled from being yanked from bed with strain around their mouths and eyes. The sound of a baby crying in the distance came through the comms link and Connor assumed it was his nephew Adam.

"What happened," Nick asked as soon as the video call shifted from Hank in the other room to Connor.

"SSMs, sir. Fired from Oak Island off the Carolina coast, Cuba, and Greenland targeting Alexandria, Boston Harbor, Port of Savannah, Quebec City, Las Vegas, Los Angeles harbors, Manta, Cairo, Hanover, and Helsinki. We fired defensive ABMs from here in Alexandria, Santa Rosa Island, and Kiev." He took in a long breath through his nose to fight the knot in his gut. *Never got easier.* "One of the ABM fired from Kiev malfunctioned in the air and Hanover was hit, sir. Kiev didn't have sufficient time to relaunch."

"Dear God . . ." VP Surimoto whispered and closed her eyes.

"Souls?"

Nick would ask later about resources, structures, and materials but that was never, ever the first question the President of the World asked. Which made the answering even harder.

"Estimated five hundred thousand, including military detail of fifteen-hundred and three hundred civilian attaché support personnel. Because much of the city and surrounding area had been relatively untouched, there had been a substantial population shift to resources and shelter available there."

"How quickly can we get personnel there to help?"

"Less than twenty-four hours, sir."

Nick rubbed his fingers across his mouth, then sighed. "Send what you can. Rescue resources are arriving this week from Aretu. We'll evaluate need and aid when they get here but get what you can there now. Coordinate with Colonels Corchan and Bertrands. Bev, is Victor with you?"

"No," she answered, shaking her head. "He felt it best to stay at Alexandria Hospital with our guests for the night."

"Connor, send a communication out to everyone – the usual suspects – to be at The Castle for 0700 to discuss coordination. Include

Victor because I want him looped in with the aid from Aretu and its distribution. Bev, pull him in with your medical and science people tomorrow." His eyes shifted from what Connor assumed would be Beverly on his screen to look at Connor. "Is the situation under control for tonight?"

"We are on high alert and no further signs of attack seem eminent. Our fighters are in the air en route to the launch sites waiting on your orders, sir."

Nick inhaled long and deep through his nose, working his jaw. "Take them out. Take them out before they can get anything else in the air."

"Yes, sir."

"Just . . ." Nick held up his hand, his eyes momentarily closed. "Just, take out the weaponry. Precision attack. Minimize collateral damage. Just because it's likely Xenos doesn't mean everyone within a radius are part of this."

"Yes, sir. Understood, sir."

The screen went black, and Connor bowed his head, inhaling what he hoped would be a calming, adrenaline-reducing breath. He wasn't going home, so rest wasn't in sight. Not until this mission was done. With a deep sigh that turned into a yawn, he opened his communication link to Evie to let her know he wouldn't be home.

3 OCTOBER 2054, SATURDAY
FIREBIRD COMMAND BARRACKS – FORMER HOTEL DISTRICT
"THE NEST"
UNITED EARTH PROTECTORATE, CAPITOL CITY
ALEXANDRIA, SEAT OF VIRGINIA
NORTH AMERICAN CONTINENT

"We sent fighters and once the exact locations of the launch sites were determined, we shut them down with extreme prejudice," Connor explained from the front of the once conference room back when The Nest was a high end, downtown Alexandria hotel.

The Alexandria contingent of Firebirds was over five hundred, and most were in the briefing, with the message being transmitted to Firebird bases all over the globe. The Xenos had stepped up their game. SSMs had been used in attacks, but never ones with the range used overnight, and never as many. Which meant they were gathering weapons or getting help gathering them. Since the SSMs had been shot down, none had been collected for forensic review, but Connor had deployed small groups of two or three to the last known impact site for debris to collect anything they could for examination.

David was curious as hell if the missiles had any non-Human origins. Would explain the sudden step up in fighting ability.

Like they didn't have enough to worry about with off-world attacks. Zealots, jingos, and terrorists had been using the name patriot as justification to kill anything that didn't think like them for centuries. Now they just had bigger guns.

The Human Race had come a long way in the decades since he'd walked the planet last, but still had a long way to go. People didn't seem to care as much anymore what color skin you were born with, or deity you did or didn't worship, or person you loved. But damn you if you believed we were part of something bigger. Damn you if you looked beyond the third planet from the sun. Damn you if you accepted the truth staring every single Human in the face and chose not to believe in it. Damn you, and for it you deserved to die. History was full of hypocrites.

Their guns just got bigger.

"Additional recon teams will arrive in Greenland within the hour, and the Cuba launch site within an hour and a half. The Oak Island launch site showed no signs of enemy combatants or any other populous. We assume at this point the only people there were the ones employing the weapons, and they either got off the island before we responded by air or were eliminated in the fallout. There were no structures to speak of, and the launcher was mobile. Because of the size and location, we don't believe any civilians – Separatists or otherwise – were living there.

"We expect findings to be different at the Cuban and Greenland sites since both have maintained a civilian population since last year. Military response to the attacks were limited as much as possible to the pinpoint location of launch to avoid innocent loss of life. But the weapons had to be permanently deactivated."

Connor concluded the briefing, letting everyone know information would be disseminated as it came in, and dismissed the crowd. While other Firebirds left the large room, David hung back. Connor had asked to talk to him after the meeting, and as he approached the table Connor drained whatever remained of the mug of coffee he'd had nearby throughout the briefing. He looked tired, but David was pretty sure he'd been up for at least thirty-six hours, if not longer.

"You look like I felt after a party weekend in college," David said, taking the empty chair Hank had vacated when he left.

Connor made a sound between a grunt and a chuckle and stared into his empty cup. "Feel about like it, too. Been here since yesterday morning but didn't really sleep the night before. Adrian is sick."

"Nothing serious I hope . . ."

"Nah, just a fall cold or something." Connor sighed and looked up. "Thanks, though. Tell me about your work on the dome upgrades."

Just like when he'd been in Unity Valley, guilt clawed at David's gut because he wasn't fast enough. In Unity Valley, he hadn't been fast enough to get the rudimentary dome installed and now he wasn't fast enough to get it upgraded. No dome had failed last night, but it could have. As if he wasn't sleeping as it was . . .

"I know the problem, and the theoretical solution," he said, hoping he'd sound more encouraged than he felt. "But I need some Areth – or at least Alliance – guidance because it might require some alien adaptations. John is connecting me with someone. He said he'd have answers for me this weekend when we're at the residence. That still happening?"

Connor was mid-yawn and rubbing the back of his neck when he tried to answer, the first words more a long groan. "For now, yes. The president knows there's always a risk, and we're hyperaware but he doesn't want Nicole to suffer by not having a birthday party even if it's small. I'm pretty sure they'd scaled back from one of his usual gatherings."

"We weren't originally going, but Nick said he needed me there to talk to someone. I don't know who he'd need me to meet that I haven't already."

Connor looked at him when he said "talk to someone," and quickly looked away.

"Do you know who it is?"

"Yeah," Connor answered. "I have a pretty good idea. Makes sense now that I think of it." He smirked, though any humor didn't make it to his eyes. "Don't sweat it. Nobody to worry about, but I get why Nick thought to bring you in."

"Well now I'm damn curious."

"It's a hell of a story." Connor shrugged. "But then again, so are you."

"That's how I want to be remembered. David Forte: Hell of a Story. Maybe I'll write my memoirs."

Connor laughed and it sounded genuine. Genuine enough David hated to ruin it. "You covered the high points, and I don't think I have any more a vested interest than anyone else here, but how close did we get to losing Alexandria?"

Connor drew in a long, slow breath through his nose and let it out before he answered, which said more to David than words could or would and the hairs on the back of his neck stood up. Nausea hit him for a second.

"Without the dome you've built and the countermeasures had failed like they did out of Kiev, we wouldn't even be talking right now. The trajectory would have brought the missile into the front yard of The Castle. Alexandria proper would have been leveled. I won't know until we retrieve any debris to confirm how big a boom it would have been to know if the damage would have gone as far as the residence, but I suspect whoever planned this wouldn't have left a chance of survival."

"No pressure on the dome efficacy, though, right?"

Connor shook his head and investigated the empty mug again, as if more coffee had magically appeared. "Didn't mean it like that. Your domes have saved a lot of lives already. I'll just feel better when it's bigger. What's your hope?" He gave up on the empty mug.

"Ultimately? Global. But . . . I can't make promises until I speak to whoever it is John can set me up with."

Connor pushed back from the table, the legs of his chair making an odd thwumping sound on the low-pile carpet. "I know you will, but let me know what you need from me, personally or from the Firebirds if anything. Otherwise, I'm going to catch thirty and I'll see you tomorrow."

David stayed in the chair after Connor left, the conference room completely empty except for the rows and rows of chairs. He'd worked at a hotel in high school, and it was his job to collect the chairs and clean up all the food wrappings and mostly empty cans of soda left behind. Nothing like that here. The chairs were still in neat rows and nothing on the floors. They probably hardly ever had to do any clean up here; the military had trained them better than that.

He sat until the motion detectors assumed the room was empty of people and dimmed the lights, and still sat there. From the moment Connor had said a missile had been on target to Alexandria, an acidic ball of dread had sat in his gut. The loss of life would have been devastating, and the disruption to the leadership structure would have sent the entire planet into a chaotic tailspin. Of course, that would have been the goal.

But the idea of dying himself didn't scare him. The idea of what would happen to the planet if the Tanners were dead, that bothered him, but it wasn't what spawned the dread in his gut.

The idea of one life being lost. One life in particular. That was what would keep him up at night until he got his act together and figured out the dome. What good would it be to save the world, if it was a world without Lucy Santos?

"Damn, you're a selfish bastard," he said to the empty room.

CHAPTER THIRTY-FIVE

3 October 2054, Saturday – late evening
Presidential Residence
United Earth Protectorate, Capitol City
Alexandria, Seat of Virginia
North American Continent

"Not exactly the White House, but I prefer this," Nick said as the side door and ramp of the military hover lowered to reveal the house. He moved down the ramp and waited at the bottom for his parents to exit.

They held hands as they came down, the way they had his entire life. If they were near each other, they were touching each other, even if it was something as simple as holding hands. Nick didn't realize until he was an adult, and especially with Caitlin, how much he'd learned from their relationship. He just wished he'd learned it younger. He wished he'd learned a lot of things younger, though he also understood the ripple effects. If he'd listened to them thirty years ago, he wouldn't have the life he had now.

He smiled as Caitlin came onto the porch, Adam against her side.

He'd grown like crazy in the last couple of weeks and was holding his head up and looking around with wide-eyed curiosity all the time.

"Oh, Nicholas. This is a beautiful house," his mother said, stopping at the bottom of the hover ramp to look at the home. "My grandparents had a house like this. I remember it always smelled of fresh bread."

"It doesn't smell of fresh bread right now, but I managed to make some oatmeal cookies while Adam took a nap."

"Those are Nicholas's favorite," his mom said with a smile.

"I know," Caitlin said with an equally bright smile. "Come inside. I think it might rain."

His mom hadn't come out of stasis with as much strength as his father, though Nick wondered if that was purely mind over body, so at the bottom of the steps she took his elbow and his father's and they helped her to the porch. She wasn't weak, but she wasn't strong yet either. Victor said it was just a matter of time.

He nodded to the Firebirds stationed on each side of the door. Since the attempted attack during the night, they had stayed more visible than usual only so they could respond faster if needed. Even if only by a few seconds. As he passed them, he leaned over and whispered to Lieutenant Juarez, "I'll get you some cookies later."

The six-foot, broad-shouldered man grinned wide but didn't look his way. Nick chuckled and they stepped inside the house, motioning for them to go to the living room to the left of the entryway. Caitlin walked past him to sit in a chair, but he snagged her wrist to stop her long enough for a kiss. He'd been gone since before dawn, and she knew it had been a scary night. Kissing her helped his world realign. As Mom and Dad sat, a squeal sounded from the dining room and Nicole rounded the corner with Dog on her heels.

"Gumpa!"

Nick crouched in time to catch her and pick her up so she could hug him and plant a loud kiss on his cheek. They'd told his parents there were children to meet beyond Adam, but the actual introductions would be tonight. Somehow, introducing them by name needed to be face-to-face.

"Did you help Lumpy make cookies?"

She nodded with such enthusiasm some of her blonde hair fell across her face and she swiped it back. "Um hum!"

Nick sat on an ottoman near the couch and set Nicole on his lap. "This is Michael and Jackie's oldest," he explained. "Nicole."

Never having a shy moment in her life, Nicole wiggled off his lap and stood in front of them. "Ah-morrow is my birfday," she said. "Do you wanna come to my party?"

"We'd love to," his mom said, then looked to Nick. "My thoughts are swimming. Yesterday, I found out I'm a grandmother of two. You told us Michael has children, but it wasn't quite real until now. We're great grandparents, and to me just a couple days ago you were younger than Michael is now." She shook her head, her eyes shining. "I know you've said this is real, but . . . it feels so unreal. I don't know how I'm supposed to reconcile it all in my head."

"I doubt anyone would know how to do that," his father said.

"Not a whole lot of people, no. But I've got someone coming by the house tomorrow who might not be able to tell you how, but he can at least sympathize." Nick chuckled as Nicole climbed onto the couch and right into his mother's lap.

Never a shy bone in her body, despite what she'd gone through.

"Is you Gumpa's Mama and Daddy?"

His mother's eyes widened, and she looked from Nicole to him.

"She has a way of knowing things," Nick said by way of the only explanation they could give sometimes. "We haven't tried to figure it all out yet. Maybe when she's older, but right now . . . she just knows things and that's about all we can say."

"Yes, baby," Mom answered, smoothing her hand over Nicole's hair. "I'm Gumpa's Mama." She winked at Nick when she said Nicole's version of his name. "I'm very happy to meet you."

"Yup," she said and scooted down, heading for the stairs with Dog beside her. "Mama's coming! Daddy's coming! Babies coming!"

"See? She knows things," Caitlin said from her chair.

Nick stood from the ottoman and sat on the arm of the couch closest to his mother, smirking slightly at all the memories of her telling him not to sit on furniture like that. He was probably teaching bad habits, but most days a kid sitting on the arm of a couch was the least of his worries. A couple minutes later, he heard footsteps descending the stairs. Bringing the Quads downstairs was a minimum of two-person job. Nicole preceded them, giggling as she came.

"Mama, come meet 'em!"

"I already met them," Jackie said, and even without seeing her Nick heard the grin in her voice. She'd come to the hospital during the day before for a quick meeting but hadn't stayed long.

He watched his parents – his mom especially – out of the corner of his eye when Michael and Jackie came around the corner. He'd told them there were four babies but hadn't delved into the full explanation. They started with the most basic bullet points of the last few years, because if that information dump was a lot to take in. The finer, crazier-though-somehow-amazing, details could be explained with time. All they needed to know right now was that Michael and Jackie had four newborns.

His mom's small gasp was his reward.

"I hope you aren't overwhelmed by the chaos that lives here," Michael said as he crossed the room to them.

"Overwhelmed? Nah," his father said. "Just . . . okay, maybe. But in an awesome way."

Michael didn't give any chance for arguing but placed the two babies he carried into his grandmother's lap. Nick doubted she'd argue since her eyes lit up as soon as he held out Victoria Grace, and Nick smiled since he fully understood Michael's choice. She took the second baby just as willingly and Nick helped her situate them, one in each arm, while Michael took each of the two babies Jackie held and gave them to his grandfather with the same lack of hesitance. Nick would bet money which of the boys his father now held.

He glanced over at Caitlin, and she smiled, winking at him.

"We didn't tell you their names before now because I wanted the introductions to be like this," Michael said as he pulled the ottoman Nick had sat on before to be in front of the couch, sitting with enough space left for Jackie to sit beside him.

"After Dad found me, he explained to me about how in the Tanner family children were always named in some way after a Tanner before them and we tried to do that, too. We had to go a little outside the family," he said with a wide smile, "but every name is important to us."

"I can see why you might have had a rough time," his dad said. "I don't know if there are enough Tanners anywhere."

"We nearly resorted to Dorcas Hortense and Elmo Aloysius." Jackie bumped her shoulder against Michael's.

"Geez."

"Thankfully, we didn't have to. After Dad told me a few things, we were all set." Michael shifted and leaned forward to rest his elbows on his knees. He nodded toward the boy his grandfather held on the far side. "That is Gideon Paul. Gideon was the name of my brother who died a few months ago protecting his family."

"One of those stories we're saving to keep from making your head explode," Nick interjected at his father's confused look.

Matthias nodded. "Okay. Sounds like a doozie."

"It is." Nick nodded back to Michael to continue.

"Paul was my father's name," Jackie provided.

"That's wonderful," Mom said, tipping her head enough to look across Dad to Gideon.

Michael alternated by pointing to the boy his grandmother held. "You have Sean Anders. Sean being after my great grandfather, your father," he added, nodding to Dad. "And my middle name."

"Anders is short for my family name of Anderson."

"Oh, I like that," Mom added.

"You're holding the only girl of the four," Michael said, pointing to the baby held in Mom's other arm. "Her first name is Victoria, named after Victor, who has been a friend to me my entire life and as close as family. We owe him so many debts we can never hope to repay, not the least of which bringing you back to us. And her middle name is Grace."

Mom didn't speak but took in a deep breath before looking down at the baby girl. He'd already gotten accustomed to the awareness he felt around them – just like he did with Michael and Caitlin and others close to him – so when the envelope around her warmed he understood. He probably wasn't safe to try to speak right now either.

"And the last that you have, Grandfather, is Matthias Matthew. You probably know that Matthias means blessed, and so does Matthew. We named him that way because we are doubly – more than doubly – blessed with all of them."

"Damn," his father said, his smile crooked as he nodded. The buffer around him shifted, to the point it was almost overwhelming to Nick. His dad looked up from the babies in his arms to look first at Michael, and then Nick. "You named them before . . ." He kind of let the sentence fade, but his expression said what he couldn't.

"Before Victor brought you back? Yes," he provided. "He told Michael that announcing their names – especially Victoria Grace and Matthias Matthew – was the final catalyst for helping him remember. It's . . . hard to explain, and I know we've said that a lot. Because of what Victor has gone through, as long as he's lived, he has a lot of *stuff* kind of crammed in his head. Sometimes it needs to be knocked loose. Naming the babies was what he needed to know he had to go get you."

Nick laid his hand on his mother's back and rubbed across her shoulders. She'd started to cry, silently and not out of sorrow, but it made his throat hurt. She looked up at him, her eyes the same color as his rimmed with more tears.

"If this really is a dream, I'm okay with it," she said with a whisper. "But I know it isn't because I never could have imagined anything so wonderful."

"I get it," Nick said, rubbing back and forth beneath her braided hair. "Most days I can't figure out how I got to be such a lucky bastard."

ALEXANDRIA HOSPITAL, SECURE WING – GENERAL CARE
UNITED EARTH PROTECTORATE, CAPITOL CITY
ALEXANDRIA, SEAT OF VIRGINIA
NORTH AMERICAN CONTINENT

Today was a day for self-punishment.

David had gone from the Nest to the hospital to check on some diagnostics he'd been running. Normally, this kind of equipment build and computer programming wouldn't be done in a hospital but since he kept finding uses for Katrina's toys, it made sense to work there. Because of the extent of data the program had to run, it was a long process and he wanted to make sure nothing had glitched in the process. It still churned away, calculating and extrapolating thousands of possible scenarios, and wouldn't be done until some time on Monday. Unable to do anything else, he could have gone home.

Lucy was at home.

Instead, he stood in a dark hospital room at the foot of a bed holding a woman he barely knew, while she slowly died because she chose to save his life. A man she didn't know. A life she had no responsibility for. And as of late, he believed at a cost that put far too much worth on his existence.

Yeah, he was in a dark place. He knew he was in a dark place. He acknowledged what put him there. He just wasn't convinced he didn't belong in the pit he was in.

He was so damn deep in the pit he couldn't go home to the woman he'd fallen in love with, and *hot damn* she loved him back, because he knew without question, and no one could tell him otherwise, that he didn't deserve her. He didn't deserve her calm. Her peace. Her beauty. Her affection. Her joy. Her body. Her smile. Her laugh. Her support. Her care. Hell, he didn't even deserve her goddamn cooking.

What the hell good did it do to be yanked out of his life, such as it was, in 2011 and dropped in 2054 if all he did was take up time and resources and cost the lives of people who deserved more?

Damn, he'd love to get good and drunk.

One of the machines hooked up to Tessera that had been beeping at a steady, slow beat since he'd arrived picked up faster, but no loud warning alarms went off and no one came rushing into the room. The slightly faster beat went for maybe thirty seconds, plenty of time for someone to come in if there were something wrong, then fell back to the slower pattern. David leaned forward with his hands braced on the footboard.

"They say coma patients can hear people talking to them. I don't know if it's true, but I know Lucy is here a couple times a week, and if you were gonna wake up to a voice I'd imagine of anyone's it would be hers since you know her. You sure as hell know her better than you know me." He huffed and dropped his head forward, staring at the back of his own hands and the pattern of the textured blanket covering her.

"I need you to wake up, Tessera. I just really need you to wake up. I need you to stop whatever you did. If that means I go back to being an invalid in a wheelchair, fine. So be it. I don't know how any of this works, but if that's what would have to happen, I'm okay with it. Just . . . wake up. I don't know what to do with this . . ."

His voice choked off when his throat tightened and he stopped talking, swallowing hard several times. His chest hurt and his lungs burned, and he wanted to curse the sky. Instead, he pushed away from the bed and headed for the door. The same machine beeped faster again, so maybe it was normal. In the hall, no one looked up or seemed to be heading for the room.

It was a relatively short walk from the hospital to the apartment, and he used every step of the way as a futile attempt to tamp down the darkness. He didn't deserve Lucy, and she didn't deserve his darkness. The evening air had a definite bite, and the sky opened with a driving rain when the building came into sight. Few people were on the street, but those that were ran for the nearest shelter.

He didn't.

By the time he stepped inside, he was soaked.

When he opened the apartment door, the smell of fresh bread and spices wrapped around him and filled his senses. He shut the door, and Lucy came out of the bedroom. Her wide smile turned quickly to wide-eyed concern.

"David, you're soaked!"

He tried to smile, looking down at himself. "Wow, yeah, guess I am."

"Very funny. Come get changed. The bread is probably still warm, and I've been simmering stew all afternoon. It feels like stew weather."

He hadn't moved from the two steps he'd taken into the apartment, and she reached him as she talked, going to work at peeling the wet cotton shirt off him. By the time she pulled it over his head, his darkness had flipped a switch and all he wanted – *needed* – was her. Maybe, just maybe the fact she loved him made him worth . . . something. Anything.

She dropped the wet shirt on the floor with a laugh, and when she raised her chin to look at him David took her face in his hands and covered her mouth in a kiss that made her gasp and slammed into his chest like an invisible battering ram. Every time he kissed her it was enough to make him tip off his orbit. Every single time.

Lucy moaned into the kiss, and she raised her arms, wrapping them around his neck to run her fingers over his short hair. She was a match on gasoline, and he wanted to burn.

He curled his fingers into her sweater, using it to pull her closer before he yanked upward, and she had to lift her arms so the sweater came up over her head. David threw it away and cupped the back of her head to pull her in for another hard kiss. When she pulled back for breath, she looked up at him with shining lips, breathing hard.

"David," she said. "What is it? What's wrong?"

"Nothing," he lied, curling a bit of her hair behind her ear that he'd worked loose of her braid. He shook his head, focusing on her lips and not her eyes. "Nothing," he repeated and kissed her again.

Damn, you're a selfish bastard.

CHAPTER THIRTY-SIX

4 October 2054, Sunday – pre-dawn
Presidential Residence
United Earth Protectorate, Capitol City
Alexandria, Seat of Virginia
North American Continent

"You're going to be too tired to stay awake through the birthday party if you don't get some sleep." Grace shifted closer to Matthias, resting her head against his shoulder and her cheek on his chest. He curled his arm to draw her closer.

"Says the man who is awake himself. I think I'm afraid to close my eyes for too long, because all this will be gone. Then I think by wanting this, did I not want what we left behind? My head won't be quiet."

"The world sure is messed up, but . . ." He shifted his head enough he could look down at his wife. At that angle he could only see the slope of her nose. "There's no doubt our son is happy."

He felt her smile, her cheek pressing against his chest, the movement familiar and comforting. "That's what makes me question, and I know that sounds foolish. One of the last things I remember before waking up yesterday was being so worried about him, so the logical voice in my head says this is my subconscious compensating. But I don't think I could have made up so much."

Matthias chuckled, rubbing his hand up and down her arm. "I've had the same internal argument. Maybe that makes it truth." He turned onto his side to face her, bringing them face to face but with her still in his arms. "One of the last things I remember is right after the accident, after we went off the road, the doctor they call Victor stood outside the car and looked at me through the window. Since I thought he was there to kill us, I don't know why my subconscious would turn him into some sort of unlikely hero. The truth is stranger than fiction, right?"

She didn't answer, and her steady breathing against his chest told him she'd finally fallen asleep. Outside their new bedroom and down the hall he heard the familiar sound of a baby declaring their need for attention. Then another, and another, until four voices were heard. They quieted again quickly, and Gracie never woke.

Considering the fact they had been in a form of stasis for nearly thirty years, Matthias recognized they had recovered relatively quickly but her quick fatigue and weakness worried him. He hoped Victor, with Michael's supporting opinion, was right and she only needed time. He'd felt the drag of his limbs, too, but had done his best to push past it so she wouldn't worry. He'd never fooled her in their thirty year – though he supposed it was over sixty now – marriage, so the fact she hadn't called him on it reflected her slower recovery.

He'd watch her close. Holding their *great* grandchildren had bolstered her more than anything else.

He didn't realize he'd drifted off himself, finally, until he woke to sunlight coming through their bedroom window and the smell of coffee and a mouthwatering combination of smells he could only define as "breakfast" hit his senses. For a small moment, he was twenty-something again smelling Ma's kitchen coming up from the apartment below him in the winter of 2001. The year he'd come home from Afghanistan to take care of Pop after his stroke, and the year he'd met Grace Meridian Pryor.

Defining moments. Defining days.

He firmed his embrace and kissed her forehead, eliciting a deep inhale and a low moan as she released it. Since the first night they spent together, when he was home, he woke her with a kiss to the forehead. She tipped back her head to look at him and smiled.

"We're still here."

Matthias smiled back. "We are. Should we go see what'll shock the hell out of us today?"

Gracie laughed and rolled away from him, sitting on the edge of the bed before standing. She did it with relative ease, so Matthias hoped it was a sign today would be a good day. Another defining moment. They didn't have much of their own by way of clothing, but Jacqueline – or Jackie, depending on who was talking about her – had loaned Gracie some short pajamas to sleep in. Matthias boosted himself up on his elbow to watch her walk.

"You're lookin' damn sexy for a near-eighty-year-old woman," he said with a chuckle.

She looked over her shoulder at him and wiggled her hips. "You don't look so bad yourself."

Dressed in more borrowed clothing, basic jeans and a sweater for Gracie and jeans and a Henley for him, they headed downstairs finding the entirety of the Tanner family except for the Quads in the dining room eating together. Nicholas looked up, a cup almost to his mouth, when he saw them and stood.

"Were we too loud?" he asked, coming to kiss his mother's cheek.

"No. The food smelled too good," Matthias answered.

"We tend to have big breakfasts on the weekend," their newly met daughter-in-law said, Adam asleep on one arm while she ate with the other. "Been a tradition since Michael came home."

"I like breakfast," he said with a smile that reminded Matthias of Nicholas. He looked so much like Nicholas it took Matthias back sometimes.

"That's an understatement," Jackie said, and Michael winked at her.

"Sit down. There's plenty." Nicholas motioned for them to sit and started to head back to his chair but stopped short and pivoted back with a finger in the air. "Vic did say you should take it kinda slow, though. Your stomachs haven't had to really eat, and all that."

"Then you shouldn't have made bacon and eggs."

Nicholas smiled, a slow grin that changed his expression. "Yeah, maybe not. I think the love of bacon might be genetic."

Gracie took the empty chair beside Caitlin, and he sat beside her across from Michael and his family. While he wanted to fill up a plate, because everything smelled tempting, after a couple bites of eggs he understood Victor's warnings. He stopped before the mild protest in his gut turned into an angry roar, and he noted Gracie did the same, leaving them to enjoy the conversation around the room. The most talkative of them all was Nicole, who spent several minutes telling them all about her party and that her bestest friend Amari was coming over.

"Amari is one of the children of Ambassador John Smith of Aretu," Caitlin explained for their benefit. "He was here when the Sorracchi attacked the first time and became father to a young boy named Silas left orphaned. A few weeks ago, he married a woman named Jenifer and together they adopted four other children ranging from a girl maybe fifteen down to a baby boy a few months old. They'll be coming today."

"Did he marry a . . . human?" Gracie asked, stumbling over the moniker of human.

He didn't blame her. It felt odd to have to make the designation in a conversation.

Caitlin nodded with an understanding smile as she swayed slightly in the chair, still holding Adam. He wasn't surprised when Gracie raised her hands, offering to take him. Caitlin passed him over, his eyes never opening, though he released a long sigh when settled in his grandmother's arms.

"So, the children are human, too."

Nicholas nodded. "There are a lot of kids left without parents or family," He set down his coffee cup after a drink and folded his arms on the table. "It's one of the many balls we're juggling right now. Trying to find them and get them safe, secure homes." He hitched one shoulder slightly. "We could all learn from the Areth when it comes to how they see adoption. They don't."

"They don't adopt?" Gracie asked. "I thought you said—"

"They just love," Nicholas said with a crooked smile. "No adopted. No half. No step. Just children. Not saying I like or agree with everything they believe, but on that I do."

"I'll clean up while you're holding him," Caitlin said, pushing back.

"*I* need to ask you something." Matthias looked up from where he sat on the couch, waiting for Gracie to return from helping with the babies, to see Nicholas standing a few feet away with his hands pushed into his pockets.

"Seems fair since we've been asking questions for two days."

Something about the tension around his son's eyes made him sit up and forward as Nicholas sat on the same ottoman he'd been on the night before when they arrived. Not for the first time, Matthias was struck by how much Nicholas looked like Gracie's father, which made sense. Nicholas had always taken way more after Gracie than him. Nicholas sat, leaning forward with his elbows on his knees and hands loosely linked.

"What?" Matthias urged.

He cleared his throat and looked over his shoulder when something banged in the kitchen, but nothing came of it, so he looked back. "Michael said he explained Talents. That's what we call them."

Matthias nodded. "We had other words for them that didn't sound as impressive."

"He's . . . amazing. He's like nothing anyone has ever seen. Even John says that, and he comes from a planet where most everyone has Talents. Victor says one of the reasons the bitch wanted Michael so bad was because of his potential. Genetics." He shifted is gaze to pin Matthias.

Prickles raised the hairs on the back of his neck. He nodded.

"Victor was around from the time the Sorrs first got here. Way before they said hello. He remembers she found out about this guy in the military whose unofficial record was pretty out there."

Matthias looked away, feeling every one of his crimes come crashing back on him and all the lies he'd told.

"I don't hear a question."

"I haven't asked it yet," Nicholas said, and it made Matthias look at him again. "Vic says she tried to get close to you, but when she found out you were with Mom – very *specifically* with Grace Pryor – she decided to wait. Because the genetic possibilities were even more impressive."

Matthias sat back and released a long breath. "Your mother had no idea what I was when she met me. She didn't even know what she was capable of. To her it was just second nature."

"You're confirming what he said then. That you have Talents."

He always seemed to stumble over the word, just like Gracie had with human at breakfast. It wasn't a natural word for him. Matthias cleared his throat and worked his palms together. "Yeah."

"Enough to draw her attention."

Matthias nodded. "Yeah."

Nicholas dropped his head forward so Matthias couldn't see his face, breathing slow and deep for a few moments before looking up again. "Why didn't you tell me?"

"Because it put us at risk. *You* at risk."

"Victor believed she assumed I'd be some super combo of the two of you. He said she tried to get at me when I was a kid, but I guess I wasn't what Barnabas wanted. So, she played the odds and waited."

The sudden pounding of blood in Matthias' ears muted everything Nicholas said after 'when I was a kid.' He curled his fists against the sudden rage of memory and realization as years of pieces fell into place. Unable to sit or face Nicholas any longer, he pushed up off the couch and went to the fireplace to brace his hands on the mantel.

"Dad," Nicholas said harder, louder beside him.

"You're exactly what she wanted," Matthias hissed through clenched teeth. He was drowning in the overwhelming slam of comprehension.

Undoubtedly drawn by his flash of anger, he simultaneously heard and felt Gracie coming down the stairs. All their years of lies were about to come home to roost.

"Yeah, for some kind of damn breeding stock like she figured it skipped a generation."

"It didn't skip."

Gracie's voice of calm gave Matthias the second of control he needed to rein in his turmoil, and he turned to slam his back against the mantel edge. It hurt, but it grounded him. She walked toward them, her brown eyes sad and he hated it. He hated she had been required to lie for so long because of him. If she hadn't met him, she might have lived a normal life. A safe life.

Nicholas waved a hand of dismissal. "Okay, yeah, I get it. I've got *something* going on. We figure I can navigate wormholes because of *it*. I'm aware of stuff I probably shouldn't be because of *it*. But that's more like hepped up intuition, it's not—"

"We trained you to forget," Matthias snapped out. When Nicholas turned a wide stare on him, he had to commit and get it out. "We knew from the time you were about three that you were gifted. By then, I'd had to come clean with your mother and she had figured out she had her own gifts she'd never understood. Neither of us had any signs of anything at that young an age, so we knew you were something special. We had every intention of figuring it out with you."

"But . . ." he led, his mouth set in a straight, angry line.

"But someone tried to kidnap you when you were five."

Nicholas visibly leaned back, but never actually stepped away, unblinking. "That's what Victor meant . . ."

"I don't know if it's what he meant or not, but it makes sense."

"What happened?"

"Exactly what your father said. Someone tried to take you when you were five," Gracie said, walking further into the room. Behind her, but in the hallway still, he saw Michael and Jackie. They stayed back but listened. "A woman and two men attempted to take you from us."

"And?"

"And I stopped them," Matthias said, swallowing down the bile that hit his throat every time he thought of that night. He was a sniper but had never been face to face with someone he killed. They tried to take his son, and that wasn't going to happen. "With extreme prejudice. For years afterwards, I stayed awake at night waiting for another attempt. After that, we trained you. To forget. And to suppress what came naturally to you. I hoped it was enough, and no one ever tried again."

Nicholas shook his head, his frown firm. "I can't believe this."

"It's true, honey," Gracie said with her soft, soothing voice that had calmed Nicholas so many times when he was a child. "We believed we were doing the right thing. I don't know if we did, but I don't know if we would have done anything differently."

"I'm not like you! I'm not like Michael!"

His decision was split second, but just like he'd acted without hesitation forty-five years earlier, he knew Nicholas would now. Without moving, without looking away, because he'd mastered the skill before ever going into the military. He didn't need to see the path, only the destination.

He knew. He had absolute faith in his son.

"Dad!" Michael shouted, rushing the room.

He didn't look to confirm, but he knew. Hovering in the air just inches from Gracie was the knife he'd seen earlier in the kitchen. He stared at Nicholas, whose intense focus was on the knife.

"Stop this!" Michael shouted.

He felt the pull. The struggle.

"Let it go, Michael," he said, his tone as firm as every time he'd told his son to stop as a child. "You don't need to intervene."

"I won't let you—"

"Let it go," Matthias snapped, still staring at his son who hadn't yet blinked. The only sign of intent the slight squint around his eyes.

He felt the release when Michael did as he said, but equally he felt the fear. The concern. The confusion.

"Take it, Nicholas. You're the one in control."

"No, you're—"

"No, I'm not. No one is in control right now, but you. Put up your hand and take the knife."

Nicholas Tanner was half a century old, nearly as old as Matthias had been when they went into their deep sleep, but at that moment he looked like the child the first time Matthias told him to stop. Now, he wanted him to let go of everything they'd told him when he was young.

He raised his hand, palm out, and the hilt of the kitchen knife slapped against his skin before he closed his fingers around it.

CHAPTER THIRTY-SEVEN

4 October 2054, Sunday
Presidential Residence
United Earth Protectorate, Capitol City
Alexandria, Seat of Virginia
North American Continent

Nick had said the party for Nicole's second birthday would be smaller than usual but based on the group of people at the residence that pretty much only meant no one was coming in from out of town. Which, for many gatherings at the residence for specific reasons, that was a downsizing. The Smiths were present, as were Victor and Beverly, and Connor and family in addition to all the Tanners. There were two new faces, a couple who didn't appear to be much older than Nick, but something about the man prickled at David like he should know the guy.

The likelihood of knowing him was slim. At the man's age, he would have been a kid when David went in the deep freeze. Like younger than David's own children.

The comparison brought a sharp pang in his chest, but he ignored it.

He smiled through the singing of happy birthday for Nicole, and managed to choke down a few bites of cake, hoping he played enough poker in his life to trick most people in attendance. The one person he knew he hadn't fooled was Lucy. Every time he looked to her, she watched him, her brow tense and her smile strained if present at all. She wasn't the poker player he was. Or he thought he was.

After the food and the singing and the few presents the girl unwrapped – it wasn't exactly easy to pop over to Toys R'Us for gifts – Nick approached him and if he had to guess there was a lot on the president's mind as well. It hadn't exactly been a calm week for anyone.

"Can I borrow you for a few, David?" he asked, angling his head in the general direction of his office at the back of the house.

"Sure." He gave Lucy's hand a squeeze but didn't look at her. He wanted to, but it hurt a little too much to see the worry in her eyes.

He followed the president down the hall to the office that faced the backyard. The entire house was wrapped in a deep porch and from the office Nick had a great view of the yard. It reminded him of Unity Valley except for the lack of livestock.

John Smith met up with them just as they reached the door, and Nick opened it to motion them inside. The couple David didn't know was already there, talking as they looked at some of the photos on the wall, smiling. They looked over their shoulders and the three men entered.

Nick shut the door and cleared his throat, going toward the couple so John and David followed. "Not really sure there's a way to ease into this conversation, but I want both of you here for different reasons. Very long story made very short, Victor did a thing thirty or so years ago and these are my parents. Matthias and Grace Tanner."

"Damn," was all David managed.

"Well, tha' explains a lo'," John said, extending his hand to Nick's father. "I've been tryin' to figure out what I was gettin' off you since I got here. Knowin' what I know of the Tanner family, it makes sense now."

Matthias took John's hand and shook it, but there was a definite play of *something* in his face.

"This is Ambassador John Smith of Aretu," Nick said. "Congratulations. You've just met your first true Areth. Not to be confused with the asshats you remember."

"No offense, but I wasn't sure what to expect," Matthias said, releasing John's hand. "When Nicholas gave the abridged version of the last thirty or forty years I guess I was expecting something more . . ."

"Dramatic?" John said with a laugh. "Sorry to disappoint. We suspect our similarities are why the Sorrs chose our name in their lie. Tha' and they hate us."

"It's nice to meet you," Grace Tanner said, and John took her hand but didn't shake it. Just held it for a moment.

"Absolutely. I'm very interested in hearin' the story here."

"We'll get around to it," Nick said with a smile, but it definitely reflected more thought than enthusiasm and David wondered what the hell was really going on.

David couldn't shake the niggling at the back of his brain. *Matthias Tanner. Matthias Tanner . . .*

"This is Lieutenant Colonel David Forte," Nick said, holding his hand out palm up to David. "Remember when you said there wasn't anyone who could have prepared you for waking up? Probably true, but David can empathize." Nick paused to clear his throat again, canting his head toward him. "David was captured by Heinous Bitch and the Sorrs in 2011 and put in stasis like you, except Bitch didn't do as clean a job as Vic. We found him floating in a derelict ship a few months back. So, if anyone gets it, it's probably David."

"Colonel," Matthias said, extending his hand and David took it.

Matthias Tanner. Matthias Tanner . . .

"Merlin!" David spurted, the name suddenly clicking.

The shake stopped mid-movement, and Matthias Tanner stared at him before releasing his hand. "It's been a very long time since I heard that name. We served together?"

"Nah," David said, shaking his head. "Not directly. I was in Afghanistan after 9/11, same time you were, but I heard of you. You were a legend."

"I was a soldier," he said. "Nothing else."

"You had the highest kill rate and successful distance shot, breaking every previous record. I mean, at least in 2011 no one had beaten you."

Merlin shook his head. "Nothing I take pride in. I was doing my job."

David nodded, letting it go. By what he'd seen, snipers had two opinions of their job. They either hated it but did it because it was always required of them, or they loved it a little bit too much. He was clearly the former.

"Small world, short timeline," Nick said. "Not sure if you have advice or anything, David."

"Buckle up and hold on."

"I spoke with Zephania and Beia Willoughby the mornin' after we discussed your research," John said after motioning for David to hang back leaving Nick's office. "They're the top researchers and engineers in psychokinetic amplification structures in the Alliance. Just happen to be life partners too," he added with a grin. "Makes it convenient to coordinate calls."

David shook his head with a chuckle. "Husband and wife team. That's great."

"I didn't say they were husband and wife."

David canted his head. "Fair enough. What did they say?"

John held out a data microslide. "Took me since yesterday to get the files since the transfer of data from Aretu is a bi' slow, and communication channels go' jammed up yesterday. Then translatin' into a language your computers could read. I think this should work. They're schematics, plans, and structural requirements for kinetic amplification in a variety of implications and scenarios. Seemed to me you had a good understandin' of wha' you wanted, so they sent this to get you started. They said they are willin' to do a long-range consult if you need it, and if tha' isn't enough they can speak to the queen about transport."

David took the microslide, staring at it resting in his palm. "You're putting a lot of faith in my last-century brain being able to decipher your advanced technology."

"Don't doubt yourself, David. The solution is there, and you're the one who figured tha' out. No' a small step. You see the end result, now you jus' need to reverse engineer back to the problem."

David folded his hand around the microslide. "Thanks for the vote of confidence. I'll let you know in a couple days if I need to speak to the Willoughbys."

"You can or go direct. I'm no' an engineer and seems it would save time to go direct. They don' need me to play interpreter."

"Thanks again."

"Of course."

"I just wish I'd figured it out earlier," David said, patting his hand on John's shoulder before deciding it was time to go find Lucy.

John raised a hand to stop him. "David, it took us nearly a hundred years after we accomplished space travel to even come up with the idea of psychokinetic enhancing structures, and another thirty years to have a prototype. You figurin' it out in a few weeks *is* impressive."

"Goodyear only produced a tire after someone else invented the wheel," David said and offered what looked more like a smile than a scowl.

"But they improved on the theme, didn't they," John said after him as he walked way.

"*E*xplain to me what happened this morning," Jacqueline asked as she settled into one of the two wide, overstuffed chairs they'd managed to find to place in the bedroom. They didn't match, but they worked perfectly for supporting more than one baby if needed. "I *saw* what happened, but I'm pretty sure I'm missing context."

Michael carried Gideon Paul to her since he seemed the most hungry and desperate for attention of the four. With him settled, Michael went back to the crib and took Matthias Matthew, the next most aware and edging on fussy. If they worked quickly enough, they'd be able to feed everyone before anyone became too cranky.

"Dad believed, even before I accepted it as truth, that the extensiveness of my Talents was a genetic trait somehow," he explained, sitting in the other chair beside hers. "He also accepted in the last year or so that he himself had some Talents, thus confirming genetics."

"I knew all that."

"I apologize. I don't mean to repeat what you know. It helps me connect the dots even for myself."

"Okay," she said, looking down at Gideon as he nursed. "Looked to me like today your grandfather drove that point home."

"I haven't spoken to Dad yet to fully understand his experience, but yes, I agree with you. We only heard part of their conversation, so I am also piecing together all the elements, but my takeaway is that my grandparents decided when my father was very young to mindfully suppress his Talents because they feared for his safety."

"Victor told us the Bitch had eyes on the Tanners back fifty years ago. Is that where we came in on the conversation this morning? Your grandparents telling Nick that the Bitch tried to kidnap him?"

"I don't think my grandparents knew who, only that someone tried. We know now that she and Barnabas had been watching our bloodline since they arrived."

Jacqueline's anger flared, a tangible push against Michael, and Gideon Paul fussed. She shushed him and smoothed his hair until he went back to nursing. Michael balanced the bottle he used for feeding Matthias Matthew against his chest and reached his now-free hand out to his wife. Her gaze shifted from looking at Gideon, to his hand, and back to the baby before she extended her own hand to take his.

"You have been troubled since Victor came back with them. Sometimes angry. Talk to me. Tell me why."

Jacqueline worked her lips together before looking at him, her mouth set and the twist of hot emotions flickering in her eyes. "I hate her."

"I don't know of anyone who holds any affection for her," he said, hoping to gain a smile.

She shook her head. "No, Michael. I mean I *hate* her. I don't understand why Nick didn't just order her put to death when we caught her. She doesn't even deserve Mel Briggs' broken body. All she's done is hurt. You. Your father. Your whole family."

"I understand." Her eyes flicked to him and she tried to withdraw her hand, but he tightened his hold enough to silently ask her to stay. Her hand relaxed. Michael waited until she looked at him again. "I do understand. But I had to stop hating her because it was doing more harm to me than it ever would to her. Do you know when I stopped hating her?"

She shook her head, her eyes shining.

"When Victor told us about the babies we hold now. Our children. Yours and mine. In her desire to possess something she would never have she gave us gifts she never imagined."

"She's been trying to get her claws into your family for four generations. Between Victor and your grandfather, we know that now."

"She's done. She has no power and no way of hurting us ever again."

The bottle against his chest shifted and Michael had to let go of her hand to catch it from falling. Barely missing a sip, Matthias Matthew worked diligently on finishing his meal. When he looked toward his wife again, her face was turned down and she focused on Gideon Paul.

Forte & Santos Residence
Civilian Employee Housing
United Earth Protectorate, Capitol City
Alexandria, Seat of Virginia
North American Continent

As soon as they were in the apartment, David went to the computer he kept at home for late night work sessions and inserted the microslide. Lucy didn't say anything, giving him time to take a look at the information while she went in the bathroom and then bedroom, changing into her nightclothes. When she came out, he still was seated on the couch, hunched forward, scanning his screen with his eyes shifting left to right and his head moving in small degrees.

"Does it help?" she asked as she went to the kitchen for a drink.

He hummed, which could have been an affirmative, a negative, or just an obligatory acknowledgment she'd spoken. Lucy took in a long, deep breath to calm her nerves. She didn't need to have any special gifts of perception to know the tension in the Tanner house had been too high for a toddler's birthday party. She knew the city had been at risk the day before, and she knew David had come home late and on edge. He'd insisted there was nothing wrong, but even the way he made love to her had a feeling of restrained . . . something. Something she couldn't name because he hadn't told her enough.

He couldn't tell her a lot of things; that was a fact she'd accepted early on and most especially after the attack from off-world, but this was more than guarding information. He was withdrawn and doing his damndest to outwardly convince her otherwise. With a drink for each of them, she returned to the couch and sat at the other end from him, close but far enough away she wouldn't unintentionally see anything she shouldn't. Not that she'd probably understand anything she saw. Getting a look at the long equations he worked told her his area of expertise was lightyears beyond hers.

Unsure what to say or do, she waited.

Twenty minutes passed before he groaned and dropped his head forward, roughly rubbing his palms over his hair. David abruptly stood and marched halfway across the living space before turning back, his hands set at his waist.

"I need you to go back to Unity Valley," he snapped.

"Why?" she asked before thinking whether it was the right question or not. Lucy stood, blinking, trying to recover from the abrupt demand. No other question formed. "David, why?" she asked again.

"Because I'm a goddamn idiot and it's going to get you killed!" he shouted with a thrust of his hand toward her, shocking her.

She had seen a range of emotions from him, including intense sorrow, but never unleashed anger. Anger, yes, but not anything he let go on her or anyone else that she ever witnessed. Lucy stood and stepped around the table where his work was always spread out, at least as much as he could. She took steps toward him, but he backstepped, and that froze her in her tracks. She inhaled slowly, fighting the sudden jump in her heartbeat.

"You aren't responsible for keeping me alive."

"Aren't I? I'm the one who asked you to come to Alexandria—"

"Yes," she pushed back, refusing to shout but also refusing not to be heard. "You asked, and I agreed. You didn't force me, and I didn't demand to come. We've had this discussion already, David. I didn't expect anything other than to be with you."

"I'm not worth the risk!"

"Stop yelling at me."

David closed his eyes and turned partially away, shaking his head before he started again. "I have to figure this out. I have to *fix* this. I told Nick I would."

"If you can't do that because I'm here, then say that. Don't lie to me because you think it's what I need to hear. Be honest with me."

"I am!" he shouted again.

"Stop. Yelling. At me."

He dropped his head forward, breathing so hard and rapidly she heard every scrape of his breath from where she stood. Taking her own fortifying pause, Lucy crossed the space until she stood in front of him. Close enough she could touch him if she wanted to. Or he could touch her. But she didn't.

"David."

He didn't raise his head, didn't acknowledge her.

"David James Forte," she said more sternly.

He made a small snorting sound before raising his chin to look at her, his face flushed and eyes red.

"Do you want me to leave Alexandria?"

"No, baby," he said, all blustering and anger gone from his voice. Just a heaviness that made her chest heavy and heart ache. "I don't *want* you to. I *need* you to."

"Why? Help me understand."

His expression softened and he took the one step toward her he needed to bring them together and raised his hands to cup her face.

Calloused thumbs stroked her face, brushing her lips. She kept her breaths shallow, watching him as he studied her face, waiting.

"Because someone wanted to blow Alexandria off the planet yesterday, and I've seen the analysis. My dome wouldn't have prevented loss of life. It would have prevented some, but too many people would have died." He sniffed, his eyes shining. "You could have died, and I wouldn't be able to take that."

"I didn't die. No one died."

"Not here, but people died yesterday. If I had figured out my screw up before now, maybe no one would have died."

"Maybe—"

"Yeah, maybe. But maybe is better than what we have right now."

"Anywhere in the world could be a target."

He nodded, changing his caress from her lips to her cheeks beneath her eyes and she realized he wiped away tears. "You're right. But Alexandria is target one. Alexandria is where they are always, always going to go after first."

"I don't want to go."

He pressed his lips together and shook his head, slow and intent. "I don't want you to. But I need you to."

"Tell me you love me."

"I love you," he said without hesitation, before she could finish the request. "Baby, I love you so much it scares me. It scares me because I can't, I *can't* let anything happen to you."

Lucy had to pull in several smothering breaths and swallow hard before she could speak, and even then her voice was a ragged, rough whisper. "I'll go."

He tipped his head forward until their foreheads touched, and Lucy closed her eyes, moving into him until their bodies touched and she could put her arms around him. David brushed his nose against hers, and with his thumbs beneath her chin, tipped her face up to meet his kiss. She tasted the salt of tears on their lips, knowing they were her own but maybe even his too. David deepened the kiss, and a conflicting swirl of sadness and need curled in her belly.

Why did this feel like goodbye?

CHAPTER THIRTY-EIGHT

7 October 2054, Wednesday
Protectorate Citizen Community — Unity Valley
Vancouver, British Columbia
Former Country of Canada
North American Continent

Heavy rain had forced Captain Ashley Stewart to slow their travel to Unity Valley, extending the trip by two hours. While the sound of the rain pelting the hover and the frequent shudders and jerks of the craft when wind gusts pushed it made Lucy's stomach twist with nausea, she took the two extra hours with David as a blessing. Even if it were mostly sitting in silence in the hover, holding hands.

But it also meant David wouldn't be able to stay long in Vancouver.

She had committed to returning on Sunday, but David needed at least a couple days to read through and interpret the data he'd gotten through John Smith. He'd started another simulation that would take a few hours to extrapolate the data, giving him time to go with her back to Unity Valley. The stress of finding the answer to a question no one had asked before – not the Areth or the Alliance – how to use their psychokinetic enhancement designs to power a defense shield, was eating him from the inside. Lucy worried more for him now than when he'd come back down the mountain with Tessa. That was physical; this was almost spiritual.

"Not a great day for a homecoming," he said when Captain Stewart confirmed they were five minutes out from the community.

"Nothing would make this a great day," she said softly, staring down at their linked hands on the armrest between them.

David lifted their hands to his mouth and kissed her knuckles.

The closer they got to Unity Valley, the more her stomach twisted and her head hurt. By the time Captain Stewart slowed the hover and gently set it on the ground, the rain had slowed to a depressing, late afternoon drizzle.

"Should I wait here, sir?" the captain asked as the hover hatch released and the hydraulics hissed to lower the ramp.

"Yeah," David said. "We can't stay long."

"Yes, sir."

Hand in hand, while David carried her only bag and her sketch materials he'd given her, they jogged through the cold drizzle to the porch of the main house where Rev and Molly waited, their baby girl in Molly's arms. Despite the dread in her heart, Lucy smiled and let herself feel the excitement of seeing her best friend again.

"Oh, it's so good to see you," Molly declared, holding out her free arm to wrap around Lucy's neck when they embraced, Baby Della between them. She kissed Lucy's cheek before giving a quick squeeze and letting her go.

"It's good to see you, too," Lucy managed to say and hugged Rev, too. "I've missed you." She turned back to Molly to pull back the blanket enough to see the baby. Her fine hair lay in waves, and she had the most adorable cheeks. Lucy smoothed her fingers over the baby's forehead. "She's beautiful, Molly."

"Thank you."

"Isn't she beautiful, David?" she asked over her shoulder to him, forgetting for just the briefest second he was practically on the hover already to leave her behind.

He stepped up behind her and curled his hand around her far hip, looking over her shoulder at the baby. "Yeah. She's beautiful. Every baby is beautiful. Especially these days." He looked to Trevor. "Feels like hope."

"I agree. In fact, we considered naming her Hope."

"No," Lucy said, shaking her head. "Della is perfect for her."

"Colonel, I am amazed by your recovery since you left us. I'm happy to see you here to know you are doing so well. Can you come inside for a little while?" Trevor asked. "We're preparing dinner and our guests—"

"No, I can't stay," David answered, his hand on her hip firming slightly. "Thanks. The rain delayed us getting here. I need to get back to Alexandria."

She couldn't meet Molly's eyes, so focused instead on the baby, fighting the desperate need to cry. She would, but when she was alone.

"Of course. We'll see you inside, Lucy," Rev said and reached for his wife's hand to go into the house.

She tried not to let the tears come, tried to deny the sob stuck in her chest, but it was as undeniable as the rain. When the house door closed behind the Tisdales, David stepped around to face her and wrapped her in his arms. She pressed her forehead on his chest and fought for control. He never tried to shush her, didn't tell her to stop, and while she was thankful he wasn't the type of man who thought telling her not to cry would somehow stop the pain she almost wished he would. Maybe she would find a way.

Instead, he held her with his cheek resting against her temple, his arms firm around her.

"I'm sorry," she forced out through her tight throat. "I'm not trying to make this hard—"

"This is on me, darlin'," he said against her hair. "I'm the ass here."

He kissed her temple and withdrew enough to take her face in his hands and she tipped back her head to look at him. David smoothed his thumbs over her damp cheeks. They'd already talked about how she could reach him, and he'd given her a comms link, with promises to reach out when he could, and he'd asked her to check on Felicia, Davey and DJ. Maybe find a way to soften Felicia's heart to his existence, because come hell or high water when he came back he would be in his son's life. His great grandson's life. Whether Felicia liked it or not.

He'd said "Or *bye, Felicia*," with a weird, lyrical tone and had laughed afterwards, so she assumed it was another one of those references no one else got. Maybe she'd try to figure it out while they were apart.

Her heart hurt so much she couldn't take a breath.

"I'm going to figure this out. As fast as possible. When I do, I'll ask you if you want to come back."

"I'll want to."

David smiled, but it was less than convincing. She understood because her heart felt the same way. "I'm still going to ask."

The choking sadness eased just enough she could take a breath and release it. Lucy licked her lips and looked him in the eyes, turning her head slightly into his touch.

"So, ask me," she told him.

"I will. When I'm done."

"No, David. *Ask* me."

The moment he realized what she meant sparked in his expression and he pressed his lips together, his focus somewhere around the end of her nose rather than her eyes. He inhaled slow and exhaled as he looked her in the eyes.

"Marry me, woman."

The same words, the same way he almost always asked. Lucy smiled, more of the ache letting go. The next few days and weeks would be hard, but in that moment – if even for just a moment – she knew it would be okay. "Yes."

He kissed her, long and deep and thorough, leaving her holding on to him to keep on her feet. Somewhere on the edge of her peripheral awareness, she heard Captain Stewart call that another storm would be rolling in soon. If they left, they could get into the clear before it blocked them. At least she sounded apologetic. David slowed the kiss, every slide of his lips on hers feeling like a study in their taste together. She curled her fingers into his jacket, not wanting to let him go when he eased away. Instead of stepping back, he kissed her forehead then touched his to hers.

"I love you," he said in the space between them. "You don't have any idea what you've done for me. To me. Don't forget that, okay?"

"I won't forget." She tipped her head up to kiss him again, far too short and far too quickly. "Don't forget I love you, too. Come back for me soon."

He nodded, his eyes closed. One more quick kiss and he stepped back from her. One more squeeze of her hand and he descended the steps, jogging back to the hover where Captain Stewart stood beneath the canopy of the hover door. The door closed as he disappeared inside. Because it was a military hover, the windows were opaque from the outside though crystal clear from the inside. She couldn't see him, but ahe knew he saw her so she kissed her fingertips and held out her hand, waving goodbye.

The hover rose gracefully from the ground, doing a near-one-eighty before heading back the way they had come. It only took seconds for the hover to be out of sight. As soon as it was, the tears came again. Lucy swiped at her cheeks with anger and frustration, wishing she hadn't been so emotional. David didn't chastise her for it, but she felt foolish all the same for it. With a shaky breath and cheeks as dry as they could be – she knew Molly and Trevor would understand – she turned and went inside the house.

The air outside had been wet and approaching raw with the driving rain and dropping afternoon temperatures. Soon, everything would be dark and it would be colder. They would have to begin heating the house with the large wood furnace in the basement or the fireplaces in most bedrooms. Some of the temporary housing structures had more efficient, clean heating options but the house was so old the furnace and fireplaces were what worked. When she opened the door, the familiar, comforting warmth hit her along with the aromas of dinner. Smelled like fresh bread and possibly chicken stew.

"Is that you, Lucy?" Molly called from the kitchen.

"I'm coming, yes," she answered. It was nearly dinner and community members who needed to eat in the main house would be arriving soon. She would make herself useful again.

She glanced into the infirmary as she passed. *Gracias a Dios*, the beds were empty. She would need to update Rev and Molly about

Tessa, though little had changed and that was the only update. Sunny the orange tabby house cat came barreling down the stairs, sounding like a herd of elephants rather than the sizeable cat he was. He circled her ankles and rubbed against her jeans and she chuckled.

"What can I do to help?" she asked as she stepped into the kitchen.

And froze in her spot, eyes wide and mouth open.

"*Hermanita*, I've never known you to be without words."

Lucy stared, stuck until her brain finally engaged again and she looked between the two men standing near the kitchen work island. "Tio?"

Ignacio Santos smiled and spread his arms as he took a step toward her. Lucy ran to him, crying when he wrapped her in a hug. He stood several inches taller than her and being embraced by him was like being embraced by a giant bear. Even when she was little Tio Ignacio had been big and strong and let her curl up in his lap when she was sad. He smelled of tobacco and coffee and she closed her eyes while he hugged her.

"It is so good to see you, Lulu," he said against her hair. "For so long we had no idea."

She just nodded, soaking him in. Uncle Leo's gentle hands rubbed her back and she opened her eyes to see him beside them, tears in his eyes. She shifted from Uncle Ignacio to Uncle Leo, hugging him too. He was her height, and as much as Uncle Ignacio was a big bear of a man, Uncle Leo was like a dancer lean and thin.

"You are as beautiful to see as ever, little one."

"I don't understand. How are you here?"

"We were contacted just two days ago by a colonel in Alexandria who said he had been looking for us for you. He asked if we would be willing to come here to this beautiful place to see you," Uncle Ignacio explained.

"We didn't just come to visit," Uncle Leo added. "We spoke with Mr. Tisdale and have asked to stay."

"Where were you? Where have you been?"

"We were in Santa Cruz until the attacks but relocated to Las Vegas and had been staying in one of the once hotels on the Strip," Uncle

Ignacio told her. "Perhaps that is why the gentleman was able to find us."

She didn't need to ask but wanted to be sure. "What was the name of the man who contacted you?"

"Forte," Uncle Leo said. "He spelled it for us and said it had an e at the end, but it was useless. David Forte. Do you know him?"

"Know him," she said with tears welling again. She nodded. "I'm going to marry him."

Firebird Command Barracks – Former Hotel District
"The Nest"
United Earth Protectorate, Capitol City
Alexandria, Seat of Virginia
North American Continent

"When you said you were moving a three-dimensional dome simulation generator I was imagining something a hell of a lot bigger."

David shrugged with his hands held out from his sides. "I said I didn't need help. The simulation generator itself isn't big, but the holograms it creates are. That's why I need to set it up in one of the ballrooms at the Nest."

Connor snarled. "Don't call it a ballroom."

He chuckled and went back to work on situating and powering up the simulator. It had been running diagnostics and analytics since Monday afternoon, and he was ready to start examining the results. But he basically needed to have his own holodeck and the largest ballroom at the Nest worked perfectly. It was unused because it was too big for any of the purposes the Firebirds would need it for, unless they needed to convert some of the building into emergency housing or something, and Connor wasn't a fan of the overdone ornate décor of the space.

Knowing that, David had to poke.

"Will this disrupt your fall cotillion?"

"Shut up," Connor said, crouching down to examine the two-foot across circular machine that served as a fancy, and probably very expensive, projector. "When will it be ready to go?"

"Probably twenty minutes. I need to set it up to scan and map the space so it knows how to adjust the environment in the simulation so we don't run into walls and stuff."

"I'm curious to see it. You hungry? I heard it's chicken tonight."

"It's always chicken," David said, standing from the crouch. "Not hungry, but I'll go with you."

He set the dimension scan to start in thirty seconds to give them time to leave. As they reached the double doors at the far end of the massive room, multiple beams of light shot from the projector to sweep the space. The cafeteria was a restaurant dining room from back when the Nest was a hotel so walking into it didn't feel like walking into the military cafeterias he'd known. Sure as hell was a step up. Probably why this particular building had been chosen for the Firebirds primary facility. Several hundred Firebirds lived in the Nest in all the old hotel rooms. Connor had lived there as commander until he married Evie, though he still had a space for times when he needed to be closer at hand.

Like he'd been the last few days since the attempted attacks.

The sooner David got the shields figured out, the better.

He sat at one of the tables while Connor picked up food. He came back with his dinner on a large plate and a piece of pie – pumpkin by the looks – on a smaller plate.

"Yep, chicken," he said, sitting down. "You know what would be good? Fried chicken. I haven't had crispy, greasy, seasoned fried chicken in years."

"Lucy made fried chicken last week," David said, hoping he kept the flash of regret out of his voice long enough to mock Connor. "Damn good, too."

Connor mumbled a string of curses, some in French, before scooping up a bite of chicken in gravy on white rice. It was basic, but it was hot and easy to make, which meant the Firebirds probably had it once a week. He turned in his chair so he could put his back against the wall and one of his feet in the empty chair beside him.

"How are you doing, David?" Connor asked after a few minutes, keeping his head down but still looking at David across the table.

He wasn't an idiot, and knew this conversation was the whole reason Connor had suggested they get food. He'd considered begging off before it even came up but knew he wouldn't be able to avoid Connor for long. He had to get someone to fly the hover, and Connor was the one to assign Captain Stewart.

"I'm fine," he answered.

Connor snorted and stirred his shredded chicken into the rice and gravy. "Liar."

"What do you want to hear?" David asked, still staring across the mostly empty dining room. "I'm gutted. I'm pissed. I'm terrified. I miss her like hell already. I hated taking her back."

"Is any of that the truth?"

"All of it's the truth."

"Then that's what I want to hear." Connor sat back and moved the plate to the edge of the table away from them. "I'm not going to give you a hard time about this, David. I know I'd be torn up if I had to do with Evie and Adrian what you did with Lucy."

Nothing, no words managed to work themselves together enough to make a coherent sentence, so David sat silent. He'd made it back to Alexandria less than two hours before and could have gone home and started the process tomorrow but going back to the apartment meant facing the fact it was empty. Her clothes were gone. Her sketches were gone. Even her shampoo was gone. The freezer was full, but he didn't know when he'd eat any of it.

When the food she made him was gone, the apartment would be void of anything Lucy. Other than his memories.

"I asked her to marry me."

Connor laughed. "Man, you were *always* asking her to marry you."

David grinned. "Yeah, but this time she said yes."

"Congratulations." Connor shoved the uneaten pie at him. "Have a piece of pie to celebrate."

"Nah, that's okay. Nothing against the cooks here, but once you've had Lucy's pie nothing else compares."

"I don't need to hear about your love life."

David grabbed a cloth napkin on the table and threw it at Connor's face. The other man laughed and yanked it off his shoulder where it landed. He picked up his fork and cut a third of the pie away from the slice, putting it in his mouth.

"I mean it. Congratulations. Best thing I ever did in my life," he mumbled around the food.

"Being a married man hasn't taught you any manners."

Connor grinned around his full cheek and finished eating the pie. When done, he put the small dish on top of the remains of his chicken and rice dinner. He sighed and set his arms on the table to look at David. "You deserve it, David. I'm happy for you."

"Thanks." With a groan he lowered his foot from the chair and stood. "I'm going to check on the scan. You coming?"

"I'll meet you there. Just getting rid of my plates."

David was about to open the doors to the ballroom when Connor ran down the hall to catch up. He waited until the Firebird commander was beside him and pushed open the door with a click of the wide bar. One foot into the room and they both stopped short. For his part, David was left stunned by the awesome transformation. What had been an ornate, elaborate, cavernous room half an hour before was now essentially a command center for what could be the global defense shield. The disk on the floor was now a circular control panel akin to the consoles he'd built for the singular domes, but this one was much larger with a six foot in circumference tower that rose to the fully imagined ceiling. Within the tower, blue and white energy pulsated and sparked and there was a low hum in the air he felt on his skin.

"*Maudire*," Connor swore.

"Yeah," David agreed, and went into the room.

His boots thumped like he walked across the sensory-fabricated metal floor rather than the low pile carpet he knew was there. He walked up to the control console and reached out a tentative hand. His fingers touched smooth, cool metal.

"David, this is incredible," Connor said with awe, his head tipped back as he stared at the tower, his mouth hanging open. "You created this?"

"I created the concept, yeah."

He walked around the console, scanning the imaginary monitors streaming hypothetical data and tested his creation by pushing a few buttons. He'd never admit it to anyone alive, which probably wouldn't matter if he did because not a whole hell of a lot of people would know what he was talking about, but the design had the smallest inspiration from a cheesy science fiction show he'd watched as a kid. The correlations were perfect since the simulation would make any space seem much larger than it was, and that show in particular liked to brag about being bigger on the inside.

The console hummed and the tower lit up.

"I just entered the command to prepare for shield initiation."

"What would happen if you completed initiation?"

"Nothing in the real world." He moved a few more steps and pushed a few more buttons. The hum got louder. "But we'd see what would happen if my idea worked."

"Well, old man, fire her up and let's see what happens."

CHAPTER THIRTY-NINE

8 October 2054, Thursday
Secure Docking Bay, Transportation Hub
United Earth Protectorate, Capitol City
Alexandria, Seat of Virginia
North American Continent

Nick and John stood at the third level observation deck window, looking down to the hub floor where Earth's Firebirds and Aretu's Surety Officers worked together to unload the teeming cargo hold of the *Aroyan*, a strictly Areth craft designed for transportation of goods and personnel while also being equipped with impressive weaponry at the ready if the need arose. The *Aroyan* hovered with perfect precision over the transportation hub structure without as much as a sound or a shift in their position. They could have just as easily been anchored and docked, powered down. The *Aroyan* cast a shadow over much of Alexandria proper.

With a ship large enough to transport a compliment of two-thousand Defense Alliance military personnel and a hundred thousand square tons of cargo, there was no way to bring anything to the surface directly. Including Envoy Callen Basselin, who had arrived herself in one of the transports.

Huge hoverlifts stacked with containers slid from the transport crafts traveling back and forth from the hub to the *Aroyan*, since the ship itself could not come close enough to the surface to unload directly. The hub in Alexandria had never anticipated something so massive.

Nick's engineers would have to get on that. It was one thing to have ships like the *Steppenschraf* hover in orbit, but ships like the *Aroyan* needed better access.

"It's an impressive ship," Nick said to John, only glancing briefly to the Areth ambassador before looking down again at the coordinated effort of Firebirds and Areth alike to empty the ship. "How many does Aretu have like her?"

"Of the *Aroyan* class, I believe twenty. But if the *Aroyan* impresses you, the true battle class would be something to see. Twice the size, two and a half times the speed, and the ability to carry a hundred of the *lichtgescheindt* Defense Alliance crafts."

"Damn."

The door behind him opened, and Connor entered with Envoy Basselin. Nick watched them in the reflection of the window security glass. She was slight in stature compared to Connor, but there was a distinctive strength about her that moved with her into the room. Black hair, cut close to her head, was a striking compliment to her medium-tone skin. Nick supposed in Earth descriptive, she'd be considered olive-toned or Mediterranean, but that didn't seem to work for someone from *away*, as his grandfather used to say. Of course, Sean Tanner was talking about people not from Maine.

"We're about a third finished, sir," Connor said, joining Nick at the observation window. "I'd say probably another four or five hours and we'll have everything to the surface. We're inventorying as we go, so at that point we can easily distribute wherever needed."

"Good. Thank you."

"If I might have a word, President Tanner," Envoy Basselin said behind them, and Nick turned. "With you as well, Ambassador. If appropriate, in that it refers to a security concern, perhaps Colonel Montgomery should also remain."

The hairs on the back of Nick's neck prickled, but he kept his expression neutral. "Sure."

"The Defense Alliance has been investigating the events of a few weeks past when your planet was attacked by the Urdo Khantan. There were certain details that concerned those in leadership of the Alliance, raising suspicions that the Urdo Khantan may have had aide on the planet to coordinate efforts."

"I know all that," Nick said, taking a couple steps toward her. "What came out of the investigation?"

"The final report was issued this morning and forwarded. The arrival of information coinciding with my arrival was fortuitous timing. Though, I doubt the information itself would be seen as such."

"Who."

"Ambassador Drucillus Clodianus Hiacyntus of Raxo."

John let go with a whole string of words Nick didn't even begin to understand, in languages he couldn't guess, but based on tone it relayed exactly what he felt at the same moment.

The chill in his blood flipped instantly to hot rage, and he fought to maintain the unchanged exterior. Clenching his jaw for two seconds before speaking, he twisted at the waist enough to look to Connor. "Get him. Because if I go get him—"

"Understood, sir."

"Take him to detainment."

"President Tanner, the Alliance would ask that you allow me to take him into custody aboard the *Aroyan* so he may face his peers and leaders for his crimes. I believe your word for his actions is treason."

"I will," Nick said, forcing his jaw to relax enough he could speak. "But I'm going to have a talk with him first. Connor," he called out just before Connor left the observation room. When Connor looked back, he said, "Maybe the good ambassador would like to spend some time in the room with his friend."

"The Urdo Khantan have no loyalty," John interjected. "If given the chance, he might kill his informant."

"Nah. We'll make sure Carnation just gets his nerves rattled."

Connor acknowledged with a short nod and left.

"Our investigation implies the ambassador sought a leverage of power to advance himself. It was likely he would have presented himself to either yourself or the council as some sort of—"

"No disrespect to you, Envoy Basselin, but I don't give a rat's ass why he did what he did," Nick snapped. "The fact is he did it, and nearly two-thousand five-hundred of my people are dead because of it. As far as I'm concerned, he's a mass murderer."

"Agreed, President Tanner. We will see he faces justice."

"Not until I'm done with him."

Firebird Command Barracks – Former Hotel District
"The Nest"
United Earth Protectorate, Capitol City
Alexandria, Seat of Virginia
North American Continent

"We have reviewed your preliminary implementations and the corresponding data and are in full agreement you've embraced the concept of psychokinetic amplification. The theoretical transfer of passive psychokinetic energy to a defense grid is actually quite brilliant," Dr. Beia Willoughby said, leaning forward to be closer to the monitor.

If David had to place an age, which was nearly impossible to do when it came to the Areth, in the Human aging process he'd put her at probably close to seventy-five or eighty. Which meant she was considerably older than that in Areth years and had lived longer than Humans were capable of since Biblical times. Zephania sat beside her, shoulder to shoulder. Both had pure white hair worn in an intricate twist of braids around their heads and deep wrinkles lined their faces. At quick glance, it was difficult to tell them apart and from across the room he might not be able to, but he'd pinpointed early in their conversation that Beia had dark green eyes and Zephania had bright purple. A color he'd never seen, though he'd have to admit he hadn't exactly had a whole lot of face-to-face conversations with Areth so their variations were unknown to him.

"Thanks. I feel like I'm kinda flying by the seat of my pants here."

Both women made almost the identical confused face, with brows drawn and slight frowns, and David had to hold himself back from chuckling. Apparently, decades of being life partners really did make people more like each other.

If he was lucky, he'd have that with Lucy.

He shook off his melancholy and sighed, making a distraction ploy of writing on his paper tablet. Scratching a pencil or pen on paper always helped him think better.

"I've run at least a dozen simulation scenarios since last night. The way I set up the program, it can run the variations simultaneously and report what would be optimal and what would make the non-optimal scenarios more . . . optimal." He winced at his apparent inability to speak coherently.

"That's quite brilliant," Dr. Zephania Willoughby said, nodding. "You may consider a self-contained control option that would allow your program to adjust and compensate as needed. For instance, shifting reserve power from one location on the grid to another based on other criteria points."

David nodded and wrote. "A thought like that came to me last night, but I hadn't gotten around to writing the coding for it yet."

The two ladies turned their heads and looked at each other and smiled at the same time. Zephania nodded and turned her attention to David again. "We are truly impressed with your knowledge and understanding of the necessary engineering, design, and programming needs for your research."

David shrugged a shoulder. "I've said before I can make just about any computer do what I want once I know the language it speaks."

"A true talent."

He assumed she meant the little-t kind of talent, not the big-T kind of Talent. "I'd like to spend a day or so working on the coding and send you the analysis. With the *Aroyan* docked for a couple days, the communication links seem to work better."

"Of course, David. We are happy to assist," Beia said. "We believe your research, along with its final implementation, will be beneficial to the whole of the Defense Alliance. The better we are protected at times of threat and attack, the better we can protect those who can't protect themselves."

"That's the goal."

With a few departing remarks, David closed the communication channel and looked down at his notes which looked more like drawings than anything else. He got it, even if no one else would. Connor had allocated an office space for him that had once been the business center in the hotel so he could continue to work on the planetary defense project from the Nest and not have to go between the research facility at Alexandria Hospital and the Nest. It was practically across the hall from the ballroom where the simulator had permanently been set up, so he could easily program the changes from the office, and they would feed to the holodeck.

Few people got the joke, and for the most part he didn't refer to the ballroom as the holodeck, but he got a chuckle out of it. So far, Nick, his father, and Michael had been the only ones who seemed to get it. Him and a bunch of Tanners, that was it.

He supposed he could be in worse company.

While he liked the idea the Drs. Willoughby had about instinctive situation power shifts controlled by the program, his next real focus was to see how much would be required to power the shield. It wasn't a dome anymore since what he proposed – if it worked – would encompass the entire planet. His questions were things like how much would it take to power the system? How much effort would be required, and could the system be powered with passive psychokinetic energy, or did it require focus? What would the difference be? How far up could he go with it? Could he maintain a mile or two from sea level? Or could they take it to atmospheric levels?

All he knew for sure was he needed to figure out the answers to a whole lot of questions, and he needed to do it quickly. Before the next threat, the next attack, the next loss of life because it wasn't ready.

David was hunched over his code when Connor knocked on the doorjamb of the open door. He didn't like sitting in a cave. David looked up and swiveled his chair enough to face Connor.

"What's up?" he said, but Connor's strained expression made his nerves tingle and he stood up. "What's wrong?"

"Hank, Sabrina, and I are on our way to take into custody the suspected fly in the ointment."

David was heading for the door before Connor finished asking if he wanted to be in in the action. "Who the hell is it, and how did we find out?"

"Raxo ambassador."

"Drucillus Clodianus Hiacyntus?"

"Yep." Connor filled him in as they headed for the front exit of the building. "The Defense Alliance, specifically Queen Bryony's people I'm pretty sure, found evidence it's him. He's in cahoots with the Urdo Khantan, and presumably the Sorrs, to gain power."

"I never liked that guy," David said as they headed for the military hover where Hank stood waiting.

"Nobody likes that guy but himself," Hank said as they moved past him into the hover. "I don't even think his concubines like him."

"Do you blame them?" Sabrina Tambour said from where she already sat inside the hover.

David shrugged and grinned. "Hey, I'm not one to judge. Doesn't he usually stay on his private ship in orbit?"

"Usually, yes, but he was informed that while the *Aroyan* is here, an invitation has been extended to dine with the Alliance liaisons."

"Do I need to guess who passed on that message?"

Connor winked. "He returned to the embassy about ten minutes ago." They walked up the ramp into the hover and Connor took the pilot chair with Hank as his co-pilot, and David behind them with Sabrina Tambour. "His concubines will be taken to the *Aroyan*, because as far as we're aware they're not directly involved, and we're taking him to detainment and interrogation. If it's determined his ladies and gents are involved, they'll be dealt with later."

"Given the chance, they might be willing to share what they know," Sabrina said.

"People love to sing when it'll save their own ass."

The ride from The Nest to the embassy was less than three minutes, and Hyacinth aka Claude aka "forget your title, bub" was slowly descending his obese body down the steps to his private transport, his concubines walking behind.

"Perfect timing." Connor angled the hover in front of the transport and was down the ramp before the hover doors were fully open, with the three of them right behind. "Yo, Hyacinth!" Connor called, a 'probably too wide to be appropriate, but who cared' grin on his face as he reached the bottom of the steps. He put one foot on the bottom step and set his hands at his waist. "What's happenin', *buddy*?"

Hyacinth stopped short and spit out "How dare you speak to me with such disrespect! Be gone from my way!"

"How dare I? How dare *I*?" Connor looked over his shoulder at them, and David really had to fight a grin. For the commander of the most elite fighting force on Earth, he had irreverence nailed. Then his face went stone cold and he turned back. "Ambassador Drucillus Clodianus Hiacyntus of Raxo, by order of President Nicholas Tanner of the United Earth Protectorate, I do hereby place you under arrest for war crimes against the citizens of Earth and its allies."

He walked up the steps and the concubines scattered to get out of his way, Hank flanking on the other side. Despite his size, Hyacinth huffed and tried to get down the steps ahead of Connor reaching him and David and Sabrina stepped in his way. Red almost to the point being purple, and already sweating profusely, the ambassador started screaming demands and profanities, flailing his arms while Connor reached for one hand.

"I am the Ambassador of Raxo as appointed by powers greater and higher than you can ever fathom! You have no auth—"

"Yada yada yada. Blah blah blah," Connor continued, getting a solid grip on both the morbidly huge man's hands while Hank stopped the man from descending further. Unable to clasp them behind him, Connor shrugged and secured his wrists in front. The guy could barely walk. He wasn't getting away. "You have the right to remain silent, but I'm guessing you don't have the ability."

"The council will hear of this! You have no right to put your vile, Human hands on me!"

"Dang, if you're not careful you're gonna sound xenophobic, Skippy. You can take it up with the judge." He snapped his fingers. "Oh, wait! We don't really have judges these days. Workin' on it, though. In the meantime, President Tanner wants to have a little talk."

"You will hear about this!"

"I sure hope so," Connor answered, propelling Claude forward.

David couldn't figure out what name he liked best quite yet.

"But first, we thought you'd like to visit your best bud we've got downtown. Let you two catch up. I don't know his name, he's not really been forthcoming, but I'll bet you recognize him when you see him."

"Fugly as hell," David said in Sabrina's direction, but plenty loud enough for the good ambassador to hear.

She shook her head and made an "oomph" sound. "Have you seen them without their armor? Even worse. I know the one we've got in detainment and interrogation is looking for a fight."

Hyacinth shook his head so vehemently his jowls made slapping sounds and his cheeks flopped. "They're savages!"

With Hank at one elbow and Connor at the other, they practically lifted Hyacinth down the last couple of steps to the bottom, him attempting to struggle the whole time.

"Make a deal with the devil and eventually payment is due," Connor said, cold and without any touch of sarcasm.

DETAINMENT AND INTERROGATION FACILITY
UNITED EARTH PROTECTORATE, CAPITOL CITY
ALEXANDRIA, SEAT OF VIRGINIA
NORTH AMERICAN CONTINENT

Nick oversaw the full process of unloading the *Aroyan* and had a long conversation with Envoy Basselin before he decided he'd make his way downtown to visit their newest detainee. Envoy Basselin expressed the necessity of taking Claude back to Defense Alliance territory for trial and punishment, since he had consorted with the enemy, and while Nick tended to see her point she agreed to let him keep Claude around until the *Aroyan* was ready to leave Earth's orbit.

He didn't need to know that was the plan. Maybe not knowing would loosen his tongue because Nick had questions.

He also knew Claude had no great affection for Phin and Daniel, seeing them as some sort of abomination, which was ironic considering he was accused of being aligned with the race that produced the Heinous Bitch who was responsible for their existence. The fact they tagged along was just a little more lemon juice with the salt he intended to rub into Claude's wounds.

Two Firebirds waited at the door of the facility, and with nods and salutes, opened the door for Nick to enter, Phin and Daniel behind him. He looked around, surprised Connor wasn't waiting for them, but Connor joined seconds later, jogging from his office.

"Sorry, sir," Connor said. "I was talking to Evie. Members of her team just came back to Alexandria with some more children—"

"That's great!"

Connor smiled. "Yes, sir. Brings the total to over fifty now. But there's one child in particular she wanted to talk to me about."

"Anything we can do?"

"Actually, I told her to reach out to the vice president and Victor on this one. Well, that was her idea but I agreed."

Nick raised an eyebrow. "Okay. If there's anything I need to do to help, tell Evie to let me know."

"Of course, sir." Connor turned toward the security door leading into the facility, with them following. "Hank is downstairs with our new guest, and John arrived a bit ago but hasn't spoken to Hyacinth or the Urdo."

"Has he said anything?"

"Nah," Connor said, touching the next bioscan to release the lock. "Nothing worth anything. Mostly how we're all pathetic and ignorant and will face the consequences of our treasonous actions. Yada yada yada. Blah blah blah."

"So, acting like he didn't get in bed with the Sorrs."

Connor nodded. They went in silence the rest of the way to the lower levels of the facility. In the basement hallway where the cells for the worst of the worst were, John stood outside the familiar door where Nick had questioned the Urdo Khantan just over a week earlier. The "conversation" hadn't yielded much other than their doom was coming and all the things he intended to do to them. As Connor said, "yada yada yada blah blah blah." Nick was curious to see if the Urdo would be willing to say more if one of his employers was ratting him out.

"Heard anything interesting?" Nick asked when they reached John and Hank.

John shook his head. "Nothin' useful. Unless you count the death threats against Drucillus Clodianus Hiacyntus."

"Has Claude said anything to set him off?"

"Nope. But my guess is the Urdo recognizes him."

"Do you want Hyacinth brought out and to an interrogation room?"

"I want to talk to him in full view of his best friend," Nick said and ticked his chin toward the next secure door. "Let's go."

CHAPTER FORTY

10 October 2054, Saturday
Alexandria Hospital – Pediatric Care
United Earth Protectorate, Capitol City
Alexandria, Seat of Virginia
North American Continent

"I had hoped to have this group of children here yesterday, but the storms over the Pacific made it too choppy for the larger transport hovers to make the trip out of Yakutsk," Evie Montgomery explained as they walked the hospital hall. She looked tired yet happy. "The northwestern part of the European continent isn't exactly balmy this time of year as it is, but we knew if we didn't get them out soon the severe winter weather would make it so much harder. And because of the location, we couldn't get any aircrafts into the area."

"I understand many of the children were afraid already, most having never traveled by hover before, at least not that they remember, so traveling in inclement weather would have been very frightening," Victor said as they turned toward the pediatric care wing.

Beverly walked with him, hand in hand, and her Firebird guards walked behind them. In many ways, he appreciated the protection afforded his wife, but in many ways and on many days he longed for the day their life became more their own. Though, having served as the vice president, he wasn't sure that would ever be the case. Time would tell.

"How many did you bring back?" Beverly asked.

"This trip we brought back seventeen, our largest group to date from one location. We weren't expecting to find so many, since the trail that started with Jenifer's information was only tracking two children. The area was so remote."

Evie paused in her explanation to shake her head, her lips pressed closely together. "I will never forget the horrible conditions most of these children are found in. Squalor. Abuse of all natures. Once – only *once* – in the months since we began actively seeking out these children have we found a child in a good home, being cared for and loved. I'm so suspicious of someone doing good I've had the family checked on numerous times to make sure what we found wasn't a lie."

"The best of Humanity came from the last two years, but the worst found footing as well," Beverly said, and Victor squeezed her hand because of the sadness in her voice.

"My understanding is all the children have been examined, and there have been some issues we'll be addressing, but most will be moved from the hospital today," Victor provided.

"We are already working out appointments with our trauma team to begin their healing process beyond the physical."

"It will be a long road," Beverly said. "I'm thankful we've been able to do what we have."

"I appreciate you coming for this special situation—"

A shrill holler of a child echoed down the hallway, and Victor sprinted toward the sound. Behind him he heard the footfalls of the four whom he'd walked with, trying to keep up. Victor reached the open hospital room door where the sound had come from and his heart jumped to his throat as he gripped the jamb to stop.

On the bed was a young girl, probably no more than five or six years old though it was difficult to tell because she was so thin and she thrashed on the bed in an attempt to escape Doctor Euan McCallum, the Head of Pediatrics, and the nurses trying to assist him. She continued to yell, but no words were formed. Just the loud wail of fear. Her eyes were closed tight, her head pressed to the pillow, mouth open as she screamed. Victor sensed the sheer terror flowing out from her. If he felt it, it had to be an onslaught for Beverly.

Doctor McCallum threw a short look at them over his shoulder. "She's inconsolable, and we can't communicate with her. My next step is sedation, but I don't dare get near her with anything."

The child tried to vocalize, but the words were nonsense, not understandable, just noise. In that moment, Victor understood why Evie Montgomery had wanted them to come. Had specifically wanted Beverly to come. His wife moved around him, relative calm in the chaos as she stepped between Doctor McCallum and a nurse and reached for the child.

Just as she had done for him what felt like years before, her touch was calming because she was calm, because she didn't seek to control but to help. Not to frighten, but to assuage fear. Her touch was soothing, because she needed to soothe. The little girl jerked, freezing, her brown eyes wide now as she stared at Beverly and huffed rapid breaths. Beverly stepped closer to the head of the bed, and without ever looking away from the girl, wrapped her elegant fingers around the wrist of the nurse nearest her and removed her hold from the child.

The girl stared, unblinking.

Doctor McCallum spoke the name of the other nurse and he stepped back as well, releasing the girl from any contact except Beverly's fingers on her forehead smoothing away her chaotically curled red hair. With her free hand, Beverly set her fingers to her temple and brought her hand forward in the simple sign for *hello*. He didn't see her face, but he knew without a doubt and would bet his unnaturally long life she smiled.

The little girl's gaze darted from Beverly's face to the sign, and back again. Needing two hands to sign further, Beverly leaned away from the bed and brought both hands in front of her to sign *My name is Beverly*. She gave her name sign, and then spelled Beverly. *What's your name?*

The girl blinked and shifted on the bed so her back was fully supported by the raised head of the bed and the pillows behind her. She tapped the ring and index fingers of both hands together, one on the other, then made a sign, and Beverly nodded, repeating it.

"She's given a sign that is likely her name sign. She said it was her name before giving it," Victor said to Doctor McCallum who had stepped back to join him, but he stepped away himself to move to the foot of the bed where he could both see the child and his wife. Beverly asked her to spell her name, and the girl did.

Mayda Jane.

"Mayda Jane," Victor repeated.

Since the little girl didn't respond at all to his voice, he assumed she was completely or profoundly deaf and likely had been her whole life based on her lack of verbal language. Beverly smiled wider and repeated the sign for the girl's name, and Mayda smiled as well.

The air in the room changed, shifted. It went from cold to warm, and Victor's nerves calmed. Mayda shifted to sit cross legged, her entire demeanor different in a blink, her hands moving so fast he could barely keep up. Manual language had served its purpose in his life with Beverly, but he had fallen out of practice since she'd regained her hearing. She'd only relied on it for a few months, but she had embraced the language, and to watch her communicating so quickly and easily with the child made his heart expand so much it felt confined by his chest. Beverly sat on the bed with the little girl to continue talking.

Not looking away, Victor turned his head toward Evie Montgomery, his focus still on his wife. "I see now why you wanted Beverly to come."

"I knew there was a chance they still couldn't communicate since manual language can be different, but I wanted to try. For the girl's – Mayda Jane's – sake."

He heard the smile in her voice when she said the child's name, and Victor smiled too. Beverly glanced back at him, her smile wide and her eyes bright. Victor drew in a slow breath, releasing it as he spoke.

"Have you found a placement for her yet?"

"No, not yet. She'll need someone—"

"Us," Victor said, then looked to Evie. "She needs us. She has us."

Evie smiled, her eyes shining. "I didn't want to put any pressure on you, but I'd hoped."

Victor looked back to his wife, who now watched him with Mayda in her lap. Beverly motioned to him to join them, and as he reached the side of the bed, Beverly introduced them.

"This is Victor," she said, providing first the spelling of his name, and then his name sign.

His intent had been to simply stand near them and perhaps absorb some of the joy emanating from them both, but when Mayda scrambled from Beverly's lap toward him, reaching for the little girl felt as natural as anything he had ever felt in his life. He lifted her with his hands beneath her arms. She was light, much lighter than he expected, and she wrapped her arms and legs around him, resting her head on his shoulder. With a long sigh that shook her little body, Mayda relaxed in his arms.

Victor closed his eyes.

PROTECTORATE CITIZEN COMMUNITY—UNITY VALLEY
VANCOUVER, BRITISH COLUMBIA
FORMER COUNTRY OF CANADA
NORTH AMERICAN CONTINENT

"Am I selfish for being glad you're back?"

Lucy forced herself to look up from Baby Della's round face and bright eyes to look at Molly, continuing her slow sway back and forth with the baby in her arms. "No, you're not selfish. I missed you. I missed it here." She had to look down again because her throat tightened and her vision blurred.

"Oh, Sis. Don't hide your tears from me. I know you miss him, too."

Lucy swallowed hard, but only managed to force a weak smile

when she looked at her friend again. She nodded and looked away, pressing a kiss to Baby Della's forehead.

"If it's anything, I'm really happy for you and David. I know he's good for you, and good to you. I mean, the man hunted down Uncle Ignacio and Uncle Leo just because he knew you'd smile."

Her lifelong friend knew what she needed to distract her from the melancholy of missing David. Molly always knew just what to say and do. Feeling her strength come back and her throat relax, Lucy sat up straighter and shifted to support her arm, and Baby Della, on the pillows around her. She'd built up plenty of strength caring for the Tanner Quads, but she probably held Della as much as Molly and Rev combined. She couldn't get enough.

"He does things like that," she said with a confident, more genuine smile. "He likes to make me smile."

"I hope we get to know him better. I'm being selfish again, but I hope he brings you back to us often. Especially since he has family here."

Molly knew the bizarre reality of how her David Forte was father to Davey Forte, and great grandfather to little DJ, but to keep things simple and not likely to cause confusion they decided in private to refer to the other Fortes in Unity Valley simply as his family. If it was revealed later, so be it, because his story certainly wasn't the most bizarre some had heard. Just the few weeks Lucy spent in Alexandria gave her plenty of stories to tell if she chose to. At the mention of David's family, Lucy shifted forward and reluctantly eased sleeping Della into her mother's arms.

"I need to take care of something before dinner," she said as she smoothed her hand over Baby Della's hair.

"Good luck."

She left the main house with determination, opting not to grab a sweater because the chilly air was a shock to her system when she stepped outside and gave her focus as she walked toward the yurt-style shelters provided to them by the Protectorate. She'd given herself a couple days home before making this house call in hopes of her own emotions being less raw, but that didn't seem likely to happen, so she was going to do as promised.

Inside the yurts was pleasantly warm and made her glad she hadn't brought her sweater. Now slowing her step, Lucy went to the door of the rooms belonging to the latter Forte generations and tapped her knuckles on the wooden frame. Inside, Duke barked and Felicia shushed him before she came to the door.

She smiled wide when she opened it. "Hey, Lucy. I heard you'd come back to the community."

"For the time being, yes. Can I come in?"

Lucy normally preferred soft approaches, but in this she believed in her gut she needed to be firm. Not forceful, but not subtle either. Felicia nodded and stepped back so Lucy could step inside. The set of rooms were designed for families with a main room for cooking, eating, and gathering with two rooms for sleeping and a bathroom. Davey and DJ sat at the table, and DJ had a tablet of paper where it looked like he was practicing his letters. Davey had blank paper he drew on, holding it in place with the halted stump of his other arm. Both boys, because mentally Davey was no older than DJ, looked up and smiled. Duke met her inside the door and nuzzled her hand with his nose, then poked her stomach as he wagged his bushy tail, and she chuckled as she pet his head.

"I know you went back to Alexandria to help care for . . ." She glanced sideways at the other two in the room and spoke in a softer voice. "David and Tessa. I suppose I should ask if everyone is okay."

"Yes, David is doing much better," Lucy answered, not matching Felicia's drop in volume. "He's much stronger. When he returns you'll see what I mean."

Felicia's cheeks colored and she glanced at her son and father-in-law again, but neither looked up from their work. "I wasn't sure he'd come back, since—"

"His son is here."

Felicia met her gaze, and Lucy held firm.

"Maybe he didn't tell you – I'm not sure why he would – but I told him I didn't think it was a good idea."

Lucy cleared her throat and shook her head. "I realize that, but when it comes down to the finest point, it's his call. Not yours, Felicia." She took a slow breath to steady herself, not wanting to give in to the anger she held against Felicia Forte. It was hard. So hard. "David is a miracle, and he is a gift to your family. Frankly, he's a gift to all of us because he's finding a way *right now* to keep us all alive. When he's done he's coming back. To get to know his son. And his great grandson."

Felicia crossed her arms over her body and took a step back from Lucy, moving closer to the utilitarian kitchen and away from her charges. "He gets to decide." Her voice was sharp, cold, and her mouth a thin, fine line. "I get no say."

"You can say, and decide, what part you want to play in this. But, yes, he gets to decide to be a part of his son's life. Three generations after him carry his name. Davey never stopped loving his father."

Felicia shot another look at the older man seated at the table. He was definitely more engrossed in his drawing than their conversation. "He's going to take them away from me."

"No," Lucy said as firm as she could without drawing their attention. She intended to be clear but didn't intend to create chaos in doing so. "He's been through so much. More than you know. He deserves the chance to have a family. And . . . you deserve a chance to know him. He's a good man."

Her throat tightened again; she had lost count of how many times that day. Felicia looked away from her, focusing on the boy and his grandfather. After a few moments, she licked her lips and focused on Lucy again. "We'll see. I won't stop him, but it's not fair to ask me to just accept it."

"None of this has been fair, Felicia, to any of us."

She took a step backward before turning to leave. She'd said her peace, and accepted Felicia would need time. It wasn't the end of the conversation, and hopefully it was a beginning. She was almost to the door when Davey called her name. Lucy stopped as he maneuvered his way off the bench seat, trying to stand free while holding in his only hand the drawing he'd been working on at the table. He smiled as he came to her, his expression bright and pure as he held out the paper.

"Thank you," Lucy said with all honesty as she took the drawing and turned it to see what he'd made. The crayon sketch blurred behind instant tears.

It wasn't a stick drawing or something rough and elementary in nature; the drawing had definition and skill well beyond what his intellect had been reduced to since the events that stole his memories, his arm, and his eye. It wasn't a perfect piece of art, but it was beautiful nonetheless, and the subject of the drawing was absolutely clear.

If there was any question, the words written across the bottom in a much more juvenile print made it obvious.

My Daddy.

She wasn't sure she could have captured his smile or his eyes any better with her pencils and sketchbook than Davey Forte Jr had done with the broken, limited crayons he owned. Lucy swallowed hard and looked up.

"This is absolutely beautiful," she said, holding it so Felicia could see. The woman's small gasp was the sign of her acknowledgment. Unwilling to risk Felicia taking the paper, Lucy held it to her chest. "May I keep this, Davey?"

"Yes," he said, nodding. "I can draw 'nother one for Daddy for when he comes home. He'll be home soon."

"He's been saying that since he woke up over a year ago," Felicia said, her tone soft and strained.

How could she not see? How could she argue against this?

Lucy inhaled slowly through her nose and nodded. "Yes, Davey. Your daddy will be home very soon. He's going to love your drawings."

Davey nodded and went back to the table. In his mind time was different. His daddy had just left and would be home soon. Unable to say anything else, Lucy opened the door to the quarters and stepped into the yurt hall. She was almost back to the main house before the tears started in earnest, but for once they weren't tears of sadness.

There was hope in the crayon drawings of a man/child.

CHAPTER FORTY-ONE

21 October 2054, Wednesday
Firebird Command Barracks – Former Hotel District
"The Nest"
United Earth Protectorate, Capitol City
Alexandria, Seat of Virginia
North American Continent

"So, what do you need us to do?"

David glanced over the top of the full-fledged, non-holographic shield generator console to where Connor stood with Phin and Daniel. They were the first he intended to introduce to the generator, figuring his kids couldn't say no. He glanced down at the energy readings and masked his expression.

His theory already showed merit. If he was right, the power and effectiveness of the shield would be way more than he originally figured. Granted, just about everything about the shield generator was more than he figured.

"For the moment, nothing. Just hang out."

Connor pulled a face and crossed his arms. "I thought this was some kind of test."

"It is. Take it easy. We'll get there."

The boys exchanged silent glances and the power level bumped up. David tried not to smile.

"Is it live?" Connor asked.

"Yeah," David answered, distracted, then shook his head and looked up to get his focus off the readout. "I mean, it's live enough that if I flip a switch the shield would engage. But I'm not ready for that yet."

"What do you need to do?"

"Geez, Montgomery. Cool your jets," David said with a frustrated laugh. "You're like a kid. Can I have it? Are we there yet? Is it on yet? Can I play with it yet?"

"It's cool. So sue me."

Shaking his head, he adjusted a gauge to release the stored energy reserve and bring it to zed. "Okay, fine. This is just you, Connor." He glanced up then back to his screens again. "See that pen I left on the console?"

"Yeah..."

"Don't touch it," David snapped when Connor took a single step forward, and the man immediately withdrew. "Just focus on it. Try to move it."

"Excuse me?"

"*Essayez de déplacer le stylo sans le toucher*," David said, tapping into his unstable memory of high school French, figuring he'd butchered it either way. He wasn't going for finesse as much as snark.

Connor's scowl said he'd at least gotten enough right. "I don't have Talents."

"That's the cool thing," David mumbled, not really paying attention to the conversation other than to half-heartedly explain. "Just give it a try."

Connor huffed. But moments later, the needle moved. Not off the charts, and some might even call it negligible, but the movement was there regardless.

"See? Nothing."

"Something." David looked up. "Phin, now you."

The sentence was barely past his lips when the pen flew off the table and into Phin's raised, open hand.

Connor huffed. "Show off."

The results were exactly what David expected. The action was small when considering what Phin and Daniel were capable of, but the exertion of psychokinetic energy created a solid spike and left residual stored energy. Not enough to power the shield, but Phin picking up a pen would brew a pot of coffee pretty quick. David had the boys flex their psychokinetic muscles a few more times, with each task more advanced, though still for them the most basic of efforts. If his hypothesis worked out, all of Alexandria could be one hundred percent protected with slight effort from Phin and Daniel, and probably John and Jenifer Smith. Everyone else was bonus.

When the first nacelle showed 80% capacity – one of a dozen in the Alexandria prototype – David finally paused in the experiment to motion Connor and the boys around to his side of the console. He stood and took a step back so Connor could see. Knowing Phin and Daniel, they'd catch on a hell of a lot quicker than most. They sure as hell didn't get their large capacity brains from him, considering how long it'd taken him to figure out the conductive power of psychokinetic energy as a storable and convertible energy source.

"What are we looking at?" Connor asked.

"Okay, so, the Areth and Defense Alliance figured out a few decades back they could build structures specifically designed to . . ." He fumbled, trying to find the right way to explain. ". . . make the use of Talents easier. They did it with buildings and eventually ships like the *Steppenschraff*. The specific designs resonate the psychokinetic energy and cycle it back to the user, I guess, for lack of a better term." David shifted forward and tapped the monitor showing the nacelle power level. "This generator does a lot of the same, but instead of resonating back to the person it stores the kinetic energy. These nacelles then convert that kinetic energy to whatever kind of power I want. In our case, a network of interatomic particles that function together to create a force shield."

"Forte Dome 2.0," Connor said.

"Yeah, except more like Dome 50.0. Because this is so far beyond what I first did it's like comparing chisels and stone to a super computer."

"Damn, David. I'm . . ." Connor nodded, his eyes shifting as he took in the array of monitors and gauges. "I'm damn impressed. So . . . you use psychokinetic energy from people with Talents." It was a question wrapped in a statement.

"Just about anyone, like I said. According to John, Talents are actually recessive. It's just that on Aretu, it's prominent recessive. More people have the recessive gene than not, and it's getting like that here on Earth. Connor, even you moved the needle."

Connor shot him a look that didn't read as convinced, but he didn't argue. "Okay, so assuming that, what's next?"

"A live test. Once the nacelle batteries are charged, they hold the energy until use. But the stored energy can also be supplemented with active psychokinetic energy. Then we test for real."

"For real?"

"Every hypothesis I've come up with has proven correct, and my last one is that the interatomic particle net created by the psychokinetic energy can also take exterior energy and cycle it back. My previous dome dispersed the energy, but this system will convert it."

"So every time we get hit with fire, it makes the shield stronger?"

David nodded, trying not to bounce on the balls of his feet. It was exciting as hell, and if it worked . . . hot damn! "My goal first is to protect us, but I think – I *think* – I can eventually create a power grid that can not only protect the planet but provide power globally. No more brown outs. No more trying to find renewable energy. *Everything* will be on a fully realized, fully self-generating grid!"

He didn't realize he was practically shouting until Connor put a hand on his shoulder with a wide grin. "Okay, buddy. That's amazing. Now, what do we do *today*?"

David chuckled and scrubbed his palms over his heated face. He'd been riding a high of potential for a week since everything started to slide together in his head like the perfect Tetris game. He took a deep breath and huffed air out his nose before staring at the console. This one was real. Not a hologram. Not a 3D prototype. With his specs, a team of engineers and manufacturing units had built it in two days. It it worked, if it *all* worked, similar teams would be put to work to churn out generators, consoles, nacelles, and projectors all over the globe.

And they'd be safe.

"We get a couple more big Talents in here and get these batteries charged. Then we flip the big switch and move to the next stage."

"What does this do to the . . ." Connor looked like he was trying to find the right way to explain. "Power providers? The people."

David shook his head. "Nothing a glass of orange juice and a couple cookies won't solve. No worse than donating a pint of blood. If that."

"Hot damn," Connor said, already heading for the door. "Let me make a couple calls."

When Connor was gone, David leaned forward to brace his hands on the edge of the console, the rush of adrenaline at the theoretical becoming reality waning away enough to leave him shaking. *If this worked . . . if it actually worked . . .*

"It works, Father," Phin said, stepping to his side to put a hand on his shoulder. "Be proud. We are proud of you."

ALEXANDRIA HOSPITAL, SECURE WING – GENERAL CARE
UNITED EARTH PROTECTORATE, CAPITOL CITY
ALEXANDRIA, SEAT OF VIRGINIA
NORTH AMERICAN CONTINENT

She pushed open the door to the private room at the end of the hallway, away from any other patient rooms. It wasn't private out of privilege, but because no one else would ever be exposed to the bitch known as Kathleen inside. The room was dark, which was apparently how she liked it, screaming vulgarities and threats at any nurse who dared turn on a light to check her vitals, feed her, or bathe her.

In truth, Kathleen could die in her own filth and no one would care, but humanitarian sensibilities won over justice.

Until today.

Darkness was appropriate.

"Get out," the Heinous Bitch hissed.

She ignored the demand, letting the door close behind her.

"I said get out!"

She acknowledged there should be some part of her that felt guilt or hesitation for what she intended to do, but there wasn't the smallest bit of her conscience telling her to leave. Telling her this wasn't justice, this was vengeance.

No, this was protection.

This was what had to be done.

Kathleen ranted, cursing at her, trying to angle her head to see who it was moving to the machines feeding her nutrients and fluids since her throat struggled to swallow food. Trying to see who crouched to find the small port intended for reprogramming microslides.

"What are you doing? Who is that? I demand you tell me!"

The sound of the Bitch's voice scraped over her nerves and made every pounding thud of her heart pulse in her temples. Her blood was hot with rage and determination. Her insides quaked, but years of doing her duty left her hands steady as she found the port and slipped in the specially programmed slide.

The instructions given with it said it would take no more than thirty seconds for the programming to upload, plenty of time to get in and out before anyone made note of her presence. The slide was also programmed to be one way only. Output. No input. Nothing would leave the room on the slide. It didn't matter the atrocities the vile creature trapped in the bed was responsible for, the act she now took in retribution and justice was a crime.

A crime she was willing to live with if it meant those she loved would be safe from the evil that poisoned the very air in the room.

"I demand you speak!"

She stood abruptly, turning to the bed with enough force the medical chart moved several inches, and got in the Bitch's face. "See me now? Know who I am?"

The Bitch hissed, trying to pull away but unable to since nothing below her neck worked. "Get out! Get out!" she screamed.

Grabbing a fistful of the blanket covering the Bitch to her shoulders, she pressed it over the Bitch's mouth, silencing her. Wide eyes stared back at her. She could complete the job by smothering Kathleen, but that was too messy and too obvious. Instead, she leaned in again.

"Listen carefully, because these are the last words you will ever hear, you filthy, steaming pile of shit that doesn't deserve the flesh suit you wear. Mel Briggs was a traitor and a fool, but she was still one hundred times better than you. Are you listening?"

The Bitch fought against the blanket over her mouth and nose. A few seconds more wouldn't kill her.

"You are a failure. A repeated failure. A colossal failure. But even a failure has the chance to possibly pull off something they attempt."

The Bitch's eyelids fluttered as lack of oxygen started to take hold so she lifted her hand. She wanted this piece of trash to hear every word. Kathleen gasped, wide eyes focusing on her again.

"You've wanted your claws in the Tanner men for generations, but you get no more chances to hurt *any* Tanner ever again. You die. Tonight. By *my* hands. Their hands and consciences are clean, and you. Are. Gone."

The machine behind her beeped and the Bitch tried to speak. The first, small delivery of paralytic slipped into the IV to steal Kathleen's ability to shout once alone again. Crouching, she yanked the microslide from the bottom of the machine. The programming was temporary and unrecorded.

"It's going to hurt," she said as she pocketed the sleeve. "Hurt like a sonofabitch. Or so I hear. Seems fitting based on all the pain you inflicted on Michael over the years. Phin. Daniel. Gideon. Countless other human beings you made into lab rats. Every single person you tortured gets their revenge."

After spewing hate and poison for decades, all the Bitch could do was gape at the mouth like a fish out of water. She wasn't suffocating. Not yet. At the door, she paused and looked back.

"I may see you in hell for this. But it's worth it."

She pulled open the door and stepped into the dimly lit hall, taking the door to her immediate left to a stairwell, the same one she'd used to come onto the floor. The rain was cold, not quite frozen, but enough to sting her cheeks. She made it to the corner before finding a broken planter she vomited in.

Alexandria Hospital, Secure Wing – General Care
United Earth Protectorate, Capitol City
Alexandria, Seat of Virginia
North American Continent

David always hoped when he went to Tessera's room he'd find something different, like her sitting up eating canned fruit cocktail and talking to a nurse rather than silent and still. But visiting her was important. She was here because of him, and once he knew that fact he couldn't stay away. Lucy used to come almost daily, and with her back in Unity Valley, it was even more important to him to go. Tessera barely knew him, but she gave up so much, he'd be a bastard if he didn't.

The blinds were open in the room, but it was nearing the end of the day so the sun was setting, the final spikes of light making their way in and across her legs and abdomen. He'd been in her room all times of the day, and noticed the nurses made sure the blinds were open during the day and closed at night. She was being cared for.

David went to the side of the bed and looked at the machines monitoring everything from her breathing and heart rate to her brain activity. He didn't know what he was looking at, but the lines had movement up and down so he figured that was good. He drew in a long breath through his nose and let it out when he looked down at her.

"So, I figured out how to make the dome work. I guess it's more than a dome now, but I figured it out."

He cleared his throat and pushed his hands into his pockets. He'd call, or Skype, or whatever it was called now . . . he'd talk to Lucy later and tell her maybe he'd done what he needed to do, but in a way he figured Tessera deserved to know first.

"I'm not saying your sacrifice was worth it. I'm not worth anyone dying for. But I'm not wasting my time either." He stared down at her hand closest to him, resting on top of her blankets with her palm turned up so one of the beams of sunlight coming in her window streaked across it. "Thank you," he said, dropping his voice low enough he wondered if she'd hear him even if she was awake. But speaking much louder wasn't going to happen. "I would have stopped you if I knew what you were doing, but I can't change that now. Thank you. It's more than I deserve, but I'm trying to earn it."

He stood silent for another few minutes before taking a step back to leave her alone. A nurse probably would be in soon, and he didn't want to be in the way. He was almost to the door when the machines went nuts, blaring and beeping with alarms sounding in half a dozen different tones. David turned back just as Tessera gasped and arched off the bed, her eyes wide and hands flailing.

David yanked open the room door. "Help! We need some help here!"

Presidential Residence
United Earth Protectorate, Capitol City
Alexandria, Seat of Virginia
North American Continent

"Your dad is his father's son," Grace Tanner said with a playful grin and sidelong glance at her husband, even though she spoke to Michael. "Stubborn, but always with the best of intentions behind it."

Matthias chuckled, a low sound that came from somewhere deep in his chest and brought their joined hands to his lips so he could kiss her knuckles. "Probably why we butted heads as often as we did. But we always found compromise of some kind. Would have again if it hadn't been for—"

"Heinous Bitch," Michael interjected, assuming his grandfather would have referred to the woman by name. Something they never did. Gave her too much importance, his father said.

"The point is," Grace said, "Nicholas is going to need urging to figure out what it means to know . . ." She paused, her eyes looking down then to her husband. "What he's capable of. I doubt anyone knows for sure. We can only say we knew from a young age he was something amazing. If things were different . . . well, things would be different now, I'm sure."

"I don't know if I know how to help with that, but I intend to do what I can. I fought against accepting what I am for a long time because I believed it was something she had done. Dad and Victor were the ones who helped me understand. It's my turn to do the same."

"Even with perfect hindsight, I can't swear we would have done anything different," Matthias said, releasing his wife's hand to push his fingers through his dark hair and stretch backward over the back of the couch in the sunroom. When he relaxed again, he draped his arm behind her on the back of the couch. "In that moment, we were doing what we honestly believed was necessary to keep him safe."

"He knows that."

Nicole came through the sunroom door at top speed, her twin braids flying behind her with Dog on her heels. Without slowing down, she launched herself onto the couch and into her great grandmother's lap, then slipped into the small space between them. She loved Matthias and Grace as deeply as if she'd known them her entire short life.

"Lumpy says we needs to get Mama," she informed Michael despite having made herself welcome on the other side of the room.

Michael chuckled and pushed up from his chair. "I'll find Mama. You keep GiGi and Papa company."

She nodded, pushing hair off her face. Finding something for

Nicole, and eventually the Quads, to call their great grandparents had ultimately been a solution Nicole provided. She informed them one morning their names were GiGi and Papa, and that was it from that moment forward. Michael was fairly sure her grandparents hoped she eventually stopped calling them Lumpy and Gumpa, but time would tell on that.

He left them in the sunroom in an animated three-way conversation, climbing the stairs to the second level, going to their bedroom door.

"Dinner will be ready in a few minutes."

Michael spoke from the bedroom doorway, watching as Jacqueline laid Victoria Grace into the crib she shared with Matthias Matthew. They'd learned early on the babies slept better when they shared a crib with a sibling. It didn't matter which, but as long as they weren't alone, so they rotated them, two to a bed. What that would look like when they got older he and Jacqueline didn't know yet, but for now it equaled better sleep for everyone.

"I just put them all down," she said, not looking at him. "They should let us eat in peace."

Since the babies had been born, and shortly after the attack on the city nearly two months previous, his wife had been different. Not so different he didn't recognize her, but different enough he felt her distance at times. She would withdraw into herself, sometimes so closed off in her thoughts she wouldn't be aware of him or anyone else until a baby brought her back to the moment. He understood the source of her turmoil and did his best to let her do and be what she needed until they all felt safe again. It wasn't easy for any of them.

He crossed the room to step behind her, wrapping his arms around her body to bring her back against his chest. She tensed, but then relaxed. His nerves prickled. Not once, not ever, had she responded to his touch by tensing or pulling away. Her guard was up; he felt it around her like a buffer pushing out as tangibly as if she'd stepped away from him.

Michael ran his nose along her cheek and kissed her neck just below her ear. She relaxed more and leaned into him, tipping her head so he could kiss again. He tightened his embrace and she ran her hands along his arms, humming.

"I'm fine," she said, angling her head so she could look at him. "I don't have radar like you, but I still know you. Don't worry about me. I'm fine."

"I can't stop worrying if I believe something is wrong."

She turned in his arms to face him, resting her hands on his chest. "The whole world is wrong, Michael."

He kissed her forehead, holding his lips there. "I can't change the world, but I won't ever let anything happen to you or our children," he said against her brow.

"I know." Her voice was almost lost between them. "I won't either." She finally raised her chin to look at him. There was still a shadow behind her eyes he couldn't interpret, yet her smile was genuine. "So kiss me already."

Michael would never turn down the chance to kiss his wife, and any doubt he might have still held about her distance was erased when she slid her hands to his shoulders, lifted her arms, and pushed her fingers into his hair to hold him close. He curled his hands into the back of her sweater, fighting the very intense and instant desire to draw it over her head. Jacqueline hummed into the kiss and he held her tighter, kissed her deeper.

"Dinner!" called Caitlin from downstairs.

He grinned, feeling her smile against his lip before she laughed. "Sometimes living with your parents has its downfalls."

Hand in hand, they left the bedroom for the Quads to sleep. The smell of chicken and spices, vegetables, and bread drifted up the stairs. Nicole ran past the bottom of the stairs from the living room to the dining room, squealing, with Dog on her heels. Matthias' laughter boomed from the dining room. Having his grandparents added to the house felt natural and right, as if it had always been and always intended to be.

With so many young ones in the house, and with Lucy back in Vancouver, some new people came by the house each day to help. Some with caring for the children, and some just to help prepare meals for the president and his extended family. The table was always full.

"Wook, Daddy!" Nicole called out, her voice either set at silent or full volume. "No 'krats!"

Michael took his usual seat across from his mother and adjacent to where his father would sit. Nicole took her seat, a special one somewhere between a highchair and a regular chair so she could sit on her own, between him and Mama. Adam had a reclined seat between his mom and dad since he wasn't quite big enough to sit up on his own, but big enough he tended to be awake more than his niece and nephews. Matthias and Grace sat on the other side of the table from Michael and Jacqueline. When Adam and the Quads were big enough to eat with them things would likely shift, but not yet. As they sat, his father's chair remained empty.

"Where's Dad?" Michael asked, scooping some zucchini onto Nicole's plate. She hated carrots but loved anything related to squash of any kind.

Caitlin handed the plate of roasted chicken legs, thighs, and wings to Matthias. "He had to talk to someone in his office. Not sure who."

The sudden prickling of nervous emotion that rolled off Jacqueline made Michael pause and look to her, studying her profile, but her focus was down on buttering half a slice of bread for Nicole. Nicole had been bouncing on her bottom, but she stopped.

"Whus wong, Mama?"

Jacqueline raised her chin and looked at Michael sideways before handing the bread to their daughter. "Nothing, baby. Mama is sad because there are no carrots. I like carrots."

Nicole screwed her face into a funny grimace. "Yuck!"

"Nothing wrong, I hope," Grace said, taking the plate from Matthias.

"I don't think so," Caitlin answered. "Didn't seem like an urgent need, and no one is rushing us from the house," she added with a small smile. "Probably just some kind of information relay."

Moments later, Nick came into the room, rubbing his hands together. "Leave me any?" He took his chair and reached for the bowl of potatoes.

"They always make enough to feed a small army," Caitlin said. "Everything good?"

"Yeah, actually," he answered, scooping mashed potatoes onto his plate. "Tessera, the woman they brought back from Unity Valley with David, woke up today. That was Victor just filling me in."

"Does he need any help?" Michael asked.

"Nah, doesn't seem to. He said she's weak, but she's talking and she's staying awake. They'll keep an eye on her but seems good. David was actually there when she woke up."

"I'm glad," Caitlin said.

"I'll check on her tomorrow when I'm at the hospital," Michael offered, taking the chicken from Jacqueline that had made it around the table. "I have a lot of questions for her."

"She might not be up to long conversations," Caitlin pointed out.

"No, of course not. I do want to make sure she really understands she's safe, though. If my suspicions about her past are right, she would likely be worried about her safety. She likely experienced trauma at the hands of Kathleen."

"Speaking of which," his father said, putting the plate of chicken on the table in front of him. "She's dead."

All conversation paused.

"What?" Caitlin asked.

"Yeah, she's dead. Died not long before Tessera woke up, I guess. It's why Victor was at the hospital. The doctor on staff at the time wanted, you know, confirmation."

"Confirmation she's dead?" Matthias asked.

"Well, more confirmation that it appears no transfer happened." He waved his fingers beside his temple in a vague indicator of the transfer of consciousness that had kept her alive that long. "Her room was on tech lockdown, and the one monitor attached to her was immediately unplugged. It will be decommissioned and destroyed. Seems legit." Nick picked up his glass of water and held it out. "Hail, hail, the Bitch is dead."

Michael lifted his glass, but all his focus was on the rolling waves of what felt like panic slamming into him from his wife. She raised her glass, but her eyes were cast down and she didn't look his way. Michael couldn't keep himself from studying her as she set down her glass and picked up her fork, touching her food but not eating.

Another tingle of awareness thrummed over him and he glanced across the table, seeing both his grandparents exchange a glance before Grace shifted her attention to watching Jacqueline.

Conversation continued, but neither Michael nor Jacqueline joined. A heavy nausea hit his stomach, a sense of dread and apprehension, and each bite of food he took was a battle.

She managed to slip out of the dining room as soon as they finished. Michael caught her escape down the hall to a door leading to the yard, but he was halfway to the kitchen with a nearly empty bowl in each hand. Grace stepped in his path, stopping him to take the bowls.

"Go," she said low so it would be only Michael who heard. "She's tearing herself up over something."

"I know," he said, relinquishing the bowls with a kiss to his grandmother's cheek. "Thank you."

The sun had set hours before, and after the rain that had come through in the afternoon, the evening air was raw and biting. Michael eased the door closed to avoid attention and stood on the deep porch, scanning the backyard until his eyes adjusted to the dim light. His wife stood a few feet from the back steps with her back to the house. He pushed his hands into his front pockets and took the steps, walking to her.

"I should have known," she said, her voice barely carrying on the breeze. "I thought I could actually lie to myself enough I could lie to you, too."

"Why do you need to lie?" he asked.

Jacqueline dropped her head forward, her shoulders hunching into a bristling posture, the body language enough to hold him back from closing the space between them.

"Because that's what we do when we do shit we don't want anyone to know we did. We lie and hope it works." She raised her head but didn't look toward him. "I actually told myself it didn't matter. Punishment be damned, I'm not sorry I did it. I'm sorry to disappoint you."

The reality was obvious to him, unless he was completely off the mark but everything since before dinner said otherwise. Michael drew in a slow, raw breath through his nose to process what he felt, and what she thought he should feel and they weren't the same.

"I'm not disappointed in you."

Jacqueline snorted. "You *say* that, Michael, but you don't even know—"

"I believe I do."

She turned in a flurry, marching past him toward the house without looking him in the face. Michael extended his hand to stop her, but she dodged his touch. "No," she snapped. "I'm not doing this. To hell with it."

"Where are you going?"

She didn't answer. Michael caught up with her when she yanked open the house door, the sound of conversation in the living room down the hall carrying to them. Jacqueline took a shortcut down the hall, Michael walking fast to catch up. She was angry, but her anger confused him to the point of silence. His wife pulled up short at the wide opening to the living room where everyone had moved to while his father started a fire in the fireplace, on one knee while he poked the embers to life.

"Nick," she snapped.

He paused mid-sentence with whatever he had intended to say, looking over his shoulder at them. Whatever he saw in her face had him set aside the cast iron tool to stand. "What's up?"

Without explanation, she turned and brushed past Michael while managing not to let her body touch his, heading the direction they'd come to the back of the house. Nick reached Michael, and with a quick look in question – a question Michael couldn't answer – followed her. She stood in the middle of Nick's office and the two of them stepped in, Nick closing the door.

"Go ahead," Nick said.

When she turned to face them, her eyes shined and an almost indiscernible tremor moved through her, but her jaw was set firm and her lips pressed tight against each other.

"Jacqueline—"

She shot out her hand, one finger raised, granting Michael only the shortest of glances. With her hand still extended, she focused all her attention on his father, who said nothing, but Michael sensed a slow, gradual easing of his stance.

Confusion warred in his chest with concern.

"Do whatever you need to after this, I—"

"I'm probably going to pour you a drink," his father said, his tone level and calm.

"I doubt it," she said with a sharp shake of her head.

"I don't."

Jacqueline finally raised her eyes to look at them both, lowering her arm. The rapid shift of extreme emotions battling for dominance in his wife was enough to make his chest hurt. Unwilling to leave her standing alone any longer, and unable to accept another refusal of his touch, Michael took the few steps needed to reach her. Her shining gaze tracked him, a tremor moving through her despite her clenched jaw.

"She killed you," Jacqueline whispered when he was close enough to hear. "She took you and I couldn't do anything about it. You *died*, and she did it. I swore I was going to kill her."

"I'm here," he said, resting his palm on her cheek. "She didn't succeed."

"Not that time, but what if she did eventually? She tried to kill Nick. She told them to take our daughter! She tried to take your father when he was a child!" she hissed through her clenched teeth, the tremor gripping her growing more violent. "She's been trying to attack, manipulate, exploit, and destroy the Tanner family for generations. She-she-"

Her argument choked in her throat and she pressed her lips together to look past him to his father. "I couldn't let her have another chance," she managed in a forced whisper.

"I know," Nick said behind him, and the weight of his voice made Michael look back at him. "Victor said there were indications her death wasn't completely natural. The body was weakening, and she probably would have been dead on her own in another few months, but there were safeguards on her life support to prevent anyone from getting access to the parasite when the body died."

"You didn't say anything about that at dinner," Michael said.

His father's full focus was on Jacqueline, and he dipped his chin in a single nod. "All I really cared about was whether anything made it out of that room that shouldn't have." He paused, a slight cant of his head. "Nothing did. She's dead. She's gone. I told Victor to let it go. Doesn't matter now."

Jacqueline sucked in a sharp breath and straightened her back, standing tall so she pulled away from his touch. "You knew."

"I suspected."

"When were you—"

"I wasn't," he said, stopping her, then shrugged a shoulder. "I figured if you needed to get it off your chest, you would. And then I'd pour you a drink."

As he explained, he walked around his desk and opened the low cabinet set against the windows. When he turned he had a bottle of amber alcohol in one hand and three glasses pinched together with his fingertips. Opening the bottle, he poured a small amount in each glass.

"Look, I'm not going to argue justification or feign some righteous indignation here," he said, coming back around the desk. "She was an infected puss boil on the ass of the universe and needed to be cauterized. Existence is better for it."

He held out a glass to each of them, but when Jacqueline reached for the one intended for her the shake in her hand was too violent and she closed her fist, shaking her head. His father set the glasses on the desk, and instead wrapped his arms around her and she sank into him, never making a sound.

CHAPTER FORTY-TWO

April 2053
Location unknown

"Come on! If we can make it past the perimeter before the soldiers infiltrate the complex, we are free."

The explosions beyond the high walls around the facility that had been home and hell for the last twelve years muffled Tessera's shouts. Beams of light from the aircrafts infiltrating the airspace over the complex searched for the new enemy. Tessera shouted over her shoulder at her sister clones, pulling Ena along by wrapping her fingers around a too skinny wrist as Pendae paused to look back at the battle. Ena's wrist were no skinnier than Tessera's, but it still felt frail in her grip. Skin too cold.

Their captor and creator had disappeared, and rumors within the complex said Michael Tanner had found his ultimate revenge by crushing her like the parasite she was, but the legacy of her experiments still lingered. Tessera's sister was frail and ashen, her breathing thick with fluid filling her lungs. Trailing behind, Pendae stumbled through the darkness to them, looking back to the horror they'd escaped.

They were the only three left, as far as they knew. Treea and Esse had died years before, and Kathleen hadn't ever bothered to create more. Theeo had been taken away before the humans fought back, before the power the Sorracchi wielded was ripped away, before Tessera and her sisters had dared fan the embers of hope.

Ena stumbled, and Tessera caught her, bringing them both to the ground at the base of a hedge, holding her in the type of comforting embrace they were so often denied. To allow contact was to allow connection, but their captor had failed to realize long ago their connection had nothing to do with physical contact. In existence was their strength, in contact was their power. She curled her arm beneath Ena's head, supporting, with Ena's brow tucked beneath her chin.

After so many years, Tessera no longer found it disconcerting to look into the exact duplicate of her own face, her own eyes. It helped once she had finally accepted she was no more a true human—a true being—than any of her sister clones. They were all quite literally carbon copies of a woman who had once been. A woman who died fighting to live for the baby thrust upon her, the baby whose heart stopped beating just moments before her own, and death claimed her body as the Sorracchi extractor ripped her consciousness into oblivion. That woman was gone, and they remained her pale shadows, her manufactured doppelgangers who never even spoke her name in honor of her life. Kathleen had insisted they all be called by the name, to spite the son she hated, but they had amongst themselves chosen names in silent rebellion against her.

Sirens and alarms wailed from the complex, and floodlights bathed the surrounding grounds. Tessera pulled Ena until the thicker foliage hid them both, cradling her dying sister to her chest. She was dying. There was no question, and it was beyond Tessera's power to stop it. Perhaps if they had been allowed to be together days before, but the damage was too great. Infection wracked Ena, weakened her, and malnutrition gave her no stores to pull from to heal herself.

But Tessera could try.

She smoothed her shaking hand across her fallen sister's clammy brow as Pendae dropped to her knees beside them, panting for breath. Flashes of weapons and shouts of battle echoed off the tall security walls around the home of nightmares they'd escaped in the chaos. The power had gone down, and backup systems had to have been damaged, because the three of them had been given just enough time to flee their cells and find each other before systems came back on. By then, they had decided to run. Regardless the cost.

"The humans have arrived. They're taking over the complex. Maybe if we'd stayed—" Pendae began.

"No," Ena wheezed, shaking her head beneath Tessera's touch, effectively breaking the subtle contact Tessera had tried to establish.

The fight had gone beyond the walls, and by the shouts Tessera suspected they had not been the only rats to escape the sinking ship. Even while the Sorracchi guards tried to escape the human uprising, they still pursued their prisoners who ran with equal—if not greater—motivation. Screams of pain could have been guards taken down by the revolutionaries, or escapees dying at the hands of their captors. All the screams sounded the same.

And they were getting closer.

"We could wait and—" Pendae tried again.

"We would be no more free with them than we were with her," Ena argued one more time.

"We don't know that," Tessera countered, her voice the same tone and rhythm, but stronger. "They might—"

"We are no more human than the Sorracchi," Ena argued, purposefully turning her head out of Tessera's touch. "We are empty husks waiting for their incursion." Tessera tried again to rest her hand on Ena's brow, and Ena pulled away. "I know what you're doing. There's no point. Save your strength." She sucked in a shallow, scraping breath. "At least I will die free."

Pendae shook her head. "No, stop talking like that. We've come this far, we'll—"

Tessera saw the flash of the weapon hundreds of feet away only a second before her sister cried out and arched, her skin and clothing sizzling from the blast. "No!" Tessera screamed, her chest squeezing painfully around her lungs.

Her sister slumped over Ena, the stench of burning skin and fibers making her eyes water. She tried to reach out, but was trapped beneath the weight of Ena and Pendae. Tears blurred her eyes. She was losing them both.

"You have to go," Ena begged, her feeble shove against Tessera's hand not enough to release her hold. "Please. One of us needs to live."

She bundled her sister close, pressing her forehead to sweat-soaked hair, weeping as her heart broke. They were pale shadows of life, but they were everything to each other. "I don't know how to be alone," she whispered.

"We've always been alone," her sister said, finding enough strength to stroke Tessera's stringy hair. "We had each other, but we were always alone. Please . . . go and be the one to live. For all of us."

A jolt, though weak and little more than a pulse, flowed from Ena to Tessera and moments later Ena released a long, slow breath as her eyes closed and her body went limp.

Even though she heard the running of feet toward her, and the clashing sound of weapons fire and shouted commands—some from the humans, some from the Sorracchi they hunted—she didn't leave the huddled spot beneath the bushes until she felt the cold seeping into Ena's shell. Keeping to the darkness, she laid her sisters beside each other and tucked their hands together, before kissing each cold forehead and sliding off into the night.

She wandered for days. After finding a road, she stayed to the forest but walked parallel and in hiding, moving mostly at night. Convoys of hover vehicles sped by on two different days, heading in opposite directions each time. She instinctively assumed they were part of the new world military order, but Ena's warning kept her from seeking help.

With her pulse pounding and her stomach twisted with the fear of being caught, she stole food from a small, abandoned store she found within her first day, and by rationing what she'd stolen, she made it several more days before the lack of food made her stumble with weakness. She gave individual buildings a wide girth, but when she reached the edge of a town, growing sparsely at first and then forming a populated community of buildings and homes, she knew she had to find food again or die.

As the sun rose, warming the air again, Tessera walked the streets with no idea where to go or what to do. Thankfully, they had escaped with shoes and clothing, barely enough to fend off the cold at night, but nothing else. She had no identity other than the name she had claimed.

As she walked, she noted the people of the town gathering in groups, their conversations all sounded familiar. They spoke of the attacks they'd heard, the insurgence of military battles all over the globe, and the name of one man repeated again and again.

Nick Tanner.

Michael had learned the name of his father just months before Tessera's original body had known him; he had confided to that soul how his mother – their torturer – had spat the name like a curse. But he had hung on to it like a treasure. He had a name. No longer was he just Michael, he was Michael Tanner. He was the son of Nicholas Tanner, and if his mother hated the man, Michael was inspired to love him . . . even if he held no anticipation of knowing the man.

Tessera had no idea what was truth and what was just wishful dreams, but some said they'd heard Michael had been rescued by his father. He now lived free. Could this man everyone spoke of in reverent whispers be the same man?

She walked behind a crowd gathered in front of some sort of eating establishment, though the windows were partially boarded up, and shattered glass crunched beneath her feet. The damage had been recent. Some stared into the building, some in front of a window where temporary vidscreens had been set so everyone could see. Too curious to continue past, she stopped to listen.

A man appeared on the screen, and her breath caught. If there had been a doubt, she doubted no more. Older, yes, with hair mostly silver and touched by the brown it had once been, he was without doubt Michael's father. They shared the same dark brown eyes, the same angled features, and perhaps even the same set expression. Michael had been a boy when her memories saw him last, not nearly a mature man, but even then there was no doubt they were of the same kin.

With him stood a woman with golden red hair pulled back from delicate features and angled, green eyes.

The screen filled with the presence of this man, and Tessera moved closer, drawn to him in a way she didn't understand. But couldn't deny. His lips were pressed together in a fine line, nearly disappearing, and anger tightened his features as he braced his arms on the sides of the lectern.

Different sensations bombarded her from all sides as the crowd filled in around her. The cold of fear battled with the warmth of hope and the heat of anger. The humans around her were all in the same place, the same situation, yet each had a unique response. There were so many it made her dizzy.

Then the man on the screen cleared his throat.

He seemed to struggle, as if speaking at all was a battle, lowering his head before finally looking directly into the camera broadcasting his words and visage. His voice was heavy, rough, and so raw it made gooseflesh rise on Tessera's arms. "The Phoenix is an immortal creature, unique, the only one of its kind. Legend says that at the end of its life, the Phoenix builds a funeral pyre, dying in the flames. From the ashes of the fire, the Phoenix rises and begins its life again. Reborn.

"My son . . ." He stopped, visibly struggling to swallow after his voice cracked, diverting his eyes again for a moment. Then he canted his head and seemed to find an inner strength. "My *son* told me this story after my return from Raxo and Aretu. I wonder if, fifty-odd years ago, the founders of Phoenix had any idea how appropriate the name would eventually be.

"We've been through hell, and we've thrown ourselves into the flames, and now it's time to dig ourselves out and get on with the job of rebuilding our world. There's no point in pointing fingers and playing the blame game. What's done is done, and what is—is."

He straightened, taking his hands from their perch on the lectern, tapping long fingers in front of him. "The Earth is in bad shape. That's probably not the way my official speechwriter would want me to lay things out, but there it is. Our population is twenty percent of what it was two years ago, but we're still here. Our environment has been damaged, but not irreparably. We're battered and bruised, but we're not defeated. Not by a long shot. I'd rather have the crap beaten out of me and live to fight another day, than be a slave or lab rat."

Tessera's heart jumped and she blinked against sudden tears. While she felt weak, Nicholas Tanner seemed to find his strength. He stood straight and tall, shoulders squared, and his voice held no waver.

"This government is new, and we're still working out the kinks, but we've got a plan. No one wants to see this planet return to the fractured and divided way it was before the Sorracchi came. Maybe that's the one good thing that has come from this. We are unified. We are one. Together we stand. Together we kick ass." He smirked, and just as quickly as he'd inspired tears, he inspired Tessera to smile. "My speechwriter just had another heart attack.

"I know the biggest question on everyone's mind is what are we going to do with the Sorracchi. They have been confined, and we are working with Areth scientists to divide the Sorracchi identities from their human hosts. The success rate sucks, but even if we only free a handful of human minds, that's better than what we had. These newly liberated humans have to adjust to a world they don't know, and deal with thousands of years of memories that aren't theirs.

"Let's remember that these new citizens had nothing to do with their capture, their possession, or the acts committed by their hands. They are not the bad guys."

A rumble of conversation moved through the crowd, some already voicing their discontent with his warning. Fear gripped Tessera, and she clutched her fingers into the front of her ragged clothing. She wasn't one of the people he spoke of. She was less.

"As I said before, our government is new. We are working on a model that will give each major population a voice. Each continent will have two representatives who will sit in council for the people they serve. From each continent, a panel of judicial representatives will be selected to help maintain and create law to keep our new world civil.

"We have formed an executive council similar to the previous government; with a president." He splayed his hand on his own chest, then looked to the woman beside him. "A vice president, and a pyramid of leaders who will provide guidance and a balanced power. This time around, all the representatives and council members, including myself, have been selected through emergency elections. This is just to get us off the ground. Next time, the choice will be yours. Every human will have a vote."

He paused, clearing his throat, taking in a deep breath through his nose. When he turned his head, Tessera was once again struck with how much he and his son were alike.

"Queen Bryony the Fourteenth of Aretu, and the Council of Seven of Raxo have promised aid and support until we are on our feet again. Before anyone worries that we'll have a repeat performance, just know we're going into this with our eyes wide open. We are making it clear that while their help is appreciated, Earth belongs to *us*. No shared government. No shared powers. A rebuilding plan has been established and initiated. We are focusing first on the areas of the world hit hardest by the attacks to gather up the refugees, the wounded, and the homeless to provide care. We'll branch out from there, and when we're confident we've helped everyone we can, we will rebuild. In many ways we're starting with a clean slate, here. I say we do it right." For emphasis, he jabbed his finger against the lectern. "Scientists, environmentalists, and a whole bunch of brains I can't name are working together to make sure we come out better than we went in. I think that's a damn good plan. Let's show them that not only are we not beaten, but we're better for the war.

"It's going to take time and a hell of a lot of sweat and tears to rebuild our world. But it's not impossible. It's not all going to happen in the next eight years, while I sit at this desk, but I'm going to do my damndest to do what I can."

"It's the government's fault we're in this shitestorm," someone near her mumbled, and she looked around until she found him, leaning toward a man beside him. "Why the hell should we just step back in line with a president willing to work with *aliens* just like the screw-ups before him."

His words and tone made Tessera's skin crawl. She blinked and focused again on President Tanner, realizing now why he was the one to address the planet.

"A few decades back, a small group of humans came together to fight the Sorracchi. They may not have known their true faces, or their true names, but they knew what they had to do. It took years, but they did it. We did it. All of us." He leaned toward the filming camera a few degrees, his jaw set. "And we'll do it again. Out of ashes, Humanity *will* rise again. Just like the Phoenix."

Then with a curt nod, he stepped away and the screen went black for a second before information began to scroll about aid locations and what to do. Tips on cleansing water and first aid. They were already trying to help.

"Sweetheart, are you okay?"

Tessera gasped and jumped when a hand—so much more gentle than any touch she'd felt, this body had felt, other than from her sisters—touched her arm. A woman decades older than her stood beside Tessera, her hair gray and a bit wild, escaping from the twists she'd tried to use to tame it, and wrinkles fanned from the corner of the woman's eyes. Eyes slightly clouded, but still a rich brown, almost as rich as her skin. Tessera could only stare, wide-eyed, until her eyes burned. She couldn't find the power to speak.

The woman moved closer, her gaze taking in everything about Tessera from head to toe, and her features softened. "Oh, precious, this world has seen some terrible things but my gut is telling me you've seen more than most. Come with me. I can't offer much, but my food is warm and I'm sure my daughter can spare some clean clothes."

She tugged on Tessera's arm, a gentle urge, but Tessera hesitated and finally found the ability to talk. "Why would you—"

"Child, we're all going to need each other. Might as well start now. I'm Della." Without Tessera having a chance to accept or deny, Della took Tessera's hand in hers in a firm hold.

"I'm called T-Tessera," she mumbled, wondering a moment too late if she shouldn't have said.

"Tessa," Della repeated, a wide smile blooming on her weathered face. "Come now, sweet child. Let's leave the world saving to President Tanner and get on with living."

CHAPTER FORTY-THREE

22 October 2054, Thursday
Civilian Employee Housing
United Earth Protectorate, Capitol City
Alexandria, Seat of Virginia
North American Continent

"Guess what today is?"

On the other side of the video call, Lucy leaned forward to bring her face closer to the camera. It gave David a pleasant view down her shirt. "Thursday?"

He chuckled and she popped a wedge of apple in her mouth, grinning. "Nah, darlin'. Today is my birthday."

Her expression lit up and her jaw fell open. "Why didn't you tell me before *right now*?"

"What would you have done? FedEx me a cake?"

She looked confused for a moment, as she usually did when he dropped a reference and realized half a second too late she wasn't going to get it, then shook her head. "I don't know. But I wish I'd known."

"It's okay. Besides, no one can really agree how old I am. Am I thirty-seven? Or am I eighty-one?"

Lucy bit off half a wedge of apple with a satisfying crunch. Juice landed on her lip, and she licked it away. He forced himself not to groan. He missed her. Damn, he missed her.

"You look good for a geriatric," she said around the apple in her cheek with a teasing wink.

"Ouch," he cried, leaning back with his hand on his chest. "You wound me, madam."

Lucy laughed and it was one of the best sounds he'd heard in a long time. It felt like she'd been gone months instead of two weeks.

"Well, happy birthday. We'll celebrate when we're together. I'll bake you a cake and everything. If you're a very good boy, I might even manage some ice cream."

"When we're together we're eating wedding cake."

Her smile was slow and sexy, that closed lip grin she'd entranced him with the first time he ever saw her. "That we are." She leaned back and he lost his view, reaching just off camera to pick up a mug. "How is everything going?"

"First tests have been successful with the expanded dome. I've worked out the power transfer and conversion. We're testing now how long the nacelles can hold the charges. Best option is for them to stay charged for weeks at a time, but probably don't need to observe that long. I'm going by the control center later today to check, and then we're taking it to the next phase."

"What's that phase?"

"Turning it on," he said on a long expel of breath. "Then we test it."

"Test . . . like . . . shoot at it?"

David nodded. "Yeah. I'm terrified," he said on an uncomfortable laugh. "The initial dome should be big enough to cover forty square miles—"

"Wow!"

"Yeah, so, I'll turn it on and the Firebirds will take potshots around the perimeter first where if the blast makes it through the most we lose are some trees and maybe swampland."

He realized a few minutes later that he was explaining the theories and the system with the same over-exuberance he'd fallen into when explaining the process to Connor. She canted her head while he talked, that slow, sexy smile still on her lips. When he realized he was rambling, he cleared his throat and waved a hand, dismissing his own talking. "Anyway, we'll see."

"You're sexy when you're talking science. Do you know that?"

"Woman, that's not fair to say to me when you're almost five-thousand miles away."

Her smile widened enough her dimples showed and she took another sip of her drink, the twinkle in her dark eyes visible over the rim as she sipped. "How is everything else going?" she asked, lowering the mug again.

"I do have good news you can pass on to Trevor and everyone. I don't have details past last night, but Tessera woke up."

Lucy gasped and set her cup down with enough force it made the video shake. "*Gracias a Dios*! That's wonderful!"

"I probably should have led with that, sorry. Yeah, I just happened to be there. She scared the bejezzus out of me, to be honest. Sat up and gasped like she just came up out of water or something. She was really disoriented, but by the time I left she'd calmed down some. Victor was with her."

Lucy pressed her hand to her chest and let out a breath. "Rev and Molly are going to be so glad to hear. They asked me when I came back, but I couldn't say much. This is great news. Thank you."

David nodded, since he didn't really have anything to do with Tessera waking or anything. He was just there. "Have you been able to catch up with your uncles?" he asked, switching conversation again.

She pursed her lips and shook a finger at him. "I'm still a little annoyed you didn't stay long enough for me to know what you'd done. Thank you for finding them. Yes, we've spent a lot of time talking. You're already on their good side for finding them and bringing us together, so I think you have their approval."

David laughed. "Good. I wish I could have stayed . . ."

"I know why you couldn't. I love you. For doing that, yes, but . . . I just love you. And I want you to know something."

"What's that?"

Her expression softened and she rested her arms on the desk to lean into the camera again, but her crossed arms blocked his view. "Your son loves you, and I don't think you're going to have any trouble when you come back here."

"You talked to Felicia." Something intense shot up his spine; he wasn't sure if it was hope or panic.

"I did, but she's not the one who convinced me. Davey did."

"I don't understand."

She leaned sideways out of the shot and came back with a piece of paper in her hand. "I went to Felicia a couple days after coming back because I didn't want to wait. The topic wasn't an afterthought, you know? It wasn't a great conversation, but she understood. The whole time we talked, Davey and DJ were at the table. DJ was working on his letters and Davey was drawing. Before I left, he gave this to me."

She turned the paper so he saw what Davey had drawn, and his chest squeezed until his lungs hurt. Lucy moved the paper closer to the camera, blocking herself out completely. Even without the words "My Daddy" at the bottom, it was obvious the drawing was him. It was . . . beautiful. He remembered both Davey and Anthony had liked to draw, and for their ages they were pretty good, but this was so much more. His face, drawn in green and red and orange crayon with shadows and light and texture and realism. A masterpiece in colored wax.

David touched the screen and sniffed, then withdrew his hand and snuffled his nose. "That's amazing," he managed to say.

Lucy set aside the paper, her cheeks streaked and she sniffed, too. "Yeah, I was stunned. I asked him if I could keep it, and he said yes because he would draw you another one. That you'd be home soon." She met his gaze through the video call. "Felicia admitted he's been waiting for you to come home . . ." Her voice disappeared in the rasp of tears and she wiped her cheeks. She cleared her throat. "I'm sorry. Um, Felicia said he's been waiting for you to come home since he woke up as a child again. His memories are jumbled, like he knows somehow DJ is his grandson and his mom is gone and Felicia takes care of him, yet he still remembers you promising to come home. Mentally, I understand he's younger than when you were taken away, but he's never stopped loving you, David."

A small flare of anger tried to take hold. Anger at Felicia for refusing to let him see his son that first night when she knew Davey waited. But there was a part of him that understood, and ultimately it didn't matter. He snuffed the side of his nose with his thumb. "You keep that safe for me, okay?"

"Of course. You keep safe and come home to us soon. Okay?"

"As soon as I possibly can, darlin', I swear."

Alexandria Hospital, Secure Wing – General Care
United Earth Protectorate, Capitol City
Alexandria, Seat of Virginia
North American Continent

The door to Tessera's room was slightly ajar, with low voices drifting into the hallway. Michael glanced through the wire mesh enforced window to see Victor standing on the side of the bed opposite the door speaking with the young, newly-awake woman. Tessera reclined on the raised head of the bed, stabilized around her shoulders and head with an abundance of pillows, but many of the connections and tubing used to monitor and nourish her were gone, only two hanging bags remaining. A nurse was across the room preparing some new IV bags and glanced up as Michael pushed open the door.

"May I come in?" he asked, shifting his attention to the bed.

"Yes, please," Victor answered, speaking louder than moments before and motioned Michael into the room. "I hoped you might come by this morning. Truly, I had no doubt you would." Victor looked again to Tessera. "Many of us have anxiously hoped for your recovery, but few as much as Michael."

While Victor's tone was upbeat and intended to be casual, the sudden wave of panic and anxiety flowing out from Tessera nearly stopped Michael from entering. She stared at him, wide-eyed with any healthy color she had gained washed away from her cheeks, pushing back against the raised head of her bed. Michael stopped walking a few steps into the room, halfway between the bed and the door, and pushed his hands into his pockets in an attempt to mimic Victor's casualness. He hadn't sensed any fear from her before entering and held no doubt he was the cause for the sudden shift.

Why . . . was the mystery.

"I was thrilled last evening to hear that you had woken," he said to Tessera, looking to her but keeping his voice level.

He focused on tempering whatever emotion she might sense from him since he didn't know the extent of her Talents beyond his as-of-yet unconfirmed suspicions. To give of herself so excessively in an attempt to save David's life, Michael's hypothesis would be she possessed a highly-sensitive level of empathy.

"We have all been very worried," he added.

"I'm not her," she said, her voice rough like dried leaves, and the sensation of Tessera retreating into herself was as tangible as the sight of her pushing herself deeper into the pillows.

Michael risked a step toward her, but no further. "Do you mean you aren't Ranae? I know," he said, hoping his tone was gentle enough. "I know Ranae died a long time ago, and we learned last year that you and your sisters existed. David said you told him your name is Tessera, and Lucy Santos said she knew you as Tessa. Which do you prefer?"

Her gaze shifted from him to Victor, who nodded once.

"I assure you we are your friends here. You have nothing to fear," he said, and Michael wondered if that was the conversation he'd interrupted.

She looked back to Michael. "Tessera. I was four of six."

Michael smiled. "I thought perhaps that was the meaning of your name. Can you tell us about your sisters?"

She tipped her head, studying him. "No one has ever called them my sisters but each other. We weren't . . ." Her emotions twisted, feeling cold and flushed on his nerves at the same time. "I'm not a person. We were not siblings. We were her creations. Nothing—"

Unable to say the truth with conviction and remain so far from her,

Michael crossed the room to her bed and curled his hands around the railing still raised beside her. "No, Tessera. No. She told you that. I know she did. Probably much worse. But please, hear me and I hope someday you will believe me. You *are* human. You are not the ugly things she called you. They are your sisters. I—"

He shook his head and looked at his hands, his knuckles white with his grip. "I can imagine what she told you. All to make you feel like less." He took in and released his breath to stay calm before meeting her wide eyes again. "You are not less. And you are so welcome here."

She stared wide-eyed until the shine in her eyes overflowed, and she blinked. Tears ran down her cheeks, but she didn't wipe them away. Finally, she swallowed, finding her voice. "I may be the last," she whispered. "Treea and Esse were gone many years ago. Ena and Pendae died as we tried to escape. The place we had been was under attack, and those who held us would have killed us if they could. Only I lived. Theeo was taken from us, and I don't know if she lives."

"We learned of you, of all of you, when Theeo was found. She's gone. I'm sorry."

She blinked again and looked down at her hands. "Then I am the only one who remains."

"I'm sorry you lost your sisters. We're happy to have you here. I'd like to tell you something."

She raised her head, confusion pulling at her brows. Her color was definitely improved, though she was still pale. Too pale, but that would change with time. Having no idea of her past, Michael restrained himself from reaching out to take her hand.

"She is dead. The one responsible for all the pain and all the lies you suffered. She is dead. I swear to you. I promise you. She will never, ever have the power to hurt you again."

Tessera shook her head, her mouth working to form the "no" she couldn't speak. Michael nodded, the shaking fluctuation of her disbelief skimming over his senses.

"It's true. I'm not speculating or assuming. We know without a doubt because she died last night, here in Alexandria, just as you woke up."

"We heard you . . ." Her whisper shuddered over the words, and she stopped to press her lips together, composing herself. "We heard you took your revenge on her long before last night."

Perhaps that was the fear . . .

"No. There was a moment when I thought I had killed her, saving someone I love, but she had found a way to live. She didn't die at my hand. She died alone and in the dark."

Tessera folded forward, her hands over her face, until she was curled on herself and shook with her crying. Victor looked over her hunched form to Michael, concern pulling his features. He didn't often rely on the manual language he had learned when Beverly had lost her ability to hear, but in this case he didn't want his words to be taken by Tessera as a reason to restrain her visceral reaction. Michael released the railing to use his hands to communicate with Victor.

"Relief sometimes looks like sorrow. Perhaps for the first time since she escaped wherever Kathleen had her, she is really free."

Victor didn't respond other than with a slow nod.

CHAPTER FORTY-FOUR

11 November 2054, Wednesday, 21:35pm
Firebird Command Barracks – Former Hotel District
"The Nest"
United Earth Protectorate, Capitol City
Alexandria, Seat of Virginia
North American Continent

"Turn it on!"

"We haven't tested it for this kind of coverage!" David shouted back over the blaring claxons and the sound of screaming aircraft flying just above the rooflines of the city. He instinctively ducked his head when the sonic boom shook the building, still working at the dome console.

"Yeah, well, it's now or never! If it doesn't work, we're screwed either way." Connor came around to David's side of the console and shoved his shoulder so David had to twist and stand, facing him. The agitation was gone, and his expression was sober. "David, turn it on."

In the last two weeks, the shield had been turned on, tested, expanded, tested more, and gone into rapid production for implementation all over the globe. But they hadn't progressed on production enough to weave coverage. He had no idea if they could expand the nets enough to offer effective protection.

Connor was right. If they didn't turn on the shields, there would be no protection at all.

He pressed his lips together and clenched his jaw, growling low in his throat trying to wring out the last sweaty drop of panic he needed to shed to turn on the damn machine. Connor nodded and stepped back, letting David turn to the machine again. From this console in Alexandria he had access to the half dozen psychokinetic generators stationed along the east coast of the continent. Even with the fast production units provided by the Alliance set to the task of creating more generators, it took days to construct one. There were another half dozen a day or two from completion, but that didn't do him a damn bit of good right here, right now.

Sweat burned his eyes and his neck ached from the clenching, but he pounded out the commands to access the other units. The powerup was passive, drawing the stored energy from anyone within a few miles of the nacelles with a modicum of Talents, latent or aggressive.

The power levels ranged from twenty-six to seventy-nine percent charged up, with Alexandria's hub being the exception at exceeding one hundred percent. They had a hell of a lot of super-conducting brains in Alexandria.

The Nest shook as another barrage of enemy ships and Firebirds flew overhead and dust drifted from the plaster ceiling. David closed his eyes and searched his addled brain for some prayer he learned in his Catechism that covered this scenario but found none.

"Hail Mary, full of grace, the Lord is with you," he mumbled, beginning the command sequence to power up the various generators. Red lights blinked yellow, then green. They were powered and ready. "Blessed are you among women, and blessed is the fruit of your womb, Jesus." He sure hoped saying his Hail Mary prayers while turning on what might be considered by some a weapon of war wasn't going to shoot him straight to hell. "Hail Mary, Mother of God, pray for us sinners, now and in the hour of our death." He swallowed hard and huffed out a breath. "Just . . . don't let that hour be right now. Amen."

He typed in the final command. There wasn't actually any audible shift in the control column in Alexandria, but he swore he heard a dimming of the thrum just before the scans registered the knitting of fields. David straightened and swiped his hand in front of a projection circle on the column base and a holographic image of the shield network along the east coast appeared over the outline of North America, the boundaries and coastlines slightly different than the one he'd learned at Saint Ignacius.

Back before he went into the deep freeze, he remembered commercials for cell service companies showing light up maps of their coverage areas, and the shield network image reminded him of those commercials.

David held his breath, not daring to blink while the grid formed and the web constructed itself, weaving and knitting together the coverage areas. The section further south, near the Florida panhandle, was the weakest section with the lower nacelle capacity, but it worked itself into the net and held.

"*Nom de dieu*," Connor said, slapping his hand down on David's shoulder, forcing him to take a breath.

"Sir, the shield is deflecting incoming fire," Captain Laramier shouted over the din in the room. Most of the command center had been shifted into the console room as a more central location.

David pointed at the hologram. The grid was brightening. "Hot damn, Montgomery. It's working! It's absorbing the energy and cycling it back into the nacelles! Holy shit!"

"Sir," Captain Laramier said again, but the shift in her tone made David look toward her. She was grinning. "Port of Savannah reports having visible confirmation three enemy crafts were destroyed when the defense web engaged." Her grin turned to a smirk. "Sheered them in half, sir."

Connor let out a "whoop!" that set the rest of the Firebirds in the room to cheering. David smiled, but didn't dare look away from the grid quite yet. His brain couldn't yet connect the image he saw here with the actual protective grid covering the majority of the East Coast currently under assault.

The East Coast was the target because here was the seat of

government, and like every war for power in the history of the universe he was pretty sure, the theory was take down the government and you hold the power.

Well, screw you. Not today, damn it. Not today.

Connor's hands came down on his shoulders again, shaking him in celebration. "David! It worked, man! It worked!"

Connor released him and fired off a series of orders, everything from getting more Firebirds in the air to scrambling to the sites where the enemy ships would have come down. Radar was online and eyes watching to see if the attack expanded beyond the original perimeter, but the security net expanded several hundred miles beyond the focused attack zone. Because Firebird crafts were already equipped with signal arrays to allow them to pass through the net without damage, the Firebirds in the air could freely pass the dome in pursuit either below or above the net.

He hoped, at least. That was the plan and initial tests had worked.

But no one had reported down crafts because they tried to cut the dome. Didn't matter; his gut would be in a knot until every single one of them reported no issue.

Hell, he wasn't going to get rid of the knot – or probably sleep – for a hell of a long time.

12 November 2054, Thursday, 08:15am
Office of the President
Robert J. Castleton Memorial Building – The Castle
Center for United Protectorate Government

"*I* am damn impressed, David. *Damn* impressed."

President Tanner studied the data on the tablet in his hand, scrolling through everything. Sometimes he paused to shake his head in what looked like disbelief, then he'd smirk and keep scrolling. He sat on one of the office couches, with Vice President Surimoto in an adjacent chair and John Smith at the opposite end of the couch. Jenifer Smith – David got a personal sense of glee using a last name with the woman – stood behind John and near the fireplace mantle. Connor stood at the desk, leaning on the edge and Hank had just stepped out of the meeting.

David hadn't slept yet, both because it had been well into the small hours of the morning before he and Connor had felt confident everything was controlled and because his mind wasn't even close to shutting down. Still wasn't. He'd crash later, but right now he rode an adrenaline and caffeine fueled high.

"I'm not surprised," Nick said, sitting back on the couch, lowering the tablet. "Seriously, not surprised. I wouldn't have asked you to come up with a bigger solution if I didn't think you could. We don't have time for messing around and seeing what happens. But this . . ." He tapped the tablet screen with a knuckle of his other hand. "This is brilliant. It's way, way more than I ever imagined."

"Thank you, sir," David said, trying to calm the fidget of nervous energy in his hands. "I'm still pissed off at myself at how long it took for my addled brain to figure out what I was missing, but after that and with John's help hooking me up with the right Areth engineers, I'm . . ." He chuckled and pressed his hands together. "Hell, I'm kind of blown away at how it all works, too."

Nick shifted forward again, bracing his elbows on his knees with the tablet held in one hand. He rubbed his other hand over his mouth, studying the tablet again. David wasn't sure what information was there, but there was a lot to cover and Connor had forwarded data, analytics, and even video surveillance and recordings taken during the fight. They'd already retrieved some of the downed Urdo Khantan crafts and had either live prisoners or the bodies of the dead pilots. All had been accounted for. Not that an Urdo could wander around without someone taking notice.

They were ugly sonsabitches.

"Zephania and Beia Willoughby are jus' as impressed as you, Nick," John said, shifting to sit more into the corner of the couch so he could put his elbow on the couch arm. "And tha' was based on David's theoretics. Once they hear about the Forte Field, I'm sure they'll be even more impressed."

"Forte Field," Nick said. "Huh . . . I like it. Seems only right we name the thing after you. But how about Forte Fortress. Or just . . ." He held up a hand and spanned the space in front of him, like highlighting a marquee. "The Forte-tress."

David chuckled and groaned, shaking his head, but before he could say anything Connor barked a laugh.

"With all respect, sir, we have a hard enough time getting his big head through the damn door now. *Forte-tress* would send him over the edge."

"Just for saying that, I'm gonna say I like it," David sneered at him.

Nick waved them off but focused his attention on David. "How many do we have functionable right now other than the hub in Alexandria?"

"Six, sir," David answered. "We have another six almost fully assembled and ready to power up as a test. Once they're confirmed good to go, we can spread further. The spacing we used seemed solid and allowed a tight knit between webs, but we can probably expand another few hundred miles between them."

"We're going to need a hell of a lot of these things to go global."

David pressed his lips together and nodded. "Yes, sir. A few thousand ultimately, but yeah. My suggestion is to place consoles in the middle of most populated areas, work out from there. Focus on landmass coverage first since we're still trying to figure out how to deal with ocean coverage. Once the net engages, if it doesn't have another to connect to, it will form a dome wherever it is and connect to the terrain, so attacking crafts wouldn't have access to the protected area."

"How does that affect anyone under the dome? I mean, how do they get in and out?"

"Well, that's going to take a lot of communication. We need to make sure everyone in the area is within the dome range and aware of the boundaries so they don't accidently take a wrong turn. Casual contact . . . like brushing near one, will sting like touching an electric fence. But if they walk into it with any kind of force, it could be fatal."

"What about when the net is complete?"

David tilted his head back and forth. "Different situation completely. Once this is global, we can literally push it upward. Increase altitude." He raised his hands like pushing a balloon to the ceiling. "It's going to be a part of the atmosphere. If I'm right, that is."

"Been right so far," Connor interjected.

"Okay, so either the trend holds or I'm due for a flustercluck."

"Let's plan for the flustercluck, but anticipate best scenarios here," Nick said, holding up his hand. "So, everyday life won't be affected by this."

"Right. Any crafts capable of space travel who want to enter our atmosphere will have to either have the correct signal arrays to allow passage through the net without damage or will have to gain clearance from the ground to come through. If not . . ." He opened his fists like small explosions, imitating the sound.

"This is global," Vice President Surimoto stated, and David nodded. "Does this then exclude the need for smaller security domes like over Alexandria?"

"I wouldn't recommend doing away with individual shields set up on a smaller scale. Never hurts to have several levels of security. Get over the fence, you gotta get past the Dobermans and sharp shooters, ya know?"

"Okay, so, what do you need?"

"Sir?" David asked.

Nick set his tablet on the table between them and David saw what he'd been looking at. While what he'd been looking through at the beginning of the conversation might have been about the performance of the net the night before, the last thing he studied was fatality statistics. "What do you need to get this done? Each stage. And how quickly can it happen?"

David puffed out his cheeks and huffed a breath. "Best possible scenario would be twenty more setups to build these. The Alliance basically sent us massive and intricate 3-D printers. They create everything we need, practically assembled, but it takes time. If I had another twenty, I could have most major populous areas at least partially protected in . . ." He rapidly ran the numbers in his head. "A month. Full global net in two."

"Two months."

"Yes, sir. Every additional machine would knock precious time off that timeframe, but I don't know what we can get."

Nick tapped one hand on his thigh, looking toward the fire burning in the fireplace. Winter had taken a solid hold on Virginia.

"Aretu is more than willin' to send as many as possible. These manufacturing devices are available, and no' likely being used for anythin' of this magnitude," John said.

Nick nodded. "I'll reach out. But it's going to have to be this morning. The Alliance has allocated four battle class ships to defend Earth until we're better equipped to do the job ourselves." The annoyance in his voice made his tone drop, almost monotone. "They're leaving Aretu tomorrow and are faster than the cruisers but slower than scouts. Will still take a couple weeks to get here. But, maybe we can manage something a little faster."

"Let me know if there's anythin' you need from me," John offered.

Nick shook his head. "No middleman, John. Nothing personal, but some of the council really needs to see my face more often."

The flat expression and equally flat tone of the president made David wonder briefly what went on behind closed doors that he'd never ever be privy to, and just as quickly he decided he didn't actually want to know. Being the leader of a planet on the edge of invasion wasn't exactly a low-stress job. Sure, David had been given the task of building a massive, never before imagined, "how the hell do we do that?" kind of defense system but at the end of the day his job was probably a walk in the park in comparison.

Nick visibly yanked himself out of his thoughts, slapped his hands on his thighs with a "Whelp!" and moved off the couch, everyone following suit who were still seated. He extended his hand to David, who took it in a firm grip.

"Damn impressed," Nick repeated. "I'll get back to you later today with what I find out. Meanwhile . . ." He released the handshake and twirled his hand to indicate some ethereal point somewhere. "You know what you're doing. I'm not going to get in the way of that."

Protectorate Citizen Community—Unity Valley
Vancouver, British Columbia
Former Country of Canada
North American Continent

Things are happening fast, baby. I don't want to curse things by putting this out in the universe, but it won't be long now before we can quit this whole long-distance thing. I miss you. I'll vid when I can. Love you. David.

Lucy smiled and set the small PAC tablet on the dining room table. She harbored some guilt for having the device when so many people couldn't make contact with loved ones, but the short messages from David were often the calm she needed. It was a basic PAC, mostly limited to means of communication, but it was enough for her.

"What is that smile for, Lulu?" Uncle Ignacio asked, taking a seat across from her at the table with a cup of herbal tea in his hand. He set it down and slid it across the wood surface toward her. "Here. This will help calm your stomach."

She picked up the mug and brought it to her nose, inhaling the ginger steam. "Thank you." It was too hot to sip yet, so she set the mug down again and looked at the tablet. The screen had already dimmed. "A message from David," she admitted. "It sounds like things are going well in Alexandria." She looked up at her uncle. "He thinks this . . . forced separation can be over soon."

Uncle Ignacio covered her hand with both his, his expression brightening. "Oh, *Princesa*, that's good to hear. Leo and I are so eager to actually meet your man."

Leo came from the kitchen, carrying a small plate with a sliced apple and some cheese, also putting it in front of her. In her family, love was expressed by feeding you and her uncles did it well.

"I can't wait for the three of you to meet," she said, picking up a wedge of apple, taking a bite. It was tart and crisp, and she immediately followed up with a bit of cheese so the tastes mingled. "There are ways you are so much alike. Mostly your humor, I think. He makes me laugh so easy."

"Sold!" Leo said, slapping his hand down on the table. "I love him already."

The tea was cool enough for her to take a sip, and she hoped the mix of ginger tea and apples – some of the few things she managed to eat most days – would calm her stomach.

"Have you decided?" Uncle Ignacio asked.

She didn't need the whole question actually spoken to know what he meant. Lucy took in a deep, slow breath through her nose and let it out her mouth. "I didn't until this message," she said. "He thinks we'll be together soon. I'll wait until then."

Tio sat back and put his big hand over his husband's but smiled at her with a nod. "I agree."

CHAPTER FORTY-FIVE

27 November 2054, Friday
Secure Docking Bay, Transportation Hub
United Earth Protectorate, Capitol City
Alexandria, Seat of Virginia
North American Continent

"Once offboarding is complete, our ships can veil between your moon and de surface. We should remain virtually undetectable to any approaching enemies," explained First Zafir AbdelKa'er Rahyan.

John had given Nick a quick primer on ranking in the Alliance and while there were parallel ranks the ranks themselves were designated by their own government. If Nick thought learning history and government in school had been a challenge, trying to absorb the civilizations, societal norms, traditions, and nuances of a galaxy of races came close to breaking his brain. First Zafir within the Sovereign of Bagdaghir, where Rahyan was commissioned, was equivalent to a high-ranking officer like lieutenant colonel. He was from the same sovereign as Njogu Anini who was on Victor's research team. Just like

Njogu, AbdelKa'er Rahyan was so tall Nick had to either crane his neck to make eye contact to stay back several feet.

The guy was seven feet tall, easy. Had to duck to enter the room. His speech pattern was close to Njogu's from Victor's team, slow and casual to the point of calming but slightly less pronounced, though his hard consonants like D and T were very sharp. Time with Njogu made the longer than human limbs and fingers, and larger and darker than human eyes, more normal than not. Sometimes it was really hard to be a grown-ass adult and not stare at some of the variations of creation he'd seen in the last year.

"All four ships can hide behind the moon?" Nick asked.

"Yes, sah," he said with a dip of his chin. "De moon is an additional layer of protection. De veil is essentially impenetrable."

"Sounds like something I'd like to hear more about."

Nick motioned for David Forte to move forward. A few of them had come together in the observation deck to go over details after the ships arrived. Beverly, David, John, Connor, and Colonel Ebben.

"This is Lieutenant Colonel David Forte," he said in introduction. "He developed the defense shield the generators you built on the way here will control. He'll provide you and your people the signal arrays and codes you'll need to move through the fields once established. Otherwise . . . *psht*." He made a motion that was supposed to resemble an explosion with his hands.

Rahyan looked puzzled . . . maybe . . . for a moment, then slowly smiled and nodded. Reading Bagdaghir facial expressions wasn't exactly Nick's strength. "Understood."

David extended his hand, and Rahyan took it.

"I am pleased to meet you, Lieutenant Colonel Forte. De Willoughbys provided details our engineers reviewed to assure de assembly units constructed correctly. It is a brilliant mechanism."

"Thanks," David said with a single shoulder shrug, then stepped back again. "I didn't invent the wheel, but I guess I might have found a new way to use it."

"We completed de manufacturing of twenty generators, which have been inspected to your specifications and stored in preparation for use. We performed preliminary power tests but were hesitant to do more while on our way here. Dey are being offboarded now. Another twenty should complete in de next five of your hour units of time measurement if our conversions are correct. At de time of completion, we can offboard dem as well as de manufacturing units to wherever you prefer."

"We appreciate the additional twenty units," Nick said. "And the bodies here ready to fight."

"Damn," David said with a sudden, wide smile and looked at Nick. "We can speed up the next rollout. I've got six ready to roll in the morning, and with another forty we can really expand the net."

"Like as far as Vancouver," Connor said, low enough it was more between them than the whole room.

David shot him a sideways stare, glaring while he continued. "We should get some of these right on long range hovers and overseas. Another couple weeks and we'll have all areas of noted population protected. We can move on to connecting the dots once we work out the water problem."

"Is dere assistance we can provide in finding a solution?" Rahyan asked, canting his head with slow blinks of his large, black eyes.

"We're floating ideas—" Nick stopped himself, realizing what he was about to say, and corrected himself by clearing his throat. "We need to work out ways to keep the generators stationary in the water to maintain the net. If we had months, we'd build platforms or recondition old ones, but time isn't our friend in this."

"Natural island formations help, but spacing is important," David added.

"We may be able to assist," Rahyan said with a dip of his chin. "De engineer on de *Barrentasi* is of de Ilgen from Oknayil."

"Primarily water planet," Nick said to David, but then looked to Rahyan to be sure. "Right?"

"Yes, dis is true. He may have guidance to share."

"That'd be great, thanks," David said. "I'd like to go down and check on the generators as they're delivered."

"Yeah, sure," Nick said, jutting his chin toward the door. "Check 'em out. You can come by later with a full report. Connor, go ahead with him and say hello to the troops."

Both men nodded in departure, in unison, before leaving. Nick fought his smirk. The word "bromance" floated around his head whenever the two of them got at each other. They were at each other worse than brothers. Somewhere around the 2030s the word bromance was termed an antiquated Millennial phrase and the Gen-Alphas mocked everything that came before them through their "enlightened" world view thanks to the benefactors from outer space they'd known their whole life. Funny how that special form of enlightenment worked out for them all.

As a young man, he'd mocked his parents too. Then he lost them and realized the void left behind wasn't worth a thousand years of wishing they'd leave him the hell alone. It wasn't until he was an adult himself that he looked back, recognizing the sacrifices they'd made for him and appreciated what that had meant. But, by then, they were gone.

He also knew he'd been given a gift he intended never to waste.

Nick practically had to shake himself to focus again. He'd be able to think about all the stuff that kept him up at night, later, while staring at the bedroom ceiling while everything he had to think about kept him up at night.

"I'd like to invite you and your officers to share a meal later today," Nick said, looking toward Beverly and the others in the room to encompass everyone. "Tonight, with my family and others you should get to know while you're here."

First Zafir AbdelKa'er Rahyan closed his large eyes and lowered his chin, hands tucked behind his back. "It would be an honor."

30 November 2054, Monday
Alexandria Hospital, Secure Wing – Rehabilitation
United Earth Protectorate, Capitol City
Alexandria, Seat of Virginia
North American Continent

Michael paused at the open doorway of the recreation room of the rehabilitation wing, taking a moment to study the inhabitants. There were only two plus one nurse since this was still the secure wing of the hospital, with a limited quantity of patients at any time. Today, a Firebird who had been seriously injured in the first Urdo attack weeks before – Captain Joseph Canon – sat in his wheelchair at a table playing chess with one of the floor nurses. In a chair near the bank of windows that looked over the central courtyard Tessera sat with her legs curled up in the chair with her, a book open on her bent knees as she read in silence.

Before he took the step to enter the room, she stopped reading and raised her head, looking to him. Her reaction to him had calmed since the first day he saw her after she woke up, but he still sensed hesitation and caution from her. She'd confided eventually it was because she had the memories of Ranae, the woman she and her sisters had been cloned from, and while she fully understood the memories weren't hers, she worried she would be seen as a liar. Especially by him as one of the few people who knew the woman she had been duplicated from.

Tessera saw herself as a less grotesque but no less freakish version of Frankenstein's Monster.

His heart – his soul – ached for her and the lies Kathleen had told Tessera and her sisters. All to keep them suppressed, feeling less, and afraid to think of more.

He crossed the room, and as he approached she unfolded herself from the chair to sit straight and closed the book in her lap. She was drastically improved, that was easy to see. She had gained weight, strength, and color. Even her hair had regained luster. It had taken two weeks for her to stand without physical support from others, and another week before she could take steps with a walking aid. But once she gained her ability to move on her own, she had improved fast. Her body had improved, but Michael knew her spirit still needed healing.

"You are looking strong today, Tessera. You're doing very well," Michael said, hunching forward to rest his elbows on his knees, his hands linked casually in front of him. "How do you feel?"

"Strong," she said, repeating his own word.

"Good, because I'd like to speak to you about your next step. What you want to do, and what options are open to you. Something to consider."

"I don't understand."

"You're strong enough to leave the hospital permanently, Tessera." Michael nodded. "You should consider your options. What you want to do. Where you want to go, or where you want to stay. Now that you are strong and healthy, you can return to Unity Valley..."

Her anxiety spiked despite her expression remaining unchanged, and he wondered if she had spent her entire life masking her thoughts from everyone around her.

"Or you can stay here in Alexandria, if you want." Michael sat up and motioned toward the large windows behind them, intending to indicate everything beyond. "Or go anywhere at all. You have friends here and you have friends in Unity Valley, but the choice is completely yours. You're free to do as you choose."

"I don't understand," she said in a small voice. "How am I free?"

"Why would you be anything but free?"

Tessera stared at him, wide-eyed and unblinking, turmoil surrounding her. Turmoil... and fear. Michael shifted to the edge of his seat to close the space between them without invading her personal space, something he knew she coveted. She finally blinked but clenched her hands together on the cover of her book.

"Tessera," he said as calmly as he was able, despite the surge of concern in his chest at her visceral reaction to the idea of returning to Unity Valley. "What frightens you?"

She shook her head and looked away from him, focusing downward at the floor. Submission. *What had Kathleen done to her?*

"You have nothing to fear here, Tessera. Did something happen there to frighten you? David told us when you cared for him, you told him you wouldn't return and he couldn't tell them where you were. Why did you leave Unity Valley? Why are you afraid to go back?"

When she raised her head and looked at him again, her eyes shined with tears and a tremor moved through her. It took every bit of restraint Michael had not to reach for her hand, but as much as he wanted to offer comfort he knew it wasn't what she'd want. And in that bit of understanding came realization.

"Did someone in Unity Valley hurt you, Tessera?"

Michael held his breath for what felt an eternity while she stared at him, the war in her heart pounding in his ears.

Her affirmation was the smallest of dips of her chin, then she whispered, "I hurt him back. I shouldn't have."

"Who," Michael asked, struggling to rein in his rage.

"They told you," she still whispered. "They had to have told you."

"No, Tessera. But if someone hurt you, then you did nothing wrong by fighting back."

"I think I killed him."

Her voice was almost non-existent, and he read the words on her lips more than heard her at all. He shook his head before she finished, sliding off the chair to crouch in front of her, still avoiding the instinct to squeeze her hands. She watched him, her eyes wide, tears on her cheeks.

"I swear to you, Tessera, neither Trevor Tisdale nor anyone else from Unity Valley has said you hurt anyone. You aren't in trouble, but you need to tell me who it was. If they tried to hurt you, *they* must be held responsible for *their* actions. Not you."

It felt an eternity before she finally said, "He was a soldier. His name was Pedadda."

Another wave of realization came to Michael with the name. A few months previous, Trevor Tisdale had reached out to Alexandria because one of the soldiers in the community had been hurt in an accident of some kind and his medical care was beyond their capabilities. His name was Kevin Pedadda. He had been in a comatose state ever since. No one from Unity Valley could explain what might have happened to him, only saying he had been found unresponsive.

"You didn't kill him, Tessera. He's here."

She bristled, and this time he did reach for her, touching her arm to keep her from bolting. "He's comatose. He can't hurt you." He waited until at least some of the tension in her body eased enough he didn't fear she'd run. "I'm sorry he tried. Believe me when I say I do not think Trevor or anyone else in that community would think you in the wrong for defending yourself. Is that why you left and stayed on the mountain alone? You thought they would judge you?"

"I was . . . normal. Human. There. They didn't know what I am. If they found out—'"

"Tessera, you *are* human. You are as human as me, or Victor, Lucy, David . . . anyone. Everyone. The fact you have abilities – Talents – doesn't separate you. There are so many who have Talents. It took me a long time to believe the truth myself, but I do now."

He partially stood so he could step back and sit again, giving her space and a moment to breathe. Tessera looked down at her hands, her fingers fidgeting with nervous energy.

"David is returning to Unity Valley in a few days for a brief stay. No more than a day, possibly two."

She looked up, eyes wide again.

"It's your choice if you'd like to return with him. Or, if you'd rather not or want to know if you're welcome, he can ask. No commitment. No explanation to them why." Michael paused, gauging her reaction. "If you are welcome to return, would you want to go back to Unity Valley?"

"I think I would, yes," she answered with a small nod. "Mama Della made me feel very welcome. I think I helped people."

"I meant it when I said you can go anywhere you want, Tessera. But, in the meantime until you decide, consider coming to our home. Stay for as long as you need."

"Your home?" she asked. "How can I be welcome in your home?"

Michael smiled, hoping it eased her concerns. "My father enjoys the house being full. We have extra bedrooms until the children are older. My wife Jacqueline would likely appreciate an extra set of hands to care for the babies. Lucy Santos frequently helped, but she has returned to Unity Valley for the time being."

At the mention of the babies, Tessera's expression brightened. "I would be pleased to help. My presence won't bother your wife?"

"No," he said, simply, not feeling the need to expand. "Not at all. If you are ready, we can leave soon. Victor has already approved your release."

She nodded, the smile remaining on her face. Michael stood and offered his hand to help her to her feet since he knew she still had moments of weakness. Once she was steady, he led the way out of the recreation room. After a few steps, she touched his arm to stop him.

"Michael . . ."

He turned to look back at her. "Yes?"

"Thank you."

"You deserve a good life, Tessera. We'll do our best to see you have one. It's no less than anyone should have a chance at."

CHAPTER FORTY-SIX

3 December 2054, Thursday
Protectorate Citizen Community — Unity Valley
Vancouver, British Columbia
Former Country of Canada
North American Continent

"Looks like we just made it, sir," Captain Stewart said as she lowered the cargo hover to the snow-covered landing field in the center of the community. "Winds are picking up and would have made our trip a bit bumpy."

David looked out the front shield as they settled, scanning the white landscape. It wasn't New England Nor'Easter weather, but enough to make the hover travel a challenge. Captain Stewart seemed to always be his pilot when the weather was unpleasant, and she did a great job.

"I'm always in good hands when you're behind the wheel, Captain," he said as he unbuckled his safety belt to stand. "Sounds like it's a good thing we're here a couple days. Give time for this to pass."

"It's November, sir."

David chuckled. "Fair enough."

Was it bad that part of him would be ecstatic to be stranded in Vancouver for a few days? *What a shame that would be* . . .

Movement at the main house caught his attention, and he squinted to make out who stepped onto the porch. He didn't even care his heartrate jumped several beats faster with anticipation. Tough to tell with the coats and hats they wore against the cold and weather, but it looked like the Tisdales, especially since they were holding hands as they stepped out of the house. Then Trevor headed down the steps, leaving his wife under the shelter of the porch roof. Forcing himself to focus on the task at hand, David moved to the back of the cargo hover, doing a quick check of the field generator strapped in for transport. It was the entire premise behind his visit, and since just about every other generator available had been delivered and installed by trained Firebirds, he needed to make himself useful.

He knew he was damn lucky Nick Tanner was some kind of romantic who decided he'd earned a reprieve of a couple days. His soul needed a pause.

Checking harnesses and readouts was the last thing he wanted to do, but he did it as he listened to the hydraulics pop and hiss as the hover door opened. Footsteps crunched in the snow outside.

"Welcome back to both of you," Trevor called, his voice muffled by the wind. "If you have no need to remain here, I suggest coming inside as quickly as you can. The sun will set in a few minutes, and we anticipate the storm getting worse. You're just in time. Dinner will be ready within the half hour."

"Yeah, on my way," David called over his shoulder as he quickly gave a glance to the power nacelle. Fully charged and holding steady.

Feeling he'd made himself useful enough to justify the trip, David headed for the open hatch. He grabbed his heavier coat as he passed the seat where he'd tossed it but didn't pull it over his heavier BDU jacket. Captain Stewart already waited at the bottom of the ramp, and as soon as David was clear she used her remote access to engage the ramp to close. The wind was brutal, carrying snow on the edge of freezing so it stung when it hit his face and his ears immediately prickled with cold. He fumbled in the pocket of his jacket for his eye shields to cut down the glare. The tint of the front window in the hover had cut down the bright reflection off the fresh snow. Trevor Tisdale extended his hand as soon as David was close and shook it firmly.

"Good to see you, David," Trevor said and motioned toward the house. "Let's get inside where the wind won't threaten to steal our breath. I'm sure you'll be much happier in the house."

David waited for Captain Stewart to take the first step toward the house with her head tucked and the wind already tugging her dark hair from her tight braid before he followed. In warm weather, the walk from the landing area to the house was a quick one but walking into the wind gust made it feel a mile long.

"Remember where we parked," he shouted over the wind to the captain. "Might not be able to find it by morning."

She smiled over her shoulder at him, but just as quickly looked away to push into the wind. They reached the porch and pounded their boots up the steps to get off the snow, the house and roof immediately cutting the wind. At least, reduced the sting of the ice carried on it. Molly Tisdale waited for them with her shoulders drawn up and her chin tucked into the scarf wrapping her neck. She waved in welcome but only briefly so she could open the house door and usher them inside.

The air inside was warm and fragrant, filled with the smells of burning wood, baking bread, and a mouthwatering blend of herbs, seasonings, meat, and vegetables that immediately made his mouth water. He had to take off the eye shields because they immediately fogged in the warm interior. With all the other advancements in technology, no one had managed to figure out a way to keep glasses from fogging.

"Oh, wow," Captain Stewart said, uncurling from her hunched stance with the welcome warmth. "It smells amazing in here."

"I don't believe we've had the opportunity to share our hospitality with you, Captain," Trevor said as he helped his wife take off her coat. "We are always happy to have friends at the table."

"You remind me of Nick," David said, hanging the coat he'd carried in on a peg near the wall. "President Tanner," he clarified. "He likes a crowded table, he says."

They took the familiar walk toward the kitchen and David didn't even try to fight the urge to check the infirmary, hoping to see a familiar face. The beds were empty, and he saw no one else. As they turned the corner to the bottom of the stairs they'd pass to enter the kitchen, the sound of rapid footsteps in the upstairs hall echoed down to them.

David looked up as whoever was running along the upper floor reached the top of the stairs, and the most amazing feeling of déjà vu hit him when Lucy Santos stopped short, looking down at them. She gripped the handrail, one foot a step down from the top, breathing hard like she'd run a marathon. The first time he'd seen her she'd been in one of those "steal his breath" sexy sundresses; today she wore a sweater and jeans. It stole his breath all the same.

"I'm sorry," she said in a rush before her lips spread in a wide smile. "I fell asleep."

Then she rushed down the stairs and he met her at the bottom with a loud groan of happiness when she came against him, lifting her off the last step so her feet dangled and her arms wrapped his shoulders, holding on tight in an embrace that he felt to his soul. Her hair fell around his face and he inhaled the scent of rosemary and the clean shampoo smell he recognized as Lucy, lowering her to her feet, still unwilling to let go.

"I have missed you," he said just loud enough for her, pressing his lips to her jaw. "I've missed you so much."

She loosened her hold once she had her feet again, but only enough to draw back and look into his eyes, holding his face in her hands. Her eyes shined bright and her smile glowed on him like sunshine. It had been eight weeks and one day since he'd held her, and her slow smile still had the power to punch him in the gut and take his breath in the best ways possible. In his peripheral he acknowledged Captain Stewart and the Tisdales had left them alone in the hallway, but it wouldn't have mattered. He wouldn't have cared if they pulled up chairs to watch. David wrapped his arms around her and pulled her as close as possible, covering her mouth with the kiss he'd wanted for two months. He both savored the intense slam of familiar need and cursed it for having such bad timing.

With a deep rumble of regret, David punctuated the deep kiss with several small, short pressing of lips before mimicking her touch of moments before with his palms on her cheeks. She was breathless, smiling, with her fingers wrapped around his wrists.

"Your lips and hands are cold," she said on a soft laugh.

"Not for long. Not if you keep kissing me like that."

"I missed you." She smiled wider, pressing closer to him. "I don't think I can kiss you any other way."

He indulged in another kiss because he couldn't not, groaning into the last moment of it. Knowing it would likely be hours before he'd be free to "express himself" in more detail, David reluctantly let her go and laced his fingers through hers to join his hosts in the kitchen. If Connor had been there, he would have been a relentless pain in the ass – of that David had no doubt – but the Tisdales and others in the kitchen preparing for dinner didn't seem to give a damn they'd been making out in the hallway.

Except for maybe Molly Tisdale, who now carried her Baby Della in the bend of one arm while setting food on the table with the other. She paused to look their way, a wide and genuine smile brightening her expression.

The usual dinner crowd filled the room, with many already seated and others moving back and forth between the kitchen and the table with baskets of bread, pitchers of water, and plates of food. While David didn't know the names of many of the community members who had been at the meals he recognized them as regular meal attendees. Likely they were the elder residents or those who needed extra care or had no direct family to help them. Then those in the community in charge of seeing to their care, from medical staff to the community elders.

As always, the room was full and the food was enough.

Overall, Unity Valley had nailed the idea of community and the concept of many hands make the work light and caring for those in greatest need. Not a bad example for the rest of the world, as far as he was concerned.

Two gentlemen David recognized immediately – not because he'd seen photos, but he'd seen the beautiful drawings Lucy had done of them – as her uncles Ignacio and Leo. She'd explained how Ignacio

Santos was like a big teddy bear, tall and wide and burly, and her description and drawings had been perfect.

"*Tio,*" Lucy called, and both men looked her way.

And in a single heartbeat, David was a nervous teenager getting ready to meet his date's family and he was pretty sure his palms started to sweat. They set down the plates they carried and crossed the space.

"Uncle Ignacio, Uncle Leo, this is David," she said, and he looked to her because of the strain in her voice. It only took a glance to know it wasn't anything to worry about; her smile said it all. "I'm so glad you can finally meet him."

David released her hand so he could extend it to them. "I'm happy to—"

He couldn't finish, because the hand was ignored and Uncle Ignacio embraced him, patting hard on his back. As soon as Ignacio released him, Leo did the same but added a deep rumble to the hug, squeezing until David thought he'd snap. For a smaller guy than his husband, Leo packed a powerful bear hug.

"We are so glad to finally meet you, David," Ignacio said when Leo released him. "We feel we know you so well already through Lulu." He patted his hand on David's shoulder and squeezed. "You've made her happy, and so we're happy."

David slid an amused look to Lucy. "Lulu?"

"Don't even think about it. My uncles are the *only* people who get away with it."

Lucy stood at her bedroom window, arms wrapped around her to keep her shawl in place against the cold seeping through the glass, watching the group of people working in the field behind the main house despite the darkness and swirling snowstorm. Her room was otherwise toasty warm with the fire burning in the small fireplace. The benefit of an old farmhouse . . .

every room had a fireplace or stove of some kind for warmth. It was below freezing and the snow of the afternoon had shifted to something closer to sleet that would probably leave a crust of ice on the surface of the snow by morning.

Which was why David and some of the Firebirds and Terra personnel were outside at nearly eleven at night completing the construction of David's field generator and the shelter to encase it. He told Rev it was too large for the cellar like the original dome, and since it was a whole unit already it probably couldn't even get down the stairs. And while it didn't need to be protected as delicate machinery it did require some shelter from the weather. The next day was predicted to be even worse weather, and David worried about getting set up if things got worse.

So they were bundled up, out in the cold storm under massive spotlights to get his generator set up.

And she watched. Waiting. While her stomach twisted with nervous anticipation. When she was little and trips to the water park in the summer were exciting adventures, she'd be up all night the night before feeling sick because she was so excited. Her body didn't always know the difference between excitement and anxiety.

Like tonight.

Another half hour passed before they seemed to be done, at least for the night, and headed in their various directions with most of the forms heading toward the barracks in the community and David the sole form heading for the main house. Lucy drew in a long, deep breath through her nose in an attempt to calm her nerves, releasing it slowly through her pursed lips.

"You're being foolish, Lucinda Gabriella Bautista Santos," she chastised herself, still staring into the storm while she strained to hear any noises from downstairs. "This is David. When have you *ever* been unable to talk to David? He's *David*," she repeated to herself.

Minutes later, footsteps came up the stairs – unusually loud in the quiet, late-night house – and along the landing to her bedroom. Lucy turned away from the window as the door eased open and David looked in, not stepping in fully until he saw her. He grinned, the dimples digging into his cheeks. She'd missed those dimples. Maybe a foolish thing to miss, but she did.

"Hey," he said, closing the door behind him. "I wasn't sure you'd still be awake. It's getting late."

Lucy crossed the room, side stepping the end of the bed, to reach him. She raised her hands as she closed the space, pressing her palms to his cheeks. "It's the first time I've seen you in weeks. I wasn't going to just go to bed without you. Your cheeks are so cold," she gasped.

He turned into her touch to kiss her palm, holding her hand to his face with his own cold fingers. "Everything is cold," he said with a chuckle. "Not our best timing, logistically."

"Come over by the fire and get warm."

He obliged and followed when she took his hand and led him to the fire and the chair positioned to face it. She'd spent several evenings since the cold set in seated there, usually reading and always missing him. David sank into the chair, hunching forward to unlace his boots. Lucy took off the shawl and after David kicked off the boots to leave them on the hearth and sat up, rubbed the shawl over his hair where melted snow hung on in droplets on his short hair. David laughed and stilled her hand, drawing her around to stand in front of him.

She hesitated for only half a second, but just as quickly dismissed her own hesitation. David shifted her until she stood between his spread knees and rested his head on her stomach, his hands around the back of her thighs. He took in a deep breath, and let it out on a long, low rumble.

"We need a fireplace," he said with a chuckle. "Nothing chases the cold like a wood fire."

Lucy pushed her fingers through his short, damp hair and smiled. "What else do you want?"

He raised his head to look up at her but didn't let go so she could move back. She smiled down at him, still rubbing his hair. "You. Everything else will be bonus."

He stood, his body pressing against and brushing up hers as he gained his feet. Lucy shifted her arms to his shoulders when he was again taller than her, leaning into him when his hands moved to her back, holding her against him. His lips were as cold as his cheeks when they touched hers.

"Mmmm, you taste so good," he said against her parted lips. "Like ginger tea."

She laughed low, nuzzling her nose along his. "I had some a bit ago."

He kissed her again, and she enjoyed the familiar shift from a kiss after too long to a kiss of what was to come. She wanted it, wanted him, but knew she had to do something first. Lucy slid a hand from behind his neck to his cheek, and to their mouths, pressing her fingers to his lips to pause the kiss and break the contact. David kissed her finger before drawing back his head so he could see her.

"I want to tell you something," she said, barely getting the words to come out of her throat, focusing on his lips as she spoke.

"Okay." He kissed her fingertips again, smiling behind the touch. She must have paused too long, because he brought a hand to her chin, tucking his finger under it to nudge her attention up, meeting his gaze. "Hey, what's up?"

She was warm, flushed, and it had nothing to do with the fire. Or his embrace. Her cheeks burned and she blinked, silently praying and simultaneously silently chastising herself.

So she said what thought came first.

"I love you, David."

He smiled, slow and wicked, smoothing his thumb over her lower lip. "I love you, too, Lucy. Meeting you shocked the hell out of me, and everything since then has kind of left me stunned." His smile ticked a little higher. "In the best way possible. I wonder what I did to be so damn lucky."

He moved to kiss her again, and as much as she really *really* wanted to meet him half way, she pulled back and pulled her lower lip through her teeth before taking the final fortifying breath.

"I'm pregnant."

David stared, and her heart thundered. Then his eyes widened, his lips opened, and he sucked in a sharp breath before finally blinking. "You're pregnant . . ." he repeated, no question in the statement.

Lucy nodded. "I think probably around nine weeks. Maybe ten, but I'm not positive. Well, I'm positive I am—"

Anything she had to say after that was silenced by the sudden and intense kiss that stole her breath and nearly took her off her feet when David wrapped his arms around her and up her back, pulling her hard against him in a soul-touching combination of most intense hug and most powerful kiss she'd ever experienced in the same moment. She forgot anything else she had to say, falling willingly into the moment.

Until she tasted the salt of tears.

Lucy opened her eyes and tried to tip her head so she could see David's expression, but he held her closer and buried his face into the side of her neck against her shoulder, sucking in hard, deep, ragged breaths. She didn't try to make him look at her but kissed his ear – the only place she could reach with him holding her so tightly and rubbed her cheek against his hair as the intensity of his emotion wrapped around them both and she had to close her eyes.

CHAPTER FORTY-SEVEN

4 December 2054, Friday
Protectorate Citizen Community — Unity Valley
Vancouver, British Columbia
Former Country of Canada
North American Continent

"Are you ready for this?"

"Oh, more than ready, darlin'," David said as he took Lucy's hand to support her descent down the house porch stairs. "I've wanted it since I knew Davey was alive, but I've been ready since you showed me that drawing. Since then, I've known it's the right thing."

"You weren't before?"

They reached the ground, and he offered his arm for her to hold onto, thinking it might be easier to walk that way. The snow had stopped in the small hours of the morning, and the temperature had already shifted back to near fifty so the snow was melting. Not so bad for walking right now, but if the temps dropped again they'd be dealing with a lot of crusty ice.

"I wondered. There are plenty of days when I stop in the middle of some crazy conversation and think damn, I'm like Buck Rogers. I don't belong here. If I can't process reality, was I asking too much of him? You know?"

"I understand, but I'm still glad you have this chance."

"Me, too." He smiled at her, then stopped long enough to lean in and kiss her cheek. She was grinning when he drew back. "I'm glad you're with me. It's important you're with me."

Lucy slid her hand from inside his elbow down to his wrist until she laced her fingers with his and squeezed. "I'll always be with you. Whether physically or not."

"Well, we're going to work that out, too. The whole planet will be under the defense shield in a few weeks, but nearly the entire continent is protected now. Will be in another week. You can come back with me now. If you want."

One of her slow smiles curled her lips and she gave him a sideways glance. "Being with you again is what I want."

"Okay, good."

The conversation carried them across the yard to the cluster of housing yurts. Snow covered the continuous roof, and smoke curled from the small chimney outlets throughout the rambling building. The yurts had more than one source of energy and warmth, and by what David understood it was the choice of the inhabitant what they used. Just like he'd told Lucy the night before, there was something special about wood heat. He held open the door that led to the hallway where his family lived, and Lucy preceded him inside.

Despite his heart and head knowing this was the right time and having no doubt Davey would be okay with seeing him, David's gut hadn't gotten the message and decided to twist up on him. He took Lucy's hand again and went to the familiar door. The sign from months before still hung on the door.

Felicia Forte
Davey Forte
David james Forte 4th

"Hang on," Lucy said as he raised his hand to knock. He paused, hand in air, and looked at her. "You're a good dad," she said, smiling.

"I didn't need to be around when Davey was little to know that. If you weren't a good dad, he wouldn't still want you to come home. He wouldn't have named his son after you. And his son wouldn't have named *his* son after you." She shrugged a shoulder. "I wanted you to hear that before you knock."

David had to swallow before he could talk and gave a quick nod. He managed a "thank you" before rapping his knuckles on the door.

The dog he remembered being named Duke sounded his alert they'd arrived and shuffling inside made him brace himself. Felicia muttered a "Duke, enough," before the knob turned. She knew they were coming. He'd made sure he wasn't taking her by surprise. The door finally opened, but only enough for her to stand in the space with the dog behind her, trying to get through. "Hi," she said, but her voice lacked any real warmth.

"Hi, Felicia," he returned and drew in a breath through his nose. "How are you?"

She looked over her shoulder, then back to them. "I don't know how to answer that." She looked him square in the eyes, her expression set. "I understand I'm on the losing end of this argument, and I'm not going to try to change what's about to happen. I'm just really hoping it's the right thing because I'm the one who's going to be picking up the pieces."

"No, Felicia. That's the point. You're not alone in this anymore." He wanted to be stern, to be confident, but his throat tightened. "We started off rough, but you're still my family. You're my . . ." He paused to find the right term because it still caught him up sometimes. "My granddaughter-in-law. DJ is my great-grandson. We're a family."

"Who is it, Mama?" came a young voice inside.

Felicia huffed and tilted her head with a shake. "Well, if that isn't a hell of a question, huh?" She opened the door, still blocking Duke. "Might as well come in."

At the table inside the small but efficient space was the young boy David had seen in a photo what felt like an eternity ago, not just four months earlier. He was eating his lunch, a sandwich and some canned apple slices, swinging his feet under the table with enough momentum to hit his heels on the bench he sat on.

"Hi," he said.

"Hey," David said, and for moment he saw Davey at the same age sitting at their kitchen table eating his favorite – bologna and cheese with mayonnaise – while their dog waited for a bite to drop. His chest tightened.

Lucy squeezed his hand, then let go and stepped back from him.

She was there, but he was on his own.

"DJ, right?" David asked. The boy nodded. David went to the end of the table and crouched so they were eye level. "When I was a kid, people called me DJ sometimes."

"They called you my name?"

David chuckled. "Well, not exactly. They call you *my* name. My name is David James Forte."

The boy's eyes widened. At the same moment, David heard movement in one of the rooms off the main room, and since he knew only three people lived in the space, his heartbeat doubled and he rose from his crouch as the door opened.

And he came face to face with his oldest child in the broken body of a full-grown man. He couldn't breathe. Davey came out with a smile on his face, then saw David and stopped. Frozen. Everything . . . everyone . . . was silent.

Then Davey gasped and yelled, running at David. "Daddy!"

He embraced the man but held his little boy.

OFFICE OF THE PRESIDENT
ROBERT J. CASTLETON MEMORIAL BUILDING – THE CASTLE
CENTER FOR UNITED PROTECTORATE GOVERNMENT
ALEXANDRIA, SEAT OF VIRGINIA
NORTH AMERICAN CONTINENT

"All this looks great," Nick said as he looked over the status reports that had been delivered at the end of the previous day.

The reports covering everything from distribution of much needed life-sustaining supplies to ongoing repair progress from recent attacks to extensive progress on the judiciary development panel. He credited the progress of the judiciary panel to Doctor Dewey. She directed the rest of the experts and steered them back to the right road when they got off track, with little more than a look. She scared him a little bit, but not in a bad way.

The report wasn't all sunshine and rainbows, but at least there weren't any huge disasters to be averted, and at least there was progress. Every step forward was something, even if was just a shuffle, as long as they weren't falling on their collective asses again.

Beverly laughed, making him look up. She sat on the other side of his desk with her elbow on the wood and her chin supported in her hand, grinning at him.

"What?" he asked.

"For someone who has been handed a thirty-seven-page report on progress, you sound exceptionally glum. I believe I heard John once call it being properly in the doldrums."

Nick groaned and laid down the tablet he'd been reading on, linking his hands over it. "I'm waiting."

"For what?"

"The other shoe."

She arched a single brow and sat back to fold her hands in her lap. "Ah, too much good can't last?"

"Which is stupid because we sure as hell have had a lot of crap thrown at us in the last two years," he said with frustration, then groaned and scrubbed his palms over his face to try to shake off the cynicism. "It feels like whenever we have a few good things, we get kicked in the—" He shuttered over what wanted to come out of his mouth and cleared his throat. Beverly grinned, so he figured she knew what he was going to say. "Kicked in the gut with something bad."

"Don't you think there have been more good things than bad?"

"Hell, yeah. And that's what scares me."

"I never knew you to be such a—"

Before she could finish, three solid knocks came at the door and Nick called for whoever it was to come in. Phin opened the door, since he and Daniel stood guard outside, letting Connor enter with First Zafir AbdelKa'er. Nick stood when he saw the strain in Connor's expression, with Beverly doing the same.

"What?"

"Sir, we've got a message coming in from the Alliance Council. You're going to want to step into the communication chamber to talk to them. We're making the connection now."

Nick looked to his vice president. "Why do I hear the echo of shoe number two?"

Protectorate Citizen Community—Unity Valley
Vancouver, British Columbia

David tapped the knuckle of his pointer finger on the doorjamb of the open door to Trevor Tisdale's office. "Do you have a second?" he asked when Tisdale looked up from the monitor on his desk.

Tisdale smiled and motioned for David to enter the room that had to have been the original library in the house because the walls were floor to ceiling, corner to corner bookshelves. And most of them were full of books. He didn't have time to scan any of the spines, but it looked to be a wide variety, both hefty and small, old and relatively new. The room had that leather and old paper smell that was a comfort, even if you weren't a reader. He had a brief thought wondering who would love this room more: Michael Tanner or Katrina Forte.

"Is there something you need, David?" Tisdale asked.

David shut the door behind him before crossing the room. There was an old leather chair on the visitor side of the desk, and David sat, bringing the ankle of one leg up to rest on the knee of the other. "Ah, not so much need but I wanted to ask you about something." He tipped his head back to the closed door. "In private in case it's information you don't necessarily want everyone to know."

Tisdale's brow pulled down and he pivoted his chair away from the monitor so he faced David directly, linking his hands on the desk. "Sounds interesting. Ask away."

"Lucy must have told you Tessera woke up a few weeks back."

Tisdale smiled wide. "She did," he said with genuine enthusiasm. "We were very happy to hear the news. How is she doing?"

"A lot better," David said, nodding. "She was very weak at first, but she's up and around now. Between Michael Tanner and Victor taking care of her, she's in good hands. Ready to figure out what she wants to do with her life."

The shift in Tisdale's expression, even though he was probably trying to stay neutral, didn't get past David since he was looking for every possible nuance. He figured that first response to anything he said would be the sincerest and would tell him the truth.

"Oh," Tisdale said, arching his eyebrows higher. "That's wonderful to hear. We'll miss her if she chooses not to come back. Especially Mama Della. She holds a special place in her heart for Tessa."

"It wouldn't be a problem if she came back here?"

Tisdale canted his head, and the brows shifted again. Downward in confusion. "Of course not. We all wondered why she had chosen to leave in silence in the first place, though ultimately it was serendipitous since she was able to be there for you. Learning she'd been living alone all that time was a surprise. If any of us had known, I've no doubt we would have tried to help her or convince her to come back."

"You never had an idea why she left."

Tisdale shook his head. "No. None."

David set his elbow on the arm of the chair, rubbing a finger across his chin. "Do you remember a Terra officer named Kevin Pedadda?"

Tisdale looked confused by the shift in topic, but in truth that's what David wanted. Not that he thought Trevor Tisdale was really going to hide anything, but he preferred to control the conversation. "Yes. I remember him. Perhaps Colonel Montgomery didn't tell you what happened?"

"Only that he had an accident. He's currently in Alexandria. Comatose."

The man nodded. "He was discovered behind one of the outbuildings much earlier this year, hurt, and we were unable to revive him. Doctor Dardashti assumed brain trauma but there was little physical evidence to imply what may have caused his injury. There were signs of some sort of fall or accident, but–"

"No one figured out what happened?"

Tisdale scowled and tilted his head again, not answering right away as he stared at David. There was a tangible shift in the air of the library. David felt it but didn't have a name for it other than instinctively knowing the dots had been connected.

The leader of the community looked away and down, but not for long. When he raised his head again, any pretense of a smile was gone. His expression was level, no attempt at masking that David could tell.

"Captain Pedadda was, by all appearances, a man committed to his duties; however, there were elements of his personality that concerned me. Nothing definitive or specific and no one had brought specific incidents to my attention. To be transparent, if there had been something specific I could name or cite in example I would have asked for him to be reassigned away from Unity Valley." The neutral, *leadership* mask was gone. "I don't know if you are aware of my education or background, but part of my training prior to the chaos that took over our world was to see and acknowledge the good, but to recognize and defend against the evil."

David nodded. "She's afraid to come back."

"She needn't be," Tisdale confirmed, his answer quick. "No explanation required. No fault assigned. Nor will any part of this discussion go beyond this room. Please, let her know that for me, David."

"I will. That's good to hear. I think she'll be happy to know."

"We look forward to her return, if that's her decision."

David nodded, a single tip of his chin, and shifted forward to stand.

"Oh, and David . . ." He paused, mid-rise. The smile had returned to Tisdale's face, but there was no careful mask around it. "Congratulations. Being the husband to Lucy's best friend has the benefit of hearing the good news early on. I've known Lucy for many years, and can honestly say I don't believe I've seen her as happy as she has been since meeting you. For many reasons. We both wish the two of you all happiness."

David smiled, knowing it was a stupid grin as his dad used to say, but he didn't care. "Thanks. I appreciate that. I feel like I've been approved by the family."

Tisdale laughed. "It's safe to make that assumption. We hope to see you and Lucy back in Unity Valley often. I know Molly missed her when she was in Alexandria, but it helped knowing she was happy."

David nodded but didn't say anything, letting a now common thought stir through his head as he stood and headed for the door.

INTERSTELLAR SECURE COMMUNICATION CHAMBER
ROBERT J. CASTLETON MEMORIAL BUILDING – THE CASTLE
UNITED EARTH PROTECTORATE, CAPITAL CITY

"They're coming."

The holographic projection of Councilmember Gozzo Torroni and Queen Bryony of Aretu faced Nick, Beverly, Connor, Rahyan, and John in the center of the chamber. John had been summoned as soon as the need for this tête-à-tête was apparent, but since he was in the building already, his arrival was quick.

"When?" Nick asked.

"It's imminent," Bryony qualified, the look of dread in her eyes enough to convince Nick he absolutely had heard the echo of that second shoe. "You need to prepare immediately."

"We have dispatched further aid from outposts closer to your system," Torroni said, his voice muffled by the moisture-infusing mask over his face. "It will be five of your days before we arrive."

Nick looked to Connor, who gave a sharp nod and jogged to the door. Rahyan followed.

"What are the coordinates of their last known location?" John asked.

"And how many are we talking," Nick added.

Gozzo relayed the information about location, and while Nick had developed a solid hand on the Alliance coordinate system his brain was still churning the information when John looked to him.

"They're within one jump from the edge of your system, and with the travel capacity we are aware of that has them reaching Earth within three hours."

"Our long-range radar estimates six transport and attack vessels with the capability of carrying up to one hundred individual crafts and up to three-thousand soldiers," Gozzo added.

In his head, Nick swore long and loud, but he kept his face as neutral as possible. The wave of anxiety bouncing off Beverly and concern off John made it hard to stay that way.

"Are we right in assuming we're facing potentially eighteen thousand Khantan?"

"Possibly, yes," Bryony said. "It's also possible the Urdo Khantan have recruited other races to fight with them on the Sorracchi payroll. They have been known to do so; however, the Khantan are the most brutal of those alliances. If other races have joined the fight, they will not be as terrifying an opponent."

"The unknown is what terrifies me," Nick said. "That and we're weeks away from a global field."

"I'm so sorry," Bryony said, shaking her head. "The combined efforts of the Urdo Khantan and the Sorracchi who still hold power in parts of the galaxy have suppressed our attempts at staying aware of their actions. While we knew it was coming, we honestly had no idea how close they were. Nicholas, you should also know we have confirmed a Sorracchi we identified by Katk Hak'Ro has been the one behind all of this."

Beverly gasped, snapping his attention to her. "Barnabas," she answered. "Victor told me his true name once."

"Damn it. I'd really hoped we'd killed him in the war," he cursed.

"He truly believes vengeance should be theirs because Humans fought back against their dominion."

"Tha' tends to happen with megalomaniac oppressors," John said.

"There was a Sorracchi scientist under his command while on Earth, and we believe he has been attempting to make contact without results," Gozzo continued to explain. "He was likely suspecting a stronger establishment of support on your planet before their arrival."

Nick's neck prickled and hated the taste in his mouth before he said the name "Tosk Rak'blon."

Gozzo nodded his head. "Yes. Are you aware of this Sorracchi?"

"Unfortunately," Nick said, letting the disgust hit his face because he didn't give a damn. He shifted his gaze to focus directly on Bryony. "Kathleen."

Bryony's eyes widened. She understood. He'd shared the story during their travel two years earlier from Aretu back to Earth. "Do you know her whereabouts?"

"Yeah," he said, sneering. "She's dead. You know the Sorracchi captured on Aretu after attempting to kill John?" he asked, tipping his head toward John. "After we got her back here we figured out she was Kathleen. Or Tosk Rak'blon. She was extracted from that woman's body, who was an unwilling participant, and put into a body we could better keep track of. That body died six weeks ago, with no opportunity for her to be downloaded again. We cremated all that was left."

"Whether she lives, or not, Katk Hak'Ro is taking action. We are coming, Nicholas. Until then, First Zafir Rahyan and the squadrons under his command will provide all support possible. May the Creator of All keep you safe."

4 December 2054, Friday
Protectorate Citizen Community — Unity Valley
Vancouver, British Columbia
Former Country of Canada
North American Continent

"There's not much you need to do for maintenance or anything," David explained as he walked around the field generator.

Trevor Tisdale and a few select Firebird and Terra personnel chosen because Unity Valley was their permanent station stood on one side of the small enclosure they'd built the night before while David went over the basics. The building was an adaptation of the yurts used throughout the community for housing, basically reduced to the size of a single-family unit with wood and metal braces, a solid door, and temperature control. They'd put on the finishing touches that morning after the sun was up and the wind had died a bit, and before his visit with Lucy to the rest of his family.

"Once the generators are fully engaged and the web has fully knit itself, they will work in tandem. Intelligently. If one generator in the network is accessing or being fed more energy than it can store, that energy will be disbursed to other spots that are lower."

As they'd created more generators, David had developed the intelligent grid that shifted power where needed when needed. It made the entire net practically self-motivated. Self-reliant. Sure, it would be monitored and there were actions that could be taken manually, but quite literally once the grid was whole – which wouldn't be for another couple months at least, even with them churning out twenty-six new generators every few days – it was a closed-circuit network.

The concept made both perfect sense to him and blew his mind at the same time.

After another hour and a half of talking and answering questions, the military personnel were excused to return to their regular duties. The generator wasn't on yet but was about to be after he initiated power-up. When other generators were set up within the needed proximity of Unity Valley and the western side of the continent, they would automatically knit. For the North American Continent, they were working around the edges and filling in as they could while generators were being shipped to other continents where marked populations had grown. The spots between generator ranges would be vulnerable, but at least the areas with people would be under cover as soon as possible.

The final stage would be protecting large bodies of water to finish the loop and bring it all together. He'd be working with the Ilgen engineer that'd arrived the week before on some ideas once he returned to Alexandria.

He hoped not to return to Alexandria alone.

The separation wasn't necessary anymore since he'd got his head out of his ass and figured out the technology, and more than that, now that he felt Alexandria was safe for Lucy.

And their baby.

The idea made his heart do a flip every time he thought of it.

Damn.

He shook himself out of his thoughts and commenced the engagement and power-up sequence for the generator. Once on, there would never be a need to shut it down, nor would it ever shut down without intent so once it was on, it was on. He wanted to do the initial power-up alone, feeling with this generator he had more personal responsibility than any other because of the precious souls it would be protecting for him. Immediately, the generator produced a low hum and the center console glowed in response to nacelle access. As soon as the energy was accessed, David set the auto checklist protocol to run, which would take less than thirty seconds, and opened the Firebird-dedicated communication line and engaged the image projector to appear above the console. Connor snapped into sharp color at eye level.

"*Nom de Dieu*, David! What the hell are you doing?"

"Nice to see you too, sweetheart," he said, focusing on his readouts and data streams rather than the image. "Stressed?"

"Just a little. We've got incoming, and it sure would be helpful if we had a defense grid up and running. Except you didn't exactly leave me an operation manual on this thing."

"Haven't exactly had time to type up one." He looked up from the controls to look directly at Connor through the holographic projection. "When you say incoming, what are we talking?"

"Hellfire and brimstone," Connor answered, shaking his head. "I left the convo to get started here, but the president passed on numbers. Thousands. Several battle transports and all the killers they can carry. ETA five seconds from now. So, again . . . a defense grid would be nice, even if it's not everywhere."

"Do me a favor, Connor."

"David, we need the damn grid!"

David watched the checklist progress bar reach near completion, then shifted his focus to the projection so he stared at Connor Montgomery. "I'll be powered up here in less than ten seconds. Are you in the main console room?"

"Where else would I be?"

"Remember that big red button under the clear shield that I told you don't ever touch unless I tell you to touch it?"

Connor scowled at him and nodded with his eyes squinted at the corners.

"Go ahead." He winked. "You know you want to."

Connor let out a long string of cursing David thought was a mix of French and possibly Arabic he'd learned from his father-in-law and moved out of screen. Seconds later, the synthesized voice of the Alexandria hub said, "Haven engaged."

"What the hell is Haven?"

"Unity Valley," Connor said as every screen, dial, gage, and readout of the newly born Unity Valley Forte Field generator came to life. "I've got control. Powering up the grid, as it exists anyway . . . *now*."

He wished he'd put in some active notification system for when the grid was online and working correctly; instead, he'd only done warning notifications. He'd feel so much more satisfied if something dinged or rang or set off fireworks that everything was good to go. Since no warning claxons went off or blaring sirens, he moved forward.

"What new locations are powered up?" he asked.

"Queretaro, San Antonio, Mexicali, Santa Fe, Las Vegas, Provo, Boise, Calgary, Grande Prairie, and Prince Rupert have reported they are on and engaged. Waiting on Juneau, Anchorage, Fort Yukon, Nome, Bilibino, Yagodnoya, and Okha."

"Okay, let me reach out from here." He accessed the multi-channel communication links but glanced at Connor as he did. "How bad is it going to get?"

Connor was looking away when David asked, shouting orders to others in the command center. He wiped the back of his hand across his brow before bringing his attention back to David. "If we didn't have what we've got with your grid, I'd say we'd be dead in the water against what's coming. With your grid, and the Alliance backup we've already got here, we've got a fighting chance until more backup arrives."

"So more are on the way?"

"That's what they say anyway."

With all communication channels open, David activated the notification alarms to get attention of anyone near the generators. Five of the seven were powered on, so he just needed to get their attention. Juneau was the first to answer.

"Captain Ungalaaq here," came a deep resonating voice as a dark haired, medium skinned man came into the video. "Good morning, sir."

"No time for chitchat, Captain," David said, shaking his head. "Time to power up and play ball."

CHAPTER FORTY-EIGHT

Bulletin For Global Broadcast

5 December 2054, Friday
Office of President Nicholas Tanner
Robert J. Castleton Memorial Building – The Castle
Center for United Protectorate Government
Alexandria, Seat of Virginia

The current and most severe attack on Earth has been coordinated and funded by the Sorracchi, who no longer have the means to come at us themselves. The Urdo Khantan are mercenary guns-for-hire sent because the Sorrs think they have the right to claim our world and our people. We're not going to let that happen.

A defensive grid known as the Forte Field is being set in place globally by our Firebirds, with support by both Earth Force Terra and Sphera. This defense grid is not yet complete because thousands of generators need to be built, but is being established as quickly as possible; aided in production by the Defense Alliance.

The Alliance is providing defensive support with thousands of Alliance military persons, some of which are already on Earth with more on the way. We're not alone in this fight. Please, if you can hunker down and stay undercover, do so. The Urdo Khantan are without morality and won't hesitate to kill any human they see on sight. Protect those near you. If you are near the location of an existing field generator, stay there. Get closer if you can. Until the field is fully established, there will be gaps the enemy can penetrate.

As hard as it may be to stay out of this fight, I am asking those who are physically able to provide protection for those who can't, please stay and protect them. We need you there more than in the fight.

We don't expect this to be over as quickly as it was two years ago when we fought back against the Sorracchi. We had the advantage of surprise. This time, we have the backing of the Defense Alliance and our allies will fight by our side.

Images will accompany this bulletin. What you see is the likeness of the Urdo Khantan. *They are the enemy.* Just because you see a non-human, *do not* assume they are the enemy. The *Urdo Khantan* are our visible, identifiable enemy. Do not engage them, and do not hinder our allies in this fight.

We will not be taken down by the Sorracchi cowards and the henchmen they hired. We're more determined than that. We're united, and we will not fail.

8 December 2054, Tuesday
Protectorate Citizen Community—Unity Valley
Vancouver, British Columbia
Former Country of Canada
North American Continent

The evening air was biting, and Lucy's cheeks were raw from the tears the wind had frozen, her fingers so cold they ached, but she couldn't make her feet move to go inside. Many evenings this time of year the night sky shifted and danced with diaphanous strands of green and blue aurora borealis light shows, but the flashes and streaks of yellow, orange, and red over the community had nothing to do with natural beauty.

They were the fires of war.

David's defense shield was doing what he'd promised. It protected Unity Valley from the fighting overhead, and the edges of the Unity Valley span were miles beyond the edge of the community. Reports, statements, and bulletins came from Alexandria a couple times a day, providing updates and guidance. When Lucy had been in Alexandria, she would watch news broadcasts each day from different regions, and the updates were being sent now the same way. Here in Unity Valley, no one watched the news so it came through Rev regularly. He had shared the enemy – the Urdo Khantan – would blanket the ground, covering several hundred square miles, with whatever form of attack their crafts carried as a means to find the edges of the field.

They'd learned early the surface was protected, but they also learned there were gaps. Holes. Ways inside.

When darkness fell, the volleys began. Everywhere. Not just here over Unity Valley. Everywhere. Searching.

And when they found a place, they attacked.

The reports broke her heart.

Terrified her.

"Promise me, David. Swear to me you're coming home."

He'd pressed his forehead to hers, the tips of their noses touching as he stroked the tears from her cheeks. *"I promise, baby. Nothing will keep me from coming back."*

Then he boarded a hover in yet another storm and went back to Alexandria. Not because he wanted to, because she knew he hated leaving with everything he was, but because he had to. The Forte Field existed because of him, and if there was any way to speed up the process or make the span greater, he'd be the one to figure it out.

"Sis, you shouldn't be out here," she heard behind her as Molly opened the house door. "It's too cold. And watching doesn't do any good. They'll keep at it whether you're here or not."

Lucy ran her fingers over her chapped cheeks and wrapped her arms around her body as much as she could over the bulky coat she wore. "It's not like I'll sleep," she said. "How can I with the noise? It's so much louder in the stillness."

"Do you want to change bedrooms?"

She turned to look at her lifelong friend, loving her for trying to help in any way she could. It was so much harder this time when David left, and Molly had tried to do whatever she could to help ease Lucy's heartache. But it was so much more than just David being gone; it was the state of war the world had been plunged into again. It felt both distant and near at the same time. Not one weapon had been fired within Unity Valley, but the constant barrage on the field a mile above their head made it close and real and dangerous.

"It wouldn't change anything but thank you. I think it's going to be a long time before I have a good night's sleep again."

"None of us will for a good, long time."

Molly stepped to the edge of the porch, wrapping the afghan she'd draped over her shoulders tighter around her body. *Here she was telling Lucy it was too cold.* She looked up just as three close bursts of red hit in a triangle configuration. They were so far up, the hits were probably miles apart, but they looked close.

"Is there any chance David is up there?"

Lucy shook her head. "No, he isn't a pilot." She chuckled softly, letting herself smile a small bit. "He doesn't even pilot hovers. He's not a fan of them in general."

"At least you know he's not in danger up there."

She nodded, because regardless whether he was in the sky or on the ground, David was a Firebird in whatever capacity they wanted him in so he was in danger.

"Trevor is eaten up by the idea the fight might come here. I mean the real fight. It was bad enough when we had those stupid-ass-idiot Xenos or whatever they're called coming down the mountain. They were bad. This . . . is worse."

New tears burned Lucy's eyes in contrast to the frigid air. She tucked her chin into the scarf wrapping her neck so the wool yarn would absorb the tears and prayed it would all be over soon.

9 December 2054 – Wednesday
Interstellar Secure Communication Chamber
Robert J. Castleton Memorial Building – The Castle
United Earth Protectorate, Capital City
Alexandria, Seat of Virginia
North American Continent

"Our ships have entered your system," Queen Bryony said, an uncharacteristic strain around her eyes. "Our jump capacity is too great to jump again, but our ships are faster than the Khantan. We will be to you within a bit less than what you measure as an hour."

The fighting was over the city and had been for days. The enemy seemed to believe if they hammered the field long enough and hard enough they would break through, not having a clue that David's design turned the energy and power of their attacks back into the field making it stronger. David had even noticed a growth of the field beyond the initial borders where there was no more field to knit together. They'd gained five miles all around the perimeter in the last two days.

But that didn't mean people weren't dying.

When the Khantan savages found a weak spot, they bombed the surface and then would land, trying to find anyone alive. The first two instances had caught them by surprise, but after that they knew what to expect and Terra Force was deployed to wherever they suspected an attack would happen.

Hundreds had died, both civilians and military personnel. Brutally.

Nick rubbed his forehead with his fingers, trying to will away the headache and the exhaustion. He'd slept probably a combined six hours in the last five days, and hadn't seen his family since the initial contact telling them the war they'd hope to avoid was on them. He'd spoken to Caitlin, and she'd assured him they were all safe in the bunker.

It helped, but only marginally.

Was this the new normal? Fighting entitled races who thought they had the right to take what wasn't theirs?

"Nicholas," Beverly said low from where she stood beside him, breaking his dark distraction.

He cleared his throat. "You can enter the upper atmosphere fine," he said, forcing himself to focus through the fatigue. He raised his head to look at the hologram. "Most of the air fighting is taking place between David's field and the upper atmosphere. You'll need his array code to get through the field to hit the ground. Colonel Montgomery will send the code on a secure, scrambled channel with the cipher. Two transmissions."

Bryony canted her head, studying him.

He wondered if someone like Bryony, Queen of the most Talented race in the galaxy, could "read" him from that far away, or was his exhaustion and strain that obvious. Nick raised a hand and waved off the concern she didn't actually voice.

"We just need to stop the dying," he said.

She lowered her chin, bowing her head. "I commit the Areth to your defense. We act in cooperation with the Alliance, but I will not let Earth fall to the Khantan and the Sorracchi. I swear to you, Nicholas."

He nodded but didn't have anything to say. The whole thing was FUBAR. He could think of dozens of things that could have happened differently, but none of them did and the hell of it was nothing probably would have changed much coming to this point. Didn't matter. They were here, now, and dealing with the shiteshow.

Woulda. Shoulda. Coulda.

30 MILES EAST OF JEFFERSON CITY, MISSOURI
NORTH AMERICAN CONTINENT

"Landing in twenty seconds, sir," Captain Stewart shouted over the cacophony around them, her voice so calm it gave David chills.

He braced a hand on the hover dash, the other holding the support bar over his head as the hover banked hard to the left. In his free time, he'd attempted a modification of the defense field on a much smaller scale to protect crafts like the military hovers and it seemed to be keeping them alive, even if the impact of enemy fire directly on and around them did still send them off trajectory.

Better that than dead.

"Just get us down alive, Captain," David said through a clenched jaw. "Take your time. Don't rush on my account."

She smirked, but it immediately disappeared when another blast shook the hover. The craft shimmied, bounced, and jerked like the worst bout of air turbulence David had ever experienced even when landing in Afghanistan under combatant fire. He let go of the "oh shit" handle to press his palm to the roof over his head, hoping not to crack his neck in the next bounce despite the security restraints. With his arms locked, he looked over his shoulder at the field generators on the rollercoaster ride with them for installation. They'd delivered one, and had two more after Jefferson City.

Hopefully before the Khantan took to the surface.

They approached the outskirts of the city, a location situated to not only encompass the city itself but a lot of the surrounding areas where people gathered. The Firebirds had a small encampment set up, providing health and medical care, food, clothing, whatever people needed and they had to provide. The goal was to protect it before the Khantan zeroed in on the potential target.

They were ruthless, merciless, and disgusting in their obscene enjoyment of killing. The Sorrs were bad enough, by what David understood, but these asshats took vile pleasure in death. Every bit of warning John and the Alliance had given was warranted, and then some.

They broke through a billow of smoke and the ground came into view. The military had removed all civilians from the area as best they could, but there were still those who hadn't been reached or were stubborn. Many were Separatists who didn't believe in the help from the Alliance. They weren't Xenos, but they weren't much smarter as far as David could tell.

"Landing area is clear," the captain relayed.

They hit the snow-covered ground with a lot less grace than Captain Stewart's usual finesse, but David was just damn happy to be on the ground. As soon as the landing gears thumped hard on the ground, half a dozen Terra and two Firebirds came running from their snowscape camouflaged cover. David released his safety harness with rapid clicks and gained his feet, rushing to the generator as his pilot released the door hydraulics. He had three of the four straps released before any boots were inside the hover, and the fourth as the soldiers reached him.

"Good to go!" he shouted, the sound of approaching fire making the air hum and his ears ring like he stood next to a claxon alarm. "Go! Go!"

Four of the soldiers grabbed the console, the one directly in David's line of sight letting surprise hit his expression at the lack of weight. Yeah, the console generators looked like they needed a forklift and Dwayne Johnson to move them but their high-tech elements allowed for lighter construction. Excellent in times like this.

He followed the men and the machine, since they knew better than him where it was going. The specs and requirements had been relayed, and every potential location made their own decisions about final placement. The other officers who had come to meet them flanked them front, back, and side with weapons ready should the need to defend suddenly show up.

David wiggled his jaw – a trick he'd figured out to engage the inner-ear communication pod – and waited for the click to let him know the channel was open and active.

"Montgomery!" he shouted, his breath curling in front of his face from the bitter cold. It had to be at least fifteen degrees below freezing.

"What's your status?" Connor came back immediately.

"On the ground, following the generator to wherever she's being planted. Will be up and running in less than five minutes."

"Try to make it four," Connor urged, the sound of blasts going on behind him. "Enemy is closing in on you fast. We've got reinforcements arriving in the next twenty, but you can take a lot of abuse in the meantime."

"Don't make promises you can't keep," David snipped back.

They ran under a white and gray camouflage canopy that blended into the snow, and the men carrying the generator paused their movement, looking back at him. "It'll work wherever you put it. I just suggest somewhere flat."

"Report when you're up and running," Connor said and the line clicked to silence.

The generator in place, the commander – a huge guy whose black eyes seemed to disappear against his skin – waved an order for everyone to step back and take up observation positions. David glanced back to the hover to see Captain Stewart had closed the door but waited for him to come back. They had two more generators to deliver before heading back to Alexandria. He circled the generator, making sure there was no visible damage before he started the power-up sequence. The engagement hum filled the space, a strange harmony to the gusting winds outside, as the nacelle access completed the process.

"Powered up in five . . . four . . . three . . . two . . . one . . ." he said more for himself than any of the soldiers within earshot.

Like someone hit the mute button on a war movie, the sound of blasts and battle became a distant, muffled rumble. David looked up, and loved when they were in just the right environment, just the right weather, when he could see the crackling play of light a mile over their heads as the field shot out hundreds of miles in all directions. From the east, he caught sight of a Firebird fighter with a Khantan craft on its tail, practically in the afterburn, firing rapid blasts while the fighter spun in evasive maneuvers.

David swung out his hand, knowing one of the men was nearby, until his fingers made contact. "Check it out. Watch this," he said, not looking in the direction of whomever it was he'd grabbed onto.

He held his breath, watching the field expand and grow, watched the angle so he knew the split second the Firebird had crossed beneath the web. And in the same nanosecond, the field sliced the Khantan craft in half in a fiery burst that disintegrated ninety percent of the enemy plane, the rest spiraling a mile to the ground in a smoldering chunk.

Every Firebird and Terra within sight let out a thunderous cry.

David's cheer caught in his throat as a weapon blast came so close to his face, it singed his skin and he stumbled back, trying to catch the man beside him who he just moments before had distracted to make sure he saw the show.

"Khantan have breached the perimeter!" the commander shouted. "Defend! Open fire!"

David dropped to his knees, lowering the pale-faced kid he hadn't even learned the name of to the ground while a hole in his chest smoked and the edges of his uniform burned with the rancid stench of charred flesh. He was already dead, his wide eyes still angled upward to the sky.

Twisting on the balls of his feet, David drew his weapon and returned fire.

War Room
Robert J. Castleton Memorial Building – The Castle
Center for United Protectorate Government

Nick stared at the holographic map spread across the space over the war room that displayed hot spots of battle all over the globe. When one blood-red area would shrink, another would show up. He stared, unable to look away to see how fast the hotspot grew. Rapid meant the defense field had been breached or wasn't active yet, slow growth seemed to imply either the attack was short-lived, small, or the shield did some of the work.

In the corner were two numbers, ticking higher and higher. Sometimes by small increments, sometimes by huge jumps. Connor tried to convince him not to use the counter, but Nick needed to know. It was known casualties. The number would be higher later, and that alone made him feel sick. One was military personnel, and one was civilian.

Way too many of both.

They'd gone from defining losses in the hundreds to in the thousands. If they didn't get things under control, there'd be no damn Human race left.

"Sir, we have visual contact," Connor relayed, scanning the three-dimensional grid displaying the planet's atmosphere. "Seven ships transmitting our array code have entered the atmosphere over the European continent and Equator."

"Do we have communication?" Nick asked.

"Yes, sir," Captain Laramier confirmed from her station.

"Put them on speaker," Nick ordered. "Not the time for private room discussions."

"Yes, sir," she replied.

A moment later the overhead projection switched to a video image and a Qacrin commander in the uniform of the Defense Alliance came into view, his bushy eyebrows reaching nearly his hairline and his chin tipped up to accommodate his shorter stature in comparison to others on the ship.

"This is President Nicholas Tanner," Nick projected so his voice would carry over the din in the room.

"I am Tama'lup'tasa of the Qacrin, Commander of the Defense Alliance Fleet. Please relay all tactical data so we may best assist."

Nick rolled a hand at Connor, who nodded at Captain Laramier. "On its way. Communicate directly with Commander Montgomery through these channels to coordinate. His people are the ones in the air and on the ground. Do your *lichtgescheindts* have the necessary array signal coded into their ships? They're not getting to the fight without it."

"Yes, all signals have been communicated." Tama'lup'tasa nodded his head, a sharp jut downward and looked again at Nick through the visual communication. "We are honored to fight at your side, President Tanner."

"Honored to have you here." He looked to Connor. "Now let's really kick some ass."

CHAPTER FORTY-NINE

Bulletin For Global Broadcast

14 December 2054, Monday
Office of President Nicholas Tanner
Robert J. Castleton Memorial Building
Center for United Protectorate Government
Alexandria, Seat of Virginia

Five days ago, aid and support arrived from the Defense Alliance in the form of seven battle ready ships bringing with them six thousand Alliance fighters known as *lichtgescheindt* and over twenty thousand Alliance military personnel. With their support in the sky, and with their people fighting along ours on the ground, we have successfully quelled what can only be described as a merciless attack by a race without any honor.

Even with their help, this planet fought hard for another three days. It wasn't until yesterday when I felt anywhere near comfortable proclaiming victory. This was not a twenty-four hour fight like it was two years ago. This was brutal, exhausting, and deadly.

We are still searching globally, and around the clock, for any enemy combatants that may have escaped vigorous dispatching or avoided capture.

We ask if you suspect you have seen any Urdo Khantan, contact the Firebirds or *any of our allies* with any information you have. Their ships have been commandeered and disabled, along with all means of communication between the Urdo Khantan amongst themselves or back to the shrinking Sorracchi command structure.

For those of us old enough to remember, the name Barnabas of the "Areth" will be familiar. He escaped two years ago when we took back Earth. I'm pleased to say he – known in the poison language of the Sorracchi as Katk Hak'Ro – has been captured and is being held in judgment of his crimes.

Crimes against not just Earth, but lives, races, planets and systems across this galaxy. His punishment will be righteous.

With this communication is included an image of the Urdo Khantan, just like I sent with the December 5th transmission. Just like I said when this started, just because you see someone clearly not Human or Areth or Umani or equally familiar, that does not make them the enemy. The Alliance encompasses dozens of planets and races, and not a whole hell of a lot of them look like us. Remember that. The Qacrin, Zibali, Pehemau, Ilgen, and Lundraids are allies, friends, and quite probably responsible for your life in some way.

We are Humanity. We are resilient. We fought our oppressors two years ago, and we won. We were beaten and bloody and our population will take generations to recover, but we will. We will be stronger. We will be better. Not just for having survived, but because we need to see this as our moment to be better. There's no going back. We aren't alone, and we will never, ever be alone again.

This fight began over fifty years ago, when the first Humans came together to create Phoenix. It's why our elite military are called Firebirds. We are the Phoenix. We rise from our ashes, stronger and renewed.

If you need help, the end of this transmission provides a radio frequency accessible with *any* device capable of sending a signal. Send the message. We will hear you. We will find you. That is my promise. We owe it to the men, women, and children who died in this war. Both civilian and military. I know we don't know every name yet, so I know the numbers will grow, but after this message the names of the 12,437 civilian and 4,476 military personnel who died will be read to honor them and remember them.

- Barnout, Christian R / Sphera 29
- Bothwell, Cheryl 53
- Carabine, Christopher Thomas / Terra 29
- Faez, Zainab / Sphera 27
- Hammerlin, Frank / Earth Force (Ret.) 84
- Knowles Sr, John / Earth Force (Ret.) 72
- Lefebvre, Jetaime 60
- Lefebvre, Sage 57
- Lefebvre, Kailani 29
- Lefebvre, Eric 5
- Lopez, Desiree Rose 32
- Mayes, Leila Ann 70
- Mayes, Phillip Ray 48
- Melendez, Steven Allen 49
- Mullins Family – Jack, Janet, Jodi (daughter)
- Petersen Sr., Robert J. / Terra Age Unknown
- Petersen Jr., Robert J. / Terra 49
- Salo, Tabatha Lynn 23
- Shariq, Muhammed / Shera 34...

15 December 2054, Tuesday
Office of the President
Robert J. Castleton Memorial Building – The Castle
Center for United Protectorate Government
Alexandria, Seat of Virginia

"We have seventy-five percent of the global landmasses now under the defense field, with the largest gaps at the poles. It's just a hell of a lot harder to get up there to install them, but I'm actually working on two sort of *super generators* that we'll literally put in Santa's front yard and they'll cover three times the square mileage as the others we've installed."

David hunched forward on the couch, skimming his notes and stats on the PAC tablet in his hand. He rubbed a hand over his hair as he thought. "If I can figure it out fast enough, we might be able to finish the planet a little faster, but I don't have schematics or output or anything yet."

"David . . ." President Tanner said.

"I'm focusing on that, but also working on the platform rigging ideas the Ilgen engineer from the *Barrentasi* shared. There have to be some adjustments made for our atmosphere and ocean floor—"

"David," Nick said more firmly.

David paused and raised his head. Vice President Surimoto sat on the couch across from him, and Nick had been until a minute before but David had been so focused on giving his status report he hadn't realized Nick had gone to stand in front of his desk.

"Yes, sir."

Nick sat on the edge of the desk, a relaxed position with his hands on either side. "Take it easy on yourself. You and your Forte Field kept the majority of this planet alive until reinforcements showed up. We've got this under control until you have the web fully formed. And then . . . if you want to make changes or improvements, you have plenty of time and all the resources you need."

He pulled in a long breath through his nose and looked down at the tablet, then set it on the table between them. "Kinda hard to let go, sir. I've been riding adrenaline for so long now."

"I get it, son. I do. I didn't actually ask you here to get a situation update."

David sat up and leaned back into the cushions, catching Connor's grin from where he stood near the door behind the president, leaning on the wall with his arms crossed over his chest. David squinted at him, getting the impression he was the only one not in on the joke.

"What is it you need?" he asked, shifting his attention back to Nick.

"For you to make a choice."

David rose from the couch, suddenly feeling odd in such a relaxed position. He didn't know where to move to, so he stood in his spot. "About what, sir?"

"You did a hell of a thing, David. Every egghead in the Alliance I've talked to or heard from has been absolutely blown away by what you created with – and don't take this wrong – very little understanding of today's technology compared to what you knew and *zero* knowledge of the Areth psychokinetic . . ." Nick waved his hand in a circle. "Stuff."

"Computer language isn't all that different," he said with a shrug. "The accent changed, but the core language is the same. Once I figured out what to listen for—"

"That's my point, David. You've accomplished a long list of damn impressive things in the last few months that effectively saved our collective asses. Without your field, we would have all been smoldering piles of human barbeque way before anyone in the Alliance could have gotten here to back us up."

"I just did—"

"What you had to do, I get it," Nick said, waving him off. "Let's just agree that we're impressed and you're humble."

"Don't let him fool you," Connor said from where he still stood. "David can be a real cocky sonofabitch." He cleared his throat. "Sorry, ma'am."

Beverly smiled and raised her hand. "No apology needed, Connor. You forget I grew up on a secret military base. I knew of a great deal worse by the time I was nine."

"Here's what I'm trying to get at, David," Nick said, after clearing his throat. "You are going to go down in the history books as the reason we're all here to write history. We haven't gotten around to our version of the Presidential Medal of Honor, but when we do you're getting one."

"Sir, I—"

"Eh titch titch!" Nick cut him off, pinching his fingers together in the space between them. "We're done discussing if you deserve the recognition. You do. What we're discussing now is how the people of the Protectorate are going to repay you."

David shook his head and looked down, setting his hands at his hips, fighting the emotion that hit his throat. Not a single word formed in his muddled brain.

"Maybe this makes it easier, maybe not."

At the easier tone from the president, David looked up again.

"Connor let me know you set up the generator in Unity Valley like an auxiliary console to the one in Alexandra, so you can control the field from either place."

"Yes, sir."

"Your lab of sorts is here. Your research. Your models, all that."

David nodded again.

"I'm not telling you I'm reassigning you," Nick said, canting his head but holding eye contact. "I'm telling you if there is somewhere else on this planet you'd rather be most of the time, then that's where you'll be. I'd like you back here once in awhile just to catch up, but . . ."

The smile hit David with enough impact he almost broke his jaw. "Yes, sir," he said quickly. "Yes, sir. I accept."

"Okay, um . . ." Nick shifted back onto the desk edge and rapped his knuckles on the wood. "I'd like you here more than there maybe just until we're closer to having the ocean platforms finished, but everything else can be coordinated with Connor. Let us know what you need to get set up there permanently. My impression is they don't have computer labs and facilities like that. If you need anything else, let us know."

A thought – one that hadn't crossed his mind until that moment, but in that moment, felt absolutely right – came to him. "Actually, sir. I do have a request. I'd need to take someone with me to show them." He looked across the room to Connor. "If you can spare the colonel for a few days, I'd appreciate it. I'd like him to stand as my best man."

Connor grinned and nodded, mumbling a "hell yeah," loud enough to be heard.

"Done," Nick said. "Congratulations. I like Lucy. I hope you bring her back to Alexandria when you visit."

"Well, she might not want to until after the baby is born."

Connor whooped, Beverly gasped, and before David could say anything else the president had one hand in a firm hold with his other hand on David's shoulder. David let out a long, slow breath as Beverly embraced him.

For the first time in weeks, he felt calm.

Alexandria Hospital, Secure Wing – Private Medicine
United Earth Protectorate, Capitol City
Alexandria, Seat of Virginia
North American Continent

"If you were any other patient, I would of course tell you to go on vacation, get out of the city for a couple weeks, and unwind. But, since you are the President of the Protectorate that doesn't seem likely."

Nick let go a long sigh as Victor set aside his diagnostic scan. "I keep putting in for vacation days, but they haven't been approved yet."

Victor smiled over his shoulder as he retrieved his secure PAC tablet, opening a program with a slide of his finger and press of his thumb. "I was curious why you chose to see me for your concerns since I'm not your regular doctor."

"I wanted to keep things a little more on the down low."

The man nodded, then turned back to face Nick and lean against the edge of the cabinet behind him in the examination room. He pushed his hands into his pockets and studied Nick. He sometimes had the same habit as Michael . . . the art of close study, and Nick wondered sometimes if that was really where Michael picked up the trick.

"In all honesty, yes, there are some things that concern me. Your blood pressure is elevated, and I suggest you increase your cardiovascular exam to every six months. If you hadn't been injured and near death just nine or ten months ago, I might not be as worried, but that is reality. Are you having trouble sleeping?"

Nick pulled a face and ticked his head back and forth, not really answering. The slight shift in Victor's expression said his lack of answer didn't go unnoticed.

"Okay, real talk. The thing that keeps me up at night – pardon the pun – is I've caught myself losing focus. Stuck in my own head."

"You've been able to move past it?"

"Yeah, yeah," Nick said. "I just have to shake it off."

Victor took his hands from his pockets and crossed his arms over his chest, shifting to put one ankle over the other. It was a relaxed stance, and Nick wondered if it was intentional. "You cannot ignore the fact that you, unlike any president – global or otherwise – have faced challenges never before seen in our history. It takes a toll. There's no doubt. However, I do not currently have any concerns about your cognitive function on any level. The stress has begun to take a toll, and you have several years left in your term. We can only hope the worst of events are behind us."

"Wouldn't that be nice."

Victor smiled and nodded. "Yes, it would. As the spouse of your vice president, I have witnessed the strain on her as well. I would also very much like to see a reduction in stress."

"Does having a young one in the house help or hurt?"

Victor smiled and chuckled. "Mayda Jane has been a challenge, that

I cannot even attempt to argue against. She has moments of terror, moments of rebellion and confusion. But we love her with everything we are, and she is a bright light. So, I would have to say she eases the strain."

"I'm glad to hear that. Kids have a way of healing in ways you never expect." He sighed, getting back on track. "Well, without being able to see into the future, what do you suggest?"

"You can't go on vacation, but you can go home for dinner. Every night. You can do what has always brought you joy. Surround yourself with those you love. Fill your home. Hold your son. Hold your grandchildren. Get to know your father again." Victor cleared his throat and made a point of holding eye contact. "Share the burden. I know that is against your instincts, but I truly believe there is not a person in that house who wouldn't step alongside you and help you carry your load."

"Easier said than done, Doc."

Victor smiled. "I know. I am aware. But they will do more to heal you than anything I can do. I also have a suggestion beyond my medical advice."

"Okay. What's that?"

"Your understanding of your own Talents has changed drastically with the knowledge of your father's abilities that were passed to you, and ultimately to Michael. Your mother as well. You aren't the missing link you've believed yourself to be for a long time."

"What does that have to do with not sleeping?" As soon as he asked the question, he knew he was playing the idiot. He knew. He knew full well. Because it was one of the bullet points on the long list of things that kept him up at night. Victor arched an eyebrow and said nothing, and Nick huffed. "Fine, point taken. Except what am I supposed to do with it now that it's in the room like a giant pink elephant?"

"Learn," Victor said, shifting his stance to cross his arms over his chest. "You have a son who has been on the same journey for years, and you have a father who spent his life both mastering and simultaneously hiding his Talents. There's no more hiding. No more need to hide. Let them teach you. I suspect developing control will lower your stress."

"Yeah, I'll head home and bend some spoons or something." Victor chuckled. "Whatever works."

18 December 2054, Friday
Protectorate Citizen Community — Unity Valley
Vancouver, British Columbia
Former Country of Canada
North American Continent

"It is not in our makeup to be alone. God didn't design us that way. He made us so that we must depend on each other. He made us so that we need one another to hold us up, and sometimes carry us through the rough stuff. He made us so that when we triumph, we triumph that much more with each other than we do alone. He gave us a vision of Holy Love."

Lucy hung on to David's hands to keep hers from shaking. They stood in the solarium of the main house, surrounded by those closest to them both in Unity Valley and Alexandria. Colonel Montgomery stood with David, and so did Davey and DJ and Molly stood with her, with Mama Della, and Tessa who had come home. Connor's wife Evie came with him and brought their young son Adrian. Uncles Ignacio and Leo were there. Felicia Forte. And David's sons Daniel and Phin, and Phin's wife Katrina. Why women ever wanted huge, elaborate weddings Lucy would never understand. This was perfect. This was enough.

"Love is patient. Love is kind. It does not envy, it does not boast, it is not proud, it does not dishonor other, it is not self-seeking, it is not easily angered, it keeps no record of wrongs," Trevor Tisdale continued. "Love does not delight in evil, but rejoices with the truth, it always protects, always trusts, always hopes, always perseveres.

"David and Lucinda, I want to urge you to hold to that vision of your love for one another because that is the kind of love God has planned for your lives. David, God has a plan for you and from this day forward that plan includes Lucinda. Lucinda, God has a plan for you and He always has. From this day forward that plan includes David."

She smiled and raised her chin, not caring about the tears that squeezed free. Especially when she saw the shine in David's eyes.

"David James Forte Senior, do you take Lucinda Gabriella Bautista Santos to be your wife through all times good and bad, through all seasons abundant and poor, through all conditions healthy or ill? Will you love, honor, and cherish her until the end of your life?"

David drew in a sharp breath and brought her hands to his lips, kissing her knuckles. "I do," he said against her skin.

"Lucinda Gabriella Bautista Santos, do you take David James Forte Senior to be your husband through all times good and bad, through all seasons abundant and poor, through all conditions healthy or ill? Will you love, honor, and cherish him until the end of your life?"

"I do."

Rev projected his voice over the gathering, his smile carrying in his tone. "Since David was unable to find a jeweler, the couple have opted to skip the exchange of rings. David and Lucinda, having proclaimed your love for one another and commitment to one another in the sight of God and all present as witnesses, by the power vested in me by God and the United Earth Protectorate, I now pronounce you husband and wife. David, you may kiss your bride."

He didn't finish before David pressed his palms to her cheeks and held her face in his hands, covering her lips in a kiss that tasted of salt and forever. She wrapped her arms around him and held on.

"It is my exceptional honor to present to you for the first time Lieutenant Colonel and Mrs. David and Lucy Forte."

21 December 2054, Monday
Protectorate Citizen Community — Unity Valley

David led the way up the steps to the deep wraparound porch of the yellow Victorian tucked away along the stream where he'd stumbled on Lucy four months earlier. He took the steps before Lucy, kicking aside the snow that had settled on the steps overnight. From inside already came the sounds of construction.

Nick told him he could have anything he wanted that they had the power to give, and what he asked for was the massive home. There were eight bedrooms and five bathrooms, though it was likely none of the plumbing had worked in decades. Every bedroom had a fireplace, and by the time the engineers and tradesmen sent by President Tanner were done, every one of them would work and there was more than enough room for everyone. He and Lucy. Felicia. Davey. DJ. Ignacio and Leo. And the baby to come. If there were more babies, well . . . they'd worry about that later.

It was warmer in the house than outside because of the portable heating units set up in each room to not only make it comfortable for the tradesmen but to acclimate the house to being warm again. The air smelled of sawdust, mortar, and paint, and it was awesome.

"David . . ." Lucy said simply, stopping in the wide foyer to look up the open staircase to the second floor landing.

The house had weeks yet before it would be habitable. Plenty of time for him to finish his work in Alexandria and come back before everyone moved in. Felicia had been reluctant, but David no longer faulted her for it. He understood. She protected her family, and even if she knew his name he was an unknown. But she'd said yes so Davey would have his father and DJ would have his great grandfather, a gift she couldn't deny was precious and rare.

"There's a lot to do, but these guys know you're the decision maker. You get whatever you want."

"But you should pick out things, too."

David laughed and brought her hand he held to his lips, kissing the back. "Darlin', I would be happy to live here with purple polka dot walls and chartreuse trim if it meant I lived here with you."

"Be careful what you wish for."

"I live a charmed life, apparently. I wished for you."

CHAPTER FIFTY

Bulletin For Global Broadcast

11 March 2055, Monday
Office of President Nicholas Tanner
Robert J. Castleton Memorial Building – The Castle
Center for United Protectorate Government
Alexandria, Seat of Virginia

Victory Day

Two years ago today, we as a people – all of Humanity – came together to rise up, push back, and without margin or yield or falter took back our world. We had lost billions but were determined not to lose any more because we'd chosen to be complacent. We started on a long, difficult road of building back from the ashes.

One year ago, I revealed the new flag of our Protectorate designed by a man named William Scarborough, who died the day of the unveiling in a selfless act of protection. He said as he described the soul of his design – the Phoenix – that we would rise from our own funeral pyre, stronger than before.

Just a few months ago, we once again found Earth in the crosshairs of the Sorracchi and their hired mercenaries the Urdo Khantan. Once again, we were knocked to our knees. Once again, we stood up and said, "No! We will not be silenced! We will not be enslaved! We will not be destroyed! We will be victorious!"

It was a harder fight this time. Longer. Deadlier. But once again, we won. This time, we had more of our allies at our back but much of the reason we exist still as a people is because we are resilient. And because the best and brightest amongst us found a way to preserve our world.

This year I introduce the "Protectorate Award of Distinction," a recognition given to those who prove themselves to be exceptional in the pursuit of greatness for our world. This first Award of Distinction is given to Lieutenant Colonel David J. Forte Senior of the Firebirds who used his knowledge to increase his understanding of technologies foreign to this planet to create what we have named the Forte Field. This field is now complete, and encompasses the entire planet beneath a tightly knit defensive shield impenetrable by anyone except those we let in.

The Forte Field was only partially complete when the Urdo Khantan attacked in full force, but the number of lives it saved are immeasurable. We would have lost so many more without it. Those who were lost will never be forgotten, but we will forever be grateful to David Forte for the lives he saved.

Let today be a day of thankfulness. A day of celebration to acknowledge how far we have come. A day of introspection of what each of us can do to make tomorrow better.

Because tomorrow, we continue our work of building back not just to what we once were, but to build a better world in defiance of those who tried to destroy us.

We are Humanity. From the ashes, we rose, and now it's time for us to soar beyond any limit. We are the Protectorate.

Forte Household
Protectorate Citizen Community—Unity Valley
Vancouver, British Columbia
Former Country of Canada
North American Continent

"Pops! Pops! I have something for you!"

David set down his cup of tea and leaned back in his chair, the older wood creaking in a way that seemed completely appropriate for the restored home the Forte Clan had moved into just two weeks earlier but didn't let go of his wife's hand when the little fireball known as DJ Forte came tearing in through the porch door.

His wife. His great grandson. His home.

His life was amazing, and he'd never get tired of it.

"Here comes Hurricane DJ," Lucy said with a laugh.

"What do you have for me?" David asked as DJ burst into the eat-in kitchen.

He barely had time to let go of Lucy's hand and lean back enough for DJ to launch himself into David's lap. He had a stained and polished box in his hands and held it up under David's nose. Moments later, Felicia and Davey came through the door at a slower pace, but Davey's grin was just as wide and genuine as DJ's.

"Where did you get this?" David asked, taking the box from the boy.

"Some of the military compliment returned from Alexandria

today," Felicia explained, walking around the table to the plate of biscuits Lucy had left on the kitchen counter. "They saw us at the house and asked if we would bring it to you."

"Let's see what it is," he said, setting it on the table by wrapping his arms all the way around DJ so he was in the space between David and the table.

DJ scooted back, his long legs hanging over each side of David's lap, and practically vibrated with excitement. The boy didn't know what was inside, but surprises were special. The good kinds of surprises, and those were the only kind David wanted in his family's life.

He opened the box, revealing a handwritten note on top.

David

I could have waited until you were in Alexandria again and done some sort of official something, but I decided there was no need. You're not into the ceremony stuff any more than I am. You already know how much we appreciate you.

Come to dinner next time you're in town. We'd love to meet the rest of the family whenever they can make it, too.

Nick

He removed the note and handed it to Lucy, who was smiling before she read it. He'd known this was coming to him at some point, just not when or how, and now was damn glad Nick had gone with the quiet route.

Nick was right. Neither of them needed the show.

Nestled in a cushion of blue velvet was a medal the size of David's palm, round with sunburst edges with a red and yellow enamel Phoenix in the middle; a duplicate of the Phoenix in the center of the Protectorate flag. In blue inlaid enamel around the edge were the words "Protectorate Medal of Distinction" with his name in the same blue enamel along the bottom. He lifted it from the velvet, and a wide ribbon lanyard trailed from beneath it. The medal was heavy, like solid gold or some other hefty metal. Gold didn't hold the monetary value it had at the beginning of the century, but it still gave substance and worth to the piece.

He turned it over and read the inscription on the back.

```
In  recognition  of  his  exceptional
contribution to the safety and defense of
Earth  through  the  development  and
implementation of the security grid that
will be recorded in history as the Forte
Field.
```

"What is it, Daddy?" Davey asked, sitting in the chair on the other side of David, leaning with his head angled so he could see the medal. "It's pretty. Did you win something?"

"I guess you could say that, Buddy," he said, rubbing his palm over Davey's arm. "President Tanner sent this to me to say thank you."

"Did you give him a present?"

"Your daddy gave everyone a present," Lucy said, smiling at the man/child. He would likely stay at the same mental age for the rest of his life. But he was loved without question by everyone in the house. "He saved the world."

"Wow," Davey declared.

"Pretty impressive," Lucy said. "I know I've said it before, but I'm so proud of you, David."

"Sure, it's great," David said and set the medal back in the box, then pushed the box toward the middle of the table out of the way. He shifted his great grandson onto one leg so he could lean toward his wife and slide his hand over her stomach. She was about half way through the pregnancy, which meant David could run his hand over her belly and sometimes get a kick back. "I'm prouder of what we have here."

Lucy smiled and leaned over to kiss him. "Me, too. Still . . ." She glanced toward the box. "Saying my husband earned the very first Protectorate Medal of Distinction sounds nice."

David laughed and DJ jumped from his lap, grabbing Davey's hand to head through the house and upstairs to play.

AMBASSADOR RESIDENCE
UNITED EARTH PROTECTORATE, CAPITOL CITY
ALEXANDRIA, SEAT OF VIRGINIA
NORTH AMERICAN CONTINENT

John looked up when the main door opened and Jenifer and Alexis came in, laughing over something as they crossed the apartment to the kitchen. The sound was wonderful and had been happening more and more frequently. Both were sweaty and dirty, but smiling, after their usual workout.

"I was beginnin' to wonder if you intended to come home," he said with a wink, handing a small cup of juice to Amari. "Silas and Simon are gettin' dressed now, and Toby is due to be up any time now."

"I need fifteen minutes," Alexis said as she tucked her staff under her arm and headed for the hallway and bedrooms.

"I need ten," Jenifer said, taking one of the crackers with peanut butter he'd made as a snack for the children, but hadn't been fully eaten.

In truth, he'd made more because he knew his wife loved peanut butter and she'd be hungry after the workout. Amari walked around him, cup to her lips, to tug on Jenifer's loose tunic. Not asking what the girl needed, Jenifer handed her a cracker.

"Thank you," the little girl said in her soft voice and went the same direction as her sister, probably to join Silas and Simon until it was time to leave.

With two crackers in her palm and one between her lips, Jenifer winked at him and headed for their bedroom. John followed, not losing an opportunity to be in the vicinity of his wife showering, even if he wasn't able to join. They didn't have time for that. In the bedroom, with the last cracker going in her mouth, she started undressing as soon as the door closed behind them. John stood in the bathroom doorway as she quickly showered, watching her through the steamed glass as they talked about the training session she'd had with Alexis. The young woman had come a very long way since coming to Alexandria, and he felt ever the proud Papa when he heard just how much.

Jenifer turned off the water and stepped out, grabbing a towel to rub her hair. "You should know something," she said, walking across the space to the vanity to brush her hair.

"What's tha'?"

"Alexis asked me if I thought you'd mind if she started calling you Papa, like the other children."

A strange, but completely pleasant rush moved over John's skin making his hair tingle.

"I told her I didn't think you'd mind at all. And maybe just try it out some time. You know . . . ease it into conversation. So, now you're warned. I think you'd need to not react too much."

John nodded, as surprised at the idea as he would be if Jenifer had just announced she was pregnant with triplets. She arched an eyebrow at him, and he realized his thoughts weren't as guarded as he thought. Jenifer laughed.

"Okay, so not *that* surprising, John. She's been moving toward it for a bit now. I think she's been considering it for a long time. She's finally convinced we're safe and we're not going to send her away."

"Perhaps taking the children back to Aretu in a few months will help," he added. "Other than Silas, they have no idea what to expect from their other home. I'm hopin' it helps them all realize."

Still naked and flushed red from the hot shower, Jenifer brushed past him with a painfully brief kiss before going to their bedroom to dress.

PRESIDENTIAL RESIDENCE
UNITED EARTH PROTECTORATE, CAPITOL CITY
ALEXANDRIA, SEAT OF VIRGINIA
NORTH AMERICAN CONTINENT

"I'll be down in a few minutes," Michael said to his grandparents as they passed in the hall on their way to the staircase. "I'm going to check on the children and see if Jacqueline needs anything."

"I know your mom has an army of people doing the cooking, but I'm going to see if I can help," GiGi Grace said as she rounded the top banister.

"I'll see if I can help, too," his grandfather said, one step behind.

"Yes, you'll see if you can help yourself to some of those cookies you were sniffing around earlier," she teased.

His rumbling laughter was the answer and Michael smiled as he turned the other direction.

The house now had twelve people of four generations living under one roof, and it felt as natural as it would if they'd lived this way every day of his life rather than just months.

They had less than two hours before guests would arrive at the house for the Victory Day party, and Michael's grandfather promised to help with the backyard play set. Michael didn't expect them to finish today, but it was exciting to watch the massive set grow. Playhouses with tables and chairs inside, slides, swings, knotted ropes, ladders . . . He had searched through hundreds of database images before he designed the set.

It would bring years of fun for all the children.

And it brought him immense pleasure building it. Never as a child could he have imagined such a spectacular structure. He couldn't imagine playing much beyond deflated balls in the dustbowl yard of the New Mexico facility. In the Colorado mountain base, he'd spent countless hours watching the children play in the grass and sand in their special play area and had been jealous of their joy.

Now, he would give his children the same joy.

He still wondered from time to time what happened to the young girl named Sabrina who had taught him how to play, and the words to 'Twinkle, Twinkle, Little Star.'

Before heading downstairs, he eased open the door to the large room where they had finally moved the Quads. They still slept two to a crib, and the cribs were very close together, but they had graduated from sleeping in the same room as Mama and Daddy. It was just across the hall, so they were close, but the move made for better sleeping for all of them. The babies were in their cribs, awake but content to be with each other without adult interference.

He closed the door and crossed the hall to open his bedroom door.

Jacqueline was curled on the bed at an odd angle, with her feet hanging off the side and her head near the bottom as if she'd only intended to sit but gave into the temptation of resting. With four little ones and a toddler, moments of quiet during the day were rare and no one begrudged her the pause.

Michael closed the door behind him and crossed to the bed, kneeling on the floor at the foot so he could rest his head on the quilt and study his wife's sleeping features.

She was . . . his world.

Their children were the center of their universe, but Jacqueline Anderson Tanner was his world.

He smoothed his fingertips over her light brown skin to brush back some of her black hair from her forehead. She inhaled a slow, deep breath and opened her eyes, smiling as soon as she focused on him.

"Hey, handsome," she said in a husky whisper. "I didn't mean to fall asleep but the house was quiet and the bed called. Everything okay?"

"Yes," he said, smoothing his thumb over her cheekbone. She was so beautiful he sometimes found it hard to breathe. "I saw the opportunity to spend a few moments with my wife – *alone* – and I couldn't let the chance pass."

She uncurled her arm from where she had it tucked beneath her body to touch his jaw. "Where are you headed?"

"To the backyard. Granddad and I are going to work on the play set for a bit before people show up. It won't be done, but it might be a good chance for Amari and Nicole to spend some time with Mayda Jane. They're learning her language at an impressive rate."

Jacqueline smiled and shifted to bring her lips closer to his. "How long until you're expected?"

The smile had been enough to make Michael's heartbeat jump and his blood warm, and he rose from his knees. Jacqueline rolled onto her back as he shifted onto the bed beside her, pushing her fingers into his hair to draw him into a kiss.

No answer was needed. The play set could wait a little while longer.

"His name is Michael Tanner. Your son."

"You look like you're thousands of miles away, Nicholas."

Nick stood on the back porch of the house, watching the final touches being made on the massive playset being built for the kids. His father and Michael had put in most of the work, and Michael was still out there even though the sun was setting and guests would be arriving soon.

"More like years. Three and a half, roughly. Distance no further than Parson's Point," he said, glancing to his father who joined him on the porch.

Inside the house, through the windows they'd opened as soon as the temperature hit sixty that afternoon, carried the sounds of laughter and conversation and children playing. Adam was nine months old and on the verge of walking, and the Quads had quickly progressed to speedy crawls. Often in opposite directions that had adults chasing them and each baby squealing with giggles.

It was amazing.

"Thinking of a vacation?"

"That'd be nice," he said, walking to the porch edge to lean his shoulder against one of the support poles. "Three and a half years ago, I'd pretty much told the universe to go to hell and I'd be happy to watch it burn. I didn't give a damn about anyone or anything. Except maybe Dog. I had no reason to care. If anyone tried to tell me this is where I'd be today, in a full house with every person I'd ever given a damn about and then some, I'd probably have shot them and not blinked." He looked to his father, whose expression was drawn, his mouth turned down. "I was in a pretty dark place."

"Things changed, but how? What happened three and half years ago?"

"Caitlin," he said, smiling when he said her name. "She knew I wouldn't want to see her. In my head, she was just as much to blame as anyone else. But she came anyway. She showed me a video and said seven words. My world tilted and nothing has been the same since."

"What were the seven words?"

He had to swallow before saying the words, because they still caught in his throat when he thought about them too long. "His name is Michael Tanner. Your son."

Michael stopped mid-swing of his hammer from the top rampart of the set and looked to the house. Nick raised his hand and waved Michael to the house. "Come on in!" he shouted. "People will be here soon."

With a nod, Michael set the hammer on the wood platform and went to the end of the walkway, taking the slide to the ground. Nick and Matthias laughed when he hit the grass, stopping himself with his heels. Michael laughed too, and dusted himself off when he stood.

"He's amazing, Dad," Nick said, watching Michael pick up some of the tools they'd left around the set. "I have looked at him so many times and wondered how the hell I could have anything to do with his existence."

"We should have told you—"

Nick raised his hand to stop his father's explanation. "It's okay. I was pissed at first, but I get it. I understand. Because if I'd had the chance to protect him – no matter what it would have taken – I would have done it. I'll still do it. For anyone in that house." He shook his head, not to negate his thoughts but because he still had to remind himself sometimes that this was his life. "It's more than what he can do, Dad. It's who he is. He grew up in a kind of hell that should have —" He cut himself off, clearing his throat. "He's a good man. One of the best men I've ever known. Considering everything . . ."

"The whole of it is wicked crazy, if you ask me," Matthias said with a laugh intended to knock Nick out of his contemplations. He bumped Nick's shoulder with his own. "I mean, come on. Aliens?"

Nick snorted. "Right? Crazy."

Michael reached the porch and took the steps two at a time. When he reached the top, Nick stepped behind him for the three Tanner men to go back inside. His father opened the door leading directly into the kitchen, and the aromas of roast beef – a rare treat – and potatoes hit them. It was Victory Day, and their celebratory dinner was a special one.

Three and a half years had built a damn beautiful life.

The End

THE NEXT GENERATION

Children of Nicholas and Caitlin Tanner
Adam Nicholas Tanner — Born in 2054

Children of Michael & Jacqueline Tanner
Nicole Tanner — Born in 2052
Matthias Matthew Tanner —Born in 2054
Sean Anders Tanner — Born in 2054
Gideon Paul Tanner — Born in 2054
Victoria Grace Tanner — Born in 2054

Children of Beverly Surimoto & Victor
Mayda Jane Surimoto — Born in 2048

Children of John & Jenifer Smith
Alexis Smith — Born in 2039
Silas Smith — Born in 2046
Simon Smith — Born in 2047
Amari Smith — Born in 2052
Toby Smith — Born in 2054

Children of Connor & Evelyn Montgomery
Adrian Chevalier Montgomery — Born in 2053

Children of Jace & Lilly Quinn
Jamie Elise Quinn — Born in 2052
Riley Quinn — Born in 2055

Children of David & Lucy Forte (and descendants)
David James Forte IV (great grandson) — Born in 2050
Sofia Hope Forte — Born in 2055

James Ignacio Forte — Born in 2058
Antonia Molly Forte — Born in 2058

Children of Phin & Katrina Forte
Lorelei Forte — Born in 2056

ABOUT THE AUTHOR

Gail R. Delaney is a multi-published, award-winning author of romance in multiple sub-genres, including contemporary romance, romantic suspense, and epic science fiction romance. She always wrote stories as a kid through her teens, but didn't decide to write 'for publication' until her early twenties after the death of her mother. While helping her father go through her mother's papers, she found a box her mother kept with everything Gail had ever written—from book reports to short stories. It was then she realized her mother saw her as a writer, and it was time to live up to her mother's vision.

You can find out more about Gail R. Delaney's body of work at:

http://www.GailDelaney.com

ALSO BY GAIL R. DELANEY

Baker Street Legacy

Baker Street Legacy is a romantic suspense series with a Sherlock Holmes bloodline.

Book One: My Dear Branson

Book Two: The Empty Chair

Book Three: Indefinite Doubt

Coming Soon

Contemporary Romance

Something Better

Precious Things

Feel My Love

Fools Rush In

A Love at First Sight novella

Made in the USA
Las Vegas, NV
13 March 2022